ALSO BY SARA B. ELFGREN AND MATS STRANDBERG

The Circle: The Engelsfors Trilogy, Book I

Fire: The Engelsfors Trilogy, Book II

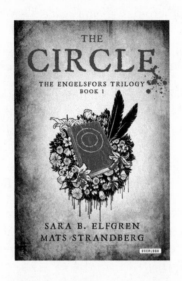

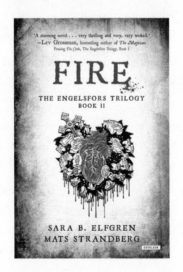

SARA B. ELFGREN
MATS STRANDBERG
THE
KEY

THE ENGELSFORS TRILOGY
BOOK III

TRANSLATED FROM THE SWEDISH BY ANNA PATERSON

THE OVERLOOK PRESS
NEW YORK, NY

This edition first published in hardcover in the United States in 2015 by

The Overlook Press, Peter Mayer Publishers, Inc.
141 Wooster Street
New York, NY 10012
www.overlookpress.com

For bulk and special sales, please contact sales@overlookny.com,
or write us at the above address.

Library of Congress Cataloging-in-Publication Data
Elfgren, Sara B.
[Nyckeln. English]
The key / Sara B. Elfgren, Mats Strandberg ; translated from the
Swedish by Anna Paterson.
pages cm. -- (Engelsfors trilogy ; book 3)
ISBN 978-1-4683-0673-6 (hardback)
[1. Fantasy.] I. Strandberg, Mats, 1976- II. Paterson, Anna,
translator. III. Title.
PZ7.E386Ke 2015
[Fic]--dc23
2015011872

Manufactured in the United States of America
ISBN 978-1-4683-0673-6 (hc)
ISBN 978-1-4683-1280-5 (pb)
2 4 6 8 10 9 7 5 3 1

WITCHES, ALIVE AND DEAD

THE CIRCLE OF CHOSEN ONES IN ENGELSFORS

 ANNA-KARIN NIEMINEN – A natural witch. **Element**: Earth. **Ability**: controlling people's minds and actions. Her familiar is a fox.

 LINNÉA WALLIN – A natural witch. **Element**: Water. **Ability**: communicating through thought. Can control water.

MINOO FALK KARIMI – A natural witch. **Element**: None. **Ability**: blessed by the guardians and able to channel their magic. Can visualize and manipulate other people's memories and remove the life-force and soul of others. Minoo can break demonic blessings and is the only one who can see the active magic of the demons and the guardians, which she sees as black smoke.

 VANESSA DAHL – A natural witch. **Element**: Air. **Ability**: making herself invisible at will. The wind occasionally behaves strangely when she is around.

 ELIAS MALMGREN – A natural witch. **Element**: Wood. **Ability**: changing his appearance. Was murdered by Max before he found out that he was one of the Chosen Ones.

 REBECKA MOHLIN – A natural witch. **Element**: Fire. **Ability**: telekinesis – moving objects using the power of her mind. Could control fire. Murdered by Max.

 IDA HOLMSTRÖM – A natural witch. **Element**: Metal. **Ability**: can communicate with spirits, receive visions and also control electricity. Murdered by Olivia.

OTHERS

 ADRIANA LOPEZ (born EHRENSKIÖLD) – A trained witch and a member of the Council. **Element**: Fire.
Ability: her talent for magic is weak, but she can control fire to a certain degree. Tried to leave the Council but was punished with the application of a magic link that prevents her from escaping and also makes it very hard for her to disobey direct orders. She is Alexander's younger sister but changed her surname to her mother's maiden name. Her familiar was a raven.

 ALEXANDER EHRENSKIÖLD – A trained witch and a leading member of the Council. **Element**: Fire.
Ability: turning the elements of other witches against each other. Led the investigation into Anna-Karin's alleged breaches of the Council's rules and was chief prosecutor in the Council's court case against her. He is Adriana's older brother and adopted Viktor and his sister.

HEDVIG ELINGIA – A natural witch. **Element**: Unknown. Member of the Council in the seventeenth century. Matilda's mother, Nicolaus's wife. Threw herself on the pyre when Matilda was burnt at the stake.

   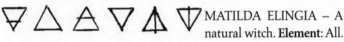 MATILDA ELINGIA – A natural witch. **Element**: All. The previous Chosen One in Engelsfors. Lived 1660–1675; daughter of Nicolaus and Hedvig. When she relinquished her powers, the Council handed her over to the civil authorities; they convicted her of witchcraft. She was burnt at the stake. Her soul has been caught between the worlds ever since.

MAX ROSENQVIST – A natural witch. **Element**: Earth. **Ability**: controlling people's bodies. Was once the demons' Blessed One. Minoo broke his blessing, since then Max has been in a coma. Murdered Elias and Rebecka.

MONA MOONBEAM – Unknown background. **Element**: Unknown.
Runs a shop called the Crystal Cave. Uses her magic power in the shop to make her customers believe what she foretells. Also has a non-magical instinct for saying exactly what her customers want to hear.

 NICOLAUS ELINGIUS – A natural witch and ex-member of the Council. Hedvig's husband and Matilda's father. **Element**: Wood. **Ability:** controlling plant growth.
Has been alive since the seventeenth century when he was the minister in Engelsfors. When his wife and daughter died, he made a pact with the guardians. He murdered the high officials in the Council's Swedish contingent in a ritual that made it possible for him to live on and so help the next Chosen One. Calls himself the guide of the Chosen Ones. No one knows where he is. His familiar was a cat.

 OLIVIA HENRIKSSON – A natural witch. **Element**: Metal. **Ability**: controlling electricity. Olivia can charge amulets with magic and use them to control others. Was the demons' Blessed One. Murdered Ida, Elias's parents and many more. The Council removed Olivia after her defeat by the Chosen Ones.

 SIMON TAKAHASHI – A natural witch. **Element**: Air.
Adriana's boyfriend and Alexander's friend. Was executed almost twenty years ago because he and Adriana had attempted to leave the Council.

VIKTOR EHRENSKIÖLD (born ANDERSSON) – A natural witch. **Element**: Water. Works for the Council, but has not yet sworn the oath of allegiance.
Ability: can detect lies, control water and communicate with other water witches by telepathy. Has a twin sister who fell ill after misusing her magic. They were both adopted by Alexander.

A NOTE ON THE SWEDISH SCHOOL SYSTEM

In Sweden, grades 1-9 comprise primary school, and secondary school (high school) lasts for three years, the equivalent of US grades 10-12. The main characters in *The Key* are therefore finishing eleventh grade when the book begins, and the characters that are about a year older are about to graduate.

The Borderland

CHAPTER 1

The dazzling white light is growing fainter.

Ida blinks a few times, looks around.

She isn't in the church anymore. She is nowhere. Surrounded by grayness, like a fog but not quite. Much more like *nothingness*.

Matilda still stands next to her in her white dress, holding her hand. Matilda's reddish-blonde hair, ice-blue eyes and freckles contrast with the grayness around them.

Ida tries to tug her hand free, but Matilda won't let go.

'Where are we?' Ida asks.

'In the Borderland.'

'What is—'

Matilda shushes her.

'Be quiet,' she whispers. Her fearful eyes scan the gray nothingness. 'Or they might find us.'

Ida suddenly feels glad that Matilda is holding her hand.

Her hand.

Moments ago, when Ida was still in the church, she had reached out for Minoo, but Minoo had walked straight through her. But apparently Matilda can hold on to her.

So maybe I'm not all that dead yet, after all, Ida thinks. Can't be.

She looks at herself and realizes that she is wearing her usual clothes. Dark jacket. Pale blue V-necked sweater and jeans.

She touches the silver heart that hangs on a chain around her neck.

Matilda's grip tightens.

'Ouch,' Ida hisses.

Matilda starts running, pulling at Ida, who stumbles until they find a shared rhythm.

The ground is hidden under the veil of mist. It is yielding, almost marshy, underfoot, and Ida can't hear their footfalls. But at least there is something like ground. She can feel it. And running speeds up her breathing, makes her pulse beat faster. The silver heart bounces against her chest.

I just can't be totally dead, she thinks. I mean, like, not *totally*.

They keep running. There is nothing to catch your eye in the grayness; perspectives disappear and, seemingly, they're getting nowhere.

Ida glances behind her. Only grayness.

No. Something else. A sound like a faint whisper.

Something is there.

Ida can't see it, but is still certain that it's there. She runs faster. By now she is pulling Matilda along. Onwards, onwards, through nothingness.

Another whisper. Now, she hears it close behind her.

Ida chokes back a cry. It feels as if all she ever feared about darkness is chasing her.

She can make out a change ahead of them, then sees that there really *is* something, though no more than a shift in the depth of the grayness, as if it were thinning out. Beyond the gray veil, she senses a hint of light, like the sun behind the clouds on an overcast day; a dull shade of yellow, of light diluted and scattered in moisture.

They have almost reached the light when Matilda stops abruptly. Her ice-blue eyes, so like Nicolaus's, drill into Ida.

'I must distract them but I'll find you again,' Matilda says. 'Time and space here are different from what you know. While you're here, you must keep on the move. Look for the lights.'

And then she gives Ida a firm push.

4

It is like falling in slow motion. The air is thick and resists her.

Suddenly, Ida is somewhere different.

A stone-flagged floor. A grand gallery. Tall columns vanish into the dark space above her head. Their shafts are decorated with patterns and shapes in clear colors: red, blue, yellow, green, black. The air is hazy with incense and the strong, spicy scent makes her dizzy.

The only source of light seems to be the teenage girl in the middle of the gallery. Light radiates from her body and filters through her white linen shift. Her dark wavy hair falls over her shoulders. Her head hangs down; her chin rests on her chest. Only her toes lightly touch the floor.

She is hovering.

'Excuse me . . . but . . . hello?!' Ida hears how shrill she sounds.

The girl's head is lifted, as if pulled up by an invisible hand under her chin. She wears a necklace, a small pottery object on a chain. Her mouth opens slowly and she starts to speak, straight out into the gloom around her.

'We are here now,' she says.

The language is alien to Ida, but she understands all the same.

From somewhere, the grating voice of an old man.

'We greet you.'

For the first time, Ida becomes aware of other people in the gallery. She can hardly make them out where they are sitting in the shadowy spaces beyond the reach of the girl's light. There are about twenty of them, at a guess. Perhaps more.

Ida is about to say something else, but holds back. Even if they are able to understand what she says, attracting attention could be an horrendous mistake. She has no clue who they might be. And no clue where she might be, for that matter.

'All of you have been called in your dreams to come here,' the girl tells her audience. 'All of you are witches. All of you are masters of magic in different forms. We called you and you came.'

'Who are you?' A woman's voice comes from somewhere in the dark. 'Are you spirits who speak through this girl?'

'Yes, spirits of a kind,' the girl replies. 'We are your guardians.'

The guardians. They must be able to help Ida. Explain what's happening here.

'Hello?' Ida walks up to the girl. 'It's me . . . Ida!'

But the girl looks straight through her.

'We have watched over you since the beginning of time,' the guardians pronounce in the girl's voice. 'We have been watching over you, seen you build your communities and fight your wars. We have not interfered. But circumstances changed.'

'Hi!' Ida waves her hand in front of the girl's face.

No response. She attempts to hold on to the girl's arm, but her hand grips empty air. It is just as it was in the church.

'Evil beings, demons, are trying to force their way into this world,' the girl continues.

'Demons?'

It is a young man's voice.

Ida backs away but doesn't want to end up in the shadows. Especially not when they're talking about demons.

'They are able to move between worlds,' the girl tells him. 'They have only one purpose: to bring order into chaos.'

'That is good,' the young man says. 'Chaos should be eliminated.'

'You do not understand. When the demons arrive in other worlds and discover its life-forms, they see taming them as their task. They attempt to reshape that world in their image. The demons despise feelings, disorder, differences. They regard themselves as flawless and eternal; no other beings can live up to their ideals. When the demons fail to tame a world according to their intentions, they exterminate everything alive there. Devastate it utterly.'

A restless, worried mumble rises from the congregation.

'So far, we guardians have succeeded in stopping the demons,' the girl says. 'But, in the battles between the demons and us, the veil between the worlds was ripped in seven places. Seven weakened areas were created. They serve as a set of doors through which the demons can gain entrance. We have managed to close them temporarily, but they must be sealed.'

Ida has heard all this before. To be precise, she has *said* it herself before, after Matilda took possession of her and used her as a medium.

'The first portal to be sealed is here, in your town,' the girl continues.

The first? Matilda had said that six of the seven portals had been closed by other, earlier Chosen Ones, and that the Engelsfors portal was the last.

A shiver runs down Ida's spine.

The *first* portal must be closed and sealed. So, the question isn't just *where* she is. It is also *when* she is wherever she is.

'The portal gives your town a special magic status. Just now, we are in a period of high magic. Its level will increase, and when the power is at its peak, the veil between the worlds will be at its thinnest. Only then can the portal be sealed. And the young woman, through whom we are currently speaking, is the only one who can do it. She is the Chosen One.'

The first portal. The first Chosen One.

'This must be a dream,' Ida tells herself, shutting her eyes tightly. 'Such a long dream, but I'll wake up soon and everything will be back to normal. I'll be in the first year of high school. There won't have been a night of a blood-red moon. Everything has to be a dream – it's so much more likely.'

She tries to make herself wake up. She even pinches her arm. But when she opens her eyes again, she sees the glowing, hovering girl.

Tears begin to flow down Ida's cheeks.

At least, if I can cry, I can't be totally dead, she thinks.

But then, she can't figure out what's worse. To be dead, or just stuck in another time.

'What is supposed to be so special about this girl?' the young man asks.

'She has a particular connection to this place,' the guardians reply. 'And she is in control of more magic than any of you ever will be.'

The irritable old man's voice speaks again.

'You are insulting us.'

'We tell you the truth. You were called here because of your magic talents. But your reach is limited because you do not truly understand your powers. You have got much to learn.'

Someone sniffs derisively. The girl turns her head slightly to look in that direction. Once more the silence is complete.

'You don't even know the most fundamental structure of magic,' she tells them.

'Really? Then do enlighten us!' the old man says.

'In this world, there are six elements,' the guardians state. 'The elements are the basic essentials of all magic. Each one of you is able to control one element.'

The girl raises her hands. No she doesn't, Ida reminds herself. *The guardians* raise the girl's hands.

Two yellow flames flare up in her palms.

'Fire,' the first of the Chosen Ones says.

The next moment, the flames are put out by a glittering fall of light rain.

'Water.'

A joint intake of breath from her audience.

The girl moves her hands in a sweeping gesture and a gust of wind makes the incense whirl in the air in front of her. Then it forms a small vortex that soon dies away.

'Air.'

She claps her hands. The slapping sound echoes through the gallery. When she spreads out her hands again, her palms are cupped around black soil.

The Borderland

'Earth,' she says. Suddenly, two frail green stems sprout from the black matter. 'Wood.'

Both plants and soil change color, become shining silver. 'Metal.'

She makes fists of her hands, then opens them. Glittering silver sand drizzles softly to the floor.

'The Chosen One is able to control all six elements. She has a connection to this place. And her powers form the Key that can seal the portal.'

'A key can also be used to open doors,' an old woman says.

'That is true,' the girl replies. 'And our enemies will try to steal it.'

'How will they go about that?' the old woman asks.

'The demons cannot act freely inside our world, but instead they will persuade witches to take on tasks for them. They use demonic magic to bless any willing witch. Once blessed, he or she has only one goal. It is to kill the Chosen One; to take over her soul and her powers in order to open the portal and let the demons in.'

Ida realizes that is why Max killed Elias and Rebecka. He needed their powers to open the portal. He actually needed all the powers of the Chosen Ones.

'For a while, the Chosen One will be protected from the scrutiny of the enemy,' the girl continues. 'But the closer we get to the time of the battle, the weaker the protection becomes. Then she will need your help. That is why we are going to teach you more about magic.'

A roll of parchment appears in her hands. As she unwinds it, six signs slowly appear on the initially empty surface. Six signs which are only too familiar to Ida.

'The signs represent the six elements. They hold their own power,' the guardians intone through the medium of the girl. 'Your task is demanding, but sacred. You are charged with saving this world from annihilation. From now on, you are no longer individuals. You are a unit. You are the Council.'

9

The Key

The first Chosen One, Ida thinks. And the first Council.

The incense smoke grows denser around her, then turns into a deep fog. The voices fade away. Suddenly, Ida is back in the grayness. The place Matilda called the Borderland.

She looks around. She can't pick up any movements or sounds, but that doesn't necessarily mean that she is alone. The invisible things that chased her and Matilda before might be watching her right now.

'Search for the lights,' she whispers to herself as she starts running.

She tries to grasp what she has just heard, what it signifies.

The powers of the Chosen Ones combine to make the Key to the portal. The Key that will either shut it for good, or open it.

All six elements are required, which means that the Key is not complete. It hasn't been since Elias died.

But then, how will they be able to lock the portal? And how could someone blessed by the demons open it? Isn't everyone stuck?

No, that's not possible, thinks Ida, because if it was useless, surely the demons would have given up? Actually, they should have backed off ages ago, the moment Minoo liberated Elias's and Rebecka's souls from Max. Then, what was the point of blessing Olivia?

Also, surely the guardians would have told the Chosen Ones that they didn't have a hope of closing the portal? Why stay quiet about something that important?

How she wishes Minoo were here to explain everything.

Further ahead, Ida spots a new light in the grayness.

She focuses on it and throws herself out into the unknown.

Part I

CHAPTER 2

Minoo opens her locker and is hit by a torrent of books, pens and notebooks. She manages to catch her biology textbook and *Crime and Punishment*, but all the rest clatters onto the floor.

As she bends over to pick it all up, her ears go hot with embarrassment. She listens out for someone snickering. But no one seems to have noticed. People are focused on something else entirely and everyone is talking about it.

. . . it'll be such fun, something is happening at last, it's been fucking ages . . . my big bro's friend will fix us up with drink . . . please, can I borrow that dress . . . whatever, everyone's going . . .

Minoo shoves her things back into her locker. Then she pulls off her backpack and starts stuffing it full to the brim.

'Paaarty!' someone roars.

It's a senior guy who comes running along the hallway.

Minoo reminds herself that she never parties – everyone knows that. So, she's never invited. It's not that they hate her, but it simply doesn't occur to them. Which is fine by her. Really fine.

She slams the locker door shut, turns and meets two cornflower-blue eyes.

Viktor Ehrenskiöld is wearing an immaculate pale blue shirt and a sand-colored cardigan. His ash-blonde hair is in perfect order, as always. And, as always, he is utterly odorless. No perfume of any kind. His body has no smell at all. It still bothers her.

13

'Here, you dropped this.' He holds out one of her pens.

'Thank you,' she says as she takes it from him.

Which amounts to their longest conversation for more than a month. Ever since their talk in his car, when he had declared that he was still loyal to the Council, she has avoided him and he has left her in peace.

Minoo tugs the backpack into place and braces the small of her back against the weight of the books.

'That looks heavy,' Viktor observes. 'Are you working during the May First holiday?'

She doesn't answer, only starts walking toward the entrance. He follows her.

'Or are you going to his . . . little soirée?'

He nods toward Levan, who stands a bit further along the hallway, surrounded by senior guys. They all laugh and slap his back, which makes him have to push his glasses back up on his nose.

Levan. So she is not invited even when one of the other nerds in the class is throwing the party. It hurts more than she's prepared to admit.

'Well, are you?' Viktor asks.

'Why do you want to know?'

'I'm just trying to keep our conversation going.'

'Find someone who's interested.'

'Ouch.' Viktor puts his hand to his chest in a theatrical gesture.

They are in the entrance hall by now and Minoo catches sight of one of the posters with Olivia's photograph.

Underneath the picture it says: HAVE YOU SEEN OLIVIA HENRIKSSON? in big letters, and gives a contact number for the police.

Olivia's face is covered in whitish foundation and framed by a cloud of blue hair. Her big brown eyes are shining. Her cheeks are full. This Olivia is someone very different from the ruined figure that Alexander picked up from the floor of the gym.

14

'Minoo,' Viktor says. 'I realize that you and I disagree about a lot of things, but surely we can still talk to each other?'

Near the front door, Minoo stops suddenly and looks straight at him.

'Of course we can,' she says quietly. 'Actually, there are quite a few things on my mind. Things I'd like answers to. Like, where is Olivia? Is she alive? Why are you and Alexander still in Engelsfors? You don't even believe in the apocalypse, or that we are the Chosen Ones. You must have better things to do than staying here?'

'You know that I can't answer your questions,' Viktor tells her.

'Then we have nothing to talk about.'

He places his hand on her shoulder to stop her from leaving.

'Do you truly believe that I'm your enemy?'

'You are certainly not my friend.'

Viktor takes his hand away.

'I see,' he says. 'You do mean it.'

It seems that his lie-detector magic has revealed to him just *how much* she means it, because he looks quite hurt. For a fleeting second, Minoo feels bad. Then she reminds herself that this is probably what he intended. She has no idea who Viktor really is, which part of him is truthful and which is manipulative. All she knows is that she has promised herself never to trust him again.

'Just leave me alone.' She walks outside and he doesn't follow her.

The schoolyard is bathed in a pale, gray light that is bright enough to make her squint. Gustaf, wearing his green army jacket, is standing by the soccer goal. The wind ruffles his blonde hair as he smiles and waves at her.

Minoo's body goes on high alert. Her ears go hot again. As she walks toward him, her wrists seem to buzz with electricity. She tries to stay calm; she must not let him see how she feels.

'Hi there.' Gustaf hugs her.

15

'Hi, Gustaf,' she says, and forces herself to let him go; otherwise she'll start clinging to him like a koala bear on a eucalyptus.

'You wanna go for a walk?' Gustaf asks.

The clouds form a lid over Engelsfors. They walk past Lilla Lugnet. Coltsfoot and crocus glow along the shoulders. They walk past the lovely white wooden house with its decorative carved details where Adriana Lopez lived until only a few weeks ago. It looks deserted; Adriana stays at the manor house now. Minoo wonders what it is like for her. How she feels. She hasn't seen her since she concealed all Adriana's memories of what's happened since she arrived in Engelsfors. Concealed them to protect Adriana from the Council.

They carry on southwards, in the direction of the canal. Gustaf talks about which universities he'd like to go to this autumn. He has applied for lots, but would prefer law school in Uppsala. Minoo tries to sound encouraging and to ignore her pain.

Uppsala. Stockholm. Lund. Linköping. Umeå. Göteborg. Every university on his list feels like another knife-cut. A few months from now, Gustaf will be off to one of these cities and no longer be part of life here. It will probably be just as well, of course. It'll be best to let their relationship, whatever it amounts to, fade anyway.

As they pass Olsson's Hill, Minoo's eyes wander to the top, where there is a huge pile of firewood. People have dragged branches and boards and things up there to be burnt.

'Are you coming along to watch the May Day Eve bonfire?' Gustaf asks.

'No . . .' she begins, but is interrupted by a small, sharp explosion that makes her jump. She turns around and spots a group of middle-school kids just down the road, laughing loudly.

'I thought kids of that age weren't even allowed to mess

around with fireworks,' she says, realizing she sounds like a grumpy old man.

Gustaf is smiling.

'Did you get scared?'

'I simply don't see the point.'

'But didn't you used to think blowing things up with bangers and crackers was the best thing ever. Like sandpit explosions. We did.'

Minoo shakes her head. Of course Gustaf had played with fireworks. And of course she hadn't.

She thinks back to the Gustaf she used to watch at a distance when they were in middle school. During lunch break, he would always be outside, usually on the soccer field, and surrounded by his friends and fans. Minoo used to hide in the school library to escape having to go outside.

It makes her uneasy to think about Gustaf and herself as children and how totally unlike each other they had been. Because it reminds her that they are fundamentally different.

What do they truly have in common? Why be friends now? And that other feeling – what is it? Something she had better not think about. Whatever it is, it made Gustaf take her hand when they were sitting side-by-side on his bed, that evening before the Spring Equinox.

'Are you coming to the party?' Gustaf asks.

New bangs echo behind them.

'Oh, do you mean Levan's party?' Minoo says, and realizes that it might come across as though she is pretending she has at least two tempting parties to choose between.

'Yes.'

'I have to work. And besides, I'm not invited,' she replies, hoping that she doesn't sound like a martyr.

'Nobody will give a damn if you're invited or not. I don't think Levan has got a clue about what's going to hit him. Maybe we ought to go just to stop it getting out of control.'

He rounds this off with a little laugh that sounds almost

nervous. Minoo glances at him and realizes that he is looking at her sidelong.

Does he really, truly, want us to go there together? she wonders. Why would he? Is it a sudden inspiration that I'd be a fun person to go partying with? Or does he pity me because I'm about to be home alone on May Day Eve? Or, maybe he means exactly what he says. I'd be just right for a little party policing?

Or is it because anything might happen at a party?

Her ears are on fire.

'Why do you think it's going to get out of control?' she asks.

'Because it's May Day Eve. Because hardly anyone knows Levan, or cares. And because it's the first big party since the gym hall business.'

The gym hall business.

Olivia had joined in with Helena and Krister Malmgren and together they had planned to sacrifice the entire school membership of Positive Engelsfors. The idea was to use the collective life-force of hundreds of people to resurrect Elias from the dead. But what Helena and Krister didn't know was that Olivia wanted to sacrifice them as well. As for Olivia, she didn't know that the demons had deceived her completely. If she had succeeded with her mass murder, it wouldn't have brought Elias back. It would have triggered the apocalypse.

But Gustaf is unaware of all that. He remembers as little of that night as all the Positives, who were wearing Olivia's amulets. Minoo has seen to it that Gustaf's memories are hidden deep inside him.

How she wishes that someone could make *her* forget.

She has seen Ida die, both through her own eyes and through Gustaf's. She has seen far too much through the eyes of others. Through Adriana's. And through Max's.

When he pointed his gun at Linnéa in the dining hall. When he made Anna-Karin pick up the carving knife and press its edge to her. When he pushed Rebecka off the roof of the school. When he forced Elias to slash his wrist with the shard of mirror glass. When he made Alice, his girlfriend, leap from the window to be crushed against the rocks below because she no longer wanted to be with him.

Gustaf lightly touches her shoulder. His touch wakes her, allows the maelstrom of Max's memories to disperse.

'Hey, where did you go?' he asks.

She would so much like to answer him honestly. She would like to tell him everything.

But the laws laid down by the Council forbid her to reveal to the general public that she is a witch, and Gustaf belongs to that general public. At this stage, the Chosen Ones must keep a low profile so they don't attract more unwanted attention from the Council. Above all, Minoo worries about what the Council might do to Gustaf if he were to know.

'Oh, I'm sorry. It's just that there's so much on my mind right now.'

'Listen, maybe I didn't sell the idea too well, but seriously, what do you think? What about the two of us crashing Levan's party?'

Suddenly, Minoo really wants to go. Just for one evening, she would like not to be good and thoughtful and do the right thing.

She turns to Gustaf, but he has seen somebody and waves. Minoo looks in the same direction.

Isabelle Mohlin, Rebecka's mother, comes walking toward them. Two little girls, Rebecka's little sisters, hold on to her hands. She has cut her strawberry-blonde hair a little shorter, but she still looks so much like Rebecka. She smiles happily at Gustaf and, when she reaches him, gives him a big, warm hug.

'Really nice to see you!' she says as she lets go of him.

'And you,' Gustaf says. Then he bends down to say hello to Alma and Moa.

'Hi,' Isabelle smiles at Minoo.

'Hi,' she replies.

19

The Key

Is Isabelle taking note and recalling that Minoo and Gustaf were two of the people who were closest to Rebecka? Is she asking herself if they might not have noticed signs she herself had failed to pick up? Nonexistent signs, in fact, since Rebecka did not kill herself.

'Mommy,' Moa says in the slightly croaky voice of a small child. 'Mommy, please, let's go. I need a wee.'

'Yes, we'll go home in a minute,' Isabelle tells her, and then turns to Gustaf. 'I've got to feed everyone before going off to work. Thank God I'm not in the ER now, what with the May Day Eve fun and games tonight.'

'Mommeee,' Moa hisses, using her body weight to pull at her mother's arm.

'Yes, sweetie.' Isabelle doesn't take her eyes off Gustaf. 'You know, don't you, that you're welcome to come around any time? Though I understand that you've got a lot to deal with now, in the run-up to the final exams.'

'Only a few more tests to go, and afterward things calm down,' Gustaf tells her. 'When it's over, you'll all be invited to my reception.'

'Sounds great!' Isabelle says. 'We'll try to come – well, one of us at least. Bye for now. Bye, Minoo.'

Minoo and Gustaf watch as they walk away.

'Gustaf, I can't go out tonight,' Minoo tells him. 'I really must work.'

She notices how Gustaf's gaze flickers. 'If you're sure.'

When they part, he doesn't hug her. She wonders if that means anything. And hates herself for wondering and for wishing that he had.

Minoo unlocks the front door, kicks off her shoes, runs upstairs to her room and throws herself on the bed. Her thoughts feel like a thousand little hooks buried in her mind, tearing at it in all directions.

She holds her hands out in front of her. Releases her magic.

The black smoke starts winding itself around her fingers. It moves slowly; the trails of smoke merge, thicken and spread until darkness floats above her like black water.

There's something wrong with you. But you know that already, don't you?

You positively stink of magic, but it's unlike any I've ever come across. Can't fucking identify it at all. And I don't like it.

The week after Ida's funeral, Minoo went back to the Crystal Cave to ask Mona Moonbeam what she actually meant by all that.

'I knew there was something weird about you even before we met,' Mona told her while she applied another layer of frosted pink lipstick. 'But I only grasped quite how peculiar the first time you turned up in the shop. Magic shows itself this way and that, but the foundation stones are always the same.'

'You mean the elements?' Minoo asked.

'Yeah, I mean the elements,' Mona said impatiently. 'Thing is, you haven't got an element, have you?'

No, Minoo thinks, as she follows the pleasing tracery of the smoke. Loses herself in it. No, I haven't. I've got something much better.

Her mind goes silent. Her emotions quiet down. She feels as if she is dissolving.

She is no longer afraid of anything. Nothing can harm her now, not inside the smoke. Nothing hurts. No matter if the pain is outside or inside her, it cannot get at her for as long as the guardians' magic pulses in her body and fills the space around her.

She had felt like this for the first time after she defeated Max. She had felt it when she hid Adriana's memories. But it was after Ida's funeral that she began to escape into the smoke. And perhaps this is the guardians' greatest gift to her: a way to set her free from herself.

Minoo sits up, opens the drawer in her bedside table and takes out the *Book of Patterns*. The smoke twists lazily around her hands as she puts the book on the bed in front of her and starts turning the pages.

Every day since Ida's death, Minoo has spoken with the guardians through the book. They rarely answer her questions, but it is a comfort that they are there.

Minoo watches as the elemental signs float across the pages, fusing and separating again to form new patterns.

We must show you something.

Minoo's hands slide over the signs.

'What?' she asks.

Suddenly she feels dizzy.

The room rotates and her head feels light, as if filled with helium.

She is floating now, first just above her own body, then rising up and up toward the ceiling. She sees herself sitting on the bed, still with the book on her lap.

Next, she sees the roof tiles below her. She raises her head and looks out over the town. The sun is a glowing disc in the sky. Immediately below her is her house. The part of town where she grew up. She sees it all, watches as it grows smaller and smaller as she continues her slow rise.

She should be frightened, surely, but she isn't. Instead, she observes Engelsfors from a bird's perspective and registers everything with cool curiosity.

It is so beautiful.

From up here, the streets look different. Some run in smooth curves that she had never noticed while walking along them. She studies the forest that surrounds the town. The waters of the canal and of Dammsjön Lake glitter in the sunlight. The hospital. The manor house.

The silence is absolute. The town looks asleep; not a movement anywhere.

Except in the sky.

Now she is looking at Engelsfors High School.

Dark clouds have piled up behind the square brick building

and are crawling up above the horizon from all directions, swelling and spreading over the sky.

But these are not clouds.

Black smoke pours soundlessly in over Engelsfors. Its tentacles stretch between the tall apartment buildings, and into the gardens of the houses, until the smoke has swallowed all the buildings, the entire town.

The sun grows pale and shrinks until it is a distant star. Then, finally, the star is extinguished. And Minoo no longer knows if she is ejected into space or left to fall.

She opens her eyes.

Dread floods into her; all the fear she had not experienced just moments before.

She gets up from the bed. Her legs tremble as she walks to the window and looks out.

And even though everything looks perfectly normal, she feels certain that what she saw was for real.

Only, it has not yet happened.

CHAPTER 3

Anna-Karin has been walking for several hours. She is inside both her own consciousness and the fox's. They have seen buds on the trees and flowering meadows on sunny slopes. They have listened to birdsong, followed hare tracks and paths of other foxes, found a blackbird's nest but left the eggs alone.

It is a perfect spring day, but restlessness tears at both their minds.

'What are we looking for?' she asks the fox.

During the last few weeks, she has asked that question of him, as well as herself, many times. The fox can't give her any answers. All he knows is that they must carry on looking.

They are following a path that divides into two at an old, fenced-in quarry full of water. Its edges drop steeply down toward the still surface of the water.

The moss that grows on the rock walls is a glowing, almost fluorescent green.

The fox pads lightly up the winding left-hand path. Anna-Karin has to smile as she looks at his thick, fluffy tail, waving as he trots along.

She wanted to give him a name, but nothing seemed to fit. Later, she realized it was wrong to name him at all. She has no right, so now she thinks of him as the fox. Maybe the same feeling had made Nicolaus use 'Cat' for his familiar.

Anna-Karin tries to push thoughts of Nicolaus away. It has been more than six months since he left Engelsfors and he hasn't once been in touch. Not even to say that he's still alive. *If* he is.

Part One

The fox suddenly stops in the middle of the path and looks up at her with his amber eyes. His tail is still.

'What's the matter?' Anna-Karin asks.

A sharp bark.

She walks toward him, but he doesn't wait for her. Instead, he leaps off the path and runs off among the fir trees.

Anna-Karin stops and looks for him. Hesitates. There are many stories of people getting lost in these forests and most Engelsforsers feel insecure about leaving the paths. Anna-Karin would rather not, but the fox wants her to come with him.

His mind tugs at hers and she sees what he sees, glimpses moss rushing past underneath, tree trunks flashing by as he speeds up.

She steps off the path. For an instant she is surprised to sense the moss giving way under her feet instead of supporting her paws. Then she hurries in among the trees.

Somewhere ahead, the fox barks. Anna-Karin follows the sound until she spots him waiting near the huge root-plate of a fallen tree. He is staring intently at her.

'What have you found?' she asks him.

And then becomes aware of the silence. No birds sing. No wind stirs the pine branches above their heads.

Now she understands.

She walks around the root-plate and surveys the scene. She ought to be used to the sight, but still the hairs on the back of her neck stand on end.

The trunks of the trees have turned gray, the fir needles a dirty brown. They look completely dry. There are no leaf buds on the bare branches of the leafy trees. Yet another dead place in the forest. Since last summer, she has seen more and more of them.

The fox barks once, then pads on. Slowly. Watchfully.

Anna-Karin follows him.

The air feels heavy to breathe. The only sounds are the

crackling noises under her feet. The trees seem to come closer. As if the forest were about to engulf her.

Only her imagination, of course. Everything is so still.

Far too still.

She jumps when the fox suddenly barks. He has stopped to look at something.

A blackbird is lying on the ground, belly up. Its beak is open a little, its wings spread out on the moss.

'Poor little thing,' Anna-Karin says.

She wants to get out of here. Now, at once. The fox sniffs the black feathers cautiously.

'Come along,' she says. And then she looks ahead.

The ground is so stony that it looks as if waves of moss are advancing on them. And now she sees all the bird bodies. All of them with wings spread out, as if they had fallen out of the air in mid-flight.

Anna-Karin takes a few steps. They are everywhere.

Magpies. Crows. Lots of small birds.

She stops by a buzzard lying on its back. She realizes from the markings on the inside of its wings that it is a young bird. And wonders for how long these birds have been lying here. The bodies look intact and show no signs of decay. With so many cadavers around, the air should be humming with insects.

The fox pads up to her side.

'Come on,' she whispers to him. 'Let's go home.'

She turns around and starts walking back, feeling safer the moment her feet are back on the path. Her cell phone pings and the fox's ears point. She is relieved to see Minoo's name on the display. Everything will feel better once she has told Minoo.

'Something has happened,' Minoo says as soon as Anna-Karin replies.

Anna-Karin has difficulty swallowing while Minoo tells her about the black smoke. How it ate up Engelsfors.

'I can't be here alone tonight,' Minoo says. 'Dad is staying the night in Fagersta. Can I come over to your place?'

Anna-Karin thinks quickly. Minoo has visited her home a few times and Anna-Karin has been as nervous every time. She can imagine only too easily what their house looks like to someone like Minoo.

Besides, Mom has been worse than usual lately. She has hardly moved from the sofa, only lain there, chain-smoking and moaning about things, with the TV on non-stop and much too loudly. This morning, when Anna-Karin asked her how she was, she just snarled: *Why don't you stop asking? You might as well: it's not as if you'd ever understand anyway.*

'Or, do you want to come here?' Minoo asks, and somehow it's clear that she understands why Anna-Karin hesitates.

Suddenly, Anna-Karin feels irritated. Why should she feel ashamed? She's not the same person as her mom.

'No, it's fine,' Anna-Karin tells her. 'Come over to us. I'll give you a call when I've cleaned up a little.'

'You don't need to clean up.'

Anna-Karin has a vision of Mom's ashtrays, the overflowing laundry basket in the bathroom. The dust balls everywhere, so large you can pick them up with your hands.

'Actually, yes, I do,' she says.

When she opens the front door, Peppar comes over to sniff her. He is always fascinated by the smell of fox.

The door to Mom's room is closed. Anna-Karin takes a long, hot shower to try to wash away the sense of a catastrophe drawing close. She finds a pair of jogging pants and an oversized T-shirt in her room and pulls them on.

The lamp in the ceiling flickers. The electricity has misbehaved for almost a whole year. Just another reminder that the apocalypse is coming closer. She switches the light off to avoid having to see it.

In the kitchen, she soaks the dishes with dried-on food,

then checks the contents of the fridge. She must ask Mom for money so she can shop. She feels bad about it because she's well aware that they live on a knife-edge. And Mom doesn't even pretend to look for a job any longer. Anna-Karin has no idea what will happen when their bank account is empty. Will she have to speak to social services? Will anybody help them?

She doesn't want to think about it now. Instead she phones Granddad.

His phone rings out again and again, but no one answers. It worries Anna-Karin. Granddad should be in his room at this time. She is just about to give up when she hears a woman's voice.

'This is Taisto Nieminen's telephone.'

'Hi, I'm Taisto's granddaughter. Is he there?'

'He's asleep. He has been a bit peaky today.'

Anna-Karin stares at the water in the sink. Its surface is turning greasy.

'How is . . . is it something serious?'

'Not to worry,' the woman replies. 'He is probably only tired. Why don't you phone again tomorrow?'

Anna-Karin ends the call. In her head, she hears the echo of Mona Moonbeam's prophetic words.

Say goodbye when you can. There is still time. Use it well.

CHAPTER 4

Linnéa sits back on the uncomfortable sofa in Diana's room at the Engelsfors social services offices.

She wonders how many times she has been propped up somewhere or other here.

Then she wonders how many times she'll come back here in the future.

Diana is sitting opposite her on a chair covered in some kind of felt. Jakob, the psychologist, is on Diana's right and, on her left, is a plump woman whose name Linnéa has already forgotten.

They are like those three monkeys. Jakob hasn't uttered one word so far. The plump woman has asked a lot of questions, but not listened to the answers. And Diana is avoiding looking at her.

This meeting is called a 'network counseling session' which is presumably meant to sound reassuring, but makes Linnéa think of a fish caught in a net, twitching as it tries to free itself.

'Now it's not long until your eighteenth birthday,' Diana says. 'The main change for you is that you can't rely on the Mental Health Service for young people afterward.'

She glances at Jakob, who clears his throat.

'That's right,' he confirms. 'Afterward, adult psychiatry takes over. But, in your case, attendance is voluntary.'

They all look expectantly at Linnéa. She doesn't need to read their minds to figure out that they hope she'll say something thoughtful and mature.

'I feel so much better now,' she tells them. 'About the panic attacks and all that.'

Jakob and Diana nod sympathetically. They believe her.

What she hasn't told them is that Erik Forslund and Robin Zetterqvist forced her to jump off Canal Bridge and that, ever since, she hasn't had a single night without nightmares. And whenever she sees anyone who looks like either of them, the panic comes rushing into her head.

She has no intention of telling Diana and Jakob what happened. For a start, they might not believe her. If they did, they would want to report the incident to the police and that is something she absolutely doesn't want. Helena is dead, but both boys are still protected by the alibi she provided. Word would stand against word, and she doesn't doubt for a second who would be believed. Erik and Robin are local hockey stars and their families belong to the pathetic social elite in Engelsfors. Linnéa is a known mental case, who wears bizarre clothes and whose father is one of the most notorious alcoholics in town.

'It's wonderful that you feel so much better,' Diana says. 'But, you know, it might be good to have that extra bit of support all the same.'

'I'll think about it, naturally,' Linnéa lies.

What is the point of seeing a psychiatrist if you must hide everything that matters to you? Like, someone trying to murder you? Or having to save the world from a demon invasion?

'That sounds sensible,' Jakob nods.

'Well, as we've agreed, for as long as you're in high school, little will change otherwise,' Diana continues. 'You can stay on in the apartment, as before. And I'll still be assigned to be your social worker. Unless you want to end our relationship, that is.'

She is smiling, but Linnéa notices the insecurity in her eyes.

When Minoo ripped the metal sign amulet from Diana's neck, right here, in the department of social services, it was as if Diana woke up after a dream. Suddenly, she couldn't understand why she had attempted to have Linnéa transferred into juvenile hall. A little later, she went on sick leave for several weeks. Linnéa has picked up that Diana thinks she was recovering from burnout syndrome. And she senses the terror Diana feels about not being able to trust her own mental stability. How she worries that her mind will suddenly break down – something that Linnéa sympathizes with.

'No, that's fine,' she says.

Diana looks relieved.

'Right. That's agreed. Now, over to you, Anette. Can you explain a little about how you two will deal with things?'

The plump lady, Anette, talks very slowly, as if Linnéa is incredibly slow on the uptake. Plus, everything she says is so predictable that, after just a few words, Linnéa can work out the rest. She has to bite her lip not to fill in the final bits of sentences.

The thing is, she knows exactly how this will work out. Anette is supposed to manage her benefits and Linnéa has to apply on a monthly basis for her student loan. All should work smoothly for as long as Linnéa attends school. And behaves properly.

The arrangement will carry on until she passes her school finals.

After the finals, she'll have to make it on her own. Or, she won't make it at all and will have to sit through meetings like this for the rest of her life. The world is full of misfits who never accomplish anything apart from having kids, who in turn become misfits and losers too.

Just like Linnéa's parents.

She tries to convince herself that she doesn't have to repeat their mistakes. At least, she is positive that she will never ever have children.

It will be tough enough not to make a bleeding mess of her own life.

'Is there anything you'd like to ask us?' Diana asks at the end of the session.

The Key

There is nothing. It is over. Linnéa nods goodbye to the three monkeys and hurries away.

The streets of Engelsfors are unusually crowded. Lots of people carry clanking bags from liquor stores.

May Day Eve. People used to believe that this was the night when witches rode around on broomsticks or goats.

No wonder I'm feeling restless, Linnéa thinks.

She pulls out a pack of cigarettes from the top of her boot; as she lights a cig, she glances at the burnt-out building that used to house the *Engelsfors Herald,* then starts off again to get to Ingrid's tiny shop, where she sometimes helps out. By the time she arrives, the glowing tip has reached the filter.

The faint ceiling lights are flickering. Ingrid sits behind the counter and smiles when she sees Linnéa.

'Nice to see you,' Ingrid says.

Her white hair is pulled back into an untidy bun with a pencil stuck through it.

'I thought I'd pick up that dress,' Linnéa tells her.

Ingrid leaves to look in the storeroom.

Linnéa stays, eyeing all the stuff: the shelves full of old toys, odd glasses and cups and collectors' plates; the piles of video cassettes. She doesn't recognize any of the titles on the back of the boxes, but the blood-spattered letters promise cannibals, zombies, blood and terror. This makes her think of Vanessa, who can't get enough of horror films. She even enjoys the bad ones.

Linnéa would like to give Vanessa a call, ask her to come over tonight. They could watch a bad horror movie. Side by side, close together. Maybe share the same blanket. Then Linnéa could smell the scent of Vanessa's hair, feel the warmth of her body.

Yes, even the thought of cannibalistic terror makes Linnéa fantasize about Vanessa. But it is May Day Eve. Vanessa is certain to have made other plans for tonight.

'It's a perfectly hideous old party dress but I'm sure you'll be able to make something special of it,' Ingrid says when she returns with an armful of black silk. It's a lovely material, but Linnéa can see that sewing it will be a nightmare.

Ingrid puts the dress in a carrier bag and hands it to Linnéa, who thanks her and puts her hand into the bag to touch the smooth fabric.

'I'll be watching the bonfire later on,' Ingrid says. 'Who knows, there might be people there to chat to.'

She smiles and Linnéa wonders whether Ingrid is lonely. And if she is, does it trouble her? Maybe she likes things as they are?

'Have a good time tonight, then.' Linnéa hopes the words don't sound as formal and unnatural as they feel when she says them.

'And the same to you,' Ingrid says. She turns the sign around to *Closed* even before the door has shut behind Linnéa.

Linnéa spots him as soon as she steps into the street.

Dad.

And he has seen her. There is no place to hide.

The last time they spoke, he was busy clearing out the furniture from the Positive Engelsfors Center. He had promised her that he wouldn't start drinking again and that he would prove it to her daily. She examines him now, and sees no sign of him having broken that promise.

People do change sometimes.

That's what Mona said in the Crystal Cave on the day of the Spring Equinox.

Although, given that Mona missed the fact that Ida would die that night, Linnéa feels less than confident about Mona's prophetic gifts.

'Hello.' Björn stops. 'Happy May Day Eve. Are you going to celebrate tonight?'

'No. I never was that keen on the May Day thing.'

Does he even remember, she asks herself, all the May Day night piss-ups with his friends? Linnéa used to hide under her bed all night. She couldn't sleep and, once, when she didn't dare go to the bathroom, she had peed herself and stayed for hours in her wet clothes. When silence had fallen in the kitchen at last, she had tiptoed down to the laundry room in the apartment building, washed herself in the sink, changed her clothes and stuffed her old things into one of the washing machines. Then she had finally fallen asleep, with her head against the drying cupboard. She had been nine years old.

'No, I suppose not,' he says. 'But look, if you don't have any plans . . . I've got some ground beef at home, just right for hamburgers. Why don't you come around?'

'I haven't eaten meat since I was twelve,' Linnéa reminds him.

'Sorry, I knew that, really. What about the veggie ones? The Ica store is still open.'

He looks pleadingly at her and tries hard to hide it at the same time. It tugs at her heart. And then she becomes angry with him for making her feel like that.

'Last time we met, you said you wouldn't demand anything from me,' she says. 'But I can't help feeling that you're pretty demanding.'

He nods. And looks devastated.

She has an almost irresistible urge to carry on. To cause him pain with her wretched memories.

But what scares her isn't the temptation to hurt him; it's her longing for him. Her feelings are pulling her in opposite directions and she feels the ground shift beneath her feet.

The first wave of panic wells up inside her.

'I'll be off now,' she mumbles, and walks away before he has had a chance to reply.

CHAPTER 5

Vanessa stares at the flames as they lick at the twigs and branches, chipped boards, an old bedframe and whatever else has been hauled up to the top of Olsson's Hill. The fire crackles and roars against the black sky.

The choir bursts into song:

Winter's fury ends in our mountains, snowdrifts' glimmer fades away and dies . . .

The conductor beats time with his arms in front of the small group of bony little old men, who are all wearing decaying dark suits. One of the old boys walked past Vanessa just moments earlier, giving off booze fumes so powerful he'd surely explode if he got too near the fire.

A gust of wind makes the smoke whoosh out over the crowd. Vanessa's eyes fill with tears.

She will be reeking of bonfire smoke when she gets to Linnéa's place. Stinking, when she turns up to tell Linnéa that . . . well, that she has been thinking . . . that she has kind of grasped . . . that she . . .

Vanessa curses under her breath. Smelling of smoke is clearly going to be the least of her problems.

Yes, I'll join you! Greetings, joyous breezes, birds and coun-tryside so fair . . .

Vanessa's little brother Melvin squeezes her hand hard and sings along, though he knows neither the words nor the tune. Mom smiles to Vanessa. Ever since they left home, Mom has been going on and on about how pleased she is that Vanessa is keeping them company.

The Key

Vanessa was twelve when she was last up here for the May Day Eve festival. The year after that was the first time that she, Michelle and Evelina had gotten drunk together.

Ever since, it has seemed so much more tempting to spend time with her friends. Vanessa has agreed to meet up with Evelina at a party tonight, but has no intention of staying on.

Tonight is the night when she will face up to it. She will tell Linnéa that she is . . . that she . . .

The choir is reaching the end:

Blackbirds' song among the pine and fir trees, water birds at play around the isles.

The old boys fall silent and acknowledge the applause with pleased expressions.

Melvin howls with delight when a burning branch falls to the ground in a shower of sparks. He tugs at Vanessa to get closer to the fire and she goes down on her haunches and puts her arm around him.

'No way, darling. Stay put,' she tells him.

'It's fire!' Melvin shouts. 'I want fire!'

Vanessa wonders if she should worry about her kid brother's pyromaniac tendencies.

'When are you off to your party?' Mom asks.

'Soon,' Vanessa says, and notes the nervous fluttering inside her stomach.

Melvin twists in her arms and she loses her balance for a moment. Her heels sink into the grassy ground.

As she looks into the flames, she remembers Matilda, the Chosen One from the seventeenth century. Nicolaus's daughter who was burnt at the stake. Alive. The heat is scorching on Vanessa's face, even though she is standing several yards away from the fire.

She pulls Melvin closer and kisses his soft, dark curls. She doesn't want to think about Matilda.

'I'm going now,' she tells Melvin, who nods absent-mindedly, fixated on the flames.

She straightens up, waits for Mom to take Melvin's hand.

'Who is giving the party?' Mom asks.

'No one you know.'

Actually, Vanessa doesn't know him either, except that he's one of the geeks who is in the same class as Minoo and Anna-Karin.

She'll just drop in and say hi. Then go around to Linnéa's.

Whenever she tries to utter the words, they vanish out of her mind.

It's time for you to wake up, sweetie.

That's what Mona had said to her. Vanessa is wide awake now and she is scared to death.

This whole situation is new to her. In the past, liking someone had felt like a game. It never made her wretched, because she never had anything to lose. Not even when she met Wille. She had checked him out at parties, kept track of what he was up to, but hadn't fallen *in love* with him until later on, when they were already together.

With Linnéa, it's different. Not only are they friends, but Fate has also joined them one to the other. If Vanessa screws up tonight, it will ruin everything.

But she has to speak out. She needs to know if she has a chance. Or if she should just find a suitably sized hole and lie down to die. Because that's how she feels. Either or.

Linnéa.

Her name is enough for that fluttering inside to start again. Linnéa's dark, dark eyes, her black hair. Her hands, her lips. Her bare skin; that time she was kissing Jonte on the sofa and Vanessa still had no clue why she couldn't stop looking.

'See you,' Vanessa says.

'Have fun,' Mom tells her. 'But not *too* much fun.'

The wooden house is painted pale blue. Now and then, raucous voices are heard from inside it. The thump of the music comes across easily and every beat makes Vanessa realize that she really doesn't want to be at this party.

Still. She checks her lip gloss. Puts a hairpin into place. She *promised* Evelina. Besides, she promised herself a drink.

Which is totally pathetic. Linnéa doesn't drink anymore. She wouldn't need alcohol to give her the courage to say something like this. She would just say it.

Which means if Linnéa felt something for me, she thinks, she would have told me already.

She opens the front door, takes a big step over the piles of shoes and jackets in the hall, and almost falls when one of her heels gets stuck inside a large sneaker. She has to plow her way past a big huddle of guys filling half the hall. One of them wolf-whistles. In the living-room doorway, a girl from Minoo and Anna-Karin's class seems to be humping the doorframe in time to the music. Vanessa carefully walks around.

The big room is full of people dancing, and so hot that the windows are coated in condensation. A boy has passed out on the stairs to the upper floor, with a dead cig still sticking to his lips. A girl comes running downstairs, stumbles on his stretched-out arm, loses her balance, falls down the last few steps and knocks the humping girl over. Everyone starts to laugh and applaud. The girl who has fallen laughs harder than anyone else.

On the face of it, it's just another party. But, somehow, it seems to be simmering. And not in a fun way, either. The whole house feels like a pressure cooker.

Most of these people were at the Spring Equinox event in the school gym. They don't remember anything from that night, apart from waking up as if from a bad dream. Helena and Krister Malmgren were lying on the floor, dead, and, soon afterward, Ida had died too.

They have forgotten how they had been breathing in the same rhythm, like a single being. How glowing circles came and went on walls and floor, and flashes of lightning hissed through the air.

But they are aware that something went *wrong*, and now they are fed up with wondering about what it was. Fed up with feeling afraid. A collective sense of frustration has built up and needs release.

The lights flicker and the music stops suddenly. There's a moment of confusion. A girl in a pink cowboy hat rushes up to the player and gets it going again.

Vanessa scans the room. There's no sign of Evelina, but Michelle and Mehmet are kissing, tucked in under a window-sill. The drooping, pointy leaves of a potted plant just above Michelle are becoming tangled in her hair. The pot wobbles unnervingly.

When she catches sight of Vanessa, Michelle pulls away from Mehmet and waves happily. A slender thread of saliva is suspended between her lips and Mehmet's, but breaks when Michelle shouts something that drowns in the music.

Vanessa waves back at her.

She spots the door to the kitchen and begins to push her way through the crowd, but comes to a halt behind a circle of boys with their arms around each other's backs. They seem to be practicing some kind of Cossack dance and their faces look euphoric. One boy's glasses are coated in moisture and his sweat-soaked hair lies glued to his skull. She tries to maneuver around them but only manages to hit her knee on a low table she hadn't even noticed.

Kevin Månsson is seated on the puffy black leather sofa with a bottle of red wine on the table in front of him. It still seems weird to see him without the yellow polo shirt he wore daily while the Positive Engelsfors rule of terror dominated the school. He is playing a game on his cell phone, prodding the screen so hard it seems he's determined to crack it.

Vanessa shoves the Cossack boys hard enough to make them loose their hold on each other.

'Hi, Vanessa! Great that you could come!' the guy with glasses shouts as she pushes past him.

'Get that, Vanessa Dahl is here! In your place!' one of the others says excitedly.

At last, she gets into the kitchen. Gustaf Åhlander is there, chatting with some of the other soccer players in EFC. Evelina is leaning against the sink. She is talking to someone in a red sweater, a guy with a shaven head and an eagle tattooed on his neck. Must be Leo, who Evelina has been on and on about, ever since meeting him at a party in Örebro. Vanessa can tell from the look on Evelina's face that she and Leo had sex before going to the party. And that it was good.

'Nessa! At last!' Evelina shouts and hugs Vanessa. 'Babes, you're so smelly. Like a barbecued sausage!'

Vanessa takes the plastic glass that Evelina hands her, drinks and feels the taste of alcohol through the Coke. Just one drink like this one will definitely be enough. One more would be one too many. She mustn't be pissed when she sees Linnéa.

'Great to see you at last,' Leo says. 'Evelina talks about you all the time.'

'She talks a great deal about you, too,' Vanessa says, and sips her drink.

Evelina looks hopefully at her and she tries to think of something to say to Leo. Her head seems totally empty.

'So, how are things in Örebro?' is the best she can do.

'Right now, I prefer Engelsfors.' Leo looks at Evelina, who titters.

'Isn't he *soo* cute?' she whispers a little too loudly to Vanessa.

'Too true,' Vanessa whispers back. 'Well done.'

Evelina titters some more and raises her glass in a toast.

Leo begins to talk about going to Rättvik next weekend to buy a secondhand car. Then he talks about cars he has owned, and cars he would have liked to have owned.

Vanessa hasn't got the strength to fake an interest. All she can think about is what she is going to say to Linnéa. Leo has apparently made a joke and she laughs without getting it. It makes her feel like she isn't supporting her friend. Not that it seems to matter in the slightest. Evelina is looking at Leo as if he could offer her all the answers to life's mysteries.

Vanessa drinks a little more, then gets her cell phone out and clicks on to the SMS she texted on the way to the party.

AT PARTY. BORING. CAN I COME OVER?

She presses SEND and drinks again, a bigger swallow this time. She wishes she could allow herself to drink some more. To drown her nerves.

Evelina is tugging at her.

'Hey, what do you think? Like, honestly?'

Vanessa realizes that Leo is off to check the fridge.

'He's great.'

'But you hardly glanced at him! Who's that text for?' Evelina looks troubled. 'Is it Wille?'

'No.'

Vanessa wonders what Evelina would say if she realized that it was sent to Wille's ex, Linnéa Wallin. Her cell vibrates and she drains the glass before opening the message.

SURE.

Just one word. But that's enough. Suddenly, Vanessa can't bear to stay for a second longer. She puts the glass down on the sink.

'I've gotta go.'

'Why, what's happened?' Evelina asks.

'Nothing really. But Mom has caught a cold and needs a little help with Melvin, that's all.' Vanessa quickly kisses Evelina on the lips. 'Take care. I'll call you tomorrow.'

She manages to get back into the living room. It's cooler now, because the windows are open. The Cossack dancers have pulled their tops off and are hanging halfway outside to chill out. The potted plant with pointy leaves has met a grim end on the red-wine-spattered wooden floor. Michelle and Mehmet have simply shifted their making out to another corner of the room.

Some new arrivals are standing in the doorway leading to the hall. Vanessa stiffens the instant she sees who they are.

Erik and Robin. And Julia, jammed in under Erik's arm. Felicia clings to Robin.

They were all Ida's best friends, once.

Erik is scanning the room. His gaze stops at Vanessa. She locks eyes with him, wishing that she had Linnéa's talent of projecting thoughts into other people's heads.

I know what you've done, she thinks. And I'll make you pay.

A plastic mug hits the doorframe near Erik. Red wine splatters over his face and his white T-shirt. Julia's scream is so piercing it cuts through the roar of the music.

Vanessa realizes what this means. It is going to trigger total loss of control. This will become the story the whole school will be talking about.

'Who the fuck did that?' Erik's voice has risen to a howl. Red flares are spreading up his neck.

Someone switches the music off. Everyone is silent. The guy who passed out on the stairs sits up and looks confused.

'Whoever did it is totally sick in the head!' Julia shrieks, and gets closer to Erik.

Emerging from upstairs, a few curious people edge a bit further downstairs. Gustaf comes out from the kitchen, closely followed by some of his FC boys. Vanessa spots Leo, who is rubbernecking to see better. She wonders how long he'll enjoy being in Engelsfors.

'I did.' Kevin steps up on a table.

By now, Erik looks more irritated than angry.

'Kevin, for fuck's sake . . .'

Kevin staggers and drinks from his bottle of red wine.

'He's pissed shitless.' Robin grins at his own wit.

Felicia giggles nervously.

'Now, listen,' Kevin says. 'You're all to . . . listen to me. Can't anyone remember what happened? No one?'

'Oh, shut up,' Julia tells him. 'You're off your face.'

'No, I'm not!' Kevin shouts. 'Drunk, yeah, sure. But I know that something happened at the Positive Engelsfors party. Look, it can't have been some fucking accident like they said! Why can't anyone remember anything? Someone must. You were there, all of you!'

Vanessa sneaks a glance around the room. Some faces have worried expressions.

Do they remember? Do they know somewhere inside what Kevin is talking about?

'Look, I know Ida . . . Ida did something,' Kevin says. 'But what, I can't remember—'

'Stop it, Kevin,' Erik interrupts. 'What happened to Ida was sad enough without—'

'Shut it!' Kevin is shouting so loudly his voice cracks. 'You fucking bastard! You pretend to miss Ida, but you're lying!'

He gestures with his arm to include Robin, Julia and Felicia.

'You're all lying!'

'Watch it,' Erik says.

He walks toward the table Kevin is standing on and people move away nervously.

'It's you who should watch it,' Kevin replies. 'I know all about you. About you and Robin. I haven't forgotten.'

Vanessa's heart is racing. Is Kevin going to say what Erik and Robin did to Linnéa, right here, in front of everyone?

'Shut it. Now!' Erik's voice is icy cold.

'You can't tell me what to do!'

Julia and Felicia shriek as Kevin leaps at Erik, who crumples onto the floor with Kevin sitting astride him. Kevin lifts his arm to hit but Erik gets in first and drives his right fist into Kevin's face so hard the blood spurts. Julia and Felicia scream in unison. Others join in.

'Go, Erik, go!' Robin shouts.

Erik shoves Kevin so he ends up on his side with his hand clamped over his nose. Blood is streaming between his fingers. Erik gets on his feet, then kicks Kevin in the stomach. Kevin moans.

'Stop!' Vanessa screams.

Erik aims a new kick, but someone jumps at him and drags him away from Kevin.

It's Gustaf, of course.

'That's enough!' he says to Erik.

Erik hits him in the face.

Chaos erupts. Some people try to get out, others to force their way in. People stumble, fall over, scream. Cell phone cameras are flashing. More potted plants crash to the floor and little clay balls are spilling out everywhere. A shelf is ripped away from the wall. Suddenly, the stench of vomit fills the room.

Vanessa catches a glimpse of a group of soccer boys as they haul Kevin away and protect Gustaf whose lower lip is bleeding. Other than that he seems OK.

Vanessa is pushed this way and that by bodies on the move in different directions, but she manages to get to one of the open windows. The guy with glasses has got his cell phone out and demands to speak to the police in a shrill, panicky voice. Vanessa jumps out, holding her high-heeled shoes in her hand. She lands softly on the lawn.

The pavement feels cold under her feet as she runs through the nice residential area. When she hears police sirens she hides in the shrubbery and slips into invisibility. If Nicke, her ex-stepfather, is in the police car, he mustn't see her.

Once the patrol car has zoomed past, she returns to visibility and gets out her cell.

ON MY WAY

CHAPTER 6

Minoo glances over her shoulder before opening the door to the apartment building where Anna-Karin lives. On the opposite side of the street is the building that used to house Positive Engelsfors. Sheets of brown cardboard cover the windows. A poster saying FOR SALE is taped on one of them. The poster gives the number to Bertil Gunnarsson, the real estate agent, but nobody is likely to ask for details of that property any time soon.

She takes the stairs almost at a run. The stench of stale cigarette smoke pours out when Anna-Karin opens the door with NIEMINEN on the letterbox. As Minoo says hello and hangs up her jacket, she knows she'll be smelling it for days afterward.

Anna-Karin goes to her room, but Minoo stops on the threshold of the darkened living room. Mia Nieminen half lies on the sofa, propped up by a mountain of cushions, watching television. She is adding to the smoky atmosphere with a new cigarette. Its tip is a glowing point in the murk.

'Hello, Mia,' Minoo says. 'How are you?'

Mia's eyes stay glued to the TV. On the screen, a woman with very white teeth pipes icing roses on top of a cake.

'No worse than usual,' Mia replies. 'My back is so bad it hurts to breathe, you know.'

She sucks energetically at her cigarette.

But smoking is no problem, obviously, Minoo thinks.

'If I had been a dog they would've put me down long ago,' Mia adds before stubbing her cig out.

Minoo can't think what to say to that. It probably doesn't matter, because Mia doesn't ever seem to expect or even want a reply.

Minoo has tried to feel compassion for Anna-Karin's mother but, if truth be told, her strongest feeling is anger. Anna-Karin shouldn't have to put up with this kind of thing day in, day out.

'Hey, Minoo, are you coming?' Anna-Karin calls from her room.

Instantly, Minoo's conscience points out that this is actually Anna-Karin's mom and that depression is an illness, not the person's fault.

The air in Anna-Karin's room is breathable and Minoo closes the door behind her.

Peppar greets her by rubbing himself against her legs. He usually hides under the bed when she is visiting.

'He seems to have gotten used to me,' Minoo says.

'Try to lift him,' Anna-Karin says with a smile.

Minoo gingerly takes hold of the cat, wondering if she's doing it the right way. Her cousin's hamsters are the only animals she has held. Shirin was forever setting up hamster circuses and making Minoo be the animal minder, while Shirin herself was the boss.

'Would you like something to drink?' Anna-Karin asks as she sits back on the chair at the desk. 'Like tea, or water? There's cranberry juice too.'

'No thank you, I'm fine.' Minoo sits down on the neatly made bed with Peppar on her knee.

Neither speaks for a while. Minoo has discovered that when she is with Anna-Karin, silences are neither scary nor embarrassing. This is one of the things she likes best about her.

'Your vision, what do you think it was really about?' Anna-Karin asks in the end. 'Do you think it was . . . the apocalypse?'

Part One

'Honestly, I can't work it out,' Minoo told her. 'I tried to check in the *Book of Patterns* but it stayed totally silent.'

Anna-Karin scratches the moon-shaped scar on her hand, a mark of where her fox bit her once.

'If it was a vision of the apocalypse, what might it signify?' she asks. 'What I mean is . . . is the message that we're bound to lose? And why should the guardians want to show you that?'

'No idea. It might mean something utterly different,' Minoo says. 'All I know is that it scared me.'

Well, afterward, she thinks. Not at the time. But that's too weird to tell Anna-Karin.

Minoo starts stroking Peppar. Beneath his silky fur, his bones seem so fragile that she shudders. What if she cracked one of his ribs by mistake? She rubs him gently behind the ears instead and he purrs.

'I found another dead place in the forest today,' Anna-Karin tells her. 'And there were so many dead birds—'

Suddenly Peppar leaps down onto the floor.

Minoo hears a scream from the living room; just for a moment, she assumes it must be some TV program. Then there's a heavy crash.

'Anna-Karin! Anna-Karin, help! Help me! Anna-Karin!'

Mia sounds in despair, almost insane.

Anna-Karin rushes to the door and pulls it open. Minoo follows her and they run to the living room.

Mia is lying on her back in front of the TV. Her wordless moans express only pain. Anna-Karin kneels by her side.

'Mommy, Mommy! I'm here!'

Mia starts to scream. She screams and screams. Minoo goes rigid, paralyzed.

'Mom!' Anna-Karin calls out. 'What's happened? Did you fall? You must tell us!'

Suddenly, Mia is silent.

Drunken voices shout in the street outside, somewhere in the world beyond this claustrophobic, airless apartment.

'I don't know what to do, I don't know what to do,' Anna-Karin wails.

Minoo kneels at her side.

Mia's breathing is harsh and fast, her face is gray. Her lips are moving quickly, as if trying to form words. Her eyes roll back inside their sockets.

'She must've fallen,' Anna-Karin says. 'She must . . .'

Mia stops breathing.

'Call the ambulance,' Minoo says, surprising herself by how calm and assured she sounds.

Anna-Karin runs to her room. Minoo shuts down all emotion.

It felt like this when she learned that Rebecka had died. Being terrified is useless. She has to take action.

She has been dreading that something like this would happen to her father, that he would just collapse one day. She has obsessively researched what she must do if she is alone with him at the time.

Following the instructions she has studied on the Internet, Minoo shakes Mia and calls to her to make sure that she really is unconscious. No response. Minoo pulls Mia's chin up and back, looks down her gullet to check that nothing is stuck inside it. She leans forward to listen out for breaths and watches Mia's chest at the same time.

No signs of breathing.

'They're on the way,' she hears Anna-Karin say. 'They're coming.'

Minoo puts one hand above another between Mia's breasts, then tries to keep her arms straight and strong.

She pushes down and feels the ribcage give. *1 . . .*

She does it again. *2 . . .*

Again. *3 . . .*

The entire hefty body is swinging under her hands as she pushes and counts, pushes and counts.

. . . 15 . . . 16 . . . 17 . . .

Part One

This is a body, Minoo thinks. A large package of flesh and bones and blood. This is not Anna-Karin's mom. I'm not to think of this as Anna-Karin's mom.

. . . 28 . . . 29 . . . 30.

She squeezes the body's nostrils together, opens its mouth and places her lips over it. It smells of smoke and of something rank, but nothing affects Minoo.

After blowing air into Mia's lungs, she checks her chest to see if it is rising. Then she inhales deeply and blows into the body's lungs again.

Minoo always imagined that mouth-to-mouth resuscitation would feel intrusive, intimate, like a kiss. But it's not like that in the slightest.

She straightens her back and places her hands on Mia's chest again. Pushes thirty times. Blows twice. Another thirty compressions.

Two. Thirty. Two.

Minoo soon feels tired. Her arms are shivering with effort. But she carries on, like a machine. She has no idea where Anna-Karin might be. She has no idea of how much time has passed. She doesn't notice when the paramedics enter the house, until they move her away from the body and take over.

CHAPTER 7

A nna-Karin edges over on the seat in the ambulance driver's cabin and avoids the gaze of the paramedic.

He introduced himself as Stian. He is strong. He and the ambulance nurse lifted Mom up on the stretcher as if she was practically weightless.

Mom.

She is lying somewhere behind Anna-Karin's back.

She is on a drip and a tube has been rammed into her throat. She might die at any moment. The thought doesn't make Anna-Karin feel anything. It is just a thought.

'It was very good that you two knew how to carry out first aid,' Stian says.

You two? What is he saying? Minoo did it, and this Stian person knows just as well as Anna-Karin. He saw it with his own eyes.

As for herself, she did nothing. Could hardly get her address out when she got through to emergency services. In fact, she didn't even think of calling 911 until Minoo told her to.

If Anna-Karin had been alone, Mom wouldn't have stood a chance. Stian is bound to realize that as well and that's why she can't bear to look at him. She doesn't want to read in his eyes how useless he thinks she is.

'Your friend will be there for you at the hospital, won't she?' he asks.

Anna-Karin nods. As soon as the paramedics had strapped Mom to the stretcher, Minoo called a taxi.

Anna-Karin looks at the reflection of her face in the side

window. She looks just as usual. Shouldn't it show that what is happening is for real? Does Stian wonder why she isn't crying?

'Your granddad and my dad are friends,' Stian says. 'My dad is Åke.'

A quick sideways glance tells her that he is smiling.

'How awful this must be for you.'

STOP BEING NICE TO ME. STICK TO YOUR JOB.

It feels as if her magic suddenly fills the closed space of the cabin.

Stian blinks and fixes his eyes on the road. He doesn't utter another word during the rest of the drive to the hospital.

The blanket flutters in the wind and Linnéa pulls it tighter around her. Engelsfors looks almost beautiful from where she is on the roof of the tall apartment building where she lives. She drags on her cigarette and looks at all the familiar places. The lines of streetlights form geometric patterns in the darkness. The fire on Olsson's Hill has started to die down. The howling sirens that criss-crossed the town earlier are quiet now.

Linnéa has one last puff and stubs her cigarette out against the tarred surface of the roof. She has been sitting here for hours, writing and sketching in her diary until the sun began to set. She stayed on because it felt impossible to go downstairs into the dark, silent apartment.

Then Vanessa's text arrived. She was at a boring party. And, as usual, Linnéa admitted immediately that she was available.

When she senses Vanessa's energy field approaching, she walks to the edge of the roof and sees the blonde hair shining in the street.

Linnéa projects a thought.

I'm on the roof. Come up.

Vanessa looks up and waves.

OK.

Linnéa sits down again. Vanessa's energy grows stronger

until the gray steel door to the stairwell opens and she steps out onto the roof. She is wearing a micro dress with only an open jeans jacket on top. She holds her high-heeled shoes in her hand. Her skin-colored tights are so thin that her legs look bare.

'Why are you sitting here?' She walks toward Linnéa.

'Why not?' Linnéa replies, smiling.

Vanessa's glittery earrings tinkle faintly as she sits down. She hardly looks at Linnéa.

It's so odd. When she is not with Vanessa, Linnéa longs for her all the time. But sometimes, like now, being with Vanessa makes the longing more intense. To have her there, so close, but still not truly to have her, not in the way she really wants to.

'You smell of smoke,' Linnéa says. 'It's almost like . . .'

'Barbecued sausage . . . I know.'

'Actually it made me think of when we dreamt about Matilda for the first time.'

Vanessa doesn't reply. She is stiff in a way that is utterly different from her usual body language. Linnéa suddenly feels worried. It's as if Vanessa has wound herself up to speak about something. Something difficult.

She would feel really bad if she had to tell me that she's going out with Wille again, Linnéa thinks.

'Please, give me a cig,' Vanessa says. Linnéa's certain now that something must be wrong. Vanessa hardly ever smokes.

'Only if you tell me what's up,' Linnéa tells her.

She lights a cigarette and hands it to Vanessa.

'Nothing special,' Vanessa says, in the way that tells you the opposite is true.

'Did something happen at the party?'

'It got out of hand.'

Linnéa tries to look into Vanessa's eyes, but she keeps staring fixedly at the glowing tip of her cigarette, rather than smoking.

'What happened?'

'Oh, please. Not now. I mean, I don't want to talk about them now.'

'*Them*, who?'

Vanessa sighs.

'Erik and Robin came. And Erik and Kevin started fighting. After that, it was a massive clusterfuck.'

Linnéa is fingering the stitched edge of the blanket. Her hands are surprisingly steady given that she goes shaky inside at just hearing their names. She detests being so weak. She detests the fact that those cowardly little creeps Erik and Robin are able to make her react like this. And she detests Vanessa's assumption that she must be treated with kid gloves.

'Why didn't you tell me straight?' she asks. 'You don't have to hide things because you worry that I'll have a breakdown or whatever. That just makes me feel worse.'

'You don't get it!' Vanessa hisses and gets up, throws the cigarette away and picks up her shoes. 'You just don't get it!'

Now Linnéa is standing, too, and the blanket slips off her shoulders. The wind catches it and tumbles it over the edge of the roof.

'What is it that I don't get?' she says. 'That you treat me like a fucking mental case?'

Vanessa stands looking at her for a moment. Then she turns and starts walking toward the door.

Linnéa stays where she is. She can't get her head around what just happened. But she does know one thing: she can't bear a repeat of last summer, when they didn't talk to each other for months.

Vanessa tugs the stairwell door open.

Wait!

Linnéa calls out into Vanessa's head and she stops.

'I'm sorry,' Linnéa says. 'Please don't go.'

Vanessa lets the door slide shut again. But she doesn't turn around.

'I am really sorry. You know how I get sometimes.' Linnéa comes closer.

'Yes, I know,' Vanessa replies quietly.

'Trust me to lose it like that. I guess I *am* a mental case.'

She has tried to use a light tone of voice, but Vanessa turns quickly to face her and looks seriously at her.

'You mustn't ever say that.'

Linnéa is dumbstruck. Both are very still as they meet each other's eyes. And something changes in the silence between them.

'I'm going to do it now,' Vanessa says.

And then she gives Linnéa a kiss.

A light kiss, on the lips.

Linnéa is so surprised that she takes one step back. Vanessa looks terrified, as if she has just realized she has made the biggest mistake of her life.

'I'm so sorry,' Vanessa tells her.

'Why are you sorry?'

'The way you looked . . . as if you didn't want to . . . that I shouldn't . . . do what I did.'

Linnéa wishes that she could express how often she has dreamt of this moment, how much she has longed for it. But words seem too small.

She takes a step forward, gently puts her hand on the back of Vanessa's neck. Her skin is warm. The sensation is dizzying, as if she is standing on the edge of the roof.

This time she feels that Vanessa's lips are as soft as she'd always imagined.

Vanessa hugs her tight and Linnéa dares – quite how, she cannot think – to let her hand slip under the jacket just where it ends at the small of the back. She senses the warmth through the thin fabric of the dress.

Their kiss becomes more intense, deepens. It feels like being in free fall, like plunging straight into an alternative universe where the impossible suddenly is possible, where fantasies become reality and you are given exactly what you have wished for.

A light slowly grows stronger, strong enough to pierce Linnéa's eyelids. As if the sun has risen again. And perhaps it has. Perhaps she has been kissing Vanessa all night long. Perhaps dawn has come.

Vanessa carefully frees herself from their embrace and Linnéa opens her eyes. Above them the sky is glowing orange.

'Look, over there.' Vanessa points at the horizon.

In the far distance, Engelsfors sawmill is on fire. It lights the town like a gigantic May Day Eve bonfire.

And Linnéa's phone starts ringing.

CHAPTER 8

It looks like the middle of the day. On Mars.

Minoo stands next to Anna-Karin. Both are looking out through the window of the small room off the ER reception that is set aside for visitors. The sky itself seems to be on fire. Far away, a huge pillar of smoke is rising from the sawmill. The one owned by Ida's father.

'Why don't they tell us anything?' Anna-Karin asks. 'Why not let us know what they're doing?'

Her voice is as tired and empty as the look in her eyes.

'It'll be OK,' Minoo replies.

Precisely the kind of stupid platitude that complete idiots utter when something terrible has happened. Clearly, Minoo is one of those idiots.

'Why do you say that? You don't even know what's wrong with her.'

'All I mean is . . . Mia isn't that old,' Minoo says.

Anna-Karin doesn't respond. For a start, Mia isn't that young. Also, she's a heavy smoker and hardly ever moves. Worse, she seems to have lost the will to live. How will she find the energy to fight?

'I miss Nicolaus,' Anna-Karin murmurs.

Her face glows in the firelight.

'Me, too,' Minoo says.

She puts her hand on Anna-Karin's arm, but feels awkward.

'Vanessa and Linnéa will be here soon.' She takes her hand away. 'Would you like a coffee?'

Anna-Karin mumbles something that might be yes. The

coffee machine is crammed into a gap between a small sofa and the wall. Minoo puts a paper mug in place, then hesitates. Did Anna-Karin actually say yes? If so, would she like milk in her coffee? Minoo doesn't want to ask. It would feel like another piece of idiotic chatter, going on about stuff like milk and coffee at a time like this.

The walls are decorated with a border showing little lambs that gambol happily in very green grass. They seem to glare accusingly at Minoo.

She guesses and picks CAFÉ AU LAIT. The machine just sits there. She tries a couple of other buttons. Nothing happens.

Then they hear the sounds of high heels and of boots in the hallway outside. Next, Vanessa and Linnéa stand in the doorway. Vanessa in a tiny dress and glittering earrings, Linnéa in head-to-toe black: jeans and a hoodie. Her eyes under long bangs are thickly outlined with eyeliner.

Vanessa walks straight over to the window and puts her arms around Anna-Karin. Minoo notes that Anna-Karin's tense shoulders relax a little.

For the first time tonight, Minoo feels close to tears. But she swallows and gets back in control. She has no right to cry when Anna-Karin isn't. The last thing Anna-Karin needs now is for one of her friends to crack.

Minoo keeps pressing coffee machine buttons at random.

I am so totally useless at this kind of thing, Linnéa's voice says inside Minoo's head. *I can't think what to say to her.*

Me neither, Minoo thinks. *Not that it stopped me. Unfortunately. I guess it's better to say nothing.*

They hear sobbing. Minoo and Linnéa simultaneously look toward the window.

Anna-Karin is crying on Vanessa's shoulder, while Vanessa is stroking her back. Minoo takes in the uncomplicated physicality that comes so easily to Vanessa, despising herself for being unable to show warmth, even when one of her friends needs it more than anything else.

'I'm off to look for coffee,' Minoo tells no one in particular.

'Get some for me too, please,' Linnéa says quietly.

Minoo takes out her cell once she is in the hallway. She badly wants to talk to her mother. But there are signs up everywhere showing an ancient cell phone scoured out with an angry red cross. She jogs along the hallway toward the door to the stairwell.

The ceiling lights are off, but the stairs are lit by that extra-terrestrial glow. Minoo dials her mother's number, hoping that she isn't on a late shift. She wishes that her mom still lived at home and did her doctoring in Engelsfors hospital. That she was here now.

'Hi, *azizam!*'

Minoo hears voices in the background. A barking laugh that could only come from Aunt Bahar.

'Mom . . .' Minoo begins.

Suddenly the full force of the night's events come crashing down on her. She chokes on the words.

'*Bacheye aziz,*' Mom is saying. 'Has something happened?'

The phone crackles, her mother's voice is so fractured that Minoo can hardly understand her.

She starts walking up the stairs.

'It's Anna-Karin's mother,' she says.

'What about Anna-Karin? It's very bad reception.'

Minoo moves toward the window and the reception improves a little.

'She collapsed. Anna-Karin's mother did.'

'Relax, Minoo. Breathe. And then talk to me.'

Minoo realizes that she is practically hyperventilating and forces herself to breathe normally. And then the words flow. Everything seems more real when she can tell Mom. She has to fight not to burst into wild tears.

'Mom, do you think I did anything wrong? Do you?'

'Minoo . . .'

The crackling drowns her mother's voice and Minoo keeps

walking upstairs to ground level. She goes out into a hallway.

'Can you hear me?' she says into the phone, but gets no reply.

Walking quickly now, she passes openings into dully lit hallways and arrives at a small café. The tables inside are decorated with plastic flowers in little vases. It is closed.

'Can you hear me now?' Minoo asks.

'Now I can hear you,' Mom says, sounding relieved.

'What if I did something wrong, if I made it worse? Do you think I did?'

'It sounds like you handled it really well,' Mom reassures her.

Minoo can tell by her voice that she is in doctor mode.

'You did exactly the right thing, Minoo.'

'But, Mom, what could it have been?' Minoo asks. 'Do you think it was a heart attack? Or a stroke? What could be so sudden?'

'There are lots . . . I can't tell without . . .'

Minoo's phone goes dead. She checks the display. Transmission error.

She tries to reconnect but fails. Then, as she pockets the cell, she spots a coffee machine just outside the café.

This machine works and the smell of instant coffee makes things feel a little more ordinary. Minoo fixes four mugs of *café latte*, then attempts to carry them all without burning her fingers.

She walks slowly to avoid the coffee slopping over, wondering how she'll manage to open the door to the stairwell.

She is aware of the darkness in the hallways leading off the main one. And the silence. Shouldn't somebody be around? Just to keep an eye out?

She takes an uncertain step and splashes coffee on her right hand. Stops and swears loudly. Blows on the hot liquid. Starts walking again.

And then she hears it. Coming from behind her in the

hallway. The sound of breathing. Minoo stops, the hairs on the back of her neck standing on end.

She has no reason to be scared. This is a public place. Presumably someone else is out hunting for coffee. Someone who breathes very loudly, with an effort.

Minoo turns to look.

The first thing she notices is his hospital-issue clothing. White shirt with the local authority logo. Floppy gray pants. It takes her several seconds to recognize him.

In her nightmares, he has always looked the same as when she first knew him.

The mugs of coffee fall from her hands and hit the floor so that the contents splash her jeans.

Max.

He seems to have aged a whole lifetime. His body is emaciated. His pale skin has a sickly yellow tinge. His hair has been shaved and his head is bare and skull-like.

It isn't possible, Minoo thinks. He has been lying in a coma for more than a year; one can't simply get up and start walking . . . He takes a step toward Minoo.

She screams, then slips in the puddle of coffee, falls and hits her tailbone so hard that she stops breathing for a moment, just like the time she fell on the ice and he helped her up.

The fluorescent lights in the ceiling start to flicker.

Minoo.

She looks up at him. His eyes are black, like crude oil. Black, like a bird's eyes.

The lights crackle.

Minoo.

His voice is inside her head. His bird's eyes are watching her. Black smoke is billowing around him.

You will not get away.

Minoo tries to concentrate. Tries to emit her own black smoke. But, just as in her nightmares, she is helpless. Against him, she's helpless.

He takes another step forward and she pulls herself backward with her hands, then tries to get up.

STOP!

Her body stiffens. She lies on the floor, supports herself on her elbows and looks at him as he comes closer.

He is surrounded by blackness now. Coils of smoke rise all the way to the ceiling. Behind him, smoke fills the whole hallway.

And he smiles.

They have blessed me once more. Their power is everywhere inside me. Soon, the portal can be opened. I am stronger than ever.

'Please . . .' Minoo manages to say.

SILENCE!

Her jaws slam shut, her lips are pressed together.

Max is standing just beside her now. His unblinking bird's eyes are fixed on her.

This time I am stronger than you are.

He kneels at her side. His face is only a hand's breadth from hers. He stinks of disinfectant, decay, and something much worse.

I am going to kill you now, Minoo.

And inside her head, she hears his command, hears him order her body to stop breathing. The muscles that move her ribcage are paralyzed. She tries to draw breath but nothing happens.

Max observes her.

At first, they promised that I could have Alice back. Then they promised me you. But you ruined everything. You chose your friends instead. You chose this worthless world rather than me.

It feels as if she is back in the bathtub when Max tried to drown her. Her lungs seem about to burst. She tries to rouse her body, tries to make it fight back, but nothing happens. Nothing helps against this.

Max reaches out with his hand and places it on her cheek; ice-cold moisture touches her arm. Minoo's field of vision is clouded with black spots.

We could have been together, Minoo. You and I. But you betrayed me. You deserve to die. Just as Alice did, back then. But they have promised that once I have helped them to open the portal, I shall have her back. And then she will be just the way I want her.

Another smile. He looks like a wild beast. And, at last, fury explodes inside Minoo.

From deep inside her, the power of the guardians erupts. In an instant, her smoke envelops them both. Her paralysis lifts and she takes a deep breath. The rush of oxygen almost makes her dizzy. She hits out at his hand.

No . . .

Suddenly, she can see his new blessing. And it is flawed; something is wrong with it. Its flaring black flames are burning too intensely. Her instinct tells her that she must not even think of trying to put the fire out; instead she must get as far away from him as possible.

You don't understand! You haven't even a chance of winning!

She manages to stand. Her head is spinning and she supports herself against the wall. Starts backing toward the stairwell. Her chest hurts with each breath.

Stop. Don't go.

Max's controlling thoughts only brush past her. She flicks them away like annoying insects. Meanwhile, she sees the black fire blazing around him where he stands with his claw-like hands held out.

Nothing is as you think.

She continues backing toward the stairwell. Sees how Max's body starts to shake.

Nothing is as you think. Noth . . .

Max's throat lets out a cracked, inhuman cry. He bends back

and howls at the ceiling as the black fire grows and grows, closes around him, swallows him. He sinks to the floor, writhing. Demonic magic is consuming him.

Minoo turns and runs along the last stretch of the hallway, then tugs open the door to the stairwell.

She hears his screaming behind her, and can still hear it as she runs downstairs and into the ER hallway. She closes the door behind her. Stops.

The only sounds now are ordinary hospital noises and her own labored breathing.

With the pulse hammering at her temples, she walks toward the visitors' room. The base of her spine aches. She can't think how to explain this to the others; can't think even how to take it in herself.

She stops in the doorway.

Vanessa sits on the sofa, holding Anna-Karin in her arms. Linnéa, who stands close by, looks up, and Minoo understands what has happened even before she hears Linnéa think it.

The Borderland

CHAPTER 9

Ida is falling through the light; she falls and falls for what feels like an eternity.

Then, abruptly, she is standing somewhere high up, with a view across a deep blue sea. The sun is a glowing, white-hot sphere that colors the whole horizon red. Far below the rock she stands on, Ida looks out over lovely, serene beaches with not a soul in sight. This could have been the perfect holiday spot. That is, if it hadn't been for the smell of manure.

She turns and sees an expanse of hilly grassland, scorched by the sun. Further up the slope above her, Ida identifies a vineyard, or something like that. Beyond it, a tower is just visible. Not far from her, several goats graze.

'What the hell is this?' she says out loud.

Then she spots a figure hurrying down the slope: a boy of her own age, with black curly hair and large, dark eyes. He would be kind of hot if it weren't for his clothes. He is wrapped in a red cape and wears a darkish-green, knee-length tunic underneath. Worse, his feet are strapped into leather sandals – and that's an absolute no-no for guys. He is carrying a bag on his shoulder.

'Hey, please,' Ida says when he has come closer. 'Is this some fucking LARP?'

No response.

A man is shouting from somewhere.

'Alkides!'

Two men appear at the crest of the hill. The guy glances over his shoulder. Speeds up.

The Key

'Alkides!' It's the same voice. 'Stop!'

Their language is completely different from the one used by the people in the grand gallery. But Ida understands this one as well.

'Alkides!'

The man sounds really angry now. Alkides stops. And waits, tight-jawed, for his pursuers to catch up.

The two men are probably both in their fifties. The man who did the shouting has thick, raven-black hair and a large beard. His cape and tunic are dark blue. He is broad-shouldered, and his large hands look strong enough to crush someone's head. The other man, who is simply dressed in a kind of white sheet, has gray hair and a gray beard. Around his neck, a small glass disc dangles from a leather strap. He holds a cylinder of leather in one hand and he looks like a schoolbook illustration of an ancient Greek philosopher.

Then it strikes Ida that he might actually *be* an ancient Greek philosopher.

Time and space are different for you now.

One couldn't accuse Matilda of exaggerating.

It is so fucking unfair that I have to be the one that this happens to, Ida thinks. After everything else.

The broad-shouldered man rips the bag from Alkides's grip and empties its contents on the ground. A loaf of bread. A silver bowl with the signs of the six elements engraved in the bottom. A hunting knife with a black handle. A leather bag with something in it.

'So, where do you think you were going?' the big man says, staring threateningly at Alkides.

'Home.'

The big man snorts and Alkides's expression darkens.

'Kimon, I'm serious,' he says.

'My dear boy.' The gray-haired man hobbles a little closer. 'His men would capture you within moments of your first steps on land.'

The goats are bleating as they start to trot slowly up the slope. They've probably picked up the bad vibes.

'I *want* them to capture me,' Alkides says. 'I want them to take me to him. So I can kill him.'

Kimon snorts again.

'Kill him? You? He's not only one of the most powerful men in Athens, he is also the demons' Blessed One—'

'And I am the Chosen One!' Alkides interrupts. 'You're to show me respect!'

The fury in Kimon's eyes frightens Ida. But, even so, she is unprepared for what Kimon does next: he raises his gigantic hand and slaps Alkides's face.

The blow is enough to fell him.

'My dear boy,' the gray-haired man says. 'I understand how hard this is for you. But, as members of the Council, it is our duty to protect you, against yourself as well.'

'You tell me to run away and hide, like a little girl,' Alkides mumbles. He uses a corner of his cape to wipe a little blood from his mouth.

'Only until the time is right for you to close the portal,' the gray-haired man tells him. 'That is when we will travel to Athens. And if you have to face the Blessed One in a fight, so be it. But not now. It is too soon.'

'You can't stop me,' Alkides gets up from the ground. 'I won't give in, so you might as well let me go!'

'Curse you, boy!' Kimon says.

'Hold it,' the gray-haired man interrupts and looks thoughtfully at Alkides. 'I can see that you are serious about this. Well then. Allow me at least to ask the guardians for advice.'

He opens one end of the leather cylinder and pulls out a roll that reminds Ida of the one she saw in the girl's hands back in that gallery.

He unwinds the roll, then lifts the glass disc to his eye. Presumably it's an older, more basic version of the Pattern Finder.

'I see . . .' he says.

He lets go of the glass lens and pushes the roll back into its cylinder. Ida can't interpret his expression.

'What did they say?' Alkides asks, still with the cape pressed against his bleeding lip.

'They said that you are ready to depart.' The gray-haired man exchanges a glance with Kimon.

Alkides looks triumphantly at them.

Kimon bends and picks up the black-handled knife. At first, Ida doesn't understand what is going on when the big man slips behind Alkides, puts one arm around his neck and thrusts the knife into his heart.

Ida screams. But she can't stop looking.

Kimon holds on to the knife, pressing Alkides's body close to his own until the young man no longer kicks and twists. The red of Alkides's cape deepens where his blood is staining it. Kimon pulls the blade out and lets the body fall. Alkides sags down onto his knees, then collapses face first into the dry grass. And lies still.

'But he was the Chosen One!' Ida screams. 'What are you doing?'

Kimon stares sadly at Alkides. Blood is dripping from the knife; it looks so small in his hand.

'So regrettable, but also essential,' the gray-haired man says. 'When our young Alkides decided to return to Athens this early, everything changed. The guardians could only see possible futures in which the demons' Blessed One would succeed in killing him and robbing him of his powers.'

He sighs deeply.

'It's all over for now. The present magic era will fade away. The next one will bring with it a new Chosen One. Hopefully, more intelligent than this one.'

'He was brave,' Kimon says.

The mist comes drifting in over the landscape. Ida can no longer see them, but she hears the gray-haired man's reply.

'Bravery without common sense never helped anyone. Don't blame yourself. You did what you had to do. The key did not fall into the wrong hands. True, we can't lock the portal now, but no Blessed One can open it either.'

He falls silent.

All is silence.

'What the hell?' Ida whispers as she spins around, but now the grayness has closed in around her. 'Oh, damn, damn, damn.'

She starts walking quickly, but looks over her shoulder now and then, trying to sense if there is someone out there.

Where the hell is Matilda? Did the invisible thing catch up with her?

Ida is running now, searching the fog around her, expecting every moment that something is going to jump at her. She releases her magic. Watches as her fingertips sparkle with lightning. And realizes that they might light up the grayness around her.

She swears and extinguishes the light at once. No need to make herself glow like a neon sign if whatever-it-is is chasing her. But at least she has a way of defending herself if need be.

She looks around. Is this where Matilda has been staying ever since her death? For hundreds of years? No wonder she has gone a bit weird.

Suddenly, she sees a yellow light source straight ahead. Ida stops and then hesitates for a moment. But anything would be better than hanging out here. After all, Matilda told her to look out for the lights.

Ida takes one step forward.

This time she doesn't fall. She just stands there.

She is in a living room. Minoo's living room.

Such a sense of relief.

I'm back, Ida thinks. I am back.

CHAPTER 10

Ida looks at Minoo, who is curled up in the corner of the sofa. Her forehead is resting on her knees. Linnéa sits close by, biting one of her bright pink nails and glancing worriedly at Minoo.

'Hi there,' Ida says.

But they can't hear her. Of course they can't.

'How do you feel now?' Linnéa asks.

Minoo mumbles something against her knees.

'What did you say?'

Minoo looks up and changes position. Her black, curly hair is dull and lifeless. She is pale; her eyes are red with crying and her skin hasn't improved since Ida last saw her.

'I said I don't know how I am,' Minoo says. She licks her lips, which are desperately in need of some lip balm. 'It's just too much to . . .'

She falls silent.

'Take?' Linnéa suggests.

Minoo nods.

'He almost killed me. Again.'

'He, who?' Ida asks. 'What's this about? What terrible thing has happened now?'

Steps on the stairs. Vanessa comes in, holding her cell phone. She, too, has been crying.

'She's asleep now,' she says. 'I told her to call us or text us if there's anything at all.'

'Is that Anna-Karin?' Ida asks. 'Listen, what *is* going on?'

Vanessa slumps down on an armchair, puts her cell on the coffee table and all three of them sit in silence for a while.

Ida walks over to Vanessa. Even before she tries to touch her shoulder, Ida knows what will happen. Her hand slips straight through her and then through the armchair.

Not totally dead not totally dead not totally dead.

'Minoo, have you told your father about Anna-Karin?' Vanessa asks.

'He wanted to come back but I told him it was better if we were alone with her just now. Besides, he's so busy writing about the fire.' She moistens her lips again. 'He had just heard about the dead body that the police found in the hospital.'

'So at least he's really dead!' Vanessa sounds so relieved.

The dead person clearly wasn't one of Vanessa's favorite people.

'The police think that he must have woken up from his coma, managed to get out of his room and then had a heart attack from sheer effort,' Minoo says.

They must be talking about Max.

'He said that *nothing is as we believe it to be,*' Minoo tells them.

'Max said that?' Linnéa asks her.

Minoo nods. A chill crawls through Ida.

'He and the demons were trying to freak you out,' Vanessa tells her. 'It didn't mean anything.'

But it did mean something. Ida is sure of it. Already, she knows so much that the others don't; all sorts of stuff that the guardians haven't told them about. Like, the Chosen Ones being a key. And that the Key is not complete.

Ida must tell them.

An electric shock should do the trick, attract their attention. She tries to release her magic. But nothing happens. She is just as out of magic as they all were when they swapped bodies once. Non-magical and utterly frustrated.

'Hello!' she shouts.

'What happened to him, do you know?' Vanessa asks. 'Why did he die?'

'You've got to listen to me!' Ida shouts. 'Just fucking focus for a moment.'

She kicks the table but her foot goes right through. She almost loses her balance.

'I don't know exactly,' Minoo says. 'But it seemed to me that the demons might have pumped too much magic into him. His body simply couldn't cope.'

Ida starts pacing up and down the floor. How come she can feel that under her feet but still not grab hold of anything?

'Shit! What's happening?' she screams.

'What do the guardians say?' Linnéa asks.

'The *Book of Patterns* refuses to talk to me,' Minoo says.

And then, from the corner of her eye, Ida spots grayness welling up.

'No!' she exclaims, but the living room has vanished already. Ida feels like screaming out loud, but she no longer dares to.

She starts running. And it doesn't take long before she catches sight of a bright bluish light in the distance.

It's an office with fluorescent tubes in the ceiling.

Minoo and Anna-Karin sit on the sofa and Minoo's father sits on a chair near them. A young woman with really short, bottle-blonde hair is seated behind a desk and checks out a bunch of papers. She has a small, glittering jewel in one nostril.

Minoo and her dad look intently at her. Anna-Karin keeps staring at her hands.

'Hello?' Ida says, though she knows it's useless.

'I do realize your present situation is very difficult,' the blonde says sympathetically.

For a brief, wonderful moment, Ida thinks she is being talked to.

'You have never heard anything from your father.' The blonde looks at Anna-Karin. 'That's correct, isn't it?'

'I don't even know if he's alive.' Anna-Karin's voice is barely audible.

'I see. And your maternal grandfather stays in a home for the elderly, doesn't he?'

Anna-Karin nods.

'Also, your mother had no brothers or sisters. Are you in contact with any other relatives?'

'No.'

An icy hand squeezes Ida's heart. Because now she understands. Anna-Karin's mother has died and that must have been why she wasn't with the others talking about Max.

'You are not yet eighteen,' the blonde woman points out, presumably because she's some kind of social worker. 'It means that we are obliged to investigate the Falk-Karimi family before we are able to agree to let you live with them.'

'Is that really necessary?' Minoo's dad asks. 'Of course it's good that you are so conscientious, but she will be eighteen in just a few months.'

'We have to, for the sake of appearances,' the social worker says. 'But it's fine for Anna-Karin to stay with you in the meantime.'

Minoo and her dad look more relaxed and Anna-Karin gives a little sigh that might have been a thank you.

The social worker keeps talking.

'Your mother had no life insurance. But she did leave you a certain amount of money in the bank. For as long as you have an independent source of income, we can't offer you cash benefits. But the Falk-Karimi family will be compensated for housing you for as long as you attend high school.'

'We'll take care of her.' Minoo's dad pats Anna-Karin's shoulder awkwardly.

Around Ida, the gray curtains are closing and she is once more alone in the fog.

Except, she's not alone. The invisible being is there, somewhere.

She runs blindly. Onwards, onwards, one step after another. Someone screams behind her. Was it really a scream? Or did she imagine it? She has no intention of stopping and investigating.

Then suddenly, there is the light. This time, a warm, rose-colored glow.

She hears the rolling of surf against a beach and the sound of panpipes, then picks up the smells of incense and cigarette smoke.

Someone coughs and clears his or her throat in the way that can only lead to a mouthful of mucus. It is right up there as one of the yuckiest sounds in the world and Ida is running straight at it.

She finds herself in the Crystal Cave. She looks around quickly, but the Borderland is nowhere and the invisible thing has vanished, too.

Mona Moonbeam is sitting on a stool behind the counter. Her arms are crossed and she stares angrily at Vanessa, who is leaning forward across the counter. Vanessa's denim shorts are so micro you can almost see the lower part of her buttocks.

'What are you really after?' Mona sounds fed up.

'I want to know why you didn't warn her,' Vanessa says.

Ida gets closer to them. They must be talking about her.

'That's exactly what I did,' Mona tells her. 'I told her to use the time that was left well.'

'But you didn't let on that it was her mother who was close to death. She thought you meant her granddad.'

Now, of course Ida feels sorry for Anna-Karin, but she wishes they'd talk about *Ida* just once in a while. Does no one remember? Or miss her just the tiniest little bit?

'Oh dear. Most humble apologies, Miss!' Mona says.

She lights a cigarette and slaps the lighter down on the counter. Her cheap silver bracelets rattle.

'What's the use of making fucking prophecies when you only ever tell half-truths? Or things that are totally wrong! Like what you said about Ida!' Vanessa says.

'Exactly!' Ida exclaims.

Mona starts, then scans the shop. Her eyes flick back and forth across the shelf next to which Ida is standing.

'Can't you see me?' Ida asks her.

She suddenly adores the grisly old bag. Steps a bit closer to the counter.

'Mona, can you hear me?'

Mona turns back to Vanessa.

'You had better get this,' she says. 'I tell people what I see. But the fact is that you don't always get the entire goddamn list of contents. Sometimes you're only given glimpses that you have to interpret to the best of your ability.'

The year ahead will be hard and dark for you. Still, you'll get what you were promised. So plodding on is worth it.

A pretty pointless forecast if you're to die later that very evening.

'If that's the case, isn't your talent pretty pointless?' Ida feels like applauding Vanessa.

'My talent pays your wages,' Mona reminds her. 'I suggest you get on with your work or get out of here. For good. And you can forget about my help next time you need more ecto.'

The bell on the door tinkles and Ida turns to see who's come in. It's Leffe, the guy who runs Leffe's Kiosk. He smells of pipe smoke and aftershave. It looks as if he has even made an attempt to dress properly.

'Look who's here! Welcome!' Mona beams ingratiatingly at him.

Leffe looks embarrassed and mumbles something. Mona gets up and walks over to the red velvet curtain in the corner. She pulls it back and hangs out a sign that says PROPHECY IN PROGRESS.

'Wait!' Ida cries out. If *anyone* can hear her, the crazy soothsayer should be able to.

Ida hurries after Leffe. But on the other side of the curtain is only the Borderland. And when she turns to look behind her, the Crystal Cave is gone.

She starts running again. Her own breathing is the only sound. She scrutinizes the mist for another source of light and finds it almost at once, though it is only a few shades lighter than the rest of the dullness. She runs on and into the light, runs until she feels gravel under her feet.

The dance pavilion in the Kärrgruvan fairground emerges from the mist. Anna-Karin and Minoo sit side by side on the stage. Linnéa and Vanessa stand on the dance floor, facing each other and holding hands. A plastic water bottle is on the floor between them.

Ida looks around, then walks closer to the pavilion.

The trees are in leaf and the blackbirds sing as though they're possessed. Spring has come. She steps into the pavilion.

A silver cross is lying on the stage near Minoo, who fingers it absentmindedly. It's the cross that protects the Chosen Ones from being found by their enemies.

It would have been plenty useful for Ida, if only she could have brought it to the Borderland.

'Go for it,' Minoo says, looking at Vanessa and Linnéa. 'See what happens.'

Vanessa and Linnéa nod and Ida watches as they squeeze each other's hand harder. The bottle begins to wobble. A light gust of wind flows through the pavilion and plays with Vanessa's freshly blonded hair. And then, suddenly, the water starts flowing out and upwards, becoming a stream that gently twists around itself until the bottle is empty.

Vanessa giggles and the water splashes on the dance floor. The bottle falls over and rolls out of the way.

'Oh, shit!' Vanessa exclaims. 'I couldn't keep it going any longer.'

'But you did do it!' Minoo sounds quite exalted.

Anna-Karin is the only one who isn't smiling. She just sits there. As Ida watches her, the mist comes drifting back and obscures them all. Ida takes a few steps toward them but realizes that she's already too late. She is back in the Borderland.

This time, she finds a light without looking for it. The source is right in front of her. She takes another step and glimpses pavement beneath the whirling veils of mist. Another step and the air clears.

Ahead of her stands the scorched, disintegrating skeleton of a large building. It seems familiar and yet isn't. Then she spots a metal sign. Badly burnt, but a part of the lettering is still readable, enough for her to recognize her own surname in the sloping font she has seen so many times.

It is the sawmill.

Dad's sawmill.

Dad.

Ida doesn't want to think about him. Doesn't want to think about where he might have been when the mill caught fire.

She hears Vanessa's voice and turns toward the sound. Vanessa and Linnéa are walking along side by side; they stop a few feet away from Ida.

'No one will see us here,' Vanessa says.

She takes Linnéa's hand. Ida assumes they are trying out some more witchcraft, but instead they kiss.

'What are you doing?' Ida asks. 'What the hell are you up to?'

They keep making out. Vanessa's hands sneak into the back pockets of Linnéa's jeans.

'Excuse me, but how long has this been going on?' Ida demands, her voice going falsetto. 'Is it, like, common knowledge? To everyone except me?'

Linnéa suddenly backs away.

'What is it?' Vanessa asks.

'Nothing. I have to go home. Some stuff I must fix for school tomorrow.'

Vanessa looks confused. Ida can't blame her; Linnéa's behavior is odder than ever.

'Fine,' Vanessa says.

The silence between them is awkward.

'When are we going to tell the others?' Vanessa finally asks.

'Tell them? What's there to tell?'

Vanessa stares at her.

'Look, I didn't mean to put it like that,' Linnéa says quickly. 'All I wanted to say was . . . I guess we don't really know . . . what this really is. Maybe we should wait a little. After all, so much is happening . . .'

'OK,' Vanessa replies, but it's obvious that she doesn't feel it's OK in the slightest.

Linnéa reaches out to her and they kiss again. Ida cannot help remembering Gustaf and the one and only time he kissed her.

The *Book of Patterns* had lured her on, promising her that kiss. It would be her reward for doing what the guardians told her. Except they must have known all along that it wasn't going to be a real kiss, but G trying to save her life with mouth-to-mouth resuscitation.

The guardians must have seen ahead and known that she was going to die.

But then, maybe they're like Mona, Ida thinks. Perhaps they can't see the whole truth, or perhaps they are bound to misunderstand what they see sometimes.

She watches as Vanessa and Linnéa start walking toward the center of town.

'But there's so much that the guardians haven't even mentioned,' Ida says out loud. 'Why are they hiding things from us? I don't understand . . .'

She looks up and down the burnt ruin of the sawmill again. The wind is whistling through the skeleton, making a hollow sound.

Dad. Surely he wasn't in there when it caught fire? He can't have . . . he mustn't . . .

The gray curtains wrap themselves around her once more. She starts running, her eyes sweeping across the grayness.

Until she suddenly halts. In front of her feet she sees a strong red light. As bright as a traffic light. As a *stop* light.

No other lights in the distance.

She closes her eyes and jumps.

When she opens her eyes, she sees it in the sky.

The blood-red moon.

Chapter 11

Ida hears a stream. She stands in a clearing in a forest, sur-rounded by spruce and pine trees. The blood-red moon glows in the sky, but its light is so bleak that the world around her looks like a black-and-white film. Frost glitters on the dead grass.

A branch cracks and she flinches. Soon afterward, she hears heavy splashing. Between the trees, she makes out a stream that reflects the moonlight. Someone is wading in the water and she catches a glimpse of a pale face and light-colored clothing.

Matilda. Now she steps into the clearing and Ida feels a surge of relief.

'Matilda!'

Matilda's light nightdress is wet and makes a sloshing sound as she walks. Her eyes stare blindly. She moves like a sleepwalker. A robot under remote control. And Ida suddenly understands.

This is *Matilda's* blood-red moon. They are in Engelsfors in the seventeenth century.

'No,' Ida says. 'Please.'

Matilda stops abruptly, kneels and stays in the same position. A black bird flies into the air above them, then lands on Matilda's shoulder. Is that her familiar?

The wind rustles in the tops of the pine trees. Ida hears whispers, by many voices and a single one at the same time.

Don't be afraid. We will not harm you. We will help you.

It is a gentle voice, full of good intent. The language has an odd ring to it but it's Swedish and Ida feels she could understand it even without her brand-new linguistic brilliance.

Matilda instantly becomes less tense and Ida realizes that she has regained control over her body. She crouches, holds the bird in her hands and strokes its feathers.

You are the Chosen One, the voices say, and seem to merge into a single one. *You will save the world from the evil forces that try to enter our world. The last portal is here in Engelsfors and you are the one who shall close it.*

'It cannot be,' Matilda whispers. 'It cannot be me . . . that I should be the Chosen One . . .'

You have felt that your abilities have become less and less predictable. More powerful. Harder to control. You have been fearful.

'Yes,' Matilda whispers, tears beginning to stream down her cheeks. 'It is true.'

You cannot risk harboring doubts about what fate awaits you. For now, you are hidden from the gaze of your enemies by strong protective magic. But it will not stay strong enough forever.

'The enemy? The demons?' Matilda sounds terrified.

Yes. If they win, flames will consume the world.

'Who are you?'

We are the guardians. We have been watching over mankind since the beginning of time. We founded the Council but the Council have forgotten us. They are too legalistic to understand. Tell them that you are called, but do not tell them about us.

Ida shuts her eyes tight.

'I don't want to be here,' she says. 'I want to go home. Back to the present.'

But, then, if one can jump about like this, from one time to the next, what is the real present? Can the past, the present and the future really overlap like this? What was it Adriana said about time being circular? And what the fuck does that mean anyway?

83

Ida opens her eyes. She sees a room with plain, white-limed walls that seem to pulsate in the fluttering glow from the hearth. A fire with blue flames. Magic fire.

Matilda stands near a table. She is wearing a simple gray dress and her long, reddish-blonde hair is falling loose over her shoulders and back. On the table in front of her lies a silver cross. Light falls on it from a candle in a pewter candlestick. Nicolaus's silver cross looked exactly like that one. Could it be the same cross? Must be, surely, because Nicolaus himself stands a bit away, near one of the small windows. His dress is clerical, a black dress coat and white collar that looks a little like a bib. His hair is longer and darker than Ida has seen it, and his face less furrowed. The Cat, his familiar, lies curled up at his feet. Its fur is thick and glossy and it still has both its eyes.

There are four men standing close to Nicolaus. Pattern Finders dangle from silver chains around their necks and the fattest of the men holds a copy of the *Book of Patterns*. Ida knows zilch about fashion in the seventeenth century, but no one could miss that these guys are expensively dressed. The colors are strong; long lace cuffs protrude from their sleeves. The fat man's dark green jacket is covered in gold embroidery. Clearly, he is the boss. Ida also knows nothing about social hierarchy in the 1600s, but she can spot a leader a mile off.

'Make haste, man,' the fatso commands. 'We cannot wait all night.'

'Indeed so, Master,' a man says.

At first, Ida hadn't noticed him, as he was hidden among the shadows. Now he takes center stage. He has the same type of moustache as the rest of them and blonde, shoulder-length hair. Unlike the rest of them, he carries off his swanky clothes with style. Actually, he's quite good-looking.

'Matilda.' He turns to her. 'Are you able to state the three laws of the Council?'

She answers unhesitatingly.

'I must not use magic without the permission of the Council. I must not use magic in order to disobey the laws of the ordinary world. I must not reveal to the uninitiated that I am a witch.'

The man who questioned her nods and looks pleasantly at her.

'Good. Now, can you explain the difference between a natural witch and one who has been trained?'

Nicolaus looks nervously at his daughter.

'All human beings can learn to control magic,' she replies. 'But most people will never acquire magic abilities unless they're prepared to teach themselves with much devoted work. If they do, they become trained witches. Their abilities may or may not flourish, according to each person's nature and talents.'

Matilda lifts her head and meets the man's eyes.

'A natural witch, be it a man or a woman, has no choice,' she continues. 'They carry within them abilities that will awaken, sooner or later. A trained witch chooses magic, but a natural witch is afflicted by it.'

There is nothing cocky in what she is saying, but she still manages to make it sound cocky. Ida can see that Nicolaus is even more nervous now.

'You chose the word "afflict", although most would regard such a talent as a great blessing.'

'Naturally, my lord Baron Ehrenskiöld,' Matilda says mechanically.

Baron Ehrenskiöld. One of Alexander's forefathers. He is paler, not as tall, and not even dark-haired. But the biggest difference is that this Ehrenskiöld looks kind.

'You have answered well,' he tells her. 'We will proceed to the practical examination. Are you ready?'

Matilda nods.

'Yes, I am.'

She looks at the candle on the table, which is burning

strongly, takes a deep breath and reaches out for it. Slowly, she moves her hand closer to the flame. When Ida was younger, she used to impress Lotta and Rasmus by prodding candle flames with her finger. What Matilda does is different, slower. Far too slow. And then she holds her hand completely still, in the middle of the flame. There is a hissing sound but her hand looks unharmed.

Nicolaus relaxes, and so does Baron Ehrenskiöld.

'The fire does not hurt her,' he says.

'Nothing is proved by this,' Fatso – also known as 'Master' – pronounces.

The mist rolls in just ahead of Ida but vanishes almost as swiftly.

A perfectly normal, white full moon is lighting the scene. Matilda and Baron Ehrenskiöld are walking along a narrow path. Ida follows them. They arrive at a lake. The surroundings look different, and there is no beach, but Ida instantly recognizes Dammsjön Lake.

'You must not worry,' Baron Ehrenskiöld says quietly. 'I believe that you spoke the truth about what happened during the night of the blood-red moon. You are the Chosen One and the element of water will protect you.'

Matilda doesn't reply; though she tries to appear calm, Ida can see how fearful she is. Her familiar is circling in the air near her.

A rowing boat is pulled up on the side of the lake. In it, a man in gray clothes sits waiting. Another man in gray stands at the water's edge, brandishing a flashlight. The fat boss and his friends have arrived, and so has Nicolaus. He stands very still, but Cat is pacing anxiously up and down along the lakeside, watching Matilda.

Matilda stops near the boat and puts her hands behind her back.

Ehrenskiöld picks up a rope from the ground and ties her hands.

'Now, pull it tight,' Fatso orders.

'This will do, Master,' Ehrenskiöld says calmly.

He bends over to tighten a loop of rope around Matilda's feet. Then he carries her in his arms to the boat. Matilda tries to catch Nicolaus's eye, but he doesn't look her way.

A huge bank of fog drifts past.

Now, they are all back in the room with the lime-washed walls. Matilda is tied to a chair, slumped helplessly against ropes that are bound tightly around her. Her head is drooping; every part of her is coated with soil and her hair is plastered with clay. She seems barely alive.

Ehrenskiöld grabs her shoulder with one hand. He holds a sharply honed knife in his other hand.

'Start immediately!' the Master orders from the other side of the room. 'One more trial and then we will be ready to decide!'

He looks quite merry. The audience has grown. Twenty or more men have crowded in around Matilda.

Nicolaus is standing just outside the group. He looks pleadingly at Ehrenskiöld.

'Master.' Ehrenskiöld turns to the fat man. 'We have already seen that she can control five elements. Surely we might now agree that she is the Chosen One?'

Fatso's smile fades as he looks from Baron Ehrenskiöld to Nicolaus.

'If the minister cannot stand the strain, he had better leave now!'

Nicolaus mumbles an apology and lowers his head.

'Set to, now,' the Master says.

Ehrenskiöld draws breath and then he plunges the knife straight into Matilda's hand where it lies on the armrest of the chair. Matilda's scream blends with Ida's as Ehrenskiöld pulls the knife out and the blood spatters all over the floor. Matilda is suddenly very silent. She has fainted.

Ida turns to look at Nicolaus. At his rigid face. His withdrawn gaze.

'Why don't you do anything?' she shouts. 'She's your daughter!'

Ehrenskiöld bends to scrutinize Matilda's hand. Straightens up.

'She has stopped bleeding.' He puts the knife down on the table. 'The wound is healing already. She is also mistress of the wood element.'

'Gentlemen.' The Master turns on the other men. He sounds thrilled. 'You are in the presence of the Chosen One!'

The mist sweeps past so quickly that Ida hardly notices.

She is back in the forest. Sunlight is filtering down between the trees. Matilda crouches on the bank of the stream and hugs her familiar.

'You must forgive me,' she murmurs, stroking the feathers of her bird. 'I have to, or the ritual would not work. This is for the sake of the world.'

She closes her eyes and pushes the bird into the stream. Its wings flap and scatter water over her face and arms. Ida sees two black feathers float away in the current.

The mist flows in over her and then Ida is back, for the third time, in the white-limed room. Cold daylight streams in through the windows. Matilda is seated in the same chair. She is staring at the tools lined up on the table in front of her. Ida recognizes one of them and instantly feels sick. So this is why Nicolaus recognized the torture instrument that Adriana kept in her office. It was another one of these.

Nicolaus stands by the open fireplace with Ehrenskiöld by his side. The so-called Master and the two gray-clad men from Dammsjön Lake loom over Matilda. The Master doesn't look in the slightest bit merry now.

'Observe these!' the Master says, pointing at the tools. 'The Council has not always been as civilized as it is today. Yet we will not hesitate if using such instruments on you is what is required to make you talk.'

Christ, how Ida hates that fat monster. He is so absolutely fucking *evil*.

Matilda seems about to pass out at any moment from sheer terror. But she looks the Master in the eye.

'A new Chosen One will come,' she tells him. 'Someone who is stronger than I am.'

The Master slams his fist against the table so hard that his torture toolkit rattles and Matilda shudders in her chair.

'Dear Matilda.' Ehrenskiöld comes closer to her. 'Answer the Master. Why did you give up your powers? Is there any way in which you can get them back?'

'I did so for all your sakes,' Matilda says between clenched teeth. 'For the sake of the world.'

'You outrageous little slut,' Fatso roars. His face has gone bright red.

Matilda flinches where she sits but still looks straight at him.

'What you do to me is no great matter,' she says. 'I will not tell you more than I have. I am sworn to silence.'

'Is that so? *Sworn*, have you?' the Master shouts at top volume.

'Yes.'

'And who has induced you to do so?'

'Go ahead and tell him!' Ida says.

She wants Matilda to speak out, wants her to save herself. But Matilda only shakes her head. And, of course, Ida knows how all this will end. In her dreams, she was there in the prison wagon with Matilda when she was transported to her place of execution. And she woke with the smell of smoke from the pyre still in her hair.

'The time was so very close,' Fatso says. 'Our names would have gone down in history, become immortal! The final portal!'

His face turns from red to purple and he is breathing heavily through the nose. Ida thinks he might have a heart attack. Hopefully.

89

'Master,' Ehrenskiöld intervenes. 'This girl has clearly lost her mind—'

'Already, there are rumors making the rounds in the village!' the Master interrupts. 'Well, let her be tried for practicing witchcraft. It would be a suitable punishment.'

Nicolaus draws breath. But he still does not speak. Just stares at the floor.

'With respect, Master,' Ehrenskiöld says, 'this is surely too harsh?'

'What? There's room for two on the fire!'

Ehrenskiöld looks down. Says nothing more.

'We will stay in this godforsaken hole until justice is done. Arrest her,' the Master commands.

His gray henchmen pull Matilda from the chair.

'Don't touch me,' she cries.

She twists and struggles but she hasn't got a chance. They are laughing as they drag her from the room. The Master follows them. Ida knows that none of them will survive their stay in Engelsfors. Nicolaus will lock the church door while they are inside and set it on fire. Good.

Fatso will end up as roast pork.

Nicolaus crosses the floor to the chair where Matilda had been sitting just moments earlier. He touches the back of the chair. Then slumps slowly down until he crouches on the floor.

'I have sent her to her death,' he whispers. 'I have murdered my own child.'

Ehrenskiöld is by his side now and pulls him upright. 'You must stay calm.'

'Henrik, what shall I do? Dear friend . . . help me.'

Henrik Ehrenskiöld glances quickly over his shoulder, then leans over to whisper in Nicolaus's ear. Ida has to get closer to hear him.

'I'll help you. I'll see to it that the judge in Matilda's trial is me. And I'll think of a way to soothe the Master's ire.'

Nicolaus tries to respond but is choking with grief. Henrik Ehrenskiöld hugs him.

Ida stares at the two men. It is so confusing. Henrik's compassion seems utterly genuine. And yet, it must be *him* . . . the man who was Nicolaus's old friend. Who told Nicolaus that he could save Matilda, only to let her be burnt alive.

'He'll deceive you, Nicolaus!' she says. 'You must act now! Save her!'

But she realizes that, if Nicolaus *does* act now, all of history will change.

Suddenly, she feels completely terrified. True, she doesn't seem able to get through to others, but what if she has and just doesn't know it?

Like in the story she read in school once about a man who time-traveled back to the dinosaur era and just happened to stand on an insect. When he returns, he finds the whole world has changed.

It is a relief to be enclosed in the fog again.

Once more, she starts running in the Borderland, as quickly as she can. She sees another light, flaring and intensely yellow, smells the smoke from over there, hears the roaring of the fire. She knows that Matilda is dying in that fire, together with her mother who has thrown herself on the pyre.

Ida doesn't run toward that light. Then it fades and everything is gray again.

I'm tired of this shit, she whispers to herself.

But she keeps running. What else can she do?

Part 2

CHAPTER 12

In the school library, the windows are open. Outside in the yard, the voices are loud, fired up with the two-weeks-to-end-of-semester feeling. The library is quiet and filled with artwork. All the students taking Fine Arts are exhibiting their favorite work from the past year. The only people up to have a look are the artists themselves.

A faint draft from the windows makes a collage rustle. Linnéa stops in front of one of the framed drawings hanging nearby. The art teacher, Petter Backman, picked it because it is one of the few pieces of Olivia's work that remained after she left school just after the Christmas holidays. This is one of her many self-portraits: a girl with blue hair and black tears running down her cheeks.

Linnéa remembers the last time she saw Olivia. Her thin hair. The dark gaps where she had once had teeth.

You've ruined everything! Elias will never come back now! He'll never come back!

The last words Olivia said to her.

And Linnéa remembers her own final words to Olivia, whispered as she bent down to take the amulet from her.

She wonders if Olivia heard her. And if Olivia is still alive. If she is, does she still believe that she is the Chosen One? Does she truly think that Linnéa sabotaged Elias's resurrection?

'It feels so strange that she's gone.'

Linnéa turns and meets Tindra's eyes. Her black and purple dreadlocks dangle well down her back and she has shaved off her eyebrows.

The Key

There was a time when they both used to hang out in Jonte's house. Tindra was one of the ones who stopped calling after Linnéa gave up partying. They ended up in different worlds, despite being in the same class and still sometimes sitting at the same table in the dining area.

'I hope Olivia got way out of town and has been having tons of adventures,' Tindra smiles. 'Like she always kept saying she would.'

Her smile can't hide the fact that she clearly thinks it's very unlikely. In her view, Olivia wouldn't be capable of 'adventures'.

Tindra has no idea what Olivia was capable of doing.

He told me to take revenge for his death! Every time I kill someone who has hurt him, my powers grow stronger!

Linnéa thinks back on the people Olivia murdered. Regina, the psychologist – the one Elias was so fond of; Leila, an elementary school teacher with two young children of her own. And a harmless old man called Svensson, who was the retired head of the high school. And Jonte. Jonte, who had himself messed up other people's lives, but in no way deserved to die like that.

'Do you know that people are laying bets on what happened to her? Like, did she get out because she wanted to? Or was something done to her?' Tindra clicks the pin in her pierced tongue against her teeth.

Linnéa can visualize the moment Alexander walked away, carrying Olivia's frail, emaciated body. Tears of blood were trickling down her pale cheeks.

Then it strikes Linnéa that now, when she is gone, Olivia has finally achieved what she always wanted: everyone is talking about her and wants to know more about her. Everyone is fascinated by her.

'Holy shit!' Tindra points to another drawing. 'Did you do that one? I *love* it!'

'Thank you.'

'I understand exactly what you felt like when you made it,' Tindra says.

Linnéa looks hard at her own work, tries to see it with the eyes of another. Asks herself what it reveals, if anything.

She had hesitated for a long time over her portfolio before deciding on an ink drawing of a heart-shaped flower arrangement around a heart, anatomically correct and bleeding.

Linnéa wonders if Vanessa had understood that the image was all about her. And that it is still true.

She had never thought that Vanessa would want her. It had made her very happy to realize that she was wrong. Happy, and then, just a little later, utterly terrified. To have Vanessa and then lose her would be unbearably painful. And she knows it will happen. That loss is certain. When she finds out just how fucked up Linnéa actually is, Vanessa will grow tired with her.

Whatever it is we have together now, I should get out of it, Linnéa thinks. It will never work out. Better end it myself, here and now. Make a clean cut, then the wound will heal faster.

Panic wells up, and with it comes a prickly chill that makes her whole body break into a sweat.

'Are you OK?' Tindra asks.

'No. Panic attack.'

'Can I get you something?' Tindra rummages in her bag. 'Look, I think I've . . .'

'No, thanks,' Linnéa says quickly. 'See you later.'

She hurries out of the library. Hears voices around her on the stairs as she keeps her eyes fixed on the stone steps and counts the fossils to get a grip on her mind.

She can't think how she'll endure the funeral this afternoon. But she must do it somehow, for Anna-Karin's sake.

When Linnéa steps into the entrance hall, someone walks straight into her so she falls over backward and drops her bag.

'Fuck's sake . . . !' she says furiously. She looks up.

It's Erik Forslund. Grinning at her.

The Key

'Gosh, I am *sorry*,' he smirks. 'So *very* sorry.'

That grin. The same expression as the time he forced her to jump off Canal Bridge.

Panic is hammering in her head.

'I do hope I didn't hurt you. Last thing in the world I'd want,' Erik says.

Robin is near him, just a step away. Linnéa remembers the scene on the bridge, how Robin hung back but still did what Erik told him to do.

As she grabs her bag, she sees Robin's hand suddenly reaching out for her. Their eyes meet and she can just pick up his thought: his strong feeling of guilt, but also something else that is close to fear.

'Oh, piss off,' Linnéa tells him.

Robin's hand drops to his side.

She stands on shaky legs, then walks away. Her heart is thumping.

'Wow, Robin. Such a gentleman,' Erik says behind her back. 'Are you in love?'

CHAPTER 13

Anna-Karin slices through the layers of the savory gateau with the edge of the server. The swampy bread alternates with gluey mayonnaise, glistening slivers of gravadlax and dull roast beef, segments of egg so hard boiled that there's a green ring around the yolk. The sight is disgusting but, at the same time, she feels ready to eat the whole gateau. She carefully lifts her portion onto a plate.

She is so very tired, as if she isn't properly awake. She could lie down and go to sleep right here, on the plastic flooring of the parish hall. Sleep and eat are what she wants to do these days, nothing else.

This is my mother's funeral, she tells herself as she collects a napkin and a cutlery set. My mom has died. She will never be back. I will never meet her again.

But she doesn't feel anything. Nothing, except a vague sense of shame that her feelings aren't stronger, and an intense wish that today would soon be over. She doesn't want to be here. Earlier on, she hadn't wanted to be in the church, hadn't wanted to listen to the minister or walk up to the coffin to place a rose on it in front of all the watching eyes.

There is a surprisingly large crowd here, though most of them are Grandpa's friends. She catches sight of Åke, and wonders if Stian has told him how useless she was.

Anna-Karin goes to sit next to Grandpa in his wheelchair. She stares at the floor, hoping that her hair will hide her face so the other people at the funeral reception won't notice that she hasn't been crying. They have been lining up in front of

Grandpa and her all day long, expressing their condolences in subdued voices. All these people must wonder about her.

Since the night in the hospital, she hasn't been able to cry. The massive lid that used to cover the well of tears inside her during all those years is back on now. Welded into place.

She puts her plate on the table with its white paper cloth and sits down.

'Are you sure you wouldn't like something to eat, Grandpa?'

He shakes his head. There is a vacant look in his eyes.

'I can't eat today,' he says quietly.

Anna-Karin looks at her large slice of gateau. Grandpa seems to understand what she's thinking because he pats her hand.

'But it's a good thing that you're eating, my dear child. You need the strength.'

Anna-Karin eats a chunk of gateau, then another. The mayo sticks to the roof of her mouth. She speeds up, determined to get through it all before her body orders a stop.

She only realized what she had been hoping for when she sat down in the church. That he would come. She discovered herself looking from face to face in the pews for an older version of the man in the photos. A man called Staffan. Her father. Grandpa had only spoken properly of him once.

I don't think he had a lot of love in him to start with. Mia was drawn to those boys. The ones who didn't have much to give.

Does he even know that Mom has died? And, if he does know, has it even occurred to him to get in touch with Anna-Karin?

The gateau is swelling in her mouth. From the corner of her eye she sees Minoo stop at the empty chair next to her.

'All right if I sit here?' Minoo asks.

Anna-Karin nods. If she keeps her mouth shut, maybe people will assume that grief has made her mute.

'I'll fetch a drink for you . . . what would you like?' Minoo asks.

Anna-Karin stays silent.

'Maybe some mineral water? Natural? Or citrus? Or would you rather have lemonade or something?'

Still no reply, so Minoo goes to scan the rows of bottles. Anna-Karin watches as her friend chooses both kinds of mineral water, an orange fizzy drink and adds a fruit soda. Minoo looks tired. She must have had nightmares about Max again. These last few weeks, Anna-Karin has often heard her scream at night.

Anna-Karin knows that she couldn't have got through the time after her mom's death – and all the practical things there were to deal with – without Minoo and her father. Throughout, they have both been there for her. Phoned people. Arranged appointments. Filled in forms. Helped her to make up her mind. Anna-Karin simply didn't know what she wanted to do; she had been her usual pointless self. As for Grandpa, he was too frail. He just cried. Cried and cried and apologized for not being stronger.

'We will have to comfort each other,' Anna-Karin would say and hug him, but at the same time, she would close her eyes and flee into the consciousness of the fox.

She only feels alive when she's with the fox. She has been with him more often now than ever before. They run through the forest together. The fox continues to search for the unknown presence that seems to call to it.

Anna-Karin swallows another mouthful. Only a little longer now. Then she is free to go home to Minoo, pull down the blind and lie down. Zone out.

'Do you mind if we sit here?'

Anna-Karin looks up. Jari's parents stand on the other side of the table and look at her and Grandpa with that pasted-on funereal expression. Like they're trying to exude compassion, but to make it clear at the same time that they're not being pushy. It is really hard to respond to. Even though people do mean well, they project a sense of demanding

101

something, as if it was up to Anna-Karin to make them feel more at ease.

'Please, sit,' Grandpa says.

'Jari sends his regards,' Jari's mother says. 'He's hard at work at the agricultural college just now, or he would have come today. Of course.'

Anna-Karin nods. And remembers the only time she saw Jari at home. The pool of vomit. The disgusted outcry. She wonders if Jari's mom knows that it was Anna-Karin who had escaped through the front door. Still, all that feels like a thousand years ago. Like something in another life.

Minoo puts bottles and glasses on the table. Just so she has something to do, Anna-Karin pours herself an orangeade. It fizzes with gas.

The minister arrives, sits down opposite Minoo and looks kindly at Anna-Karin, who avoids meeting his eyes. She catches sight of Vanessa and Linnéa, sitting together without speaking. Anna-Karin wishes that Vanessa, if no one else, would behave as usual. Giggle. Talk a little too loudly about boys she has never heard of.

She thinks about the night in the hospital. Vanessa had held her and she had cried. Why was it so easy then?

Jari's parents and Grandpa are talking about the farm, Anna-Karin's childhood home, which burned down. Afterward, Mom sold it to Jari's parents. Grandpa asks politely about their pig-breeding business and they reply at length.

But, inevitably, they move on to the funeral. Anna-Karin registers that Jari's mother tries to connect. She has worked herself up to say something dutifully appreciative about Mia.

'Sorry, I'm going to the bathroom,' Anna-Karin mumbles as she gets up.

She accidentally gives the table a push, making the glasses and cutlery rattle and the bottles wobble. She walks quickly toward the bathrooms, locks herself into a stall, goes down on her haunches, leans her back against the door and closes her eyes.

And she arrives straightaway. She is with him in the sunshine, somewhere near the manor house. She feels ashamed about her sense of liberation, but convinces herself that the two of them have something they must do. That she and the fox are charged with keeping an eye on the Council.

The fox vanishes into a shrubbery when its sensitive ears pick up the low, purring engine sound of an approaching car.

The sound grows stronger. A little later, they hear the crunching noise of a car driving across the graveled yard. It stops in front of the large, white-painted wooden building; the engine is shut down and Viktor gets out of the car.

He hasn't been seen in school since May Day Eve. Today, Anna-Karin caught a glimpse of him in the church. Unlike most of the funeral congregation, he looked perfectly natural in his black suit. But there is nothing natural about him being here, and Anna-Karin wonders why he has turned up.

He walks toward the main entrance but stops at the bottom of the steps, sits down and pulls a pack of cigarettes from an inside pocket. Anna-Karin has never seen him smoke before. His hands shake a little as he lights the cigarette.

The fox hears the steps of someone walking inside the manor house before Viktor does. He lowers the cigarette when the door behind him opens.

Adriana.

She looks like a complete stranger, Anna-Karin thinks at first.

Then she changes her mind. Adriana looks just as she did when they first saw her up close. They had been in the first year and had been called to her office. At the time, they suspected her of Rebecka and Elias's murders. Watching as Adriana crosses her arms and stares sternly at Viktor, Anna-Karin feels a pang of fear, triggered by this unexpected echo of the past.

'Where have you been?' Adriana demands. 'Why didn't you answer your cell?'

'I've been at a funeral,' Viktor says. 'Anna-Karin's mother died.'

He looks keenly at her, but Adriana is indifferent. The name Anna-Karin no longer means anything to her.

'I am sorry to hear that. However, you should have informed Alexander of your whereabouts. Come along now.'

Viktor drops his cigarette and rubs it out on the gravel. Adriana glances disapprovingly at him.

'Do pick up your cigarette butt, please.'

Viktor bites his lip, does as he is told, and then follows Adriana into the house.

Anna-Karin opens her eyes, goes to a basin, soaks a paper towel under the cold-water tap, and pats her forehead and temples with it. She meets her face in the mirror and notes the emptiness in her green eyes.

She wishes something shattering would happen, something that could wake her from this cold, dulled state. Maybe she could finally feel again. Maybe even be able to revise for tomorrow's big biology test. If only qualifying for veterinary college felt important to her again, she could make herself study.

Anna-Karin leaves the bathroom and finds Minoo standing there. Perhaps she has been hovering outside, listening out for sobs and preparing to come to the rescue.

'I was with the fox,' Anna-Karin says quietly. 'We saw Viktor go to the manor house. And we saw Adriana come outside for a bit.'

'Did she seem all right?' Minoo asks.

'She was like she used to be. You know . . . earlier.'

Minoo looks troubled, but says, 'Good.'

'But I don't understand why Viktor came to the funeral.'

'Maybe he has a bad conscience about what he did to you. He should have.'

Part Two

They are silent for a while, absently listening to the distant murmur of voices.

'People are asking for you,' Minoo tells her. 'But if you'd rather, I'll get Dad to collect us and drive us home. Everyone would understand.'

Minoo looks uncertainly at her. Anna-Karin longs to say yes. But knows she shouldn't leave Grandpa to face all this on his own.

'No, don't worry. I'm coming,' she says.

CHAPTER 14

Minoo looks at Gustaf. They stand so close that their big, padded winter jackets touch.

'I think about you all the time,' he tells her.

The cold makes their breath turn into white clouds of frozen vapor. His lips are so near hers that the clouds merge.

'At first, I thought it was because you remind me so much of her. But now I finally understand. I understand.'

She knows his words so well but can't recall when she heard them for the first time.

'I care so much for you, Minoo. So much.'

He bends over her and kisses her.

Now she remembers.

She pushes him away.

Max fixes her with his black bird's eyes. His thin skin is tightly stretched over his skull and face. Minoo takes a step back, but he moves faster. His claw-like fingers reach for her and then close around her neck.

He smiles.

She tries to release the black smoke, but it is no longer there inside her. She cannot scream, can hardly breathe.

She can't breathe.

Max's voice thunders inside her head.

Nothing is as you think.

Minoo is woken by her own screaming.

She has fallen asleep on the living-room sofa. When she stretches and sits up, the notebook in her lap slides to the floor.

She picks it up, then listens for sounds from upstairs. All is silent. Maybe Anna-Karin didn't hear her screams. Or else she has become used to Minoo's nightmares about Max.

The papers wrote up the story about the patient in a coma, who had woken up after more than a year and then died of a heart attack. Max had already been splashed on the front pages as the math teacher found unconscious in the 'suicide-pact school'. Cissi, a trainee journalist at the *Engelsfors Herald*, wrote quite a few of these articles. So far, her career has been based on reporting the mysterious events in Engelsfors.

Minoo holds her hands out and checks that she can still release the black smoke. It's a relief when it works.

If only the *Book of Patterns* would start communicating with her again. She wishes that the guardians would explain what Max meant with his *Nothing is as you think*. If he meant anything at all.

She opens her notebook, tries to focus on more ordinary worries. Ove Post always adds questions about stuff he has gone through in class that isn't in the biology textbook. The real problem is that he can forget which class he has told what.

She puts her feet up on the table and leans her notes against her knees. Usually, she prefers studying at her desk, but when she tried that earlier tonight, all she did was listen for noises from Anna-Karin's room and wonder what she was doing in there.

When they came home after the funeral reception, Anna-Karin said she wanted to be on her own, but Minoo isn't convinced she meant it. Besides, even if she meant it at the time, Minoo suspects that being alone isn't good for Anna-Karin. Perhaps she should go to her and simply sit at her side. Or ask all the right questions, so that Anna-Karin can at last speak about how she feels. Next, Minoo worries that she is a useless friend because she doesn't have an automatic sense of what would be for the best.

She almost looks forward to the next day, when they have

agreed with Vanessa and Linnéa to meet up in Anna-Karin's apartment and clear it out. At least that will give Minoo something practical to do to help.

She leafs through a few pages and then stops at her copy of one of Ove's drawings on the whiteboard. A cross-section through the main body artery. It carries the body's life-sustaining blood supply. The aorta.

Mom told her that people can have an inherited tendency to develop aortic aneurysms and that they can occur at any time. Mia's lifestyle needn't have been the cause. But at the funeral reception, the guests would again and again utter the phrase *she has always been unwell*, like an incantation. As if people were trying to reassure themselves that death can't strike anyone at any time.

Until two years ago, Minoo had little idea about death. Her dad's father died before she was born and she has no memory of his wife, her grandmother, who died when Minoo was three years old. As for her mother's parents, her father had been killed by the regime in Iran and her mother had been too ill to come with her daughters when they sought asylum in Sweden. She had died before they could arrange to bring her here.

Minoo's first encounter with death was when she saw the dead body of her classmate Elias in the school bathroom. It wasn't the last.

She hears Dad's car, then listens as he walks toward the house. She imagines his sweating forehead and red face. His belly bulging over the waistband of his pants.

Now, he opens the front door. She can hear his heavy breathing.

Minoo can't stop herself and bursts into tears. When he enters the living room, she turns away so he won't see her face.

'How did it go today?'

She tries to suppress her sobs but can't. He comes to sit next to her, puts his hand on her back.

'Sweetheart, how are things?'

Part Two

She suddenly feels very small. She is angry with him, but at the same time she wants him to comfort her. He pulls her close and she presses her face against his shoulder. Her tears soak into the material of his shirt. Suddenly, she is crying wildly. She hopes Anna-Karin won't hear her.

'Was the funeral so sad?'

She pulls away from him and looks him in the eye.

'I don't want you to die. Don't you get that?'

Dad looks shocked. There is a little moisture on his glasses, near his nose.

'Minoo . . .'

'And I hate you because you don't listen to me.'

Her voice is thick.

'What do you mean?'

He seems completely at a loss. It makes her even angrier.

'You know I've learned first aid. That's why I was able to try to resuscitate Mia. I'll tell you why I learned it. It's because every single day I dread finding *you* flat out on the floor.'

Dad tries to say something, but Minoo gets in first.

'You seem set on killing yourself. Your father was younger than you are now when he had a heart attack and died. And you do nothing to stop the same thing happening to you. Always tons of stress at work. And you don't think twice about what you eat. And take the car everywhere. And sleep max five hours and . . . can't you see it will kill you?'

She can't hold back the sob and is almost too choked to speak.

'So, you see . . . if you die, I'll never forgive you,' Minoo finishes.

She expects Dad to get angry, as he always does when anyone mentions his health. He will sigh or say something cutting or actually start shouting.

But he doesn't do anything like that. Instead, he doesn't utter a word, just hugs her and strokes her back.

CHAPTER 15

Vanessa inspects her face in the mirror in Linnéa's bathroom. Her eyes are swollen and red-rimmed.

She went home after the funeral and cried in her mother's arms. And while Mom hugged her and tried to comfort her, Vanessa was thinking about Anna-Karin, who no longer had a mother to hold her. A mother who didn't seem to hold her even when she was alive. And then it struck Vanessa that her mom would die one day and she cried even more. She had to pull herself together in the end, because she knew that Linnéa was waiting for her. But, as soon as Vanessa arrived at Linnéa's, she started crying again.

Vanessa blows her nose and returns to the living room. Music is playing and Linnéa is fixing something in the kitchen.

The music comes from a laptop that is far too new and expensive for the apartment. Vanessa remembers the day it was presented to Linnéa. Vanessa had come over for a serious talk but didn't manage to get a word out, only watched Linnéa clean the floor. They had been so close to kissing, and maybe they would have if Viktor hadn't turned up carrying the laptop, saying she needed a replacement for the one that had been destroyed in the break-in.

Vanessa checks out the room. Minoo's parents found the beige sofa and teak table in their attic and lent them to Linnéa. The china panther has had its broken head glued back on and looks like a Frankenstein's monster-version of its old self. The worn wallpaper with its pattern of little flowers is slowly becoming covered once more with a new selection of drawings, posters and pictures. Linnéa has managed to repair the wooden cross that was a gift from Elias.

A wave of hatred against the fuckers who destroyed every-thing washes through Vanessa.

'Would you like to eat something? All I've got is spaghetti.'

Linnéa carries two mugs of steaming tea from the kitchen.

'Spaghetti is fine.' Vanessa sits down on the sofa.

Linnéa opens the window. A blue tit that had perched on the window ledge flies away. Then she lights a cigarette. She is still wearing the dress from the funeral, black with puff sleeves, but she has pulled off her tights and walks about in bare feet. All her nails are painted the same dark purple. Her long black hair has been pulled back into two bunches. She is so beautiful it almost hurts just to look at her.

How could it take so long for me to understand? Vanessa thinks.

Still, there is a lot she doesn't get. In the movies, everything reaches a conclusion when the lovers kiss. Problems have been solved, questions answered. Time for the titles to roll. By now, Vanessa and Linnéa have kissed hundreds of times but, as far as Vanessa can see, problems are still around and questions are far from answered.

Like, where does Linnéa want to go with this? If she wants anything at all, that is.

Vanessa tries to drink some tea, but it is still scalding and she puts the mug down again.

Linnéa stubs out her cigarette, closes the window and comes over to the table. She touches Vanessa's mug. The steam vanishes.

'Now try it,' she says.

The tea has cooled. It is perfect. Vanessa sips it and then, suddenly, something clicks. She realizes that she can't stand another second of uncertainty. She must know.

'This isn't working.' She puts the mug down.

'What? Still too hot?'

'No, I meant all this,' Vanessa says. 'This thing we have together. We have to talk about it.'

A light seems to switch off in Linnéa's eyes.

'Do we really have to?'

'Don't you think so?'

'I guess,' Linnéa says quietly.

She settles back at the other end of the sofa.

'Look, don't get me wrong. I usually don't have anything against just hanging out and having sex and having fun,' Vanessa tells her. 'But, with you, it's not fun. I feel . . . I feel too much.'

Linnéa only looks at her. Her corner of the sofa seems miles away. Vanessa forces herself to continue, even though she feels that the gap between them widens with every word.

'You said you aren't sure what this thing we've got means,' she says. 'And I can't stand not knowing anymore. Either we are together or not. Aren't we?'

'What do you think?' Linnéa's face is a mask.

Now Vanessa isn't nervous anymore, she's angry.

'Don't ask me! We used to talk about everything. Now . . . I feel less like we're a couple now than before we got together. The atmosphere can turn all stiff and edgy in an instant. No, fuck the atmosphere . . . it's *you* who goes all stiff and edgy. I wonder sometimes if you even like being with me, or if you have – like – nothing better to do. And it doesn't help that you don't want anyone to know about us, so I can't even talk to someone about how I feel. It's fucking with my self-confidence and that's not OK.'

She is almost breathless.

'So true,' Linnéa says. 'It's not OK at all.'

'If you don't want to be with me for real, please tell me now,' Vanessa says. 'Then we'll ditch all this and agree to meet up as little as possible, except when we're saving the world together with the others.'

Linnéa studies her hands.

'Please, look at me,' Vanessa says.

Linnéa looks up. Her bangs almost hide her eyes.

'What I don't get is how come you're asking . . .' Her voice is hoarse. 'Surely, you must realize . . .'

She stops and looks pleadingly at Vanessa, who simply waits. She won't let her escape. Time passes. Then Linnéa hides her face in her hands and keeps her fingers pressed against her forehead.

'I'm so useless at all this,' she mumbles.

'How do you mean, "all this"?'

Linnéa takes a deep breath and lowers her hands. She is crying. Not as Vanessa cried moments ago, sobbing and snorting. Linnéa's tears just flow.

'Do you know the most fucked-up thing of all?' she says. Her voice is faint. 'Some part of me is out to ruin everything. It's always like that when something good happens.'

'Wait. So you think what we have is good?' Vanessa asks cautiously.

Linnéa sighs deeply. 'Vanessa, I think you don't understand . . .'

She stops talking for a moment and looks seriously at Vanessa. 'I love you. I have been in love with you for ages.'

Silence. The words seem to hang in the air between them.

'How long is "ages"?'

'Like, a year and a half.'

A year and a half. Eighteen months. And Vanessa felt it positively hurt to bottle up her own feelings for just *one* month.

'How could you bear it?' she asks.

Linnéa laughs a little. 'I couldn't. It was awful.'

'Why didn't you say anything?'

'Because you're fantastic and deserve someone who is fantastic, too.'

Vanessa wiggles along to Linnéa's end of the sofa.

'I love you too.' It's a relief to say it out loud. 'And I think

I've been in love with you for a long time. It just took me some time to realize it.'

'Shame you're so stupid,' Linnéa says with a little smile.

'Shame you're so chicken.' Vanessa grins broadly.

Linnéa wipes her tears away with the back of her hand.

'I want to be with you,' she says. 'But could we wait to tell people for a while?'

'Sure, we'll wait. For a while.'

Vanessa plays with the silky-smooth hair in Linnéa's bunches, then sweeps her bangs to the side and looks into her dark eyes.

And then there is nothing more to talk about.

Linnéa's mouth tastes of smoke and tea and Linnéa. Somehow, it feels as if they are kissing for the first time.

Vanessa is kissing Linnéa's neck when she suddenly feels warmth spreading along her own neck. She slides her hand in under Linnéa's dress and starts stroking her hip. Her own hip is tingling delightfully, and then a shiver spreads all the way down to the back of her knees and onto the soles of her feet.

Vanessa looks up and sees Linnéa gazing at her.

'I think I just felt exactly what you felt,' she says.

'And I felt what you were feeling,' Linnéa replies. 'As well as feeling what I felt myself, of course.'

They keep gazing at each other. And then start to laugh at the same time.

This must be explored, Linnéa thinks.

She straightens up and slips out of her dress. Reaches for the back of Vanessa's neck, pulls her in close and sucks on her lower lip. It is wonderful, and then Vanessa feels the wonder of it again as the feelings echo between them. Vanessa pulls off her top and Linnéa unhooks her bra and kisses the base of her neck, her breasts.

Christ, Linnéa thinks. *This is almost too much.*

Vanessa can only agree.

Especially when Linnéa slides her fingers into Vanessa's panties, when she begins to caress her.

They kiss.

Vanessa reaches behind Linnéa's back and undoes her bra, while Linnéa tugs at her bright pink panties.

Every nerve in Vanessa's body buzzes and crackles like a lit sparkler. She kisses Linnéa's knees, then carries on upwards, along the insides of her thigh.

Her own body is her guide.

CHAPTER 16

When Linnéa wakes, it is night outside, but still light enough for her to make out Vanessa's naked body on the other side of the bed.

'Did that just happen?' Linnéa whispers, unsure if Vanessa is asleep or not.

'I think so.'

Vanessa moves over and lies close to Linnéa.

'If this is what sex will be like from now on, I don't think I'll ever want to do anything else,' Vanessa tells her. 'Ever.'

'I know what you mean.'

Linnéa cannot recall when she has felt so calm before. So light. And the nightmares had stayed away.

'Do you remember the first time I came here? When I was going to borrow clothes from you?' Vanessa asks. 'If someone had told us back then that this would happen . . .'

Linnéa smiles and lets her hand slide over the contour of Vanessa's hip. Her skin is so indescribably soft.

'I wonder what Wille will say when he hears that his two exes are together,' Vanessa continues. 'Think about it. Total horror.'

They laugh.

'By the way, Minoo knows already,' Linnéa says. 'I mean, she knows that I am in love with you. Once, I happened to project my thoughts about you.'

'What did Minoo say?'

'She said she thought it wasn't hopeless at all.'

'Oh, my God, even Minoo got it before I did.'

They both laugh again. Somewhere nearby, someone is driving a motorbike without a muffler.

'Though I think the worst thing is that Mona knew before I did,' Vanessa continues. 'She told my fortune once and said that I had already met the love of my life. And that it wouldn't be easy, but we would be tied to each other until the end.'

Hearing Vanessa say *until the end* makes Linnéa hold on to her even harder.

'Listen, Linnéa. I am really sorry about the way I went on about all the guys I was seeing last spring. Hearing about the whole sad parade must've been like torture for you.'

'Of course you needn't apologize for that,' Linnéa says.

'But it can't have been much fun for you when I turned up here and went on and on about Jari?'

'Don't think about it,' Linnéa says. Meaning that *she* doesn't want to think about it.

'Anyway. What time is it?' Vanessa asks.

She rolls over to the other side of the bed and reaches for her cell phone on the floor.

'Shit. It's twelve o'clock. Mom has called a lot.'

She gets up and disappears, holding her phone.

Linnéa closes her eyes, listens to Vanessa in the living room, hears her mumbling voice as she talks to her mother. She tries to steel herself for the moment when Vanessa will end the call, start dressing, and then say she must go now.

She doesn't want Vanessa to leave. She doesn't want to be alone with her thoughts. She knows herself too well; she'll start twisting and turning all the beautiful, fantastic things that have happened. Try to spot something wrong and ugly. Her brain will be back on old, familiar tracks. She will become convinced that if something seems too good to be true, it's because it is.

She listens as the footsteps come closer. The bed moves under Vanessa's weight as she lies down.

117

'I told Mom I'm sleeping here.' She crawls close to Linnéa again.

'I love you,' Linnéa tells her.

She is amazed at how easy it is to say now. And how easy it is to go to sleep when Vanessa lies next to her.

* * *

'I love you too,' Vanessa whispers and feels that she has never meant anything so much in her whole life.

She listens to Linnéa's rhythmic breathing until she, too, falls asleep.

* * *

Minoo's eyes are fixed on the page in *The Golden Compass*. She has reached one of her favorite passages in the book, but still she seems to read the same sentence over and over again. She must be tired.

She puts the book away and turns the bedside light off. She hopes she won't be haunted by nightmares tonight. And then she goes to sleep.

* * *

Anna-Karin wakes when Peppar strolls across the bed and then curls up on her stomach.

For a moment, she thinks this is her old room in the house. The house that never quite felt like home.

But it could become a home if she moved there with Grandpa.

Anna-Karin knows that's unrealistic, but it is a fantasy she allows herself late at night.

'I'd look after both of you,' she mumbles, burrowing the tips of her fingers in Peppar's fur. He starts to purr.

She falls asleep again.

* * *

Part Two

The darkness that envelops Minoo is unvarying, like black velvet. It offers nothing for the gaze to fix on. Her eyes hurt.

She holds out her hands to test the space in front of her. Nothing there. She takes one cautious step, then another. Under her bare feet, the surface is soft and cool. Grassy.

Two flames flare up, making the ground glow orange. The flickering light confuses and dazzles her, and makes the shadows dance over the stones and roots.

Further ahead, another couple of small fires are lit, and then another couple and another. She understands now that the flares mark the edges of a path. A path that she has to follow.

A light breeze gently touches her face. She looks at herself and realizes that she is wearing pajamas, the same ones that she wore the night of the blood-red moon. She had thrown them away as soon as she'd got back home, because she didn't want either of her parents to find them and start wondering about all the dirt and the torn hems on the pants.

More flames spring up, and now she sees the dance pavilion in Kärrgruvan. It is surrounded by a meadow, not the usual gravel. Minoo looks up at the familiar pointy outline of the roof, the railing, the raised stage.

I'm not here, she thinks. This is a dream.

But as she climbs the steps to the dance floor, she feels the wooden boards under her feet, as unmistakably as she had felt the grass earlier.

Suddenly, Matilda is there, standing in the middle of the floor. She is dressed in her white dress and her reddish-blonde hair is swept forward across one shoulder. A rook is perched on her other shoulder. It opens its beak and utters a croaking noise.

Now Minoo sees the others.

Anna-Karin sits on the floor, curled up. Her nightdress is torn and dirty and her bare feet are covered in mud.

Linnéa and Vanessa stand together, hand in hand. Linnéa is wearing her black hoodie and jeans; Vanessa is wrapped in a blanket but Minoo catches a glimpse of her leopard-print underwear.

It is like being thrown right back into the past. To the night when it all began.

But Rebecka and Ida were here, too, Minoo thinks. And Nicolaus, Matilda's father.

She glances over her shoulder. The flames are gone. The pavilion seems suspended in endless darkness.

'This is no ordinary dream, is it?' Vanessa asks.

'No,' Matilda replies, her voice clear and distinct in the silence. 'This is no ordinary dream.'

CHAPTER 17

Vanessa observes Matilda's pale, freckled face. She looks so young and, in a way, she is. She will always be fifteen years old. Caught between worlds, she belongs neither among the living nor the dead. She doesn't know what awaits her if she crosses over into the realm of the dead; doesn't even know if it exists.

Vanessa pulls the blanket tighter around her. Looks at the others, who all look so real. Can this be a dream they are all experiencing together? Her scalp prickles as she tries to grasp the idea.

'What are we here for?' Minoo asks. 'Has something happened?'

Matilda doesn't reply, just looks at them all in turn.

When her gaze lingers on her, Vanessa feels the same tingling sensation that she used to feel before Ida became possessed. The smell of burning wood tickles her nose.

'First of all, I have to ask you all to promise me something,' Matilda says. 'You will not leave this pavilion before I have finished telling my tale. Do you promise me that?'

'Yes, I promise,' Minoo says, and Anna-Karin nods without speaking.

'Of course,' Vanessa agrees.

'Why do you want us to promise that?' Linnéa asks.

'I have to make sure that you hear and understand all that I have to tell you, instead of . . . just lashing out.'

'Obviously you don't have good news for us,' Linnéa says.

'Please, I beg you, just hear me out,' Matilda pleads. She sounds even younger than she looks.

121

Vanessa looks at her and thinks of everything Matilda has been through. They belong together. Which was exactly what Matilda said, here in Kärrgruvan during the night of the blood-red moon, when she spoke through the medium of Ida.

I am you. You are me. We are one.

'We must trust her,' Vanessa tells Linnéa.

'OK, whatever,' she replies with a glance at Vanessa. 'I promise not to leave. But that's not to say I like the vibes.'

The rook flaps its wings and the tips of its black feathers nudge Matilda's face when it flies away.

Vanessa's eyes follow it as it vanishes into the compact darkness. She wonders what is out there. If there is anything at all. That thought alone is enough to give her vertigo.

'This will be difficult for us,' Matilda says. 'But . . . I haven't told you everything.'

* * *

Minoo understands why Matilda made them promise not to walk away. As far as she's concerned, all she wants is to make herself wake up and get out of this dream. She is afraid of what they are going to hear.

'Are you saying that you've been lying to us?' Linnéa asks.

Matilda hesitates. 'It's not that simple. Please, let me explain before you judge me.'

Minoo looks pleadingly at Linnéa. Everyone is scared, but they must be patient.

'This world has always contained magic,' Matilda continues. 'Six elements. Earth. Fire. Air. Water. Metal. Wood.'

As she names each element, she draws its sign in the air. Each one appears, one after the other.

'Witches have always existed. In the beginning, they used magic to meet basic needs. They found ways to make fires, locate sources of water and edible plants, and build shelters against the wind. And to track animals for hunting, deflect lightning during thunderstorms and so on. All skills that helped the tribe to survive.'

'When was all this going on?' Vanessa says. 'Back with the Flintstones?'

The mystified look in Matilda's ice-blue eyes makes her look even more like Nicolaus.

'I do not know of whom you're speaking. But it was a very long time ago. Before the demons entered our world.'

Entered? Minoo can't quite believe her ears.

'Hey, what do you mean by "entered"?' Linnéa asks.

'Yes,' Minoo says. 'Earlier, you said that the demons *tried to* enter, but that the guardians and humans stopped them. And then, at some point in time, the seven portals appeared—'

'I simplified the truth.' Matilda looks apologetic. 'You were not ready.'

'You've no right whatsoever to decide when we're ready!' Linnéa says.

'Let her finish,' Minoo says.

Matilda glances gratefully at her.

'You see, the demons tore open seven gaps in the boundary layer and entered through the gaps. What they found seemed chaotic and primitive to them, a world that needed demonic reorganization. They brought with them their own magic, powerful enough to civilize the most advanced of the Earth's species, the humans. And human beings did change. Settled down and started building communities.'

Minoo thinks back to the history lessons about the Neolithic revolution, when human development took the same great leap forward in every corner of Earth. When people invented farming, kept herds of tamed animals and organized themselves into separate communities.

Is *this* the explanation?

'But with the settlements came warfare, oppression, epidemics,' Matilda continues. 'As humans became more sophisticated, the chaos grew worse in many ways. The demons decided to leave our world alone and come back later to examine the outcome of their experiment. But they didn't all leave. Some stayed behind. As supervisors, one might say . . . they came to call themselves "the guardians".'

Minoo is feeling sick. In a second or two, she might vomit.

Max's words resound in her head.

Nothing is as you think.

Linnéa is as still as a statue. Minoo expects her to have one of her outbursts any minute. She actually wants her to do so. But nothing happens.

Anna-Karin gets up from her place on the floor. 'Are guardians and demons the same beings?' she asks.

'They *were* the same,' Matilda replies. 'In the beginning, when the first wave of demons came here. But something happened to the demons left behind in our world, something quite unexpected. They changed.'

'Did they now? Surely that's impossible?' Vanessa says acidly. 'Aren't the demons supposed to be unchanging and perfect?'

'Well, yes, that is how they see themselves,' Matilda replies. 'But it's not true. When the demons arrived here, the balance of magic shifted so that some places became more magical than others. The levels of magic also ebbed and flowed periodically. Everything changed. And so did the demons that stayed behind. They began to feel part of our world and, with that, to want to protect it from their old kin.'

Minoo thinks she hears whispers rising from the compact darkness that surrounds the pavilion. The voices seem to back what Matilda is saying, as if to reassure the Chosen Ones.

'The guardians managed to strengthen the portals so that they could only be opened and closed from inside our world. To seal them completely proved impossible for them, because it required our world's own magic, so they needed a special witch. Someone who could control all six elements and was born during an epoch of high magic, near one of the portals.

He or she is the Chosen One. And the guardians formed the Council to help and support the Chosen One.'

'Of course, the very wonderful Council,' Vanessa sneers.

'The guardians shouldn't be blamed for the corruption of the Council. It has been going on for thousands of years. As the guardians have grown weaker, communicating with humans has become more difficult—'

'Why didn't you tell us the truth from the start?' Linnéa interrupts. Her voice sounds frosty.

'It might be hard for you to understand . . .' Matilda begins.

'Hard for you to explain away, you mean,' Linnéa says.

Matilda ignores her.

'The future is in constant motion, you know that. It is affected by all the choices people make, and by natural events. The guardians are always trying to read the future, trying to interpret the effects of different choices, see where all the different routes will lead.'

She looks at Minoo as she continues to talk.

'When I was the Chosen One, the guardians told me that I had no hope of closing the portal and that there was a huge risk that the demons would get in. The guardians asked me to relinquish my powers and allow the next Chosen One to try.'

Minoo knew already that Matilda had given up her powers, but she had always wondered why. Now it's clear. The guardians had told her to let her successors take over.

'And then the Council had you executed,' Linnéa says. 'Apparently, the guardians weren't on the ball enough to warn you?'

Matilda looks grief-stricken and Minoo wishes Linnéa would go easy on the sarcasm just for once.

'Random events can always disturb the course of the future. The guardians cannot predict everything – for instance, that there would be seven Chosen Ones this time, instead of only one.'

She gazes at them.

'Throughout, the guardians have aimed to guide you so that the future would become as favorable as possible. They tried to supply you with the right information at the right time. And sometimes you had to find out what you needed to know on your own.'

So this is why Matilda and the guardians have been so cryptic at times; this is why they have provided clues for the Chosen Ones rather than straight answers. Because, if the Chosen Ones were able to figure out certain answers for themselves, this would have a better effect on the future.

'The guardians have done everything to protect you. But sometimes it just hasn't been possible to avoid tragedies. They have been too deeply rooted in the ongoing events. Or it could be that other choices could have led to even more catastrophic situations.'

Minoo tries to understand the true meaning of what she hears.

Did the guardians foresee that Elias, Rebecka and Ida would die? Did they see these deaths and just let them happen?

'You fucking shits!' Linnéa leaps at Matilda and grabs at her dress. 'You let them die!'

Black smoke wells out of Matilda and its tentacles wind themselves around Linnéa; it pulls her away and holds her still.

'What's happening?' Vanessa, who can't see the black smoke, sounds terrified. 'Linnéa?'

Linnéa makes a choking noise. It's all she can do. By now, Anna-Karin is terrified.

'Let her go!' Minoo orders.

'Unless she calms down, she will expose us all to danger,' Matilda warns. 'You don't know what exists out there, what she could have alerted to our presence.'

She gestures at the surrounding darkness. A chill runs through Minoo.

'The guardians do not know everything.' Matilda looks at Linnéa again. 'Nor do they see everything. You think that we have lied to you. Very well, we haven't told you the whole truth. But I am not lying when I tell you that, throughout, our endeavor has been to protect you, to protect this entire world. You have to believe me.'

The smoke withdraws and sets Linnéa free.

'You're not exactly making it easy,' she says between clenched teeth.

She gives herself a shake, takes a few steps to the railing and leans against it.

Minoo no longer knows her own feelings.

She should be angry with Matilda and the guardians, sure. But it is strangely difficult to get really worked up. She knows only too well herself how hard it can be to make the right decision. How much harder must it be if you have insights into so many different futures – or at least parts of them?

'If the guardians can see the future,' Anna-Karin asks, 'what about the demons? Can they foresee things, too?'

'It's hard to know. But we suspect that they can foresee a great deal – probably more than us at times.'

Something irks Minoo. It is something Matilda said.

'When you gave up your powers, how could you be sure that the demons couldn't get in? Their Blessed One could surely have opened the portal when the time came?'

Matilda blinks and looks away and Minoo suddenly understands.

'The Blessed One needed your powers to open the portal.'

'Yes,' Matilda says. 'The powers and soul of the Chosen One make up the Key to the portal.'

'So that was why Max wanted to kill us,' Vanessa muses. 'He not only saw us as threats, but he needed our powers as well.'

Matilda nods.

'But he lost the souls of Elias and Rebecka,' Minoo says. 'They're gone.'

'And so is Ida,' Anna-Karin adds.

'All six elements are needed to open the portal, or to close it – isn't that so?' Minoo asks.

'That is so,' Matilda replies.

'So it's been over from the start?' Linnéa says. 'Ever since Elias died.'

'But then it's over for the demons, too,' Vanessa points out.

'But they don't act as if it's over,' Minoo says. 'They seem to carry on despite everything. For instance, why bless Olivia?'

'We don't know,' Matilda says. 'It should be over, as you say. But we could see futures when the portal was closed, even after Elias's death. And even after Minoo had defeated Max, we became aware of futures in which the demons managed to open the portal.'

'So, there must be other options,' Minoo suggests.

'You're right. The rules seem to have changed. The demons must also have noticed it. If Olivia had succeeded with her human sacrifice at the Spring Equinox, she would have acquired your powers and your souls. And, by carrying out mass-murder, she would have set free so much life energy that she might have been able to affect the portal . . . but we're not sure. It's just speculation.'

'We've noticed,' Linnéa says coldly.

'But what about me?' Minoo asks. 'If the six elements make up the Key . . . ?'

Matilda looks at her.

'Then strictly speaking you are not needed to open or close the portal. Which is why the demons were able to promise Max that you would live. Perhaps they even hoped that you would cross over to them.'

When she had faced Max in the dining area, he had said that they belonged together. Minoo had felt a wave of revulsion sweeping through her. He seemed to believe that she would let him go ahead and kill the other Chosen Ones. And let him destroy the whole world. What could have made him and the demons even consider such a thing?

Now a chilling insight comes to her. The demons might have discovered a future in which she would choose to be on their side.

'But, if so, what is my role?' Minoo asks.

'You are blessed by the guardians,' Matilda replies. 'That means you can defend the other Chosen Ones against those who are blessed by the demons. But that is not all.' She looks seriously at Minoo. 'As I said earlier, the rules have changed. Now that the Key is no longer whole, your function in the closing of the portal has also changed.'

'How?'

'That is not yet clear.'

'You mean, you're not going to tell us,' Linnéa says.

Matilda doesn't even glance her way.

'The demons will try to attack you again,' she continues. 'It was easy to take over Max, because he had already been blessed once, but his life energy was so weak. They had to fill him up with their energy and he received too much, too quickly.'

'Like an overdose of magic,' Vanessa says.

Minoo remembers the black fire, how it consumed Max, annihilated him. His inhuman cry, which has echoed in her dreams ever since.

'Have the demons blessed anyone else in Engelsfors?' Anna-Karin asks.

Matilda shakes her head. 'Not as far as we can see. But someone else will return.'

'Olivia,' says Linnéa. 'So she survived?'

Matilda nods.

'Do you know where she is?'

'No. But we do know that she will return to Engelsfors. She will be blessed again. And then she will come here. And she will be strong – much stronger than Max.'

Matilda's ice-blue eyes sweep over their faces.

'You must practice your powers and become stronger, because you are the last hope of this world.'

129

'The last hope?' Linnéa asks. 'Why? If we don't close the portal, surely the next Chosen One will have a go?'

'Makes sense,' Vanessa says. 'You left it for later, Matilda, and we could do the same, couldn't we? We'll just have to make sure that the demons' Blessed One doesn't get to open the portal. Whoever is the next Chosen One might get to shut that fucking portal for good. Maybe in another three hundred years or so.'

'There will be no "next Chosen One",' Matilda tells them.

A sound of beating wings is coming closer. Minoo feels a puff of air as the rook lands next to her and perches on the railing.

'What do you mean?' she asks Matilda.

'There is no uncertainty about this. It is quite clear that there will be no more Chosen Ones to follow you. Either you are the last because you will succeed in closing the portal . . .'

She falls silent.

'Or else, we are the last because the demons will get their apocalypse,' Vanessa says.

Minoo recalls the vision of the black smoke engulfing Engelsfors. Her town sunk into total darkness. Did she see the apocalypse?

'Time is running out,' Matilda states. 'The last battle will take place within a year from now.'

Minoo has heard so often that the apocalypse is close, and that the fate of the world is in the hands of the Chosen Ones.

But right now, and for the first time, she truly believes it.

'There is hope for the future,' Matilda tells them. 'We have seen that clearly. And we have also seen a new possibility.'

She comes close to Minoo.

'A stranger will make you an offer. You must accept it. And you must do what is demanded of you and do it wholeheartedly.'

'What kind of offer?' Minoo asks.

'You will understand.'

Part Two

Matilda takes Minoo in her arms and hugs her. Minoo is surprised how warm Matilda is, how alive she feels.

Matilda's voice whispers inside her head.

I wish things were easier for you.

CHAPTER 18

Minoo wakes up with the smell of smoke making her nose prickle. She sniffs a strand of her hair, realizing that that is where the smell comes from.

The morning light filters in between the slats of the Venetian blinds. She reaches for the notebook and pen on the bedside table. Starts to write down everything Matilda said before she forgets any of the details. Writing usually helps her to think more clearly. However, this time, when she is finished, her head still feels overloaded.

Her cell phone vibrates. It's a text from Linnéa.

DID YOU DREAM?

YES, Minoo texts back.

The reply arrives almost instantly. Linnéa wants them to meet up in Nicolaus's apartment before setting out for school. She asks Minoo to tell Anna-Karin.

Minoo puts the cell phone down and tries to remind herself that she is not alone. She can lean on the others. Together, they will be able to sort this out.

* * *

Anna-Karin lies awake in the darkened room, aware of the smell of smoke lodged in her hair. Peppar jumps down from her bed when the door opens. Minoo stands there, outlined against the light in the hallway.

'Morning,' she says. 'May I come in?'

'Of course.'

Anna-Karin shifts into a sitting position.

Peppar meows and slips out of the room before Minoo closes the door.

'You dreamt it, too, didn't you?' she asks.

'Yes,' Anna-Karin replies.

Minoo sits down on the end of the bed.

Anna-Karin knows that she ought to be scared, upset, sad, angry. Matilda and the guardians didn't tell them the truth. The guardians were demons once and the demons are still plotting to kill them. Olivia is coming back. The Chosen Ones might not be able to close the portal at all. Still, they are the last hope for this world. No more Chosen Ones will ever come. And they only have a year.

She had thought that her numbness would give way if only something happened to shake her. But nothing has changed.

'At least it's good to know the truth at last,' Minoo says. 'Must be for the best, right?'

Anna-Karin nods.

What would Minoo and the others think if they knew the truth about *her*? What if they knew that she has lost it to such a degree that not even this has made her feel anything?

'I wonder who that stranger might be,' she says – just to say something.

'Me, too. And what that offer might be.'

'I'm sure it's nothing to worry about. I mean, it's something that's meant to help us.'

Minoo glances quickly at her, and Anna-Karin asks herself if it's too obvious that she doesn't care one way or the other.

'Linnéa wants us to meet in Nicolaus's apartment before school starts,' Minoo tells her.

It is a strain even to think that she has to get up, shower and dress.

'I don't think I've got the energy,' Anna-Karin replies. 'I'll probably miss out on school today, too.'

'But the biology test is . . . ' Minoo begins. And stops.

She looks embarrassed and it has clearly struck her that

The Key

Anna-Karin buried her mother yesterday and is feeling exhausted. Of course she won't be worrying about biology tests.

'OK.' Minoo gets up from the bed. 'Text me if there's something you want. I'll be home for lunch if you like.'

'No need,' Anna-Karin mumbles, crawling in under the duvet again.

'Do you think you can bear to carry on clearing the apartment this afternoon?' Minoo asks. 'I realize it's tough, but if we do it together it's quicker. And imagine how good you'll feel when it's all done . . .'

'Yes, you're right.'

As soon as Minoo has left her alone, Anna-Karin closes her eyes. She disappears into the fox's consciousness, where she doesn't have to think.

* * *

Minoo stops for a while outside Anna-Karin's room. Somehow, nothing she had said seemed to reach Anna-Karin. Should she go back in?

Minoo knows what it is like to be listless. After her victory over Max, she had felt utterly switched off. Perhaps she should tell Anna-Karin. But might that not sound as if she thought what happened with Max mattered as much as Anna-Karin's loss of her mother? Besides, was Anna-Karin as detached from her emotions as she seemed? Perhaps she cries her heart out when Minoo isn't there to watch?

Minoo showers, washes the smell of burning from her hair, and gets dressed. In the kitchen, a voice on the radio talks about how someone has discovered a large batch of rocket leaves contaminated with salmonella. Probably another sign that the apocalypse is near.

Dad is breakfasting on a big bowl of yogurt, a banana and a cup of coffee. Minoo is amazed. Both he and Mom usually skip breakfast.

She gets herself coffee and yogurt. Dad is leafing through the latest issue of the *Engelsfors Herald*. He always tries to read it as if for the first time, like their subscribers would.

'Is Anna-Karin awake?' Dad asks.

'She's taking the day off.'

'I see. Of course.'

He scrapes up the last of the yogurt and washes it down with coffee.

'Would you like to come along before school starts and have a look at our new editorial offices? I thought I'd walk there.'

He looks almost shy as he says this.

'I've got to meet Linnéa first thing,' Minoo says. 'But I'd love to, some other day. I mean, I almost always walk to school, it's just that today . . .'

'Minoo, that's fine.' Dad puts his hand on hers.

Minoo walks toward the center of Engelsfors. The scent of hawthorn flowers hangs in the air. The trees are in full leaf. The birds are singing. Summer is almost here. It could be the last summer ever.

The last battle will take place within a year from now.

She hadn't expected the day to be so warm. By the time she arrives at 7 Gnejs Street, Minoo has shed both her jacket and her cardigan. As she enters the building, she fishes in her pocket for the key to the apartment. It is the only one on the ground floor.

In the living room, the Venetian blinds are pulled down. Linnéa and Vanessa are sitting on the sofa. They look up at her at the same time with identical expressions of guilt. Minoo wonders if they have been talking about her.

'Where is Anna-Karin?' Vanessa asks. She is definitely dressed for the hot weather. It is a pale blue shift – so short that Minoo would have assumed it was a top if she had seen it in a shop.

'She couldn't face coming.' Minoo sits down on one of the hard wooden chairs.

'How is she?' Vanessa asks.

'Honestly, I'm not sure.'

Impatiently, Linnéa changes position on the sofa.

'I just can't get my head around the way Matilda and the guardians lied to us.'

'I know,' Minoo says. 'Still, they had good reasons for not telling the truth.'

Linnéa's eyes narrow and Minoo immediately regrets putting it the way she did.

'I mean, they *believed* they had good reasons,' she continues quickly. 'I'm not saying I agree but, after all, they're trying to save the world, just as we are.'

She falls silent and remembers what Viktor said when they sat together in his car.

To you, everything is straightforward. Right or wrong, good or bad. But it is the goal that matters, not the route you take to get there.

Now, she is arguing practically the same thing in her answer to Linnéa. Does that mean Viktor was right all along? Or that she is as wrong as Viktor was?

'The number one question is: can we trust that Matilda told us the truth this time?' Vanessa looks from Linnéa to Minoo and back.

'I don't know,' Minoo says. 'But I think so.'

Actually, she feels almost certain they can, but can't explain why.

'I won't believe a single word from them anymore,' Linnéa says. 'Not from Matilda, or from the guardians – you know, the *good* demons who wish mankind all the best ever.'

Minoo wants to contradict her, but can't think how, because Linnéa has a point.

'What do you think we should do, then?' Vanessa asks gently.

Linnéa doesn't reply. Only stares stubbornly down at the sofa table.

'OK,' Vanessa goes on. 'I think we should buy into whatever Matilda said. We shall choose to believe that she and the guardians are truthful this time. Which means we have to worry about Olivia, for a start.'

'What about trying to speak to Viktor?' Minoo suggests. 'Maybe I can persuade him to tell me what the Council has done with her.'

'No,' Vanessa says. 'We can't risk having the Council snapping at our heels again. We'll have to be extra alert instead. And we must practice our powers so we can defend ourselves. We need to be as strong as we can be, if we're to stop the demons and close the portal.'

'It would be a terrific help if we knew exactly what we were supposed to do,' Linnéa says crossly. 'If the powers of the Chosen Ones make up the Key, then what does the lock look like? But I suspect we aren't "ready" to be told.'

'It would be good to have a guide, that's for sure,' Vanessa agrees. 'Where is Nicolaus?'

'When he recovered his memories, I guess he thought the most sensible thing he could do was to get as far away from Engelsfors as possible,' Linnéa says. 'We can't count on him coming back to help us.'

In his letter to them, Nicolaus had written that he believed and hoped that he would return. Minoo, too, had believed and hoped. But now she thinks of him more and more rarely. And she wonders if Linnéa is right.

'Vanessa, how much do you think Mona knows about the portal and all that?' Minoo asks.

'Not a clue. I've tried to ask her, and I guess I'll have to try again. Perhaps she'll take me seriously if I tell her that we only have one year to sort things out.'

CHAPTER 19

The morning drags. Minoo checks her biology notes under the table during Patrick's English lesson. She is worried that nothing has actually stuck in her mind.

It's a very familiar feeling that creeps into her mind before every test and exam. Rationally, she knows that she usually does very well. Even so, she can't help thinking that *this time* might be the exception.

She changes the lead in her mechanical pencil. It strikes her that she ought to reflect on why she still cares. How come ordinary life still matters, despite everything she has learned about the future? But maybe focusing on these everyday, manageable issues is what stops her from going crazy.

When the school bell rings for lunch, she walks down the main staircase alone. She stops when she sees the entrance hall filling with people wearing white graduate caps. She had forgotten that today was the day the seniors would put on the white cap signifying they're ready for graduation. There is just a week to go before their last school year ends.

Minoo looks at the crowd. The good-looking people look even better with their caps on. It's unfair but a fact. Naturally, Gustaf is one of them. And so are the two girls he's with. Minoo's inferiority complexes kick in. She'd like to hide before he has a chance to compare her with the gorgeous creatures close to him. But it's too late. He smiles and leaves the girls to come and meet her. He hugs her and the stubble on his cheeks rasps lightly against her skin.

For a fraction of a second, they seem alone together, in the middle of the packed hall.

'I like the cap,' she says when he lets her go.

'Thanks,' he says with a little smile. 'Did you get my invite?'

'I did. Thank you.'

She has stuck the white A5-sized card under the frame of the mirror in her room. The card is printed on thick, matte paper. There is a drawing of an undergraduate's cap on one side. On the other side, Gustaf has written her name, together with the date and time of his reception, in his angular handwriting.

She has examined the card so often it might be a test in graphology that she has to pass. As if the way he wrote her name would reveal what he feels for her.

'You're very welcome to come to the running-out ceremony as well,' Gustaf tells her. 'I hope you'll make it.'

'I'd love to!' Minoo knows she sounds as frantically happy as the women in laundry detergent commercials.

'Great,' Gustaf says. 'And Anna-Karin is invited too, of course. How is she, anyway?'

'Not that good, I don't think. She's staying at home today.'

Gustaf nods. 'I was thinking seriously about going to the burial service, but then I thought that Anna-Karin and I hardly know each other. But, since she's your friend, I would have liked to . . . If you had wanted me to, I would've come. Though of course, I didn't ask, so . . .'

He falls silent. Minoo realizes that he has been *rambling* in just the way she does when she's nervous. But maybe, in Gustaf's case, it means something quite different. Maybe he's simply stressed out.

'Thank you for your concern,' she tells him.

Your concern? She hates herself. Who talks like that?

Gustaf's face suddenly takes on an odd expression. A moment passes before Minoo realizes that it isn't to do with her. He has caught sight of someone or something behind her. She turns and follows the direction of his gaze.

A guy with dark hair. Wearing steel-rimmed glasses.

Rickard Johnsson.

Rickard, the soccer club obsessive, who was always training. And who introduced the message of Positive Engelsfors to the school. Rickard, who must have been one of the first students to be given a metal amulet by Olivia. Before Olivia revealed herself, the Chosen Ones had suspected that Rickard was the demons' Blessed One.

And then, after the collapse of Positive Engelsfors, he had ended up in hospital, mentally and physically shattered after being controlled by Olivia for so long. No one had seen him since his discharge from hospital – not even Gustaf, who used to be one of his best friends.

Rickard has changed. He is wearing all black, making him look like an ink blot among the sea of white caps. His hands are plunged into his pockets and he walks hunched up, his eyes fixed on the ground.

'Rickard!' Gustaf shouts.

He looks up. His eyes darken when he sees Gustaf and Minoo and he walks on toward the front doors of the school.

Gustaf hurries after him.

'Wait!'

Minoo follows. She has to know why Rickard looked at her like that. When she gets outside, Rickard is running across the pavement. He crosses the dark line of the filled-in crack.

'Wait!' Gustaf shouts again.

Rickard stops. His entire body language, even from the back, radiates resentment. When he turns toward them, Minoo is close enough to see the dark rings under his eyes.

'Were you at the capping?' Gustaf asks. 'I didn't see you—'

'Does it look like I'm wearing a cap?' Rickard interrupts.

Gustaf is confused. He looks wonderingly at Rickard.

'I've tried to contact you,' he says. 'Are you back at school now?'

'I've been to see the head about graduating. He says I've done enough to graduate with everyone.'

'Wow, that's great,' Gustaf exclaims.

'It will stop my old man from nagging. That's all,' Rickard mumbles.

He sounds aggressive, but Minoo pities him. No one has been able to explain to him why he suddenly fell ill in the winter. His head must be full of questions. And he wore Olivia's amulet throughout almost all of last year. It must feel as if an entire school year has vanished into a black hole in his memory.

'How are things, really?' Gustaf asks. 'How do you feel?'

Rickard's face goes very pale.

'Why don't you stop pretending to care!' he hisses. 'I know you're trying to check up on me! Come on, that's why you kept turning up at the hospital – right?'

He is not just aggressive, but scared as well, Minoo thinks. And she has a sense of danger lurking.

'What are you talking about?' Gustaf asks. 'What do you mean, "check up on you"?'

'I don't know how you've managed to make the rest of them forget,' Rickard says. 'But I remember fine now, so you'd better be careful and watch your fucking step. I know what you did at the Positive Engelsfors party.'

The ground seems to open under Minoo's feet.

He remembers.

'What do you mean?' Gustaf looks perplexed. 'What did we do? Do you really remember what happened?'

He sounds genuine. And he is, because he truly doesn't know. Rickard must realize this, because he stiffens and looks hard at Gustaf.

'If you remember what happened, please tell us,' Gustaf adds.

Minoo wants to put a stop to all this. Rickard must not tell Gustaf. He mustn't tell anyone. She becomes conscious of the curious glances from people who are walking past them. Is Rickard going to say, right here in the schoolyard, that witches exist?

Rickard looks at Minoo and then looks back at Gustaf.

'I am sorry,' he says. 'I saw you with them, you see, and thought that you, too . . .' His eyes go unfocused.

'Rickard, what is the matter?' Gustaf asks. 'I'm worried about you.'

By now, the anger has drained away from Rickard's face. His expression is just fearful now.

'Please, leave me alone,' he says to Minoo. 'I won't say anything to anyone. It's a promise. Just let me be.'

He turns and starts running away from them. Disappears out of sight once he is through the gates. Minoo and Gustaf stand looking after him, at first without speaking.

'Shit!' Gustaf says. 'What should I do? Should I phone his dad?'

How much of what happened in the gym hall does Rickard remember? How much of what he remembers does he understand? And what is she going to have to do about it?

'Shit,' Gustaf says again. 'Do you think he might suffer from some kind of psychotic delusion? When he joined Positive Engelsfors, he had this total personality change. He must've been ill even then. Or . . . ?'

He looks helplessly at Minoo, who is nearly suffocating under the weight of all her secrets.

'Look, I'm sorry,' she manages to blurt out. 'I must run. I'll call you.'

She hurries back to the school building.

* * *

Elias, so much has happened, I don't even know where to begin.

I spoke out yesterday. I told V what I felt for her. I uttered the words, said them out loud and she didn't run away and I didn't die. And afterward, we had sex. And I honestly don't think anyone else has experienced it the way we did.

She stayed the night. And I was happy when I woke up.

How is it possible to be so very happy and so very scared at the same time? I have switched my cell phone off because I feel sure she is going to phone or text to tell me it was all a mistake.

I wish I could wind the clock forward and get to a time when I know precisely what will become of us. I wish I could truly believe in a happy-ever-after for V and me. It is not just because we only have one year left to save the world. I have never been able to imagine a future me – and especially not me together with somebody.

When will we speak out about us? Why am I so frightened at the thought that everyone will know?

OK, I admit I know why. It frightens me to think that V might not hack it. All Engelsfors think they know who she is, and the notion that she is together with the biggest freak in town (look, this isn't megalomania – without you around, the competition isn't so hard) definitely doesn't fit into their image of her. Besides, we're talking about a female freak.

On the other hand, I may not ever have to face up to that.

Perhaps none of this matters in the slightest. Everything could end tomorrow. And I mean end, forever. The whole world. Finished. Done with. And that makes me so fucking scared.

I wish I could talk with you, E.

Love you.

Linnéa closes her diary. She is sitting in her usual place, a window recess in the bathroom on the top floor of the school.

She looks out over the strip of asphalt linking the yard to the staff parking lot. The only people in sight are Erik and Julia, who are strolling along, hand in hand. Even seeing him at this distance and from this perspective is enough to make Linnéa feel the beginnings of a panic attack. She manages to force the feelings down. Even so, when the front door to the bathroom suddenly opens, she almost screams.

Minoo's face is flushed, as if she has been running up the stairs.

'Great, I've found you,' she says, quite out of breath. 'I've been trying to call you.'

'What's happened?'

Minoo shuts the door and looks around.

We are alone here, Linnéa thinks. *But if you want to make quite sure nobody can hear us, let's talk this way instead.*

'I'd rather not have anyone inside my head right now.' Minoo goes a shade redder in the face.

Linnéa sees a flash of Gustaf Åhlander and, attached to it, an emotion that is not entirely unlike her own when she thinks of Vanessa.

So, Minoo is in love with Gustaf, just like two of the other Chosen Ones. What is it about that guy?

Linnéa listens as Minoo runs through what just happened in the schoolyard with Rickard.

'That's fantastic,' Linnéa says when Minoo has finished. 'More great news.'

'Still, what can he do? Even if he remembers every detail . . . who would believe him?'

'It is not hard to trigger a witch-hunt. As we know. Me, I would quite like to recover from the latest one before they start off again.'

'I have to do something about him. Don't I?' Minoo sounds pleading, as if she hopes Linnéa will let her off.

Linnéa understands. To root around inside other people's minds doesn't feel too good. 'Yes, you must, I'm afraid.'

Minoo lets her finger slide along the edges of one of the tiles.

'I thought you would tell me that I shouldn't do it.'

'Why?'

Minoo glances quickly at her.

'Because, now we know where my powers come from. That the guardians and the demons are – or were – of the same kind. So it's like I've been blessed by the demons as well.'

'I hadn't really thought about it,' Linnéa says. 'Somehow, it felt like one thing too many.'

Minoo looks frightened; seeing it, Linnéa realizes that she is, too.

'Perhaps it doesn't matter where your powers come from,' she tells her. 'If you use them to reach good aims.'

'But is it good to remove Rickard's memories?'

'How I hate this fucking set-up,' Linnéa says. 'Why can't it all be a little less complicated? Why not straightforward, like in *The Lord of the Rings*? You know, like Orcs are bad, Elves are good?'

'Except, the Orcs were Elves originally. Before Evil corrupted them,' Minoo says. 'Nothing is ever that simple, I suppose.'

Linnéa can't help smiling. Suddenly, she realizes how fond she is of Minoo, never mind how often they aren't on the same wavelength. And she will never forget the time Minoo prevented Diana from locking her up in an institution. Nor that Minoo told her that she had picked up what Linnéa felt about Vanessa.

'Look, Minoo, I couldn't help seeing just now that you were thinking about Gustaf when you came in. So, I thought . . . you know, in a way . . . it was a bit like when you heard me think about Vanessa that time in the dining area. Though you didn't come across as anywhere near as crazy as I did.'

Minoo's face turns a deep red.

'I thought I had better tell you,' Linnéa adds. 'If you feel the need to talk to someone, I'm . . .'

She falls silent, aware that she is probably hopeless at what she is trying to do. But she means what she says and hopes that Minoo understands.

'Thank you,' Minoo says.

She looks as awkward as Linnéa feels.

'We don't have to decide what to do about Rickard right now,' Linnéa says. 'We must talk to the others first. Let's do it when we're clearing Anna-Karin's apartment.'

CHAPTER 20

Vanessa tears another page from the *Engelsfors Herald*, flattens it on Anna-Karin's kitchen table and starts to wrap a leaf-shaped glass plate. She places it in the cardboard box. Her fingers are stained black with printer's ink.

From Mia's room, she can hear Minoo and Anna-Karin stuffing things into trash bags. Vanessa is relieved that she and Linnéa are in charge of the kitchen cupboards. The smell of Mia's cigarettes is at its worst in the living room and in her bedroom. It hangs in the air, coating your face and sticking to your clothes. Vanessa hasn't had an issue with cigarette smoke before, until now when she is spending such a lot of time with Mona and Linnéa. She is utterly sick of it.

Anna-Karin comes in, picks up the newspaper and tears out a few pages.

'How are things going?' Vanessa asks her.

'We're almost done,' Anna-Karin replies before disappearing again.

Vanessa's eyes follow her. She looks so lonely. And it strikes Vanessa that Anna-Karin has very few people in her life. Her grandfather. And the Chosen Ones. Where is her father? All Vanessa knows is that he left when Anna-Karin was little. How much does Anna-Karin know about him? she wonders. Has she fantasized about him now and then, hoping that one day he will turn up? As Vanessa used to do herself, when she was little and mad at her mom. She would dream that her unknown father was an actor and a billionaire, and one day would rescue her from the tedium of Engelsfors.

She washes her hands under the kitchen tap. Linnéa is wrapping coffee cups at the workbench. Vanessa watches her, feeling warmth spreading through her body. Mona had been talking about 'the love of your life', and it really feels like that. Vanessa wants to share her life with Linnéa. The fun parts, as well as the sad, the everyday routine and the out-of-this-world fantastic moments. Together they will explore the world. Conquer it.

Linnéa is so strong. She is a warrior. She is never afraid to speak up and say what she thinks, and she always fights to protect the weak.

And, at the same time, she is soft, so vulnerable, which is something not many are allowed to see. But when she lets you in, you feel chosen.

Linnéa looks into Vanessa's eyes and smiles. Vanessa knows that she is thinking about what happened last night. And that she, too, longs for the moment when the two of them are alone together again.

* * *

Minoo heaves the last black bag out of Mia's room, placing it in the hall with the others lined up along the walls.

Inside them are the remains of Mia Nieminen's life: odds and ends that Anna-Karin has decided should go either to Ingrid's shop or into the bins. Apart from some pieces of furniture, a couple of milk crates are enough to hold the few objects Anna-Karin wants to keep.

'Are you sure you won't want some of her clothes?' Minoo asks when Anna-Karin comes out into the hall.

Anna-Karin nods. In her cupped hand lies a Dalmatian made of china. One of its ears is broken. She dumps it into one of the black bags.

'Are you really sure . . . ?' Minoo begins, but gives up.

'It's broken.'

'I know, but . . . I just didn't want you to regret it later.'

'I won't,' Anna-Karin says.

Minoo bites her lip. Why can't she stop meddling? Why not leave Anna-Karin alone to make her own decisions? Why does she always have to be so unbearably . . . Minooish?

'I'm sorry.'

'Don't worry,' Anna-Karin replies. 'And I am so grateful to you all for helping. I don't know what I would do without you.'

She says this without any emotion in her voice.

'Of course we'll help you. Come on, let's clear out the last things from your room.'

The sagging mattress looks naked in the light from the curtainless window. The wardrobe door is ajar. The wardrobe is nearly empty, because most of Anna-Karin's clothes are already in Minoo's home.

Minoo goes over to the window and looks out. A little girl on a skateboard scoots past the old, closed-down Positive Engelsfors Center. The sound of wheels on pavement echoes across the street.

Minoo hears Anna-Karin pull out a drawer in her desk and turns around to see her tip its contents into a trash bag. Then she crouches down in front of one of the cupboards below the desktop, pulls out folders and notebooks, and throws everything into the bag.

This is how she has been ever since they started clearing the apartment. One moment she stands around looking utterly helpless, the next moment she turns into a human hurricane.

'The things in this bag, are you keeping them? Or not?' Minoo asks when Anna-Karin dumps an old photo album.

'Not.'

'Anna-Karin . . .'

Anna-Karin looks up. She looks at Minoo but somehow doesn't see her. Instead, she seems to be observing the air between them.

'There's no need for you to make all your decisions now,' Minoo says. 'We have plenty of space in the basement.'

'Yes, I know. Thanks,' Anna-Karin replies tonelessly. 'But I simply want to get rid of all this.'

'Anna-Karin, if you feel like talking . . . I'll listen. I don't want to nag at you, but I truly mean what I say.'

'Thank you.' Anna-Karin opens the other cupboard under the desk and pulls out a worn box with a thousand-piece jigsaw. The lid shows a picture of elephants on the savannah. The box rattles as she throws it into the bag.

Minoo stands still. Her instinct tells her that she must not give up now.

'You know how frightened I have been that my dad will die suddenly. I have thought about it so much. But even so, I can't really imagine how it feels when someone close to you dies.'

Anna-Karin does not answer. In the silence, the words reverberate inside Minoo's head. They seem selfish, a reminder that her father is still alive. That *both* her parents are still alive. And that Anna-Karin doesn't have anyone now.

Anna-Karin has found a Scrabble box. Minoo feels she must say something. Something better, this time. Something that isn't about herself.

'I hope you don't feel guilty or anything like that?'

'No.' Anna-Karin throws the game away. 'There was nothing I could do. The hospital people said so.'

Now, why did I have to say that? Minoo thinks. What if Anna-Karin hasn't even thought about it until now, and I planted the idea in her head? All because I have to be the sympathetic, understanding friend who always says such wise things.

'I'm sorry,' Minoo says. 'I don't know what's best to say, so I talk too much instead.'

Anna-Karin draws a deep sigh. Gets up and leans against the desk.

'There is no need for you to feel sorry about anything,' she says. 'I am glad that you care. I really am. It's just that . . .'

She is quiet for a while. Minoo waits.

Part Two

'When any of you ask how I feel, I don't know what to say,' Anna-Karin finally says. 'Because I don't know how I feel. Or if I feel anything at all. Not even what we were told in the dream got through to me . . . I mean, I know I should be scared. But it seems that things happen and I just stand there, watching.'

'That's just how I felt during freshman year in high school,' Minoo tells her. 'After Max. As if there were a pane of glass between me and the rest of the world. I couldn't feel a thing.'

Anna-Karin suddenly looks at her.

'How long did you feel like that?'

'For months.'

Minoo sits down on the bed. She had almost forgotten how long it had been before she'd dared to tell anyone about the black smoke.

'Linnéa made me talk about it. It actually did make the memory easier to deal with. And then, it was like that sheet of glass disappeared.'

'But what if I break down completely when it disappears?' Anna-Karin asks.

'You'll be all right,' Minoo says. 'You get through these things, even though you don't think you can. And maybe you should go and talk to somebody.'

'I know. At the hospital, I was given this number to call. Grandpa thinks I should do it, too.'

Their eyes meet.

'I only wish there was more I could do to help you.'

'You do so very, very much,' Anna-Karin replies quietly. 'All the time.'

Minoo feels a strong wave of love for her friend. As if she were her sister. She would like to tell Anna-Karin, but doesn't want to embarrass her, or perhaps make it seem as if she is then expected to say something emotional in return.

'I'm thirsty,' Anna-Karin says. 'Do you want something to drink? I'll go.'

'I'll come with you.' Minoo gets up.

151

They walk through the living room. Minoo looks away from the place where she tried to save Mia's life.

'I think there's some cranberry juice in . . .' Anna-Karin says, and then stops in the kitchen doorway.

Minoo also stops the moment she sees what Anna-Karin has seen.

Linnéa is sitting on the worktop. Her arms are around Vanessa's neck. Her legs are wrapped around Vanessa's waist.

They are kissing.

Minoo has time to think that they should creep away, but it is too late. Linnéa and Vanessa have already noticed them. They separate.

No one says anything for what feels like an eternity.

Finally, Vanessa speaks. 'This wasn't exactly how we planned to tell you.'

'We are together,' Linnéa tells them.

'What?' Anna-Karin exclaims. 'Since when?'

She is bright red in the face.

'A while,' Vanessa says. 'Sort of.'

Minoo catches Linnéa's eye and can't hold back a smile. She feels very happy for Linnéa. And for Vanessa. So happy she might explode. But Anna-Karin looks shocked. She sobs and slides to the floor with her back against the wall. She pulls the sleeves of her tracksuit down over her hands and hides her face behind them.

'Anna-Karin, what's the matter?' Minoo asks.

Anna-Karin's body is trembling and she sobs again. Minoo, Vanessa and Linnéa exchange glances. Minoo crouches down next to Anna-Karin.

'What's the matter?' she asks again.

Anna-Karin takes her hands away from her face. It is flushed and swollen, and tears are trickling down her cheeks.

'I . . . am . . . so . . . happy,' she says between sobs.

'You are?' Vanessa asks.

Anna-Karin looks up.

'Yes, I really am. Because, at last something *good* has happened.' She sobs again. 'This is . . . the first good thing . . . that's happened for ages.'

Linnéa slides off the worktop.

'Too right,' she says. 'How often do we get any good news?'

Minoo tries to think but her mind is a blank.

'Ain't that the truth?' Vanessa says. 'Hard to believe that we're the Chosen Ones, considering everything that's gone wrong for us.'

Minoo snickers suddenly. Laughter has bubbled up inside her without warning.

'I'm trying to think of one good thing but I can't.'

Linnéa laughs out loud.

'I got my life almost sorted,' she says. 'Only to be told the world is coming to an end.'

'And my first love wanted me,' Minoo reflects. 'Shame that he turned out to be a murderer who had killed my best friend.'

'And my best friend,' Linnéa adds.

Vanessa, too, is smiling by now.

'And then Minoo managed to defeat him. Though he woke up from his coma and came after her to kill her.'

'For the second time.' Minoo bursts out laughing because everything is so absurd.

Linnéa is laughing and Vanessa, too, so hard she makes a loud snorting noise that makes all three of them laugh even more.

'I was freed in the trial,' Anna-Karin says, and starts smiling hesitantly. 'But instead the Council sentenced Adriana to execution.'

'And now the demons are trying to kill us again.' Linnéa is wiping away tears of laughter.

'And the only ones we thought we could trust have lied to us all along,' Vanessa puts in. 'Or else they've vanished.'

'And it's more than likely that we won't even be able to stop the apocalypse,' Anna-Karin says.

'Perhaps it's all been hopeless from the start,' Minoo sputters between her cackles.

Linnéa is struggling to breathe.

'But, even so, we're – like – the world's last hope,' she stammers.

They carry on listing everything that has happened since the night of the blood-red moon, as well as everything that the future might bring: all the frightening things, the dangerous and dark secrets. They drag it all out into the light, competing with each other to put their terrors as plainly and brutally as possible.

And none of them can stop laughing.

CHAPTER 21

Linnéa empties the glass of cranberry juice and puts it down hard on Anna-Karin's kitchen table. She is feeling wiped out, as if she has laughed away half her brain cells.

'I'm exhausted,' Vanessa says, as she fills her own glass. She is sitting next to Linnéa.

Minoo nods. 'Me, too. Is it all right if we call it a night?'

'Yes, of course,' Anna-Karin says. 'Anyway, I think I should think about this a little more. Work out what I should keep and all that.'

Under the table, Linnéa's foot lightly touches Vanessa's.

'There is one thing we must talk about first,' Minoo says. 'Rickard.'

'What about him?' Vanessa asks.

She takes Linnéa's hand on the table top and their fingers intertwine. At first, Linnéa wants to pull her hand back, but then she realizes that Vanessa hasn't forgotten about having to be discreet. It's Linnéa who has forgotten about *not having to.*

Vanessa strokes her thumb across the palm of Linnéa's hand. Every nerve-ending sends signals criss-crossing Linnéa's body. She can barely take in what Minoo is saying but, after all, she has already heard it. Vanessa feels what she herself feels, Linnéa can sense it. Sensations zoom back and forth between them, twisting, spiraling . . .

This won't do, I can't concentrate at all, she suddenly hears Vanessa think at the same moment as she lets go of Linnéa's hand.

Linnéa comes back to reality, as if she had been in a trance.

155

'What do you think we should do?' Minoo asks.

'There's no choice,' Linnéa tells her. 'You have to remove his memories.'

Minoo stares at the table top.

'Wouldn't it be better if I tried to talk to him first?' she asks. 'We don't know how much he really remembers.'

'Easy for you to find out if you go into his head and check his memories,' Linnéa suggests.

'Hey, go easy on her,' Vanessa says. 'Don't pressure her.'

Linnéa knows that Vanessa is right.

'I understand that it's not exactly fun for you,' she tells Minoo.

Minoo straightens up.

'No. You don't understand at all. None of you do. Gustaf was really shocked by what he saw in the gym. When I removed his memories, his shock has become *my* shock. When Max killed Elias and Rebecka . . . Look, at times it feels as if *I* killed them.'

A chill crawls through Linnéa's body. It is the first time she has had some insight into what it has been like for Minoo. She remembers what it was like for her, when her own power had just awakened. How it was when everybody's thoughts were crashing into her head, jumbled and unfiltered. She could hardly stand it. And what Minoo is describing sounds even worse.

Part of Linnéa feels that Minoo should be let off having to go through that process again. But is she prepared to run the risk of Rickard speaking out?

'If I have to sort out what is inside Rickard's head, I'll do it,' Minoo says. 'But, please, give me a chance to find out.'

'I think Minoo should talk to him first,' Anna-Karin says.

'Me, too,' Vanessa agrees.

'Fine by me,' Linnéa adds, though she thinks it will be a waste of time.

Minoo looks relieved.

'I have a feeling I could calm him down. He's just frightened.'

'I would be, if I were him,' Vanessa says.

'I wonder how long it will take for people to grasp what is actually going on here in Engelsfors,' Minoo muses. 'So far, they've come up with "natural explanations" for everything. Everyone who lost it during the night of the blood-red moon, the problems with electricity and water . . .'

'And the weird weather, and the forest,' Anna-Karin fills in.

'Yes, exactly,' Minoo says. 'But how much more can they explain away? There must be a limit somewhere. And everything that's happened until now . . . it's presumably just the beginning. The intensity of the magic is increasing; the veil that separates the worlds is getting thinner . . . and then . . .'

She falls silent. Linnéa is convinced that they are all thinking about the same thing. Matilda's words.

The final battle will take place within a year.

Suddenly, it feels impossible to laugh at the apocalypse.

'Then we will lock that fucking portal and live happily ever after, ' Vanessa says. 'Right?'

Linnéa can almost believe it when Vanessa says it. Almost.

Minoo smiles.

'Of course. We are the Circle, after all.'

What little is left of it, Linnéa thinks.

But that thought, she keeps to herself.

CHAPTER 22

Vanessa steps out into the street and draws a deep breath. After too much time spent in Anna-Karin's apartment, the fresh air is cleansing her lungs.

Behind her, she hears the familiar click of a lighter. Linnéa has put a cigarette between her lips and is lighting it, sheltering the flame with her hands.

'It's beyond me how you can smoke after being in the apartment.'

'I don't get it either,' Linnéa replies and inhales.

They start walking along the street. A swallow takes off from a gutter, plunges down and almost crashes into the road but, at the last second, swoops upwards with a whoosh.

'It actually feels good that they know now,' Linnéa says.

'Yes, it does,' Vanessa answers.

And she means it: one secret fewer to guard. Though before she understood why Anna-Karin had started crying, she had been scared. The fear was instant, and she understood that it had been there all the time, that she has underrated it.

'I must tell Evelina,' she suddenly says, and stops.

'What? Straightaway?' Linnéa asks.

'Yes, now. Is that okay? I'll come to your place directly afterward.'

Linnéa drags on her cigarette.

'Are you worried what she might think?'

'No. I don't know. But she has to be told, whatever.'

Actually, Vanessa badly wants to know how Evelina will react.

'Naturally,' Linnéa says, and Vanessa senses a smile playing around one corner of her mouth. 'But, look, you don't have to ask me when you want to tell somebody. Let's just do this. For real.'

'Are you sure?' Vanessa asks.

'I'm sure.'

'You don't have to ask, either.'

Linnéa smiles sardonically.

'Who am I supposed to tell? Diana from social services? Olivia, when she comes to kill us?'

Vanessa nearly mentions Linnéa's dad but holds back just in time.

She moves closer to Linnéa and gives her a kiss. It feels unbelievable to kiss her like this, in the middle of town, where anyone might see them. It's almost wasteful that no one does; that the streets of Engelsfors are as deserted as ever.

* * *

Minoo is standing in front of the ground-floor board with the names of people who live in the upstairs apartments. JOHNSSON is the only entry for the third floor, which is the top floor of the building. There is no elevator and she starts walking upstairs. The higher she gets, the stronger the smell of cooking.

They have stuck a small plastic sign on the door.

WE CARE FOR THE ENVIRONMENT! NO JUNK MAIL PLEASE!

Minoo presses the doorbell. From inside comes a deep male voice.

'Rille, please answer the door!'

Far too soon, Minoo hears steps in the hall. Before she has had time to get her act together, the door swings open and she is overwhelmed by the smell of frying.

Rickard is in the doorway. Their eyes meet. He tries to push the door shut but she gets her foot in the way. It hurts so much she has to choke back a cry.

159

'Please, Rickard, just a quick word.'

'Who's that?' the man calls out from inside the apartment. The frying pan sizzles and the smell intensifies. Despite everything, Minoo suddenly feels very hungry.

'Back in a moment,' Rickard shouts over his shoulder as he steps out onto the landing. 'What do you want?'

His hand is still on the door handle. It is obvious that he is frightened.

Minoo keeps her voice as low as she can but, even so, it seems to boom in the stairwell.

'I don't know exactly what you saw in the gym that time. And I don't know exactly what Olivia did to you—'

He interrupts her.

'I don't want to have anything to do with you or your friends. Leave me alone.'

'Can't we go somewhere, just to talk?' Minoo asks. 'Give me a chance to explain in peace and quiet.'

She tries to look as calm and unthreatening as possible. Rickard backs toward the door.

'We could go to your room if you like,' Minoo suggests.

Rickard presses the door handle down.

'OK, fine,' she says. 'Think about it. We can talk some other time. And if you don't want to, don't worry, I'll leave you alone . . .'

Rickard gets back behind the door and retreats quickly into the apartment. Minoo hears him lock it and put on the safety chain.

She stands still for a moment while the sound of his footsteps fades.

And if you don't want to, don't worry, I'll leave you alone . . .

The lie seems to reverberate in the stairwell.

If he doesn't want to talk to her, she will have to break into his mind. And then use magic, to alter his memories.

Rickard is absolutely right to be frightened of her.

CHAPTER 23

Belinda, Evelina's mom, has a green watering can in her hand when she opens the door. She smiles widely when she sees Vanessa.

'Nessa! It's been such a long time!'

She lets Vanessa in, hugs her, and manages to splash some water on the floor.

'We really must stick together now,' Belinda says in a low voice.

Vanessa only makes a ho-hum noise while she takes off her outdoor shoes.

Belinda has a habit of catching Evelina's friends practically in the doorway. Especially when she and Evelina have had a fight.

'We simply must work at this together,' Belinda continues. 'You've heard about Örebro, haven't you?'

Vanessa doesn't want to go there. The only thing she knows that connects Evelina and Örebro is that Leo lives there, but she isn't sure that Evelina's mom knows about him.

'Anthony is about to start a new job as a truck driver in Örebro. And now he has told Evelina that she can come and live at his place. Do her last year at school there. It's typical of him. I am landed with bringing her up, right to the end of puberty, and then, when the worst bit is over, he suddenly remembers that he has an almost grown-up daughter. Nessa, whatever am I supposed to do? I mean, I'm not stupid, I realize that Evelina has got some guy from there, otherwise she

161

wouldn't even dream of leaving this town and all her friends. Do you know who it is?'

'Look, I'm sorry but I must . . .' Vanessa says.

Belinda sighs and waves her hand hopelessly.

'Yes, yes. Just say if you want to stay for dinner.'

'Thank you.' Vanessa escapes to Evelina's room.

Evelina half lies back on her bed with her bashed-up laptop resting against her knees. Back in middle school, she covered the lid with sticky labels, and last year she had a go at picking them off. Vanessa almost ruined her nails trying to help.

'One second, I'll just say bye to Leo,' Evelina says, without taking her eyes off the screen.

Vanessa sits down on the bed. Looks around the room while Evelina taps on the keyboard.

A string of heart-shaped fairy lights hangs across the window. Michelle and Vanessa bought them for Evelina after she'd been dumped by her last-but-one boyfriend.

A glittery gold top sticks out from the pile of clothes on the chair at the desk. Vanessa borrowed it once. They were going to a New Years party in Sala, the party where she met Isak, the younger guy she had a one-night thing with.

On the wall above the desk hangs a framed photo of Evelina, Michelle and Vanessa on the roller coaster at Liseberg. Vanessa and Evelina are sitting in the front car. Their arms are stretched up in the air and they are holding hands, hair flying around their laughing, screaming faces.

Evelina snaps her laptop shut.

'Look, take no notice of Mom,' she sighs. 'I get so fucking fed up with her.'

'Örebro?' Vanessa asks. 'Seriously?'

'I haven't made up my mind yet.' Evelina puts her computer on the floor. 'It would be nice to live with Dad for a bit. And be close to Leo, naturally. But having to start in a new school isn't so great. Maybe I can stay there just for the weekends. I don't know.'

'But why haven't you said anything?' Vanessa asks.

Evelina shrugs.

'Anyway, what did you want to talk about?'

Vanessa looks at Evelina, remembers the many, many times they have been together in this room, exchanged whispered secrets, chewed over problems, teased dirty old men online, planned outfits, tried to concentrate on homework, gone to sleep drunk and wept over guys they never give a thought to anymore.

She should be able to tell Evelina.

'I'm together with Linnéa now.'

Evelina sits bolt upright on the bed.

'What? You . . . what?'

'Linnéa and I. We are together.'

Evelina still looks completely baffled.

'Are you saying that . . . with Linnéa?' she asks. 'Like, you're . . . an item?'

'Yes.'

Vanessa smiles but the smile feels tense and odd and trembles on her lips. Evelina doesn't smile back at her.

'But, for heaven's sake, how? What I mean is, when did it start? Was it, like, overnight?' She sounds almost angry.

'No. I've been in love with her for ages. But I didn't understand what I felt until this Easter. And then, on May Day Eve, we kissed, but we hadn't been together for real until—'

'I *knew* it,' Evelina interrupts and jumps off the bed. 'I just *knew* there was something going on when you turned up to that May Day eve party!'

'Nothing had actually happened by then.'

'It didn't stop you from lying to me, did it?'

Evelina is screaming and Vanessa becomes angry, too.

'What's your fucking problem?' She gets up from the chair.

'What's *my* problem? What's *your* fucking problem? What's been the fucking matter with you for the last *two years*?' Evelina is spitting with rage. 'Like, "Oh, please,

Evelina, say that I'm staying the night with you." "No, I'm just tired, nothing special at all." "No, nothing is wrong, it's just that I've had a fight with Wille." "No, I must go home 'cause my mom isn't well *though actually I'm off to make out with my ex-boyfriend's ex-girlfriend!*"'

Vanessa can't think of anything to say. She is far too shocked.

'I am so totally fed up with having to lie to cover for you and I am so totally fed up with you lying to me and *believing I don't even see through it!*' Evelina carries on.

Vanessa realizes how long Evelina has been keeping all this bottled up. No wonder she's erupted like this.

'We used to tell each other everything. And then, suddenly, you're keeping secrets from me. Any idea how that makes me feel? I told myself that we were best friends and you'd tell me about whatever it is when you were ready. But, oh no, you're hanging out with your new friends and I can't even figure out what it is you're all *doing* together. You never ask me to come with you – it's like you're ashamed of me. I bet they already know about you and Linnéa. Am I right?'

Vanessa looks away, feeling so guilty she can hardly stand it. How could she have been taking Evelina for granted for so long?

'And that's not the only thing,' Evelina continues. 'As soon as something happens to *me*, in my life, and I try to tell you about it, I feel I'm just being a nuisance. You only took one look at Leo when you met. I've never been so in love with anyone and I want to tell you everything, but you never listen! And now you sit here and wonder why I haven't told you about Örebro! It's because you don't seem to give a shit what goes on in my life!'

Evelina snivels a little. And falls silent.

Vanessa doesn't know what to say. She has no defense. Guilty as charged. She has been lying and she has used Evelina; always expected her to back her up.

And Evelina *has* always backed her up. She has been the

best friend you could ever wish for, while Vanessa has been the opposite.

Most people only see Evelina's superficial self, the good-looking, feisty girl with tons of self-confidence. One of those people who always do well and never seem to need any help. Now, Vanessa realizes, she has been guilty of doing the same thing.

Why did she? Because it was easier that way. Easier for herself, that is.

'Please forgive me,' Vanessa says.

Evelina doesn't answer, but she bursts into tears when Vanessa puts her arms around her. They cry on each other's shoulders.

'Forgive me,' Vanessa says again. 'I've been a god-awful friend.'

'You have so.'

But Vanessa can sense that Evelina is smiling against her cheek.

We belong together, Vanessa thinks. The Chosen Ones and I may well be bound together by fate, but Evelina and I are as much tied together. Bound by friendship.

CHAPTER 24

The spine of the photo album crackles when Grandpa puts it on the table and opens it. His arm moves stiffly as he turns the pages.

'It was very kind of you to bring me this,' he says.

Anna-Karin's smile is a little forced. Just a week ago she had thrown it into a trash bag. She is glad now that Minoo made her think again.

Grandpa has placed his wheelchair at the short end of the table, and she is seated on the wooden kitchen sofa that has been painted grayish-blue. She munches on a chocolate ball while they look at the pictures.

They are taken at the farm and look idyllic. The sun always seems to be shining. Grandma is sitting outside, in front of the big house, with a cigarette between her lips while she peels potatoes over a basin. A much younger Grandpa is mending a cattle fence.

Here and there, her father turns up. In one photo, he is holding a crayfish in one hand and a glass of schnapps in the other. In others, he leans on a rake in front of an enormous pile of fallen leaves. Or stands on a snow-covered field, laughing with his eyes screwed up against the sun and pretending to aim a snowball at the person holding the camera. Anna-Karin wonders if it is her mother. And if she, too, was laughing.

Inside her, something flickers. A twinge, just one breath away from tears. But then she sees that Grandpa's eyes are shiny. The flicker dies down.

He turns a few pages.

166

'I thought Mia looked so nice in this photo,' he said in a choked voice.

The picture was taken at Midsummer and Mia is pregnant with Anna-Karin. Her hair has been curled and she is wearing make-up. It is one of only a few pictures of her mom smiling with her eyes as well as her lips. She looks so full of hope. As if she were looking forward to the future. Did she feel like that because of the child in her belly?

'It really is a nice picture,' Anna-Karin says.

'It was Staffan who took it.' Grandpa wipes his eyes.

They leaf through more of the album. Anna-Karin is born. She grows teeth. She learns to walk. Soon, Dad will be gone. Lost from the pictures.

In one photo, Mom is decorating the Christmas tree, turned away from the camera. She is wearing a flannel nightdress with a flower pattern. Suddenly, Anna-Karin remembers a night when she had a nightmare. She was four or five years old then. She woke and went into Mom's bedroom. Mom let Anna-Karin crawl in under the covers and lie down close to her. She had felt so safe; Mom was warm and her nightdress, that nightdress, was soft. Mom had probably understood that, for weeks afterward, Anna-Karin had only pretended to have nightmares every night so she could come to sleep in the big bed.

Until, one night, Mom said no.

Was Mom happier during that period? Was that why Anna-Karin was allowed to sleep in her bed? Could she still have been saved back then? Was it the last chance, before she was finally pulled down deep into a well of bitterness and self-pity?

Anna-Karin looks out through the window. It is a warm morning; the sun is shining over Engelsfors. She can hear a group of seniors walking past on their way to school after a champagne breakfast on Olsson's Hill.

* * *

'Your turn next year,' Dad says when he and Minoo stop outside the school gates.

Minoo looks out over the sea of friends and relatives, many holding up placards with pictures of the graduates as children. All are more or less embarrassing. A whiteish-blonde girl with red jam all over her face. A naked little boy on a potty.

Minoo reminds herself to hide all old photos of herself until her own finals are over and done with.

She has always aimed for top marks and she has got them, but never been able to decide what they are for. Both Mom and Dad quietly hope that she will follow in one of their footsteps. But Minoo has no idea what she wants to do as an adult. She doesn't even know if she will be given the chance to become one.

'It feels way in the distance,' Minoo says.

'Yes, of course, at your age time moves slowly. Later on, you'll see, life whizzes past.' Dad smiles at her. 'I sound like an old fogie, don't I? Well, say hello to Gustaf and congratulate him for me as well.'

Minoo watches him walk away toward the center of town. He walks every day and has stopped working until late into the night. He has even been to see his doctor. But Minoo hasn't dared to tell Mom yet, because she doesn't want to give Mom false hope. This has only been going on for a week. His new regime might stop as quickly as it started.

She walks through the gates and scans the placards. The sun is heating her hair. She longs for a shady corner to wait in.

Rickard's placard catches her eye. The picture shows a plump little boy with round glasses sitting on a red plastic tractor. Rickard hasn't been in touch and she still doesn't know what she should do for the best.

Finally, she spots Gustaf's placard. It says CONGRATS GUSTAF! On the picture, Gustaf is perhaps three years old. He holds a black kitten in his arms and has a huge smile. Minoo suddenly aches inside in a way she can't explain.

She pushes on between the clusters of people, asking herself if she really has any business being there. But he did ask her to come. He even said he *hoped* she would come. Presumably she had better believe him. Though it's incredibly hard.

'Oops, someone's in a real hurry,' a woman's voice says when Minoo's bag bounces against a person in the crowd.

'I'm sorry.' Minoo turns toward the voice.

It belongs to a middle-aged woman who is chewing gum energetically, though no peppermint flavor in the world could hide the smell of alcohol that seems to exude from every pore of her body.

Robin is standing next to her. He holds a placard that says CARRY ON ADDIE! The boy in the picture is perched on the lap of a fat man in a Father Christmas mask. His hair is neatly combed and he looks terrified.

Robin seems barely conscious. His eyes are glazed over, as if he hasn't slept for weeks.

'Which of the students do you know then?' The woman has exaggeratedly precise diction. 'My eldest, that's Andreas, is finishing today . . . My husband couldn't come. He's away on business.'

'I'm so sorry,' Minoo mumbles again before hurrying on.

'*So sorry,*' she hears Robin's mother say, imitating Minoo behind her back. 'Is that all she ever says?'

Minoo homes in on Gustaf's parents, Lage and Anita. They stand together with two young women, both about twenty-five, one as blonde as Gustaf, the other with the same dark hair as their mother. Both wear flowery dresses and sunglasses, and look terrifically glamorous, without trying too hard. They must be Jossan and Vicky. One of them works in Berlin, the other is studying something at Lund University. Minoo has seen their pictures in Gustaf's home but can't remember which is which.

'Hi, Minoo!' Lage shouts and waves.

She joins them, hugs Lage and Anita. Then she says hello

to Gustaf's sisters, trying not to think about what they will make of her.

'Oh, so *you're* Minoo,' the one with the dark hair says. She has just introduced herself as Vicky.

'Stop it, you're embarrassing her,' admonishes the blonde, before she introduces herself as Jossan.

Minoo feels the blood rushing to her face. Luckily, she doesn't have to think of anything to say. A distant shrieking noise is growing in volume and everyone turns toward the school building.

The front doors swing open and the seniors run outside, yelling and whooping. They stop at the top of the steps and start to chant the immortal lines for the benefit of the expectant audience.

'Cause we have graduated! 'Cause we have graduated! 'Cause we have gradua-a-ated!

Cell phones and cameras click. People are shouting and applauding. And Gustaf is standing in the middle, halfway up the steps, with the same smile on his face as the three-year-old holding his black kitten.

He is so unbelievably good-looking in his white cap and light suit. She feels as if small electric currents have been triggered in her wrists and spread along her arms, making them powerless.

She thinks of all those years when she knew who Gustaf Åhlander was but only at a distance. And of how it is hard to believe that she is standing here now with his family.

The graduates stream down the steps to mingle with the crowd in the schoolyard. Gustaf has to stop all the time to have his back slapped and to shake hands, but he finally reaches their small group. Suddenly, his arms are around her and he kisses her on the mouth.

He lets her go. They look at each other and he seems as surprised as she is.

The next moment, Vicky throws her arms around his neck,

and he is surrounded by his family and friends who have managed to work their way through the throng.

Minoo stands fixed to the spot. She can still feel his lips against hers.

As soon as they arrive at the Åhlanders' house, Minoo sneaks off to the upstairs bathroom and locks the door behind her. She lets cold water flow over her wrists. Mom has said it helps if one is overheating. But it doesn't make any difference.

Gustaf was driven back in his aunt's sports car and Minoo went in the car with his parents and sisters. She was almost too dazed to answer when they spoke to her; she must have seemed drugged.

But it wasn't a *kiss*, was it? More a kissie-kiss, the kind you give a friend without meaning anything more. Maybe Gustaf had just aimed for her cheek but missed . . . or had she turned her mouth to meet his? Was that why he looked so astonished?

But he looked happy, too. He really did.

But why shouldn't he look happy? He had just graduated.

'Oh, so you're Minoo.'

What did she mean by that? It might not have meant anything at all. Or it might have meant *Oh, so you're Minoo, the chick who's always running after our brother.*

She looks at her face in the mirror. Tries to see herself as Gustaf saw her this morning, standing in the schoolyard. Tries, as she has so many times in the past, to decide what she truly looks like.

Once, Anna-Karin told her she was beautiful. But that is the only time anyone, apart from her mom and dad, has ever complimented her on her looks. Parents don't count. As for Max, he was obsessed with her because she reminded him of his first murder victim. Which doesn't count either.

If Minoo looked like someone who was right for a guy like Gustaf, surely she'd know it? She is convinced that he would

171

never be interested in a girl just because of her looks. But there are lots of good-looking girls around who are also fun to be with – and smart, and generally great.

Everyone says that it's what's beneath the surface that matters, but then Minoo isn't particularly impressed by her own personality either. Especially now, when she hangs out in the bathroom and ruminates about her looks instead of being with other people.

Minoo hears voices from the hall. New guests. She ought to join them, but she's pretty certain she doesn't know anyone apart from Gustaf and his parents, and they are bound to be too busy to look after her. She will just end up in some corner, feeling like an imposter.

I should go home, Minoo thinks as she unlocks the bathroom door. I'll leave my present on the gift table and slip away before anybody notices. I can always claim I got sunstroke or something after waiting in the schoolyard.

She walks downstairs and into the hall, smiling politely at some people she's never seen before. Through a doorway, she glimpses people filling their plates at the buffet in the kitchen. The room shimmers with green light because the sun's rays are filtered through the fresh birch leaves in the garlands that frame the open veranda door. Lage smiles broadly toward her and raises his glass in a toast.

It would be very rude to leave now. She simply can't.

Minoo takes the present from her bag and walks along to the living room. It is immaculately tidy and quiet. Not a soul is inside; everyone is in the garden.

She goes over to the gift table. She has been pondering what to give Gustaf for weeks but now her choice feels so utterly wrong. Sure, Gustaf reads quite a lot, but *The Master and Margarita*? Perhaps he'll think that she is trying to impress him. Or that it is the most boring book in the world and, if she likes it, she must be the most boring person in the world.

Minoo places her parcel among the other ones, then glances

into the garden. Anita has just greeted Rebecka's mother with a hug before taking her to join the others.

Rebecka ought to have been here, Minoo thinks. Gustaf ought to have kissed her in the schoolyard. None of what has happened between Gustaf and me would have happened if Rebecka had been alive.

Someone gives her a sharp tap on the shoulder and Minoo turns around.

Rickard. He is wearing a suit and, around his neck, a blue-and-yellow ribbon with a miniature white cap as a pendant. But he doesn't exactly seem to be enjoying his Graduation Day.

'I want a word with you,' he says.

'Now?'

He nods.

'But . . . there are so many people here,' Minoo stutters. 'Someone might hear us.'

As if to back her up, Lage pops his head around the door.

'Glad you could make it, Rickard! Great! Both of you, come and get something to eat!'

'We'll be there in a moment,' Minoo replies in a far too enthusiastic tone.

Then she looks at Rickard again.

'Come with me,' he says.

They go into the empty kitchen and he walks over to the basement door and opens it.

'You first,' he says.

CHAPTER 25

The basement air is cool. Cross-country skis are neatly lined up in a rack. Next to them, a set of wall-mounted tools are all in their correct place on the board and Minoo feels certain that the contents of the white cupboards are just as well organized.

The enormous table supporting Lage's model railroad occupies the center of the room. He is building a miniature Engelsfors. Everything is there, but it is a nostalgic version of the town, harking back to a time when Engelsfors was at its most successful. Many of the railroad tracks are no longer in use. Minoo didn't even know they existed until she inspected Lage's impressive reconstruction.

She looks at the model of the high school. The site of evil seems very small from her giant's perspective.

'Don't you have a graduation reception of your own?' she asks, and looks at Rickard, who has remained near the stairs.

'Sure do,' he says, sounding weary. 'My relatives are out in force. Ready with the gravadlax. But I felt I had to come here first. I knew you would be here.'

He looks steadily at her.

'At first, my memories were a mess. I thought you and your friends and Gustaf were in with Olivia in some way. Today, everything sort of fell into place and I remembered everything. You stopped Olivia from killing the lot of us, didn't you?'

Minoo realizes that Rickard remembers far too much.

'Who are you, really?' he continues. 'You and your friends . . . *What* are you? Or is the whole thing a hallucination? Am I completely unhinged?'

He looks desperate. And utterly alone.

Minoo makes up her mind.

'We are witches.'

Her mind is reeling with the fact that she has admitted the most forbidden thing of all to an outsider.

She had no idea what kind of reaction to expect. But Rickard actually looks relieved.

'I'm not mad then?' he says.

'No, you're not.'

Rickard sits down heavily on the stairs.

'Witches,' he says, and seems to taste the word. 'Olivia, was she a witch, too?'

'Yes.'

'But she was . . . an evil witch. But you are . . . good witches?'

'Well, sort of. I don't know if Olivia was truly evil. But she did evil things . . . Are you all right?' Minoo asks, and instantly hears how silly it sounds. 'I realize it's a lot to take in.'

'It was much worse worrying that I was going nuts. I knew, of course, what I had seen, but it all seemed so impossible.'

Minoo nods. She understands perfectly. In the beginning, it had been hard for her to believe in everything they were taught. And she had, after all, been able to share the knowledge with Rebecka and the other Chosen Ones, and with Nicolaus. Without them, she would definitely have worried about her sanity.

'At first I didn't remember anything,' Rickard says. 'I woke up in hospital. They said I had been picked up unconscious and that it was because an electrical fault had caused a lot of accidents in the school. I couldn't answer a single question about what had happened. I didn't remember much from my entire senior year. But later on, I started dreaming about it . . . Then I saw snapshots when I was awake as well. Like flashbacks in a film.'

There is a large thump in the kitchen. Minoo and Rickard look toward the door at the top of the stairs, but it stays closed.

'I've done so many horrible things,' he says.

'No, it wasn't you. It was Olivia. She used your amulet to control you.'

Rickard nods.

'Sometimes she was only a small voice whispering somewhere in the background. But at other times she would take me over. Only, I would still be present, but couldn't do a thing. Like, when you know it's a nightmare and are aware that you're dreaming but it doesn't help because you can't wake up and can't do anything about what's going on in the dream.'

Minoo shudders. She knows way too much about nightmares.

'Why did Olivia choose you? Do you know?'

Rickard looks troubled.

'We had a thing going.'

'A thing? Did you go out together?'

'Not exactly,' he says, still avoiding her eyes. 'It started at the Spring Ball, when she was in her last year of middle school. I went along because I hoped she would be there. She seemed so self-assured and cool. Different. Earlier, I had wanted to talk to her but didn't dare. Girls like her think boys like me are hopeless weirdos. At the ball, we were both drunk. Afterward, we got together now and then, but she insisted on keeping it secret.'

He takes his glasses off and polishes them slowly with a corner of his shirt.

'I understood from the start that she didn't really want me. She was after Elias. But I kept hoping that she might change her mind. Even if it was humiliating, it was better than nothing. I loved her. But, after Elias's funeral, she told me that . . . that she didn't want to go out with me anymore.'

He puts his glasses back on and Minoo waits, lets him tell the story at his own pace.

'Last summer, she asked me to come and see her at home. She said it had dawned on her that I was the right one for her after all and that she wanted to be my girlfriend. For real. I was pathetic enough to say yes immediately. And then she gave me this gift. A token to show we belonged together.'

'The necklace with the amulet,' Minoo says.

Rickard nods.

'That same evening, she took me along to be introduced to Helena and Krister. I heard her say to them that I was a perfect choice for persuading people at school to join Positive Engelsfors. Popular, but not too popular. Of course, her control over me was especially strong because I was in love with her.'

Minoo had known all along that Olivia killed the innocent. Still, it had been easier to think of her as a victim of the demons and their lies, blinded by her longing for Elias.

What Minoo hadn't realized was how cynical and calculating she actually was. How deliberately she exploited people around her.

'It was the worst part of it,' Rickard continues. 'Whatever she did, I couldn't stop loving her. Not until Ida stopped her. I got the message then. Saw her for who she truly was.'

He looks straight at Minoo.

'Minoo, what happened to her? Do you know where she is? Is she alive?'

'She is alive, but I don't know where she is.'

Rickard says nothing. Two children run shouting through the kitchen above them and disappear outside.

'Why doesn't anyone else remember what went on in the gym?' he asks eventually.

'Because they were all wearing Olivia's amulets. What I don't understand is how you can remember anything.'

'To what extent is Gustaf mixed up in this?'

'Not at all. He didn't wear an amulet. But I took away his memories of what happened in the gym. I had to.'

All the color drains from Rickard's face.

'I won't tell anyone. I promise.'

She believes him. She doesn't even have to scare him with the Council, because he is scared enough already. Everything in her shies away at the thought of manipulating his memories. She can't bring herself to put him through that. Not after all he had to endure from Olivia.

'I trust you,' she says. 'But I shall have to talk to the others about this.'

'The others?' Rickard asks. 'Linnéa? And Vanessa? And that big girl who usually goes around with you? Are there more?'

'There were more of us,' Minoo explains. 'In the beginning, we were seven, with Ida, Elias and Rebecka.'

'Elias? And *Rebecka*?'

'That's right.'

Telling the truth, just for once, is irresistible.

'But they were murdered,' Minoo adds.

She and Rickard jump when they hear glass breaking. Minoo looks around and realizes for the first time that the basement is divided into two rooms.

The door between the two rooms is too near one of the white cupboards to be easily seen. She notices it now, as Gustaf comes through it. He is holding a champagne bottle and his light slacks are splashed.

He looks straight at her.

He has heard them. He has heard everything.

Behind her, Rickard gets up.

It is so silent down here, it is difficult to imagine that a noisy reception is going on outside the house. That guests in bright clothes are mingling and chatting about their plans for the summer, and probably wondering where the man of the moment has disappeared to. The man who is looking at Minoo as if she were a stranger. Somebody *alien*. A creature from space who has just ripped off her human disguise.

'I've wanted to tell you for so long . . .' Minoo says.

'Go right ahead,' Gustaf says evenly. 'Do tell me everything.'

She is dying inside now, when he looks at her like that. She fights to stay detached, to keep a cool head. Of course Gustaf is upset. She must take her chance and explain. If only she can put it clearly, he will understand. She *must* make him understand.

'There is a war going on,' she begins. 'Demons are trying to enter our world here, in Engelsfors. If they succeed, it means our world is finished. We, who are called the Chosen Ones, can stop this from happening. Nobody else can.'

She stops talking and looks at Gustaf.

'Go on.'

'It all began with Elias.'

She tries to explain without getting bogged down in details. It is surprisingly easy. Even when she describes their suspicions of Gustaf and how they pursued him and made him take truth serum, she talks on. She can't stop now until she has confessed everything. Even how much she loved Max.

The words are flowing, even though a part of her tells her to stop. This is too big. Too much. And much too dangerous for them to know. What will the Council do if they find out?

But another part of her drives her to reveal all, and that part is the stronger. She *must*. Lies are unsustainable: that has been proven to her again and again.

Gustaf and Rickard listen intently while she talks. She loses all concept of time. Then, suddenly, she has reached the part about Matilda and the dream. And, after that, there are no more words.

Somewhere in the house, one of Gustaf's sisters calls his name. He doesn't seem to have heard.

'You said to Rickard that you removed my memories of what happened in the gym.'

'I'm sorry. But it was the only thing I could do to protect you from the Council.'

'I want them back,' Gustaf says.

'I don't know if it's possible. I've never—'

Gustaf interrupts. 'Now.'

The look in his blue eyes is steely.

She swallows hard.

179

She comes close to him, puts her hand on his forehead and allows the smoke to well out. She doesn't even have to enter Gustaf's consciousness. It is as if she has created a loop around the bundle of his memories and all she has to do is *pull* . . .

On the walls and floor of the gym, circles of light emit a ghostly glow. Ida stares in terror at Olivia, who is announcing Ida's love for Gustaf to everyone in the hall. Flashes of lightning. Ida, dying in Gustaf's arms. His lips against hers as he tries to blow air into her lungs.

Minoo opens her eyes and takes her hand away. Gustaf is as still as a statue. His eyes are fixed on the model of Engelsfors.

'It was all true,' he says in the end. 'Everything you've told us is true.'

'I've wanted to tell you,' Minoo says. 'I've wanted to tell you for such a long time. Rebecka, too, always wanted to tell you. But Matilda said we must not, and urged us not to trust anyone—'

Gustaf interrupts her. 'You knew all along that she did not take her own life.'

'Yes,' Minoo says in a strangled voice.

'I never want to see you again.'

He says it plainly. As if it were any ordinary sentence.

The adrenaline is rushing into her system. Her arms and hands are shaking.

'Please,' she says.

'Leave, now.'

He looks at her and she knows that she truly has lost him.

She walks toward the stairs. Rickard is speaking but she doesn't listen. She walks past him. When she opens the door to the kitchen, the first thing she sees is Vicky's grinning face.

'Minoo! We were beginning to wonder why Gustaf never came back from the basement,' she begins teasingly. But her smile fades quickly. 'Has something happened?'

Minoo doesn't answer.

The walk back from Gustaf's house has never felt so long. Ahead of her, the streets seem to stretch like elastic.

Halfway home, she has to stop to vomit into a lilac bush.

She feels no better afterward.

Pain corrodes her whole being, vibrates throughout her body as she places one foot in front of the other, moving herself step by step toward home.

Lying on her bed, she allows the black smoke to swallow her up until her mind is freed and silenced; until every trace of Minoo Falk Karimi has dissolved and vanished.

CHAPTER 26

A light breeze ruffles the surface of Dammsjön Lake. Linnéa sits in the shade of a tree, looking at Vanessa, who is lying on the sunny side of their blanket. She has turned onto her front to tan her back and has removed her bikini top. Linnéa studies her spine and the contours of her shoulder blades under the skin.

'I wonder if Michelle and Evelina minded that we left so early?' Vanessa says.

'Don't think so,' Linnéa replies.

They only stayed half an hour at Mehmet's reception. Michelle had been absorbed in cuddling his little cousins, while Evelina was being at least as cuddly with her boyfriend.

'You must meet up with them sometime,' Vanessa says.

'I have met them,' Linnéa says.

Vanessa turns her head to peer up at Linnéa. 'I meant, like, really get to know them,' she says. 'They asked if we'd come with them to Olsson's Hill tomorrow after assembly. We might hear of any last-day-of-school parties for later.'

'Super,' Linnéa says.

She is determined not to be the kind of girl who wants to be with her girlfriend 24/7 and won't socialize. All she wishes is that she might at least look forward to going out, because if there's one thing she's useless at, it's faking enthusiasm.

She reaches for the bag of pick 'n' mix that Vanessa had placed between them on the blanket. Most of the sweets contain gelatin, but Linnéa doesn't want to ruin the mood by pointing it out. She roots around and finds a hard, salty licorice bonbon. The heat has made it go sticky and she licks her fingertips after touching it.

A little further along the beach, someone is playing a song that's tipped to be the song of the summer. Vanessa is clearly already hooked because she is moving her shoulders and humming along. Linnéa smiles. She can't hate the song as much as it deserves, now that Vanessa likes it.

She takes another sweet from the bag and scans the people on the beach. Most of them are freshmen and sophomores, trying to get the first tan of the summer while the school is shut for Graduation Day. And most of them can't keep their eyes off Linnéa and Vanessa.

Once Vanessa told Michelle, the news spread like wildfire through the school. If Wille hasn't heard already, he is bound to very soon. For one thing, Lucky is here, sitting some distance away with some boys from the middle school. They are passing a joint between them and Lucky, who seems well into his high, is ogling Linnéa and Vanessa. Linnéa waves and he looks away, embarrassed. She remembers how broken he was the night Olivia killed Jonte and wonders how he is these days.

Linnéa looks at Vanessa again. Her eyes are closed, as if she has fallen asleep. Linnéa longs to lean forward and kiss her sun-warmed neck, but doesn't want to seem like an overeager lapdog.

She is addicted. She wants to touch Vanessa all the time. She, who always used to roll her eyes when couples couldn't keep their hands off each other. Now she understands them only too well. She needs to be better at hiding how obsessed she is or she might scare Vanessa away.

Linnéa's cell phone pings. She finds it in her handbag and reads Anna-Karin's text.

'Vanessa,' she says. 'I think we'd better go. Right away.'

At Minoo's house, Linnéa barely has time to press the doorbell

183

before Anna-Karin opens the door. Her eyes are wide and fearful.

'Come with me,' she says. 'Quickly.'

Linnéa and Vanessa glance at each other before hurrying upstairs behind Anna-Karin. They almost fall over Peppar, who is on his way down.

'We didn't understand your text,' Linnéa says. 'Is Minoo ill?'

'Something is wrong but I don't know what,' Anna-Karin says. 'She was like this when I came home.'

She opens the door to Minoo's room and they troop inside, Linnéa first.

Minoo, still in a sky-blue party dress, is lying on her back on the bed. Her eyes are open but unfocused. The mascara has run down her cheeks.

'Do you think it could be the demons?' Anna-Karin says. 'Could they have taken her over somehow?'

Linnéa sits down on the edge of the bed. She concentrates on trying to reach Minoo's thoughts. It's like banging her head against a wall. She is positive about one thing, though. It is Minoo herself who is mounting the defense.

'No, it's not the demons,' Linnéa says, and snaps her fingers in front of Minoo's eyes.

'Minoo! Hello!'

No reaction. She grabs Minoo by the shoulders and shakes her.

'Hello!'

'Be careful!' Anna-Karin says.

Linnéa slaps Minoo's cheek, not very hard but hard enough. Tears well up as she looks at Linnéa.

'I'm sorry,' Linnéa says. 'But it was a slap or a bucket of water.'

'Go away,' Minoo mumbles. She curls up with her back toward Linnéa.

Does anyone have a clue what might have happened? Linnéa thinks, looking at Anna-Karin and Vanessa.

She went to Gustaf's reception, Anna-Karin thinks. *That's all I know.*

Gustaf. Did Minoo tell him how she feels but was rejected? Linnéa can't believe that Minoo would choose to bare her soul at Gustaf's party. Or, in fact, tell him at any time.

'Please, Minoo, tell us what happened,' Vanessa says in her gentlest voice.

Minoo's back is shaking now.

'Forgive me,' she sobs. 'I've ruined everything . . . I can't . . . I . . .'

Linnéa cautiously puts her hand on her friend's arm.

Think it instead, she pleads. *If it's easier that way.*

'You'll all hate me,' Minoo sobs.

And then her thoughts come pouring into Linnéa's head. Every word Minoo uttered to Rickard and Gustaf. Every secret revealed.

The look in Gustaf's eyes when she had finished. His icy stare. His words. *I don't ever want to see you again.*

Linnéa tries to fend off Minoo's feelings of intense self-disgust and backs away mentally.

'What's the matter?' Vanessa asks.

Linnéa feels the self-disgust – for once not her own – start to fade away.

'She has told Gustaf and Rickard about us,' she explains.

'Told them what about us?' Anna-Karin asks.

'Everything,' Linnéa says. 'Absolutely everything.'

She still can't get her head around this. Compared to the other Chosen Ones, Minoo has always been the most cautious, the most disciplined. She is the type who always thinks before she acts.

And then she goes and does this. How could Minoo ignore what the Council does to law-breakers?

'Holy shit,' Vanessa exclaims. 'How did the guys take it?'

'Gustaf hates me,' Minoo mumbles.

'Stay cool,' Linnéa says, making an effort not to sound

angry. 'It's easily fixable. You can take their memories away again.'

'I can't . . .' Minoo is sobbing again. 'I can't.'

'Minoo, listen. I know you're desperately sad now, but think about it,' Vanessa says, as patiently as if she were talking to Melvin. 'It's dangerous for them as well as for us—'

'They deserve to know the truth,' Minoo interrupts.

'Don't you remember how it felt when we were told?' Linnéa asks. 'Suddenly, you're informed that magic is for real, and demons too, and that the world will be destroyed some time soon and—'

'Of course I do!'

'But Gustaf and Rickard don't have anything to balance against all that,' Linnéa continues. 'They are not witches. They can't do a thing. Totally powerless.'

'He thought all along that Rebecka took her own life and that he was to blame,' Minoo says, turning to Vanessa. 'You were there when we gave him the truth serum. You saw how shattered he was. Because he couldn't bear his feelings of guilt, he even let PE brainwash him for a while.'

'Do you truly believe that telling him what really happened has made it easier for him?' Linnéa asks. 'I'd say not, given how he reacted.'

Vanessa gives her the evil eye but Linnéa doesn't regret having a go. She knows she's right.

'So, it's suddenly just fine to feed people lies?' Minoo says. 'You're such a hypocrite!'

'And what are you exactly? Who gave you the fucking right to make such a huge decision?' Linnéa says harshly. 'You might at least have talked to us first!'

'Stop it,' Vanessa says.

Anna-Karin backs her. 'Yes, stop it!'

Linnéa will not let Minoo look away.

You are in love with Gustaf, she thinks. *That is why you can't think clearly about the situation.*

Minoo stares at her. 'Neither of them will repeat a word of what I told them.'

'Are you sure about that?' Anna-Karin asks.

'Yes, I am. For one thing, I told them about the Council. They realize what a threat it is. And, besides . . . don't you understand, this is just the beginning? Remember what we talked about earlier! Everything is changing. More and more people will be affected.'

She meets Linnéa's eyes.

'I take responsibility for what I did. The way I see things, *everyone* should be informed. It would undermine the Council's power, for one thing.'

Linnéa can't answer. Suddenly, *she* is the cautious, conservative one.

'I am not going to alter their memories,' Minoo says. 'You can't force me.'

'No,' Vanessa says, glancing at Linnéa. 'It's a fact, we can't.'

Minoo turns her back to them again. Suddenly, Linnéa feels a pang of conscience. What if Gustaf had been Vanessa?

I understand why you did it, Linnéa thinks.

But she has no idea if Minoo is listening.

* * *

Anna-Karin is sitting in bed with her laptop in front of her and the headphones on. She is watching a movie with a female lead who is trying to figure out who her father is before she gets married. But Anna-Karin can't concentrate on the ins and outs of the plot.

She doesn't quite understand how Minoo's magic works. Clearly, Minoo can use it as a means of escape. It's all very worrying. Anna-Karin knows from her own experience how easy it is to misuse magic and how hard it is to admit one's dependency on it.

She shuts her eyes. Escapes in her own way.

Now, she is with the fox.

The Key

This early summer night, he is running among the tall trees. What he feels cannot be put into words. But if she were to try, his mind is urging him to *search, search, search, look, look, search, search, search.*

* * *

Minoo is standing in front of Rebecka and Elias's graves. The stones gleam faintly in the dark. A few rows further away, there is a third source of light. Ida's grave.

'Minoo.'

She turns toward the voice and sees Matilda's freckled face. Her reddish-blonde hair falls loose over her shoulders; strands are lifted by a light wind that Minoo can't feel.

'Everything changes,' Matilda says. 'And soon they will change even more.'

Minoo nods. She recognizes the truth of this.

'Have you come to show me something?' she asks.

Matilda holds a skull in her hands and Minoo takes it from her. It is surprisingly light. She looks into the empty eye sockets.

'Is this the stranger you told me about?' she asks.

'No.'

'Does it have something to do with death?'

Matilda doesn't reply. When Minoo looks up she sees that Matilda's face is streaked with tears.

'Will someone else die?'

'There is always someone who must be sacrificed,' Matilda says. 'Remember that. Promise me.'

And Minoo knows that she will have forgotten this dream when she wakes up, but Matilda's words will stay inside her and be there for her when she needs them.

CHAPTER 27

A choir of monks singing in Latin, backed by a synthesizer and sexily whispering female voices, is coming from the Crystal Cave's loudspeakers. Vanessa eyes the clock on the wall and flicks the duster. Two dolphins are tumbling in a never-ending circular movement in front of the sea horizon painted on the clock face.

The restlessness inside her feels like an exploded ant heap. She longs for Linnéa. But Linnéa is in the school and Vanessa is stuck here. The clock dolphins move so unbelievably slowly.

Her cell vibrates in her pocket. A text from Linnéa.

JUST SAW M IN SCHOOL. SHE SEEMS OK.

That's a relief. After yesterday, Vanessa has been worried about Minoo.

'You're not paid to stand around tapping away on your cell phone,' Mona says, and looks at Vanessa across the rim of her reading glasses.

She is perched on the high stool behind the cash register, with a gossip mag open on her crossed legs. Today's outfit consists of denim-look leggings and a peach sweatshirt with Minnie Mouse printed on the chest.

'I've finished dusting,' Vanessa tells her.

'No, you haven't, you haven't done the bookshelf,' Mona says, noisily turning a page. 'Oh my God, he looks crazy these days. It's like his face has shrunk in the wash. If he isn't Botoxed within an inch of his life, I'll eat every scented candle in stock.'

And this is the woman who is our only source of independent information, Vanessa thinks. The only one that doesn't have some connection to the Council or the demons or the guardians.

She takes a book from the shelf – *Find Your Inner Shaman* – and wipes it carefully with the duster. Trying to get Mona to talk will probably get her nowhere – but then, she has nothing to lose.

She replaces the book and takes out *Diet with Your Aura* instead.

'Mona,' she says. 'How much do you know about the apocalypse?'

'Quite enough to want nothing to do with it,' Mona replies as she turns another page. 'Wow, what the fuck does she think she looks like in that?'

Vanessa sighs. Whenever she has tried to take up the subject with Mona, she has gotten this far and no further. But she is not going to give up. Maybe she has never asked the right question. Maybe a roundabout approach would be better.

'Are you a natural or a trained witch?' she asks, and tries to look super-focused on the duster as she sweeps it over *Karma as a Weapon*.

'That's no question to ask a lady, surely you know that much?' Mona cackles. 'But since you ask, I'm a natural.'

'How did you find out that you're a witch?'

'It wasn't too hard for my parents to work that out,' Mona replies. 'Seeing that they were both witches too. And clairvoyants.'

Not exactly a complete autobiography, but this is more than Mona has ever said about her life. Vanessa tries to hide how eager she is for more. She knows showing it would make Mona shut up like a clam. If for no other reason than to piss her off.

'Were they Council members?'

Mona looks up from the magazine.

'What are you going on about?' she snaps. 'My parents were free witches – miles different from that crew of snot-nosed suits. Fucking brown-nosers, all of them. The Council always delude themselves that they can make witches do what they say, no questions asked. Sure, one doesn't want to cross them if one can avoid it. But we don't give a shit about whatever they're up to.'

She tries to light up, and swears loudly when her lighter won't work. Vanessa has never seen her so angry. Clearly, this is a sore spot. She should keep prodding at it.

'I'm sorry,' Vanessa says, trying to look innocent. 'All I thought was . . . I've heard that the Council runs schools and thought maybe that's where you learned about magic.'

'You think those fucking bureaucrats have anything to teach me?' Mona inhales deeply and blows smoke through her nostrils. 'We free witches teach each other.'

'What about the *Book of Patterns*, then?'

'*That thing*,' Mona sneers. 'Strictly for Council nerds to sit and stare at through their sad little spy-glasses.'

'So you don't have one yourself?'

'In your dreams! I don't even stock them, even though they're selling like fucking hot cakes on the black market. That book has always given me a nasty sinking feeling. Bad vibes. Just like that very proper friend of yours.'

'Minoo?'

'That's the one. Something's not right with that magic.'

Vanessa wonders what Mona would say if she knew that the magic of the guardians doesn't belong to this world at all.

'You don't think we should trust the *Book of Patterns* then?' she says.

'Now, you take the advice of an experienced woman,' Mona says, fixing her with a steely eye. 'Don't trust *anything*. Or *anyone*.'

'Not you, either, then?'

'Especially not me, sweetie.'

Mona falls silent. Her gaze follows the column of smoke that rises from her cigarette and mixes with the sandalwood incense.

'Things are gearing up,' she says. 'But you know that, too.'

'Within the year, apparently,' Vanessa agrees.

Again, Mona peers at her above the rim of her reading glasses.

'Now, look, sweetie. I know you lot are all worked up into a froth about that portal. Yes, sure, it would be nice if you closed it. But the way I see it, everything will end sooner or later anyway. I try to catch the day when I can. And the night, for that matter. But, to be honest, I feel quite sorry for you and the other junior witches. I know you're trying hard but, frankly, the odds against you are fucking terrible.'

Vanessa is amazed. Coming from Mona, all this sounds almost like a declaration of love.

'You'd be very welcome to help us, you know that,' Vanessa says.

'What will be will be,' Mona replies.

She stubs out her cigarette, starts studying the magazine again and points to a picture of a smartly dressed couple at a party.

'Those two, what they've got going won't last.'

'So you can tell the fortunes of people in gossip mags as well?'

'No need to be a psychic to spot that,' Mona sniffs. 'Just check her out. Eyes so wide apart she looks like a hammerhead shark in a wig. Now, look at him . . . now, him I wouldn't kick out of bed.'

You wouldn't have to, Vanessa thinks. He'd run a mile.

Mona turns another page and lights another cig.

'Of course, you've kicked all males out of *your* bed. And hitched up with that little shoplifter. I don't want to say "I told you so", but I told you so.'

Vanessa looks at her, annoyed. Mona is back to her old self.

'You should work for one of those magazines, Mona. Since you're so brilliant at sticking your nose into what's none of your business.'

Mona grins and sucks on her cigarette.

'I suspect you'd like us to change the subject,' she says. 'Not everyone is as up with all the latest developments as I am.'

The bell on the door tinkles and Vanessa turns around. Her mom enters, carrying a dripping umbrella. Mona removes her reading glasses and puts the magazine away.

'Hello, girls. What weather we're having,' Mom says. 'But you're all cozy in here.'

'Oh, yes,' Vanessa mumbles while Mona and Mom hug.

'Your energy is in good shape today, Jannike,' Mona says.

'Do you really think so?' Mom says happily. 'I tried to meditate a little this morning.'

'Yes, I can feel your chakras are becoming balanced,' Mona says. 'Have you tried keeping some crystals of rose quartz in your room?'

Mona blathers on about Mom's chakras. Now and then, she casts meaningful glances in Vanessa's direction. Vanessa knows exactly why. By now, Mom is probably the only person alive in Engelsfors who doesn't know that she and Linnéa are together.

Some people don't understand. But, as Linnéa says, it's a fail-safe idiot test.

Vanessa hopes that Mom will pass the test.

She notes that her mom buys a rose quartz crystal, and then can't resist a small Buddha figurine and a vial of ethereal oil that Vanessa knows will make their apartment stink.

'I hardly dare to come here,' Mom says, and laughs. 'I always leave having bought more than I'd intended.'

She turns to Vanessa.

'You're not sleeping over with one of your friends tonight, are you?'

'No,' Vanessa says. She stands staring after her mother as she leaves the City Mall.

'Who's a little coward, then?' Mona says.

'Shut it,' Vanessa says.

CHAPTER 28

'Only a week left before summer vacation! And that's why we are going to have an *especially* great time today!' their gym teacher, Lollo, says, spreading her muscular arms in a wide gesture.

Anna-Karin stares at the obstacle course that runs the full length of the gym. Even the scheduled softball game would have been preferable, but it is raining too hard.

All the worst torture instruments have been hauled into place. The beam. The pommel horse. The ropes are dangling from the ceiling. One of the thick mattresses with sweat-stinking plastic covers has been placed across two low benches. Presumably they're meant to crawl under it.

Anna-Karin's mind feels just as switched-off as usual but her body responds instinctively. The palms of her hands are moist.

'Jump to it, everyone!' Lollo shouts and claps her hands. 'Let's start with a warm-up round!'

Anna-Karin reminds herself that Lollo is *not* a sadist. Her problem is that she can't get into her head that not everyone loves exercise.

They start by jogging in a wide circle, following the walls of the hall. Kevin smacks Hanna H's bottom as he passes her and she screams irritably. Only a few months have passed since they were all in this gym with gleaming amulets on chains around their necks.

Anna-Karin runs past the stands and thinks about the moment when Ida stepped forward and saved them all. She

194

showed strengths that Anna-Karin had never expected in her. She was courageous. Loyal, unselfish. And then she died. It was so totally unfair, as Ida would have said. What would Ida have been like if she had survived? Would they ever have become friends?

Minoo sits in the stands. She told Lollo that she wasn't well; after one look at her, Lollo asked if she should have come to school at all.

As she runs past Minoo, Anna-Karin looks up at her but Minoo just stares at the floor.

'Now, let's go!' Lollo cries. 'I'll sort you into teams . . . and I'll time you. It would be a shame not to have a bit of a competition!'

Anna-Karin is told to join Levan and two all-around athletes, Anchalee and Lina. Anna-Karin senses the eyes of the two girls drilling into her and almost wants to apologize. With her on the team they haven't a chance of winning.

Lollo blows her whistle and the first team sets off toward the pommel horse, led by Hanna A. While they work their way around the obstacle course, Levan stands scanning the hall, hands on hips, looking as if he were calculating a physics formula that will get him into goal with minimum loss of time. Then he turns to Anna-Karin.

'We'll do great,' he says and smiles encouragingly at her.

The lie feels almost as humiliating as Anchalee and Lina's staring. Lollo blows her whistle again. It's their turn. Levan, Anchalee and Lina all clear the pommel horse smoothly and continue on to the beam. Levan runs across it without having to look where he puts his feet. Anna-Karin hasn't even gotten to the horse and then, just as she is about to jump, she hesitates for a microsecond too long. She lands on her knees on the worn leather and has to slide down the sides.

Lina snakes under the mattress and practically throws herself at the wooden bar frames. Anchalee and Levan are already climbing and all three are too busy to keep an eye on

Anna-Karin. But she is very aware of the eyes of the others. At least she manages to get across the beam without falling off.

She gets down on her belly and starts wriggling into the dark space under the mattress. Her heart is beating far too hard. It feels as if something inside her is about to burst. A wave of panic almost makes her stand up and heave the mattress away. She tries to calm down.

'Are you stuck?' Kevin shouts.

This isn't dangerous, she tells herself. Nothing bad can happen.

The stench of the mattress and the floor is nauseating. She keeps on crawling. And finally, she is out.

She gets up and jogs toward the frames. Her team is already waiting for her between a row of small plastic cones where they are to run a relay race.

'Go, go, *go*, Anna-Karin!' Anchalee calls out. Lina jumps impatiently up and down on the spot, making her bunches of blonde hair bounce.

Anna-Karin puts her foot on the lowermost bar of the frame. It still feels as if something is about to break inside her. Like what happened to her mom. After looking around on the web, Anna-Karin knows that a tendency to develop aortic aneurysms can be inherited.

But she starts climbing. It isn't hard. It isn't dangerous. What she is feeling is just her imagination. All she has to do is grab the top bar and then clamber along the wall-mounted frames to the other end of the hall. She reaches with her right hand, feeling the bar against her palm. She grips it and it breaks.

She falls and lands heavily on the floor.

'Time for that diet!' Kevin yells.

'Don't be so fucking horrible!' someone else calls out. 'Her mom just died!'

Anna-Karin sits up and sees Lollo and Minoo come running toward her.

Part Two

'Goodness, Anna-Karin! Are you all right?' Lollo says.

'Did you hit your head?' Minoo asks.

'No . . .' Anna-Karin mumbles. 'I'm fine.'

It's a fact that she doesn't hurt anywhere. She brushes the fragments of wood off her hand.

'I can't tell you how many times I've been nagging the school management about new equipment,' Lollo says. 'All the old things are death-traps.'

Anna-Karin looks up and sees the broken wooden bar. She begins to realize what has happened. Her team crowds worriedly around her.

'Gosh, that looked awful,' Lina says.

'Are you sure you're all right?' Minoo says as she holds out her hand.

'Yes, I'm fine,' Anna-Karin says and gets up without taking the offered hand.

'I think you should go and see the school nurse all the same,' Lollo says.

'I'll go with her,' Minoo says quickly.

Lollo blows her whistle and announces that she will take Anna-Karin's place on the team.

In the changing room, Anna-Karin sits down on a bench and looks at her hands. They look perfectly ordinary. She feels the same as ever. It would be easy to tell herself that the bar really was about to break, but she knows it is not so.

'What actually happened?' Minoo asks.

Earth is associated with strength. That was what Adriana had said when she explained to them about the elements for the first time. *Physical as well as mental.*

'The bar was in bad shape,' Anna-Karin says.

She is ashamed. Ashamed because now she will cause a new problem for the others. She won't manage to control this new power. She will become a threat to herself and everyone else. Again.

The ceiling lights flicker, go dark and then come on again.

Anna-Karin walks to the lockers and turns the key gently so she doesn't break it. She gets her clothes out.

'It was quite a shock, though. I think I'd better go home,' she says.

'OK,' Minoo says. Her eyes have an inward look.

If she was her usual self, she would have seen straight through me, Anna-Karin thinks.

When she walks upstairs to the entrance lobby, habit makes her reach for the handrail. She remembers just in time and pulls her hand back.

* * *

Rain is hammering against the windowpanes. Minoo leans her head in her hands and stares at the lab bench. The cow's eye lies in its dish and looks back at her. The others are already busy separating the iris from the cornea. Minoo hasn't been able to bring herself even to lift her scalpel.

She didn't lie when she told Lollo that she felt unwell. Whenever she thinks about yesterday, which she does incessantly, it feels as if she has a red-hot iron ball in her stomach. She can hardly sit upright.

She wishes that she dared go home and lose herself in the black smoke. But her experience yesterday frightened her. The depths she had disappeared into made her fearful because, next time, maybe not even a slap would bring her back.

There's a knock on the door. Ove Post, who has been dozing at his desk, wakes with a jerk.

'Come in,' he says.

He straightens up when the principal, Tommy Ekberg, steps into the classroom. Tommy's flushed face matches the color of his shirt and he can't quite hide his breathlessness.

'Minoo?' he asks while his eyes scan the room.

The ball catches fire. Something has happened.

It mustn't be Dad, not Dad, not Dad.

'You have a visitor,' Tommy says once he has spotted her. 'A relative. Your uncle, I believe. Apparently he has come about quite an urgent matter.'

Minoo has no uncle. It must be a misunderstanding. Could it be her titular uncle, Bahar's husband? But why would Reza turn up in Engelsfors? And why come and see her at school?

All eyes are on Minoo as she gets up and leaves the classroom.

'What's happened?' she asks as they step into the stairwell.

'He wants to speak to you face-to-face,' Tommy says in a gentle voice.

Minoo follows him downstairs. Her eyes fix on the large keyring in his back pocket. The keys rattle with every step he takes. Her brain is churning with nightmare scenarios, one hooking onto the next. Mom and Bahar might have been involved in a terrible accident in Stockholm and Reza came all the way here to break the news. Maybe he spoke to Dad first and Dad had a heart attack because it hasn't been at all good for him to start exercising so suddenly and now he's in hospital and no one knows if he is going to pull through. Maybe he is dead already. Mom and Bahar might be dead, too.

She tries to block these thoughts. Tries to persuade herself that all this is completely unrealistic, but her dread is too tangible, feels too real for reasoning to be effective.

Tommy escorts her into his office.

'You can talk in peace and quiet in here,' he says pleasantly and leaves.

A man in his fifties is standing in front of the desk. His graying hair is slightly ruffled and his eyes are keen. He examines Minoo intently. He wears a navy-blue suit and the top buttons of his light blue shirt are casually undone.

She has definitely never seen him before.

'I apologize for the theatricals,' he says. 'But I thought you might prefer that we meet here. On neutral ground, as it were.'

He smiles boyishly.

'My name is Walter Hjorth,' he says. 'I'm chairman of the Council.'

CHAPTER 29

Walter Hjorth holds out his hand and Minoo forces herself to take it and squeeze it with a decent amount of pressure, while not allowing herself to faint from utter terror.

Gustaf and Rickard. The Council has found out that she has told them everything.

'Shall we sit down so we can relax while we chat?' Walter says.

He settles on the sofa and Minoo sinks down on the armchair. Her pulse is beating so hard that her field of vision vibrates.

'Just to let you know, I told Tommy that I'm here because of a family crisis,' Walter explains. 'I do hope it won't cause you any trouble.'

Minoo is aware of how close she is to babbling hysterically, to going on about how it wasn't Gustaf and Rickard's fault and that she will do everything to put it right and of course she will take her punishment for revealing things to the people from the non-magic world but they must leave Gustaf and Rickard alone. But she manages to keep her urge under control. Better let Walter do the talking.

'Relax,' Walter says and smiles boyishly again. 'I've come to sort out this mess.'

What mess? Minoo wonders. The Gustaf-and-Rickard mess? Or some other mess?

'I've led the Swedish section of the Council for almost twenty years,' Walter says. 'But I must admit I've never experienced anything like this. Everything has gone completely out of control. And, as my father used to say, when things get out of hand, your first job must be to find out *why*. So that's what I'm trying to do. I want to get a grip on what actually went wrong here. It's far from easy, I assure you.'

He is still smiling but a little sadly now. What *is* all this about?

'I don't do conflict if I can avoid it,' he continues. 'Frankly, it's not how I operate. But now, well, it is as if we were at war. It is an awfully miserable situation, in my view. So unnecessary, for all involved. And it is entirely my fault.'

He places his hand on his chest and looks at Minoo with a frank expression on his face. She understands less and less by the minute.

'I should have come here at a much earlier stage,' he says. 'But I believed Alexander when he assured me that he had control of the situation.'

Minoo notes that it has stopped raining.

The clock on the wall is ticking loudly.

'The court case was a disaster,' Walter says. 'A colossal mistake. Alexander shouldn't have started the process, but he's so obsessed with following all the rules he never takes the consequences into account. You have surely heard the tragic story about Adriana as a young woman?'

Minoo wonders if this is a trap, if he is trying to make her admit that Adriana has told them too much about her past. But Walter talks on, apparently untroubled.

'It happened just after I had taken on the chairmanship. Adriana had a love affair with a very talented natural witch, guy called Simon Takahashi. They planned to leave the Council and escape together. Alexander turned them in.'

Minoo only knew that Alexander carried out the torture-style punishment that bound Adriana to the Council forever. She hadn't thought it would be possible to dislike him even more, but it's clear that isn't the case.

'He believed he did the right thing back then as well,' Walter says. 'And I knew no better. As I've mentioned, I was new to the job at the time and really feeling the pressure. I was trying to live up to what I construed as the expectations of the world. I have bosses, too, the members of the joint board of the European Councils in Paris. But I'm not trying to blame anyone else. We punished Adriana and Simon far too harshly. If only I could turn back time . . .'

He seems to withdraw into himself and sits in silence for a while. Minoo has seen through Adriana's eyes how Simon died and she has experienced Adriana's suffering. Even so, she finds it difficult to link these events to the man sitting opposite her. It seems unreal.

Her pulse is beating more slowly now. There is nothing threatening about Walter's manner. Besides, being frightened is so exhausting.

'My belief is that this tragic incident has hung over us ever since,' he says in the end. 'It certainly influenced what went on here. One error led to another. Now I hope we'll be able to put all that behind us. Start afresh. We agree about what we want, after all.'

'And what is that?' Minoo asks nervously.

Walter looks at her, pins her down with his intense gaze. She notices that his eyes are gray.

'We want to stop the apocalypse.'

Minoo tries to understand.

Adriana has told them that most of the Council members believe neither in the apocalypse nor in the Chosen Ones. That they regard the whole narrative as some sort of myth or fairy tale. The Council's own court announced that the Chosen Ones in Engelsfors were nothing but a bluff invented by Adriana.

'But, the court—' Minoo begins.

'Ah, the court,' Walter interrupts contemptuously. 'Those dinosaurs are precisely the kind of ancient Council members that make my job so goddamn difficult. You mustn't see me in the same light. They belong to the old generation who refuse to get on board with where the world is going now. Though, in this case, that's just as well. If the rumor that the end of the world is near started making the rounds . . . well, you can imagine what would follow.'

Minoo hasn't thought a lot about that angle. She has mostly focused on the end of the world itself.

'Of course, many would choose not to believe it,' Walter says thoughtfully. 'Others would go out to spread the news of impending doom around the world. And some would kill their families and then themselves. But the majority would simply decide that nothing mattered anymore. And these people would become the real threat, Minoo. Because, for them, there would be no limits. Everything would be allowed. Vandalism. Theft. Rape. Murder.'

He looks at her again and his expression is sad.

'When you think about it, it's a good thing that the court insisted that the apocalypse isn't real. Don't you agree?'

Minoo finds herself nodding in agreement.

'Which is the reason I try to keep this operation secret,' Walter continues. 'I have not informed my superiors in Europe and elsewhere. It would just lead to a lot of internal chatter. They might even set out to stop us, which would mean we wouldn't be able to help anyone. We must be left alone to carry out our task. You and I.'

'What do you mean?' Minoo asks.

It feels as if it should be obvious but she cannot make the connection.

'I thought the guardians had given you a heads-up,' Walter says.

The burning pain that she has endured all day ceases immediately.

She is icy cold now.

A stranger will make you an offer.

No, not that. Not the Council. Minoo presses herself against the back of the chair until it feels as if she is practically disappearing inside it.

'Now I understand how unexpected this must be for you,' Walter says. 'Not that the situation was expected by any of us. Especially not by me.'

He looks calmly at her and leans forward.

'A while ago, I found I could study the *Book of Patterns* in a way that was entirely new. The book spoke to me. It told me the history of the world. How the demons came and how some of them stayed, were influenced by our world and decided to become our guardians instead. The book spoke of the portals. About the Chosen Ones. And about the origin of the Council. An origin which, very regrettably, we had forgotten all about.'

'So you know . . . *everything*?' Minoo says.

'That's what the guardians claim, anyway,' he says and smiles.

Minoo doesn't know what to make of this. All the time, Matilda and the guardians have urged the Chosen Ones to stay clear of the Council. And now she is faced with the Council's leader sitting here and saying the *Book of Patterns* has insisted that they must collaborate.

'What do you want from us?' Minoo asks.

'This is hard for you to accept, I know Minoo, but the fact is that your group will not be able to close the portal.'

'We might . . . there's a chance at least,' she says, and hears how feeble she sounds.

Walter shakes his head.

'Not a hope, I'm sorry to say. Ask the *Book of Patterns* if you don't believe me. All the elements are required to close the portal. And though it should be the Chosen Ones, now that three of you are dead . . .' He pauses.

'I wish I could make you believe how terrible I've felt about that. If we hadn't been entangled in all that bureaucracy . . . in my world, there are no excuses for what has happened.'

'Nor in mine,' Minoo says.

'I realize that.'

'But, as I asked earlier,' Minoo says, 'what do you want from me?'

Walter sits back in the sofa again and watches her. She forces herself not to look away.

'I am trying to form a circle that will include some of the most powerful natural witches I can find,' Walter says. 'One representing each element. Together, we can close the portal.'

'The Chosen Ones cannot be replaced. You said so yourself just a moment ago.'

'Another circle can take the place of the Chosen Ones,' Walter says. 'If you are part of it.'

Minoo feels the chill spreading throughout her body.

'No.'

'I thought that would be your first reaction,' Walter says. 'But you really do not have a choice.'

You must accept it. And you must do what is demanded of you and do it wholeheartedly.

'If what you say is true, then why not invite other witches into *our* circle instead?' Minoo has difficulty keeping her voice under control. 'We only need three more.'

'The guardians considered that alternative as well, of course,' Walter says. 'But when they look at all the different ways the future can go, whichever way the guardians twist and turn, the alternatives . . . everything always ends in doom, Minoo. For some reason, your circle cannot be completed by adding new witches. Our only hope, *the world*'s only hope, is that you join us.'

'But Vanessa, Linnéa and Anna-Karin—'

'They have no role left to play,' Walter interrupts.

'You're lying.'

But somewhere deep inside Minoo, a certainty that Walter is telling the truth starts to grow. This *is* what the book has told him.

'I realize that this turnaround is very difficult for you,' he

206

says. 'But you must try to look on the bright side. The guardians have decided that, with you joining our circle, we will have a very real chance of stopping the demons once and for all.'

'Why me?'

'Because you are completely unique.'

He makes it sound like a compliment but Minoo has never before wanted so much to be totally ordinary.

'Our technicians were baffled when they analyzed a sample of your hair. You don't have any trace of an element,' Walter continues.

'I know.'

'But I'm not sure you realize just how exceptional this is. In all of history, there is no record of any other case. All human beings belong to an element. All, except you.'

'What I don't understand is why not having an element is supposed to be such a good thing,' Minoo says.

'You know, of course, how it came about that the demons entered our world. How the magic they brought with them started off a reaction with the elemental magic that was already present.'

Minoo nods.

'If natural witches are blessed by the demons or by the guardians, their powers can become very strong. But they also become unstable.'

Minoo thinks about Olivia and the way she was broken down by the demon magic. And then she thinks about Max in the hospital.

'There is no instability with you, because you have nothing of our world's magic in you,' Walter says. 'You can control the guardians' magic in its purest form. Add to that your special bond to the portal here in Engelsfors and that makes you the most powerful witch who has ever existed.'

Minoo gapes at him. Almost bursts out laughing.

'With you in our circle, we need none of the other Chosen Ones. With you we can win this battle.'

If what Walter is saying is true, if the Chosen Ones are replaceable, this explains how the guardians foresaw futures in which the portal is closed . . . as well as futures in which it is opened.

'But, then, all this should apply to the demons as well,' Minoo says. 'They still have a chance, because their Blessed One can open the portal by having me killed and killing six other natural witches, one for each element. No need to target the Chosen Ones especially. Isn't that so?'

Walter rubs his chin.

'You are very sharp, Minoo. Yes. You're right.'

Minoo doesn't know what to say. Or think. She can find no footholds anywhere.

'I realize that this is a lot to take in,' Walter says. 'Talk to the book to confirm what I have told you. And, Minoo, do remember that this must be *your* decision. Only you have the whole picture. The others may not see the situation as clearly.'

'I won't act one way or the other until I've discussed it with them,' Minoo says.

'Goes without saying. In fact, I *want* you to talk with them. But, before you do, think over what we have talked about carefully. Make up *your* mind. That's more important than anything else. I will respect whatever decision you make, but see to it that you make it for solid reasons. You cannot turn your back on the world because you feel you can't disappoint your friends.'

He leans toward her again and she catches a whiff of his aftershave. It smells expensive.

'Eventually, one reaches a point where one must stop messing around and decide what to believe in,' he says. 'Sometimes things really are as simple as they seem. Do you understand what I'm trying to say?'

Minoo isn't entirely sure that she does, but nods all the same.

Part Two

'I must return to Stockholm now,' Walter says. 'But I will come back once our circle is complete. And, Minoo . . .'

He places his hand on her shoulder.

'I am perfectly aware that you and your friends will find it hard to trust me. I have done nothing to earn your trust. Please, offer my apologies to the others. They don't have to forgive me. But we don't have much time. If we are to save this world, old conflicts must be left in the past. You agree with that, don't you?'

'I will tell the others you said so,' Minoo replies.

Walter nods and gets up. When he gets to the door, he turns and smiles one last time. Then he leaves, closing it quietly behind him.

As soon as she comes home, Minoo takes out the *Book of Patterns*. And for the first time since May Day Eve, the contact is instant.

She knows what the book will say, even before it confirms every single thing Walter has told her.

She puts it away and listens to the noises from Anna-Karin's room. She is shuffling about doing something. Minoo could go and talk to her. And then to Linnéa. And Vanessa.

But she can already guess how they will react: Linnéa protesting. Vanessa being conciliatory. Anna-Karin worrying about what would be best for Minoo. And Minoo herself, swinging like a weathervane in a gale.

Eventually, one reaches a point where one must stop messing around and decide what to believe in. Walter is right. This must be her decision. She alone must work it out. And find out who she is and what she believes.

You are the most powerful witch who has ever existed.

A shiver runs through her body when she recalls what Walter told her. She is not sure whether it is pleasure or fear that she feels. Perhaps both.

CHAPTER 30

The sun dazzles Anna-Karin as she gently pushes Grandpa's wheelchair out onto the terrace of the Sunny Side nursing home. The view is dull, just a few pine trees scattered among a group of brick buildings, but the day is warm and little fluffy clouds are floating in a blue sky.

It is National Day and Anna-Karin and Grandpa have had Sweden cakes with their morning coffee. They were so sugary it hurt her teeth, but she ate Grandpa's cake all the same, after he had said he didn't want it.

She places the wheelchair under a shading parasol and pulls up one of the white plastic chairs, worrying all the time that it will break in her hands. She hasn't visited for a week. She hasn't dared to.

Yesterday, when she tried to tie her shoelaces, she tore them off instead. When she had a drink of water in the evening, she crushed the glass in her hand. When they hauled the last of the removal boxes out of the apartment she had to pretend that they were heavy. This morning, a light squeeze on the shampoo bottle sprayed the contents over the tiled walls. It made her scared to turn the shower off herself in case she pulled the tap to pieces and landed the household with enormous repair bills. She almost told Minoo at that point, just so she could ask her for help.

'Isn't the weather lovely?' Anna-Karin says as she sits down cautiously.

'Yes, yes,' Grandpa says. 'Bit chilly, though.'

'Would you rather sit in the sun?'

'Don't worry. This is just right.'

His eyes scan the terrace anxiously. It gives Anna-Karin a queasy feeling to watch him. Grandpa always used to enjoy being in the open air, but ever since he moved into Sunny Side, he rarely goes out. It seems to make him nervous. He mutters about the sunshine being too hot, and the wind too cold. Her grandpa, who never complained about anything.

It's this place, Anna-Karin thinks. This place is making him like this.

'Shouldn't you be in school today?' Grandpa asks for the second time.

'No, it's *National* Day today,' Anna-Karin replies, trying to sound as if she hasn't already told him. She doesn't want him to feel as if he's going senile.

'Yes, yes,' Grandpa says. 'Soon it will be end-of-semester assembly and all that.'

'Yes, tomorrow.'

Grandpa mutters something in Finnish.

'You lose count of time here,' he says then.

For a while, they are both silent. The scent of lilac is floating past on the light breeze. Anna-Karin wonders if Grandpa senses it. He has told her that his sense of smell is not what it used to be.

'How is it going with the apartment?' Grandpa asks.

'We have cleared everything out,' Anna-Karin says.

She looks at his face with its sunken cheeks and eyes set deep in their sockets. His body no longer fills his checked shirt. The material is flapping around his arms and chest.

Suddenly she has to say it out loud, the idea she has thought about so often, even if it is unrealistic.

'But I don't know if I want to get rid of that apartment. If you and I . . .'

'Anna-Karin . . .' Grandpa says and shakes his head.

But now that she has started to talk about it, she can't stop.

'There is plenty of room. It's easy to adapt for a handicapped person, the doors are already wide enough for a wheelchair. I could ask the school to let me have a sabbatical year. Or maybe I don't even need to do that. You have a right to personal assistance, don't you? Or to home carers?'

The more she talks, the more certain she feels that it would be wrong to give notice to the landlord and leave Grandpa in this place.

'No,' Grandpa says decisively.

'But, listen—'

'Come, come, my girl. It wouldn't do,' he interrupts. 'Now I'd like to go back inside. I had better rest for a while.'

She nods quietly, gets up and releases the brakes on the wheelchair. She pushes Grandpa through the French windows and along the hallway.

The lights in the ceiling are flickering and the alarms are piping monotonously.

The door to the unit next to Grandpa's is open. Anna-Karin glimpses the outline of a bent figure. His thin, wild hair makes his head look like the crown of a dandelion.

She stops outside Grandpa's door, unlocks it gently and opens it wide. Then she swings the wheelchair around, gripping the handles as lightly as she can, and pushes Grandpa inside. He flips the wheelchair table back and holds out his hands toward her.

She has helped her Grandpa into bed many times before, but now she hesitates.

'Maybe I should call for the staff instead,' she says.

'Sweetheart, what's the matter?'

Anna-Karin doesn't want to worry him. But the worry is already there in his eyes.

'You know that I can do . . . some special things,' she says. 'Now, it seems I can do . . . even more.'

She tells him about her new strength and that it comes and goes. Grandpa listens with interest.

'I'm scared that I'll hurt you by accident.'

'I understand that you are scared,' Grandpa says. 'But I'm not.'

'Grandpa . . .' Anna-Karin begins.

'Now you listen to me,' he says. 'That's a wonderful gift you've been given. Right now, you can't quite control it. That's why it scares you. But you mustn't be scared of what is inside you, Anna-Karin.'

He once more holds his hands out. Anna-Karin has a lump in her throat.

'I can't,' she says.

'Yes, you can. I trust you.'

Anna-Karin takes a deep breath and comes to stand in front of him. She puts her hands under his arms. Her pulse is drumming in her ears when he places his hands on her shoulders and pulls himself up from the wheelchair, moaning a little with the effort.

Grandpa's body feels so frail when she holds it upright. It would be so easy to crush his ribs by mistake.

It will not happen, Anna-Karin thinks. I can control myself.

But she doesn't feel too sure.

She moves a few steps so that Grandpa can follow while supporting himself on her.

'This is going just fine,' Grandpa says.

What if she handles this wrong? What if the joints in his arms tear as easily as her shoelaces?

But, finally, Grandpa sits down on the bed. She helps him swing his legs up and then tucks him in.

'There, you see,' he says and smiles. 'I'm not made of china.'

Anna-Karin smiles back at him. Relieved.

'I am an adult,' Grandpa continues, more seriously now. 'I need help with a lot, but you are not responsible for me. I enjoy your company when you come to see me but I will never accept becoming a burden on you. You are young, Anna-Karin. Lead *your* life. That's the best thing you can do for me.'

Anna-Karin presses her lips tightly together. Must not cry.

Doesn't he understand he is a part of her life? Perhaps the most important part of all?

'Now, tell me something,' he says. 'How is your little fox getting on?'

'Just fine, but we haven't been out in the forest together so much recently. But he has been there. So in a way I've been there too . . .'

Grandpa nods a little absently.

'I'll tell you, Anna-Karin, that when I lived on the farm, I could sit and stare at the forest for hours on end. But now, I'm glad I can't see it.'

He glances at the window as if to make sure that the forest isn't there.

'Gerda never liked it,' he adds.

It is rare for Grandpa to mention Grandma, who died from cancer. Anna-Karin has only faint memories of a woman who talked and talked but didn't seem to be there with you.

'You see, she had this friend who vanished.'

'Grandma's friend?' Anna-Karin asks. 'Who was that?'

'She was called Ragnhild. Mother of Leffe, that's him who runs Leffe's kiosk. Ragnhild went skiing a lot in the winter. One day, when she was out on one of her tours, she dropped in at the farm and stayed for a cup of tea. She was much more silent than usual. Didn't seem to listen properly; allowed the coffee to go cold. Just sat there and looked out at the forest. Suddenly, she got up and left. Gerda and I watched as she skied away out of sight between the firs. And that was the last time anyone saw her.'

Goose pimples are spreading over Anna-Karin's arms. Grandpa has never told her this story before. She thinks about all the people who have disappeared in the forest around Engelsfors. They are part of the local folklore. But she has never really thought about the lost ones as people, more as ghost stories or newspaper items.

'All my life, I believed that the forest was my friend,'

Grandpa continues, almost as if talking to himself. 'I used to think that people who said that you should always keep to the paths didn't know what they were talking about. I thought I knew better. I carried on walking freely in the forest, even after Ragnhild's disappearance. And allowed you to do the same. I had sat for so many hours listening to the wind in the trees that I thought we understood each other, the forest and I. But lately, it has dawned on me . . .'

He looks at Anna-Karin and his gaze is deeply serious. 'I knew nothing about the forest and still don't.'

The only sound in the room is their breathing.

'I know nothing of what the forest wants and what it holds,' Grandpa continues. 'And I wish I could advise you to be very careful. But, then, I think you know more about what is happening than I do. All I know is that there are difficult times ahead.'

Difficult times ahead.

That is exactly what Nicolaus wrote in the letter he left when he disappeared.

A scream slices through the silence. It comes from the room next door. The man with the dandelion-hair is screaming and screaming.

'Poor Sven-Olof,' Grandpa mumbles. 'He has been in a poor way for many days now.'

Anna-Karin hears the staff come running along the hallway. Soothing voices murmur on the other side of the wall and finally the screaming stops.

But the neighbor's words still ring inside Anna-Karin's ears when she walks through the front door of Sunny Side.

It's coming! It's coming!

Chapter 31

Linnéa is walking through Engelsfors. She has put her sunglasses on but the light still stings in her eyes. She has been sitting at home with a saucepan full of water in front of her, practicing for hours to freeze and thaw the water, make it boil and cool down.

This morning, Vanessa called to say she couldn't see her tonight. She was going to have National Day supper with her Mom and Melvin.

'She has even gone and bought some kind of Sweden cakes,' Vanessa said. Linnéa could almost hear her eyes rolling upwards.

Linnéa hadn't said anything much. She didn't want to risk revealing the pain it caused her. She can't get her head around just why it matters so much to her that Vanessa has not yet told Jannike about them. She knows that it isn't because Vanessa is ashamed of her, but still it feels like she is.

'What are you going to do?' Vanessa asked.

'Nothing special,' Linnéa had said.

She might have said what was on her mind. But, suddenly, she didn't want to.

She strolls past The Bag. He is sitting on the hood of a rusty old Volvo. He waves and shouts at her.

'Where's your old man these days? He ain't making the rounds no more!'

Linnéa doesn't answer. She tries to swallow the happiness that bubbles up inside her. Dad must be staying away from his drinking buddies.

Part Two

The playing fields are still a bit away when she hears the slapping sound of feet kicking a ball. Whistle blasts cut through the air. Excited shouting.

Linnéa can't be certain that either Gustaf or Rickard will have turned up for the EFC training session today. But she hopes they have. She has to find out what is going on in their heads. She needs to check that they really will keep their mouths shut. If not, Minoo will have to accept that she must do something about it.

The soccer field glows emerald green in the sunlight. Linnéa strolls along the fence, letting her fingers run across it, searching among the players. Kevin Månsson does a poor pass and his muscle-bound dad, the team coach, roars at him to sharpen up. But Linnéa can't see either Gustaf or Rickard.

She has gotten to the back of the stands and is just about to walk home when she hears somebody call her name.

Rickard is leaning against an electricity box on the other side of the street. His duffel bag is at his feet. He picks it up and walks toward her.

She remembers that night, when she came into her apartment. The thumping music at top volume. Rickard pulling the balaclava down over his face. He was not his real self. Olivia controlled him. All the same, Linnéa's body reacts at once. Wants to flee.

'What are you doing here?' he says, and dumps his duffel bag on the pavement between them.

She instantly senses that he is nervous. Much more nervous than she is. And that calms her down.

'I was looking for you,' she says. 'And what are *you* doing here? Not playing soccer, as far as I can see.'

Rickard gives the bag a light kick.

'My dad gave me a ride. With him I try to make like everything is as usual.'

Of course, Linnéa knows nothing about Rickard's life. But he has always come across as one of the super-normals. Nothing will have prepared him for what has happened. She was ahead of him in that respect, at least. She has never trusted anyone, always expected the worst. And she has fought demons all her life, though of a different kind.

'Linnéa, I've wanted to talk to you about what happened that time at your place. I had an idea what Erik and Robin were going to do when they ran after you. Olivia hadn't planned it but she didn't want to do anything to stop them. All she thought was, it wasn't her fault.'

That sounds like Olivia, Linnéa thinks.

'It must have been horrible,' she says. 'To see bad things happen and not be able to do anything about it.'

'I'm not the one you should be feeling sorry for. I want to tell you how sorry I am.'

When Linnéa reads his mind, his thoughts exactly echo what he has just said. He is brimming with the sense of having done an unforgivable thing. The worst feeling of all.

'It wasn't your fault,' Linnéa says. 'Let's just forget about it.'

'It's not fair that they got away with what they did to you,' Rickard says. 'I'm going to the police. I don't mind being charged with taking part in the trashing of your apartment. The thing is to get Erik locked up. He is fucking dangerous.'

Linnéa looks at Rickard. His dark hair, glasses, his ordinariness. But his eyes have the look now of someone who has seen too much. The look that no one should have to have. A wave of fury and grief strikes her. The demons have already ruined so much.

'I mean it, seriously,' he adds.

If she hadn't been able to read his mind, she would never have believed that anyone could be that noble and self-sacrificing. But Rickard does mean what he says.

'I believe you,' she says. 'But it won't get us anywhere. Sure, Helena is dead, but the alibi she gave Erik and Robin still stands. What you and I say won't wash.'

'I think you're wrong about that.'

'You don't know the police force in Engelsfors like I do,' Linnéa says. 'So thank your lucky stars.'

'I must do this.'

'Please, drop it. When all that happened, you were the only one who was controlled by Olivia. It was her doing, not yours.'

Rickard shakes his head.

'I should have worked out how to escape her. After all, I knew she was in my head, making me do things. If only I hadn't been so weak . . .'

Fragments of love for Olivia are still in his thoughts, even now.

'You weren't weak. You were exploited.'

A gust of wind from the soccer field carries more shrill whistles.

'I have to ask you something,' he says. 'Did you know that she and I . . . ? What I'm wondering is . . . did she ever talk about me?'

When she had heard that Rickard and Olivia had a secret relationship, it had come as a complete surprise. And, once more, Linnéa was amazed at how she had underestimated Olivia's capacity for keeping secrets.

But she is pretty sure Rickard doesn't need any more truths right now.

'She never spoke about it, not in so many words. But there were times when she gave it away. You know, that she was seeing someone.'

'Thank you. I don't actually believe you. But it's nice of you to say it.'

The sounds from the soccer field are dying down. Practice must be over.

'Why did you want to see me, anyway?' he says.

Linnéa can't think why she should lie to him.

'I wanted to check that you weren't thinking of telling people what you know now.'

'Have you been reading my mind?'

'Only as much as I have needed to. What about Gustaf? Do you think he might tell?'

'He won't say a word,' Rickard says, and his thoughts reveal no doubt at all.

'How is he doing?'

'Not good. But at least we have each other.'

Linnéa can see why Minoo trusted Rickard. She is surprised at how much she likes him already. And it saddens her to think of how he had been used by Olivia.

'Tomorrow . . . are you going to the final day assembly?' Rickard asks.

'Yes,' Linnéa replies.

Rickard frowns.

'But, why? I mean, what's the point of going to the assembly? Or, rather, what's the point of doing anything at all? Now that we know the world is likely to end some time soon.'

Linnéa is on the verge of saying that it's pretty obvious the world is going to hell anyway, with or without the demons to push it over the brink. But then she sees the desperation in Rickard's eyes.

'We're trying to stop it,' she says. 'And, in the meantime, we have to . . . keep living, I suppose.'

'If I had been in your shoes, I would've left school ages ago.'

Linnéa laughs a little.

'We figure school is part of our job, you see. We have to keep an eye on what's going on in the place of evil.'

Rickard nods.

'Thank you,' he says.

'For what?'

'For all you're doing, of course. Saving the world and everything. I suspect you don't get many thanks for that?'

'You're so right,' Linnéa says with a little smile. 'But, you're welcome.'

Part Two

* * *

Minoo is lying on her back, staring up at the ceiling.

She has been lying on her bed like this every evening for a week, ever since the conversation with Walter. At least it has made her obsess a little less about Gustaf.

Another circle can take the place of the Chosen Ones. If you are part of it.

The guardians have said so. But can one trust the guardians? Do they have any alternatives?

You really do not have a choice.

'Minoo!' Dad shouts from downstairs. 'Do you want gazpacho?'

'Fantastic!' she shouts back.

'Does Mom like it?'

'Dad! You've known her for longer than me!'

He has spent his day off planning the family meal for tomorrow, after the final assembly. So far, he has been through about a thousand ideas. As soon as he has made up his mind about a dish, he has started to browse cookbooks again and changed his mind.

Minoo hears the door to Anna-Karin's room open and steps going into the bathroom. They have hardly exchanged a word during the past week, as if they have both been avoiding each other. But, from time to time, Minoo has felt as if Anna-Karin wanted to tell her something. As for herself, she hasn't even got near to wanting to tell. She has to reach her decision first.

Her cell phone on the bedside table starts ringing. It's Linnéa.

'I've been speaking to Rickard,' she says straight off when Minoo answers. 'You're right. He won't give anything away. Nor will Gustaf.'

'How are they?' Minoo asks, feeling Linnéa will understand that she is really asking about Gustaf.

'They're coping,' Linnéa says. 'And Gustaf is getting on all right.'

'Is he, truly?'

'Well, no, not exactly *all right*. But they have each other.'

But I have lost him forever, Minoo thinks. For him, I will always be the person who ruined his life.

CHAPTER 32

Vanessa steps down from the bus and the doors close behind her with a noisy *shoosh*.

The heat is oppressive and black thunderclouds are piling up in the sky. She looks at the school further along the street. Students, dressed up for the last day of school, are hurrying across the schoolyard. Her phone rings in her handbag and she rummages around in it, irritated with herself for always carrying so many pointless things. Finally, she finds her cell phone.

A text from Linnéa.

OVERSLEPT. SAVE A SEAT FOR ME.

Vanessa puts the cell phone away. Imagines Linnéa waking up alone. Wishes she had been there.

She tugs at her dress as she walks toward the school. She discovered only this morning that she had nothing clean to wear. In the end she found a dress from last summer at the back of the wardrobe. Now she remembers why she stopped wearing it. It had shrunk in the wash and is far too tight around the chest. It's almost hard to breathe.

The text tone sounds again. She rummages for a second time.

Evelina.

CAN'T BE BOTHERED TO GO TO FINAL DAY! SEE YOU ON OLSSON'S TONIGHT!

Vanessa is hungry for a party. It has been such a long time. But she is nervous as well. She hopes Evelina and Michelle won't get *too* pissed. And that she doesn't either. Linnéa doesn't touch booze, of course, and Vanessa has a distinct feeling that the three of them drunk would be unbearable to a sober person.

She goes through the gates and catches sight of Viktor, who is just hanging around, doing nothing. She hasn't seen him in more than a month and she hopes he doesn't spot her now. But just as she thinks she has gotten away, he calls her name.

She sighs and turns to him.

'What do you want?' she asks.

Viktor has taken up his usual pose. Long-suffering and handsome in his posh clothes. Vanessa would lay bets on him practicing the stance for hours.

'I heard about you and Linnéa,' he says.

'So?'

'Nothing, I guess.'

'Oh, good. The Council doesn't object, then.'

Viktor pushes a strand of hair from his forehead. Glances at her. An especially self-pitying look, clearly rehearsed.

'It seems that things always go wrong when I try to talk with you,' he says.

'Maybe you shouldn't try so hard.'

'No, maybe I shouldn't,' he says, pulling his car key from his pocket and toying with it. 'Well, take care. I don't think we'll meet for a while.'

'Why is that? Are you and Alexander off somewhere? Like, leaving town?'

She makes no attempt to hide how hopeful she feels.

'No. But I've left school for good. Other things are on the agenda this autumn.'

He observes her watchfully. As if he expects her to understand something.

'What are you talking about?'

Viktor still scrutinizes her.

'Nothing. Forget it.'

'Happy to,' Vanessa says.

When she crosses the schoolyard, she feels Viktor's eyes on her back.

* * *

As the black car zooms past her, Linnéa just manages to see who is behind the wheel. Viktor. She throws her cigarette butt on the pavement and a lady rolling past in an electric wheelchair stares irritably at her.

When Linnéa walks through the gates, the schoolyard is empty. The air is heavy with heat and her skin feels clammy. A huge thundercloud hangs over the sky like a lid. She is longing for a storm to clear the air, as it surely must, soon.

Closer to the school building, the piano playing grows more distinct. As she pulls the front door open, the choir starts to sing.

Walking through the lobby, Linnéa feels weirdly off-balance with lack of sleep. She ought to be used to sleepless nights, but now they come for a different reason. It's no longer panic that keeps her awake. It is longing for Vanessa. The nights when she doesn't sleep by her side make Linnéa burn with restlessness. The only thing that can soothe her is Vanessa's skin against her own.

If Linnéa had been her old self, she would hardly have been bothered by missing the final day assembly. She would just have turned over in bed and gone back to sleep.

But now, Vanessa is there.

She pushes the door to the assembly hall open a fraction and slips inside. Light is pouring in through the tall, unwashed windows. The room is airless. The choir is lined up on the stage and Kerstin Stålnacke, dressed in a tie-dyed tunic, is directing with lots of arm-waving.

Linnéa scans the audience for Vanessa and catches sight of her blonde hair in one of the rows near the back. She is wearing a strapless, turquoise dress. Minoo and Anna-Karin sit on one side of her and, on the other, her large handbag keeps one seat for Linnéa.

Suddenly, Vanessa turns her head and looks straight at her. And smiles. Linnéa feels warmth flow through her body. She pushes her way to the free space, pulls the folding seat down. Once she is seated, Vanessa kisses her on the mouth. Very softly. It is quite enough to make Linnéa's heart rate double. From a few rows behind them, some people wolf-whistle. Vanessa doesn't even look to see who they are, just flips them the bird. Then she kisses Linnéa again.

'Another academic year has passed and summer is waiting just outside the door. I, for one, will open the door joyfully and let it in.'

Tommy Ekberg has taken the place behind the lectern. His bald head is shining with sweat. He is wearing a shirt with oversized daisies on a cornflower-blue background. If Linnéa hadn't disliked him so much, she might have thought it almost touching that he had chosen it for today. He must have chosen it because he thought it was summery and nice.

Tommy clears his throat loudly. The microphone makes it sound like a dog's bark.

'The summer vacation is a time to recoup,' he says. 'For my part, I like to spend the time pottering in the garden and relaxing with a few fat volumes of biography. But I have a feeling that what you long for during the vacation is not another pile of books.'

A handful of teachers take pity on him and laugh a little. Vanessa puts her head on Linnéa's shoulder and sighs.

'What the fuck are we doing here?' she whispers.

Linnéa smiles. Waves a little to Anna-Karin and Minoo. Anna-Karin smiles back but Minoo seems almost unaware that Linnéa has joined them.

'At your age, I'd cycle down to Dammsjön Lake to check out the birds. The non-feathered ones, that is,' Tommy says. 'I can't think that it's not done these days. Or what do you say, guys?'

Linnéa's mentor and arts teacher, Petter Backman, cackles with laughter. The rest of the assembly hall is dead quiet. Tommy strokes his moustache.

Minoo seems totally devastated, Linnéa thinks to Vanessa.

Yes, I think she's in love with Gustaf, Vanessa thinks in return.

Linnéa glances quickly at her. She neither wants to lie to Vanessa nor give away Minoo's secret.

Why do you think that?

It's been obvious for quite a while, Vanessa replies.

'After the summer, the new year of study will start off again,' Tommy says. 'I am sure we all hope it will be less . . . turbulent than these past two years.'

I am so sorry for them both, Vanessa continues her line of thought. *Gustaf is going through a bad time, too. Like, when I was angry with you because you hadn't let on that you were a mind-reader. I wanted to forgive you and hated you at the same time.*

Linnéa doesn't want to think about last summer, when Vanessa refused to talk to her and even seemed unwilling to look at her. She pulls at her cuticles so hard it hurts. Vanessa puts her hands across Linnéa's.

But I got over it, Vanessa thinks. *Gustaf will, too, I'm sure.*

'The past year at school has been difficult,' Tommy carries on. 'I won't deny it. We lost, for instance, a highly valued colleague when Adriana Lopez handed in her notice.'

Linnéa and Vanessa exchange glances. So this is the way Tommy is rewriting history.

'Then the terrible electrical malfunction which caused one of our students, Ida Holmström, to lose her life.' He looks out over the assembly hall and pauses to let Ida's name sink in. 'During her time here in Engelsfors High School, she was a role model to us all.'

Linnéa recalls when Ida read a poem to Elias in front of the

227

whole school. Linnéa had gotten out of her chair, even though panic was rushing through her.

You gave them the scissors, Ida! It was you! I saw it! And so did the rest of you, you sick, fucking hypocrites!

'Ida will always live on in our hearts and our memories,' Tommy says.

Linnéa realizes he is right. She and Ida had been fighting the same enemies and had both been part of the Circle. However fiercely Linnéa had hated her, there was a bond between them. And there had been moments when she had even liked her. At least toward the end.

Naturally, that coincided with the time when the rest of Engelsfors High School began to detest her. Some of those who let her down most, like Julia and Felicia, are sobbing the loudest now. Linnéa almost feels like getting up again and speaking her mind.

You sick, fucking hypocrites!

'I regret to say that Olivia Henriksson has still not been found. I must remind you to get in touch with the police if you know anything that might have a bearing—'

A chair seat snaps loudly back when Robin stands up, a few rows in front of Linnéa. Tommy looks irritably at him.

'Right, Robin. Are you going somewhere?'

Robin is swaying slightly, but doesn't move from the spot. Felicia pulls at his sweatshirt and hisses something at him.

'Robin, sit down,' Tommy says.

'Erik Forslund and I forced Linnéa Wallin to jump off Canal Bridge last winter. We tried to kill her.'

Robin rattles off the words as if it were his homework to recite the sentences aloud. Then he falls abruptly silent.

All faces turn toward him. People's glances bounce between Linnéa and Robin and whispering spreads throughout the hall. She feels paralyzed.

Erik gets up from the chair next to Robin and forces a tight smile.

'Robin has a pretty morbid sense of humor,' he says. 'But, Robin, this is well beyond funny. Nowhere near.'

'I'm not joking!' Robin shouts. 'We did what I said!'

Linnéa takes Vanessa's hand and feels a reassuring pressure back. Another seat snaps when Kevin stands up in the front half of the hall.

'It's true!' he says. 'They did it! They tried to kill her!'

This isn't happening, Linnéa thinks. It simply isn't happening.

'Stop it,' Julia shrieks. 'You're all lying!'

She casts a dark glance at Linnéa, as if all this is her fault. Erik doesn't turn around. But Linnéa can sense his hatred of her. It is radiating from him and its rays enter her. She can hear his thoughts.

I knew he couldn't hack the pressure. I'll have to make him take all this shit back. And then I'll wipe that bitch out for good.

It feels as if she is falling again, tumbling down into the black water.

'He can't get at you,' Vanessa whispers.

She must have sensed what Linnéa is feeling. And Linnéa realizes that she is not alone. She has Vanessa. And Minoo, and Anna-Karin.

'What the fuck, phone the cops now,' Tindra screams. 'He confessed, right?'

The noise grows in the hall. Now Linnéa realizes that several students are on their feet, holding up their cell phones to take photos and videos.

'That's enough!'

Tommy's howl into the microphone is so loud it causes feedback in the speakers and everyone claps their hands over their ears.

He points to Petter Backman.

'You take these boys to my office, please, Petter. Everyone else stay put until they've left. Then, go back to your classrooms!'

Petter steps down into the aisle, crosses his arms on his chest and stares hard at the boys until they slowly walk toward him. Julia starts sobbing loudly. Felicia is crying, too, and tries to pat Julia's back. Julia slaps Felicia's hand away.

'Wow!' Vanessa says. 'Shit, they'll be locked up for this!'

But not only them, Linnéa realizes suddenly. The only one of that gang who had not willingly gone along to her apartment will also be hauled away.

Rickard, she thinks to the Chosen Ones. *We can't let Rickard be had for the break-in.*

Minoo nods.

'I'll fix that,' she says.

Chapter 33

Minoo holds on to Anna-Karin's arm as they walk through the entrance lobby and on toward the hallway that ends with the spiral staircase. Everywhere, they hear excited voices. They pass people who are pushing to get through the crowds. Minoo picks up fragments of talk.

. . . the police have been called . . . remember May Day Eve, that party, how weird Kevin was . . . I've heard Robin is on something, maybe he's shooting up with Linnéa . . . I think Erik did it, I've always believed he did . . .

Minoo keeps her eyes fixed on Linnéa and Vanessa who are walking ahead of her along the hallway.

'Are you quite sure?' Anna-Karin asks quietly. 'Do you really want to do this?'

'Yes, I do,' Minoo replies.

It is a half-truth. Of course she doesn't want to have their memories in her head. But she is sure, all the same. This is different from hiding Rickard's and Gustaf's memories.

This is about fairness, getting things right. About helping someone who is innocent.

All very noble. But Minoo can't help hoping that a side-effect of doing this for Rickard will be that Gustaf hates her a little less.

'We will help you,' Anna-Karin says when they catch up with Linnéa who is holding the door to the spiral staircase open. Vanessa is already on her way upstairs. 'We will sort this out together.'

Together.

Minoo thinks of everything the Circle has done together. All the times they have risked their lives, side by side. And realizes that soon she might not be part of their circle. Soon, she shall have to decide.

* * *

The door slams behind Anna-Karin and she follows the others up the spiral staircase.

When Erik rose in the assembly, she had felt anger rushing to her head. It would have been so satisfying to give in to it. To draw strength from her hatred as she has done before, when everything was going so badly.

She remembers all the times Erik has terrorized her, with Robin and Kevin backing whatever he did. When she was starting to grow breasts in elementary school and they started pinching and squeezing her whenever they got close. When they started shouting 'B.O. Ho' after her. When they put dog turds in her schoolbag.

Though the worst thing wasn't what they did but her fear of what they would do next.

What if she loses control when she sees them? Orders them to jump out through the window? Or uses her newfound strength to throw them out? She has hated them for as long as she can remember. How will she be able to resist the temptation to hurt them?

They stop at the floor of the principal's office.

Petter is alone with them, Linnéa thinks to them. *Vanessa can make herself and Anna-Karin invisible. Anna-Karin makes Petter leave and makes sure the boys stay calm.*

She looks quickly down the hallway.

I'll keep look-out here in case someone comes this way while Minoo does her thing. Everyone ready?

They all nod, Anna-Karin too. Vanessa holds out her hand and she takes it, ever so cautiously. Then she feels the light air movements fanning her skin, so familiar from the practice sessions when Vanessa wraps her in invisibility.

They step into the deserted hallway. Vanessa looks at Anna-Karin before she knocks on the door to the principal's office. Petter Backman opens the door. Stares straight through them.

'Hello?' he says.

Behind him, they see Erik seated in the armchair. Robin sits on the sofa next to Kevin, who hides his face in his hands and weeps quietly.

Petter Backman looks annoyed, swears, and is just about to close the door when Anna-Karin releases her power.

STOP.

He freezes in mid-movement, just like in the play-school game.

GO DOWN TO THE ENTRANCE HALL, Anna-Karin orders.

Stone-faced, he walks out into the hallway in the direction of the main staircase.

'Where are you off to?' Robin asks shrilly.

SAY NOTHING. DON'T MOVE.

Robin, Erik and Kevin stiffen where they sit. Anna-Karin and Vanessa step into the office and close the door.

Anna-Karin feels the fanning on her skin again when Vanessa lets go of her hand and they both become visible. Robin, Erik and Kevin look shocked but say nothing and don't move. A solitary tear runs down Kevin's cheek.

'We could do anything we like with them now, right?' Vanessa says. 'Like, I could pick up that pair of scissors on the desk and use it to cut off their tiny little balls.'

Terror glows in their eyes. They are entirely at the disposal of the Chosen Ones. Anna-Karin is savoring every moment. She opens the door and lets Minoo in.

'Now it's your turn,' she says, and goes back into the hallway.

* * *

Minoo looks at the wax figures seated in front of her. Only when she looks really closely can she see that they are breathing.

She stands in front of Erik. Looks into his eyes. He doesn't even blink. Her distaste for him is so strong it makes her dizzy. She emphatically does not want to know what's in his head. But, if what Walter said is true, if she is that powerful, surely she can handle it?

Vanessa takes her hand and makes them both invisible. Then, Minoo releases the black smoke. It makes her feel serene.

She puts her hand on Erik's forehead and observes the weave of his memories.

Darkness. Minoo feels Erik kissing somebody. Moist, slow kisses. He gets a hard-on. R & B in the background. Erik fumbles with his bedside lamp, switches it on. Says that he wants to see her. Julia is screwing up her eyes against the light. Erik pulls her top off; she is wearing a white lace bra. She has passable boobs, not as nice as Ida's, but Julia is more willing to do stuff. He grabs her left breast hard. She pushes his hand away but she likes it well enough. She's just pretending, he's sure of that. He kisses her before she gets to say anything.

Back in time.

'Don't you worry,' Helena says. 'I'm backing you one hundred percent. You were here all night. No one is going to believe Linnéa, even if she survives.' Helena hugs him. Her perfume smells nice, sweet and flowery. Erik is relieved. It's all going to be OK.

'We didn't want to hurt her, of course,' he says, trying to make his tone of voice quite worried but without sounding like a wimp. 'She caught us at it. I didn't want her to call the police. She might have ruined everything for us all . . .' Helena caresses his back. 'I know,' she says. 'Not to worry.'

Back in time.

He swings the baseball bat. It feels so good in his hands, so heavy. Linnéa's scream gives him a high. She is really scared of him now; he owns her and she knows it.

Back in time.

Erik turns up the volume. Linnéa's playlist is perfect for when you destroy, mangle, crush. He is going to wipe out every trace of that psychotic whore to the sound of her own music.

Back in time.

Erik looks at Helena, wondering if he had heard her right. 'What was that?' he says. 'Do you mean you want us to wreck her apartment?'

'Correct,' Helena says as she hands him a key. 'We've waited far too long. Time to teach her a lesson.' That soccer-crazed blockhead Rickard stands behind her and nods.

Minoo starts to collect all the images in Erik's memory of the evening that include Rickard. She unravels the weave, ties the threads together, hides Rickard away. Then she moves on, forward to the very latest memories, and makes Erik forget he has seen her, Vanessa and Anna-Karin here, in the principal's office.

The black smoke is still whirling as Minoo opens her eyes and takes her hand away. She moves to Kevin, and Vanessa follows her, still holding her hand firmly.

'Hurry,' she says.

Kevin's red-rimmed eyes are shiny with tears. As Minoo puts her hand on his forehead, she feels nothing but a mild interest, neither hatred nor compassion.

Kevin stands on the makeshift stage in the gym and looks at Helena who is bathed in light. She holds an envelope containing the results of the vote. It has to be him; no one has been more loyal. She pulls a card from the envelope and her smile widens. 'Erik Forslund!' she almost screams. Thunderous applause. Kevin feels his face go hot but he tries to smile. Fucking Erik. Erik who always gets stuff. First Ida, and now this.

Back in time.

Music at top volume. He watches Robin and Erik run after Linnéa. They'll kill her. Erik is a total psycho. 'What shall we do?' Kevin says. 'Phone the police?' Rickard hesitates for a moment. 'No,' he says. 'If something happens, it isn't my fault, it's Helena's.' He picks up Linnéa's laptop, lifts it above his head and smashes it against the floor. The music stops. 'Fuck Linnéa, she's only got herself to blame. It's not my fault,' Rickard mumbles, and stamps hard on the laptop.

Back in time.

Kevin drives through Engelsfors on his moped. He thinks maybe he has lost sight of Linnéa, but then he spots her. Minoo sees her own home. There she is, letting Linnéa in. Kevin drives off, hoping that Linnéa will stay at Minoo's place all evening. What he and the others are going to do is exciting, but he is scared as well, scared of the police and even more scared of his dad and what he might do if he hears about it.

Minoo has little idea of time but feels that she works faster now. It seems easier to find and hide all the memories that link Rickard to that evening's events.

When she opens her eyes, she hears Vanessa again. Has she been talking all this time?

'Linnéa thinks that Tommy is on his way here, bringing Nicke and a policewoman. If she has to, Anna-Karin can probably keep them away, but hurry up!'

Minoo places her hand against Robin's forehead.

Linnéa sits astride the railing of the bridge. She is in tears. All Robin wants is for her to jump. For this to be over soon. He can't take anymore. Why won't she jump?

Minoo sets to work with the memory weave.

She has just completed her task when something catches her attention. She has found a thread that is glowing strongly.

She follows it, senses the terror this memory holds.

Robin is getting out of the shower, wrapping the towel around his hips. He notes a word that is written in the condensation on the mirror. CONFESS!

Forward.

A permanent marker is floating in the air, next to a wall, and then Robin hears the moist, rasping sound as it starts writing a word in spiky, hate-filled letters on the light-blue wallpaper. CONFESS!

Forward.

The stairwell in the school. Linnéa has tripped; she is lying at Robin's feet. She is looking at the hand he is holding out to help her up. He is so frightened. He must confess. But what will happen when he does?

Forward.

Robin stares at his computer screen. Words are sliding across it. The keys depress themselves in a series of soft clicks. DEAR MOM, DAD AND ADDE. I AM SORRY THAT YOU WILL FIND ME LIKE THIS BUT I CANNOT STAND LIVING WITH WHAT I KNOW. ERIK FORSLUND AND I TRIED TO MURDER LINNÉA WALLIN. PLEASE FORGIVE ME. IT IS NOT YOUR FAULT. IT IS JUST THAT I CANNOT LIVE WITH THE GUILT. NOT ANYMORE. ROBIN. A suicide letter. Robin turns, looks around the room. He is terrified out of his mind. Then he leaps forward and slams the lid of his computer shut.

Vanessa calls Minoo's name. She opens her eyes, and looks at Vanessa who is disturbing her concentration.

'They're here now,' Vanessa says. 'Should Anna-Karin . . . ?'

'I've finished,' Minoo says, and retracts the black smoke.

Vanessa nods, just as the door to the office opens.

Minoo jumps, before she remembers that she and Vanessa are invisible.

'. . . you were to wait in here with them!' Tommy Ekberg says.

Behind him, Petter Backman enters with Nicke and a police-woman with short dark hair.

'Yes, you did,' Petter says tonelessly. 'I just . . . felt like . . . it seemed a good idea to leave, that's all.'

Nicke snorts. Arms crossed on his chest, he examines Kevin, Robin and Erik in turn.

'Right,' he says. 'What do you guys have to say for yourselves?'

The wax dolls blink. Anna-Karin must have released them.

'These guys are acting up with some fucking awful joke that's gone wrong,' Erik says.

'We tried to kill her,' Robin says.

Kevin snivels and Nicke looks contemptuously at him.

'You'd better come along to the station,' his colleague says. 'We need statements from all three of you.'

Erik gets up and looks menacingly at the others.

'Let's go. You'll have a chance of making assholes of yourselves in front of the police as well.'

Minoo observes him and feels sick. She has been inside his mind now; she knows what it feels like to *be* Erik. How cold his mind is, and how capable of what can truly be called evil.

He will never confess.

CHAPTER 34

Vanessa hears the rumble of thunder. The world outside Linnéa's apartment is washed in a strange, grayish-blue light. She is sitting on the sofa with her arm around Linnéa's shoulders. On the opposite side of the sofa table, Anna-Karin and Minoo sit on chairs.

Minoo seems like the real Minoo again, with her intelligent eyes and her pimples partially covered with badly applied concealer. But Vanessa will never forget the look in Minoo's eyes that moment in Tommy's office. She can't describe it to herself. The only word that comes anywhere near is 'contempt', but that isn't right either. It felt as if, to Minoo, Vanessa was too unimportant for her even to feel contempt.

'Could Robin have gone a little mad?' Anna-Karin asks. 'If he had, he might have hallucinations that made him think he saw all that. And memories of hallucinations would look real to you as well, wouldn't they, Minoo?'

'Or, someone was there, someone Robin didn't see. Someone invisible, is what I mean,' Minoo says, glancing quickly at Vanessa.

It takes a second or two for Vanessa to see what Minoo means. She straightens up.

'Do you really think I'd run around spooking Robin without telling the rest of you?'

'Sorry,' Minoo says, and her ears go bright red. 'I thought, you know, that since it was Linnéa he had been going for—'

'I see,' Vanessa says and suddenly feels ashamed. 'I didn't

but I should have. Fuck it, I'm so stupid. I should've thought of it myself.'

'No, don't say that,' Linnéa says evenly. 'It's good that you didn't. We don't want to have the Council at our throats again.'

Vanessa looks at her impassive face, the ink-stained hands that are twisting in her lap. Linnéa has been like this ever since they got here.

'But, in that case, who could it have been?' Anna-Karin says. 'Surely it must have been an air witch. Like Vanessa? Or could it have been an earth witch? Who could've made him believe he saw things?'

'Perhaps we should ask ourselves *why* instead,' Minoo says. 'Who, except us, would have a reason to make Robin confess?'

An all-too-familiar, annoying face turns up in Vanessa's mind. But it can't be him.

'It must be someone who hates Erik and Robin for real,' Anna-Karin says. 'Or else someone who is really fond of Linnéa.'

He has helped us before, Vanessa reflects. And he saved Linnéa's life that time.

'It could be Viktor,' she says.

Minoo stares at her.

'Do you really think that's possible?'

'I met him in the schoolyard this morning,' Vanessa says. 'He said he was leaving school for good. He seemed shifty, somehow. As if he was trying to get out of saying something.'

They hear the first true thunderclap. It is followed by hail. Vanessa watches the little white grains bouncing on the outside windowsill.

'But, do you think Viktor could do the things Robin saw?' Anna-Karin asks. 'After all, he's a water witch.'

'We haven't got a precise idea of what powers Viktor really has,' Minoo says, speaking loudly to be heard above the hailstorm. 'And he has said himself that his powers have grown stronger here in Engelsfors. Besides, we know it isn't the first time he has shown a taste for revenge. Do you remember what he did in that chemistry lesson, to get back at Kevin? The thing with the acid and water? And that was just for a skirmish.'

Vanessa looks at Linnéa, wondering if she is even listening.

'What do you think?' Vanessa asks her. 'Could it be Viktor?'

'I don't know,' she replies. 'There's something about all this that doesn't make sense.'

'That just about sums up Engelsfors,' Minoo says.

The thunder rumbles again and the hail is turning to rain.

'What matters is that they've been caught,' Anna-Karin says.

'Erik will never confess,' Linnéa says.

'Oh, yes, he will,' Anna-Karin says. 'And the judge will give him a very tough sentence. And Robin, too. I'll see to that.'

She looks determined. Vanessa feels both touched and worried.

'If you use your magic power like that you'll be breaking the laws of the Council again.'

'I don't care,' Anna-Karin replies.

'I can't let you run that risk,' Linnéa says.

'Maybe it won't be necessary anyway,' Minoo suggests. 'Robin and Kevin have confessed already. And Viktor is a witness to Linnéa's state when he found her.'

Linnéa's cell rings on the table and she reaches for it. Answers the call. Vanessa hears a woman's voice but can't distinguish the words. Linnéa's answers are so monosyllabic that Vanessa can't even guess what the caller wants.

'Fine,' Linnéa says in the end. She switches the cell phone off, then sits for a while, clutching it so hard it creaks worryingly.

'Who was that?' Vanessa asks.

'That was Diana. The police will be here shortly. They want to question me. So you had better leave.'

'I'll stay,' Vanessa says.

'You don't need to,' Linnéa says, still in that toneless voice.
Vanessa wants to scream that she's an idiot.
'Yes,' she says instead. 'I need to.'

CHAPTER 35

The storm dies away as suddenly as it had built up. Linnéa lies curled up on the sofa with her head in Vanessa's lap. She keeps her eyes closed while Vanessa caresses her hair.

Linnéa wishes she could press a pause button and stop time at this moment. Escape what will happen next. Soon, Diana will arrive with a police person in tow. Soon, Linnéa will be made to tell them everything.

The doorbell rings.

'Don't open it,' Linnéa whispers.

She feels Vanessa's lips against her temple.

'You can get through this. And I will be here for you, all the way.'

Reluctantly, Linnéa sits up and leans back in the corner of the sofa while Vanessa opens the door.

She hears Diana and another woman in the hall. At least it isn't Nicke. Linnéa looks at the panther on the floor next to the sofa, strokes the china head and fingers its glued-together edges.

She forces herself to look up when they come into the room.

'Hello, Linnéa,' Diana says.

The pity in her voice makes Linnéa wince. She looks at the policewoman instead. She is tall and looks like someone who swims several miles every morning. Her chestnut hair is pulled back in a ponytail.

'Good to meet you, Linnéa,' she says.

Her voice is deep and authoritative. A police voice. Linnéa

immediately feels that this woman won't believe a word she says.

'My name is Patricia Tamm and I am a detective.'

'Hello,' Linnéa mumbles.

Vanessa sits down next to Linnéa, takes her hand and squeezes it.

Is she the one who had it off with Nicke? Linnéa thinks.

No, Vanessa thinks.

Linnéa is almost disappointed. If it had been, she would have been able to dismiss Patricia completely.

Diana sits down on the sofa at Vanessa's other side.

'You're going to do most of the talking, so you might need a drink of water,' Patricia says. 'Do you mind if I fetch a glass of water from your kitchen?'

'Sure,' Linnéa replies and points.

When Patricia returns, she puts the glass in front of Linnéa, then pulls up a chair and sits down opposite her and begins to explain why she is there. Linnéa nods like an automaton but the roaring of panic in her ears makes it hard to focus on what Patricia is saying. She watches as the detective puts a small tape recorder on the table and presses Record. Then she takes out a notepad and a pencil.

'This is the first time we'll question you,' Patricia explains. 'If you don't remember everything, don't worry about it. And if you want to take a break, just say so.'

Linnéa regrets agreeing to being interviewed in her apartment. Diana had told her the police had suggested it because it would save her having to come down to the station. But now she's afraid that, by talking about it here, her home will become contaminated again.

Linnéa?

Vanessa puts her arm around Linnéa, but it feels so distant, as if even her own body no longer belongs to her. She is locked in by her anxiety.

Linnéa, she has asked you something.

'Sorry, what did you say?' Linnéa feels confused as she looks at Patricia.

'Please tell us what happened that evening,' Patricia says calmly.

Tell. Tell them what happened.

She has never told anyone before, not in detail. Not even Vanessa.

Linnéa realizes that she will have to tell it all now. Patricia will keep asking about everything they did, every word, every blow.

I don't want you to hear, she thinks to Vanessa. *I don't want you to hear what they did.*

Why not? Vanessa thinks.

Linnéa doesn't want to admit that she is ashamed. She knows that it's common for victims of crimes to feel like this, but she can't make the feeling go away.

I am not going to leave you alone on that fucking bridge, Vanessa thinks.

Linnéa's eyes meet Vanessa's. So much love in her gaze. Linnéa can't take it in, not now when she can feel nothing but roaring panic. But she knows that it is there.

'Start at the beginning,' Patricia says. 'What did you do before going home that afternoon?'

'I was with Minoo,' Linnéa replies. 'Minoo Falk Karimi. A friend of mine.'

Patricia makes a note. Linnéa falls silent, doesn't know how to continue.

'When did you leave your friend's home? Do you remember?'

Linnéa tries to answer but it was almost three months ago. She wonders if Minoo knows. It would be so typically Minoo to have kept a record of all the times and dates in one of her notebooks, just in case Linnéa would one day go to the police after all.

'Did you notice anything or anybody special on your way home?' Patricia asks.

Linnéa remembers how relieved she had felt. It was the first time she had spoken to someone about her feelings for Vanessa.

'No, I don't. But all day, I had this odd feeling that someone was following me. Just when I got to Minoo's place, I heard a moped.'

It hadn't come back to her until today when Minoo told them about what she had seen among Kevin's memories.

Patricia writes something on her notepad.

'Shall we go on to when you arrived at your house?' she says.

Linnéa takes a deep breath. Starts by describing the crushed windowpane by the front door to her apartment building. The music. The heavy bass. She feels it now or maybe it's the beating of her heart that is making her whole body vibrate.

'I took the elevator. I realized that the music was coming from my apartment. So I went in.'

She has hit a block.

The seconds tick by. One after the other.

'Do you remember if the door was locked?' Patricia asks in the end.

'It was locked,' Linnéa says. 'I was so furious I didn't think. I shouldn't have gone inside. I can be so stupid when I'm angry.'

Vanessa squeezes her hand.

'You weren't stupid at all,' Patricia says. 'None of this is your fault.'

Linnéa bites her lip hard. Tries to believe what Patricia is saying. Tries to hold her tears back.

'What happened next?' Patricia asks.

'I went into the hall . . . the music . . . it was so loud. The whole place smelled of drink. Like a party that's got out of hand. They had . . . had trashed the entire apartment.'

It sounds petty when she says it. So petty, but she had seen her whole life smashed to pieces.

'Do you have any idea of how they got into your apartment?' Patricia asks.

Linnéa has more than an idea. Erik got the key from Helena, who must have got it from Olivia, who must have had a copy made of Diana's key during the period when Olivia controlled Diana. But of course she can't say any of that.

'The apartment is on loan from social services, so I don't know who has keys and who doesn't.'

'Did you see anyone when you went into the apartment?' Patricia asks.

Erik in the blood-red light of the lamps. The splinters of glass all over his black sweater. The baseball bat in his hands. His thought arriving inside her head.

You fucking cunt.

'Erik,' she says. 'Erik Forslund. He stood by the window.'

She points.

'And then the others came in. Robin . . . Robin Zetterqvist and Kevin Månsson.'

And Rickard. Whom she mustn't mention. Must remember not to slip up. Patricia's pencil scratches away.

'How did they react when they saw you?'

'They looked surprised. Shocked. Kevin just stood there. Robin pulled down his balaclava. They all had balaclavas but they weren't covering their faces when I came in.'

'What did Erik do when he saw you?'

Linnéa bites her lip again. And tastes blood.

You fucking cunt.

'He just . . . looked at me.'

Her voice sounds choked. She has to swallow so that she can carry on speaking.

'He smiled. And pulled his balaclava down.'

She takes a deep breath. Breathes out slowly. Breathes in again.

'How did you feel?' Patricia asks.

'Frightened,' Linnéa says, almost sucked back into the

remembered emotion, the feeling that time seemed to have stopped, that she couldn't move. 'He had a baseball bat in his hands. And I ran . . .'

She can't hold her tears back any longer. She presses her free hand against her eyelids and tries to draw strength from Vanessa's presence. She manages to continue, tries to describe the route she ran. She can almost hear the smack of her boots against the pavement, the breaths tearing at her lungs, her heart beating so fast she fears it will stop pumping.

'I cried for help,' she whispers. 'But no one heard me.'

She can sense how Vanessa is trying to stop herself from crying.

'Did any of the boys say anything to you while they were chasing you?' Patricia asks. 'Can you remember anything?'

Linnéa can't tell Patricia that she has perfect recall of every thought in their heads. But she nods, because what they shouted after her is also engraved on her mind.

'Erik shouted, "You fucking cunt".'

Cold sweat is breaking out over her body. She continues, telling them how she hid under the bridge.

'I had dropped my bag in the stairwell so I didn't have my cell. I thought I'd try to cross the canal . . . Viktor Ehrenskiöld, who helped me later on, lives in the manor house.'

Patricia makes another note.

'I went up on the bridge.'

She has hit another block.

Linnéa looks at the windows with their new panes. How she wishes it had been as easy to fix herself. Maybe Minoo can do it? If she asked her, could Minoo take all these memories away?

'I went up on the bridge,' she finally says. 'And then they saw me.'

Caught! She's so fucking caught! So fucking caught!

'I told Erik to go to hell. Then . . . he laughed. And said that this wasn't the idea from the start, that I wasn't supposed to come home . . . he said he thought whores worked all night. But that this was fine, that it was . . . *better.'*

Linnéa senses a black wave of emotion that comes from Vanessa.

'Then, what happened?' Patricia asks.

'I tried to run away. But Robin grabbed me . . .'

She can still feel his hands, as if they had never let go of her.

'He held me. I tried to pull free but he . . .' She suddenly laughs; it comes out like a strange snort. 'Both of them are hockey players. He dragged me along easily. And I realized . . . exactly how strong they are. What a big difference in strength there was between them and me. I didn't have a chance.'

She knows that is how it was. Still, she can't get rid of the thoughts. *I should have done something. I should have been smarter, run faster, screamed more loudly.*

'Then what did Robin do?'

'He dragged me along toward Erik. And Erik said I was boring, that he had thought I *liked a good time.* He took hold of my hair, the bangs, and tugged hard . . . he asked me if I was frightened.'

'What was your answer?'

Linnéa looks up and meets Patricia's eyes.

'I lied. I said I wasn't.'

She hears Vanessa's thoughts. They come straight into her. *Fucking bastard.*

'He pulled my hair again,' Linnéa says hoarsely. 'I screamed. And kept saying . . . "Robin, please let me go." Lots of times. That was when Erik said that I had . . . had to . . . jump in.'

Her lips tremble and she stutters.

'Or else they would . . . throw me in.'

The black water below the bridge.

Breathe. She must remember to breathe.

'Then what did Robin do? When he heard Erik threaten you?'

'He said . . . he said something like, "Come on. I mean, seriously" to Erik. And Erik told Robin to be a man, not a wimp . . . and "you hate this slut as much as I do".'

Linnéa falls silent and wonders suddenly if Patricia thinks she is lying. Maybe it's abnormal to remember as much as she does. Would she have sounded more credible if she had pretended to have suppressed it all, so that Patricia would have had to probe more, help her to remember?

'Would you like to have a break now?' Patricia asks.

Linnéa shakes her head. She is not sure how much more of this she can take but, above all, she wants this to be finished.

'Erik threatened you,' Patricia says. 'At the time, did you think he meant it?'

'Yes, I was absolutely sure.'

'How could you be so sure?'

. . . I'll kill you, you fucking slut, you cunt, I'll fucking kill you . . .

'He hates me. This wasn't the first time . . . that he and Robin had been after me.'

Patricia nods. Another note on her pad.

'And what happened next?'

'He said . . .'

Breathe.

'He said . . . he thought all psychos wanted to kill themselves.' Her voice sounds so faint. As if it might soon fade away completely. 'This was my chance to do it, he said.'

Why does it hurt so much to repeat aloud the things he had said?

'Then he hit me,' she whispers and points to her thigh. 'With the baseball bat.'

Not much left to go. Soon over now. Soon she will have told them everything.

'I screamed. And then Erik grabbed hold of me . . . he pushed me against the railing and then he said . . . that they should . . .'

She closes her eyes. Tries to pretend that the words have

nothing to do with her, that the words were directed at someone else.

'He said that "someone should fuck you first, but we don't feel like catching AIDS".'

She struggles to catch her breath.

'Then he gripped . . . . he . . . he twisted my arm and it was so damn painful. I thought he'd carry on twisting forever and that either way it would all end with them killing me. So, I thought that if I jumped I'd have a chance to survive. A small one. And I climbed up on the railing and looked at Robin and said, "Please", and he said, "Just do it." And Erik said, "That's right. Just do it, Linnéa." And I did. I jumped.'

She has run out of words now. The tears are streaming down her face. She can taste them in her mouth.

'Why didn't you inform the police of all this at the time?' Patricia asks.

'Surely you can figure that out!' Vanessa tells her.

'No one is accusing Linnéa of anything,' Patricia says calmly. 'She is making a statement. But I must ask these questions.'

Don't worry, Linnéa thinks to Vanessa. *I have to go through with this.*

'I was afraid of them,' she says. 'Besides, I knew that nobody would believe me.'

'I understand that's how you felt,' Patricia nods.

Linnéa looks at her and realizes that she means it. Patricia does understand her. The relief she feels is indescribable.

'What will happen now?' she asks, reaching for the glass of water and drinking in deep swallows.

'Happen to Erik and Robin?'

Linnéa nods and wonders if this had been explained to her in the beginning, when she couldn't listen. If so, Patricia doesn't let on.

'They are being held for questioning and a preliminary investigation is under way,' she says. 'The prosecutor who is leading the investigation is a man called Hans-Peter Ramström, from the district attorney's office in Västerås. He will request that they are arrested. Because the alleged crime is so serious they will almost certainly be kept under lock and key for as long as the preliminary investigation is ongoing.'

'In other words, they will be rotting in jail in Västerås until the trial,' Diana tells her. 'You won't have to see them until then.'

'Kevin is held on suspicion of aggravated damage to property and has confessed,' Patricia says. 'Robin and Erik are held on suspicion of aggravated damage to property and attempted murder. Erik denies the charges. But I wouldn't be too worried about that, if I were you.'

She smiles. Just a little. But it is enough.

'Why do you think they wanted to destroy your apartment?' Patricia continues.

Linnéa gets hold of the glass of water again. It will buy her time. She mustn't give anything away. Her head feels dull and her thoughts move so slowly. Of course Helena had given the order. But she isn't meant to know anything about that. She swallows. Puts the glass down.

'I don't know exactly what they were after. But they were members of Positive Engelsfors, and I was openly anti-PE.'

'Earlier, you said that it wasn't the first time Erik and Robin had gone for you,' Patricia says. 'What were these previous occasions?'

Where to start? Which of the thousands of times that they had shouted things after her, threatened her, smashed her stuff, grabbed her and held her, hit her?

'Does it matter?' Linnéa asks. 'I mean, could it affect the case against them?'

'Absolutely,' Patricia replies. 'The issue here is whether they acted with intent. If their acts were premeditated or on an impulse.'

Part Two

'Does it mean that every single thing they've done to me . . . that they all count?'

Patricia looks seriously at Linnéa.

'Yes, indeed, Linnéa,' she says. 'Every single thing counts. Every little thing.'

Chapter 36

Minoo opens the packet of quinoa and pours the contents into the strainer. Dad is dashing about in the kitchen and tries to avoid stumbling on Peppar. A powerful smell of onion is rising from the bowl of gazpacho.

They have tuned in to the local radio station and the host is talking about the continued electrical problems in Engelsfors and how the mysterious related accidents might have contributed to the marked increase in people leaving town over the past year. Furious listeners phone in and rant.

'How many more victims have to die before the authorities pay attention?' demands an anonymous woman who sounds suspiciously like Kerstin Stålnacke.

Minoo wonders how quickly people would be leaving town if they knew the real reason for the problems.

If the rumor that the end of the world is near started making the rounds . . . well, you can imagine what would follow.

The host changes the subject and starts a discussion about the video clips of what happened in the assembly hall today. The clips have already attracted tens of thousands of hits. Minoo wonders how Linnéa is feeling. How the interrogation went. When a listener phones to agonize about what will happen to 'the poor boys', Minoo quickly switches to another station.

Mechanically, she washes the quinoa under the tap. Her shoulders feel tense. She must be prepared. Any time now the memories might come back to haunt her. The events she saw inside the heads of Erik, Robin and Kevin. Any time soon, these repulsive images are going to leap into her mind.

She tries to comfort herself by saying that it was worth it. She has helped Rickard. She phoned him as soon as she could, told him what had happened and assured him that nobody would point the finger at him. Rickard was silent for a long time and then he thanked her. It was heartwarming to hear the relief in his voice.

Yes, she thinks, it was a good thing to do. But if I were truly good, would I be hoping that Rickard tells Gustaf as soon as possible?

Minoo pours the quinoa into a saucepan and measures out the water. She glances through the window. The sun is shining as if the storm had never been. Anna-Karin is in the garden, wiping the rain off the garden furniture.

When she comes inside, she looks around uncertainly.

'What would you like me to do now?'

'It's cool,' Minoo says. 'We're fixing the rest.'

Anna-Karin leaves the kitchen and disappears upstairs. Minoo wonders how much time it will take before she stops behaving like an acquaintance on a visit.

'Damnation,' Dad curses as the metal ring on the can of chickpeas breaks. He finds a can opener in a drawer.

'How late did your Mom say the train was?'

'About half an hour,' Minoo replies. She puts the saucepan on the heat.

Robin and Erik's memories haven't swallowed her up yet, not even when she was telling Mom about the events in the assembly hall.

Maybe I have more control now, Minoo thinks.

She goes upstairs to change, feeling a small flicker of hope.

* * *

Linnéa wakes up as suddenly as she had fallen asleep.

As soon as Patricia and Diana left, she had put her head

down on the sofa cushions and gone out like a light. Now, she is wide awake. She sits up and realizes that Vanessa has spread a blanket over her. Linnéa folds it and puts it away.

Vanessa comes in from the bathroom.

'How are you?' she asks.

'I'm not sure,' Linnéa replies honestly.

She is drained of feelings. It seems as if she might never feel anything ever again. Vanessa sits down close to her.

'I felt some of what you went through.'

'I didn't mean to make you.'

'I want to share everything with you, not just the good bits,' Vanessa says. She places her hand on Linnéa's knee.

She has changed into pants and sweatshirt and washed off her make-up. Now she sits quietly, screwing up her eyes against the evening sunlight that pours in through the windows.

It is the last day of school. Vanessa shouldn't be sitting around in this depressing apartment, keeping company with her depressed girlfriend. Besides, Linnéa doesn't want to stay here either. She wants to go out.

'Are we going to Olsson's Hill, or what?'

Vanessa just stares at her.

'Aren't the others waiting for us?' Linnéa asks.

'Do you really want to go?'

'I do. I don't want to sit here and hide.'

* * *

Anna-Karin pulls her hair back into a ponytail and checks herself in the mirror.

She is wearing jeans and a dark green T-shirt that's almost new. She straightens up. Tries a smile. It looks more as if she is pulling a face.

She sits down on the lid of the toilet. Her eyes wander over the map of Engelsfors on the wall in front of her. Noises from the kitchen filter upstairs, the clatter of cooking and strains of classical music. From Minoo's room comes the sound of clothes hangers being pulled along a rail.

It's the first time Anna-Karin is going to have a meal with the entire Falk Karimi family. She has barely seen Minoo's mother in the past. She feels in the way already because it is so rare for the family to be together. They would surely prefer meeting up without having to be nice to an awkward, silent stranger. A stranger who is also costing them a lot of money. This morning, she had been given the same end-of-semester present as Minoo, a gift certificate for books. The sum on the certificate made her so panicky she almost forgot to thank Minoo's father.

I must remember to thank Farnaz as well, Anna-Karin thinks. And to make an effort to talk and laugh and behave like somebody halfway normal.

The front door opens and Farnaz calls out, 'Hello, everyone!' Her voice is strong and clear. It sounds as if she is the kind of person who never mumbles.

Minoo runs past the bathroom and down the stairs. Anna-Karin hears them talk together in the hall.

'Anna-Karin!' Minoo shouts. 'Dinner is ready!'

Anna-Karin tries to give herself an encouraging look in the mirror. All she sees is a pair of eyes full of contempt.

They are to eat in the garden, where drops of water are still glinting on the lawn. The table is laid with a pale blue tablecloth and delicate blue-and-white china.

Minoo and her mother are already seated at the table. They look so alike. Suddenly, Anna-Karin is reminded of all the times people have told her that she looks like her mother. She never liked it, but now it strikes her that no one will ever see them side by side again; no one will ever again look from one to the other and say, 'Wow, you're so alike!'

'Hello, Anna-Karin!' Farnaz says.

The Key

She gets up to hug Anna-Karin and envelops her in scent, a mixture of fresh air, shampoo and a spicy perfume.

'Hello.' Anna-Karin hopes it doesn't show just how overwhelmed she feels.

She becomes aware that both Minoo and her mother have put on a dress. She hadn't realized that she should wear something extra nice. But how could she not have realized? After all, Minoo had told her that they were celebrating. They must think that she looks like a tramp.

She sits down on the free chair next to Minoo. Erik comes out of the kitchen carrying a large bowl of quinoa salad and a dish with oven-baked chicken breasts. Then he walks back to the kitchen and returns with a tray of bowls filled with gazpacho, olives and dressings.

'There you are, folks!' he says, sitting down beside Farnaz.

'That's fantastic, Erik!' She smiles toward him.

Minoo looks pleased and proud. Anna-Karin is happy for her because she knows how much it means to her that her father has listened to her worries about his health.

'I'm trying to extend my repertoire of dishes,' he says. He piles salad on his plate. 'I want you know, I've started to walk to work. I plan to start running later on but the doctor advised me to take it easy in the beginning . . .'

'Hey, wait,' Farnaz says. 'Have you really consulted a doctor?'

'Yes, I have.' Erik's voice suddenly sounds harsher. 'Incredible as it may sound, I am capable of changing my mind.'

A tense silence follows. The only sounds are the tinkling noises from serving spoons on china. Anna-Karin looks fixedly at a blue tit that has flown in and settled on the lawn near the table, where it hops about, its head turning this way and that.

'I wasn't being critical,' Farnaz says. 'I'm delighted, Erik. A little surprised, but happy.'

She puts her hand on his and looks at him with eyes full of affection.

'Thanks,' he says quietly.

He clears his throat, gets hold of the bottle of wine and tops up his own and Farnaz's glasses.

'Minoo told me about Bosse Forslund's son and those other boys,' Farnaz says.

'It's an appalling business.'

'It is. And utterly typical of this town.'

'What do you mean?' Eric asks, and the edge is back in his voice.

Anna-Karin notes that Minoo stiffens.

'I meant that I understand very well why she didn't dare report them at the time,' Farnaz replies. 'Given her background, no one would've believed her. And the boys are probably used to getting away with things just because they grew up on the right side of the tracks.'

She is truly beautiful, Anna-Karin thinks. She looks like Minoo, but she has such a clear self-confidence. It is as if she would never apologize for herself, for being the person she is. Is this who Minoo will become when she grows up?

'You're right,' Minoo says. 'They usually get away with everything.'

She fills their glasses from the carafe with its clinking ice cubes. The sun glitters in the water.

'Have you girls known about the bridge business for a long time?' Minoo's dad asks. 'Did Linnéa tell you?'

'Yes, we knew,' Minoo tells him. 'But Linnéa was very clear that the police wouldn't believe her, and she was scared of Erik and Robin. It meant we couldn't say anything either.'

'You ought to have told us,' Farnaz says. 'Perhaps we could have helped you.'

Anna-Karin can't help comparing Farnaz with her own mother. She knows just how Mom would've practically smacked her lips, how her eyes would've lit up. *You see! The posh ones are the worst every time.*

She cuts her chicken breast in tiny pieces. One mustn't

speak ill of the dead. Or think badly of them. And especially not of one's own mother.

A cracking sound. Her plate breaks into two pieces. The different dressings seep through the crack and soak into the pretty tablecloth. Anna-Karin tries to mop up the stain with her napkin but it only seems to make it worse.

'Sorry!' she says. 'I'm so sorry.'

'Not to worry,' Farnaz tells her. 'I've spilled worse things on this cloth. Why don't you take the plate through to the kitchen and we can fix the rest later.'

She doesn't sound mad at all but Anna-Karin still doesn't dare look at her.

She stacks the two pieces of her plate and walks toward the house. Low music is playing in the kitchen, something from an opera. She puts the ruined plate in the sink and washes her hands. What should she do with the bits? Will Minoo's parents want to try to mend the plate? Or is throwing the pieces away the obvious thing to do?

'Anna-Karin,' a voice says behind her. Farnaz.

Anna-Karin turns toward her, but still can't bring herself to look at her.

'I am so sorry. I'll pay for another one or maybe try to mend it.' Anna-Karin only manages to sound silly.

'No, really. Just throw it all away. Honestly, these old plates break the moment you touch them. It wasn't your fault.'

Anna-Karin looks up cautiously. Farnaz smiles warmly.

'I wish that we'd had time to talk properly earlier,' she says. 'But now I want to ask you to regard this place as your home. I do understand that what you are going through now is very hard to bear.'

The look in Farnaz's eyes is sympathetic and far from the cloying pity that Anna-Karin can't handle. Far, too, from the concerned expression that makes her wonder about herself and just how wrecked she really is.

'Is there someone you can talk to?' Farnaz asks. 'Minoo has told me that you and your grandfather are very close.'

This surprises Anna-Karin. It hadn't occurred to her that Minoo and her mother might have been talking about her.

'Yes,' she says. 'But he is very old and I don't want him to worry . . .'

She stops there, because she doesn't want to say that – with Grandpa – she is ashamed of her lack of feelings. Unwilling to give away how dulled she is; how her loss only strikes her at times, like the painful flash of lightning caused by seeing Farnaz and Minoo sitting together just now.

'When I was young, I lost so many people who were close to me,' Farnaz tells her. 'I know something about grieving. And I also know that no two people mourn in the same way. Nothing is right or wrong, Anna-Karin. You must live through this your own way. But you're not alone.'

The lump in Anna-Karin's throat seems so large she can hardly breathe.

'You can talk with me or phone me whenever you feel you need to,' Farnaz says. 'And if you want me to help you find a therapist, you need only ask.'

'Thank you,' Anna-Karin manages to say.

Farnaz hugs her and then walks back into the garden. Her perfume still fills the air.

Anna-Karin rinses the two pieces of the plate but can't bring herself to throw them away, so she leaves them in the sink. When she turns around, Minoo is waiting in the doorway that leads to the garden.

'What did Mom say?' she asks.

Anna-Karin can't speak. The lump in her throat is in the way. But even without it, she could never have expressed how much it meant to her, what Farnaz had said. Suddenly, she feels less of a freak. Maybe she will be able to deal with this after all.

Minoo walks off to look through one of the windows in the

living room. It's not until a car engine is switched off outside that Anna-Karin notices it.

'What's he doing here?' Minoo asks.

Anna-Karin goes over to stand next to her.

Viktor is walking toward the house. He moves quickly and his body language seems to shout that he is a bearer of bad news.

Anna-Karin has an awful premonition that everything is falling apart and that she triggered the disaster just because she relaxed for a moment.

Has the Council decided to round them up, once and for all? Have they found out that the Chosen Ones used magic in the school today? That Rickard and Gustaf have been let in on all their secrets? Or perhaps Viktor has come to tell them that it was he who made Robin confess?

'Come on,' Minoo says, and Anna-Karin follows her into the hall.

Minoo opens the door before Viktor has time to ring the bell.

'Minoo, you must come with me to the manor house,' he says. 'You must help us.'

The fear in his voice makes Anna-Karin even more alarmed.

'What's happening?' Minoo asks.

'It's Clara,' Viktor tells her. 'My sister.'

So, her name is Clara. Viktor had told Anna-Karin a little about his twin sister last winter, when they were standing near the locks of the canal. He had said that his sister's magic had made her ill.

'She is dying,' Viktor continues. 'Please, Minoo. You must come. The *Book of Patterns* told Walter that you can help her.'

'Who is Walter?' Anna-Karin asks.

'I'll explain later.' Minoo looks evasive. 'Sorry, I have to go with him.'

Viktor sets out for the car and breaks into a run. Anna-Karin looks anxiously at Minoo.

'I'll be fine,' Minoo whispers. 'Anyway, I won't be there alone, will I?'

Anna-Karin understands. She nods. The fox will be there, keeping an eye on the manor house.

Viktor has jumped into the car and started the engine.

'But . . . what will I tell your parents?' Anna-Karin asks.

'Tell them I went to see Linnéa. That she felt bad and I had to go.'

Anna-Karin nods. Her eyes follow Minoo as she runs off and jumps into the passenger seat of Viktor's car. He drives off before she has time to close the door.

CHAPTER 37

Olsson's Hill smells like wet grass and cigarette smoke. Vanessa pulls a bottle of raspberry cider from Michelle's bag. She glances at Linnéa, who is sitting cross-legged, cig in hand, next to her on the picnic blanket. Vanessa hopes that she truly meant that she wanted to be here. And that she'll tell her if she wants to go home.

Vanessa unscrews the bottle top and drinks.

It wasn't just for Linnéa's sake that she would have preferred to stay at home tonight. She feels exhausted. She had realized that the interview with the police would be tough, but it was something else completely to have to hear Linnéa describe every detail. To feel what Linnéa felt.

There is so much she still hasn't had a chance to process. While Linnéa slept afterward, Vanessa had just sat and stared unseeingly at the room.

'Move over.' Evelina waves with her cell phone. 'Michelle, you must sit with them.'

Vanessa puts her arm around Linnéa and pulls her close. Michelle leans against her other side and pouts at the camera. She smells sweetly of hairspray, powder and raspberry cider. Evelina's cell goes *click*.

'You all look fucking great,' she says, and shows them on the display. 'Linnéa, is it OK if I upload it?'

'Fine by me,' Linnéa says.

'Now, tell me honestly!' Michelle drawls. 'Of me and Evelina, who is the hottest?'

'I don't know,' Linnéa says.

'Ignore her,' Vanessa tells her.

'It's cool,' Linnéa replies stiffly.

'Come *onnnn*,' Michelle persists. 'If you had to make out with one of us, who would you pick? I wouldn't be upset at all if you say Evelina.'

'Yes, you would,' Evelina says. She laughs raucously.

Vanessa makes herself laugh, then has another drink from the cider bottle. Just for tonight, she wishes that Michelle had some kind of social filter. Already, she has asked Linnéa why she has stopped drinking, then if she misses it, and also if she'd maybe go off the deep end straightaway if she had a mouthful of cider. And then she launched into an account of how they used to pay Linnéa's dad to buy alcohol for them while they were still underage. And just when Vanessa thought it couldn't get any worse, Michelle fired off far too many questions about what had been going on in the assembly hall today.

Of course, all of Engelsfors is talking about it tonight.

People keep glancing at them. Whispering. Some are staring openly. Someone did a thumbs-up when Vanessa turned to look. And others sit clustered around a cell phone checking out clips from the assembly. At regular intervals, Vanessa hears a repeat of Tommy's, 'That's enough!', followed by gales of laughter.

But the false friendliness is the worst.

Several of the people who, the day after the Canal Bridge incident, had been calling Linnéa a psycho and a liar, have come up to her tonight and told her how pleased they are that Robin has confessed. And that they thought all the time that he and Erik had been guilty. As if that made things better. It was the other way around, of course. If they had it all worked out, why didn't they speak up at the time?

Vanessa drinks some more cider and looks out over the grassy slope with its scattering of groups from Engelsfors High School. In the distance, the canal is glittering in the evening sun and, beyond it, the cemetery.

It seems unbelievable that only a year has passed since

Vanessa left another last-day-of-school party here on the hill and went off to meet the other Chosen Ones at Rebecka's and Elias's graves. Now, the urn with Ida's ashes in has also been lowered into the ground over there. And there could have been a gravestone bearing Linnéa's name.

Vanessa moves closer to her and leans her head against Linnéa's shoulder.

Michelle lies down with her head in Evelina's lap and announces that she is positive she and Mehmet will spend the rest of their lives together.

'It must seem crazy, the number of times we've ended it and then got together again. But now everything is great between us. I think we've finished fighting about all the big things a couple can fight about.'

'This must be the first time none of us is single,' Evelina says.

'Do I hear "a toast to that"?' Michelle shrieks, and holds out her cider bottle.

Glass clinks as she toasts with Vanessa and Evelina.

Linnéa just drags on her cigarette. Her bottle of Coke stays untouched in the grass. Vanessa looks quizzically at her.

I thought it was a private toast between the three of you, Linnéa thinks.

But she leans forward a little, as if she wants to get across that she is part of their talk.

'Eugh, the grass is still fucking wet,' Evelina complains. 'It goes right through the blanket.'

'Probably you've just wet yourself,' Michelle says.

'In that case you're lying in my piss now,' Evelina tells her. They laugh.

Michelle's cell phone pings and she picks it up.

'Oh no, Mehmet is in Götis,' she sighs. 'Shame you're banned, it would've been brilliant to meet up with him.'

Banned? Linnéa thinks, lifting one eyebrow.

It's a long story, Vanessa thinks, and smiles.

'What's that, you're not going to abandon us now?' Evelina says. She smacks Michelle lightly.

'Of course I won't,' Michelle assures her, lifting her head to have a drink. 'Listen, we mustn't ever become the sort of girls who always put their boyfriends first. Or, like, their girlfriends. Linnéa, you have to get this, the three of us have always been best friends. And it will stay that way. Evelina and I are part of the Vanessa-package.'

Linnéa smiles and, for the first time in the evening, looks relaxed.

'I know.'

'And it means that we're your friends, too,' Michelle says. She lowers her voice to a whisper. 'I'll be a witness for you, Linnéa, if you need one. I'll back you all the way – like, I could say I walked past Canal Bridge and saw the whole thing.'

Vanessa sneaks a worried glance at Linnéa, but she just keeps smiling.

'I don't think—' she begins.

'Hold it, I know, I know!' Michelle interrupts. She fumbles with her hand for Linnéa's knee. 'I could say that I heard Erik and Robin talk about it in town!'

'Thanks,' Linnéa says. 'But I don't think it'd be a good idea to lie to the police for my sake.'

A freshman is staggering past them on his way to a shrubbery and has already started to pull his zip down. He catches sight of Michelle in Evelina's lap.

'Are you all dykes now, or what?'

'No, we dig *men*,' Evelina says sweetly. 'So you haven't got a chance with us.'

Michelle laughs. 'A toast to *that*.'

Vanessa's phone pings.

'I hope that's someone calling to tell us about an awesome party tonight,' Evelina says.

'I doubt it.' Vanessa frowns, seeing Anna-Karin's name on the display.

She can feel the eyes of the others glued to her as she talks. She tries to respond to Anna-Karin as neutrally as possible, but it's hard when what she's saying is so odd.

'OK. We'll be in touch,' she says.

What's happened? Linnéa thinks.

Viktor's twin sister is ill and Minoo has gone with him to the manor house to help her. The Book of Patterns *told some guy called Walter that she must go.*

Linnéa stares at her.

What?

The fox is keeping an eye, Vanessa thinks. *And we aren't that far away if something happens.*

I don't like any of this, Linnéa thinks.

'Why so quiet all of a sudden?' Evelina asks Vanessa. 'Has something bad happened?'

'No, it wasn't anything special.' Vanessa puts her cell phone back in her bag. Avoiding Evelina's eyes, she raises the bottle again.

'Can you believe it! Summer vacation's here!'

Michelle sits up, sticks her arms up in the air and yells so loudly that people turn around to have a look.

Vanessa laughs but can hear how false it sounds. She notices the way Evelina looks at her. Evelina hears it too, she realizes.

CHAPTER 38

Viktor swings the car into the yard in front of the manor house with a fast half-turn that makes the gravel spray around the wheels. He brakes hard and Minoo is jerked forward so that the safety belt cuts into her shoulder. He turns the engine off and throws the car door open.

'Come quickly!'

Minoo isn't sure if her legs will carry her. By the time she has climbed out of the car, Viktor is already at the front door.

'Hurry up!' he calls, before disappearing into the manor house.

Minoo jogs after him. In the hall, the unnaturally clean smell hits her. It is dark, only pale strips of light coming through the cracks between the shutters. The hallway on the left leads to the library where they were interrogated, and then on to the big room where the court had sat. Viktor has turned right, toward a part of the house Minoo has never seen.

Her footsteps on the flagged floor echo as she follows him. Perhaps she should worry more about the possibility that she has been tricked into coming here. But not even Viktor is that good an actor. Something really has gone wrong. And he really does believe that she can help.

'Come here!' Viktor shouts. He pulls a door open further along the hallway. 'Please, please, hurry!'

She runs through the door after him. They are in a dimly lit hallway lined with dark, moss-green wallpaper. Now their footsteps are softened by a burgundy wall-to-wall carpet.

'Is Walter here?' she calls out to Viktor. He stops and waits impatiently for her.

'No, he's in Stockholm,' he says. 'Alexander is there, too. But I called him when Clara got worse. That's when I spoke to Walter.'

Viktor starts walking again and Minoo does her best to keep up with him. It isn't easy. He turns a corner and walks up a narrow wooden staircase.

'Adriana, what about her? Is she here?' Minoo asks.

'Yes, but she won't disturb us.'

They are now in an identical hallway on the first floor.

'Won't you tell me what the matter is with your sister?' Minoo asks him.

Viktor doesn't reply. Minoo suddenly feels very scared. All she knows about Viktor's sister is that she somehow had too large a dose of magic too quickly. Has the magic broken down her body? Has she gone mad? Violent, perhaps? Is her magic like an infectious disease?

Viktor opens a door and they go through into a hallway with a dark brown carpet. It has windows along one side. The tops of the trees look strangely twisted when seen through the bulging old panes. Along the other side of the hallway are several white doors with the outlines of small signs still visible. They must have been put there at the time the manor house was an inn.

Viktor opens one of the doors. Minoo takes a deep breath and follows him.

The dark blue blind has been pulled up a little. The white wallpaper has a pattern of golden fleur-de-lys. The air is stale. Clothes and books are scattered on chairs and on the floor. The bed is unmade. Viktor walks up to the bed and stops.

'Here,' he says.

Minoo comes closer. It's just possible to see the outlines of a body under the duvet.

'Clara has been stuck in an invisible state since we were little,' Viktor tells her.

270

Minoo looks at the hollow in the pillow where Clara's head must be. And remembers the first time Adriana had them all gathered around her in Kärrgruvan. And her warning to Vanessa.

One day you'll make yourself invisible and discover you can't reverse the process. You might be forced to spend the rest of your life as a shadow.

That is what has actually happened to Clara.

'But now her condition is worsening,' Viktor says.

In front of them, the air shivers like it does above hot asphalt on a summer's day. And then the entire bed is gone. There is only a bare floor in front of Minoo. The next moment, the bed is visible again, along with the mattress, sheets and pillows. Everything except the body that is lying there.

'She lost consciousness an hour ago,' Viktor goes on. 'I think Engelsfors is making her worse. The levels of magic are rising constantly and she can't control her uptake. While we've been here, she has felt unwell for most of the time, but she has never admitted just *how* unwell.'

His voice breaks and he looks away.

'But what can I do to help her?' Minoo asks.

His voice is still choked when he replies.

'I don't know. But, please, try.'

'Of course I will,' she says, even though she has no clue what to do.

Still, if the guardians have let it be known that she can help Clara, then she must be able to. She must try.

'Can you please see to it that we're not disturbed?'

Viktor nods and quietly leaves the room.

Minoo releases the black smoke. She lets it wrap itself around her fear and suffocate it. She approaches the bed. It shivers again, disappears entirely and then reappears.

She gently touches the pillow until she feels Clara's hair. Then, her cool forehead.

Minoo shuts her eyes. Immediately, she becomes aware that

something is wrong. It is like hearing a false note, a dissonance. She has to make an effort not to let that discordance interfere with her concentration. It is essential to get beyond it.

Suddenly, she sees Viktor, and knows she's inside Clara's memories. Viktor is only a child, maybe of elementary school age. His eyes are scared and fixed on two bigger boys who are standing in front of him. 'Junkie kid,' one of the boys says. The other one laughs and slaps Viktor around the head.

'Where's your yucky kid sister?' he says. Minoo feels how anger flares inside Clara, and then a light fanning sensation over her skin. She runs at the boy who hit Viktor and crashes into him. He stumbles into the other boy who falls over, hits his elbows on the pavement and starts howling. *You promised you wouldn't do anything like that,* Viktor's voice says inside Clara's head. *I don't care,* Clara thinks. *I won't let them hurt you.*

Forward.

'What have you done?' the woman called Malin screams. She wants them to call her 'mother'. They are in a kitchen that is all chrome and gleaming white surfaces. Water is overflowing the edge of the sink and forming pools on the floor. Viktor is soaking wet. Clara can't allow Malin to look at Viktor as if she is about to hit him. 'I did it!' she shouts. 'It's me, I did it!' Malin whirls around and fixes her eyes on Clara.

Forward.

Clara stands in a dark room and watches Malin through the gap in the open door. 'It's terrible,' Malin is saying into the phone while she keeps fingering the strings dangling from the hood of her purple top. 'I just don't understand her. She *frightens* me, even though she's just a child. I can't cope with the two of them. The way I see it, they should be made more independent of one another. It would be for the best; they're too close.' A claw of iron grips Clara's heart. Malin wants to separate her and Viktor.

Forward.

She is standing near a sofa where Malin and Viktor are sitting. Malin has turned to the two policemen who are in the room with them. 'I am so worried,' Malin says. 'Could someone have kidnapped her?' Clara is thrilled. Malin is getting what she deserves. And she has been over-the-top nice to Viktor ever since Clara disappeared. *Serves her right*, Clara thinks. She focuses on Viktor. *Where are you?* he says, lifting his head. His face is streaky with tears. Viktor is brilliant at acting. As for herself, she can't ever hide what she feels. *Just next to the sofa*, she tells him. He looks her way and smiles so fleetingly that no one else notices.

Forward.

Only Viktor's image in the mirror. However hard she tries, only Viktor is visible. He does his best to seem calm but he can't deceive her. *It will pass*, he thinks. *And if it doesn't, I promise to look after you.*

Forward.

In the anonymous office, Clara shifts along on the hard upholstery of the sofa to sit closer to Viktor. 'I've got someone here who wants to talk to you,' the social service official says. She opens the door to a tall man with dark hair. Alexander. Ten years younger than he is now. Minoo realizes that this is the first time Clara has seen him. Alexander exchanges a glance with the official and hands her an envelope. She leaves the room. Alexander sits down on the desk and examines Viktor. *Don't say anything*, Clara thinks, and Viktor doesn't. 'I've been given to understand that you are a very unusual young man,' Alexander says. Viktor stays silent. 'For instance, I'm told that you've been involved with numerous incidents of water damage.' *Don't say anything*, Clara thinks. She is even more frightened now. 'I see,' Alexander says. He holds out his hand and a blue flame flares up in his palm. It makes his brown eyes glitter. Viktor leans forward and stares at the flame with absorbed fascination. 'You're not alone,' Alexander tells him. 'Nor are you, Clara.'

Minoo moves on, into Clara's later memories. There are glimpses of large, beautiful rooms with high ceilings. Views over Stockholm. A razor-blade gleams and she wonders how much she will feel it . . .

Forward.

She is held in Viktor's arms. They are sitting on the bathroom floor. Both are soaked in water. *You must never ever do this again*, Viktor thinks. *Promise me.* He has gripped her wrist and is pressing hard on the tight bandage. She only had time for one cut before he kicked in the flimsy door. He hasn't asked why she did this. He has felt her pain, the pain of leading a life as a shadow. Of being a secret and a burden. The pain remains, but so does Viktor's love for her. She can sense the love in his thoughts and realizes that she must not leave him alone here. *I promise*, she thinks.

Forward.

A powerful smell of some cleaning product. A message scribbled on a wall in Engelsfors High School, a message that they've tried but failed to remove. IF U WANNA SAVE THE PLANET. KILL UR FUCKIN SELF. Minoo sees herself walking along the hallway toward the janitor's office. Clara is curious. She creeps closer to Minoo until she suddenly makes a shuffling sound against the floor. She stiffens. The magic here in Engelsfors is very strong but also very unpredictable. Minoo looks straight at her and, for a brief moment, Clara thinks she has been seen. But the door to the janitor's office opens and Nicolaus's head appears in the gap. 'Minoo?' he says. Minoo steps inside.

Forward.

A school photo of Elias is projected onto a screen in a darkened room. Clara stands among the shadows. *Elias Malmgren was the first to die,* she thinks, and Viktor repeats her words aloud for Alexander, whose face is pale in the light from the screen. He looks tense, attentive. *Elias's element was wood. His powers were unclear; it could be that he had not yet developed them.* She changes to the next image. Rebecka,

274

the second victim. *Rebecka Mohlin was a fire witch. We know that she was psychokinetic. She was also able to set fire to objects.* She projects another image. The blonde girl in the picture makes Clara's heart do a double beat. *This is Vanessa Dahl.* Clara hopes that Viktor won't pick up what she is feeling because it might make him worry about her. *Her element is air and she can make herself invisible. So far, no signs of any other powers.* Clara struggles to seem neutral and untroubled but envy is gnawing inside her. Vanessa has the same talent as Clara but it hasn't taken her over. Also, she is lovely. Her beauty is of the kind that is even more attractive in reality than in photographs because Vanessa glows with the joy of life. Clara has observed her as she has followed her around to collect information for Alexander. Viktor looks fixedly at the photo on the screen. Clara notices that he is already a little in love, even though he has never met Vanessa. 'Well, none of this adds anything new to what we have already learned from Adriana,' Alexander points out impatiently. 'Speaking of Adriana, any information about her?' *I haven't found any indications that she's disloyal to the Council,* Clara thinks. She is doing her duty but doesn't like that Alexander wants her to spy on his own sister.

Forward.

A train rumbles in the distance. The grasshoppers are chirping. Linnéa stands on the road to the cemetery and stares into the darkness. Clara backs away and tries to protect her thoughts from the mind-reading one.

Forward.

Nicolaus holds Cat in his arms, rocks it like a child. The cat is meowing so loudly that Clara can hear it from where she is lurking, close to a large gravestone. 'Forgive me, forgive, forgive . . .' Nicolaus whispers and Clara has to look away when Cat dies.

Forward.

Clara sneaks over to the workbench in the chemistry lab

and swiftly switches the places of the acid and the water. When Kevin starts yelling, Clara can't believe that no one can hear her laughing. *Clara, that was highly unnecessary*, Viktor thinks, but he can't stop himself from smiling just a little. Clara carries on laughing as the scene develops: the blah girls in Kevin's lab group are screaming their heads off and Kevin is going 'Fucking crap acid rule! I did it right!' at the top of his voice. She has taken him down a notch or two for being so annoying in the hallway before the lesson.

Forward.

It's cold and Clara pushes her hands deep into her jacket pockets as she walks toward the canal. Viktor just laughed when she asked him if he wanted to go for a walk. But she likes the fog. This winter, it has been good not to have to deal with snow, where she always leaves a trail. She stops when she hears a scream from Canal Bridge. 'I'll jump. I'll do it!' It is Linnéa. Clara can see her now. There are two figures with her on the bridge. Both are masked and one of them holds a baseball bat. Linnéa swings her leg across the railing. She says something but Clara can't make out the words. 'Just do it,' one of the masked men orders. 'That's right. Just do it, Linnéa,' says the other, the one with the baseball bat. Clara turns around and runs back to the manor house, shouting to Viktor in her head. She hopes it won't be too late. Then she hears a loud splash from the canal.

Forward.

Clara watches as Viktor half drags, half carries Linnéa to the manor house. When she sees Linnéa's pale face with the blue lips, Clara feels a wave of fury. She hates the men who did this. She doesn't know who they are, but she's quite clear why they dared to do what they did. There was no risk involved, because even if Linnéa survived and tried to speak out, nobody would believe her. Nobody believes girls like her. Clara knows what it is like to be in Linnéa's shoes. She promises herself that she will find out who the balaclava men are, and make them pay.

Forward.

She presses the marker pen hard against the pale blue wall-paper and takes pleasure in watching Robin's terrified face as the word is formed: CONFESS!

Everything flickers and shivers.

And then Minoo realizes that she is doing this all wrong. She is not helping by being inside Clara's memories.

She withdraws from Clara's mind but stays inside the smoke. Suddenly, she can see Clara. She is lying under the covers in the fetal position. Minoo takes in Clara's profile, her long, ash-blonde hair spread over the pillow, the scar on her left wrist.

Clara isn't as similar to Viktor as Minoo had expected, but it is easy to see that they're brother and sister. Clara's skin is grayish, her breathing is quick and shallow. Her life-force is very weak. Minoo knows that she is close to death.

The dissonance is there again, a sharp note that vibrates through Minoo. She allows it to lead her on. Hopes to locate its source.

Suddenly, she *sees* it.

Clara's magic. It has gone badly wrong.

It looks like a milky-white fog, like the thick whiteout that covered Engelsfors last winter. And it seems about to swallow Clara, to suffocate her. The sound has grown loud and excruciating; it is jamming Minoo's mind and she must use all her strength not to let it paralyze her. She makes the black smoke whirl into the whiteness and begins to prod into Clara's magic. She finds what is wrong with it: the knots and tangles, a mess that she can't find words for. But she can try to untangle them.

Step by step, the sickly fog thins and Clara's magic grows stronger and sounder, until it looks like a shimmering, pale blue aura.

Everything is as it should be now. Minoo can feel it. Clara's breathing is calm.

Minoo hauls the black smoke back and looks at Clara in her bed. She is fully visible now. And she will live.

Minoo opens her mouth to call Viktor, but she is completely drained. She is surprised to feel her legs give way and wonders if she going to faint.

CHAPTER 39

Anna-Karin is sitting on the floor in her room. Her eyes are closed. She feels the hard surface of the parquet underneath her, touches the object she is holding and listens to Minoo's parents chatting in the garden. At the same time, she is with the fox. He is snooping around in the light summer evening, circling the manor house again and again, but cannot sense what is going on in there.

Without opening her eyes, Anna-Karin's mind returns to her room. Clutches the china dog with the broken ear a little more firmly. She has rescued it from a trash bag, but only because Minoo had looked so shocked when she was about to throw it away. In fact, the barking Dalmatian with a red velvet ribbon around the neck does not represent a memory she wants to keep.

Mom hadn't even tried to look pleased when she opened her Christmas gift. Grandpa had gone on about how nice the dog was, even though he was with Anna-Karin when she'd bought it in Ingrid's Hidey-hole. Mom placed it dutifully with some other china ornaments. Just a few days later, she managed to knock it over. Anna-Karin had thought Mom had thrown it away.

But Mom always had this block against getting rid of things, she thinks. At least in that, I'm not like her.

Her fingers are sliding over the smooth china surface. She thinks about what Grandpa had said and tries to make his words her own.

My new power is a fantastic gift.

I mustn't be afraid of what is inside me.

I shall learn to control it and, when I can, I'll not be afraid anymore.

But the fear is stronger. It tells her she shouldn't have been given her new power, that it is a mistake. Minoo or Vanessa should have received it instead. Even Linnéa would have handled it better, even if she is the one who gets angry the most often. All three of them are mentally stronger than Anna-Karin, and would be much better able to cope with having great physical strength.

But she has no choice. It will become truly dangerous unless she learns to control it.

Anna-Karin clenches her fist around the Dalmatian, trying to imagine how it will break with a cracking sound, how white china dust will fall from the cracks. But nothing happens and her head immediately begins to throb.

She opens her eyes and puts the dog away. The headache is like a pounding inside her skull.

Suddenly she sees a red spot on the floor and another spot on the Dalmatian. She rubs the skin under her nose with a finger. It becomes sticky with blood. She remembers that Vanessa had a nosebleed in the beginning when they tried to use their magic. It was never like that for Anna-Karin. Her power was just there without any coaxing. Stopping herself from using it was the hard bit.

Anna-Karin gets up and finds a packet of tissues in her desk drawer. Minoo had given them to her for the funeral, but Anna-Karin never needed to use them. She presses a tissue against her nose while she cleans up the blood on the floor with another one.

Her phone starts vibrating. Number withheld. The worry about Minoo returns.

'Hi, it's Viktor.'

He sounds different now.

'She did it!' His tone tells Anna-Karin how relieved he is. 'Clara is well again.'

'What about Minoo?' Anna-Karin asks, pressing the tissue against her nose. 'How is she?'

A little blood dribbles down her throat and she almost chokes.

'She's fine,' he says.

'Why doesn't she phone herself?'

'She's asleep,' Viktor replies. 'But don't worry. I've seen witches exhaust themselves before. It's not at all dangerous but she must rest. I think it's better if she stays here overnight.'

Anna-Karin fumbles about for something to say. She sits down on the bed. From the garden she hears Farnaz laugh. Of course, Minoo's parents think that their daughter has gone to be with Linnéa and presumably will also think it is fine for her to stay the night.

'Why don't you come over here tonight?' Viktor says. 'Then you can see for yourself that she's OK. But, Anna-Karin, there is something you have to understand. Minoo saved my sister's life. I will *never* allow anyone to harm her.'

And for the first time, Anna-Karin feels she can trust Viktor. All the same, she is going to make the fox stay in the vicinity of the manor house until Minoo has left.

'I believe you,' she says quietly. 'Please ask her to phone me as soon as she wakes up.'

'I promise. And when you talk to Linnéa, tell her that I will be questioned by the police tomorrow. I am going to tell them that I saw the entire Canal Bridge attack.'

'But . . . did you?'

'No, Clara did. But the police don't need to know that.'

* * *

Linnéa reads Anna-Karin's text for the second time as she and Vanessa walk down Olsson's Hill.

Minoo is safe. She has cured Viktor's sister from whatever

it was that was wrong with her. And Viktor is going to lie to the police and say that he saw much more than he actually had.

'I wish I knew whose side Viktor is on.' Vanessa has been reading over Linnéa's shoulder.

'I'm not sure he knows that himself,' Linnéa says, deleting the message and putting the cell phone away. 'Not that it matters. Not for as long as you're on my side.'

'Forever yours.' Vanessa smiles drunkenly.

Linnéa kisses her. Vanessa's mouth tastes of chewing gum, cider and lip gloss. Linnéa hopes that hers doesn't taste like an ashtray.

They walk along, arm-in-arm, and leave the drunken voices on Olsson's Hill behind.

Linnéa is surprised at how much fun the evening has been. It was lovely to be reminded that there is a life without guardians and demons. She looks forward to spending long summer nights with Vanessa.

Last summer was her worst ever. The first summer without Elias. The summer she and Vanessa didn't speak. She almost longed for school to begin. To be surrounded by people she didn't much care for seemed a better option than being so terribly lonely.

'Did you have a good time tonight?' Vanessa asks as she slaps at a hungry mosquito.

'Yes, I did.'

'Didn't you think Michelle was a bit of a pain?'

'Of course she was,' Linnéa says with a laugh. 'But she's a good person.'

Vanessa smiles. And everything feels so simple just now.

'It feels really weird to think that just a few hours ago I was utterly miserable.' Linnéa pulls Vanessa closer and puts her arm around her waist. 'I couldn't have gotten through the questioning without you. I can't tell you how glad I am that you were there.'

'I'm glad that you let me be there for you,' Vanessa says, and kisses her.

The kiss deepens and Vanessa's small sigh spreads throughout Linnéa's body.

Do you know what? Linnéa thinks. *At this moment, it feels like everything might turn out all right.*

'I know exactly what you mean,' Vanessa agrees, kissing Linnéa again.

Chapter 40

Minoo opens her eyes and sees wallpaper with a pattern of red clover flowers. She is lying on top of a made-up double bed. She has slept in her clothes. Her mouth is dry.

Where is this? She can't think clearly, her head seems full of a thick, gooey mass. The only thing that really matters now is finding a bathroom.

She sits up and looks around the strange room. Daylight comes through the thin curtains. There is a white-painted desk and a wardrobe, both in a rustic style. Her light canvas sneakers are neatly placed on the floor by the bedside table. She puts them on.

There are two doors in the room; she tries one of them and turns the light-switch on its other side. Pleasant, toned-down light shows her a small but very clean, newly tiled bathroom. She pees, washes, drinks a little water from the tap and dries her face on a luxuriously fluffy towel.

Then she steps back into the bedroom. Stands still. Her brain is clearing.

She is in the manor house.

Suddenly, it feels as if the room is shrinking. From every direction, the red clover flowers are dancing in on her. She leaps at the other door and pushes the handle down, expecting it to be locked. It isn't.

Minoo stops in her tracks and looks around. The hallway is lit by old-fashioned windows looking out over the tops of trees. It has a dark brown carpet. On the opposite long wall is a row of white doors with painted-over marks of small signs. It looks like the hallway that leads to Clara's room. But it might not be, of course – only another, identical-looking one.

She takes her cell phone from the pocket of her dress. It is 5.17 a.m. She shuts the door behind her quietly and tiptoes along the hallway, hoping that she will find her way out.

A door somewhere behind her opens and she turns around. Viktor.

He looks tired. Exhausted. But he smiles at her and, before Minoo has time to respond, he hugs her.

'Thank you,' he says. 'Thank you.'

Minoo goes as stiff as a post but Viktor doesn't seem to notice. She picks up a faint smell of sweat and at first thinks it must come from her. Then she realizes that it's from Viktor. Perfect Victor, who is always abnormally odorless.

'She wants to meet you,' he tells her.

And Minoo realizes that she also wants to meet Clara.

Viktor holds the door open for her and she steps into the room, which is still in semi-darkness.

Clara sits up in bed, supported by a pile of pillows. Her eyes are closed and her face is pale but it's a healthy pallor that no longer shades into gray. Her hair cascades over the pillows. The paintings in Minoo's book about the Pre-Raphaelites suddenly come back to her. She rejects the thought at once because it reminds her of Max.

'Clara, Minoo is here,' Viktor says in a gentle voice that is new to Minoo.

Clara opens her eyes. The irises are a clear, dark blue, just like Viktor's. She glances at Minoo and then looks away and tugs at her duvet as if she wants to hide under it.

'Clara, you can say it yourself now,' Viktor says. 'She will hear you.'

'Please, forgive me,' Clara says. 'I'm so unused to people hearing me speak.'

She looks quickly at Minoo, then turns away again.

'Or seeing me,' she continues, and a smile lights her face for just a moment. 'It feels so . . . unusual.'

'I understand,' is all Minoo can think of saying.

Clara fixes her eyes on her again and Minoo can see that it takes a lot of willpower. 'I am very grateful.'

'I'm glad I could help you.'

Should she to admit that she has seen Clara's memories? Minoo recoils at the thought. She doesn't want to upset Clara now. On the other hand, there is so much Minoo would like to know. How often has Clara been following the Chosen Ones? How much has she seen? And what has she been telling Viktor? And how much have they told Alexander?

Then it dawns on her that it wouldn't matter. The guardians have already told Walter everything.

Another circle can take the place of the Chosen Ones. If you are part of it.

Footsteps are approaching in the hallway. Minoo turns around as Adriana comes in.

Her glossy black hair is styled in a pageboy cut. Her cream-colored blouse is buttoned all the way up and her dark suit fits so perfectly it must be tailor-made. Her face is without expression, just as it used to look before Minoo got to know the real Adriana.

'Good to meet you,' she says, looking at Minoo. 'Adriana Lopez.'

They shake hands. Adriana doesn't show a glimmer of recognition. Maybe she has suppressed the memory of when she woke up in her bedroom and saw Minoo and Alexander there.

I feel so peculiar . . . Have I been asleep?

'Minoo Falk Karimi.'

Adriana lets go of her hand and looks inquisitively at Minoo.

'Such a remarkable change,' she observes. 'How did you do it?'

Minoo casts around for something to say.

'Minoo is in a hurry,' Viktor says. 'I'll drive her home.'

Part Two

Adriana turns to him. 'Alexander will expect a complete report when he comes back.'

'Of course,' Viktor replies coldly.

Minoo looks at Clara, who turns away as soon as their eyes meet.

'Take care,' Minoo says. 'And maybe you shouldn't . . . you know . . .'

Clara smiles. 'Not to worry. I'm not going to use magic again for a long time.'

Minoo nods, then mumbles 'Bye' to Adriana, whose eyes seem to scorch her back as she follows Viktor from the room.

He leads the way back through the manor house.

So far, Minoo has tried to avoid thinking about Adriana, but now the questions are flooding in. How has the Council explained her partial amnesia to her? What if Minoo has left any forbidden memories behind? Is there something still lodged in the back of her mind that she doesn't understand?

Viktor opens the front door for her. They walk together across the graveled yard.

'Viktor, you must tell me about Adriana,' she says in a low voice. 'How is she?'

Viktor doesn't answer, just keeps walking toward the car, which he opens with the remote key. The car bleeps softly and the headlights blink. Minoo hurries to catch up with him.

'Viktor . . .'

In a sudden movement, he turns to her, puts his arms around her and whispers with his lips close to her ear.

'Not here,' he mumbles in a barely audible voice.

He lets her go. As she opens the passenger-side door, she glimpses Anna-Karin's fox in the bushes on the other side of the yard.

They drive away. Viktor's fingers drum lightly on the steering wheel.

Once they hit asphalt, Minoo becomes aware of how quiet the engine is. The car glides noiselessly along the streets of

Engelsfors. They pass the turning that leads to Minoo's home and drive on eastwards. When Viktor suddenly leaves the main road, Minoo realizes that he is driving toward the abandoned industrial area.

'What are we doing here?'

They swing around a corner and drive past old brick-built factories.

'We'll talk,' Viktor replies. 'By the way, Anna-Karin wanted you to get in touch when you woke up.'

Minoo sends a text to Anna-Karin. When she looks up again, the old steel plant towers rise above them. The pride of Engelsfors' past.

Viktor drives around the huge building and pulls up on the parking lot. He turns the engine off and takes the key from the ignition.

'Come with me,' he tells her.

Avoiding the puddles, which glitter in the sun, they cross the old lot. Here, it feels as if they are alone in the world. The steel plant's chimney casts a long shadow.

Viktor follows the old, overgrown rail track, unused since the plant closed. Probably, though, it will be remembered in Lage's model railroad. The grass tickles Minoo's ankles. She steps more carefully when she notices the litter scattered everywhere. Plastic bags. A glint of sunlight on a vodka bottle. Used condoms.

A few freight wagons are left on the track and Viktor walks toward one of them, slides the door open and climbs inside in one agile movement. Then he holds out his hand to help Minoo. She is not as agile.

The air inside is stale and cold. It smells of damp and dirt. Light enters through a couple of ventilators near the roof. The interior is empty apart from some old beer cans and some rags which might once have been clothing.

'What are we doing here?' Minoo's voice is a tinny echo against the bare walls.

Viktor pulls the door almost shut.

'Clara found this place. We used to come here when we wanted to be left in peace.'

He looks intently at her. 'After what you did . . .' he begins, then pauses, before starting again. 'Minoo, I'd do anything for you. Anything at all.'

She shivers a little in the chilly morning air. Viktor pulls his jacket off and drapes it over her shoulders. 'Have this for a start,' he says.

For once, this doesn't come across as one of his empty gestures.

'Thank you.' Minoo wraps it closer around herself.

'I know you have many questions to ask,' he says. 'Ask away.'

'Haven't we done this before?'

'I'm serious. And I'll try to answer everything.'

'Then, please start with Adriana.'

Victor nods.

'She has been told that she came to town to find the Chosen One. But the stress was too much for her and after a while she began to behave . . . irrationally. Using magic she couldn't handle. Then things went really wrong; she failed to carry out a particular ritual and ended up losing a lot of her memories. The medics on the Council claim that major magic efforts had to be made to save her.'

It pains Minoo to hear this because she understands how ashamed Adriana must have felt when she heard these lies. Yet another failure for someone who has always been told how useless she is because of her poor magical abilities.

'Does she believe everything she's been told?'

'No, she doesn't believe it,' Viktor says. 'But questioning Council statements simply is not part of her mental make-up. I suspect she tries hard not to think about it at all.'

Adriana has again become the person she hated being.

'Does she remember anything about the court case and the trial?'

'Not a thing.'

289

'How is it possible to keep all that from her?' Minoo asks. 'There were so many Council members present.'

'Adriana meets no one not vetted by Alexander. And everyone is given strict orders not to bring up her past. She isn't even allowed to go out without Alexander's permission. She is employed as his secretary and housekeeper.'

Minoo thinks of Adriana. So lonely, caught in the hellish situation she tried to escape from. Minoo saved her life, but instead she has been sentenced to a lifetime of imprisonment with her brother as her jailer.

Adriana is held captive, not only by her oath of allegiance to the Council but also by the way they punished her for trying to run away with her lover, Simon. They chained her for life with a magic link that makes it hard for her to disobey orders and impossible to try to escape again.

Perhaps it's just as well that she doesn't remember how she once wanted to help the Chosen Ones. She is much safer, as long as she is loyal and willing. But Minoo can't stop wondering whether what she did to Adriana was right; if there really was no other way to help her.

'I think I know what's on your mind,' Viktor says. 'But, Minoo, you did save her life. This existence is better, after all, than not existing.'

Minoo nods and hopes Adriana would have agreed.

'You wanted to know what happened to Olivia,' Viktor goes on. 'I don't know where she is now. But Clara was in the school that night in the gym. She was the one who got the message through to Alexander. He picked up Olivia and went away for a few days. My guess is that he took her to the Council's headquarters in Stockholm.'

'What will they do to her there?'

'Don't know. I don't even know if she's alive.'

Minoo knows she is. The guardians have seen Olivia return. But she isn't allowed to tell Viktor that.

'Alexander won't speak about it,' Viktor continues. 'There's so much he doesn't want to speak about, ever since you and I helped Adriana.'

He looks sad and Minoo feels sorry for him.

She knows that Viktor and Clara's biological mother was a heroin addict who died when they were seven years old. Now she has seen Clara's memories, she understands that, to Viktor, Alexander must have felt like a savior. He knew about Clara, and accepted her, and he gave Viktor a more secure life.

Minoo realizes that she must tell Viktor what she knows about him and Clara.

'When I was trying to cure Clara, I happened to see some of her memories. I didn't intend to snoop; I just didn't know how to help her and I got off to a wrong start.'

Viktor stares at her.

'I didn't intend to,' Minoo says again.

'How much did you see?' he asks. 'Or, actually . . . no. Don't answer. It would be like sneakily reading her diary. I'll tell Clara and she can decide what she thinks.'

Minoo feels guilty, even though she knows that there was no other way. At least, she's not the only one who has been spying.

'One of the things I saw was that she had been following us about.'

Viktor looks embarrassed. 'Yes, she came here first for a few short reconnaissance trips. Alexander sent her to investigate what Adriana was up to in Engelsfors, because he didn't trust her reports. But it was difficult for Clara. Adriana had her raven and animals can see invisible people.'

'Did she live here all the time with you and Alexander?' Minoo asks.

Viktor nods.

'How much did she really see?'

'Less than you'd probably believe. She hasn't been out all that much because she's been unwell a lot, ever since she came here.'

That explains why the fox didn't spot her, Minoo thinks.

'But she went after Robin. I saw that in her memories.'

Viktor sighs.

'I tried to persuade her to stop. Not because Robin didn't deserve all he got, but because it was such a strain on her. Also, I didn't want Alexander to find out.'

'You've always protected each other,' Minoo says.

'Yes. Nobody else did.'

She sees a small bird flitting past the gap in the door and soon afterward she hears it land on the roof.

'What do you know about Walter?' she asks.

'Not much. He's Alexander's boss and I'd only met him a couple of times before he came here. But it seems you and I will see a lot more of him in the autumn.'

'Are you the water witch in the new circle?' she asks.

'Yes, I am.' She looks at Viktor, trying to imagine what it would be like to be in a circle with him.

'Do you know who else is in Walter's circle?'

She wonders briefly if Alexander will be one of them, but then she remembers that he is a trained witch.

'No. Well, Walter himself.'

If Walter is going to be part of it, he must be a natural witch. A strong one.

'Do you really think it's going to work?' Minoo asks.

'I think it's the best alternative. The *only* alternative,' Viktor says slowly.

He is silent for a few seconds, before he speaks again.

'I have sworn allegiance to the Council.'

Minoo stares at him.

'But I thought you didn't need to . . . ? Didn't the Council make an exception for you?'

'When Walter came here he told me that the guardians had selected me as one of the members of the new circle. But in order to join, I had to take the oath.'

He meets Minoo's eyes. 'If someone tells you that you're

selected to help save the world . . . you have to go along with what is required of you. Don't you agree?'

Minoo has no answer to give. Viktor has given up his freedom in order to become a member of the Council's circle. And the risk he is running by telling her everything and exposing his superiors to outsiders, is even greater than she'd imagined.

'You haven't spoken to the other Chosen Ones, have you?'

'No, I haven't,' Minoo replies. 'I have to make my decision first. I don't even know how to explain it to them. Everything is turned upside-down.'

'I know. Just to be told all this stuff about demons and guardians and the end of the world . . .'

'You didn't believe any of it before, did you?'

'Not when I first came to Engelsfors. I thought the tale of the Chosen Ones and their great task was so much fairy-dust. But now . . .' He shakes his head. 'So much has changed for all of us, hasn't it?'

'I don't know what I believe in anymore,' she says and, to her surprise, tears come to her eyes.

Viktor gingerly puts his arm around her.

'I believe in *you*,' he tells her. 'No one has powers that can hold a candle to yours. If there's anyone who can stop the apocalypse, it's you.'

Minoo blinks the tears away. She is so tired. Tired of turning everything over and over, of trying to see all the options from all possible angles. Tired of questioning and resisting.

Eventually one reaches a point where one must stop messing around and decide what to believe in.

And, suddenly, she knows what to say to the others.

'Thank you,' she says. 'I must go now.'

Viktor takes his arm away. She hands him his jacket.

'I just have to ask you something.' He hesitates. 'Did you see our mother in Clara's memories?'

'No.'

Viktor looks relieved. Minoo thinks of when Clara was

watching him in that darkened room and the image of Vanessa came up on the screen. Viktor had looked very vulnerable then. And he looks vulnerable now.

'I know you're in love with Vanessa,' she says. 'I just want you to know that I know and that I will never tell anyone.'

Viktor blushes from the base of his throat all the way to the top of his forehead.

'Right . . .' he says. 'Listen, it's not that strange, is it? How can one *not* be in love with Vanessa?' He looks bashful for a moment. 'I know I haven't a hope. And I accept that. It's enough . . . just to be in the same town as her.'

He falls silent and the color in his face deepens. Minoo feels just as embarrassed. But he has told her so much now. Not telling him wouldn't have been right.

Viktor slides the door back and the light pours in. He jumps down and then holds out his hand to help her. She lands softly on the grass.

The air outside is warmer now. The sunlight is brilliantly bright and small clouds sail across a clear blue sky.

'One last secret,' Viktor says.

Minoo hears the sound of wings flapping and the bird that perched on the roof suddenly flies down to them. It's a blue tit.

Viktor holds out his hand and the bird lands on it, puts its head to the side and looks at them with black peppercorn eyes.

'My familiar,' he explains.

The blue tit flies back to the roof again.

'So you have been able to see Clara through its eyes?' Minoo asks.

Viktor nods. 'I suppose you'll tell the others about it?'

'I have to,' Minoo replies.

'Perhaps you might mention to Vanessa that I can't always keep tabs on it,' Viktor says and blushes again. 'She will know what I'm referring to.'

*

Part Two

Viktor drives her downtown, and from there she walks the few blocks to Nicolaus's apartment. She lets herself in, slumps down on the sofa in the living room and sits there for a while, listening to the silence.

Then she reaches for her cell phone and texts the others.

CHAPTER 41

Minoo has no sense of how long she has been talking. All she knows is that when she has finished she is hoarse. The room is as silent as the grave. Nobody has asked any questions, nobody has made any comments. And even now, when Minoo has nothing more to tell them, nobody speaks.

Anna-Karin sits on one of the wooden chairs, leaning forward, her hair falling across her face. Vanessa sits cross-legged on the chair next to Anna-Karin and stares at the bare brown wall in front of her. Linnéa, who settled down on the floor near Vanessa, is the only one who looks at Minoo, but her expression is inscrutable.

If Ida had been there, she would have spoken up. Minoo can almost hear her.

Collaborate with Council? Good luck with that, Minoo. You'll probably enjoy every minute. Until they figure you've made some mistake and decide to execute you on the spot. Or whatever.

'Come on, say something,' Minoo says. 'What do you think?'

'Creepy,' Vanessa responds. 'I've been stalked by both Viktor's sister and his blue tit.'

'He did say he couldn't always control his familiar,' Minoo says. 'Besides, that's not what I meant when I asked.'

'Of course I realize that, Minoo.' Vanessa looks straight at her. 'But you have already made up your mind, haven't you?'

'Yes, I have.' Minoo's voice is low.

'The guardians have told you that you must,' Vanessa says.

'And we have already decided that we have no choice but to trust them.'

'But maybe there'll be an alternative,' Minoo muses. 'You can carry on practicing and grow stronger . . .'

'Sure,' Linnéa agrees, chewing on a poison-green nail. 'We'll practice.'

Minoo feels worried. 'Linnéa, I know you don't like this at all.'

Linnéa snorts.

'You bet I don't like it. I don't like it one little bit. The *Book of Patterns*. The guardians. Matilda. The Council. This fucking Walter character. I don't trust any of them. But, Minoo, I don't know what to say. What could I say?'

She spreads her hands in a helpless gesture.

'You must do it.' Anna-Karin looks at Minoo. 'But you will still be one of us.'

It is a relief to hear her say that.

'No one can replace you,' Minoo says. 'We are friends.'

'Sure,' Linnéa says, getting up. 'I'd better be off.'

Vanessa looks at her. 'Where to?'

'Just something I've got to do.'

'Now? But we must talk.' Vanessa sounds confused.

'I've talked enough about this.'

Linnéa leaves the room. The front door slams behind her. They listen to her boots on the stairs, then to the main door opening and shutting with a bang.

Vanessa pulls her knees up and rests her chin on them.

Minoo isn't surprised at Linnéa's reaction. She hadn't expected anything else. She only wishes it hadn't made a target of Vanessa as well.

CHAPTER 42

W hen Linnéa crosses the little wooden bridge at the canal locks, she avoids looking at the Canal Bridge. She finds her cell phone and sends a text to Vanessa, promising to phone her soon.

But, first, she must have a talk with Viktor.

She is walking across the meadow behind the manor house when she hears the ringtone. Diana's name appears on the screen.

Linnéa feels sick. What if Diana is calling to say that Robin has backtracked?

'Hi, Linnéa,' Diana says. 'How are you? All right after the questioning and all that?'

'Fine. Anything else?'

'Well, yes. Your father just phoned the office. He asked for your phone number.'

Another wave of nausea.

'Surely you didn't give it to him?'

'Of course not. And he took that as read. But he had heard what happened and wanted to talk with you. He was very careful to say that he'd understand if you didn't want to.'

He must be sober. If he had started drinking again, he wouldn't have called Diana. He knows where Linnéa lives and would have turned up to hammer on her door. Would have become more and more noisy on the landing. Would have babbled. Pleaded. Called her *the light and joy of his life*.

It occurs to Linnéa that it has been almost a year since he

stopped drinking. He hasn't stayed off the booze for that long before.

'I don't want to talk to him,' she says.

'That's all right,' Diana says. 'If you change your mind, remember that I have his number.'

'Sure. But I must get on now.' Linnéa ends the call.

She walks through the overgrown garden behind the manor house, following the outline of the building while she keeps an eye on the shuttered widows and wonders if someone in there is watching her.

She reaches the front, walks up to the entrance and rings the doorbell. Viktor looks surprised when he opens the door.

'I want to talk to you,' she tells him.

Viktor glances over his shoulder, then steps outside and closes the door behind him, pulling out a pack of cigarettes. Now she is the one who is surprised. They sit down on the stone steps and Viktor lights two cigarettes with a gold-plated lighter and hands her one of them.

'Thank you,' she says, 'for what you're going to say to the police.'

Viktor smokes, then rolls the cigarette between his fingertips.

'You don't have to thank me. It's simply about justice. They should be punished.' He drags on the cigarette again and the smoke glows almost purple in the slanting sunbeams. 'And I'm glad there is something I can do for you to make amends for all the hassle I've caused you.'

'True, you have quite a few things to make up for,' she agrees. 'But you're doing fine.'

His car, looking as immaculate as ever, is parked in the yard. Linnéa remembers when he drove her, wrapped in his coat, back home that night. Suddenly it comes to her that the shoes he had lent her were probably Clara's. They are still in a bag at the back of her wardrobe.

'Minoo told us about your sister,' she says. 'You must say hello to her from me. And thank her for everything she—'

'I'll tell her,' Viktor interrupts.

He doesn't sound unpleasant, but it's very obvious he does not want to talk about Clara. Linnéa has no problem with that. She has something else to discuss. But it isn't suitable for speaking about.

Is it true what Walter says? she thinks. *Does Minoo have to join your circle in order for the portal to be closed?*

Yes, what he says is true enough, Viktor thinks. *As far as it goes. All it means is that the guardians have told him so and he believes what they say.*

Can you find out if the guardians are telling the truth?

I have never actually managed to read the Book of Patterns. *And I don't know if it would work anyway. The guardians aren't human.*

No, they are not human, Linnéa thinks to herself.

The guardians don't think the way people do and perhaps people cannot really understand how the guardians function. But the guardians claim that they understand people. That they are on humanity's side. That they try to help people. That everything they do is with this world's interests at heart.

Linnéa's instinct is screaming that they are not to be trusted. Trouble is, when one is as paranoid as she, it's hard to know when to rely on one's gut feelings. In her case, her gut feeling is always that the absolutely worst possible thing will happen. And it hasn't improved matters that the absolutely worst thing has happened to her so many times.

Suddenly, she realizes what a relief it would be not to have to care about this whole affair anymore. If the guardians are right, stopping the apocalypse isn't up to Linnéa anymore, but to Minoo. Minoo – otherwise known as the most powerful witch in the world. It's her job now. Minoo, together with Viktor, Walter and the rest of the Council's circle, have to pull it off.

Part Two

Linnéa is excused. Vanessa is excused. Anna-Karin is excused. None of them asked for this. In the beginning they were seven and now only four of them are left. Why should she want to hang on to this task at any cost? Shouldn't she *want* to be shot of it? Why is she clinging to it?

'The Chosen Ones are meant to be the ones who close the portal,' Linnéa says.

'No,' Viktor tells her. '*A* Chosen One was meant to close it. Instead there were seven of you, and there has never been anyone like Minoo before.'

'What's your point?'

'That the rules have obviously changed.'

Linnéa wraps her arms around herself. Chill from the stone steps is seeping through her body.

'It can't be right that the Council is going to save the world,' she says.

The Council is not a perfect organization, he thinks. *Far from it. But I believe that the Council is useful, even necessary. Without it, there would be chaos. Those with magic powers would exploit those without.*

And you don't think that the Council exploits its power? she asks.

I think it could be worse and I am also sure it could be improved. I believe the Council can change and I want to be part of that change.

Naturally, she thinks. *You hope to bring about change in a corrupt organization without letting it corrupt you. All I can say is, good luck.*

Why should it be impossible?

Linnéa looks at him disbelievingly. Is he that naïve?

Because, Viktor, you're a part of the organization. Your noble ideas won't change anything as long as they're only ideas. Only what you do can bring about change. But what can you actually do, now that you have sworn the oath of allegiance? How much are you free to do?

'The oath makes no difference,' he says.

'Face facts,' she says. 'You belong to them.'

Viktor produces his cigarettes again, and again she accepts one. When he bends forward to light it for her, sheltering the flame with his hands, she picks up thoughts that he wants to hide from her. Viktor is aware that he is no longer free to choose, that his life is now dedicated to the Council, and it frightens him. He is not only fearful for himself but for his sister. She, too, has sworn the oath now.

Linnéa doesn't hesitate anymore. To land someone else in all this portal shit would be lovely. But it is not an option.

'They had no right to make you take that oath,' she tells him.

'And you have no right to pity me.'

She knows exactly how he feels. She also knows that they have nothing more to say to each other.

Putting on her sunglasses, she gets up and starts walking. For the first time in ages, she no longer feels doubtful. She has a goal. A goal that is more important than anything else.

She can't believe in the pronouncements by the guardians and the Council. She can't trust those who have lied so many times. She has to carry on with the fight. And never give up. For her own sake, for the sake of the other Chosen Ones and for the sake of the entire fucking world, she has to be strong enough.

She can't stop Minoo from joining the Council's circle, because there are no alternatives that she can offer. Not now.

But I can go all out to find some, Linnéa thinks. It's true what Viktor says. The rules have changed There must be other ways to save the world. And I shall find them.

CHAPTER 43

Vanessa goes straight from Nicolaus's apartment to the Ica supermarket. She has promised to help with the weekly shopping before Mom goes back to work.

It's the last thing she needs, especially as she has a banging headache. She isn't sure if it's yesterday's cider drinking, or what Minoo has said to them, or the way Linnéa reacted that's caused it.

She'd felt a little better when Linnéa texted her. But Vanessa can't forget how Linnéa looked at her; as if she were a stranger, someone with no rights whatever to ask anything from her.

Vanessa drags herself between the shelves with the shopping cart.

Frozen broccoli.

She doesn't have to save the world now.

Boxed macaroni.

It is no longer a task for her.

Paper towels.

At least, so it seems.

She tries to think what leading a normal life again might actually entail. It's tempting. A lovely dream. But Vanessa knows too much. She knows that it is too late to put on blinders. She can't ignore demons and the apocalypse; can't just sit back, cross her fingers and hope for the best. Hope that someone else will fix it. It's like she said to Minoo. Right now, there are no alternatives.

But when they find an alternative, she will be ready.

Vanessa puts a box of tampons in the cart and pushes it

along to the registers where Mom is waiting, deep in one of the evening papers. Vanessa checks out at the only open register. No sign of Sirpa. Perhaps she's still on sick leave.

Vanessa wonders if Sirpa knows that two of her son's ex-girlfriends are together now. In which case, she would know more than Mom.

'Are we done now?' Vanessa asks. 'I'd like to go home and have a nap.'

Mom lowers the paper and Vanessa realizes at once that something is wrong.

And then she sees the double-page spread.

A large photograph of two young men standing in the packed assembly hall. Robin's and Erik's faces are pixilated.

Above it, a screaming banner headline.

CONFESSED TO ATTEMPTED MURDER DURING SCHOOL ASSEMBLY.

Vanessa has time to catch a few of the phrases in the text below the photo. *Break-in. Vandalism. Miraculous survival.*

'Vanessa,' Mom asks. 'What's all this about?'

'Let's talk about it outside.'

Vanessa starts loading their shopping onto the conveyor belt. She doesn't even look at the man at the register. Mom is silent. The only sound is the barcode scanner.

Blip. Blip. Blip.

Vanessa packs the carrier bags while Mom pays. She puts the evening paper in last.

'It's Linnéa, isn't it?' Mom asks once they are outside the shop. 'The person whose apartment was done over?'

'Yes,' Vanessa confirms.

They walk to the stop for the number five bus.

'Dear Lord,' Mom says. 'It must have happened just before the time she stayed the night with us.'

Vanessa nods. Mom is both right and wrong. Linnéa did stay overnight with them, but she was in Vanessa's body. The Linnéa Mom thought she had met was in fact Minoo.

'All you told me was that someone had broken into her place,' Mom continues. 'Didn't you know that all these other dreadful things had happened?'

'Yes, I did, but I had promised Linnéa that I wouldn't tell anyone.'

Mom stops to wait for the bus, puts the bags down and looks earnestly at Vanessa.

'This isn't the kind of thing you keep secret, Nessa! Those boys tried to kill her!'

Vanessa parks her bags next to Mom's and tries to keep calm.

'Nobody would've believed Linnéa. Remember what Nicke said to you about how he was positive that Linnéa threw some crazy party. And that it ran out of control so she tried to make the police believe that there had been a break-in. The whole investigation was canceled on the spot.'

Mom looks worried.

'But, in that case . . . you and the other girls lied to Nicke when you only told him about the break-in. Isn't that perjury?'

Yesterday, Vanessa asked Patricia almost exactly the same question. All the same, she becomes irritated.

'No, it isn't because we weren't under oath.'

Mom still looks worried.

'I promise you, it's OK,' Vanessa says. 'We probably won't even be called in as witnesses.'

'How is Linnéa feeling? How has she felt all this time? God, I just had no idea, never guessed . . . she was so nice and well-behaved when she stayed with us . . .'

Vanessa thinks back on what Linnéa had told her about Minoo-as-Linnéa, who sat and conversed politely with Mom at the kitchen table.

'She is very good at hiding her emotions,' she tells her.

'But how could she keep it up after something like this had happened to her?'

Mom starts crying and Vanessa has to pull herself together,

or she'll start as well. An elderly couple walk slowly past them, each leaning on a wheeled Zimmer frame. They turn to look inquisitively at them.

'It's so awful,' Mom says. 'Poor, poor Linnéa. She seemed such a lovely person.'

'She *is* a lovely person,' Vanessa agrees. It's tough to keep the tears back.

She realizes that she must say it now. The moment has come.

'Mom, Linnéa and I have . . . we are . . . well, like together.'

She had believed that a weight would be lifted off her shoulders if only she could bring herself to tell Mom. But the weight stays put, because Mom dries her eyes only to stare uncomprehendingly at her.

'Right . . . well, together with whom?'

'With *each other*.'

Mom looks baffled.

'It's quite a new situation,' Vanessa says.

'Well . . .' Mom says. And then the meaning of it all seems to begin to sink in. 'That's unexpected.'

'I know.'

Mom is silent for another long while.

'Or perhaps not . . .'

Vanessa glances at her. It's obvious that Mom is struggling not to give away how shocked she is. Not to make any mistakes.

'I mean, it's just me – I'm so out of touch. You know, if she had been a guy I would've started to wonder ages ago. You've been seeing such a lot of each other . . .' Mom loses the thread for a moment. 'Were you an item already when she stayed with us?'

'No. She was in love with me but I hadn't figured out what I felt by then.'

Mom blushes suddenly.

'And there was I, more or less forcing you to sleep in the same bed. It must have felt really strange for her.'

Part Two

Vanessa blushes too, because Linnéa has told her about that night and precisely how strange it was.

'I'm so glad you've told me.'

'I'm glad, too.'

'You never know . . .' Mom speaks with rather forced cheerfulness. 'If I had met the right girl for me, maybe I'd have tried it out. Lord knows, men make me sick sometimes . . .'

'Stop it, Mom. Linnéa is my girlfriend, not an experiment.'

'No, of course. That's not what I meant. I'm sorry, Nessa. What I did mean was just that . . . it wasn't so terribly long ago that I was your age. I had already had you then. But now it must be easier than it was then to . . . try out other . . . to dare to go for different . . . without making a big thing of it. And that's really good.'

She looks so embarrassed, bordering on panic. Vanessa has to throw her a lifeline.

'I know just what you mean,' she says.

It works. Her mother relaxes.

Chapter 44

Anna-Karin knocks cautiously on the door to Minoo's room.

'It's me,' she says. 'OK if I come in?'

'It's fine,' Minoo replies.

Anna-Karin steps inside and closes the door behind her. Minoo is sitting on the floor. In front of her is a pile of socks.

'I'm trying to sort them into pairs,' she says. 'But I'm about to give up.'

Anna-Karin looks at the mass of dark blue and black socks and sympathizes. She sits down in front of Minoo and shows her the china Dalmatian.

'I have to show you something,' she tells her. 'Or try to, anyway. It hasn't quite worked so far.'

She focuses, releases her power, closes her hand around the small figurine and concentrates on how it will . . .

The hard china shell caves with a crunching sound. Minoo catches her breath. Anna-Karin opens her hand and the little Dalmatian lies crushed to pieces in her palm.

'Was this what happened in the gym?' Minoo asks.

'Yes,' Anna-Karin replies as she puts the pieces on the floor. 'I'm trying to learn to control my new power, but it's hard. I need help – yours and the others' as well.'

'Of course I'll try to help.'

'I think we should meet regularly,' Anna-Karin says. 'I could so easily hurt people by mistake. So it is very important that I master this. And we must use the time that's left before you . . . join the other circle.'

'You're right,' Minoo says. 'We must.'

Their eyes meet.

Anna-Karin isn't sure which of them starts crying first.

The Borderland

CHAPTER 45

Ida is running through the grayness. She has no idea how long she has been running but the areas of light that used to show up all over the place are now nowhere to be seen.

Maybe I've gone in the wrong direction, Ida thinks. Though I'm not convinced this place has any directions at all.

Ring, a ring o' roses . . .

Ida stops. She doesn't know if she heard the song or imagined it. But why should she imagine *Ring o' roses*?

A pocket full of posies . . .

She tries to follow the sound but it disappears again. This is all so humiliating.

'Where are you?' she whispers. 'Where the hell are you?'

She turns around and faces a wall of white light. It is blindingly strong.

The light swallows her a moment later.

She screws up her eyes but it doesn't help. The powerful brightness comes through her eyelids.

The ground under her feet disappears. Then, suddenly, it is as if someone has switched the light off. She opens her eyes.

She is floating. Surrounded by the darkest darkness she has ever experienced. This must be the source of all her nightmares. It is where all scary things are hiding. Like murderers, pedophiles, crazed fighting dogs, druggies, ghosts and demons. It is the darkness under the bed. The darkness inside the wardrobe. The darkness in her bedroom mirror.

Then the dance pavilion suddenly appears. It seems to float in the darkness, too, like herself. Vanessa, Linnéa, Minoo and

Anna-Karin are there, wearing the same clothes as on the night of the blood-red moon. And there is Matilda, standing in the center of the pavilion. She is drawing in the air with her finger and the signs of the elements appear one after the other.

Ida wants to call out to Matilda but can't make a sound, can't move either. She can only watch.

She forces herself to concentrate on the pavilion, on what is going on there. Mustn't think about the darkness.

Matilda is talking. Talking, talking, talking. At one point, she declares that the guardians were demons originally.

Ida isn't even surprised anymore.

Matilda goes on, explaining things that Ida knows already, sometimes has even seen herself. True, some of it is stuff she hadn't quite understood. Like, it was the guardians who made Matilda give up her powers.

Then Matilda starts on how the guardians try to read the future. And how they've tried to guide the Chosen Ones.

'. . . sometimes it just hasn't been possible to avoid tragedies,' Matilda says. 'They may have been too deeply rooted in the ongoing events. Or it could be that other choices might have led to even more catastrophic situations.'

Ida feels anger bubbling up inside her.

'You let them die!' Linnéa jumps at Matilda.

Too right.

Ida explodes. Now she is certain. Certain that the guardians cheated her, using that book of theirs. They knew she was going to die, and exactly when and how, so they used the false kiss to lure her into the trap.

She hears the others droning on but can't concentrate anymore. She is too consumed with her own fury.

The guardians sacrificed her like a useless pawn in a game of chess.

Matilda said it was all for the best, it served the world. Is that so? Of all the thousands of millions of routes they could take, did all of them have to lead to a point where Ida must die so that the world could survive?

Because, even though she doesn't feel properly dead, she finally accepts that she is. In the ordinary world, Ida Holmström doesn't exist anymore and will never exist again. Her body is rotting somewhere underground, or else it has been burnt. She doesn't know which is the worst option.

Ida starts listening again when Matilda speaks about the powers of the Chosen Ones making up the Key, but saying that the game may be lost – perhaps has been lost for a long time. And then Matilda tells them that they are the last chance this world has got.

Thanks for that.

The grayness closes in on Ida. She can move again. But she stands completely still in the grayness and feels the tears run down her cheeks.

She has never felt so alone. And she no longer wants to find Matilda who is obviously siding with the guardians and actually *defended* them.

The King has sent his daughter . . .

'What the fuck!' Ida hisses.

To fetch a pail of water . . .

Ida starts to run toward the song and sees a blue light illuminating the mist. It grows stronger the closer she gets and then, suddenly, she is dazzled by the sun. She is standing on a bright green lawn and at her feet is a plastic mug with a slurp of coffee left. Whenever she's got to now, they've at least invented plastic.

A-tishoo, a-tishoo, we all fall down . . . A-tishoo, a-tishoo, we all fall down . . .

Ida turns around and sees the familiar red-painted timber cottages. She's in the Engelsfors open-air museum. There are the rabbit cages. And there is the stall selling caramelized almonds and disgusting sweets that taste like hair conditioner.

And down there, by the water's edge, is the maypole.

Grownups and children, all in summery clothes, are dancing around it. When Ida was little, she used to despise dancing around the maypole. She always felt so embarrassed. But Mom and Dad said it was the traditional thing to do.

Mom. Dad. Are they there, dancing with Rasmus and Lotta? Dad, is he even *alive*?

'We felt horrible about what we did to you,' Vanessa says.

Ida swings around to face her. Vanessa is crowned with a wreath of wildflowers and a fascinated wasp is buzzing among the drooping buttercups. She is talking to Gustaf.

G.

Seeing him makes Ida feel that familiar pang somewhere inside her.

'We only did it because we had to. I felt disgusted afterward,' Vanessa continues.

Gustaf has been crowned with flowers, too, and he looks so gorgeous Ida could die. All over again.

'I know that Minoo felt just the same,' Vanessa goes on.

Ida observes Gustaf's lips. Remembers how they felt against hers for that first and only time. That not-kiss. Just one of the guardians' lying tricks, but still she remembers it as a kiss. The memory is so powerful, it doesn't matter that it is false.

Could things have been different if she hadn't started going out with Erik? If she had told Gustaf much sooner that she loved him? Her pride had been pointless anyway, because Felicia and Olivia, and probably everyone else at Engelsfors High School, had spotted it anyway.

Why had she wasted so much time?

'We agreed not to tell the others more than absolutely necessary,' Vanessa says. 'We just said that you were innocent.'

Ida is taken aback. Innocent? Of what?

'And Minoo . . .' Vanessa continues. 'Before we left she said to you that Rebecka had not taken her own life. She hoped that you would remember, somewhere inside you, that it was in no way your fault . . .'

'Please, stop it.' Gustaf presses his hand against his eyes.

Vanessa falls silent and Ida tries to grasp what this is about. Why is Vanessa telling G that Rebecka didn't commit suicide? How come she is talking to him as if he knew the whole business with the truth serum?

'She thought it was me,' he whispers. 'She believed I was the one who killed her.'

Rebecka. Rebecka, who was murdered by Max disguised as Gustaf. How come G knows this? It must be such an appallingly awful thing to know. She reaches out with her hand. Holds it so that her fingertips almost but not quite touch Gustaf's arm, which allows her to pretend to herself that she could still touch him if she wanted to.

'She didn't believe it was you,' Vanessa says.

Gustaf takes his hand from his eyes. They are shining with tears.

'But she *saw* me,' he says, sounding almost angry.

'Yes, she did,' Vanessa replies. 'But she couldn't make herself believe it was you.'

'It's true,' Ida agrees. 'I could feel what Rebecka felt, so I know it's true.'

But, of course, Gustaf doesn't hear her.

'That's what Minoo said, too, but I still can't stop thinking about it,' Gustaf says. 'I don't know what to believe anymore. I don't know what to feel. I don't know anything anymore. Sometimes, I'm angry with Minoo because she didn't tell me earlier. The next moment, I'm angry with her because she told me at all.'

So it was Minoo who told Gustaf?

It makes Ida furious. Why didn't Minoo leave him in peace? Did she have to drag him into all this shitty business? Hasn't G suffered enough?

'Look, I do understand that this must be awful for you,' Vanessa says. 'But think about Minoo and how she feels for a moment. You don't know what it's like having to lie all the time. It becomes like a wall separating you from everyone who means most to you.'

How can she sound so harsh? How can she stop herself from touching him, she who can? Can't she see that he needs it?

'We've tried our best to do the right thing,' Vanessa continues. 'And all things considered, I think we've done a bang-up job. We identified the killer of Elias and Rebecka. We prevented the slaughter of half the school this spring. And we saved Adriana from execution.'

'I know.' Gustaf looks away.

Minoo has told him *everything*, Ida realizes.

'She didn't want to lie to you,' Vanessa says. 'By telling you the full story, she took a big risk.'

Gustaf looks at Vanessa again and his eyes say everything. He cares for Minoo. He really does care for her.

'How is she?'

'How do you think?'

Vanessa doesn't sound accusing; she just says it straight, the way only she can.

'I was angry with her,' Gustaf says. 'But, more than anything else, I was angry with myself because I was angry with her. Her situation was impossible, I see that.'

'I understand exactly how you felt,' Vanessa tells him. 'But it isn't me you should say all this to.'

Gustaf shakes his head. A buttercup works loose from his wreath and falls through Ida's hand.

'I can't talk to her, not yet,' he says. 'It will just go wrong. I'll try to take all these things on board. But please tell her that I understand. And that I don't hate her and that I'm sorry I can't deal with this better.'

Vanessa doesn't speak. She looks despondent.

'I must get back to my family now,' Gustaf says. 'Got to pretend everything is normal.'

'Me, too.'

'Does it get easier with time?' he asks. 'I mean, to pretend to everyone around you?'

Vanessa stops to look at him, as if she is really thinking about it.

The fog is welling up and separating them from Ida. It is so thick she can't see her hands anymore.

'You're a horrible, lying slut!' Julia says behind her.

CHAPTER 46

Ida turns to look behind her.

Julia, Hanna A and Hanna H are standing in the City Mall. At first, Ida thinks they are staring at her. But of course they aren't. When Ida turns the other way, Linnéa is there.

'And you're a liar and everybody knows it!' Julia says. 'You haven't got any proof. None.'

'I haven't lied,' Linnéa says. 'And your boyfriend would hardly be locked in a jail cell unless there was proof.'

Julia's boyfriend? It must be Erik. Arrested? Erik locked up!

For the first time since she died in Gustaf's arms, Ida feels happy again. And she so wants to find out what they got Erik for. She wishes she could have seen his face when the cops took him away.

'He says he's innocent and that's good enough for me,' Julia tells her. 'I'm not going to let my boyfriend down just because you're delusional.'

'You must think Robin is delusional too, then?' Linnéa says. 'And Kevin as well?'

'All three of them spent the whole night in the PE center,' Julia says.

'Then why should Robin and Kevin say they didn't?'

'They have always been jealous of Erik! It's typical of weak people that they try to drag the strong ones down to their level. Just to try to make themselves feel better!'

This makes Ida ashamed. She used to go around saying stuff like that. Julia is quoting her.

'And you might as well know something else,' Julia carries

on. 'My Dad is a lawyer and he says that Erik will never be convicted!'

'Precisely,' Hanna A agrees.

'If your father was any good as a lawyer, he wouldn't have a practice in Engelsfors,' Linnéa responds.

Ida can't help laughing. She sees a shadow fall over Julia's face. A sense of insecurity that no real leader would show.

'But then, you couldn't ever lead anyone,' Ida says. 'Maybe Felicia could, but not you.'

Julia takes a step closer to Linnéa. And spits in her face.

'Very classy!' Ida says.

She notices that the two Hannas seem to think the same thing. They glance quickly at each other. It's only a matter of time before they get completely fed up with Julia. They're already questioning her authority over them, Ida sees that clearly. But, for now, they follow Julia as she stalks off toward the exit.

Linnéa stays. Her eyes are closed. There's a concentrated wrinkle between her eyebrows.

A few drops of water hit the tiled floor. The next moment, the sprinkler system in the ceiling starts spraying water in all directions.

Julia and the Hannas scream and run to the exit door. Ida observes Linnéa, who stays calmly in place, letting the water pour over her face and wash her make-up away. Then she sighs a little. The water cuts out at once. Just a few last drops fall into the puddles on the floor of the City Mall. Ida is completely dry.

A bell rings. Vanessa runs out from the Crystal Cave.

'What's going on?' she asks.

Linnéa smiles a little and pushes her wet bangs off her forehead.

'*You* made it happen?' Vanessa asks.

'Yep,' Linnéa says. 'Now, watch this.'

She closes her eyes again. The wrinkle between her

eyebrows returns. And Ida can see clouds of steam rising from Linnéa's hair, clothes, skin.

'What do you think you're doing?' Vanessa hisses, looking nervously around her.

'What are you worrying about?' Linnéa asks her. 'The Council? Minoo is about to start working for them.'

'What?' Ida exclaims. 'Minoo working for the Council? Has everyone gone completely mad?'

Vanessa stares at Linnéa and Ida wonders if they are sending thoughts between each other. Looks like it, because Vanessa leaves abruptly and walks back into the shop. Linnéa looks at her disappearing back; she looks as if she wants to call out to her, but she doesn't. Her boots splash on the wet floor as she walks toward the exit.

The gray sweeps around Ida like a veil.

She is on the path along the canal. Minoo is standing next to her, watching the manor house. A tall white fence has been put up along the back of the big house. Ida wonders what it is hiding. Minoo looks as if she is wondering, too.

'What's this I hear about you going to work for the Council?' Ida asks.

The next veil of mist drifts past.

She stands on the dance floor in the pavilion. It's raining and the roof is leaking. Vanessa, Linnéa and Minoo are sitting on the edge of the stage. Linnéa holds the silver cross.

'We ought to find out more about it,' she says. 'Find out if it has any other uses.'

'Like what?' Minoo asks.

'We could try out a few rituals or something,' Linnéa suggests.

'We can't just try things at random,' Minoo says. 'It might be dangerous.'

Linnéa sniffs. Footsteps on the gravel are coming closer. Anna-Karin steps into the pavilion; she is carrying a pile of roof tiles.

322

'Do you think these will work?' she asks. She puts them down on the floor.

'Don't ask me,' Linnéa says.

Anna-Karin picks up one of the tiles with both hands. The others watch her but are obviously thinking about other things. They don't even react when Anna-Karin breaks the tile in her hands. And it strikes Ida how lonely they all look, even though the four of them are together.

As the mist sweeps past again, Ida hears Linnéa laugh.

'Do you remember?' Vanessa says.

'Of course I do.' Linnéa laughs again.

Ida smells the incense. Now she is in Linnéa's living room. It is dark outside and there are lit candles on the table by the sofa. Vanessa and Linnéa are half lying on the sofa, each leaning against an armrest. Their legs are intertwined.

Linnéa holds a china figurine in her hand. A fat angel playing a harp. The angel has a pointy nose and oddly swollen cheeks and is shiny all over with fake mother-of-pearl. It's so screamingly tasteless that Ida feels she could break out in hives just looking at it.

Are they *terminally* out of their minds?

'Happy birthday!' Vanessa says.

'Thank you.' Linnéa places the china angel on the table.

Vanessa looks at Linnéa with eyes full of love. No one has ever looked at Ida like that. Especially not G.

Vanessa wriggles closer to Linnéa, leans over her and gives her a kiss.

And Linnéa pulls Vanessa toward her until Vanessa is on top. They are kissing, slowly. Gently. Their lips caress each other. Where have Linnéa's hands actually gone to?

No way does Ida want to see them have sex. She turns away, hoping for a drift of gray mist, but sees only Linnéa's kitchen. Behind her back, the sound of their kissing is growing more intense. Ida hurries into the kitchen and sits down on the floor with her hands over her ears. Waits.

'Please,' she whispers. 'Please.'

The mist finally returns and she gets up.

She can't stop thinking of the way Vanessa looked at Linnéa. The mist dissolves again.

White walls. White light. A white, limed wooden floor. Every knot in the boards is familiar. She is in the kitchen at home.

Ida clutches the silver heart around her neck. The kitchen table and the chairs have gone. That was where they sat at their last, dreadful breakfast together. It seems like only yesterday.

She looks into the hall. It is piled high with boxes from a moving company.

'Stop that, Rasmus!' It's Mom's voice coming from the garden.

Ida runs into the living room and then out through the open French windows to the terrace. It's an evening in late summer. A swarm of midges dances in the slanting rays of the sun. Ida goes to lean on the railing. Lotta sits on the steps of the playhouse, holding a cell phone. She was always said how much she wanted one. Mom stands on the lawn, by her beloved rose bushes. Her eyes are empty. Dazed. Not at all as usual.

Rasmus hacks at the grass with a rake.

'Where's Dad?' he asks, and Ida holds her breath. She is terrified that Mom will say something vague about how Dad is in heaven now.

'I told you, he's at the gas station,' Mom says.

'I don't want to move to Borlänge. I want to stay here.'

'I'm not in the mood to discuss all that with you again,' Mom tells him. 'What would we do here in Engelsfors, did you think?'

.'Wait for Ida to come back,' Rasmus says.

Ida lets go of her silver heart. Looks in utter amazement at her little brother.

Then, the mist swallows the garden and the terrace and everything becomes one great big nothing again.

'Mom!' Ida calls, but without expecting an answer.

And then she sees Anna-Karin. She is sitting on a bed with a photo album on her lap. Ida goes to stand next to her and looks at the faded, yellowing images. She recognizes Anna-Karin's mother as a young woman, because she is so like her daughter. Then she grows older. Suddenly she is holding a baby. It's Anna-Karin and she is so cute. Her green eyes are enormous. But her mother looks at little Anna-Karin as if unsure what to do with her.

Ida observes how Anna-Karin's hands clutch the album covers, squeezing them like she squeezed those roof tiles. Ida expects the album to break apart any second.

Then Anna-Karin's hands relax their grip. She is crying. Large tears are falling on the shiny photos. She is sobbing and blubbering and Ida feels she, too, will burst into tears any moment now.

And then she is back in the Borderland.

She starts running. The need to weep is growing stronger; she must force it down, because if she lets out her grief she wouldn't be able to take another step. She has to keep running. She must. Not cry. It would suck all the strength from her. She would have to lie down. Not give a shit about anything. Let the invisible thing find her.

So what? Could anything be worse than this?

It strikes her that perhaps this existence is what Mona saw that time in the Crystal Cave, though Mona didn't see the whole picture.

The year ahead will be dark and hard for you.

Does that mean she's stuck here for a whole year? In this totally fucked-up situation?

Besides, 'a year', according to what time scale? Time in Engelsfors, where everything seems to happen much more quickly than here? Or a year in limbo time, which seems to make no sense at all? And , after that year, what then?

The Key

But you will get what you were promised. So plodding on is worth it.

The guardians promised her that if she collaborated with the Circle until the final battle had been fought, she would be relieved of her powers and everything else that had to do with the Chosen Ones. At this moment, it feels more like a threat than a promise.

Ida does the only thing she can do. She leaps into the next source of light.

Part 3

CHAPTER 47

Minoo reaches in under the bed and pulls out her backpack, which has been lying there all summer. She brushes the dust off and opens it. Stares into its gaping interior.

This should have been her first day as a senior.

But it is not to be.

Two weeks ago, she received a letter. Her name and address were printed on a stick-on label. The letter was from Walter, asking her to come to the manor house. Today. She is going to meet the others.

The others.

Minoo wonders who they are. She keeps staring into the backpack, as if hoping to find clues inside it.

She hears wardrobe doors opening in Mom and Dad's bedroom. Then the metallic shriek of clothes hangers being pushed back and forth on a rail. Dad is packing. He is off to a conference in Malmö. Minoo has no idea what it's about, even though he has been telling her for a week. All she's been able to think about is this day.

And now it has arrived.

She opens the drawer in her bedside table and takes out the *Book of Patterns*.

It has been quiet ever since she asked it about Walter, but she puts it into the backpack all the same, together with a notepad and a pen. She hesitates for a second and then puts the Pattern Finder in, even though she has never found it of any use. There's still plenty of room, but she doesn't know what else she should bring for a day like today.

Minoo fastens the flap and gets up. Looks quickly at herself in the mirror and wonders if Walter's circle will be like the rest of the Council members. Cool, self-assured, smartly dressed, with spotless skin and expensive haircuts. Minoo can't bear to even think of how her clothes, skin and hair will compare. Has anyone in the Council ever worn jeans?

Outside in the passage, she meets Mom stepping out of the bathroom. She smiles at Minoo.

'*Fadat sham, vaghean bavaram nemishe*,' she says, giving Minoo a hug. 'The final year has begun.'

Her dressing gown feels so soft against Minoo's cheek. She doesn't even want to think about the fact that what Mom has just said might be literally true.

'What do you think, shall we order a pizza from the Venezia and watch a film tonight?' Mom asks, letting her out of the hug.

'Great,' Minoo says. She tries not to obsess about what might happen before this day is over. 'I've got to run. Anna-Karin is waiting for me.'

Dad comes out of the bedroom carrying his red roller-case. He has changed so much this summer. His jawline has firmed up and his cheekbones, which Minoo only remembers seeing in old photos, have reappeared. But, above all, he looks healthier. His whole being shows that, for once, he has taken a proper holiday.

He puts the bag down, puts his arm around Minoo and gives her a squeeze.

'Good luck, Minoo,' he says.' Not that you need it.'

Oh, yes I do, Minoo thinks. You've no idea just how much.

The sky is bright blue. The sun is shining but it's cold for August. This year, the summer never seemed to get started and now it is almost at an end. Everyone has been complaining about the cool weather, as if they had suppressed all memories of last summer's heat wave.

Part Three

Minoo and Anna-Karin navigate between the slugs that are invading Engelsfors. The creatures crawl on the pavement, plump and glistening, leaving slimy trails across the cement. Minoo and Anna-Karin pass many gardens where people have rigged up slug traps – mostly just plastic buckets. In them, drowned slugs are fermenting in the sun into a repulsive, soupy mess. Minoo is so pleased that her parents gave up fighting them long ago, leaving the slugs to eat their greenery undisturbed.

Minoo and Anna-Karin stop at the corner where their paths will separate.

'I doubt much will happen in school today, but I'll take notes in case. They might have new information or something.' Anna-Karin pauses. 'Are you nervous?'

'Of course,' Minoo says. 'But nowhere near as nervous as when I had to drop truth serum in Max's coffee. We have another scale for nervousness now, don't you think?'

Anna-Karin laughs, something she's been doing more often these days. 'Text me as soon as you've left the manor house.'

Minoo nods. They have planned to meet in Nicolaus's apartment afterward. All she has to do is get through the next few hours. Whatever happens, she'll meet the others when it's all over.

'Shame the fox can't keep an eye on things,' Anna-Karin says.

Her fox is refusing to come near the manor house because of a strange smell.

'I wish I could come with you,' she adds.

Minoo sees that her friend means it, even though a return visit to the manor house is probably just about the worst thing Anna-Karin could imagine.

Minoo smiles at her. 'I'm glad you don't have to.'

Anna-Karin smiles, too. 'Good luck, then.'

'And you.'

Minoo walks toward the canal. She hasn't missed the first

331

day of school ever before, not once. She wonders how she'll manage to fit everything in from now on. It has been hard enough to combine the tasks of the Chosen Ones with homework and other school commands. Now she's meant to give up time to *another* circle as well.

Her cell phone pings just after she's crossed Canal Bridge.

GOOD LUCK. L & V.

She quickly sends them a thank-you text. Checks the time and realizes that she is far too early. She walks more slowly, following the canal.

The lock gates are closed but water dribbles through gaps between the enormous timbers and falls gurgling into the water below. This area stirs so many memories of Gustaf and their walks last summer. She sees the wooden seat where they had their row about Positive Engelsfors.

Vanessa has assured her that Gustaf doesn't hate her and that he is struggling to forgive her. Maybe he will. It's hardly going to make him want her in his life, though.

She looks at the seat as she walks past it. Wonders if he will ever sit on it again. She has heard that he is going to study law in Uppsala, which was his first choice of university. If he hasn't moved already, he will soon.

He will be taking his life to a new stage while she will still be plodding on here.

Of course, she reminds herself, this is good for him. He'll learn lots of new things. Get to know lots of new people. Like new girls. Normal girls who don't give him truth serum and mess around with his memory.

Minoo stops. Suddenly she longs for Gustaf so much that she loses all her strength. All her energy is focused on her loss and there is nothing left for moving arms and legs.

She stands still for a while until, finally, she can walk again.

During the summer, the manor house has been renovated. The whole building is freshly painted and gleams bright white in the sun. The shutters are open but she can't see any movement inside.

Minoo considers knocking, but feels awkward about turning up too early. Instead she walks out of sight of the manor-house windows, and starts playing a pointless game on her cell while she waits.

Chapter 48

Vanessa almost steps on a slug as she and Linnéa follow the flow of students into the schoolyard. She jumps back.

'Ugh! What are they doing here? It's not as if there's any food for them,' she says, looking around at the dead trees. 'The place of evil must appeal to them, like it does to every other disgusting thing.'

Linnéa doesn't say anything. She seems not to have heard.

The summons arrived yesterday. The date is set now. Three weeks from now, she has to face Erik, Robin and Kevin in the Västerås courthouse.

This is a new world, and a new language that makes everything sound so abstract and bureaucratic. The three boys and Linnéa will each have a lawyer arguing their case. Vanessa is alarmed by it all. She's worried that what happened to Linnéa will be dismissed; that the court won't even try to understand the effect it has had on her.

Although she's managed to grasp the facts of the trial, she has no idea how Linnéa feels about it. She has mentally pulled down the shutters, and Vanessa is on the outside. But, worst of all, Linnéa seems to think that Vanessa hasn't noticed.

Vanessa spots Kevin in the stream of people and senses how tense Linnéa becomes.

At least there's no risk that Linnéa has to meet Robin or Erik in school. They are still under arrest in Västerås. Vanessa has no illusions about Erik feeling any remorse about what he did. But she is certain that he very much regrets that he kept the baseball bat he used to terrorize and hit Linnéa. It was taken away from his home by the police for analysis in the National Forensic Laboratories. Getting the results often takes months, particularly in the summer. If only Erik had limited himself to beating and kicking Linnéa, the case would probably have been heard in June.

When they come closer to the steps, they see Julia, together with both Hannas. All three stare openly at Linnéa and Vanessa. What they are talking about is glaringly obvious.

'Look, we can just get out of here if you like,' Vanessa says. 'If you can't stand it.'

She immediately regrets saying the last bit. Sure enough, Linnéa looks at her, annoyed. But at least *looks* at her.

'I'm not going back now that they've fucking well seen me,' Linnéa tells her.

'So they won't think you care?'

'Exactly.'

'If you truly didn't care, we might as well leave.'

Linnéa stares at Vanessa. 'What are you trying to do?'

Vanessa sighs.

'Do? I'm just trying to say that it's OK if you're not up to being here,' she says. 'We can go to your place. Watch a horror movie. Eat sweets in bed.'

'And then?' Linnéa asks. 'Are we supposed to carry on hiding until Engelsfors becomes a nice, cozy place where everyone adores each other? Besides, if I start skipping school, I'll lose my student loan on top of everything else.'

It's hurtful when Linnéa rants like that. But it hurts less now, because Vanessa has grown used to it. Although she doesn't like being used to it.

They come into the entrance lobby. It is full of new faces, but everyone is talking about the same old things. And the smell of school is eternally the same.

Vanessa stops at the hallway where her locker is. She almost expects Linnéa to wander off on her way, but instead she stops, too, and takes Vanessa's hand.

'I'd love to stay in bed with you,' she says. 'But I can't.'
'I know.'

Linnéa seems to hesitate, but then she pulls Vanessa close to her. And Vanessa puts her arms around Linnéa's neck, closes her eyes and feels Linnéa's body against hers. How is it possible to be so close to someone one moment and so far away the next?

'Everything will be all right,' Vanessa whispers.

It must be.

* * *

Linnéa drags herself upstairs to the art class. It's as if she has lead weights in her boots.

Vanessa wants to help her, to be there for her. Linnéa knows that. And she wishes that she could be helped. Initially, when they were first together, life had seemed so easy that she had almost dared to believe that she had changed, that she was an easier person to be with.

But she hasn't changed one bit – the same old crap was just waiting to catch up with her. The more Vanessa tries to be supportive, the more Linnéa's instinct tells her to withdraw. Is this the way it's going to be from now on? Vanessa trying to get her to open up, Linnéa raising even higher walls around herself, Vanessa trying harder to get through, and so on: round and round in a vicious circle.

She is so fed up with her fucking self. She knows exactly what's wrong with her. The ladies from social services, the psychologists and therapists, the teachers – everyone has told her just how damaged she is by her childhood. But none of these well-meaning souls have told her what to do about it.

As she walks upstairs, people are turning to look at her.

She knew it would be like this, so this morning – despite the fact that her supplies were running low – she had put on more make-up than usual; anything to make it easier to face the idea of coming in at all. She needs to stock up, and it would be so much cheaper if she could shoplift, but it's a risk she can't afford. Especially not now.

Linnéa feels a hand on her bare shoulder. The hand is floppy and slightly moist, rather like a lukewarm fish. She turns around. It's Petter Backman. She withdraws a little.

'Hello, Linnéa.' He puts his hands in his pockets. 'Welcome back. Hope you had a nice summer.'

'Sure.'

Petter has grown a beard during the summer, presumably for added masculinity and general gorgeousness. It doesn't suit him at all.

'Could we have a word in private before the class starts?' he asks.

'Fine. We can talk here,' she says, without moving from the spot.

Petter doesn't remember how he grabbed Linnéa in the school bathroom last winter. He was zombified by Olivia at the time and she had picked up his thoughts easily. And learned just how much he enjoyed his newfound power over the chatty little bitch who always seemed to know what he was thinking.

Petter remembers nothing, but Linnéa can't forget. He was right about one thing, of course. She knows all too well the kind of fantasies he entertains about his female students, day in, day out.

'I hear the court case is starting soon,' he says.

Linnéa nods.

'All I wanted to say was, you know, don't worry about your schoolwork. We'll adjust that to suit your situation. If you need time off, just have a word with me and I'll see what I can do.'

'Thank you.'

'I was genuinely shocked when Robin confessed. What happened sounds awful. I'm so sorry for you.'

He looks at her, waiting for a reply, preferably a gush of gratitude.

But Linnéa can't bring herself to thank Petter for pitying her. She just wants to get away from him.

'I do understand that it isn't easy,' Petter tells her. 'But you must be strong now and stand up for yourself. Guys mustn't treat girls like that.'

'No,' Linnéa says. 'I don't think so either.'

'Now, I've heard them call girls whores. If it was up to me, we would have a zero tolerance rule about words like that in our school. But that they'd be capable of that kind of thing—'

'I don't like talking about it,' Linnéa says, and Petter looks ashamed.

'Oh, of course not . . . I didn't mean to . . .'

She hurries on up the stairs ahead of him. In the classroom, she goes to her usual place without looking at anyone. But she has to make an effort not to hear people's thoughts. Over the years, many of her classmates have been victims of the rule of terror imposed by Erik, Robin and Kevin. Especially the boys who avoid soccer and hockey, and show a suspect interest in art.

It frightens Linnéa to realize how many of the others think of her as a hero now. They see her as a fighter. The truth is that she feels small and weak whenever she thinks about the court proceedings; she's far from ready or willing to take on the role of Joan of Arc, fighting for the world's misfits.

After all, look how it ended for Joan.

* * *

Vanessa enters the classroom at the same time as Betty, the class mentor. Michelle and Evelina are sitting in their usual places, furthest back. Michelle droops over her table, resting her head on her crossed arms.

Everything seems as usual but everything has changed. They have hardly seen each other all summer. Usually it was Evelina who canceled at the last moment because she had decided to stay over with Leo in Örebro. And Mehmet got a new apartment downtown, and Michelle hardly ever wanted to leave it.

Vanessa sits down between her friends. Michelle lifts her head.

'Hi, darling,' she says before closing her eyes again.

Evelina just nods in her general direction.

Betty looks at them while she opens her worn briefcase on the teacher's table. She seems annoyed.

'Michelle,' she says. 'I hope I'm not disturbing your beauty sleep.'

Michelle seems completely untroubled.

'I've turned day and night around,' she explains. 'I couldn't sleep last night.'

Betty sighs, as if she has never regretted her career choice more than now. The ceiling lights buzz. Go out. Light up again.

'It was because of Lucky, you see,' Michelle whispers. Her speech seems even more languid than usual as she leans closer to Vanessa and Evelina. 'I was saying to Mehmet: baby, listen, I'll move in only if Lucky isn't there all the time. Now it's like *he* is the one trying to move in with Mehmet. Though it might be as well if he does, because my parents are so anti me moving in. I hate being eighteen and they still won't let me make up my own mind about anything. They're talking about how they won't pay me an allowance if I leave home before my school finals. If I could do a part-time job I might be able to manage, but there just aren't any in this town. So, why can't they just give me the money, that's what I want to know? I mean, I cost them anyway when I stay at home. But, no way. They think it's fun, being like my prison guards.'

Michelle goes on and on, and Vanessa can't help thinking about when, a year ago, she and Michelle and Evelina were sitting here, on these chairs, in this room, and planned moving in together.

The few times they've met this summer, they have mostly

swapped old memories. They haven't created any new ones; haven't done anything that's worth remembering.

And Vanessa can't talk to them about the truly important events in her life anymore.

Vanessa?

Linnéa's voice in her head.

Yes? she replies, and tries to listen to Linnéa despite Michelle, who carries on moaning.

I'm sorry, Linnéa thinks. *I won't make a habit of stalking you, I promise. It's just that I'm losing my mind up here.*

It's OK, Vanessa thinks.

Does it sound crazy if I tell you I'm missing you already?

The familiar wave of warmth that only Linnéa can set off is spreading inside Vanessa. She has to force herself not to grin foolishly.

I love it when you go crazy.

Linnéa laughs inside Vanessa's head.

You're in luck, then. Lots to love. Seriously, I am sorry I was so grim. It's just that . . . you know.

'But Evelina, I'm telling you, I'll never sleep over at Leo's house again. Can't cope with the way you keep making out all the time.'

Vanessa loses the thread. Has Michelle been to stay with Evelina in Örebro?

'Stop it! We weren't that bad, surely?' Evelina snickers.

Vanessa? Still there?

Vanessa tries to think, but it's so hard to keep what's going on outside her head separate from what's going on inside it.

Sure, yes, I am, she thinks, rubbing her forehead.

When she takes her hand away, she realizes that Evelina and Michelle are looking fixedly at her.

'You look weird,' Evelina says. 'What are you thinking about?'

'Nothing. All I . . .'

She tries to find something plausible to say and can't.

Notices that Michelle and Evelina are exchanging significant glances.

Sorry, such a lot going on here, Vanessa thinks. *I can't concentrate.*

'Hey,' Michelle says in a low voice. 'Have you heard? Or . . .?'

'What?' Vanessa asks, and probably looks weirder than ever.

Michelle and Evelina glance at each other again.

'Look, Nessa, there's something . . .' Evelina says at the same time as Linnéa thinks something.

I didn't catch that, she replies, but Linnéa is gone.

Her head is in a spin.

Evelina looks strangely at her.

'What did you say?' Vanessa asks.

'Never mind,' Evelina replies.

CHAPTER 49

A few minutes before meeting, Minoo walks across the graveled yard to the manor house. The building seems to grow bigger the closer she comes. It feels as if the whole edifice will collapse and bury her when she presses the doorbell.

The door opens. Alexander is standing there wearing a dark blue suit and white shirt. She hasn't met him since she hid Adriana's memories. She had almost forgotten how tall he is. His dark hair is graying at the temples and his eyes are colder than ever when he looks at her.

'Come,' he says. 'Follow me, I want to talk to you.'

He turns and starts to walk away without waiting for an answer. She quickly looks around the hall. There is a vase of magnificent white roses on the old wooden counter that served as the reception desk when the house was an inn. Their sweet scent fills the air.

'Minoo,' Alexander calls.

He has stopped halfway down the left-hand hallway that leads to the library and the gallery where Anna-Karin's trial was conducted. Minoo can't help herself; her heart starts galloping.

'Come along, Minoo.'

They walk along the hallway in silence. Minoo observes Alexander's very straight back. She feels certain that he still hates the Chosen Ones because they shamed him in front of his superiors during the trial. And now, the chairman of the Council has included Minoo in his new circle. A circle that Alexander cannot join because he is not a natural witch.

However talented he is, however strong his powers, Minoo thinks, he'll never be as strong as I am.

But, once they are both in the library, her attempts at talking herself up ring hollow. She is not used to seeing the room in daylight. She looks at the chequered floor. The bookshelves. The armchairs facing each other. The closed doors to the gallery.

'Do sit down.' Alexander settles into his usual armchair.

'The others are waiting for me.'

'This will be quick,' he says. 'If you just listen to me.'

Reluctantly, Minoo sits back in the same armchair as last time and, as it did that time, it almost swallows her.

'I wanted an opportunity to speak to you alone,' he tells her. 'Now that we're forced to collaborate under these . . . exceptional circumstances.'

She makes herself meet his eyes. And suddenly she feels a little calmer. They are back in the same room, sitting in the same chairs, but everything else is different.

Despite his arrogance, she is certain that Alexander is perfectly aware of it too.

'Do you believe it all now?' she asks. 'Do believe in the Chosen Ones? The demons? The apocalypse?'

'I believe in our chairman, Walter Hjorth,' Alexander replies.

He speaks with complete conviction, as if Walter is his religion.

'As for all the rest, let us agree that the truth was somewhere between my perception of the situation and yours,' he continues. 'It would seem, for instance, that the Chosen Ones are replaceable.'

'Apart from me,' Minoo says.

A shadow crosses his face.

'What do you want to talk to me about?' she asks.

'I need to assure myself that you are aware of the continued need for you all to respect the laws of the Council. Just in case, for example, you feel tempted to use magic to manipulate the magistrates in the case of the young men who attacked Linnéa Wallin.'

Minoo tries to look relaxed. She mustn't let on that this is exactly what Anna-Karin wants to do.

'I will be present at the proceedings. If I detect that you are deploying magic, it will have grave consequences for you.'

His face is very calm as he continues.

'I made quite a few mistakes in the trial against Anna-Karin Nieminen, but the biggest one by far was that I allowed the case to be heard in court. It should have been dealt with by a less cumbersome process. The kind of quick, discreet approach that leaves no loose ends.'

At first, Minoo doesn't grasp the full meaning of what he is saying. When she does, she goes as cold as ice.

Alexander had been terrifying enough as the prosecutor. Now he seems to regret not having taken on the role of executioner.

'Let me put it this way.' He adjusts the strap on his wristwatch. 'I have learned from my mistakes.'

'There's no need for us to manipulate the proceedings. Robin has already confessed, after all,' Minoo says. 'And we have a witness in Viktor.'

She can tell that Alexander doesn't like to be reminded of Viktor.

'Now, I would also like to discuss Adriana,' he says. 'Specifically, how we are to manage this situation so that she is not damaged.'

Not damaged?

Minoo looks at Alexander. The man who informed on Adriana. Who branded her with the sign of fire just below her collarbone, using a red-hot iron. Who tortured her again, here in the manor house, until she revealed the secrets of her own and of the Chosen Ones. Disgust for him rises inside Minoo and threatens to choke her.

'It is important that we agree on what has happened to her.'

Alexander goes on to describe, coolly and factually, how the Council has explained Adriana's position to her. When Viktor told the story, Minoo had felt sympathy for Adriana. Now, she only feels hatred for Alexander. It's his fault. He is the origin of all the suffering in his sister's life.

'I have asked Adriana to keep a low profile, but you will inevitably run into her. Nonetheless, everyone has been told to avoid her whenever possible. This rule applies to you in particular. You and your friends have already inflicted more than enough damage.'

Minoo's heart is thumping. Her hatred of him is stronger than ever before. She wants to hurt him. Make him suffer, too, and as terribly as she can. She senses the black smoke beginning to stir inside her. It wants out and she wants to let it loose. Would he be able to turn it against her? Probably not. The magic of the guardians isn't connected to an element.

She must not do it. But maybe she can still hurt him in another way.

'Is this how you manage to live with yourself? By pretending that *we* are to blame for everything? After all that *you* have done to her?'

Alexander opens his mouth to speak but Minoo plows on.

'It must please you that Adriana isn't aware that you killed her familiar. Or that it was you who forced her to stand as a witness, even though you knew she would be tortured.'

'Adriana knew the kind of risk she—' Alexander begins.

'Shame that she remembers the other time you betrayed her,' Minoo interrupts. 'Her, and Simon.'

Now, he can't hide his shock.

'Did Adriana tell you this?'

'No, she did not. Walter told me.'

Minoo watches as this fact sinks in. Alexander struggles to control his expression. She didn't know that he could look so totally shaken. It is so satisfying.

'This discussion is completely irrelevant. And I have no

intention of prolonging it,' he says stiffly.

He gets up, and Minoo follows his example. She sees that his hands are trembling, then that he has noticed that she has noticed. He quickly puts his hands in his trouser pockets.

'Even though you might be under the chairman's protection at present, the others are not,' he points out. 'Do remind your friends of this in good time before the court proceedings. You may go. The rest of the group is waiting for you in the garden.'

Minoo gives him a final glance. He looks defeated now, but she knows that is an illusion. She has probably turned him into a more dangerous enemy than ever before.

CHAPTER 50

Minoo steps out into the hallway. Someone is in the hall, a girl in a pale pink dress. Closer up, Minoo recognizes Clara. She has changed during the summer. Her hair is glossy, her still-pale skin has a rosy tinge. She looks more like Viktor now.

'There you are!' Clara says. 'I got worried you were lost. It's easily done. There are so many rooms that a lot of them aren't even in use.'

Clara's eyes meet hers for just a second or two before looking away. Clara blushes several shades pinker.

'I'm sorry . . . I'm practicing this eye-contact thing. It's still kind of new to me.'

She glances at Minoo again and smiles. 'But it's a problem I'm really happy to have. Thank you very much for helping me.'

'You're welcome,' Minoo says, sounding as if Clara had thanked her for handing her the milk at breakfast.

Clara checks to make sure she can't see anyone around who might overhear them.

'Viktor told me that you saw my memories,' she says in a low voice. 'And also that I could trust you not to say anything to anyone. Or, at least, nothing that doesn't directly affect the Chosen Ones.'

'I promise.' Minoo feels relieved that she has kept quiet. 'Would you like to know what memories I saw?'

Clara shakes her head. 'No, I don't. I feel better not knowing.'

She fingers the wide bracelet that hides the scar on her

wrist. Minoo is disconcerted by how much she knows about Clara, even though they have hardly ever met.

'Come along,' Clara says. 'The others are waiting for us.'

Minoo follows her along the hallway and through a door into a room with one long table in the middle. The linen table-cloth is such a pure, perfect white that Minoo knows if ever she was asked to eat in here, she'd spill something on it.

They continue through a series of impersonally furnished rooms and Minoo soon loses all sense of where in the building they might be.

Then she sees Viktor in a doorway.

'There you are.' He steps forward to give Minoo a quick hug. Now, he is completely odorless again. 'We almost started to worry that you wouldn't come.'

They carry on walking through the seemingly endless spaces in the manor house. Minoo becomes more and more convinced that she'd never learn to find her way.

'Minoo, I'd just like you to know that I've started to use my magic again,' Clara says.

And Minoo instantly understands.

'Have you joined the circle, too?'

'Yes. It has just been decided.'

Viktor casts a quick glance at Minoo, a glance that tells her he doesn't like this decision at all. Clara notices as well.

'Alexander and Walter are sure it's perfectly safe,' she says crossly.

Then she smiles a little at Minoo. 'Besides, we've always got you if something should go wrong.'

Clara means it jokingly, but Minoo can't help feeling that she has been burdened with yet another thing.

They enter a large, unfurnished room with tall windows and three grand chandeliers hanging from the ceiling. Presumably a ballroom, Minoo thinks, and then tries to imagine a time when balls were held in Engelsfors. It seems impossible.

In here, the air is fresh and cool. The double doors are

opened wide to the garden behind the manor house. Viktor stops to let Clara and Minoo go outside ahead of him.

Minoo stops for a while at the top of the stone steps.

Not a trace is left of the untamed greenery that used to grow there. Surrounded by the tall white fence, the garden looks cared for, with an evenly green, immaculately trimmed lawn and pruned apple trees. The white roses in the border along the wall give off an intoxicating scent. A leafy hedge in the middle of the garden reaches high up in the air and forms a near-compact wall. Minoo hears voices from behind it.

'Isn't it lovely?' Clara says.

She crosses the lawn with light steps and disappears behind the hedge, but Minoo is suddenly immobile. As if she is fused to the stone step.

She listens to the voices. The other circle. The strongest witches Walter has been able to recruit. Probably all from the highest echelons of the Council. The elite of the elite.

Viktor stands next to her.

'You have nothing to fear,' he tells her.

'I'm not afraid,' Minoo responds, but she hears how nervous she sounds. How silly she is to pretend.

'Who are the others?'

'Two of them were in my class at school, Sigrid and Felix. They're OK.'

Minoo nods. Viktor went to one of the Council's boarding schools, which means he has lived in their company. He must know them really well.

'There's another girl who seems quite harmless, too,' he continues. 'Come on, let's go.'

They cross the soft lawn toward the hedge. There isn't a single slug in sight. And definitely no plastic buckets. Minoo is sweating under her jacket but doesn't dare take it off. She is certain there will be damp patches under the arms of her T-shirt.

She follows Viktor as he steps through a gap in the hedge.

It is like entering a room with green walls, the bright blue sky for a ceiling and dark stone flags for a floor. There are two circles, one inside the other, outlined in a lighter stone. Five people stand around the inner circle.

Walter's eyes are hidden behind a pair of pilot's sunglasses, but she can still feel his gaze directed toward her. He is tanned; his graying hair is swept back. His clothes are casually elegant: sand-colored chinos and a thin, slightly burled cardigan.

'There she is!' he says with a welcoming smile. Clara, on Walter's right, smiles too.

The talking stops. Everyone looks at her.

'Well, it feels great to have the whole gang in one place at last.' Walter waves to Minoo and Viktor. 'Over here! Felix, move over a bit.'

A boy with black hair, standing on Walter's left, shuffles sideways.

Minoo avoids looking at the others as she steps across the circles and goes to stand next to Walter. Viktor is on her other side.

She wonders what Walter has told the others about her. Did he use the same words as he used with her?

The most powerful witch who has ever existed.

A wave of performance anxiety makes her sweat even more.

'You already know some of us,' Walter says. 'But this is Nejla Hodzic.'

He gestures toward a plump, bored-looking girl who stands next to Clara. Her long dark hair is very straight with a center part. She is wearing a black T-shirt with the word BATHORY on the chest. Minoo has no idea what that might mean and she has the feeling that Nejla would despise her for that. The girl glances at Minoo, then returns to doing something on her cell phone.

'This is Sigrid Axelsson Lilja,' Walter continues.

Sigrid stands next to Nejla. She is petite, with glasses and blonde curly hair that reaches her shoulders. She is wearing a 1950s-style dress with a leaf pattern, and her smile is warm and genuine, if a little curious. Minoo likes her instinctively, even though the elfin Sigrid is the type of girl who usually makes her nervous.

'Hi, Minoo,' Sigrid says.

'Hi.'

'And this is Felix Nowak.' Walter points to the boy with black hair.

Minoo takes a closer look at him. Felix is wearing a gray polo shirt and black jeans. His eyes are brown. He looks intently at Minoo with narrowed eyes and his eyebrows drawn together. She can't work out if it's she who irritates him, or the sunlight.

'Today, we won't have a long session,' Walter says. 'First and foremost, I wanted Minoo to meet you all. But also, there is something I want to show you . . .'

He stops and checks his watch.

'The time has almost come. Viktor, are you ready?'

Viktor nods and holds up a small object not unlike a lipstick. Minoo recognizes it. Adriana also used one of those ectoplasm tubes. The silvery metal glints in the sunlight.

'The fate of the entire world is at stake,' Walter tells them. 'But you're young and need to sleep. Some nights we will be here until late. I suggest that nine would be a reasonable time to start in the mornings. Agreed?'

Minoo looks around the circle. They all nod. She feels that she has somehow missed something. Possibly a lot of things.

'Good,' Walter says. 'That's it, then.'

'Sorry,' Minoo says, and feels everybody staring at her again. 'But when do we work together?'

'Nine o'clock.'

Walter takes off his sunglasses and looks down at her with a quizzical smile. Minoo isn't used to feeling short, but she does now, standing between Viktor and Walter.

'Yes I know but . . .' She hesitates. 'At nine o'clock but, but . . . which day?'

'Tomorrow,' Walter tells her. 'And every day for the rest of the week to come. Better book us in for the weekend as well. That will help us get off to a good start. Later on, I hope it will be possible to give you the weekend off, or at least Sundays. If you're to deliver at peak ability, it's so important to have time to relax and recover.'

'But I . . .' Minoo begins, but can't see her way to completing the sentence.

But I must go to school. I haven't got time to save the world.

She can't say that aloud. But she can see that Walter has already realized how little she understood of what would be required.

'Right,' he says slowly, and she notices a hint of disappointment in his eyes. 'Now, I can't quite follow your thinking, Minoo. You had a choice. And you chose to join us and help us in our work. I must say I assumed your priorities were clear to you. Was I wrong?'

Minoo feels all her blood rush to her face.

'No, not at all,' she says. 'Absolutely. It's just that I . . . was thinking along the wrong lines. I'll arrange . . . things.'

She falls silent. How will she arrange being away? The collective gaze of the others burns more strongly than the sun's rays.

'Excellent.' Finally Walter takes his eyes off her. 'Now, the time has come. Please see to it that you stand inside the outer circle.'

Viktor steps forward, bends over at the edge of the inner circle and slowly draws the sign for the element of water.

She will have to leave school. Take a sabbatical year. How does one do that? Does she have to speak to the principal? Or can she just stay away? Are there forms to fill in? Mom and Dad, will she have to tell them? Or could she carry on coming

352

here and use school as her alibi? Tricky to get out of once it's time to graduate, but by that stage the world might be annihilated anyway.

'Now. Soon,' Walter says.

Viktor puts the top back on the ectoplasm tube. From the inside pocket of his jacket, he pulls out a small silver bottle engraved with two concentric circles.

Minoo wonders who makes all these things. Does the Council run boutiques for magic accessories?

Viktor shuts his eyes briefly, then opens them again and turns the bottle upside-down over the elemental sign.

Water flows as slowly as syrup from the neck of the bottle, spreads in a thin layer over the flagstones and settles into a perfect round, reflective surface in the inner circle.

Viktor puts the bottle back and straightens up.

'Come closer,' Walter instructs.

Minoo takes another few steps forward until the tips of her shoes almost nudge the water's edge. The others are also moving toward the center of the circle. She can smell Walter's aftershave.

The surface is dark now and completely still, like tinted glass. Although Minoo knows it is only a thin sheet of water, it is like looking into a very deep well. In the center of the surface, the sun is reflected as a bright disc. Their silhouettes are little more than shadows.

'Whatever you do, don't look up,' Walter says.

At first, the stirring is so slight that Minoo thinks she has made a mistake. Then she thinks she sees a small flake of rubbish floating across the water.

'Fucking hell,' Nejla whispers.

A blackness is moving in over the bright sun. The process is so slow it's barely noticeable, but soon there can be no doubt about what is happening.

The sun is slowly being obscured by a black mass.

Minoo sees how the light in the garden is changing now,

growing duller, first to matte gold and then to bluish gray, as if every color in the world is disappearing. As if twilight is falling far too rapidly.

Then darkness falls.

Viktor takes her hand and she clasps it gratefully as they stare into the water's surface.

The sun flickers, a star's last desperate flash of light before darkness swallows it whole.

* * *

'Don't look up!' Ove Post, the biology teacher, shouts to the students who are standing at the windows or clustering by the front door. 'It could blind you!'

Anna-Karin won't look. She doesn't want to see darkness take over, as it did in Minoo's vision. That must be it, mustn't it? The world is ending right now. And people are just staring at it.

She scans the packed entrance lobby, looking for Vanessa and Linnéa in the crowd.

'Get away from the windows!'

Inez, their chemistry teacher, is shouting and, small as she is, her voice can be heard everywhere in the hall.

Anna-Karin!

Linnéa's voice in her head. Anna-Karin probes the crowd to locate her friend's energy field. She finds Linnéa's and Vanessa's energies at the same time, and follows the trail until she spots them, hand in hand by the steps to the dining area.

'People usually know about solar eclipses in advance, right?' Vanessa says quietly when Anna-Karin joins them.

'Yes,' Anna-Karin agrees. 'People do.'

'Thought so,' Vanessa says.

'It's going away!' someone shouts.

Anna-Karin turns to the windows and sees the world outside growing lighter.

Part Three

'For heaven's sake!' Ove screams. 'Don't look, I'm serious!'

The sun breaks through the dullness outside. All over the lobby, people applaud and cheer.

'There now,' Ove Post says from somewhere. 'It's all over.'

Why do I have the feeling it's precisely the other way around? Linnéa thinks.

CHAPTER 51

'That's it folks,' Walter says.

Minoo automatically follows the movement of the others as they back a few paces away from the water's edge. She looks around. Everything is as it was. No trace of anything alien in the blue sky.

Sigrid has taken her glasses off and is fingering the frame. Felix shades his eyes with his hand and scans the sky, as if looking for clues to what happened. Viktor looks at Clara with worried eyes. All color has drained from her face.

But Nejla is beaming.

'That was massive,' she says. 'So *fucking* massive.'

'What we have just observed is a portent,' Walter says seriously.

Minoo expects that somebody will ask, *A portent of what?* and that someone else will answer, *Nothing good, that's for sure*, but no one interrupts Walter.

'The red moon in the sky over Engelsfors showed that the veil separating the dimensions has started to weaken,' Walter continues while looking at Minoo. 'The red moon could only be seen by the Chosen Ones and certain ordinary people in, as it were . . . sensitized states. That's right, isn't it?'

She recalls some of the many things that happened during the night of the blood-red moon. The accidents. The fights. The nervous breakdowns. She remembers what Rebecka's mother had said about how several of the ER patients had been speaking about a red moon, but that none of the staff had seen it.

'Then there were other significant events,' Walter says.

'The elements reacted, one way or the other, to the height-ened levels of magic. Minoo, perhaps you could tell the others something of what went on?'

He looks expectantly at her.

And suddenly, the logic of the chain of events strikes her. She knew of course that the strange phenomena in Engelsfors signified increasing levels of magic. But she had never twigged that the reasons were elemental reactions.

'The crack that appeared in the schoolyard,' Minoo begins. 'That was the first thing that followed. Actually it happened during the night of the blood-red moon. And that was . . . an "earth" reaction?'

Walter smiles more generously now and she feels reassured.

'Precisely,' he says.

Sigrid has put her glasses back on and looks expectantly at Walter and Minoo.

'Then the water began to behave very oddly,' Minoo con-tinues. 'That was due to the water element, of course. And the endless electrical problems must have been linked to metal. The sawmill burnt down. That was a fire reaction.'

Walter nods.

'Anna-Karin found dead birds in the forest,' Minoo continues. 'It looked as if they had fallen out of the sky. So, air. And we have all found new areas with dead trees. That's wood, isn't it?'

'Sounds like it,' Walter agrees.

'And, also, there was a period of unnaturally warm weather – last summer and the winter that followed,' she goes on. 'But I can't work out which elements were reacting then. Perhaps several together?'

Oh my God, how *keen* she sounds. Far too eager to show off to Walter.

But nobody looks impatiently at her. There's no Linnéa to say something sarcastic about how much Minoo adores suck-ing up to teachers.

Minoo realizes that here, she has no need to hold back.

Everyone here is like her. It's so relaxing she feels almost guilty. Because this isn't her true circle. This is not where she belongs and she must keep reminding herself of that. Especially now, when Walter looks at her with such approval.

'There are no absolute distinctions,' he says. 'The important fact we have observed is that all the elements have responded to the increase in the level of magic. And now we have observed the next significant event. That is, what we have just seen.'

'It can't have been a solar eclipse,' Felix says. 'That's impossible.'

'Indeed, Felix. Obviously it was no regular eclipse,' Walter snaps. 'Perhaps you should have refrained from interrupting us to point that out.'

He turns back to Minoo with a complicit smile. Felix sends her a dirty look.

'What we have just experienced is the first sign that we are entering a new phase,' Walter explains. He pauses to make sure that he has everyone's attention.

'Another six signs, or portents, will occur. One for each element, and all concentrated around the portal. And then a great darkness will envelop Engelsfors.'

Was this the scene Minoo had watched in her vision? The smoke that snaked down the streets and coiled itself around the houses, swallowing them. Swallowing everything.

'You must be ready by then,' Walter instructs them. 'Ready to close the portal.'

No one speaks.

Minoo doesn't really dare to speak either, but there is one question she must ask.

'How do we do it? How do we close the portal?'

'It is a complex process,' Walter replies. 'We must generate a high output of magic energy so we must develop our powers and become as strong as possible.'

Minoo's heart is beating fast. She longs to tell the others about what he has just said. Make them see that there's a plan. That Walter knows what he is talking about.

'Where is the portal?' she asks.

'Sorry, I thought it was obvious,' Walter says. 'In the high school.'

Of course, Minoo thinks. It *is* obvious. No wonder Max and Olivia were stronger there than anywhere else. They could connect directly to the demons.

The school *is* the site of evil. And Anna-Karin, Linnéa and Vanessa go to that school every day.

'How will the elemental signs manifest themselves?' Minoo asks.

'We don't know.'

'But ought we not . . . it seems to me . . . it might not be safe to keep the school open.'

'I realize that you're worrying about your friends, Minoo,' Walter says. 'It's very commendable. If this had been an operation officially sanctioned by the Council, we might have pulled something off. As matters stand at present, that route isn't open to us. But I'm sure your friends are quite capable of looking after themselves.'

But what about the others? Minoo thinks. People without magic powers?

But she doesn't say it.

'Do you know where in the school the portal is?' Viktor asks.

'We aren't sure about the exact place,' Walter replies. 'And we can't just root around in the attic looking for it. The portal won't become accessible until all six portents have shown themselves and the darkness is falling in Engelsfors.'

He looks at his watch. Minoo reckons it would cost an average citizen's annual wage.

'That's it for today,' he says. 'See you tomorrow at nine o'clock.'

He walks out into the garden and Nejla, Felix and Sigrid follow him like a tail.

'See you tomorrow, Minoo.' Sigrid waves before walking away out of sight.

Viktor puts his hand on Minoo's arm.

'Wait a moment,' he says quietly.

Minoo stays and listens as the voices of the others become more distant.

'How do you feel now?' Viktor asks. 'You were so nervous earlier.'

'No problem,' Minoo says. 'As soon as I saw a sign of the apocalypse, I felt right at home.'

Viktor looks baffled for a moment, then laughs. For once, she has managed to be funny when she tried to be.

'You must ask if there's anything you're unsure about,' he says. 'The Council has so many established ideas about things which we probably don't even realize could look eccentric to an outsider.'

Minoo nods. She catches sight of Clara, who has gone up to the inner circle where the blue sky is reflected on the surface of the water.

'Take this.' Viktor pulls a key from his jacket pocket. 'Walter told me to give it to you, so you can come and go as you like here.'

'Do you all live here?'

'Yes,' Viktor says, rolling his eyes. 'It's like being back at school again.'

Clara kneels and holds her hand out over the pool of water. Her hair is blown about as if in a breeze and the water begins to swirl. Then she takes her hand away and all becomes still again.

'Everything seems so much more tangible now,' Clara says. 'Do we truly have a chance of closing the portal?'

'It's been done successfully six times before,' Minoo tells her.

'But each time it was done by a Chosen One,' Clara replies, staring at the water as if hypnotized. 'Not by some last-minute emergency circle.'

'The guardians tell us that there is hope,' Minoo says.

But Clara doesn't seem to be listening. She is resting her head in her hands. Viktor is watching his twin sister intently.

Minoo has no idea what is passing between them.

'I must go,' she says.

'I'll walk you to the front door,' Viktor says.

They leave the garden in silence. Viktor looks grim. Minoo wonders if he is deep in thought, or if he's still talking with Clara in his head. How far does their mind-reading connection stretch? she wonders.

'How is Clara now?' she asks as they cross the ballroom.

'She isn't well.' Viktor's voice echoes in the large, empty room.

'No one would be, after what we just saw happening to the sun.'

Viktor doesn't reply, just holds a door open for her.

'Or, is it something else?' Minoo adds, although she has a strong feeling she shouldn't ask anything more.

'I don't want to talk about it.'

She shuts up, feeling as if she's been told off. Instead, she tries to concentrate on memorizing the layout of the house. But since Viktor takes a different route to the one Clara did earlier, she becomes more confused than ever.

They enter a hallway with a carpet the color of oxblood and dark-red wallpaper. The walls are hung with gloomy portraits in oil. The subjects look familiar, and Minoo realizes that it's because so many of them look like Alexander and Adriana. She has seen these portraits before. In Adriana's old house.

Viktor stops and turns to her.

'I'm sorry. That was rude of me.'

A strand of his ash-blonde hair has slipped down on his forehead and he puts it carefully back in place.

'This thing with Clara is so complicated,' he says quietly. 'People have always known that I had a twin sister, but they always thought she must have gone to a different school. I've never answered questions about her. Just talking about her makes me feel like a traitor.'

He looks at Minoo. It feels as if the portrait behind him is staring at her too. It shows a man with blonde hair and clever, gentle eyes. A small golden plaque informs her that he is Baron Henrik Ehrenskiöld.

'I do worry about Clara,' Viktor goes on. 'I know she is an adult who makes her own decisions, but I have an awful feeling that all this might be too much for her.'

He looks over his shoulder and lowers his voice a little more.

'I have trained in the Council's schools and know my way around this world. But Clara has stayed with Alexander all the time. She has been sheltered and alone a lot of the time. She isn't used to having people around her. She has no . . . armor. You noticed how the others reacted to what we have just seen, right?'

Minoo tries to understand what he is getting at.

'They didn't react much at all, I would've said.'

'Exactly,' Viktor says. 'They saw a portent foretelling the end of the world and nobody showed any fear. Not openly, anyway. They know that the Council has nothing but contempt for weakness. They . . .'

He stops. He has caught sight of something behind Minoo. She turns and just has time to see Adriana go through a door further along the hallway. Then, the sound of a key turning in a lock.

The Council has nothing but contempt for weakness.

Adriana once said something like that.

Minoo realizes that she wasn't surprised by the others' lack of response. She had assumed that they actually felt as shaken

362

as she did but that keeping a calm face came naturally to them. As it did to her. This thing about not being seen to be weak was clearly deep-rooted in her as well.

* * *

Vanessa stands in the schoolyard together with Linnéa and Anna-Karin. They are looking at the students pouring out through the front door. Tommy has announced a half-day and added that anyone who looked at the sun during the eclipse must go straight to the hospital for a check-up.

Vanessa has no idea what all this has been about. Still, she has a strong feeling that the horror is stepping up.

Her cell phone pings at the same time as Linnéa's and Anna-Karin's. Minoo is finished with the manor house for today and wants to meet them in Nicolaus's apartment now.

'You go ahead,' Vanessa says. 'I'll pop around to Mona's and ask her if she has an angle on the eclipse story.'

'Do you really think she'll have something useful to add?' Linnéa asks.

'Maybe. And maybe not. But I know how these sessions usually end. Like, "Vanessa, why don't you ask Mona?" Seems just as well to get it out of the way.'

She gives Linnéa a quick kiss and hurries off to the City Mall.

The smell of incense is so strong it reaches her the moment the automatic doors slide open. The ceiling lights are flickering. Leffe, who owns Leffe's kiosk, is coming out from Sture & Co. He stops to shake hands with Sture, who has followed him to the door. Under one arm, Leffe holds a big bundle of cigarette cartons with the warning notices in Cyrillic script. Vanessa looks the other way, just as she used to when the stoners came to Jonte's house.

The Crystal Cave is completely dark and there is a notice on the front door.

The Key

CLOSED FOR HOLIDAY

When Vanessa was working at the shop yesterday, Mona hadn't said a thing about going away. But it's typical of Mona to disappear without warning, so she's not worried, just irritated.

CHAPTER 52

Linnéa looks at Minoo, who sits on one of the wooden chairs in Nicolaus's living room and drinks in deep swallows from her glass of water. She has told them about the other circle in great detail and answered every question. Linnéa asked most of them.

The air is stale but they don't dare open the windows in case some passerby hears their conversation. The Venetian blinds are closed.

Linnéa is twitching with irritation. She would like to see all these characters for herself, so she can inspect the new players. The only one Linnéa has a clear opinion of is Walter. Even though she has never met him, she hates him passionately. Especially when she can see how impressed Minoo is by him.

'Seems to me this stuff about how to close the portal is pretty fucking vague.' Vanessa chomps on her chewing gum. 'Like, you know, "Generate a high output of magic energy". What does it mean?'

Linnéa glances at her and almost forgets to be annoyed with Minoo. During the summer, Vanessa has become deeply tanned, and with her blonde hair and light pink lip gloss she almost looks like a *ganguro* girl. A very, very hot *ganguro* girl, which is confusing because Linnéa has never cared for that look.

Minoo puts the glass down and wipes her mouth. 'We do know at least that there's a point in practicing our magic and working up our powers.'

Linnéa wonders if Minoo is talking about the Council's circle or the Chosen Ones.

'It is so totally obvious that the portal had to be in the school,' Vanessa says.

'I never thought of the portal as a physical place,' Minoo says evenly, as if she was thinking aloud. 'I guess I just thought that all of Engelsfors was the portal.'

'You know, Minoo, I can't get my head around you dropping out of school.' Vanessa takes her gum out and drops it into Minoo's empty glass.

'I can't either,' Anna-Karin says.

She seems sad, and Linnéa realizes that Anna-Karin will be very much alone without Minoo in her class.

'I'll just take a sabbatical year, not drop out,' Minoo says. 'But I don't know how I'll explain it to my parents. Maybe I won't say anything at all.'

'They'll hear about it anyway,' Vanessa tells her. 'The best student drops out of school in her senior year. The daughter of the editor-in-chief and his doctor wife. Students from the posh end of town don't usually do that. You must realize what a juicy piece of gossip this is!'

Minoo blushes. 'I'm not the best,' she mumbles, but Linnéa feels sure she only protests because she feels it's the right thing to do.

'Yes, you are,' Anna-Karin says. 'And you must brief me about what to say to your parents if you do walk out of school, or I'll end up saying something wrong.'

Linnéa looks at Minoo's unhappy face and feels her irritation rising again. So, it's tough for Minoo. She can see that. But the reason Minoo has a hard time is because everyone expects her to be the best at whatever she does. For Linnéa, it's the other way around. Everyone, including herself, expects her to fuck up.

It would be great to be able to say fuck it, drop out of school and not worry about social services and the student loan and being homeless.

What will happen to Minoo if she takes a year out? Her

parents would *worry* about her. Maybe even get *really mad*. Perhaps even cut down on her *weekly allowance*. Big fucking deal.

'I don't know what I can tell them,' Minoo says. 'I have to find an excuse that works but doesn't worry them.'

'Perhaps not the worst problem we've got just now, wouldn't you say?' Linnéa remarks.

'Hey, easy,' Vanessa says.

'I just don't get why we have to keep fucking going on about it,' Linnéa goes on. 'Have we finished now?'

'Not quite.' Minoo looks uncomfortable. 'Alexander wanted a word with me. He is going to be in court during the hearing. And if any one of us uses magic to affect the conduct of the case, he's going to kill us.'

Panic grips Linnéa by the throat. She makes herself take a deep breath.

'*Us?*' she says. 'He'll hardly be planning to kill *you*, will he? Because his boss isn't going to like that, is he? Lucky you, Minoo. You're friends with such high-ups these days.'

Minoo opens her mouth to say something, but she shuts it again.

Linnéa turns to Anna-Karin. 'I told you. It's far too dangerous. You mustn't do anything.'

Anna-Karin looks shocked.

'Linnéa's lawyer says that everything points to Erik being convicted, even if he doesn't confess,' Vanessa says. 'So . . .'

She stops abruptly at the sound of a key turning in the front door. Linnéa fixes her gaze on Minoo as the door opens.

Where is the silver cross? she thinks.

In my house, Minoo thinks, and looks at Linnéa with terrified eyes. *I am so sorry. I should have brought . . .*

The door is shut. Shoes are cleaned on the mat. If it is the Council's reps, they are at least polite.

All four sit frozen in their seats as Nicolaus comes into the room.

CHAPTER 53

Linnéa stares at Nicolaus, framed in the doorway. She hardly recognizes him. His hair has become even grayer and yet he looks younger than he did. His hair is smartly cut, his tasteful and discreet clothes actually fit him. No more eye-watering color combos. No scruffiness at all – not even a wrinkle.

Nothing about him gives a clue as to his feelings. But they are so overwhelming that Linnéa senses all of them. Amazement. Relief. Joy. Love. Concern. Nicolaus fears what they might say to him. How they will react. He remembers the last time he saw them a year ago, on the night when they had dug up the grave.

His emotions are so powerful that Linnéa has to force them out of her mind. What is left is a hollow space, like a deafening silence.

Nicolaus walks into the room, stops at one of the empty chairs and puts down his brown suitcase.

'Where is Ida?' is the first thing he says.

'She is dead,' Linnéa tells him.

Nicolaus's face goes very pale. Linnéa thinks the shock serves him right. She is surprised at how angry she is with him. How angry she has been with him during all the time he has been away.

'You've missed a lot by going off like that,' she goes on. 'Things happen when you're absent for a year.'

'Don't,' Minoo says. 'We don't even know why he left!'

'True,' Linnéa agrees. 'He didn't tell us. And didn't let us know later on either.'

368

'What's wrong with you?' Vanessa says. 'Give him a chance to speak to us!'

It's humiliating to be told off, but Linnéa knows that Vanessa is right.

She sits tight.

Anna-Karin stares at Nicolaus, as if he'll disappear unless she keeps her eyes on him.

'Are you back with us now?' she asks.

'Yeah,' Vanessa says. 'Are you in transit, or staying?'

'I'm staying.' Nicolaus slumps down on a chair. 'Nothing could make me leave again.'

* * *

Minoo has imagined many times what it might be like when Nicolaus came back. Sometimes, she imagined him regretful or sad, or at least full of explanations.

In her dreams, she has sometimes been furious, sometimes forgiving, and at other times just relieved. But in all her fantasies, the reunion has led to emotional turmoil. Now, though, it just feels unreal. As if Nicolaus were a hallucination. The fact that his appearance is so different doesn't make it any easier to believe that he is real.

'What happened?' she asks. 'Why did you decide to disappear?'

'When you left me that night, I dreamt about my daughter,' Nicolaus says. 'But it was no ordinary dream.'

'We know what kind of dream you mean,' Vanessa says.

'She told me that the Council was coming to Engelsfors,' Nicolaus goes on.

'Which seemed a good reason for you to get out, right?' Linnéa sounds harsh.

'Matilda urged me not to stay. She said that if the Council caught me, I would become a danger to you.'

Minoo shudders at the thought of how true that is. If Nicolaus had been dragged into the trial against Anna-Karin, it would probably have ended with him being forced to reveal their secrets, or else being killed by the Council. Most likely both.

'But why didn't you tell us that in your letter?' she asks. 'You might even have warned us that the Council was coming.'

'Matilda said I wasn't to tell you why I left. She said that if you knew certain things too early, it could affect the future in an unfortunate way. Unfortunate for you – and for the rest of the world, too.'

Minoo notices that Linnéa sits up on the sofa. Thankfully, she keeps quiet, allowing Nicolaus to carry on talking.

'But it wasn't just because of the Council that I left,' he says. 'Matilda sent me on a mission.'

He pulls his hand through his hair; he has kept this old gesture, even though his hair is shorter now.

'I have never come across any sources that describe how the Chosen One is to close the portal. That information has always been concealed and available only to the top echelon of the Council. But I had heard of three objects that were essential for the control of the portal. Matilda asked me to find them.'

He bends over his suitcase and opens it, pulling out a ball of bubble-wrap. Delicately, he starts undoing the tape holding the parcel together.

'The Chosen One who closed the sixth portal was a young man who lived in Florence in the 1400s. By the time he had finished his task, an internal power battle had broken out within the Council. A breakout faction stole the objects and hid them in different places around the world.'

'What's the Council's fucking problem, really?' Vanessa says.

'You might well ask,' Nicolaus says. 'Anyway, they planted clues so that only the conspirators would be able to find the objects. I followed the clues.'

He cautiously unwraps the plastic and places the object on the table.

It's a skull. Its empty eye sockets stare at Minoo.

'OK,' Linnéa nods. 'So this is one of the objects, right?'

'It is. One might even say that it contains the other two,' Nicolaus tells them.

Minoo picks the skull up. It is lighter than she had expected. She has never been scared by the skeletons that feature in films or books. They always seemed a bit ridiculous, because she could never see what a skeleton could actually *do*. But it is very different to hold a cranium in her hand and know that it was once part of a living man or woman. It is both fascinating and unnerving, as is the fact that her brain, which holds her thoughts, lies protected inside a skull just like this one.

'Feel about inside the eye sockets,' Nicolaus says.

'What?'

'Try it,' he urges, and nods.

Minoo pokes inside the skull and tries not to think of the eyes that were once in the way of her probing fingers. She can feel the others watching her tensely.

Then she finds something. A rounded surface under her fingertips.

'There's something in here,' she says. 'It feels a little like a button.'

'Try pressing on it,' Nicolaus tells her.

Minoo presses and the button-like object comes loose. By shaking the skull gently, she dislodges a small cylinder of bone that falls out of the eye socket and lands in the palm of her hand. A thin join divides it in half.

'Hand that to me, please,' Nicolaus says.

He unscrews the two halves of the cylinder and turns them upside-down.

Glittering grains of jet-black sand trickle down and, as they fall onto the table top, they arrange themselves into a pattern. A pattern Minoo recognizes. It's an image of the silver cross.

'How would the silver cross help us close the portal?' Anna-Karin asks.

'Unfortunately I do not know that yet,' Nicolaus says. 'But that isn't all.'

'Let me guess,' Vanessa says. 'There's a fabulous prize in the other eye socket?'

Minoo finds the button immediately and presses it. Another bone cylinder pops out. She hands it to Nicolaus, who again lets the sand fall next to the image of the cross.

Minoo leans forward to see the image as it takes shape. She hardly dares to breathe for fear that she might blow away some of the grains of sand.

When she sees the image, she feels a sudden, inner flicker of anxiety.

A man with closed eyes is portrayed standing inside a circle with his arms stretched out. A vertical line runs right across the image and divides it down the middle. On one side of the line there is a city with strange buildings. On the other, only a spinning, threatening chaos.

The flickering anxiety grows into a shudder that runs through her whole body. There is something about that image.

'What is that?' Vanessa says.

'I'm afraid I can't work it out,' Nicolaus frowns. 'But I've got something to ask you. A few nights ago, I dreamt about Matilda again. She told me that I must return to Engelsfors. She said that the chairman of the Council is here and that I should go and see him. I must hand over the skull and the silver cross to him.'

Minoo puts the skull down on the table. She feels that Linnéa is observing her.

'What is going on here?' Nicolaus asks. 'I don't understand.'

'Neither do I,' Linnéa says.

'As we were saying,' Vanessa tells him, 'quite a lot has happened since you disappeared.'

Minoo starts talking and then they take turns to explain.

Nicolaus listens silently and intently. He only shakes his head in answer to Vanessa asking if he remembers Olivia from his time as the school janitor.

He interrupts once. When Minoo tells him about Alexander. He asks her to repeat Alexander's full name, as if to make sure that he heard it right. Then he just listens again. Looks absently at the skull.

'So our only hope now is the Council,' he says when they have finally stopped talking. 'And that this new circle will succeed in closing the portal.'

'That's what the guardians have ordered us to do,' Linnéa says. 'For our own good, of course.'

Annoyance with her flares up inside Minoo. The guardians haven't issued any *orders*. They are trying to be helpful.

'We agreed that the new circle is the only way to go ahead,' she says.

'No, we didn't,' Linnéa replies. 'As you said yourself, there might well be alternatives. And, look, here is one.'

'I don't trust Matilda,' Nicolaus suddenly interjects.

They all stare at him.

'What do you mean?' Anna-Karin asks. 'She is your daughter.'

'She was my daughter. And I loved her. When she showed herself to me in a dream for the first time a year ago, I was overwhelmed with happiness. I would have done anything she asked of me. But in this latest dream, I saw signs . . . signs that I think I willfully ignored the first time.'

'Signs of what?' Vanessa asks.

'I can't quite explain,' Nicolaus says. 'She is Matilda. And yet, she isn't.'

Minoo doesn't want to hear this. Doesn't want any more doubt and uncertainty.

'But Matilda has been caught between worlds for several hundred years,' she says. 'Surely it's not so strange that she has grown different, at least to some extent?'

'It's only a feeling,' Nicolaus continues. 'But one I cannot rid myself of. After all, I am her father. I know every expression, every change of tone in her voice. Even so, I can't put my finger on what it is that jars. But I'm certain there is something. That is why I cannot trust her, even though the thought that she should lie to me is almost unbearable. What you are telling me only confirms my worries. You are saying that the guardians communicate with you through Matilda and the *Book of Patterns*; that the guardians were demons in the beginning and that they also lied to you about it at first. So, how do we know that we can trust them now?'

'My point precisely,' Linnéa says, sounding satisfied.

Minoo looks at her and at Nicolaus. It is as if they have both betrayed her.

'So, what should we do?' Her voice is trembling with anger. 'Should I leave the circle set up by the Council? Because Nicolaus has "a feeling" that something isn't quite right? I'm not arguing that this is an ideal situation, but the guardians have in fact been right before!'

Her whole body is tense. She expects everyone to turn against her.

'Hell, this is about more than just feelings,' Linnéa says.

'You *want* the guardians to be dodgy in some way . . .'

'You mean like the fact that they've been demons? And played games with our lives?'

'Just because you can't hack authority,' Minoo plows on, refusing to let herself be interrupted.

'And *you* desperately want someone to give you orders! Like this *Walter* character.' Linnéa leans forward and fixes her eyes on Minoo. 'If it's true that the guardians have been talking to him, how come they haven't told him about these objects?'

'Of course they have!'

Linnéa smiles triumphantly.

'So why didn't he even mention them today at the manor

house session? When he told you how to go about closing the portal? If he withheld info like that, how can you fucking believe anything he says?'

Minoo can easily think of reasons why Walter wouldn't mention the objects today. They had hardly got to know each other – there must be tons of things he hasn't told them yet. But saying this won't have much effect on Linnéa and her eternal paranoia. Minoo isn't even convinced that Linnéa is interested in learning the truth. All she wants is to win this discussion.

'Linnéa is right about one thing.' Nicolaus turns to Minoo. 'You shouldn't trust Walter Hjorth. You don't become the head of the Council unless you're skilled at duping people around you.'

'If he's unreliable, it doesn't really matter anyway. Our goal is the same,' Minoo says. 'He, too, wants to stop the apocalypse.'

'True,' Nicolaus replies. 'I don't doubt it. And, for now, you must stay a member of the Council's circle. As things stand, there is no alternative.'

'The alternative would be that we go out to find more witches for our own circle,' Linnéa says. 'You're a natural witch, Nicolaus, a wood witch. We only need another two, fire and metal.'

'Our circle hasn't a hope of closing the portal,' Minoo says. 'Even if we do recruit more witches.'

'Yeah, according to the guardians!' Linnéa tells her. 'What is it you don't get? They lie to us, remember!'

'But why should they lie to us? If we did have a chance to close the portal, why not simply tell us?'

Linnéa shrugs.

'Maybe they don't want to close the portal! Who knows? Maybe they want to suck up to their old demonic cousins. Apologize and hand over our world as a sorry-we-let-you-down present!'

Minoo hates her a little. She feels fearful, too. Fearful, because if you looked at the world through Linnéa's eyes, nothing and nobody could be trusted, and there would be no point in doing anything.

'Listen, we must keep calm,' Nicolaus says firmly.

Minoo looks gratefully at him. He isn't completely on Linnéa's side.

'The guardians do want to close the portal,' he continues. 'I can assure you of that. And if they claim that the Council's circle can do it, then that's so. But, it doesn't mean that we cannot.'

'Why tell us that we can't, in that case?' Minoo asks. 'Why make us believe that our efforts would fail?'

'They may simply prefer the Council's circle.'

'Why would they?'

'It could be that they have seen something that has persuaded them that the Council is the safest bet, at least compared to us,' Nicolaus says. 'They go for the best odds, in other words. Or it may be that the guardians find the Council easier to deal with than us.'

'I don't want to have anything to do with either the Council or the guardians,' Linnéa says. 'Let's run our own circle.'

'But where could we even begin to look for two natural witches?' Anna-Karin asks. 'They're so rare.'

'But they do become more common during magic epochs, and especially near portals,' Linnéa goes on stubbornly. 'Mona is probably a metal witch, right? What with her fortune-telling and things? Maybe she's a natural witch? If the whole world is at stake, perhaps she'll join us when she comes back?'

Vanessa laughs a little.

'Can you imagine what it would be like, having Mona in our circle?'

'Sorry I spoke,' Linnéa says. 'I'm obviously thick.'

Vanessa's smile fades.

'At present, this discussion isn't taking us anywhere useful,' Nicolaus puts in. 'We do not have any replacements.'

Minoo can't understand how they can even consider it.
Even if the guardians don't always tell the whole truth, they
have access to so much more information than Nicolaus and
the Chosen Ones. Nicolaus and Linnéa are just speculating.

'But, for me, it goes against the grain to hand over the
silver cross and the skull to the Council,' Nicolaus says. 'For
one thing, I would like to find out more about the third object
first.'

Minoo looks closely at the image of the man with his eyes
closed. She realizes that it is familiar. But why?

'What's the matter?' Anna-Karin asks.

'I'm trying to think. Something tells me I've seen this
image somewhere.'

Her voice is angry, and it makes her feel guilty, because
it is Anna-Karin she is talking to. Minoo tries to give her an
apologetic look, but Anna-Karin is scrutinizing the image.

'Any idea where?' Vanessa asks.

'Don't know. I can't remember.'

'Can't you have a look?' Nicolaus asks. 'I mean, into your
own memories?'

The idea is so obvious that she becomes irritated again. She
should have thought of it herself.

'What if it's dangerous?' Anna-Karin says.

'Yeah, what if Minoo gets stuck inside her own head?'
Vanessa says.

Minoo thinks that it wouldn't be the first time.

'I'm not even sure it can be done.' But she closes her eyes
and allows the black smoke to pour out, while she puts her
hand against her own forehead. It makes her feel awkward but
soon the feeling is lost in the smoke.

Minoo enters her own mind from outside. Memories are
rushing toward her now. It is like seeing her own life through
the eyes of a stranger.

She looks for the image, tries to find the right thread in the enormous weave. Suddenly, she has the flashlight in her hand, hears the creaking floor under her feet. She picks up a smell of paper and old leather, then of something burning and also an odd, stinging smell. Then, in the light of the flashlight, she sees a small table and an old, worn leather armchair. On the table is a dark red, round wooden box.

Minoo pulls the smoke back and opens her eyes. The others are looking at her tensely.

'It was when we broke into Adriana's house,' she says, pointing at the table. 'That image was carved into a box in the locked room.'

'Wow,' Vanessa says. 'That break-in was *two years* ago. What if you could do that in exams?'

'Why does Adriana have it?' Anna-Karin asks.

'Because she is an Ehrenskiöld,' Nicolaus says grimly. 'Everything begins and ends with that family. Or, so it would seem. I followed the clues all across Europe, Asia and North Africa. I wasted an entire month in Liechtenstein. All that time, the skull was in the south of Sweden in an Ehrenskiöld-owned stately home in Skåne.' He looks at the images on the table.

'Now I'm beginning to see how it all fits together. When the stolen items disappeared, the Council kept searching for them for hundreds of years. One of my friends from my years of study was looking for them, too. I didn't know that he had located them, but he must have. Because he was the one who brought the silver cross to Engelsfors. He was the judge I told you about, the man who said Matilda would live if only she confessed. Baron Henrik Ehrenskiöld.'

Henrik Ehrenskiöld. The same Henrik Ehrenskiöld whose portrait Minoo had seen in the manor house? Was the man with kind eyes also the man who betrayed Nicolaus?

'If Adriana has the box, it should be easy to get hold of.'

Linnéa looks at Minoo. 'Adriana lives in the manor house and you're meant to be there every day. You can lift the box during lunch break.'

'I can't steal the box,' Minoo says.

One of Linnéa's eyebrows is raised. 'Think of it as "borrow" if that makes you feel better.'

'You need only find out where it is and investigate it a little more,' Nicolaus tells her. 'We can start with that.'

Minoo stares at him. *We*? In this situation there's no *we*. She has to do it. Alone. By now she's furious. Tears of anger sting her eyes. She blinks them away, telling herself that she mustn't come across as emotional when her aim is to be perfectly rational.

'This discussion is pointless,' she says. 'It doesn't matter what we tell or don't tell Walter. Matilda knows that Nicolaus has found the skull. It follows that the guardians will know, too. And that they'll tell Walter.'

'The guardians don't know that we've got these objects,' Nicolaus replies. 'I told Matilda that I didn't find them – for safety's sake, in case my suspicions about her should turn out to be true.'

'But she'll surely know that you're lying!' Minoo says.

'She might,' Linnéa says. 'But remember what she has told us more than once. That the guardians do not know everything, nor do they see everything.'

Her voice and manner are so self-congratulatory that Minoo has to clench her jaws not to scream at her.

'As far as I could interpret her reaction, I think she believed me,' Nicolaus says. 'She seemed very disappointed.'

'Then we have the upper hand, for once,' Linnéa asserts. 'We know something the guardians don't.'

Minoo feels trapped, as if the others are pushing the walls in on her.

'Well, I suppose I shall have to investigate this. To keep you all happy.' As she speaks, she hears just how martyred she sounds. She's disgusted at her tone, but she hopes the others feel bad now.

'But it's a waste of time,' she continues. 'The Council's circle needs these objects to close the portal. We must hand them over, sooner or later.'

'I don't think so,' Linnéa says.

'You don't even know what to do to close it!' Minoo tells her. 'You haven't a clue how to use these things!'

'I guess you'd better get the info from inside Walter's head, then.'

Minoo is fed up. She wishes Linnéa would read her mind so she could see just how fed up Minoo is right now.

'No need to decide that yet,' Nicolaus says. 'We'll postpone any further decisions until we know more about that box.'

Minoo can't decide if she's angrier with herself or the others. All she knows is that she can't stay here. If she does she'll explode with fury and self-pity.

'I have to go.' She gets up.

'Would you like me to come?' Anna-Karin asks. She starts to get up too.

'No, I'm fine.' Minoo tries to sound calm.

She feels Linnéa's eyes scrutinizing her and knows she sees straight through her.

'Minoo, I do realize that you are in a difficult situation,' Nicolaus says. 'You are very strong to take this on.'

'It seems I don't have much of a choice,' Minoo says, and looks at Linnéa. 'I'm clearly outvoted.'

'Stop feeling so fucking sorry for yourself,' Linnéa snaps.

Minoo grabs her backpack and leaves without a word, even though she knows her behavior confirms what Linnéa has said.

She has reached the next block when she hears Anna-Karin call her name. Reluctantly, Minoo slows down and waits.

Part Three

'Minoo, please don't feel like we're picking on you,' Anna-Karin says. 'You know how Linnéa—'

'Why didn't you support me then?'

Anna-Karin looks shocked.

'I'm sorry . . .'

Minoo feels awful, and now her anger has nowhere to go. She has to swallow it instead. It tastes bitter.

CHAPTER 54

Vanessa waits on the pavement outside Nicolaus's apartment building and watches Linnéa light her cigarette.

Vanessa hates the side of Linnéa that has been on display just now, in Nicolaus's apartment. She truly hates it when Linnéa uses words as if they're hand grenades. She can cause maximum damage in a minimum amount of time. Her words wound and crush, and cause more pain than most because there's always some truth in what she says. Linnéa has a sharp eye for other people's weaknesses. So she draws attention to what they would most like to hide. Reveals what they had hoped was concealed.

'What the fuck were you trying to do in there?' Vanessa asks.

Without saying a word, Linnéa starts walking toward Storvall Square. For a moment, Vanessa can't move at all, her fury is so strong it paralyzes her. Then she takes off and runs until she is at Linnéa's side.

'So you're just going to leave?'

'I thought you were coming. And here you are, aren't you?'

Vanessa takes a deep breath and tries to calm down enough not to explode on the spot, but her anger is too strong.

'Did you have to treat Minoo like that?'

'She's wrong!' Linnéa says. 'Or do you think she's right?'

'I don't give a shit who's right or wrong! Not now. What I want to know is, did you have to be such a bitch to her?'

'I wasn't a bitch – just told her the truth as I see it.'

'That's more or less exactly what Ida used to say when she was at her worst.'

Linnéa stares into the distance in silence for a few seconds.

'All right,' she says. 'Next time I'll shut up. If Minoo is so keen to become the Council's new pet, I won't try to stop her.'

'Just as well, because after this she'll love Walter more than ever!'

'She's free to fucking marry him if that's what she wants.'

'You're behaving like a spoiled baby,' Vanessa tells her.

'I see. So that's why you told me off in front of everyone?'

'What are you talking about?'

'Oh, Linnéa, do stop saying wicked things to Nicolaus. Now we must all be nice because he's *soo* kind and has brought us things to play with,' Linnéa says in a squeaky voice.

'Oh, wow, you're really being mature now,' Vanessa says. 'Fuck's sake . . . how can you stand yourself?'

Linnéa stops at the edge of the square. Her face is an ice-cold mask.

'Maybe we had better call this the end, then,' she says in a voice that is completely empty of feeling.

Vanessa feels a horrible, sinking sensation.

'You can't just say things like that unless you mean it.'

Linnéa opens her mouth to reply just as a couple comes around the corner.

Shit, she thinks.

The first thing Vanessa notices is that the woman is pregnant. And clearly she wants people to notice it. She wears a tight black top in a stretchy material, so nobody can miss her belly swelling out from her slender body. It looks as if she's swallowed the entire planet.

Wille walks by her side. The woman is Elin, his new, very pregnant girlfriend.

Wille has a crew-cut and Vanessa can't help noticing that he looks very fit.

They stop and look at Vanessa and Linnéa.

'Hi there,' Wille says.

Vanessa wonders if they have heard her and Linnéa fight.

She hopes desperately that they haven't. She wants Wille to think they are happy together. Really fucking happy. Why couldn't he see them when they were making out and as happy as fucking larks?

Elin holds out her hand and introduces herself. Her nails gleam, her cuticles are perfect.

'Good to meet you.' Her voice is as soft and cool as her handshake, as if Vanessa and Linnéa were nothing more than a couple of customers in the bank where she works.

'Congratulations,' Vanessa says to both of them. 'I didn't know that you were expecting a baby. That's great.'

'Yes . . . right. Thanks.' Wille looks alarmed.

Elin places her hand on her huge belly. Vanessa has to force herself not to stare at it.

Wille's child is in there.

The idea is so sick that Vanessa can hardly stop herself from laughing. She has a vision of a baby Wille – like he looks now, but in mini-format and sucking his thumb.

'When is it due?' Vanessa asks, wondering at the same time why she keeps conversing with these people.

'At the beginning of November,' Elin replies with her professional smile.

Vanessa notes that Elin doesn't seem bothered in the slightest about standing on a street corner and chatting with two of Wille's exes. Most likely she doesn't regard either of them as real girlfriends. In her mind, Vanessa and Linnéa belong to another phase in Wille's life – just a couple of girls he partied with until he was ready to turn serious and settle down.

Due in November. The baby must have been conceived . . . when? In February? Elin will have known that she was pregnant by Easter. At Easter in the playground. Wille had wanted to know if Vanessa would take him back if he left Elin. Did he know then that Elin was expecting his baby? Could even Wille be such a swine?

Part Three

'How are you two getting along?' Wille asks, glancing at Vanessa and Linnéa while he puts his arm around Elin.

His two former girlfriends. And his new one.

Vanessa has to swallow another laugh. All three of them know what he looks like naked. All three have slept with him. She wonders if he, too, is thinking along these lines. And is he trying to imagine her and Linnéa together?

'We're fine,' Linnéa says briskly.

Wille looks nervously at her.

'Yes, Lucky said that . . . you're an item?'

Vanessa nods, but the bad feeling inside her has returned, because right now it's hard to feel that she and Linnéa belong together.

Come to think of it, they haven't felt this far apart since that terrible summer last year.

'Great,' Wille says.

'It is,' Linnéa says. 'One grows up. Fortunately.'

Wille looks even more nervous now. Elin strokes her belly slowly.

'I had better go home and rest now.' She looks at Wille.

'Of course, darling,' Wille says.

Vanessa gets the impression he will do whatever Elin tells him to. He says an awkward goodbye while Elin waves and smiles politely before taking his arm. Looking at her from behind, one would never guess that she was pregnant.

Vanessa searches her mind. Is there any little hint of jealousy or resentment of Wille and his Elin? She can't find anything. Only relief that she isn't in Elin's place.

She wants to go home with Linnéa and be close to her again. They have too many important things to talk about to waste their time together on stupid fights. And what they have together is too wonderful to ruin. She turns to Linnéa to tell her this.

'I'm going home now,' Linnéa says.

'I'll come with you.'

'I'm tired. I'd rather go to sleep.'

Vanessa looks at her. If Linnéa leaves now, something between them might be ruined forever.

'We must talk,' Vanessa persists.

'Don't you think we've done enough of that for one day?' Linnéa sneers.

That sinking feeling. Sinking all the way down into her shoes.

'Yes,' Vanessa says. 'I guess we have.'

It is only when Linnéa has disappeared out of sight that Vanessa is struck by a new thought.

Evelina and Michelle are bound to have known all along about Wille and the baby. And neither of them has said a word.

CHAPTER 55

Minoo curls up in her corner of the sofa and pulls the blanket up to her chin. She would prefer to pull it over her head. By now, she is about to implode.

All the way back from Nicolaus's apartment, she longed to get home. Longed for a quiet, ordinary evening, thinking about something that had nothing to do with Walter, or the guardians, or dropping out of school, or Nicolaus, Linnéa and the box she now has to find.

You should be careful what you wish for.

All her blood seems to have rushed to her ears and made them hypersensitive to the slightest sound. They pick up every groan, every little moist slurp, with crystalline precision. She fixes her eyes on the lowermost left-hand corner of the TV screen. All she sees are fluttering close-ups of assorted nakedness.

Aren't they ever going to finish? How long can people actually keep at it for?

The film evening has turned out to be the perfect end to the day. When she wakes tomorrow morning, her face will be a mass of stress pimples. She can feel them rising now, like bubbles popping up to the surface of boiling water.

Mom sits at the other end of the sofa. She is completely silent. Anna-Karin hasn't moved at all in the armchair since this apparently never-ending sex scene started. The tea that Minoo rushed away to make when the previous never-ending sex scene began is cooling in their cups.

She asks herself if it's silly of her to feel so bothered. Does watching this sort of thing become less embarrassing after one has had sex oneself? Less dramatic, somehow? But then again, sex never seems to be *not* dramatic. Certainly not for the couple in this film, that's for sure. They get excited by throwing china at each other.

A sad, tinkling tune from a piano and the screen goes black. Then, at last, the credits start to roll.

'Sometimes I simply don't understand the critics,' Mom says. 'What do you think? Wasn't it unbelievably banal?'

'I'm just going to get some water,' Anna-Karin mumbles. She disappears quickly to the kitchen.

Minoo stays where she is while Mom zaps between the channels, then stops for a news item about the phenomenon in the sky over Engelsfors. They watch a clip that someone has filmed with a cell phone, and listen to a woman talk excitedly to a child in broad local dialect. The reporter is speaking vaguely about the remains of an ash cloud after a volcanic eruption.

'This is so strange, don't you think?' Mom's eyes are glued to the screen.

'I suppose,' Minoo says. 'But what else could it be?'

'No idea. But it's quite spooky, whatever it is.'

A doctor at the hospital in Engelsfors is the next to be interviewed. She explains that several children and young people have suffered lasting eye damage after looking directly at the sun during the dark phase.

The report finishes. The news anchor carries on with the next item, unaware that she has just discussed a portent that heralds the end of the world.

'You're sure, aren't you, that you didn't look at the sun?' Mom asks. 'The adverse effects don't necessarily show until hours later.'

'Not to worry,' Minoo replies. 'I didn't look at all.'

She hears Anna-Karin stacking the dishwasher.

'How was your first day of senior year, Minoo?'

'Fine,' Minoo says. She starts plaiting fringes on the plaid.

'Fine? Can't you tell me a little more than that?'

Minoo looks up from the plaid and regrets it immediately. Her mom is looking at her with an expression that always makes her nervous whenever there's something she'd rather not talk about. But she has to say something. Mom returns to Stockholm tomorrow.

'How are things, Minoo?'

Minoo realizes just how much she will miss going to school. She will miss doing homework. And doing tests. She will even miss her class, even though Anna-Karin is the only person she really likes. She will miss everything that makes her feel like an ordinary teenager.

From now on, until the portal is closed, her life will be focused on one thing only.

'You must take care,' Mom says. 'I worry about you. You demand so much of yourself. I know, I was just the same. And so was your dad. I know that senior year is tough – you're chasing exam results all the time – but everything will be all right. You'll find your way. I know you will.'

Minoo undoes the plait. And starts again.

'*Khayesh mikhonam, be man negah kon,*' Mom says, and Minoo looks up unwillingly. 'Would you like it if I moved back here? At least until you've left school? Would life feel easier if I did?'

'I want to have a sabbatical year,' Minoo tells her.

She didn't realize she would say this until she hears her own voice utter the words.

'I mean, I am *going to* take a year out.'

Mom looks shocked, but only for a moment. She has clearly realized that Minoo is serious.

She pulls herself together. 'Has something happened?'

'I feel I must,' Minoo says. 'I've been so stressed for such a long time . . .'

She looks down at her lap while she tries to remember all the warning signs that Mom has talked about in the past when she has been worried about Minoo.

'It's so hard for me to concentrate on anything and I feel a sort of pressure on my chest as soon as I think about school. It seems as if I never have enough time for everything. I feel like I'm treading water, just managing to stay afloat.'

'This is exactly what has been worrying me, Minoo. But taking an entire year off seems a bit drastic. Perhaps we can work something out together to ease the burden of work.'

Mom is in 'doctor mode' now.

'But it's not just that,' Minoo says, hesitating before using her most effective weapon. 'Rebecka and Ida. And everything that's happened to Anna-Karin and Linnéa . . .'

She can't go on. She has never before manipulated her mother so deliberately. She feels so guilty her skin crawls.

'Oh, my darling.' Mom puts her arm around Minoo and pulls her close.

'I'll talk with your dad tonight,' she says. 'And then all three of us can discuss this tomorrow when he is back. We'll sort it out, Minoo.'

The doorbell interrupts them. Minoo hears Anna-Karin open the door, and then Rickard's voice.

The door closes, and Anna-Karin comes back into the living room.

'Rickard and Gustaf are here,' she says. 'They are waiting in the garden.'

CHAPTER 56

Moths are fluttering around the lamps by the garden door. Gustaf and Rickard have settled down on chairs. Minoo hasn't seen either of them for months. And she hardly dares to look at Gustaf now. Instead, she concentrates on not putting her foot on any of the slugs on the lawn.

'Hi, Minoo,' Gustaf and Rickard say in unison.

'Hello,' Minoo says, checking that no slugs have got into the hammock before she sits down on it with Anna-Karin.

She glances at Gustaf. Just quickly, but long enough for her to take in every detail. Even in this dim light, she notes that his hair is bleached by the sun. He is wearing a gray college sweatshirt and his military green jacket.

'We want to help you,' he says. 'I should have moved to Uppsala this week but I've decided to stay in Engelsfors.'

He appears to be sincere and full of determination. Minoo imagines that young, idealistic soldiers look like this when they join up, before they realize what war entails.

But she is being unfair, of course. Gustaf has already suffered in the war. More than once.

'Me too,' Rickard adds. 'How can we just leave this place when we know what's about to happen here?'

He looks as determined as Gustaf.

A wave of panic washes through Minoo. This could end in catastrophe. It could end in death. She can't have it on her conscience.

'You mustn't stay here,' she says.

'It's not like it matters where we are when the apocalypse

comes,' Rickard says. He swats at a mosquito that has landed on his neck.

'There won't be an apocalypse.' Minoo is trying hard to sound authoritative. 'We will stop it. It's our job. But so much will happen here before we do. Engelsfors will be dangerous.'

'So much more reason for us to stay, then,' Rickard says. 'There must be *something* we can do.'

Minoo takes a deep breath. She must make them understand. Even if it means ditching her last chance to keep Gustaf as a friend.

'Do you really want to help?'

'Yes,' Gustaf says, and Rickard nods.

'In that case, please leave. Because we will do a much better job if we don't have to worry about you running around playing at being superheroes.'

'Minoo . . .' Anna-Karin interjects.

Minoo ignores her.

'Don't you see, you have nothing to offer in these battles? Not against the demons and not against the Council either. Being the best soccer players in Engelsfors doesn't help: this is about *magic*. You are not witches – you haven't a hope. If you insist on staying, you will cause more harm than good.'

She stops speaking.

Gustaf and Rickard stare at her. Anna-Karin's hair is hiding her face. Minoo's heart is hammering hard in her chest.

'It doesn't matter what you say. You don't decide this,' Rickard says. He gets up. 'Let's go, Gustaf.'

'I'll stay for a while,' Gustaf says.

Rickard wanders off through the garden. Anna-Karin mumbles something about going to bed and walks away.

Minoo can't bear to look at Gustaf again. She feels the hammock swing when he sits down next to her.

Once, he had spoken of the energy between two people who love each other. And now, Minoo can feel an energy field between them. She isn't sure if it's just her who feels it, but it is so strong it is difficult to think of anything else.

'I understand what you're trying to do,' he tells her. 'But it won't work. Your only hope of making me leave town is to take my memories away again.'

'I don't want to do that,' Minoo says. 'Do you want me to?'

'No, I don't. I have thought about it, I really have. But knowing the truth is better.'

He sits in silence for a while and swings the hammock lightly back and forth.

'I'm sorry I haven't handled all this very well,' he says at last.

'You don't have to apologize.'

'Maybe not, but I want to do it anyway,' Gustaf goes on. 'I shouldn't have stayed away from you for so long. Everything feels better now, just because I can see you.'

'I feel the same,' Minoo says, and feels blood rushing to her face.

Another silence.

'I understand so much more now,' Gustaf says. 'Things keep falling into place. Once, when I was with Rebecka at her house, a candle seemed to light itself. Of course, I thought it was my imagination.'

'She told me,' Minoo says. 'But she hoped you hadn't noticed.'

'I noticed, but didn't grasp what was going on. I bought the easy explanation. As I kept doing, over and over again.'

Minoo looks at him.

'I believed that she had taken her own life,' he tells her. 'I just believed it without questioning. I never asked if anyone might have killed her.'

Gustaf sighs deeply.

'When you watch a film, you want to be like the hero. You like to think that you would be the guy that demands answers, sees the truth when no one else does . . . and then you find out that you're not him at all.'

'But you are him. Only, you expect too much of yourself.'

'And you don't?'

Minoo laughs a little. Gustaf smiles.

'It's so good that we can talk about all this,' he says. 'It's almost like last winter . . . except, I wasn't talking to you, but to Ida. Christ, this is all so weird.'

'I know,' Minoo agrees.

When she looks at him, the energy between them is so strong. She can't be the only one to sense it.

'Minoo, what happened to the sun today?'

She tells him. More and more. All about the other circle and about Nicolaus and her conflict with Linnéa. It is wonderful to tell someone. Correction, it's wonderful to tell Gustaf. There is something special about the way he listens.

'You guys have to make such difficult decisions all the time,' he says. 'I don't understand why you don't crack up under the strain.'

'I'm not sure that we won't,' Minoo says. 'It feels as if everything is falling apart.'

Today, Linnéa was so much like the person she had been in the first year at high school, when Minoo first got to know her. Hard. Unrepentant. Quick to judge and to wound. Now, her tactics are doubly painful because Minoo had thought they had moved on and become friends.

'Today, when the sun disappeared, I woke up to what you told me,' Gustaf says. 'I realized that it is *happening*. It made me feel utterly helpless, until I thought that perhaps I could do something, even if it's something small.'

'I understand.'

And she does now. She has no right to try to make him go. Besides, she is past being selfless. She wants him to be here, with her.

'Another thing I understood today is that I've wasted far too much time,' he continues. His voice trembles a little.

Their eyes meet and something vital inside her seems to contract.

394

'The world might collapse around us tomorrow,' he says. 'Every day might be our last.'

She knows exactly what he means.

Suddenly, the moment has come when it might happen. Minoo feels sure that they both sense it.

And then it is gone again.

Gustaf puts his hand on hers and presses it lightly.

'Let's be in touch soon, all right?'

'Yes, let's,' she replies.

The hammock rocks when he gets up.

Her eyes follow him as he walks through the garden. Out in the street, he stops under a streetlight and raises his hand. She waves back and stays looking after him as he disappears into the darkness.

* * *

Anna-Karin sits on the bed in her room with Peppar on her lap. Minoo and Gustaf have stopped talking in the garden.

Anna-Karin hasn't heard what they've said, but she doesn't need to. She feels stupid that she hasn't realized before what they feel for each other. Tonight, when she saw them together, it was impossible not to notice.

She feels awful for being envious.

If the world ends tomorrow, she will never have experienced what Gustaf and Minoo or Vanessa and Linnéa have. Though it's also true that she can't imagine finding someone, even if the world doesn't end.

When she hears Minoo climb the stairs, she gets up. Peppar leaps onto the floor, meows and follows her, waving his tail, as she walks to Minoo's room.

Minoo is sitting on her bed with her legs crossed, typing on her cell phone.

'Is Gustaf staying in town?' Anna-Karin asks.

'Yes, he is.'

Anna-Karin is relieved. She had been so happy that Rickard

and Gustaf wanted to help them, even though they didn't have to.

Minoo's phone beeps as her text is sent.

'I texted Vanessa to let her know,' she says. 'She can tell Linnéa.'

Minoo is still angry, Anna-Karin thinks, her stomach twisting.

'I know I was hard on Gustaf and Rickard,' Minoo says as she puts the cell phone away. 'But I was worried about them.'

'I understood that,' Anna-Karin tells her. She did, but she had also been scared by Minoo's coldness. And how convincing she was. Minoo is so strong, but she doesn't seem to realize it herself. She doesn't understand the effect she has on people around her. Linnéa is just the same. Perhaps that's why they clash so much.

'How was school today?' Minoo asks.

'A lot of stuff happened – with the eclipse and all.'

Anna-Karin's stomach twists again when she thinks of what it will be like every day from now on. She has to get used to being alone again.

'I heard you telling your mom that you want to take a year out,' she adds.

'That's right,' Minoo says.

Anna-Karin wants them to have a talk about it. And to talk about Nicolaus and Linnéa and the new circle, and about the tension between Linnéa and Vanessa. This morning, they could have talked about any or all of these things. Can they really have grown so distant in just a day?

'I'd better go to bed now,' Minoo says.

'Me too,' Anna-Karin replies. 'Good night.'

* * *

Linnéa sits on her haunches, leaning back against the warm, vibrating metal cover of the tumble-drier. She stares at the window in the washing machine. A few tops belonging to

Vanessa are churning around in the foam. Round, round, round.

Rather like Linnéa feels inside.

Vanessa still hasn't been in touch. And why should she be?

She had looked so desperately fucking hurt that Linnéa's whole body twitches with guilt when she thinks about it. How could she do that to Vanessa? Just leave without another word? And especially just after they'd met Wille and Elin?

How could I say that I wanted to end what we had together? Linnéa thinks.

But she knows why. She is so terrified of losing Vanessa that it would be a perverse kind of relief if she did. Then she could stop fearing it.

Fuck's sake . . . how can you stand yourself?

Linnéa has no answer. She has no idea how she will stand being herself all her life. It is a life sentence. And Vanessa deserves better than being a fellow prisoner.

Linnéa forces herself upright, grabs the heavy bag full of clean laundry and walks into the basement hallway outside the block's communal laundry room. The timed light has gone out and she has to press the red switch several times before the light comes on again. The sudden sound of water rushing along the pipework in the ceiling makes her jump and she realizes how tense she is. Her grip on the bag's handles tightens as she starts walking, her eyes fixed on the gray-painted metal door at the end of the passage. With every step, the bag bounces against her leg. She has to keep reminding herself that the noises she hears are not made by someone following her.

She pushes the handle down with her elbow and shoves the door open. Outside is the brightly lit basement level in the stairwell. The elevator is there, and she presses the button for the eighth floor. The elevator shakes a little before it starts its slow upward journey.

Her thoughts turn to the events of the day.

The Key

The so-called eclipse. Nicolaus. The skull. And the fight with Minoo.

It makes her angry again just thinking about it. Angry and frustrated. What disappointed her most of all was that Minoo wanted to take the objects straight to Walter. That she didn't even want to consider giving the Chosen Ones a chance to find an alternative.

The empty landings come and go outside the elevator's window.

But, when all is said and done, perhaps it's all her own fault? After all, she is the common denominator in today's arguments.

The elevator stops with a jerk and Linnéa steps out onto the landing and is just about to unlock the door to her apartment. But stops. Goes stiff. Suddenly, she is terrified that Erik and Robin are inside, waiting for her. With baseball bats. She can almost hear Erik in her head.

You fucking cunt.

Linnéa has to force herself to turn the key in the lock and open the door. She dumps the laundry bag in the hall and walks about the apartment. Even checks the wardrobe. No one. Of course.

She locks the door, opens a living-room window and lights a cigarette. Tries not to think about having to go back down to the laundry room.

She drags on her cigarette and feels anxiety rushing through her body, wondering if she will ever stop longing to smoke joints or get drunk at moments like this. She hates the way her cravings always surface, like reflex responses. It would be such a relief to not have to think, just for a while. To silence her mind, stop the thoughts that keep chasing each other, like a dog chasing its own tail. Round and round and round.

Linnéa leaves the window open and carries the ashtray back to the sofa. She sits down and opens the laptop Viktor gave her and puts on a playlist. She hears guitars. Then Hizumi of d'Espairs Ray starts to sing. She has to skip the song immediately. The memory of when she and Elias tried to learn the text by heart is still too strong. It is his birthday tomorrow. He would have been eighteen. Something else she must not think about.

She checks on her profiles, opens her messages. Nothing from Vanessa. And Vanessa is nowhere online.

Linnéa's fingers hover above the keyboard.

She knows she shouldn't. Feeling bad, then doing something that makes her feel even worse is dangerous.

It is self-destructive, she thinks as she opens up the web page.

INNOCENT!

The photo shows Erik Forslund seated on a bench in the open-air museum. His eyes, which look straight into the camera lens, are calm and frank. This is a guy you can trust.

FREE ERIK FORSLUND!

A total of 627 people have liked this group.

Julia started the group when Erik was arrested and it has grown steadily. Her version of the story seems to have struck a chord. According to her, Erik, Robin and Kevin were in the Positive Engelsfors Center all night. Just like Helena Malmgren said when she provided their alibi. But, since then, Robin and Kevin have come up with their sick story, probably constructed together with Linnéa, and their aim is to harm Erik.

For a lot of people it seems easier to believe this tale than that a really nice guy like Erik would ever do anything so awful.

A middle-aged lady who lives in Riddarhyttan has written the latest message on the wall only a couple of hours ago.

ERIK, WE TRUST YOU! NEVER STOP THE GOOD FIGHT. HUGS FOR STRENGTH!

The comment just before comes from a teammate on Erik and Robin's hockey team.

GODAWFUL, THIS WHOLE STORY. L IS A MENTAL CASE OBVS BUT

WHERE THE FUCK ARE R AND K COMING FROM?!

Julia writes:

THANK YOU FOR YOUR SUPPORT! <3

Linnéa clicks on the album.

That photo is back again. Julia has taken it from Evelina's blog. They've complained more than once, but it still keeps turning up.

Linnéa, Vanessa and Michelle together on Olsson's Hill after the final day assembly. Linnéa is well aware of what onlookers will make of her. They will see the cold smile on the heavily made-up face of a girl with jet-black hair and a pentagram pendant on a chain around her neck. There couldn't be a bigger contrast to the wholesome-looking Erik.

The caption nails the message to the wall.

HERE THEY ARE CELEBRATING THE ARREST OF AN INNOCENT PERSON

Hanna A's comment – WISH THERE WAS A *DISLIKE* BUTTON – has had lots of thumbs-up.

Linnéa clicks along. New photos of Erik, and of him and Julia. And there is a picture of Erik's lawyer. He is a well-known Stockholm jurist who has won several high-profile cases.

Linnéa forces herself to leave the site.

Her heart is beating very fast.

Patricia hasn't put it into so many words but she clearly thinks that Erik will be convicted. Linnéa's lawyer, a man called Ludvig, is also optimistic. He has told her that the prosecutor, Hans-Peter Ramström, is a real 'pit bull' and pointed out that both the judge and the senior magistrate don't come from Engelsfors. In other words, they will have no idea about who Erik Forslund is, or what is supposed to be special about the Forslund family. All they will see is an arrogant young man clinging to an unsubstantiated alibi.

But, despite their encouragement, Linnéa can't bring herself to believe that she will win. And now she can't even comfort herself by thinking that, if things go badly for her, Anna-Karin will control the minds of the magistrates.

Panic stings and itches everywhere. It would be so good not to feel it. Just for a brief while.

There's a ping and at first she doesn't understand why. Then she notices that Vanessa has logged on. Linnéa shuts her laptop.

She gets up, piles the freshly washed clothes on the sofa and takes the elevator back to the laundry room, with panic eating into her mind.

CHAPTER 57

The birdlike twittering of Anna-Karin's cell phone wakes her up. She turns off the alarm and forces herself out of bed. If she doesn't get up straightaway, she will just go back to sleep. She has slept badly, slipping in and out of the fox's consciousness. He is very close now to what he has been looking for in the forest.

He wants Anna-Karin to come.

At some point in the small hours of the morning, she made up her mind. She will play truant and go into the forest to join her fox.

The door to Minoo's bedroom is open and her bed is made. When Anna-Karin comes down into the kitchen, Farnaz is there alone. She sits at the kitchen table, leafing through a medical journal. The smell of freshly made coffee fills the air.

'Where is Minoo?' Anna-Karin asks.

'She texted me to say she's off on a long walk,' Farnaz replies. 'She left before I woke up.'

Anna-Karin nods and wonders how Minoo feels after everything that happened yesterday. What must it be like having to face whatever awaits her in the manor house?

She makes herself a mug of tea, then a bowl of cereal, and sits down. Farnaz being there makes her nervous. She tries to eat as discreetly as possible. Even so, she seems to produce lots of revolting slurps and gurgles.

'Anna-Karin,' Farnaz looks up from her magazine. 'Please say if you'd rather not talk about all this but . . . I understand that it's a tricky situation for you, especially since you live here with us. You are Minoo's friend and I am her mother. I don't want you to feel pressured.'

Anna-Karin already feels pressured. But she nods in vague agreement.

'This idea of Minoo's – about taking a sabbatical year – came on so suddenly. Do you know if she has been thinking on those lines for a long time?'

'Quite a while, I think,' Anna-Karin tells her.

'Why hasn't she said anything?'

'Perhaps she was worried about how you guys would react.'

Farnaz looks even more deeply concerned, and Anna-Karin realizes that she has just made matters worse.

'But you mustn't worry,' she says quickly. 'Taking a year out could make all the difference for her. Give her time to process stuff. So much has happened over the last couple of years.'

Farnaz looks thoughtful.

'I can't help feeling that I'm to blame,' she sighs. 'If I had come home more often, I would surely have picked up the warning signs and made her talk about this much sooner. Minoo always behaves in such a grown-up way – one tends to be fooled by it. Even as her mother, I am . . . Please forgive me, I really shouldn't talk to you about these things. But the news came as quite a shock . . .'

Her cell phone rings and she replies in Farsi.

Anna-Karin gets up quickly and rinses her plate under the tap. She suddenly feels so utterly lonely She longs intensely for someone to talk to, someone who listens. And then she realizes that there is someone she can turn to.

Anna-Karin takes the key from her pocket and is about to insert it in the lock when she stops herself and rings the doorbell instead. She listens intently and hears footsteps on the other side of the door. The safety chain is unhooked. She feels enormously relieved. Only now does she realize just how much she had dreaded that he might disappear again.

Nicolaus opens the door wide and smiles at her. It still feels odd to see him look so neat and clean. His new style suits him, but Anna-Karin misses the old Nicolaus a little.

'Good morning.'

'Am I disturbing you?'

'Not at all. Come right in.'

In the hall, Anna-Karin takes her shoes off, puts her back-pack down and opens it to produce the envelope she has brought with her. She hands it to Nicolaus.

'This is what's left of the money you gave us. I thought you might need it. In your letter you wrote that you had paid a year's rent for the apartment and, well . . . that was about a year ago now.'

'Thank you, Anna-Karin.'

Nicolaus walks ahead of her into the living room. The skull is still on the table by the sofa but the black sand is gone. Anna-Karin wonders where it went. Has he managed to put it back inside those tiny cylinders?

'What would you like? A cup of tea?'

'Yes, please.'

Anna-Karin follows him into the kitchen. He pours two mugs of tea and they sit down at the kitchen table.

'I want you to know how sorry I was to learn what happened to your mother,' he says.

Anna-Karin stares into her mug. She sits quite still but, inside, she has withdrawn to a faraway place.

'Thank you,' she replies mechanically.

'Is it all right living in Minoo's home?'

Anna-Karin isn't sure what to say. She is grateful, of course. Minoo and her parents have been very generous – it's more than she can ever repay. She likes them, but she doesn't feel at home there. She doesn't feel at home anywhere.

'Absolutely,' she says.

'I have thought about you often,' Nicolaus tells her. 'Of all of you, naturally. But I was especially upset about leaving you at a time when you had to endure so much. Your grandfather was ill, your home up for sale. Had I known that the Council came here to take you to court, I don't know that I—'

'You had no choice,' she interrupts. 'Whether you knew or didn't, you had to go. So it doesn't matter, right?'

Her voice sounds so odd and strained. She smiles to make him understand that she didn't mean to sound angry. She isn't angry. Not in the slightest.

'That is indeed true. But, hearing the whole story yesterday grieved me deeply. I understand that it must have been—'

She interrupts again.

'No, I don't think you'll ever understand that.'

Nicolaus's eyes meet hers. In the weak sunlight, his eyes are icy blue.

'How do you feel? Truly?' he asks.

'Do you care?'

It sounds harsh and hurtful, and she is surprised at how pleasing that is.

'Of course I do, Anna-Karin. I do care.'

'I ask, because it hasn't seemed so to me. I accept that you had to leave, but you might have phoned. Or sent an email. Or sent a message by effing pigeon post or whatever you used back in your days.'

This isn't like her at all. More like Linnéa. Or Ida.

'Matilda did not allow me to get in touch,' Nicolaus says. 'Or I would have, I promise. You were in my thoughts so very often.'

His voice reveals how hurt he is. She feels terrible about it but, at the same time, it's liberating not to have to be the kind, grateful Anna-Karin.

'You know what, my mom used to talk non-stop about how often *she* thought about me. And told me how she fought to protect me from suffering when Dad left us. But it was all talk. She never showed it. Never did anything. You are just the same. If you'd cared, you would have contacted me, whatever Matilda had said. And you would have returned much sooner.'

She is talking very quickly now so that she gets to say all the forbidden things before she has time to pull herself together and stop the flow.

'Everything is going straight to hell. What happened earlier was so bad I . . . thought it couldn't be worse. The trial and Ida's death and Linnéa almost killed . . . and Adriana . . . and just about the entire town going crazy. But at least we had each other. We were the Chosen Ones and we trusted each other. But . . . but now . . .'

She gasps for breath and stumbles on.

'Minoo is no longer with us, or she is still there but, as you can see yourself, she's slipping further and further away and I'm not at all sure that she is right to collaborate with the Council – it was only that she was told Matilda and the guardians wanted it . . . and now you, too, feel that they are not to be trusted. And Minoo fought with Linnéa yesterday; well, you know that, but it wasn't just the two of them, something strange was happening between Linnéa and Vanessa as well and I can't stand it if what they have is ruined. I don't want it to be another thing that seemed so good only to . . .'

She falls silent.

'I understand your frustration.' He looks serious. 'And I am very sorry that I have caused you pain. You're right. I should have questioned what Matilda demanded of me. But we should all have asked more questions before we acted. Asked where precisely our orders came from. Who we were actually obeying.'

Anna-Karin feels her anger draining away. She can't rage against him any longer. Instead, sadness fills her, and hopelessness.

'I wish I could help you more, Anna-Karin,' Nicolaus says. 'But I don't know how.'

She looks at him and remembers how she had thought that

if he would only return, it would make things easier. He would help them stay together.

Now, she realizes that she is the only one who can take on that heavy responsibility. And, strangely enough, knowing that makes it a little easier.

Chapter 58

The sky is gray and rain hangs in the air. Minoo has been walking through town for hours, avoiding areas where she might meet people she knows. Now, she is simply walking up and down along the canal.

When she went to sleep last night she was only thinking of Gustaf, but she woke angry after stressful dreams about Linnéa. It's as if she had been floating on rosy clouds and then been pulled into the muck below.

It is drizzling now and Minoo walks faster toward the manor house. She doesn't want to arrive covered in runny mascara and with all her concealer washed away. She is mad at herself for not bringing an umbrella.

Yes, she understands that Linnéa must feel horribly stressed about going to court and all that. But does that mean she should be forgiven for everything? Minoo was almost murdered by Max – not just once, but twice – and still she hasn't used that as an excuse for being horrible to Linnéa.

But Linnéa has had a hard life from the beginning, a small still voice says inside Minoo. You should know – you've even been inside her body and shared her life for a while.

She dismisses the voice. This need to understand Linnéa irritates her. Why should she be so sympathetic, when Linnéa doesn't seem able or willing to understand Minoo's situation for one single moment?

It's all so damn easy for her, Minoo thinks as she walks up the manor house front steps. So damn easy to see life in black and white. Linnéa isn't the one being pressured into being a double agent. She doesn't have to run all sorts of risks to snoop around for a magic box. Quite unnecessarily as well, because they'll have to hand over the skull and the cross to the Council's circle in any case.

Minoo unlocks the front door and steps inside.

At first she thinks it's a dog that's staring straight at her. She has never seen a real lynx before. The big cat looks sternly at her. Minoo realizes that it must be somebody's familiar. And that somebody wants her to follow the lynx.

So she does. To see such a wild animal indoors is strange. Anna-Karin has never taken her fox inside, and not just because foxes mark their territory with turds. It simply wouldn't feel right.

The lynx pads on soundless paws along hallways and through rooms. Minoo thinks that it is the same route that Clara followed yesterday. Finally it stops in front of a closed door and its ears point straight up. It turns to Minoo and waits until she has pushed the door handle down. Then it leaves her.

She enters the ballroom. Rain is beating against the tall windows. The garden looks like a watercolor that has started to run.

Seven chairs have been placed to form a circle. Felix is sitting on one of them with a thick, well-worn paperback open on his lap. He is wearing black slacks, a white shirt with rolled-up sleeves and a loosely tied black tie. His eyebrows are the same deep black as his hair. When he looks at her, daylight falls on his brown eyes.

'Hi, Felix,' Minoo says.

Felix just looks at her. One second passes. Then another.

'Hi,' he says in the end.

'Whose lynx is that?' she asks. She tries to smile.

'She is the *spiritus familiaris* belonging to Chairman Hjorth,' Felix informs her without returning her smile.

The parquet floor creaks loudly as Minoo walks to a chair. She feels large and clumsy. Her sense of awkwardness isn't

409

helped by the way Felix stares, as if her every step irritates him. She pulls her backpack off and sits down on a chair, leaving an empty seat between herself and Felix.

'What's that you're reading?' she asks.

Her voice sounds tinny in the huge room. It's as if she hears herself through Felix's ears. She sounds annoying.

Felix doesn't answer, only holds up the book so she can see the front cover.

'Right,' she says. It's all that comes to mind.

She has never heard of the title *Atlas Shrugged*, or of the author Ayn Rand, but she isn't going to tell him that. Felix returns his attention to the book. Minoo puts her hands under her thighs and looks out through the window. Minutes pass. She can't even breathe normally – every breath she takes is so loud.

The only other sounds are the rain and the rustling of paper when Felix turns a page. She wishes she too had brought a book. She always used to bring one to school, in case there was no one to talk to. Perhaps she should take up her old habit again.

She looks around. The room has several doors. The double doors to the garden are matched by a double door just opposite. The way Minoo came in was through a single door, which also has an opposite number at the other end of the room. The walls are painted pale yellow and the ceiling is decorated in lovely white stucco. There is no other decoration, no pictures or curtains. Only a dry potted plant in one of the windows.

The door that Minoo came in through opens. Sigrid enters. She is wearing a white blouse with blue dots and a gray pencil skirt. Low-heeled, red shoes. No glasses today. She carries a small animal in her arms. Its fur is dark. It could be some kind of mink. Or a weasel, or a stoat.

'Hi, everyone!' Sigrid smiles warmly. The parquet barely squeaks under her feet.

'Hello, Sigrid,' Minoo responds.

Felix says nothing. Sigrid sits down on the empty seat between them and crosses her legs. Her every movement is elegant and precise. Minoo guesses at a lifetime of ballet lessons.

Minoo takes a look at Sigrid's animal. It has a small area of white fur under its chin. It is asleep but its little pink nose is twitching.

'This is Henry,' Sigrid tells her.

'He is very cute,' Minoo says, though she isn't sure she thinks so. 'What is he?'

'He's a mink.'

Minoo starts trying to calculate the number of Henrys that would go into making one mink coat.

'There, Henry, did you hear that?' Sigrid coos. 'Minoo thinks you're cute.'

'Cutest little murderer in the world,' Felix says, without looking up from his book. 'For your information, minks eat birds' eggs and kill baby birds – often way more than they need to survive.'

Sigrid reaches out a hand for Felix's book, turns it over and rolls her eyes when she sees the cover.

'Not *again*?' she says. 'Seems you can't get enough of that load of fascist crap.'

Felix quickly pulls the book back. Unfazed, Sigrid glances at his wristwatch.

'Gosh, is that the time? Where is everyone?'

'Clara and Viktor are with the chairman.' Felix looks down and starts to read again. 'That other girl . . .'

'Nejla,' Sigrid reminds him.

'*Nejla*. I'd be surprised if she's left her room.'

'Maybe she would leave it more often if you were just a fraction nicer to her. Try to remember her name for a start.'

Minoo smiles and Sigrid smiles back at her.

'Felix, Viktor and I were in the same class at school,' she says. 'I think Nejla feels a little bit like an outsider. And she's only sixteen.'

Minoo notes gratefully that at least one of them is younger than her. Viktor is twenty, so presumably Sigrid and Felix are as well.

'I've tried to talk to her,' Sigrid continues. 'She says she wants to be left in peace but I think she's just shy. We should all try harder to make her feel at home.'

She turns to Felix. 'Did you know that she's going out with Sanke's kid brother?'

'Such thrilling news,' Felix responds, turning a page.

'Sanke is a rather odd guy who went to our school,' Sigrid tells Minoo. 'You must let us know if you've had enough with our private jokes and jargon and things. We didn't just go to the same school, we boarded together, and I'm sure you know how cliquey it can get.'

Minoo nods wisely, as if she shared their experiences. In fact, her ideas about boarding schools are based on Harry Potter and scandalous reports in the tabloids about bullying and worse.

'I simply can't get over this development with Clara.' Sigrid lowers her voice and has a quick look around the room. 'We knew Viktor had a sister, but always thought she went to another school. She's incredibly like him, don't you think?'

'Yes, she is.'

'It's utterly fantastic that you saved her,' Sigrid says earnestly.

Minoo tries not to look too flattered, but also not too dismissive.

'All this, you know, with the circle, it's so overwhelming,' Sigrid says. 'When Chairman Hjorth told me about it . . . I truly couldn't believe my ears at first. I thought the story about the Chosen Ones was just that. A myth. And I can't even imagine how it's been for you to live here in Engelsfors.'

'Couldn't agree more.' Felix's eyes are still glued to the book. 'After a close look at this town, one begins to think the apocalypse isn't such a bad idea after all.'

Sigrid ignores him.

'You must have had such a strange impression of the Council.' She is speaking so quietly that Minoo has to make an effort to hear her. 'They can be so stiff and narrow-minded. But Chairman Hjorth isn't like that at all, I think. He seems a good guy and really fair. Has he been fair to you?'

'Yes, he has,' Minoo replies.

'Good,' Sigrid says. 'Do tell me if something troubles you. We must stick together.'

She places her hand on Minoo's. Sigrid's nails are nicely groomed, varnished blue with white, perfectly spaced white dots.

The double doors suddenly swing open. Nejla's long dark hair swings from side to side as she stamps across the floor. Minoo picks up an amazingly loud mix of crashing, shouting and thumping from the large earphones on Nejla's head. She settles on the chair opposite Minoo. Today's T-shirt has got ENTOMBED on the chest.

They are such an odd collection of individuals. Minoo speculates on the difference between this crew and the Council members who gathered for the trial held here in the manor house. All of them, men and women, wore very proper, sober suits. Almost as if they were in uniform.

'Hi, Nejla,' Sigrid says.

Nejla pulls her headphones off and looks at Minoo.

'Can you show us something?'

'How do you mean?' Minoo asks.

'Apparently you can do, like, totally amazing stuff. Show us some of your tricks!'

'I think we had better wait for the chairman,' Sigrid says.

Nejla rolls her eyes. 'Come on,' she urges Minoo.

'Why don't you show something?' Felix suggests.

Nejla smiles and a flame suddenly bursts out from Felix's open book.

'Are you out of your mind?' he screams, throwing the book down.

The flame has turned into a small fire that scorches the pages until they are blackened with angrily glowing red edges.

'Stop it!' Sigrid says.

Nejla laughs and stares at the book. The fire goes out, the glow fades and disappears. The smell of burning hangs in the air.

Minoo has given up on Sigrid's notion that Nejla is shy.

'So mature,' Felix says as he picks up his book.

Henry has woken up in Sigrid's lap. He slips quickly up to her shoulder and drapes himself over it, while Felix carries on talking.

'The guardians made a big mistake when they picked you to . . .'

He falls silent at once when the door on the other side of the room is opened. Viktor and Clara enter, followed by Walter. Felix, Nejla and Sigrid immediately get up from their seats. Automatically, Minoo follows their example.

'Hey you guys,' Walter says with a smile. 'That is really not necessary.'

Clara sits down between Felix and Nejla, Viktor next to Minoo. He looks at her and smiles. She is glad he's here.

'What's that smell?' Walter says, and then he sees Felix's book. 'Aha!'

Walter sits down on the last free chair between Viktor and Nejla.

'I see that Nejla was anxious to get started.'

Nejla grins.

'Not much harm done, it seems.' Walter glances at what remains of the book jacket. 'Oh, that one. Definitely no harm done.'

Sigrid and Nejla laugh. Felix puts the book away under his chair and then brushes the soot from his hands.

'Before we begin today, let's agree to do away with formalities,' Walter says. 'I don't care for that kind of thing.

Call me Walter and drop the "chairman" bit. The idea is that we're doing this together.'

He pauses, and it is as if all the energy in the room is focused around him alone.

'We have less than a year,' Walter continues. 'I expect you to give your all. The fate of the world depends on our circle.'

At the end of his last sentence, his eyes are fixed on Minoo. The way he looks at her makes her feel proud. And nervous, as she thinks of all the secrets she must keep from him.

'All right,' Walter says. 'Time to get to know each other a little better. Let's start by telling each other about our powers. We'll go around each of you in turn.'

Chapter 59

'I guess you've already worked out that Nejla is our fire witch,' Walter says and smiles. 'Nejla, tell us a little more. Perhaps you can show us something?'

Minoo watches Nejla, who stands up. Her laid-back pose is gone. She looks focused. She lifts one hand with the palm upwards. There is a sharp glint of light, then they see a glowing, bright red ball of fire, the size of a ping-pong ball, floating just above her palm. It rotates and grows until it doubles in size. Nejla's eyes glitter in the light of the fire.

A narrow pillar of fire emerges from the ball and shoots straight up in the air until it reaches the ceiling, where it begins to divide soundlessly into a branching tree. Minoo watches, fascinated. It is so beautiful.

The tree contracts back into a ball. Nejla abruptly turns her palm downwards. The ball hits the floor and branches into a burning root system that snakes across the parquet. Minoo pulls her feet away when the fire comes closer to her.

Nejla makes a fist of her hand and the fire goes out at once. The parquet is unmarked. She looks at the others, breathing heavily. The pride in her eyes is unmistakable.

'Magnificent!' Walter claps. 'Thank you, Nejla. You can sit down again. Clara, please!'

Clara stands. Her expression is uneasy.

'I believe you all know already what my element is and what I can do,' she says quietly.

'Show us!' Nejla insists.

Clara disappears. Minoo senses Viktor turning rigid next

416

to her. A few seconds pass. The only sound is the rain beating against the windows.

Until Nejla suddenly screams. Clara stands behind her with her hands on Nejla's shoulders.

The whole group bursts into relieved laughter. Except Viktor. Clara shoots him an irritated look on the way back to her seat.

'And I can communicate telepathically with my brother,' she adds. 'And control the wind, at least a little. That's all. Nothing much.'

'You are too modest,' Walter says. 'Felix, the floor is yours.'

'My element is earth.' Felix gets up. 'I can . . . control earth and stone.'

He sighs and feels for something in his pocket. It is a small black stone. He holds it tightly and concentrates. When he opens his hand again, the stone has changed shape into a perfect, five-pointed star.

'Nothing special,' Felix says in a low voice.

Minoo looks intently at the stone star. What he has done is truly wonderful and, yet, in their strange world it is not very impressive – not compared to the others and their show-stoppers.

A wave of anxiety sweeps through her but she isn't sure why. She is embarrassed, and she suddenly feels so ashamed she wishes she wasn't here. She would like so much to have Clara's power.

'Thank you, Felix,' Walter says, and then turns to Sigrid. 'Your turn.'

Sigrid gets up.

'This is my familiar. His name is Henry.'

'I bet the lynx would like to munch on him for breakfast,' Nejla says.

Walter laughs; Sigrid's smile goes a little stiff. She gently lifts Henry from her shoulder and puts him down on her chair, before going to stand in the center of the circle.

'My element is metal,' she says. 'Nejla and Clara, could you please move a little apart?'

They do, and their chairs scrape noisily against the floor.

Sigrid turns to Walter with a smile, before facing the gap between the chairs. And vanishes. Suddenly, she appears standing by the doors to the garden.

'That is totally cool,' Nejla is leaning forward excitedly. 'So you can teleport?'

Sigrid dissolves into nothingness and stands in the center of the circle again.

'Sadly, no,' Sigrid admits, but looks pleased with herself. 'I can move exceptionally quickly, but only over short distances and when there's nothing in my way. I can charge certain amulets as well and shape metals up to a point. It seems I have a certain aptitude for clairvoyance, but it's not at all well developed.'

'Not yet,' Walter says. Sigrid's smile broadens.

He is looking at Minoo now. She feels quite anxious because she is so used to hiding her powers from the Council. But then she remembers what Matilda said in her dream. *You must do what is demanded of you and do it wholeheartedly.*

'Do you mind if I take this?' Walter asks.

Minoo shakes her head gratefully.

'Minoo is unique,' he says. 'She has no element, which means that she is able to control the magic of the guardians in its purest form. Up to this point, and I emphasize, only *so far*, we already know that she can break a blessing by the demons, pull the life-force from a human being and even get hold of his or her *soul*.'

It is very strange to hear oneself described so enthusiastically. Minoo can imagine how impressed she would be if she had heard Walter describe someone else in the same glowing terms.

'We have also established that she can manipulate other

418

people's memories. If this circle is to succeed in closing the portal, it will be thanks to Minoo.'

'Won't she show us something?' Nejla asks.

'You can look at Clara,' Walter says. 'A few months ago, you wouldn't have seen her.'

But nobody looks at Clara. They are all looking at Minoo with admiration. Not even Felix can hide it.

'Viktor,' Walter says, 'it will be hard for you to top that.'

'I can't.' Viktor smiles a little. 'My element is water. I can manipulate it in all its forms. I do have a familiar, perhaps not a particularly noble one . . .'

There is a light flapping of wings from the ceiling where his blue tit must have been hiding among the stucco ornaments. It lands on Viktor's hand. Henry sniffs the air with renewed interest. Minoo wonders if he wants a snack. Does it ever happen that one familiar attacks another?

'I am able to detect lying,' Viktor continues. 'Unfortunately, I can't make out what the truth is. I can communicate by thought with other water witches. And with Clara. At least in our case, the old saying about telepathy between twins is actually true.'

The blue tit flies back up to the ornamental ceiling.

'There we are. Now I'm the only one left,' Walter says. 'You have all met my familiar, the lynx. My element is wood.'

He gets up, walks to the pot plant on the windowsill and holds his hand out over it. With little crackling noises, the dry stems straighten up and grow fresh green leaves. Then, a deep red flower opens up. It is a quietly beautiful sight.

'As you can see, I'm able to influence living things in different ways. One might say that I've got green fingers.'

He grins boyishly at his poor joke and everyone laughs. Minoo, too.

'Next, I need a little help from someone. A volunteer. It's nothing dangerous. But I must warn you that it might hurt a little.'

419

The Key

He watches them smilingly while they eye each other.

'Felix, come and help me.' Walter goes to the center of the circle.

Felix stands up and eyes him hesitantly.

'Not to worry,' Walter says. 'Give me your hand.'

Felix holds out his left hand and Walter takes it between both his.

'This will be quick. Promise. Just look at me now.'

Felix looks up. Clenches his jaw.

There is a dull cracking sound. Felix screams. Minoo feels a sudden, sharp pain in her left little finger. It hurts so badly she is almost sick. She sees that the others are grimacing with pain, too. And then the sensation is gone.

Confused, she looks at Walter and Felix. Felix's eyes are brimming with tears. Walter holds up his hand. The little finger protrudes at an impossible angle. It is obviously broken. Minoo feels another wave of nausea.

Walter looks concerned and grabs hold of Felix's hand again.

'And I thought you had learned to control that,' he says. Minoo doesn't understand what he means. Felix mumbles something.

'Very well, we'll deal with that issue later.' Walter lets go of Felix's hand.

Relief spreads across Felix's face.

'Show the others,' Walter says.

Felix holds out his hand so they all can see it. He wiggles his fingers. There is no sign of any damage at all.

'How do you feel?' Walter asks.

'I don't feel anything at all,' Felix says in a fascinated tone.

'There, you see.' Walter pats Felix on his back. 'You survived.'

Felix sits down, still examining his hand.

'This is all so awesome,' Nejla says.

Walter looks around the room and smiles.

'Yes, it is, isn't it?' he agrees. 'All of you are unusual, special. We are in a magic epoch and natural witches are becoming more and more common, most of all here in Engelsfors. But I must say I can't imagine any others measuring up to our gang!'

Minoo looks at him. When he says it, it feels so reassuring. And simple. As if they really could hope to succeed.

'We're a team now,' Walter continues. 'We must be straight with each other and trust each other. Keep the channels of communication open between us all and be completely honest. I'm here for you. If you experience any problems at all, with anyone or anything, just come and talk to me.'

He meets the eyes of everyone in the circle, but looks for a little longer at Minoo.

'It's time to start our training now,' he continues. 'It will be exciting to see what we can do together!'

He walks over to the garden doors and opens them wide. The air flows in, smelling of damp, freshly cut grass. It has stopped raining.

'I think we should take the opportunity to spend time in the fresh air,' he says.

They all get up.

'Minoo, please stay here for a moment,' Walter says.

She stays, feeling the others glance at her. Walter waits until they have all gone outside. He closes the doors after them and goes to stand by one of the windows, looking out into the garden. He plunges his hands into his pockets.

Minoo waits, wondering if she should come closer to him. She crosses the creaking parquet.

Walter looks thoughtful. The pale light shows up the stubble on his cheeks.

'We need you. Have you solved the problem of how to be here every day?'

'I have talked with my mother about taking a sabbatical year from school,' she tells him, but can hardly bear sounding so ridiculous.

She can hear the scrape when Walter strokes his stubbly

cheek with his fingertips. He clearly doesn't want to say what he's about to say. Her nerves begin to tie themselves into knots.

'The guardians have informed me that Nicolaus Elingius is back in Engelsfors,' he says.

Minoo is thankful that her hair hides her ears. She thinks of everything she can't tell him: the cross, the skull, the box. Things she actually *wants* to tell him.

'I believe he has been away for a whole year,' Walter says. 'That's right, isn't it?'

'Yes, it is.'

What does Walter know? Have the guardians told him about the nature of Nicolaus's mission? Why would they *not* have told him?

'It must have been hard for you all,' Walter observes.

Minoo nods silently.

What if this is a test? He is offering her one last chance to tell him the truth before he confronts her with the fact that he knows it already and demands that she hands over the skull and the cylinders.

'I do understand that Nicolaus isn't likely to have much confidence in the Council, given his history,' Walter says. 'But, if you see him, please give him my regards.'

'I will, of course,' Minoo replies.

Walter opens the window, then turns and looks up at the ceiling.

'Viktor, don't think I haven't noticed you're eavesdropping. Come on, you! Off you fly!'

The blue tit hastily flies out through the window and finds an apple tree to perch in. Minoo had completely forgotten about it.

Walter closes the window and turns back to her.

'You can see if someone has been blessed by the demons, can't you?'

'I can see when the Blessed One uses their demonic magic,'

she tells him. 'And, when I use my own magic, I can see the actual blessing.'

Walter looks intrigued.

'What does it look like?'

'Like a black light. A black halo.'

'Can you see other forms of magic, too?'

'It has only happened once. When I healed Clara.'

'Very interesting. Why haven't you explored this further?'

'I . . . don't know,' Minoo says.

Walter looks thoughtfully at her. 'Could the answer be that the other Chosen Ones make you afraid of your own powers? That perhaps they haven't allowed you to practice?'

Minoo is not sure what to say. True, they haven't exactly encouraged her to work with her magic.

'People are always frightened of those who are different,' Walter says. 'I have my own experiences of that. The worst thing about it is that one loses heart oneself. I was just like you when I was young, Minoo. I wasted such a lot of time trying to conform. I truly regret that. Even so, I was only an exceptionally strong natural witch. You are unique. More powerful than anyone else. I understand that it might frighten you, but we must put an end to that now.'

She feels that Walter is seeing straight through her. Minoo's ears go hot again.

'I am not afraid,' she tells him. 'At least, I was in the beginning, but . . . I just feel that I can't always control it.'

'I think it sounds as if you're afraid.'

He takes a step closer to her. She has to bend her head back to look into his eyes.

'Minoo, you're special. But that is good. Don't let anyone make you believe anything different. And you must not hold anything back when you're here. There is no time for that kind of thing. Far too much is at stake.'

'I know,' she says.

'Of course you do. You're a smart girl. I tell you what, we'll make a slow start today. Begin by observing the others in the circle. Practice seeing their magic.'

Minoo nods, relieved that Walter hasn't asked her to boost her self-confidence by sucking out somebody's life-force.

'All right,' she agrees.

'Great. But don't tell the others what you're up to. It would only make them nervous. As a matter of fact, it might arouse envy. It gets that way so often among the Council's young witches. They become very competitive. There's no need to remind them about all the things you can do that they can't.'

Minoo wishes that Walter hadn't laid it on so thickly when he praised her earlier. She wonders if they hate her now. And then she realizes that this is just the kind of self-doubt that Walter has told her there is no time for now.

'I do hope you will all become friends,' Walter says. 'It's all to the good, for us and for what we're trying to do. But think carefully about what you let them know. For instance, they know about Max and Olivia, but they don't know all the details. I haven't discussed the trial of Anna-Karin with them, but I'm sure they've heard about it. There are so many from the Council here and they all gossip. Anyway, we don't speak about it because of Adriana. I have been careful about providing them with correct information. I don't want old conflicts to ruin the chances of this circle. I want a fresh start. Please don't undermine my work.'

'I promise,' she tells him.

And she hopes that she will be able to keep that promise. She is good at secrecy. All the same, she is terrified of saying the wrong thing in this world of gray areas and layer upon layer of forbidden topics.

Walter opens the double doors and steps out into the garden ahead of her.

Minoo stops at the top of the steps for a moment and watches as he says something to Sigrid, who laughs. Within a fraction of a second, she has vanished and transferred herself to the high hedge in the middle of the garden.

Minoo walks across the lawn. It is damp and slippery under the soles of her shoes.

Nejla stands near one of the apple trees and watches a ball of fire that floats in front of her at eye level. Minoo wonders what she is practicing. If it is to keep the ball burning for as long as possible, or as still as possible, or both.

Minoo releases the black smoke.

The world grows more obscure and, at the same time, more translucent. But she still can't see Nejla's magic. And she can't very well walk up to her and put her hand on Nejla's forehead.

Minoo slides just a little deeper into the world of the black smoke.

She loses track of time, doesn't know how long she has stood there, but finally she sees that Nejla is surrounded by a shimmering aura, a red sheen that glows strongly around her. It is her magic. Minoo sees it only for a brief moment, but now she knows that she can do this.

She slides more deeply still into concentration.

CHAPTER 60

V anessa doesn't duck in time. The dense cloud of hairspray lands on her arm and forms a gluey second skin. She lowers her eyeliner and glances irritably at Michelle via the mirror in the girls' bathroom.

'Hey! Can't you aim somewhere else? Like, at *your hair?*'

'Sorry, sweetheart.' Michelle puts the can back on the edge of the basin.

She checks her hair in the mirror and starts meticulously patching up her powder. Evelina emerges from one of the stalls and washes her hands.

'This soap smells fucking disgusting,' she grimaces.

'Just be thankful there's soap at all,' Vanessa says.

Tindra from Linnéa's class comes in. Her purple and black dreads dangle over her bare shoulders. She has painted eyebrows on today – two slim black lines on her face caked in pale powder.

'Hiya,' she says to Vanessa as she goes into one of the stalls.

'Hi,' Vanessa replies.

Vanessa doesn't think that Linnéa is in school today. She has searched for her energy field but can't find it anywhere. She has been on the verge of calling to make up after yesterday's fight so many times, but each time she stops herself.

She just wants everything to be okay again. But why should she always be the one to take the first step whenever they have an argument? Why is it always her who is locked out and has to hammer on the door to be let back in? Just thinking

426

about it makes her feel tired. And it is going to happen again
and again.

'Are you coming?' Evelina asks.

They leave the bathrooms, go to the dining room and line
up for lunch. The small, semi-secluded room in the dining area
has filled up with new faces. The popular elite among the freshmen has already figured out that it's the place to sit. Maybe
older siblings have briefed them.

Linnéa had been tied up in there by Max. What if that
wasn't by chance? Maybe Max picked it because that is where
the portal will open?

Suddenly the apocalypse feels inevitable, as if their attempts
to stop it are ridiculous.

'What's the matter?' Evelina asks. 'You look really down.'

Michelle is looking at her, too.

'Is it because . . .' she begins with a sidelong glance at
Evelina.

'No,' Vanessa says. 'It has nothing to do with Wille and his
girlfriend expecting a baby.' Her voice is harsh, but they hurt
her so much by not telling her about it. She wants to hurt
them in return.

'We're sorry, we should've said.' Michelle piles hash browns
on her plate. 'We were worried about how you'd react.'

Vanessa goes over to the salad buffet. Pale, damp, grated
carrots. Chick peas in a dressing that looks like vomit. Limp
lettuce leaves going brown at the edges.

Evelina and Michelle follow her.

'We didn't know how to tell you,' Evelina says. 'And we
haven't met up, so . . .'

Her voice fades. Vanessa looks at them and it feels as if they
are strangers.

'He's such a total loser,' Michelle goes on. 'I simply don't get
why she trusts him when she knows that he was unfaithful to
you. With her. It must be horrible for you.'

It says a lot about how far apart they've grown if Michelle really thinks she's broken-hearted because Wille has moved on with his life . . .

'I felt nothing,' Vanessa says. 'I met the two of them in town and it was like . . . nothing. That's the truth.'

Evelina stares at her. 'But what's the matter with you then?' she asks. 'It's definitely something. Are you going to tell us, or what?'

Vanessa is shocked. Evelina uses that tone when she picks fights with people. People who aren't Vanessa.

'Maybe she and Linnéa have had a fight.' Michelle looks troubled. 'Vanessa, is that it?'

Vanessa wonders whether to tell her, but she can't. Hers and Linnéa's problems are so mixed up with the Chosen Ones and all their shared secrets. But even if they weren't, telling them still wouldn't feel right. Linnéa isn't just her girlfriend, she's a friend. And Linnéa hardly ever opens up to anyone. To talk about her would be to betray her.

'No . . . I'm just tired,' she says.

And the moment she says that, she knows that the rift between them might never heal.

Michelle doesn't say anything. Vanessa can't even look at Evelina.

CHAPTER 61

Anna-Karin pulls her backpack off, shoves some dried fir cones out of the way and sits down on a large stone. She opens her lunch box. The fox comes padding along, the needles crackling faintly under his black paws. He sniffs the air when Anna-Karin unwraps the foil from some slices of ham.

'All yours,' she says.

She places the ham parcel on the ground. The fox goes for it at once, putting one paw on the wrapper and tugging eagerly at the ham with his teeth. Anna-Karin empathizes. Her own hunger is like a gaping hole inside her.

She starts on the sandwich she prepared in Minoo's kitchen; bites into the wholegrain bread, tastes the salty butter and ham. It is unbelievably tasty. She drinks thirstily from the large PET bottle she filled with mixed elderberry cordial and water.

She watches the heavy clouds gathering over the town. Out here in the forest, the sun is shining. She turns her face toward it, lets it warm her face while she eats. Afterward, she packs everything back into the backpack and stands and brushes down the back of her jeans.

Suddenly, the fox lifts one paw; his ears twitch and align themselves in different directions.

Anna-Karin shivers as she is sucked into the mind of the fox. He has discovered something. It isn't a sound or a scent or a movement, but something different, irresistible and instinctively important.

He runs now, fleet-footed.

'Wait!' she calls out. She starts running after him.

The Key

The fox has already left the path and she has no choice but to follow him.

Her backpack bumps against her back. The fox is so excited, he tries to pull her into his consciousness; she has to make an effort to stay self-aware. She can't run when she sees the world through the fox's eyes; it's hard enough already to avoid stumbling over stones and tree-roots.

The fox races between the tree trunks and up a steep slope. Anna-Karin follows as best she can, breathing heavily by now. She hauls herself up by grabbing large roots; she feels them under her fingers at the same time she is aware of the ground under the fox's paws.

She clambers on up the slope, her T-shirt clinging to her sweaty back. The forest grows denser and she has to crawl under the low, intertwined branches of a cluster of fir trees. The soft needles scrape against her scalp. Finally, she reaches a ledge.

The ledge is surrounded by steep rock faces. The fox has stopped at an opening into the rock. It is clear what he wants to do.

Go inside.

'Wait,' Anna-Karin gasps. 'Wait.'

The fox stands still. His small body is quivering with tension. His black nose is moving restlessly from side to side. Anna-Karin finds the flashlight she always carries when she walks in the forest, just in case she ever finds herself here after dark. She crouches down and directs its light into the gap in the rock.

A passage leads into the mountain, sloping down toward an inscrutable darkness.

She switches the flashlight off and slips back into the fox's consciousness. She uses his senses to pick up the faint sounds of snapping and dripping, the whispers of the wind from inside the mountain and the smells of stone, moss, damp and something metallic. But no trace of any animals. None.

Part Three

I could come back later, Anna-Karin thinks. But she fears that it might be too late.

She takes out her cell phone and tries to send messages to the others, but there is no signal.

Anna-Karin places her bright-red backpack outside the opening. It should be visible from the air if the emergency rescue people decide to look for her by helicopter, as they have done in so many other cases of people disappearing in the forest. She doesn't want to think of the ones they never found.

She looks at the hole and takes a deep breath.

'Let's go,' she says and the fox shoots off into the darkness. Anna-Karin switches the flashlight on, kneels and crawls in after him.

The knees of her jeans quickly become wet and cold. The rough stone surface feels sharp, presses against her knees and shins. Holding the flashlight at the same time as she crawls is hard; the cone of light shakes and makes the shadows leap and dance on the walls of the tunnel.

It slopes downwards and grows steadily narrower. The stone scrapes against her back and shoulders now. She presses on, despite feeling the mountain closing in around her like a gigantic fist.

She enters the fox's mind again and glimpses a bigger space, a cave. Only a short way to go now. Only a short way.

The passage narrows even further, the walls pressing in on her body from every direction.

Anna-Karin lies down flat in the chilly wetness. A shudder runs through her. She wiggles forward. Every breath she takes seems to bounce back at her. She braces herself with feet and elbows. Carries on.

How far in is she now? It is as if she can feel every foot of rock above her. Tears fill her eyes. If she gets stuck here, the others will never find her. She isn't sure that she'll even be able to scream. The mountain is suffocating her.

Anna-Karin kicks out with her feet and her heels hit the stone surface above her. She wants to go back but isn't sure she can.

Her sudden panic attack triggers her magic and it flows through her; her new strength fills every muscle, making her want to fight her way out of there, to crush the stone that is pressing against her.

She forces herself to breathe calmly and not give in. If she doesn't stop panicking, she could end up crushing herself against the rock instead.

Moving forward is her only option.

It feels like an eternity, but finally she gets to the end of the tunnel. The fox's eyes gleam in the light of her flashlight. He stands waiting for her in the cave. She crawls out and the pressure around her shoulders and ribcage lightens. Halfway out, her tracksuit jacket catches on something, but she places her hands against the edges of the opening and pushes until the material gives and she falls to the cave floor.

Anna-Karin gets up on her hands and knees, tries to catch her breath and tries not to think of having to go back up through that passage. The fox comes up to her and rubs his nose lightly against her cheek.

'Thank you,' she whispers.

She stands up and looks around her in the torchlight. It is a tall space, at least twice her height. As the cone of light sweeps across the walls, she thinks she detects several other dark passages opening into the mountain.

The fox pads toward something and barks loudly and shrilly. Anna-Karin follows him and her flashlight shows up two whitish lines against the dark rock wall. It takes a few moments for her to realize that it is a pair of old-fashioned ski poles.

She comes closer, goes down on her haunches. Other objects are piled up nearby, thrown higgledy-piggledy. Near the ski poles, she sees a teddy bear that may have been white once upon a time. Anna-Karin touches it cautiously. Its fur is stiff with dirt. She looks around and sees large, sharp pieces of lime-green plastic. It takes a little while to realize that it was once a kid's sledge. A solitary jogging shoe lies in a puddle.

Anna-Karin picks up a ruined red wallet, opens it and extracts the half-dissolved remains of discontinued bank notes. A plastic compartment contains a photo of a man with a large, dark moustache and receding hairline.

She examines it. The paper has softened and feels almost like cotton. The man's features are blurred but she thinks he looks vaguely familiar.

The fox's bark echoes through the cave. Anna-Karin lets the torchlight sweep over the pile of things and sees something glint. She moves closer. It is a plastic compass. The needle is spinning

And then she hears the rustling sound.

It comes from the ski poles. From a stack of books that have swollen with damp so much that the covers are bulging. From an upside-down wicker basket. The old shoe in the puddle is moving. Black beetles are crawling over it. They form a black shiny mass covering it. One ski pole falls against the other. The books are disappearing under the crawling bodies. The mass rustles and clicks and hisses, as if in a wordless, vowel-less language.

Anna-Karin stands as if turned to stone. More beetles pour out from crevices in the cave's walls. The teddy bear falls over, as if it's had a few too many drinks, and vanishes under the black hordes.

Something touches Anna-Karin's wrist. She leaps backward and hears a squelchy, crackling sound under her shoes. She shines the flashlight on her legs. Beetles are creeping up her sneakers; one is on its way in under her jeans. She screams and shakes her legs violently, then runs to the tunnel opening. The fox is already on his way out. She hears herself crunching beetles with every step she takes. Her skin is itching as if beetles were already all over her.

433

The fox is growling and barking in the tunnel. She prays that there are no more beetles in there.

The hard mountain fist is squeezing her again. She wiggles forwards, upwards, forcing herself on, on, on, until she can crawl on all fours and her breathing becomes easier. She bursts into tears and notices that there is some light on the walls, and there, there is the opening. She aims for the spot of daylight. It grows larger and larger, although it is somehow still just as far away. Until, suddenly, it is right in front of her. And she gets out on the ledge, into the sunshine.

She straightens and starts brushing herself down: her jacket, her jeans and her shoes. But there is no sign of beetles, apart from the black goo of crushed carapaces under the soles of her shoes.

The fox looks at her.

'Come,' she says, grabbing the backpack and starting the descent.

CHAPTER 62

Minoo stands on the lawn behind the manor house. The sun is shining on the garden, but its light seems dulled to her, as if seen through a tinted windowpane.

She has been observing the others, one by one. She can visualize the magic of each one of them quite clearly now. Not only that, but she has begun to understand what she sees. She can identify each element and read the power of the magic.

Alexander watched them silently for a while from the top of the steps into the garden. She saw his aura. It was red, like Nejla's, and strong, but it's not *as* powerful. Minoo would never be able to explain why, but it is so *obvious* to her that he isn't a natural witch.

Now she observes Felix, who sits on a stone seat and stares at the lawn. His magic, which has the same green color as Anna-Karin's eyes, flutters like a candle flame. Whatever magic experiment he is trying out, it is clear to her that it will fail.

'Minoo?'

The voice disturbs her. She is busy.

'Minoo?'

She turns toward the voice. Walter stands beside her. His aura has a strong but still pleasant glow, with a dark golden sheen. He is without any doubt the strongest witch in the Council's circle.

He looks inquisitively at her. She should reply in some way.

'I'd like to talk to you,' Walter says.

She looks at her hands and becomes aware of the black smoke that is whirling around them. It feels so natural to have it there; it makes everything so much cleaner and clearer and simpler. Why should she want to make it disappear?

Can she make it disappear?

Walter puts his hand on her back, between her shoulder blades, and she becomes aware of her body again, aware that she is partly out of it.

Suddenly, she loses her focus.

The sunlight dazzles her and the blood seems to drain from her head. It feels like the sensation you get when you stand up too abruptly. Walter leans over her and looks inquiringly at her. There is the scent of his aftershave again.

'How are you?' he asks.

She has almost forgotten how to speak, and has to consider how to shape the word before she can pronounce it.

'Fine,' she says in the end.

'Let's go inside.'

He keeps his hand on her back as he escorts her into the manor house. It is reassuring. Minoo has never been drunk, but she suspects it might feel like this.

The gentle light in the ballroom is a relief. Cartons of juice, jugs of water and dishes stacked with sandwiches in plastic packs have been set out on a table. Walter leads her past it and through the single door through which he and the Ehrenskiöld twins entered the ballroom that morning.

There is an office next door. A large mahogany desk stands in front of the tall windows; a few low bookshelves are placed along the walls, with pictures hanging above them. A sofa, two armchairs and a low table are grouped at the far end of the room. Walter propels her over to the sofa and helps her to sit down. Her legs tingle unpleasantly, as though they've fallen asleep.

'I'll be back soon.' He smiles. 'Don't faint.'

Minoo tries to focus her mind on the room. She notes that

all the pictures are oil paintings showing ships. Ships at anchor in calm harbors and tossed on stormy seas; ships at war and ships silhouetted against sunsets. Minoo wonders if Walter perceives himself as a captain. She isn't quite sure where this thought comes from.

Walter comes back with a glass of juice.

'Here you go,' he says.

She drinks obediently, even though she detests the bitter aftertaste of grapefruit. The fruit sugar helps perk her up a little.

'What happened?' Walter asks. He settles down in the armchair next to the sofa.

'I did as you told me,' she says. 'It was just that I found it hard to . . . to get back.'

She catches a glimpse of Walter's wristwatch and realizes that she has never stayed for so long inside the black smoke. And that she has never been so deeply absorbed in it, not even the time after Gustaf's reception.

If she had been alone, would she ever have been able to pull herself back out? Or would she have stayed there, not caring to eat and drink?

She twists the glass round and round in her hands. Observes the tiny slivers of fruit stuck to its edges. The bitter taste rises in her throat. Suddenly she is afraid that she will throw up.

Walter takes the empty glass from her grip and puts it on the table.

'Minoo,' he says. 'Look at me.'

Minoo meets his gray eyes.

'Now you are afraid again,' he says. 'You have been hard at work and feel tired afterward. Nothing stranger than that. But still, your first reaction is fear. Just because you have experienced something new. Something strong.'

Minoo nods.

'It's like all training sessions,' Walter continues. 'Think of what it's like when you start running. If you stop as soon as you begin to feel tired, your fitness will never improve. You will never get better at it. It's when you are tired and still push yourself that things begin to change.'

Minoo nods knowingly. It's clear that Walter is keeping fit; she doesn't want him to know that she has never gone jogging willingly in her entire life.

'Do you really believe that I would have allowed you to carry on for all that time if I had believed it to be dangerous for you?' he asks smilingly.

'Oh, no, of course not.'

He leans back in the armchair with his hands in his pockets. He is so relaxed. So fearless. So much a *leader*.

'What do you feel when you use your powers?' he asks her.

Minoo hesitates. She has spoken with the other Chosen Ones about what she can do, but never admitted to anyone what using her magic does for her, what it makes her feel or, rather, not feel.

'I feel free,' she says.

The grapefruit taste is back in her mouth. She feels as though she has said something forbidden. But Walter simply looks interested.

'Go on,' he encourages her.

'I'm not afraid of anything. I feel safe, untouchable.'

Walter nods.

'Power. That is what you experience.'

Minoo instinctively wants to protest, but deep down she knows that Walter is right.

'Not only that, but . . . it's like I'm freed . . . from myself.'

'Or perhaps, for once, you can be yourself,' Walter suggests. 'Your *true* self.'

Minoo has never thought about it in those terms.

'Many people believe that they want power,' Walter says. 'But, in truth, they don't. As soon as power is in their hands, they are at a loss about what to do with all the new possibilities that open up to them. And that scares them. I don't think you're like them, Minoo. You are just a well-behaved young woman, who believes that she must always please everyone. Now, I think it is time for you to find out what you want for yourself. Find out who you would be if only you let go.'

Let go.

That was what Matilda had said just before the battle against Max in the dining area. Words that made Minoo use her powers for the first time.

'You mustn't allow your own development to be hampered because those around you are less advanced than you,' Walter continues. 'Or because you know that they will never reach your level, however hard they try. You mustn't be so fearful of being superior. Because, to be honest, in this case you *are* superior. And that is nothing to be ashamed of. You didn't choose this. Everyone has different aptitudes.'

Minoo stares at him. Wants to contradict him. But all her arguments seem to slip out of her grasp. Does it mean that he's right?

'I think this has opened up several new lines of thought for you,' he says. 'Now, do tell me. What did you see when you observed the others?'

Minoo tries not to feel ashamed about her account of the auras, even though it sounds really odd.

'This is wonderful,' Walter says. 'You will have all our technicians out of a job. Tell me, who is the strongest witch in the group? Apart from me, that is.'

Minoo must have looked startled, because he laughs.

'Look, I prefer the truth to polite modesty. It's more efficient. Which you, too, will come to realize, I hope.'

She smiles nervously at him.

'Both Viktor and Nejla are really strong,' she tells him. 'But so are Sigrid and Clara . . .' She falls silent.

'Come on, be honest,' Walter says.

'I'm not quite sure how strong Felix really is,' she admits.

Walter nods and, seeing his sad face, it is clear that he knows Felix is their weakest link.

'It's important to prop Felix up when we can,' Walter says. 'But I won't pamper him or anyone else. We can't afford that. *The world* can't afford that.'

Minoo just nods. She wonders if Walter thinks he has had to pamper her. She must sharpen up. Make sure that he won't have to do it again.

'I want you to carry on observing their magic,' Walter goes on. 'Keep an eye on how they develop. But only speak to me about it. I don't want them to feel like they're under surveillance.'

'I'll do my best,' Minoo agrees, and then realizes that she has accepted yet another spying assignment.

'But, above all, learn as much as you can about your own magic,' Walter says. 'Try to understand your own powers, just as you are learning about that of the others. As for me, I will help you as much as I can.'

He gets up.

'We had better get out and about before the others begin to wonder what we're up to in here.'

He opens the door. Minoo follows him into the ballroom.

'Have a break, everyone,' he shouts into the garden. 'You have an hour off.'

He smiles at Minoo and vanishes into his office. She picks up a plastic-wrapped cheese sandwich and sits down to eat it. Sunlight warms the room and is refracted in the prisms of the chandelier, casting rainbow reflections on the walls.

Clara is the first to come in from the garden. She is very pale and there is a feverish look in her eyes. When she bends over to pick up a sandwich, Minoo sees that her dress is marked on the back by a thin line of sweat.

'How are you?' Minoo asks.

Clara doesn't reply at all, just disappears through a door.

Minoo tells herself that Clara is just tired and doesn't hate her. She gets the sandwich out and takes a bite. It tastes of margarine and the bread is stale.

Viktor and Sigrid enter together, chatting quietly. Henry is dashing in and out between Sigrid's feet, but she seems untroubled by the possibility of stumbling over him. They move in perfect harmony.

Sigrid's laugh is so sudden that Minoo jumps.

'It's nothing to laugh about,' Viktor says with a smile. 'I'm serious.'

'You're never serious.' Sigrid smacks his arm lightly. 'You're just out to provoke. And *everyone* knows that.'

'Ouch,' Viktor says, picking up two sandwiches. 'I'm busted.'

He glances at Minoo. 'Have you seen Clara?'

She makes herself swallow the gooey mass in her mouth.

'She came in and left again just a moment ago.'

A shadow of worry falls across Viktor's face. Then it changes again, back to the aloof expression he used to have all the time when Minoo first got to know him.

'Where is Nejla?' Sigrid asks as she tears the plastic pack open. 'God, I'm starving.'

'The moment Walter called us in, she got her cell phone out and called her boyfriend,' Viktor says.

Sigrid rolls her eyes and goes to sit next to Minoo. Henry scurries a few circuits around their feet before shooting out into the garden.

'What have you been doing this morning?' Sigrid asks.

'I . . . watched.' Minoo is grateful to be able to hide behind a sort of half-truth.

Sigrid takes a big bite and her cheeks bulge like a hamster's.

'Easy, easy,' Viktor says. 'The food won't vanish suddenly, I promise.'

Sigrid laughs and a piece of cheese falls out of her mouth. If it had been Minoo, she would have felt disgusting, but Sigrid just looks charming.

Felix comes in and goes to pour himself a glass of water, drinks it and fills it up again. Minoo senses how careful he is to avoid looking at the others.

'It's amazing how much stronger one becomes here in Engelsfors,' Sigrid says between mouthfuls. 'I feel the difference already. Viktor, you must have developed a lot during the time you spent here.'

'Yes, I'm well ahead – you'll have to do some work to catch up,' he tells her.

Sigrid lifts her eyebrows and eats some more of her sandwich.

'Guys, do you remember when we were in Las Vegas?' she says.

'Hard to forget,' Felix mutters. He busies himself picking the lettuce out of his cheese sandwich.

Sigrid turns to Minoo. 'Our school arranged for a couple of weeks in the US on a student exchange, and one of the activities they had planned for us was to visit a totally non-magical place. Just to get a feel of what it's like.' She shudders. 'One felt utterly helpless. Like . . . ordinary.'

'When did you find out that you were a witch?' Minoo asks.

Sigrid takes another bite.

'I've always known,' she says, as if that was quite natural. 'My parents sent in samples for testing just after I was born. I started to practice using my magic when I was four, but my powers didn't really awaken until I was fifteen. Felix, you were thirteen, weren't you?'

Felix looks pained. He only nods in response.

'The Chosen Ones were like, sixteen, weren't you?' Sigrid asks Minoo. 'That seems to be the average age. How old were you, Viktor?'

'I can't even remember.' Viktor shrugs. 'All I know is that I was an obnoxious little kid.'

'You still are,' Sigrid giggles.

Minoo thinks about what she has seen of Clara's and Viktor's childhood. She wonders how early their powers really woke, with no one there to help them. And she realizes suddenly that she is probably the only one in this circle who has seen something of Viktor's true self. She knows him even better than Sigrid, who has been to boarding school with him for several years.

It is a strange insight. She feels tenderness for him. True, everyone puts on a show from time to time, but to never be able to drop one's guard must be tough.

She glances at him. And suddenly feels a familiar prickling at her wrists.

She can't understand what is happening.

She looks at Viktor and she feels . . . *in love.*

She can't stop staring at his blue eyes, blue as cornflowers, his ash-blonde hair, his perfect features, his warm, soft lips. She wants to feel his arms around her, feel that he will protect her against the world; she wants to touch him and wants him to touch her, wants to be alone with him. Why can't the others just go to hell and let her be alone with him, because she is the only one who understands him and he is the only one who understands her; the only one, ever.

Felix drops his glass on the floor and walks quickly out into the garden without saying a word.

The glass rolls along the parquet. Minoo hardly dares to look at Viktor again, but when she does the sudden wave of feeling drains away. He is just Viktor. And he looks uncomfortable. But not as uncomfortable as Sigrid, who has gone bright red in the face.

'That was awkward . . .' she says.

'I'll go and talk to him.' Viktor hurries outside after Felix.

Minoo watches him go. Then she turns to Sigrid, whose blushing has begun to fade.

'Poor Felix,' she says.

'What happened just now?' Minoo asks.

'Didn't you feel it?'

'Feel . . . what?' Minoo asks. Her ears are starting to glow.

Sigrid looks teasingly at her.

'Come on. Or maybe you feel like that all the time? Fair enough. At school, *everyone* was crazy about Viktor. I was too, for a while. But it passed.'

'I'm *not* in love with Viktor,' Minoo says.

'Fine,' Sigrid says and shrugs. Then she takes another bite of the sandwich. 'But you did feel in love with him just now, didn't you?'

Minoo stares at her.

'I did, too.' Sigrid suddenly looks thoughtful. 'What I'd like to know is, does Viktor himself feel it? Does he fall in love with himself? Come to think of it, it's probably his natural state.'

She laughs and then becomes serious again.

'Lucky Clara wasn't here. That would've been so gross.'

'I don't get it,' Minoo says. 'What happened?'

Sigrid glances at the garden door before leaning closer to Minoo.

'Did your hand hurt when Walter demonstrated his power on Felix?'

Minoo had almost forgotten that pang of sharp pain. It had come and gone so quickly that – compared to the other extraordinary events of the day – it seemed insignificant. She nods.

'Felix, he . . . *infects* people,' Sigrid says. 'What I mean is, he can affect other people's feelings, but only by influencing them to feel what he feels. And he's pretty hopeless at controlling it.'

'So, when Walter . . .'

'. . . we all hurt from Felix's pain. And what you felt just now was Felix's crush on Viktor.'

Minoo looks outside, but the only person she sees is Nejla, who is walking up and down with her cell phone pressed to her ear.

444

'How awful for him.' She can't think of anything worse. To be completely exposed. And Felix developed his powers in *middle* school.

'Oh, yes,' Sigrid says. 'It must be especially grim for someone like Felix. You may have noticed that he doesn't care for . . . well, people.'

'Perhaps that's why. I mean, of course that's why he wants to keep himself to himself, with powers like that.'

Sigrid looks at her and doesn't speak at first. Minoo wonders how she can stand sitting so straight-backed all the time.

'You know, I never thought of that angle. You might be right. What I do know is that Felix had a terrible time at school. Everyone knew that he was in love with Viktor. It didn't improve one bit when he and Viktor had a thing senior year. At least, people say they did. If it's true, I think it was wrong of Viktor, since it didn't mean anything to him.'

She glances quickly over her shoulder before leaning close to Minoo again.

'What Walter did this morning was awful,' she whispers in such a low voice that Minoo can hardly pick up individual words. 'I mean, he busted Felix's finger, and he must have known that we'd all feel it.'

When Minoo thinks back on that episode, she has to agree. It *was* an awful thing to do. But when it happened, it didn't seem so bad. It even seemed *normal*. After all, Felix had agreed. But she realizes that if she were to try and explain that to the other Chosen Ones, they would never understand.

The double doors open. Clara and Adriana come in.

'We will have a group meeting shortly,' Adriana says. 'Sigrid, would you please tell the others to join us in here?'

Sigrid gets up at once and calls to the others from the top of the steps to the garden.

Adriana starts arranging some of the juice cartons on the table. Minoo suspects that she is the one who put them there in the first place.

Minoo speculates about where Adriana might be keeping the box. She hopes it won't be at the bottom of one of the moving company's big boxes, stuffed away in some closet. She has to try to lay hands on it as soon as possible, get that task out of the way.

She suddenly feels that Adriana is looking at her. Minoo turns her head and meets Adriana's dark eyes. An antique brooch, pinned to the lapel of her suit jacket, glints in the sun. The brooch belonged to Adriana's mother, whose surname Adriana uses. Her mother saved her from execution, but died herself soon afterward.

Everyone who has shown Adriana love and loyalty has disappeared from her life now.

The door to Walter's office opens and Walter enters, immediately followed by Alexander. Both men look stern, and when Minoo meets Walter's gaze, she feels frightened. Something has happened.

The others have all returned from the garden by now.

'We have an exceptionally serious situation,' Walter announces. 'Olivia Henriksson has escaped.'

Minoo feels cold all over. Matilda told them that Olivia would be back; even so, she is shocked.

'Who's Olivia?' Nejla asks.

Walter casts an irritated glance at her.

'You should know that, Nejla. Before you joined us, you were given the same briefing as everybody else,' he tells her, while Nejla stares sourly at the floor. 'But since I obviously need to repeat myself, Olivia Henriksson was the one to be blessed by the demons after Max Rosenqvist.'

'And she's escaped from where?' Viktor asks. He is leaning against the wall near one of the tall windows.

Walter sighs, then turns to Alexander.

'Over to you. This was your little project.'

Alexander looks taken aback but recovers quickly.

'We have been holding Olivia Henriksson in secure

446

conditions at the Council headquarters in Stockholm. We provided necessary medical care and kept her under constant supervision until she was due to be taken to court.'

'And now she's on her way here, isn't she?' Viktor asks.

'But surely we can't be certain of that?' Sigrid has a shrill note of panic in her voice.

'I'm afraid Viktor is right,' Walter says. 'The guardians inform me that everything indicates that Olivia will be blessed by the demons once again. It means that every member of this circle is at risk. All natural witches are. And we know that she will definitely try to get you, Minoo.'

Minoo stares blankly at the piece of sandwich she's still holding. What is it like to be blasted with thousands of volts? Is it like being burned from the inside? Is that how it was for Ida?

'I suggest that we disperse for the rest of the day,' Walter continues. 'As I'm sure you understand, I've got quite a few calls to make. We have already started hunting for Olivia and I expect we will capture her without much delay. She won't have gotten far.'

But Minoo knows that he is wrong. They will not capture Olivia; she feels that in every cell of her body. And she is just as certain about who Olivia will be coming for first when she arrives in Engelsfors. Everyone who stopped her the previous time.

'Tomorrow we'll meet here at eight in the morning, to make up for lost time today,' Walter says before leaving the ballroom, accompanied by Alexander and Adriana.

'How do you feel?' Sigrid asks Minoo.

'I'm fine,' Minoo says. 'I'm kind of used to people wanting to kill me.'

She smiles but nobody smiles back.

'I'd better go now.'

'Do you really want to walk back on your own?' Viktor asks. 'Let me drive you.'

'No thanks,' says Minoo. She hurries out of the room and switches on her cell phone in the hall.

Seven missed calls and three texts from Anna-Karin. She wants them all to meet in Kärrgruvan.

CHAPTER 63

Linnéa swears when the sewing machine needle chews up a length of the black silk and makes it scrunch up like an accordion. This is why she had left Ingrid's gift of an old party dress on the shelf for so long. She is tempted to rip the fabric to pieces. Far too tempted.

The intruders ruined her old sewing machine and she misses it. It was her best skip-find ever, a solid model that had been going strong for maybe fifty years. She bought her current machine in a flea market. The former owner had claimed that she had hardly used it. Obviously she had used it enough to mess up the thread tension.

Linnéa gets up, opens the living-room window and fingers the pack of cigarettes on the windowsill. But she has smoked too many already and has too little money left.

Engelsfors almost glows in the afternoon sunshine. Linnéa tries to lose herself in the music from her laptop. The playlist is the one with Elias's favorites. It's his birthday today, but she hasn't had the strength to visit his grave. She hasn't even been able to write to him in her diary.

She still hasn't heard from Vanessa. Does it mean that it's all over? Linnéa feels nothing when she thinks about this. She is completely numb.

The doorbell.

Is it Vanessa?

It rings again. She goes to the hall and unlocks the front door.

He is drunk. She sees it before she smells it. She used to

449

think that he couldn't disappoint her anymore, but now it burns right through her numbness.

'I'm sorry,' Björn Wallin says. 'I'm sorry, for just turning up like this.'

Linnéa tries to pull the door shut, but he grabs the handle and keeps it open.

'Please, please, let me say this one thing,' he persists. 'I've felt like shit ever since I heard about what those boys did to you.'

'Go away,' Linnéa hisses.

She tugs at the door as hard as she can but he is stronger.

'Don't be like that,' he says. 'I'm so fucking angry for your sake and you must believe me, I knew nothing. I saw them often in the PE center with Helena, but I had no idea, and if only I got hold of them, I would fucking well . . . I would . . . my darling little girl. I hope they get it. A hard sentence. Fucking hard. That's only fucking right.'

He stops suddenly.

Linnéa lets go of the handle and he staggers backward, but regains his balance fast. He stinks of stale alcohol. Probably hungover this morning. Then a top-up or two before coming to see her. This is when he is the most remorseful. This is when he weeps over his own failings as a father, as if blaming himself would somehow make him innocent.

'I'm moving from town,' he says. 'To Köping. I've met a nice woman, you know. We're moving in together. I've got a job as well, shifting stock in a warehouse.'

He smiles tentatively and Linnéa's disappointment turns to anger.

'You said that it was entirely up to me if we were to get in touch again,' she tells him. 'And then you show up here, drunk.'

'It's different this time. Just a kind of leaving party, a couple of beers with my old friends from the sawmill . . .'

'And one thing led to another, and you hit the booze all

night long, and when you woke up, you went to Sture's and had another couple.'

Björn sighs.

'Yes,' he says. 'I relapsed, I admit it, but . . .'

'And then you come here to tell me you had no idea that some members of your old cult tried to murder me, just so you can feel less bad about it.'

Björn shakes his head and tries to interrupt, but she is on a roll.

'And then you go on about your new dream life with this new girlfriend, and you will fuck everything up again and you expect me to be *happy* for you! You're so fucking disgusting!'

Her eyes fill with tears and flow down her cheeks, but she makes them evaporate so that all that's left are tight trails of salt.

'I don't give a shit that you're drinking again!' she screams. 'I don't give a shit that you're screwing your life up. But you've screwed my life up and I'll never forgive you for that! I don't know why I bothered to stop drinking and taking drugs because I'm totally fucked up anyway! I'll never be whole! Never! And it's you who have made me like this. You ruined me!'

She hears the echo of her own voice die away in the stairwell.

'It's not true,' Björn says.

Linnéa slams the door shut, locks it and goes back to the living room. Stops and notices the fast beating of her heart. She feels as though she has been running. And then the numbness fills her again.

She catches sight of her cell phone. Several missed calls and three texts, all from Anna-Karin. She reads the messages. Anything rather than having to think about what has just happened.

CHAPTER 64

Vanessa rolls a vault into the gym store cupboard. She is sweating so much that her tank top is glued to her body.

Vanessa hasn't had Lollo as her PE teacher before, but she had heard about Lollo's notorious obstacle courses. Now, for the first time, she has experienced one. The losing team is given the job of putting the kit away afterward.

Vanessa went for the obstacle course as if the demons were snapping at her heels. Not because she wanted to win, but because she needed release for her nervous energy, to sweat out the stress. She could have kept going forever. She only noticed afterward how her arms and legs shook.

She and Evelina would have won if Liam hadn't been on their team. Liam, who can't even utter one word without going red in the face and who went dark purple when he tried to do the rope climbs. He looks miserable when he comes to hang up the trampette on the wall near Vanessa. She wants to tell him not to worry. That losing doesn't matter at all. But she suspects it would only make him feel even more ill at ease.

Vanessa leaves the store and goes back to the main gym. Evelina stands by the climbing frames and types quickly on her cell phone. The bar that Anna-Karin broke last spring when she suddenly turned into The Hulk has still not been fixed.

'What if we both take the mattress?' Vanessa suggests, and Evelina puts the cell in her pocket and nods without looking up.

They grab one corner each of the orange mattress that over the years has got a patchy black pattern from all the shoes

452

running over it. A cloud of ancient ingrained sweat billows up when they start dragging it across the floor.

Behind her, Vanessa hears a scraping sound that sets her teeth on edge. She looks over her shoulder and sees Liam hauling the beam up toward the ceiling.

She and Evelina drag the mattress into the store, count to three, heave it upright and lean it against the wall. And then she meets Evelina's gaze. Only to see her best friend look away quickly, as if the mere sight of Vanessa hurts her eyes.

If only there was something Vanessa could say to make it better. But there are only more half-truths and outright lies.

Vanessa's body reacts before her mind grasps that something is happening. Every small hair on her arms stands on end. Goose pimples are spreading on her back, up the back of her neck. Her scalp crawls.

The air is warm, almost hot.

And full of magic.

The trampette falls off the wall and lands with a dull thud.

Vanessa and Evelina stare at it.

Something is rattling behind Vanessa; when she turns to look she sees the indoor hockey goals jumping and shaking on the floor.

Then handballs, volleyballs, medicine balls, basketballs and indoor soccer balls fall off the shelves and begin bouncing across the floor toward them in a seething mass.

Vanessa takes Evelina's hand, pulls her out of the store and closes the door. The balls carry on bouncing about in there.

Evelina looks terrified.

'Shit,' she says as she follows Vanessa into the gym hall. 'Shit, what is—'

She is interrupted by a high-pitched screeching sound as the beam falls like a heavy guillotine blade on the floor in front of Liam's feet.

'Liam! We have to get out of here!' Vanessa screams.

Liam stands as if rooted to the floor and stares at the beam.

The magic is growing stronger and stronger. It shimmers in the air.

The first in the next chain of portents, Vanessa thinks. It has to be.

Someone in the girls' changing room is thumping on the door, trying to get in.

A loud bang echoes in the gym and is followed by the sound of a body collapsing.

Liam is lying on the floor with blood trickling from his forehead. One of the strip lights lies next to him. Vanessa checks the other lights. They are all shaking in their sockets.

'Liam!' she calls, but he doesn't answer. He doesn't move at all.

The ropes hanging from the ceiling begin to wriggle and writhe about like snakes. A pommel horse rolls slowly across the floor.

The first of the elements is flipping out of control. Must be the fire element. Some kind of psychokinesis, like Rebecka's power. The stands start shaking and rattling and yet another strip light works loose and falls.

'We must get Liam out of here,' Vanessa says. Evelina nods.

The magic makes their limbs feel heavy. It is like moving in treacle, as if in a nightmare. Sweat is pouring from Vanessa as she runs toward Liam, and when she turns to see where Evelina is, she isn't just behind her, but struggling a good way back.

Vanessa hears a creaking sound from somewhere near the ceiling and looks up. The net in the basketball goal is swaying, as if in an invisible wind. The wooden board is bulging, then suddenly it breaks away from its attachment and zooms through the center of the hall. Straight at Evelina.

Vanessa tries to run toward her, but she won't make it, she won't . . .

Evelina raises her hands to protect herself.

And the board stops in mid-air in front of her.

Everything falls silent. The stands are still. The light fittings stop rattling. Movement becomes normal again.

But Vanessa can sense a weak magic radiating from Evelina.

Evelina takes one step back and the goal falls heavily to the floor just in front of her feet.

The changing-room door is suddenly opened wide and Lollo comes running out. Her eyes are wild with anxiety.

'What is going on in here?' she screams.

Then she sees Liam, runs and kneels next to him while she pulls her cell phone from her tracksuit pocket.

Vanessa tries to grasp what has happened.

She has witnessed the first portent.

And Evelina stopped the basketball board.

With her own magic.

Does she know? Vanessa wonders, and looks at Evelina. Has she known for a long time? Have both of us been walking around, hiding from each other that we are witches?

The rest of the class comes along to see. Michelle is wrapped in a towel and has shampoo all over her hair. She clutches the towel with one hand and wipes foam from her eyes with the other.

'It sounded like you were trashing the place,' she shouts. 'What the fuck happened?'

'We have no idea,' Vanessa says. 'But it's over now.'

It's far from over. That was the first sign and there are five more to go.

Liam groans and everybody's attention focuses on him.

Vanessa takes Evelina's hand and pulls her toward the exit, then up the stairs to the entrance lobby and out into the schoolyard.

She scans the place, but there are too many people around and too few places where they have a chance of being left in peace. She leads the way to the back of the school and they stop next to the spiral staircase that runs up the full extent of the wall. There isn't a soul in sight, but Vanessa is so paranoid she checks the parked cars for faces.

Her sweat-soaked tank top clings coldly to her skin. She looks at Evelina, who has wrapped her arms around herself. Her dark skin is pimply with cold.

'Was that the first time for you?' Vanessa asks.

'What?' says Evelina, staring at her.

'That basketball goal.' Vanessa speaks quietly. 'You stopped it.'

'Yes, I . . . I did, didn't I?' Evelina looks confused. 'I stopped it. But I have no idea . . .'

She wraps her arms more tightly around her body. Vanessa remembers what Rebecka said that first night in Kärrgruvan.

I can't explain it. But the accident in the auditorium today . . . it was me who did it.

'Did it truly happen?' Evelina asks.

Vanessa nods. 'It happened.'

'What's wrong with you?' Evelina says almost angrily. 'Why aren't you freaking out? Do you think this is normal?'

Vanessa opens her mouth to deny everything. It's a reflex. Lies feel more natural than the truth. Finally she says, 'You are a witch.'

Evelina blinks.

'I am, too,' Vanessa continues. 'I found out in freshman year. Linnéa and I, and the others. That's why I've been so weird. I couldn't tell you the truth – it would've been too dangerous.'

It is such a relief to speak about this to Evelina that it feels as if a huge load has been taken off her shoulders.

'Am I . . . a witch?' Evelina asks her.

'Yes,' Vanessa confirms.

Evelina contemplates this.

'Is *this* your thing?' she asks in the end. 'You and Linnéa and Minoo and Anna-Karin. Is this what you've been up to?'

Vanessa nods.

Evelina giggles. It's like the attacks of laughing she and

Vanessa used to have in elementary school when they couldn't stop. Vanessa is getting worried. Is Evelina coping?

'Sorry,' Evelina moans and has to support herself against the railing. 'It's not funny. It's crazy. I can't believe it, even though I saw all that happening. Actually, what the fuck *did* happen?'

Vanessa tries to imagine how Minoo might have gone about explaining everything to Rickard and Gustaf. She would have been well organized and lucid. Given an account in a logical sequence that was easy to follow.

But Vanessa can't even think where to begin. The one thing she is sure about is that she won't start by telling Evelina that what they just saw was a portent that the end of the world is nigh.

'It's a long story . . .' Vanessa says.

Evelina, who is about to say something, falls silent and stares at Vanessa's feet.

'Err, Nessa . . .' She points.

Vanessa looks down. She is floating a couple of inches above the ground.

'Oops,' she says. 'That's new.'

She lands again, the soles of her shoes touching down softly on the pavement. And she feels thrilled, in the middle of everything else, because she remembers flying in her dreams.

She looks back at Evelina.

'Would you like to come to my place tonight and I'll explain everything to you? I must go and find the others now, and tell them about this.'

'*We*,' Evelina tells her. '*We* must go and find the others.'

'Evelina . . .'

'*What?*'

Vanessa realizes that she doesn't even want to try and stop her. 'Let's go,' she says.

On the way back to the school, they catch a glimpse of Liam.

He is being carried out on a stretcher and looks embarrassed by all the fuss.

The changing room is empty. Vanessa takes her cell phone from the locker. There's a text from Michelle to say that she had to go but Vanessa *must* phone her and tell her what happened. There are seven missed calls from Anna-Karin and three texts saying that Vanessa has to come along to the fairground because something has happened.

That's an understatement, Vanessa thinks. She pulls her sweater on and waits while Evelina clears out her locker.

'Fuck, I'm starving!' Evelina pulls a bar of chocolate from her bag. 'I'm so hungry it hurts.'

'At first, it was like that for us, too,' Vanessa says. 'It's the magic—'

The changing-room door opens and Lollo runs in with her whistle bouncing against her chest.

'For heaven's sake, what happened in there?' she asks. 'You must tell me exactly. And if Tommy doesn't listen to me this time, I'll go straight to the *Engelsfors Herald*.'

'I don't know what happened,' Vanessa says. She starts pulling Evelina toward the exit. 'Everything was shaking.'

'Yes, that's exactly it.' Evelina says, before gobbling up the last of the chocolate. 'It was like a small earthquake. Or something.'

Lollo calls after them, but they run upstairs together. As they emerge outside, the ambulance is driving away with Liam. Groups of students are standing about and talking excitedly.

Vanessa and Evelina push through the crowd. As they get outside the gates, they see Rickard and Gustaf. The self-appointed sidekicks of the Chosen Ones.

'What are you doing here?' Vanessa asks. She carries on walking with Evelina.

The boys follow them.

'We were nearby and saw the ambulance going toward the school,' Gustaf says.

'The guy on the stretcher said there's a ghost in the gym,' Rickard adds.

Vanessa sighs. Stops and checks that nobody else is close enough to hear her.

'It was magic,' she says quietly. She doesn't want to make a big thing of it, since Evelina hasn't heard about the apocalypse. Not yet.

'What's this?' Evelina asks. 'Do these guys know too? Are they also witches?'

Gustaf and Rickard look baffled. And then all three of them stare at Vanessa.

She has no resistance left. What does it matter? All the old rules have ceased to be valid. If they want to be part of this so badly, they might as well be part of it all the way.

'Whatever,' she says. 'Come on. I'll explain everything while we walk. Just as well it's quite a way to Kärrgruvan.'

'To where?' Evelina asks. She looks confused.

Vanessa sighs again.

'Like I said. I'll explain.'

CHAPTER 65

Minoo walks under the arched portal bearing the name KÄRRGRUVAN, then past the old ticket booth with a board nailed across the hatch.

Someone stands near the dance pavilion.

Nicolaus.

He turns toward her and, suddenly, the memory of the night of the blood-red moon is so strong that she has to stop. Two years have passed since then. In comparison with the centuries that Nicolaus has lived through, two years are nothing. But, to her, they feel like a lifetime.

'Good day,' says Nicolaus.

'Hi.'

They walk together up the few steps to the dance floor. The fox is curled up on the floor. Anna-Karin is on her way.

Minoo sits down on the stage. Nicolaus goes over to the railing and looks out over the park. A gust of wind stirs up a cloud of dust from the graveled yard.

'What are you thinking about?' Minoo asks.

'I'm trying to remember . . . but everything looks so different now and it was such a long time ago . . . I don't know where I . . .'

He stops speaking and turns to Minoo. His eyes are shining with tears. She understands.

'You wonder where you buried Matilda,' she says.

Nicolaus only nods.

'I can help you to remember.'

'Thank you,' he replies quietly. 'Another time.'

Minoo looks at the fox, who observes them both with his amber eyes. She wonders if Anna-Karin is looking through them just now as well; if she is listening through the fox's ears.

'I have been thinking about when you met Matilda in the dream,' Nicolaus says. 'Specifically, what she said about the guardians making her give up her powers.'

Minoo realizes that it was only yesterday that Nicolaus learned *why* Matilda let her powers go. After all these centuries, he finally knows.

'Do you think the guardians knew what would happen?' he wonders. 'Did they know what it would cost her, once the Council had found out what she had done?'

'I don't think so, listening to Matilda. They probably didn't know.'

Nicolaus nods, a distant look on his face.

'But if the guardians knew . . .' he goes on. 'The fate of the world was at stake. The world balanced against my daughter's life. The world against Elias's life. Against Rebecka's. Against Ida's.'

The wind is whispering in the trees around Kärrgruvan.

'Every day, people die. Every moment,' he continues quietly. 'Right now, someone passes away quietly in his sleep. Right now, someone bleeds to death in childbirth. Right now, someone is hit by a bullet. Lives are taken all the time. If you must choose between sacrificing one human being and letting the world go under . . .' He stands in silence, his hands resting on the railing. 'I know that you're trying to be rational. But, Minoo . . . The guardians themselves will say that they're not all-knowing and all-seeing. Which means that they gamble with people's lives. One life is a small matter. And yet it is everything.'

What Nicolaus is saying both frightens her and makes her furious.

'What are you trying to say?' she asks. 'That the situation isn't black and white? That the guardians aren't good through

461

and through? Or entirely trustworthy? I know that already. But eventually one reaches a point at which one must stop messing around and decide what to believe in.'

Nicolaus looks thoughtfully at her.

'Maybe so,' he says. 'But some things *must* be difficult. They are *supposed* to be difficult. If we switch off our doubts and our emotions and excuse ourselves by insisting that we are acting rationally . . . that is when we make some of our most dangerous decisions.'

'You do not agree with the opposite argument, then?' Minoo says. 'That to allow yourself to be ruled entirely by your emotions is dangerous?'

'Yes, I do.' Nicolaus looks toward the park entrance, where Linnéa is coming toward them. 'I do indeed.'

Linnéa's boots clump up the steps and across the wooden dance floor. She only mumbles a reply to Nicolaus's greeting, then leans against the railing and lights a cigarette.

Seeing what kind of mood Linnéa is in, Minoo wishes that she didn't have to tell her about Olivia now. But Olivia used to be Linnéa's friend, and that's why she will probably go for Linnéa first of all.

'I must tell you something.' Minoo turns to her. 'Olivia has been held by the Council. Until now. She has escaped.'

She waits for Linnéa to speak. She doesn't.

'I expect she'll be on her way here then,' Nicolaus says.

'So do I,' Minoo agrees.

The fox runs along to the edge of the stage and barks once. Minoo looks at the entrance and sees Anna-Karin. The knees on her jeans have large, dirty patches.

'Sorry I'm late,' she says breathlessly when she walks up the steps. 'It was further than I thought, somehow. But I heard what you said about Olivia. Well, the fox heard.'

Minoo glances at Linnéa again. She still seems utterly unmoved. Blows out a cloud of smoke.

'Linnéa?' Minoo asks.

'Honestly, I really don't want to talk about this,' Linnéa says.

Minoo exchanges a quick glance with Anna-Karin, who sits down next to her on the stage. She hopes Vanessa will be here soon so they can talk it through and she can finally go home.

* * *

Linnéa lights her fourth cigarette, even though she feels slightly sick, and even though she can't afford a new pack. She tries to avoid looking at Nicolaus, who has gone to sit next to Anna-Karin, and tries even harder to avoid looking at Minoo and Anna-Karin, who are both nervously fiddling with their cell phones. Only the fox seems relaxed. He is lying at Anna-Karin's feet, snoozing, his eyes half shut.

Linnéa drags on her cigarette and waits for what happened with Dad to really sink in. She expects it will hit her like a sledgehammer some time soon.

She wants nothing more in the world than to see Vanessa come walking down the gravel road, to see her smile and realize that all is well again and all the problems out of the way. That Vanessa has forgiven and forgotten all the unforgivable things Linnéa said yesterday.

But she knows it won't be like that.

The real question is, how bad will it be?

Already, she sees the abyss opening. And now it seems that Olivia is on her way back to Engelsfors to kill them all, and take their souls and their powers.

Linnéa feels Vanessa's energy coming closer. She straightens up and looks toward the entrance. And can hardly take in what she sees.

Vanessa isn't alone. That Gustaf and Rickard have come along maybe isn't so strange, but . . .

'Why is she bringing Evelina?' Minoo asks.

Linnéa's heart is beating hard now. She wants to know what this means. Now.

'I don't get it. How can the whole town *forget* that this place exists?' she hears Evelina say as they cross the open space next to the pavilion.

'Hi, everyone!' Vanessa calls out. 'I should've called and warned you, but I had such a lot of things to tell Evelina on the way. She's also a witch by the way.'

Her voice sounds light and happy. And Linnéa understands how good it must feel to finally be able to tell the real story. Perhaps what went on yesterday doesn't matter anymore; perhaps she isn't angry anymore.

Then Vanessa meets her eyes.

And she has obviously forgotten nothing.

* * *

Minoo watches the quartet stepping up to the dance floor. That Gustaf is here seems so unreal to her that she can hardly take in what Vanessa has been saying.

Vanessa stops in the middle of the floor, with Evelina next to her, while Gustaf and Rickard sit down next to Minoo.

'Hi,' Gustaf says. Their knees touch lightly.

That fleeting touch is enough to make her feel faint all over, rather like earlier today when she looked at Viktor. The difference is that, this time, the feeling is her own.

'Hi, Gustaf.'

'How did you make this discovery?' Nicolaus asks Vanessa. 'How did you find out that Evelina is a witch?'

'The fire element went crazy in the gym,' Vanessa says. 'I'm sure it was the first portent. And that was when Evelina's powers kicked in. Telekinesis.'

Just like Rebecka, Minoo thinks.

Almost two years have passed since Rebecka sat here and told Minoo how she wished she could tell Gustaf the truth about herself and the others.

Now he knows.

Now he sits here himself.

That is what Rebecka wished for and Minoo is the one who gets to experience it. It is so unfair. And yet, at the same time, she is so happy that he is here.

'But . . . the sun went dark only yesterday,' Anna-Karin asks. 'How can the first portent manifest itself already?'

'If the apocalypse keeps advancing at this pace, we must be ready to close the portal in five days,' Vanessa says.

'It will take longer,' Minoo tells her.

Everyone looks at her.

'How do you know that?' Linnéa asks. 'Did *Walter* say so?'

Minoo is determined not to get angry. She doesn't want to give Linnéa the satisfaction. Especially not in front of Gustaf, Rickard and Evelina.

'No. It's just what I think.'

She can't explain how she can feel so certain. It's the same kind of feeling as when she stood in front of Elias's and Rebecka's graves in the cemetery and *knew* that they were where they should be.

'Sorry, but I just have to ask,' Evelina says. She points at Nicolaus. 'You used to be the school janitor, didn't you? And that's not a dog, right? It's a *fox*?'

'Yes, he was the janitor and, yes, that's a fox and, yes, there's still quite a lot I must tell you about,' Vanessa says.

'It's probably just as well I don't get told everything in one go,' Evelina reflects. 'My brain is close to meltdown.'

She looks at the others.

'I don't think I've got my head around this apocalypse thing yet. But we're witches . . . we're like . . . superheroes. Isn't that pretty fucking awesome? You must have done so much cool stuff!'

Minoo feels caught out, somehow. She wonders if the others feel the same. For Evelina is right, in a way. But in this group, they have never talked about magic as something positive because, right from the beginning, it has always been linked to the end of the world and other dangers. It makes her think about what Walter said in the manor house earlier today.

'Like, right before we went here, Vanessa started to float!' Evelina continues.

'Yeah,' Vanessa smiles. 'That *was* cool.'

'Maybe you won't think it quite so cool that Olivia has escaped and is on her way,' Linnéa says.

Total silence. Vanessa stares at Linnéa, who puffs on her cigarette and refuses to look at anyone.

'Escaped . . . how do you mean?' Rickard asks in the end.

'The Council kept her locked up in their headquarters,' Minoo says. 'I got it confirmed today.'

'And now she's on her way here to gobble up the souls of some natural witches. Engelsfors is like a fucking buffet for her,' Linnéa goes on. 'And you're the main course, Minoo.'

It doesn't hurt as badly as it would have done yesterday. Actually, Minoo is almost pleased. Linnéa is making a fool of herself in front of everyone.

'Calm down,' Gustaf tells her.

'Yes, please,' Vanessa says.

'I'm calm.' Linnéa drops her cigarette butt and grinds it slowly under her boot. 'By the way, Evelina must be a natural witch if her powers just went off like that. And it seems as if fire is her element.'

She says this with her hard little smile. Minoo knows what she is after. She wants a fire witch to replace Rebecka in the Circle. But what she doesn't know is that Minoo could easily check if she's right. Minoo looks at the floor with its rough boards. She knows it's childish. But she doesn't want to give Linnéa this.

'Minoo,' Nicolaus says.

She turns to him. He is looking hopeful.

'You saw Clara's magic when you healed her. Perhaps you could investigate Evelina's magic, too?'

Minoo bites her lip. Obviously, Nicolaus would figure it out.

And it would be too selfish to refuse. Evelina deserves to know.

'I can try,' Minoo says.

'How?' Evelina asks. 'Like, does it hurt?'

'No,' Minoo tells her. She releases the black smoke.

By now, it works almost instantaneously. The light around her fades and all the magic auras stand out radiantly.

She is almost dazzled by the strength of the auras around the Chosen Ones, Linnéa's dark blue, Vanessa's light blue and Anna-Karin's green. Compared with theirs, Walter's aura is positively weak. Still, it could be that the Chosen Ones are at their strongest here in the park. It is their special place, after all.

She observes Nicolaus next. She knows that he is a natural wood witch, but now she sees the golden-brown radiance around him. Sometimes it is strong, but now and then it flickers, fades, even disappears, before it returns. Magic is linked to life-force. She recalls what Nicolaus said last autumn. The human being isn't designed to live for as long as he has.

Something white and blurry flutters past behind Nicolaus, but Minoo ignores it. She observes Evelina. Yes, there is a pulsating red shimmer around her. Her potential is great, but it will take a long time for her to develop her powers to be as strong as Nejla's.

'Evelina is a fire witch,' Minoo says. Her voice sounds distant to her.

She notes Linnéa's triumphant face, but she doesn't care, not when she is inside the black smoke. It doesn't matter that Linnéa knows. Evelina still can't replace Rebecka. Minoo knows this.

She observes Gustaf next and is a little surprised to see strong, silver light forming a halo around him. Then she realizes that she has made a mistake. Rickard sits on Gustaf's other side, and it is Rickard's aura she sees.

'Rickard, too, is a natural witch,' she says. 'His element is metal.'

She notes Rickard's shocked expression. She bends closer to Gustaf to get a better look and notices that he flinches. She wonders if she looks strange to him when she is inside the black smoke.

Gustaf's aura is practically invisible – just a weak, dark blue sheen. If he were prepared to work hard, Gustaf might, at best, become a middlingly competent trained witch.

'Gustaf's element is water,' she goes on. 'But he has hardly any potential to speak of.'

Gustaf looks hurt. She doesn't care, not until she has pulled the smoke back and the light has become bright again.

'I'm sorry,' she says. 'All I meant was . . . you see, the others are natural witches but you aren't.'

Gustaf doesn't say anything. Nobody says anything. But they are all staring at her.

'What's the matter?' Minoo asks.

'You didn't look like yourself,' Anna-Karin tells her.

'You looked fucking scary!' Evelina adds. Vanessa looks irritated, but Evelina persists. 'Excuse me, but she did!'

'You looked like a scientist observing ants or something,' Linnéa says. 'Which fits rather well with how the guardians look at us.'

Minoo glances at Linnéa. She is so pathetic. She doesn't understand anything.

'Perhaps we should talk about the fact that Rickard is a natural witch too?' Vanessa says.

'Yes, please,' Rickard says. 'That's something I'd really like to talk about.'

He looks as if his life has been turned upside-down, Minoo thinks. True enough, it has. Again.

'Have you noticed anything before?' Evelina asks.

'No.' Rickard shakes his head.

'I don't think you're right about that,' Nicolaus says.

Surprised, Minoo turns to him.

'I have heard what happened to you,' Nicolaus goes on,

with his eyes fixed on Rickard. 'And I have thought about it a great deal. One extraordinary fact about your story is that you survived what Olivia subjected you to. And then your memory of the events came back when nobody else involved could remember anything about their time under her control . . . this is startling evidence that you're a natural witch.'

Rickard sighs deeply, takes his glasses off, breathes on them and uses the hem of his T-shirt to polish them.

'I'm at a total loss,' he murmurs. 'I had just begun to get a handle on all the rest.'

'I guess we'll have to help each other,' Evelina says.

'There is much to talk about,' Nicolaus says. 'But we mustn't forget why we are gathered here. Anna-Karin. What is it you've found?'

* * *

Anna-Karin bends to rub the fox behind his ear to gain a moment's thought. She doesn't want to start rambling incoherently.

When she and the fox investigated the cave, it had all seemed important and meaningful. But she's not sure why, nor how she can explain it.

She begins her story.

When Anna-Karin reaches the part about the beetles, Evelina makes retching noises.

'Shit, that's so gross!' she says. 'So fucking gross! You're so fucking brave!'

Anna-Karin suddenly feels ashamed about the anonymous comments she left on Evelina's blog a few years ago.

'How could you go in there alone?' Minoo asks her. 'Just imagine if something had happened to you. We would never have found you.'

'Minoo is right,' Nicolaus says. 'That was foolhardy.'

'No,' Anna-Karin says. 'I had to do it. And I found this. I recognize him.'

She hands the photo to Nicolaus, who glances at it, shakes his head and passes the photo on to Vanessa and Evelina.

'I recognize him too.' Vanessa studies the picture carefully.

'I do, too!' Evelina says.

On the way to the park, Anna-Karin had periodically looked at the photo. It is so frustrating to recognize him and still not be able to name him.

Linnéa almost tears the photo from Evelina's hand. Stares at it, shrugs, and hands it on to Rickard and Gustaf, who share it with Minoo.

'But, wait . . .' Gustaf says. 'It's Leffe! Leffe who has Leffe's kiosk!'

Anna-Karin leans toward Minoo to see the picture again, then tries to reimagine the man's face thirty years on, without the hair and the moustache.

'You're right. It is him,' she agrees.

'Okay,' Vanessa nods. 'But, what was Leffe's photo doing in the cave?'

Anna-Karin straightens up.

She was called Ragnhild. Mother of Leffe, that's him who runs Leffe's kiosk.

'Because his mother kept it in her wallet,' Anna-Karin says.

She goes on to tell them about her grandmother's old friend, who disappeared after going skiing in the forest. And she recalls the old ski poles in the cave.

'What if all those things belonged to people who have disappeared?' she concludes.

'Have you thought about how many people disappear in Engelsfors?' Rickard asks.

'Rather hard not to,' Linnéa says.

'Yes, sure, but I meant, *thought* about it, properly,' Rickard goes on. 'I hadn't until I got my memories back . . . I started to look for information online. Did you know there's a forum where people discuss Engelsfors? True, they discuss UFOs as well, but in one of the threads there was this list of everyone who has disappeared in the forests around this town since the early 1900s. And when I saw it . . .'

He pauses to swallow.

'I was scared shitless. It was so very, very long. I didn't used to like, really think much about it when someone disappeared. I mean, nobody does. There will be something in the papers and people worry about it for a while and then forget . . .' Another pause. 'Almost like they did after the Spring Equinox party.'

Anna-Karin shudders. Rickard is right.

'People disappeared in my day, too,' Nicolaus says.

'So you think it's something . . . supernatural that makes people vanish like that?' Evelina asks Anna-Karin.

'I don't know. But I know that the cave is important. The fox and I have been searching for something in the forest for a long time. And now we have found it.'

Anna-Karin looks around the group.

'We must explore the cave,' she says.

'Let's do it.' Linnéa takes a step forward. 'And now we have a natural fire witch and a natural metal witch, the Circle is whole again.'

Hearing this, Anna-Karin gets a nervous knot in her stomach. There's nothing 'whole' about this circle.

'You haven't even asked Rickard and Evelina if they want to join us,' Minoo says.

'Well, do you?' Linnéa asks.

'I want to do all I can to help,' Rickard confirms. 'You know that already.'

'Do you mind if I take some time to digest all this first?' Evelina says.

'Do we have to go over this again?' Minoo asks grimly. 'The guardians have stated that the Circle of the Chosen Ones cannot close the portal, even if we replace the dead. Our only chance is that I stay a member of the Council's new circle.'

'Yeah, we've understood that you prefer to believe in the

guardians and the Council rather than in us,' Linnéa tells her. 'Why not take their oath as well while you're at it?'

'That's fucking unfair!' Vanessa says.

'Minoo is faced with an exceptionally difficult choice,' Nicolaus agrees.

'I don't give a shit if it's difficult!' Linnéa shouts. 'She has to choose! Us or them!'

The silence is total now. Anna-Karin senses how the raised voices have stressed the fox. She hopes her own fears won't infect him and make him feel even worse. She must not be frightened. She must think clearly now that nobody else seems to be doing so. Linnéa can't force Minoo to choose. It might end with the wrong choice. Not that Anna-Karin is sure what the right one might be, only that this is the wrong time to make the decision.

'The box,' she says. 'Minoo can't leave the Council's circle before she has found the box. And she must try to find out how we use the objects to close the portal.'

'Sure,' Linnéa says. 'Minoo hangs on in the manor house until she has sorted the box problem and found out what we need to know. Meanwhile, we'll investigate the cave and train until we're ready. We have a real chance, don't you understand that, Minoo?'

'It's you who doesn't understand.'

Anna-Karin hardly recognizes Minoo's voice. She even looks different. There is pure hatred in her eyes as she looks at Linnéa.

'You don't care about what the guardians have seen in the future. But let me tell you what I've seen here and now,' Minoo continues. 'The powers of Evelina, Rickard and Nicolaus are nothing compared to those of Nejla, Sigrid and Walter. The Chosen Ones are strong witches but, as a unit, the Council's circle is stronger. It isn't enough to be a natural witch. This task can't be completed by just anyone.'

'No, of course not,' Linnéa says. 'One must be chosen. By

the Council. It must be so nice for you to hang out with other elitists. To be told how special and important you are. It's what you've always dreamt of, right?'

Linnéa speaks slowly, as if she wants every word to have maximum impact. It works, Anna-Karin can see that, as she watches Minoo.

'Linnéa, stop,' Vanessa tells her.

'No, I won't stop!' Linnéa responds. 'She is ruining everything! We have fought for this group and we've been through so fucking much together and now the guardians turn up from nowhere and say "must change circle, off you go, Minoo", and she does what she's told, no questions asked. What do you think Rebecka would've said about that, Minoo? Rebecka, who always wanted us to stick together! Can't you see you're betraying her by even *thinking* about what you're doing now?'

Minoo seems to have lost the power of speech and just stares blankly at Linnéa.

'That was low,' Gustaf says.

Anna-Karin can see that Linnéa is working herself up to a counterattack and realizes that she actually can stop her.

SHUT UP!

Linnéa is unprepared and hasn't a chance to defend herself against Anna-Karin's magic. Her lips move without making a sound.

'What's the matter?' Nicolaus asks.

Linnéa points furiously at Anna-Karin.

'Yes, I did it,' Anna-Karin says. 'And I'll do it again if I have to. You said it yourself, we must stick together now.'

Her voice is breaking. 'I'm not going to let any one of you destroy this. Don't you understand that you're important? Not just because you're the Chosen Ones. Don't you understand that I've got no one . . .'

She is surprised when tears well up into her eyes.

'I have no one else.'

Again, complete silence in the pavilion. Anna-Karin's pulse hammers in her ears. She doesn't dare look at anyone.

'You're right.' Vanessa speaks up. 'We must do this one step at a time. And we can't mess this up.'

Nicolaus pats Anna-Karin's arm.

'I think this is enough for one day,' he says. 'We are all tired. Allow me to remind you that Olivia might turn up here at any moment. Don't be outside on your own. Take care of each other.'

He looks around the group and singles out Linnéa and Minoo as he says the last few words.

Chapter 66

Minoo lingers on the stage in the dance pavilion. She doesn't want to stay. But she can't move.

She feels as if Linnéa has exploded an atom bomb inside her. All is devastated now.

Linnéa and Vanessa were the first to leave. Then the others wandered away. All except Gustaf, who still sits next to her on the edge of the stage.

'Is this how it usually is?' he asks.

'No,' Minoo says. 'OK, we argued now and then, but we're . . .'

A pause.

'You're friends?' Gustaf finishes.

'That's what I used to think, anyway.'

Minoo draws her finger across the wooden stage floor. Her fingertip gets dirty and she wipes it on her trouser leg. Glances at Gustaf. He leans forward and his hands lie clasped on his lap.

'Sorry if I was a little too direct about your powers,' she says.

'No problem,' he says with a faint smile. 'I didn't think I had any. But of course it feels tough that Rickard and Evelina but not me . . . I really do want to help, you know.'

She had believed for a long time that she had no power at all, and wonders if Gustaf feels now as she did then. He, more than anyone, is so used to being the best at everything, including things that Minoo had never been successful at, like sport and popularity.

'Do you think I'm doing the right thing?' she asks. 'Or is Linnéa right?'

She doesn't dare look at him. She regrets already that she even asked the question. Another condemnation would be beyond bearing.

'I think Linnéa went too far,' Gustaf says. 'Way too far. Having said that, I can understand her, too . . .'

She glances at him again. He looks thoughtful.

'Look, Minoo, I don't know what's right and wrong here. But what you're going through seems very hard. And lonely.'

Amongst all the debris inside her, something stirs. A small, living shoot rises out of the ashes.

'This is how I see it,' Gustaf continues. 'I can't do very much to help save the world . . .'

He straightens up and turns to her.

'But I am your friend.'

At his words, Minoo suddenly feels utterly present and aware, even as, at the same time, the world around her is dissolving.

Gustaf looks closely at her. His eyes scrutinize her face. But it doesn't make her nervous. Not at all. She doesn't want him to stop looking at her, ever.

She places her hand on his. It is warm under her cold fingertips. He puts his hand on top of hers. Warms it.

And then he leans toward her. She feels his breath on her lips before he kisses her.

CHAPTER 67

Vanessa walks beside Linnéa along the gravel road. Neither has uttered a word since they left Kärrgruvan.

Vanessa doesn't know where to begin. She is so angry with Linnéa. She loves her so very much. And she is so very worried about her.

It seems to her as if Linnéa has decided to cut them all off. Vanessa, too. It has happened so quickly. Vanessa is not even sure that she can stop her. But she knows she must try.

'Linnéa,' she says, 'we really have to talk.'

She hopes that the way she says it will signal how seriously she means it. Hopes, too, that Linnéa will take it seriously.

'What do we have to talk about?' Linnéa asks, and stops.

She tries to look untroubled but Vanessa picks up a hint of fear in her eyes. Not only that, she *feels* how frightened Linnéa is.

It is the Linnéa who dreads being abandoned who does all this. That Linnéa is a pain in the ass; she is a coward and stupid as well, but Vanessa loves her all the same.

'I know you're scared,' Vanessa tells her.

'What?'

'Lay off. You can't hide from me, don't you get that?'

Linnéa turns her head away. Stares into the forest. Vanessa is cold with worry. Is Linnéa already too far gone? Is it even possible to reach her?

'I don't know what it's like to feel the way you do,' Vanessa says. 'But I want to understand it. Because I love you.'

A truck is driving along the highway.

'I know you have many battles to fight. And I want to fight them at your side. I want to help you. But you won't let me in.'

She puts her hand on Linnéa's arm.

'Please Linnéa,' she begs. 'Please, don't disappear. I want to help.'

Linnéa finally looks straight at her. Her eyes are lifeless.

'You can't,' she says. 'We'd better end it now. What's the point of being together when it's so fucking hard?'

* * *

When Linnéa hears her own voice, panic rises within her.

'You can't just say stuff like that,' Vanessa tells her. 'We will never be able to talk about anything that matters if you threaten to break up all the time.'

Linnéa wants nothing more than to put her arms around Vanessa, ask her for forgiveness. Forgive me for ruining everything; forgive me for being so fucking . . . me.

She sees how hurt Vanessa is and hates herself. And then it all becomes clear. Vanessa doesn't deserve this.

However much Linnéa tries to behave better, be better, it's useless. She will never succeed. The only outcome will be that Vanessa grows more like her. Vanessa will be wrecked.

'I mean it,' Linnéa says.

Vanessa shakes her head.

'It isn't true. You said yourself that you always try to mess up anything good that ever happens to you. But it's not okay for you to behave like this. You hurt people. You hurt *me*.'

Her voice is sad and small. It makes Linnéa even more certain that she is doing the right thing. She makes Vanessa feel miserable. So, she must set her free. Because Vanessa apparently thinks that Linnéa is a riddle she can find the answer to, but the answer is too obvious for her to see it: Linnéa is fucked up. And always will be.

Make a clean cut. Then the wound heals faster.

'Do you think this is good?' Linnéa asks. 'I don't. I can't

478

cope with this in my life right now. We must focus on what is important.'

'But this . . .' Vanessa's voice barely carries the words. 'Us. That's what's important. Isn't it?'

Linnéa forces herself to keep her eyes fixed on Vanessa, even though it is almost unbearable.

'No. It's not.'

She looks away. The others are coming along the road from Kärrgruvan. Evelina and Rickard, then a little behind them, Nicolaus and Anna-Karin. They will take care of Vanessa.

She pulls herself together, gathers the last of her strength to look at Vanessa again, ready to say that it's all over, that it's all for the best.

'Then you can fuck off,' Vanessa tells her.

Linnéa looks at Vanessa in shock. She has seen her angry before. But not like this.

Vanessa looks as if she can't stand the sight of her.

This is Linnéa's worst nightmare. And she herself has made it a reality.

'I can't be with someone who backs out the moment things get tough,' Vanessa says. 'I'm better off on my own, because at least then I can *be myself*. I hate being the person I become when you're like this. And I hate the way you behave, as if I'm being unreasonable when all I want is for us to talk. It feels like I'm constantly running after you, trying to be helpful, and do the right thing and say the right thing and—'

'I never asked for any of that,' Linnéa interrupts.

'Fuck you!' Vanessa says. 'I really wanted to . . . I've never . . .'

She falls silent and shakes her head. 'It doesn't matter anymore.'

The others are getting closer. Linnéa must go. She couldn't bear to see them now.

'I'm sorry it came to this,' she says.

Vanessa doesn't reply.

The Key

Linnéa climbs up the railroad embankment, crosses the tracks and hurries toward the highway.

She is going home.

Home to her empty apartment. Home, to a bed where the sheets still smell of Vanessa.

For every step Linnéa takes, she becomes more and more aware of the choice she has made. And that it is irreversible.

The Borderland

CHAPTER 68

I da stands in the dance pavilion. Alone at last. At last.

Nicolaus has returned. He has had a haircut. Olivia is on her way. Evelina and Rickard are witches. There are caves in the forest with beetles and pictures of Leffe. They all want to get hold of a box that seems to be super-important. Minoo has joined another circle now. And she's making out with Gustaf.

Was that the first time they kissed? It looked a bit like it, so uncertain at first. Hesitant. But, later on, not hesitant at all.

Ida shouldn't have watched them but she couldn't stop herself. Even though every kiss they gave each other reminded her of every kiss she would never get. She kept hoping that one of them would break it off and say something like, *No, no, this isn't right, it's a mistake*.

It was even worse, in a way, when they walked away together. Gustaf put his arm around Minoo and she leaned against him. They looked as if they belonged together. Where were they off to? What were they going to do?

She mustn't think about it anymore. It's pointless. She should concentrate on all the other things that have happened, all the things she'd heard about.

It is so hard to keep up. And it seems just as hard for the others, even though their time runs more slowly than hers.

Start with Minoo. She has become a member of a circle set up by the Council. She has joined because the guardians say that only that circle can save the world, and only if Minoo joins it.

Ida hasn't a clue if that's true or not. But she does know for a fact that even when the guardians tell the truth, they could still double-cross you.

They did that with their promises to her, after all.

Ida had hoped that, when Minoo went into the state that lets her observe magic, she would be able to see *her*, Ida. All the time, she tried to move to where Minoo was looking. But, no. Minoo clearly hasn't become that much of a super-witch.

Ida badly wants to tell the other Chosen Ones about how the guardians tricked her; about the kiss they used as bait. What if that's the piece of information that the others need to be able to make up their minds?

Suddenly, the grayness falls ahead of her, like a curtain being dropped. When it dissolves again, it is dark.

'Hey, look, an old raincoat!' a male voice says.

Ida sees two dancing beams of light. Flashlights. Rickard and Anna-Karin have one each. Rickard, whom some of them want to use as a stand-in for Ida. Just because he's a metal witch and alive. But there must be snags in any plan based on the notion that Ida is replaceable.

The lights shine on rough stone walls and piles of old, dirty things. This must be the cave Anna-Karin had told them about.

'Anyway, no beetles as far as I can see,' Rickard says.

'Don't talk about them,' another voice adds.

So, Evelina is here as well. Ida totally agrees with her. She doesn't want to think about what might hide in the pitch-black spaces around them.

More cones of light come toward them. Ida sees Vanessa's blonde hair. A little further along, Linnéa's face with its dead-pale make-up seems to float free in the darkness. The fox's eyes gleam in the torchlight. Nicolaus's deep voice echoes against the stone walls.

But no Gustaf. And no Minoo.

Perhaps they're together. Kissing. Doing much more. Who

knows how much time has passed since she last saw them? They might well be married by now.

'Here's a tunnel!' Anna-Karin calls out.

'There's another one here!' Rickard swings the flashlight around and almost dazzles Ida. 'And another one!'

'We'd better have a look then,' Nicolaus says.

His face and clothes are filthy. Ida realizes that he must somehow have crawled through the narrow passage that Anna-Karin described. Hard to imagine.

Anna-Karin shines her flashlight at one of the gaping holes leading into the mountain.

'Do we really have to?' Evelina asks. 'What I'm trying to say is, what do we hope to find? More beetles?'

'What if we do this in pairs?' Nicolaus suggests. 'Anna-Karin and I will take the left-hand tunnel. Vanessa and Linnéa can have a look at the middle—'

'I should probably go with Evelina,' Vanessa interrupts.

'Oh, yes, good,' Nicolaus agrees. 'Of course it's better if the more experienced ones accompany the new members of the group.'

'That's not what she means,' Linnéa says. 'Vanessa and I have broken up.'

'What?' Ida exclaims.

The others say absolutely nothing.

'It isn't a problem,' Linnéa continues. 'I mean, it won't affect the stuff we're doing here. But I think it's better if Rickard and I do this together.'

'Let's go,' Vanessa says. She tugs at Evelina to go with her into one of the tunnels. Before she disappears, Ida has time to see that Vanessa's eyes are shiny with tears.

Linnéa just stands there, chewing on one of her nails, looking untroubled. Ida cannot understand how she can give Vanessa up so easily. If Ida had been her, and if she had met anyone who looked at her the way Vanessa looked at Linnéa . . . then she would've done anything on earth to keep them.

The Key

Suddenly, Ida hears birdsong behind her. She turns and, as the gray mists drift away, sees a beautiful garden. The air is clear. In the distance, a blackbird is singing.

She looks around. The building overlooking the garden is the manor house.

She walks up the steps. The garden doors are closed and she can't open them, of course. Instead, she peeps in through one of the tall windows.

Minoo stands in the middle of the floor of a large room, facing a tall man with tousled, graying hair. He comes across like one of those middle-aged men who refuse to accept that their glory days are over.

Minoo's eyes are open but that weird expression is back. She's in that state where she sees things that no one else can. Perhaps she will spot Ida this time? Ida waves with both hands but Minoo doesn't seem to notice.

Now Minoo's hair is moving, lifting as if in a wind. A wind that grows in strength, tears at their clothes and then dies away. Then all is still again.

The man claps his hands and, as Ida watches, Minoo seems to wake up. And she smiles at the man.

Ida goes back to check the doors. How hard can it be? If she can't touch things, maybe she's able to walk through them?

She takes a few steps back, then leaps at the door. She slides through with a triumphant shout.

In front of her, she sees Linnéa, Rickard and Nicolaus lined up. All three are wearing padded anoraks and are shining their flashlights straight through Ida. Reflected light dances over the cave walls and illuminates their faces, glinting in Rickard's glasses.

Ida looks over her shoulder.

A subterranean lake. The surface of the water glitters in the light from the flashlights.

A rustle from an anorak as its owner moves. It's Rickard, who is walking to the water's edge. One of the arms of his glasses has been taped together. Ida wonders if he has hit his head while exploring.

He shines the flashlight on the water's surface.

'I can't even see the bottom. We'll have to turn back.'

His voice bounces between the walls.

Linnéa joins him.

'Move over,' she says.

Rickard backs away. Linnéa goes down on her haunches, puts her flashlight and her gloves away and closes her eyes. Then she reaches out to the water so that her fingertips are just a few millimeters above the surface, nearly touching it.

A crackling, creaking noise echoes though the cave. A film of ice forms on the water under Linnéa's fingertips and then spreads across the lake. The surface hardens and turns milky white.

Linnéa pulls her gloves on and gets up.

'Wow,' Rickard says quietly.

Linnéa takes a step forward.

'Linnéa . . .' Nicolaus begins.

But Linnéa has already placed one foot on the ice and now she steps out on it with both feet. Ida hardly dares to look.

'We don't know if the ice will hold,' Nicolaus warns her.

'We're about to find out,' Linnea responds.

She takes few more steps. Stops, and suddenly sways, as if she feels dizzy. Then she goes down on her knees.

Rickard and Nicolaus rush out on the ice to help her.

'I'm fine.' Linnéa pushes their hands away. 'I was just over-doing it a bit. Have you noticed how fucking tired you get down here?'

'Yes,' Rickard says, frowning. 'I know exactly what you mean.'

'So do I,' Nicolaus agrees. He directs the light out over the frozen lake. 'There's something odd about these tunnels . . .'

His voice is cut off. Ida is no longer in the cave. She stands in a red hallway in front of a portrait of Henrik Ehrenskiöld.

The Key

Once more, she is amazed that someone with such kind eyes could be so treacherous.

She hears cautious steps from the end of the hallway and sees Minoo come along it, stop outside a closed door and look around nervously. She carefully tries to open the door.

It doesn't budge. Minoo tugs at the door handle a couple of times before starting to go back the way she came. She stops abruptly when the man she had been practicing magic with turns up in the hallway.

'Hello, what are you doing here?' he says, sounding surprised. 'I thought you had gone home?'

'Yes, but I just . . .' Minoo falls silent.

Her back is turned to Ida, but Ida can easily guess at just how guilty she looks. Minoo is probably the worst liar ever.

'I just wanted to ask you if I can take time off to attend court?' Minoo continues.

'Absolutely,' the man says. 'No need to ask, really.'

The gray mist sweeps past. Then too many impressions crowd in simultaneously. Lots of voices talking. Laughter. Clatter of cutlery. The air is thick with the smell of greasy fry-ups. And someone must have smothered themselves in cheap perfume.

Ida is in line at the hot food counter in the dining area of Engelsfors High School. It is packed with students and many of the faces are new to her. Must be the new freshmen.

Ida touches her silver heart with her fingertips.

Her family has moved from town. Soon everyone she used to hang out with will have graduated and will surely leave. Before long, there will hardly be anyone left in Engelsfors who knew Ida Holmström. Though soon there might not be an Engelsfors left at all.

A shrill scream cuts through the noise. Hanna A stands at the salad buffet and screams and screams.

The screaming spreads across the whole dining area. People are jumping away from the tables, overturning chairs. A guy in the food line throws his plate away. It spins straight through Ida and the macaroni scatters all over the floor.

No.

Not macaroni.

Maggots.

Repulsive, whitish larvae are writhing on the floor.

Now Ida screams, too. Those larvae *passed through* her. When she looks around, the maggots are everywhere. They well up over the edges of the hot food containers. Crawl across the tables.

At one of the tables, someone is throwing up noisily. Several more follow suit. Others spit out porridgy mouthfuls of chewed food and maggots.

The large room is filling with a stench, a heavy smell of rotting. Of *death*.

In the distance, Ida catches a glimpse of Anna-Karin's stricken face and then the grayness thickens and whirls around her.

'What did you want to talk about?' It is Viktor's voice.

Viktor and Minoo are standing in semi-darkness inside an old freight wagon. It looks like a drugs den, or a place where a serial killer might drag his victims. It's probably both. On the upside, it's free of maggots.

'Just before the summer, you said you'd do anything for me,' Minoo says.

'Yes,' Viktor replies.

Is he in love with Minoo *as well*? How insane is that? And can't she just have him instead of Gustaf?

'What would you like me to do?' asks Viktor.

'I need the key to Adriana's room,' Minoo tells him.

Ida sighs. She is so fed up with never understanding what people are talking about.

'Why?' Viktor asks.

'I understand if you don't want to give it to me,' Minoo says. 'Now that you've sworn the oath—'

'I'll do it,' he interrupts. 'Is it urgent?'

'Yes, it is. Sorry.'

Viktor nods and pats his already perfect hair into place.

'I cannot believe that the wood element has reacted, too,' he says. 'Things are moving very quickly. Only four portents to go. Have they reopened the school yet?'

'Anna-Karin told me that the whole dining area has been fumigated. And that they are blaming the whole thing on the caterer.'

They must be talking about what Ida has just seen.

Viktor kicks an old beer can that's lying around on the floor. Ida can't think why they want to meet in this horrible, filthy place.

'How is everyone?' Viktor asks. 'Anna-Karin and the rest?'

'Just fine.' Minoo doesn't look at him.

'I know you're lying,' he says softly.

Viktor's power is so annoying, Ida thinks.

Minoo smiles sadly.

'I don't want to talk about it.'

'Can't you tell me what you want to do in Adriana's room? If I knew, I might be able to help you more.'

'Viktor, I'm sorry, but I can't say more. The others wouldn't be pleased if they knew I'd said as much as I have.'

'But *you* trust me?'

Minoo meets his eyes.

'Yes,' she says, and sounds almost surprised. 'I actually do.'

Viktor's smile shows that Minoo has been truthful.

And then the mist rolls in.

Ida scans her surroundings. She is confused. Large stagnant puddles on a cement floor reflect tall windows with many broken panes. Square concrete pillars support a ceiling so high above her she can only guess at the massive beams and huge pipework up there. In one corner, an entire spiral staircase has worked loose from its attachments and collapsed sidewise onto the floor. When she turns around, enormous machines loom in the dark like prehistoric animals.

If Ida hadn't heard a train rumble past in the distance she might have thought that the apocalypse had already struck. In here, it is very easy to imagine a lifeless planet.

She goes to look out of one of the windows. More dejected-looking buildings with broken windowpanes. Overgrown railroad tracks and rusting freight wagons. The shadow of a huge chimney falls across the parking lot. She knows where she is now.

The steel plant. The pride of old Engelsfors.

Ida jumps when she hears a crackling sound.

A blue light flickers near the spiral staircase. Someone is sitting there.

Slowly, Ida advances, passing through a fire extinguisher and a pile of rusty steel-reinforcing mesh.

More crackling. The fluttering blue light fades away near the wall but Ida has time to catch a glimpse of her.

A girl in a black parka jacket and a black cap pulled down over her forehead. A girl with large, brown eyes.

Olivia.

Flashes of lightning flare again and again between the palms of her hands. Some meet in the air, twist around each other, form a ball that unravels and becomes new flashes.

Ida stares at them, as if hypnotized. Remembers what it felt like to be hit by one of them. How she was thrown backward and slammed into the floor. The tingling that spread throughout her body and turned to chills.

Flashes of lightning leap high into the air, all the way to the ceiling, where they wind and twist around the pipes and strike sparks from the steel beams.

Olivia turns her face up to look. In the electrical glow, Ida sees the same hate-filled eyes that she had met in the gym.

Olivia is so strong. Much stronger than she was when she killed Ida.

I must warn the others, Ida thinks. There must be some fucking way.

The mist rolls past so quickly she hardly has time to react.

She is in a bathroom. She has been here before. The door is open a little and outside someone is listening to some really annoying music. And she remembers. This is Linnéa's place.

The door opens and Linnéa comes in. She is wearing soft fitness shorts and a worn T-shirt with the logo DIR EN GRAY. She goes to the mirror, pins her bangs back and starts washing her make-up off. It takes time. The basin fills with black splashes.

Ida looks at Linnéa's back. Knows that she must try.

'Linnéa! Hello! It's me, Ida! You've got to listen to me! It's important! Olivia is in town and she is hiding in the old steel plant!'

She reaches out with her hand and swallows the uneasy feeling when she sees it disappear into Linnéa's back. She forces herself to keep waving it around.

But Linnéa just picks up some cotton-wool pads and starts wiping around her eyes. Far too roughly. You need to be gentle, because the skin there is really sensitive. Tug too much and you get wrinkles and bags under the eyes.

Ida looks into the mirror.

And sees a glimpse of her own face. Just for a brief moment.

Of course. They talked about it before the séance. Ghosts are attracted to mirrors. It made Ida terrified of mirrors. Now she's a ghost herself. Irony of fate stuff again, how she loves it.

'Linnéa!' she shouts. 'Look up!' Then, 'Look up! I'm here! In the mirror!'

And Linnéa does look up. And screams.

Ida shouts for joy now. Linnéa turns around.

'You saw me!' Ida says. 'You . . .'

Linnéa looks straight through her.

'Shit,' Linnéa mumbles. She presses her wrist against her forehead. 'I can't cope. It's too much.'

'No, you're not crazy!' Ida shrieks. 'You did see me! It's true, I'm here! Linnéa!'

'I need to get some sleep,' Linnéa mutters to herself, turns back to the mirror where Ida is no longer visible. 'I *really* need to sleep.'

She reaches for a jar on the cabinet shelf, pours out a couple of pills and washes them down with a mouthful of water. Ida stands there, helpless, as Linnéa leaves the bathroom and turns off the light.

'Come back!' Ida calls after her. 'Come on, let me try again!'

But now she is back in the Borderland.

Her heart is beating fast as she looks around. Was she shouting here? Would the invisible monster have heard her?

Nothing.

But, suddenly, she becomes aware of something new.

It feels as if a thread is tugging at her. Pulling her closer. She begins to follow it.

The grayness around her is unchanging but, all the same, she is sure. She is on her way to somewhere.

Whatever is there, whatever she has to find, it is not something that she can perceive with her normal senses. All the same, she doesn't hesitate. It is so clear. And so *familiar*. It is like something important that she has lost.

For the first time since she landed in this mess, she feels certain of something. Somewhere in the Borderland, there is something she must find. That is where she is going now.

Part 4

CHAPTER 69

Anna-Karin walks along the path leading into the forest, behind the new estate where Gustaf lives. She moves some low-hanging branches out of the way and holds them so that they won't bounce back into Nicolaus's face. After him, Vanessa, Evelina, Rickard and Gustaf follow in a single line.

They pass the ring of large blocks of stone linked by heavy chains. Anna-Karin casts a sideways glance at the sign stating that this is a mass grave for people who died in the 1853 cholera epidemic. It is a place that always makes her feel uncomfortable.

Autumn has come early this year. The leaves of birch and mountain ash are changing color already. The September sun shines over the forest but doesn't warm the air. For the last few days, Anna-Karin thinks she has smelled snow on the wind. They carry on walking deeper into the forest.

They have been exploring the system of caves for three weeks now. Thankfully, they have found other, easier entrances. Like the one they are heading to now.

The fox is walking lightly at Anna-Karin's feet. Now and then his tail brushes her leg. She senses that today he is keener than usual to explore and his eagerness infects her. He is certain that, today, their search will be worthwhile. Still, Anna-Karin won't tell the others. Even though nobody says it out loud, she knows that their patience is wearing thin.

All the time, tension is simmering below the surface. Once the wood element reacted in the dining area, there are only four more portents to go. Also, Minoo hasn't managed to find out more about the box and has learned no more about how to close the portal.

The ground is sloping upwards now. Anna-Karin's back is dripping with sweat as she struggles to negotiate the dense growth of ferns. The sweat, she knows well, will turn ice-cold as soon as they are in the damp, chilly darkness of the caves. She shivers just thinking about it.

They have left chalk marks near already investigated entrances and tried to draw maps of the system. One of the problems is that compasses don't work inside the mountain. All they have truly learned is that the system extends much further than they had first thought, and includes old mine shafts and natural passages that run in every direction underneath Engelsfors. Some tunnels have been blocked by rock falls and Anna-Karin has had to clear many of these. Most of the tunnels so far have ended blindly, or narrowed so much that exploration has become impossible. Now, there are only two untried tunnels left.

Step by step, Anna-Karin starts the descent on the other side of the ridge. It is a steep slope that ends on a ledge above a rock face.

'God, I hate nature,' Evelina groans from somewhere far behind.

Finally, Anna-Karin stands on the ledge. It is so high that she looks down on the treetops; she is terrified of falling every time she looks.

They had spent a whole day in the tunnels when they found this opening. At first, they thought it was another dead end. But then they saw faint beams of daylight outlining a giant boulder that blocked the way. Despite Anna-Karin's new strength, it took several tries before it gave way and they were suddenly dazzled by the sunlight that entered. The boulder tipped over the edge and fell to the bottom of the rock face. The mighty crash echoed around the forest.

'Is it OK if you take the same route as you did yesterday?'

Anna-Karin asks Vanessa and Evelina when they have climbed down to the ledge. 'And we will test the tunnel underneath the town?'

'Whatever,' Vanessa says. She pulls on her mom's hot pink, quilted winter jacket. 'They're all the same.'

'We don't know that yet,' Nicolaus says.

'Don't we, though?' Vanessa asks, and then she sighs. 'Sorry, just being bad-tempered.'

No need for her to explain why. Tomorrow, they are going to court in Västerås. Anna-Karin can't imagine how Vanessa feels about that. Not to mention Linnéa.

'And there's definitely nothing to cheer you up inside the caves,' Vanessa adds.

Anna-Karin nods. She still isn't sure if it is the cold, the monotony or the lack of real light that makes their time in the caves so exhausting. She hopes this will be their last day here.

Vanessa and Evelina switch their flashlights on and step into the dark opening first.

Anna-Karin follows them with her eyes while she opens her backpack and pulls out the woollen sweater and duffel coat she has stuffed into it.

The zip on Rickard's anorak makes a ripping noise when he pulls it right up to his chin. The frame of his glasses had to be mended with tape after he fell over an old camping stove in one of the passages. Rickard, Gustaf and Nicolaus have spent more time underground than the rest of them. Rickard's powers have developed quickly. Now, he can sense human energy fields and determine when he is underneath populated areas.

Anna-Karin turns her own flashlight on and goes inside, followed by the others. Gustaf and Nicolaus have to bend over to move in there. These last few days, Nicolaus has been trailing a strong smell of muscle balm.

She thinks of the time when Engelsfors was a mining town, and remembers photographs of the workforce who spent every day of their working life underground. The ghostly old pictures on display in the local museum, where rows of miners stare gravely into the camera with tired, empty eyes. Little boys, sometimes no older than nine or ten, are lined up in the front row. Their eyes look unnaturally light in their dirty faces.

Anna-Karin allows the darkness and the cold to enclose her as she continues into the mountain.

* * *

The light from Vanessa's flashlight plays over the rough, craggy walls of the tunnel.

She shivers despite her jacket, which is so bulky she can hardly move. She has always detested winter clothes. So clumsy, and they don't even help much. Here, the raw chill quickly finds a way in. And wraps itself like a wet blanket around your body. All warmth is just sucked out. All energy, too. She feels tired already.

Evelina makes her flashlight float in front of them. She always was a slouch about schoolwork, but seems never to tire of practicing her magic powers. Vanessa has also tried to practice but hasn't managed to levitate again.

'Do you remember that horror movie we watched, about girls going climbing inside caves?' Evelina says. 'And then they got lost and were eaten by monsters? Time to watch it again, don't you think?'

'Why not a double-bill with the one about the St Valentine's Day murderer who hides in old mine shafts?' Vanessa suggests.

They laugh but their laughter rings false. No amount of laughing can take away the fact that they are living a horror movie. It's probably a sequel, since Olivia is on her way back, like one of those serial killers who are impossible to kill and never give up.

They have tried to locate her by suspending a pendulum above a map of Engelsfors, but it swung wildly in a way they have never seen before. Mona Moonbeam might have been able to help, but the Crystal Cave is still shut.

Vanessa feels certain that Olivia will have a go at Linnéa first. Minoo might well be the most important, because she is the only one of them that can't ever be replaced by another witch. But between Linnéa and Olivia it's personal.

And Olivia isn't the only threat. There is the court case as well.

Vanessa worries so much about Linnéa. And is furious with her as well. Sometimes, her anger makes her sleepless. Her heart keeps beating too hard.

'What's wrong?' Evelina asks.

'I was thinking about Linnéa,' Vanessa says. 'She must feel terrible about tomorrow.'

'I don't get why she broke up with you,' Evelina says. 'If I were in her position, I'd want to have someone by my side just now.'

'But I get it,' Vanessa tells her. As usual, it's impossible to stop talking about Linnéa once she has started. 'She's such a fucking coward. She's scared of being hurt. And part of me knows that she has all these issues to cope with. But another part says . . . What the fuck, come on! Who isn't scared of being hurt? I mean, does she think that anyone likes it?'

They have arrived at the place where they stopped exploring yesterday; they crawl past the pile of stones that blocked the passage before Anna-Karin shifted them out of the way.

'She could trust me,' Vanessa continues. 'I would have done absolutely anything to help her and it's so fucking tragic that she won't see that.'

'It really is,' Evelina says.

'Thanks for listening,' Vanessa says.

'No need to thank me. Seriously.'

'Yes, there is. I don't know what I would've done without you. What if this had happened when I couldn't talk to you? I would have been a wreck. I mean, who else could I have talked to? I never see Minoo these days and Anna-Karin is lovely but isn't exactly experienced with relationships.'

'Looks like Nicolaus, then.' Evelina grins.

The tunnel ceiling is lower now and Evelina allows the flashlight to land in her hand.

'Listen,' she adds. 'I'm sorry I was such a bitch. Before I knew.'

'You didn't have any choice.'

'Maybe not. But now I know so exactly what it was like for you. Just look at me and Leo.'

Leo had realized immediately that something had changed for Evelina. And drew his own conclusions when she started producing feeble excuses for not being able to see him, had less and less time to talk to him, and obviously had her head full of thoughts that she wouldn't tell him about. The previous Saturday, he'd got drunk and then called her to say it was over between them.

'Have you heard any more from him?' Vanessa asks.

'Nope. And I don't think I'd speak to him if he phoned me. It's impossible to talk to him when he's convinced I've slept around with half of Engelsfors.'

The ceiling rises again and they straighten up. Vanessa rolls her shoulders a little, tries to stimulate the circulation.

'I thought you'd take it much harder,' she says.

'So did I. But the way he behaves is so unsexy. I just can't take it . . . Michelle is upset because we don't hang with her any longer. And Dad is bitter because I've stopped going to Örebro. Mom and I have fought more than ever because I'm skipping school all the time, and all I want to say to all of them is like, *Hello, I'm busy trying to save your life and everybody else's.*

'You don't get any gratitude in this job,' Vanessa tells her.

'Too true.'

They walk around a bend and suddenly the passage stops.

'Oh, fuck,' Evelina says.

Vanessa scans the stone wall with her flashlight.

'Maybe the others have found something,' Evelina suggests, but she doesn't sound convinced.

Vanessa almost hopes that the others have also hit a dead end. Then they would have run out of places to investigate.

'Vanessa, look!' Evelina shines her flashlight on the cave floor. A wristwatch.

She makes it float up through the air and land in her palm. Once, the watch was gold-colored, but that outer coating has pretty much disappeared.

Vanessa wonders whose arm used to wear that watch, and where that arm is now. She shudders. Where are all the people whose belongings they have come across?

Vanessa and Evelina search the whole area but find nothing more. Only stone, stone, and more stone.

* * *

Anna-Karin walks along the dark passage beside Nicolaus.

The fox runs ten to twenty yards ahead of them. Now and then, she shares his senses and his curiosity, too.

They are close.

'There is something different about this tunnel,' Nicolaus says. 'Isn't there?'

'I think so,' Anna-Karin replies.

She hears Rickard's and Gustaf's voices behind her.

'Have you talked with Minoo recently?' Nicolaus asks.

It seems weird that he should ask that, since she and Minoo live in the same house. But they have hardly even seen each other during these last few weeks. Minoo is at the manor house all the time. She hasn't once come to the caves.

Anna-Karin hears Gustaf laugh at something Rickard has said. Gustaf hasn't seen much of Minoo either, even though they are together now.

'She wasn't back when I went to bed last night,' she says. 'And when I got up this morning, she'd already left.'

Secretly, Anna-Karin had felt relieved. These days, their conversations are stilted. Anna-Karin tries to make everything feel as it was before and wants to show Minoo that they're still friends, still belong together. But it is hard when Minoo won't speak about what is happening in the manor house. Whenever Anna-Karin asks, she's evasive, saying that they 'are just practicing'.

'She doesn't answer the phone when I call,' Nicolaus says. 'She is withdrawing in a way that concerns me very much.'

'I suppose she might feel she has no choice,' Anna-Karin says. 'After that fight . . .'

Then she stops. And asks herself why she should defend Minoo when she's actually hurt by her behavior.

'Things can become very intense in closed groups like the one in the manor house,' Nicolaus observes. 'Also, Walter Hjorth seems to be an exceptionally charismatic man.'

Anna-Karin wishes that she could keep a closer eye on the manor house. But the fox is becoming more and more reluctant to go anywhere near it. She understands that it has to do with Walter's familiar. Lynxes are higher up the food chain.

At least it's good that Viktor is there. He has promised that he will never allow anyone to harm Minoo.

Suddenly there's a white flash in front of Anna-Karin's eyes. She is inside the fox's mind. His sensitivity to light has responded to something further ahead. Something that shouldn't be there.

Light.

The fox's curiosity turns instantly into fear. Anna-Karin opens her eyes and stops. 'There's something ahead of us.'

Nicolaus has stopped next to her.

Gustaf catches up with them. 'What's up?' he asks.

'The fox saw a light.'

'A light?' Rickard asks. 'Are you sure?'

'Yes, I am.'

Then Anna-Karin hears something move and come closer. She just has time to be frightened before she realizes that it's the fox.

'I have no idea what's there,' she says. 'Maybe we shouldn't all go on from here.'

'I'll join Vanessa and Evelina,' Gustaf says. 'If the fox comes with me, you can make him bark if you need help.'

She nods. Gustaf knows just as well as they do that if something dangerous is waiting for them, he is the one of least use. Anna-Karin wonders how it feels to be the only one in the group without powers.

Gustaf walks around a bend and the beam from his flashlight vanishes in the darkness.

'Let's go,' she says to Nicolaus and Rickard.

The stone floor is slippery here. The walls are dripping. Now and then, drops run down the inside of her duffel-coat collar.

Then, she sees it, this time with her own eyes.

A faint light further along.

'Could it be an opening of some kind? ' Nicolaus asks. 'An old mine shaft?'

'No.' Rickard shakes his head. 'We are still beneath the town.'

'And that can't be daylight,' Anna-Karin says. The light is far too blue.

She hurries now, almost slipping on the stones. Nicolaus calls her name but she doesn't care, doesn't care that the fox was frightened and that she, too, should be. She has to see it. Has to finally find out what it is they have been looking for all these weeks. What has tempted her into the forest, again and again, for such a long time.

Now she sees that the passage ends in a cave. The closer she gets, the stronger the light becomes.

She steps into the cave. And stops.

The ceiling is high. Ten feet, maybe more. On the rock wall opposite her, two circles are painted with ectoplasm. One outer, one inner. The circles emit a strong ice-blue radiance that glitters in minerals and deposits on the rock.

Anna-Karin moves toward the circles and steps straight into a puddle.

'Incredible,' she hears Nicolaus say behind her.

Anna-Karin walks all the way to the wall and reaches out her hand toward the innermost circle.

'Be careful,' Nicolaus says.

The ectoplasm has hardened. Its consistency reminds her of congealed candle-wax. It is very cold. Colder than the mountain itself.

Anna-Karin turns around. The blue light makes Rickard's and Nicolaus's faces look sculpted in ice.

'Look.' Rickard points at the ceiling.

Anna-Karin's eyes follow his pointing finger. Above the circles, the signs of the elements have been carved into the stone.

Fire. Earth. Air. Water. Metal. Wood.

Fire and wood glow faintly. These are the elements that have already reacted in the school.

And below the elemental signs, letters form before her very eyes, creating words she doesn't understand.

TENEBRIS APERIAR.

'Is that Latin?' Rickard asks.

Nicolaus nods. 'When darkness falls, I will open,' he translates. 'Walter said that the portal will become accessible when darkness falls over Engelsfors.'

Anna-Karin places her hand on the wall. Now she senses the presence of something on the other side. Something that vibrates, resonating in her body.

'This is where it is,' she announces. 'This is the portal. Behind this wall.'

'Yes,' Nicolaus agrees.

'That makes sense,' Rickard says.

Anna-Karin observes him. His face is turned up and his eyes are closed. The blue light gleams in his glasses.

'We are under the school,' he says, and opens his eyes. 'Somewhere between the gym and the dining area.'

'Are you sure?' Anna-Karin asks.

'Positive.'

'You must not tell Minoo about this,' Nicolaus says.

Surprised, Anna-Karin turns to him. He looks authoritative, in a manner that reminds her that he was once a minister of the church.

'We must not let the Council know that we have found the portal,' he continues.

'But Minoo won't tell anyone if we ask her not to,' Anna-Karin says.

'Can we be absolutely certain about that? We don't know where her loyalties lie any longer. She spends almost all her time with the members of the other circle.'

Anna-Karin wants to protest. But she can't. She is not at all sure who Minoo would be loyal to. She wonders if Minoo herself knows.

'Gustaf would never agree to keep a secret from Minoo,' Rickard points out.

'In that case, we won't tell him either,' Nicolaus says. 'We'll say that this was another dead end.'

'I'd feel terrible about lying to him,' he says.

'If the Council finds out that we know where the portal is, they will see to it that we never come anywhere near it.'

'But what if it is the Council that's meant to close it?' Rickard's voice echoes in the cave. 'I know that Linnéa is sure it isn't. But the rest of us have put off the whole debate while we've been running around down here. Now that we've found the portal, isn't it time we made up our minds?'

He looks from one of them to the other. Anna-Karin knows that he is right.

And then, suddenly, everything becomes clear to her.

'This place wanted us to come here,' she announces. 'It called us. Not the Council's circle.'

'Yes,' Nicolaus says. 'Perhaps the Council's circle has a chance to close the portal. But so do we.'

'I'm with you.' Rickard sighs. 'And I won't tell Gustaf.'

It's such a relief to have made a decision. Anna-Karin just hopes that Vanessa and Evelina agree.

And that, when the time comes, they will be able to convince Minoo.

CHAPTER 70

Two years.

That's how long you've been gone. That's how long I've missed you.

Now I'm sitting here again, at the place where you died. And I try to fool myself that I feel your presence.

But I don't. I am alone here.

And, E, there is something I must confess.

I have forgotten your voice. I have forgotten the sound of it. I see your face almost every day when I look at the photos we took. But it is becoming ever harder to remember how you moved, your posture, how the shadows fell on your face.

I have tried to draw you but every picture is crap. Flat and lifeless. The opposite to all that you were.

Tomorrow, I face them in court. Those who hurt us so many times. I tell myself that I do it for you, too. I try to draw strength from that thought. That I do it for us.

I wonder what you would do if you were here now. You would not tell me to be strong. You would just hold me.

I was stupid to tell V that it all was over between us. I should have let her in, let her be with me throughout this time.

I regret it every day. But I did do it. And that alone – that I could bring myself to shut V out – proves that I'm the wrong person for her. Someone who deserved to share her life wouldn't be able to act as I did.

If you can hear me despite everything, you must be sick of my whining.

When you lived, we could at least laugh at it together.

And that is perhaps what I miss most of all.
That together, we could laugh at all the shit that happens.
I love you,
L.

Linnéa closes her diary. She has settled down on the floor next to the sink and can look up to the windowsill. The tokens, the photos and flowers – there are not as many as last year. But she isn't the only one who tries to keep his memory alive.

She wonders if Olivia is also thinking about him right now.

Her cell phone pings. A message from Anna-Karin, who has just arrived at the school. She has to see her tutor and wants to meet in the entrance lobby immediately afterward. Then, she and Linnéa will go to the cave together.

Linnéa wants to see it with her own eyes. The place deep inside the rock beneath her. Where the portal is.

It surprised her that Nicolaus wanted to keep it secret from Minoo. Not that she's complaining.

Linnéa went too far in the park, she's perfectly aware of it. She gave her feelings free rein at a time when she should've been clever and controlled. Because, however wrong she thinks Minoo is, they need her. Without her, they won't be able to save the world. And they must make Minoo understand that and make her believe more in the Circle of the Chosen Ones than the Council's circle and the guardians.

Vanessa was right all along. Linnéa has driven Minoo straight into Walter's arms and now she worries that they won't be able to persuade her to come back to them.

Still, if they can't convince her, there are other ways. If the end of the world is nigh and only the Circle knows where the portal is, surely Minoo will have to join them? It is blackmail, but Linnéa tells herself that it is only a last resort. Desperate times call for desperate measures.

She hears steps outside the door to the bathroom and gets up. No one comes in, though.

'Here it is,' a girl's voice says on the other side of the door.

'And today, it's exactly two years ago. My big sis says that they've taken all the mirrors away so that nobody can do it again. And if you speak his name three times and turn quickly, he stands there. With a piece of glass dripping with blood in his hand. Do you want to check it out?'

The door handle goes down. Linnéa gets ready to shout at the stupid brats to go to hell.

'Shit, no!' a boy's voice responds with a little laugh. 'I'm too fucking scared.'

The girl giggles and the door handle goes up again.

'Let's write something anyway. It's like, traditional.'

Linnéa hears the squeaking sound of a marker pen on the outside of the door. Then the steps disappear and she opens the door to have a look.

The two kids have dyed their hair the same shade of green. They jog toward the main stairs hand in hand. It is obvious that they are best friends.

Linnéa's eyes follow them. And then suddenly fill with tears.

The marker ink hasn't quite dried when she touches the letters on the door.

R.I.P. ELIAS

* * *

Anna-Karin walks upstairs. The tiredness that always hits her in the caves is still with her, and now she can also feel the resonance from the rock wall deep beneath the school.

When darkness falls, I will open.

She, Vanessa and Linnéa have taken turns to be at school these last few weeks. The idea is that one of them is on hand to recognize the next portent of the apocalypse. It's Linnéa's turn today.

But Ylva wants to have a talk with Anna-Karin, who already has a pretty good idea of what it is her tutor will say.

Kevin comes downstairs. His baseball cap is pushed well

down over his forehead, but Anna-Karin notices that he's glancing at her from underneath the peak. She has a feeling that he wants to say something, but he continues down the stairs without saying a word.

The classroom door is open.

Ylva sits on the desk, looking through an evening paper. She looks up when Anna-Karin enters.

'Hello, Anna-Karin,' she says. She puts the paper down. 'Good that you could come. Please close the door behind you.'

Anna-Karin does as she is asked.

'Why don't you sit down?' Ylva suggests. Anna-Karin sits down on the desk opposite her.

'Anna-Karin,' Ylva begins, 'I realize that you have had a difficult time since . . . the spring.'

Ylva looks at Anna-Karin with a questioning expression. As if wanting to assure herself that she doesn't need to put the phrase into words. *Since your mother died.*

Anna-Karin nods.

'We need to discuss your marks,' Ylva says. 'You have told me that you want to go on to study for a degree in veterinary medicine.'

She goes on to explain gravely about how difficult it is to get into popular fields of study in general, and how the competition for places is growing tougher every year. Anna-Karin is perfectly aware of all that. It used to worry her. Now, she realizes how long it has been since she thought about the future in those terms.

'You're one of my ablest students,' Ylva tells her. 'I know that you can do so much better than you have been recently. As for your attendance . . . well, Anna-Karin, I am terribly disappointed.'

Ylva looks sternly at her. Anna-Karin wonders what she is expected to say next. Should she say that she misses her mother so much that she hasn't been able to focus on school? Or perhaps excuse herself by saying that, since Minoo left, it has been especially tough, because she has no other friends in her class? Should she promise to get her act together? Promise that she will make a real effort from now on?

But what promises can she make? She can't postpone the apocalypse to make sure she gets a decent grade in math.

'Is there anything I can help you with?' Ylva says.

'No, but thank you for talking to me about this,' Anna-Karin replies.

Ylva stands and looks relieved. As though she feels that she has done all she can for Anna-Karin.

'Well, we'll let it rest for now. And I'm always around if you need to talk.'

'Thank you,' Anna-Karin replies. At last she can get out of the classroom.

She hurries downstairs with her cell phone in her hand, ready to text, when she sees Linnéa waiting in the lobby.

People glance at Linnéa as they pass. The atmosphere is charged. Whatever happens in tomorrow's court session, it will go down in the history of Engelsfors High School, and will be told to each new generation of students.

Linnéa doesn't respond to the curious looks. Anna-Karin knows no one who can look as unapproachable. Her black bangs almost hide her heavily made-up eyes. The purple skirt that stands out around her might have looked girly on anyone else, but the black lace around the hem looks razor-blade sharp, a defense against any approaches.

They have been distant with each other ever since the time in the pavilion, when Anna-Karin used her magic to stop Linnéa talking. Anna-Karin has no regrets. Or, maybe one, that she didn't do it sooner. The possibility that they might have lost Minoo worries her. But then, she is worried about Linnéa as well. She is in free fall, and Anna-Karin is concerned both for her and for the people she might drag down with her. By extension, that would be all of humanity.

Are we leaving? Linnéa thinks, and Anna-Karin nods.

The Key

They follow the flow of people leaving through the front door and down the steps.

Anna-Karin is completely unprepared when Julia and Felicia intercept them.

* * *

They must have been waiting for me, Linnéa thinks, and backs up, feeling the bottom step push against her calves.

Julia and Felicia stand close together, once more a united front. Linnéa's anxiety, a constant presence inside her, suddenly increases.

If Julia and Felicia are friends again . . .

'Hi, Linnéa,' Julia says.

'What do you want?'

Julia doesn't reply, just smiles. This isn't the weak, almost hysterical Julia who spat at Linnéa in the City Mall. This is the smile of someone who holds a trump card.

Felicia smiles, too.

If Julia and Felicia are friends again . . .

Linnéa releases her power. Directs a probe toward Felicia.

Felicia thinks about Robin. How she held his hand and pleaded with him. 'Don't you get it? Just think of what you're doing to yourself. You'll ruin your own life. And mine. Julia won't talk to me anymore. And think about your mom. She has been out in town, off her head on drink. *At midday*. One of our neighbors met her in ICA and she couldn't *speak properly*.' Robin looked shaken. It was the first time either of them had mentioned his mother's drinking openly. Felicia noticed the effect. 'It's you who doesn't get it,' Robin said all the same. 'I can't get away. I must confess.' Felicia felt so frustrated that her grip on his hand tightened. 'But you've confessed once already,' she said. 'And you've been stuck in here for ages. Even if that stuff with Linnéa is true, you've taken your punishment now, haven't you? It's enough.' And Robin hesitated. 'Don't totally destroy your future for her sake,' Felicia said. 'Linnéa Wallin is

514

trash. Why let yourself become like her? Look, tell them that you and Kevin were scared of what Linnéa might do. Everyone knows that she's a junkie and a mental case and hangs out with criminals. You'll be let off.' Robin hid his face in his hands. But he nodded.

Linnéa leaps out of Felicia's mind. Only a moment has passed but everything has changed. Her heart is beating hard against her ribcage, as if trying to get out.

He is going to do it. He is going to take it back.

Linnéa feels the waves of a panic attack surge through her. Each wave is larger and more powerful than the previous one.

Robin has changed his mind, she thinks to Anna-Karin.

Anna-Karin shudders as if someone has pricked her with needles, and Linnéa understands that her panic has been transmitted with the thought.

'What's wrong with you?' Anna-Karin says to Julia and Felicia. 'You must have realized that it's all true. How can you stick up for them?'

Linnéa hardly grasps what Anna-Karin is saying. All she can think of now is what Erik thought in the assembly. It is something that has pursued her in her nightmares.

And then I'll wipe that bitch out for good.

If Erik and Robin are freed . . .

The ground is rocking under her feet. Panic has taken her sense of balance.

'See you tomorrow in Västerås,' Felicia says.

And then I'll wipe that bitch out for good.

Felicia turns and leaves with Julia in tow.

As soon as their backs are turned, Linnéa grabs Anna-Karin's arm. The ground tips. She hasn't even time to notice what happens before she finds herself lying down with her head in Anna-Karin's lap.

'Linnéa, how are you feeling? Would you like some water? I think I've got a bottle in my bag . . .'

Linnéa shakes her head.

'What can I do?' Anna-Karin asks. 'Call the ambulance?'

'No, no don't,' Linnéa manages to say. 'No point, it's a panic attack . . .'

She reaches for Anna-Karin's arm again.

Did they see me? See me faint?

Anna-Karin doesn't reply at once and Linnéa knows that they saw.

Help me up.

Anna-Karin lifts her with a firm grip under her arms. Linnéa is ashamed when she feels how cold and wet her arm-pits feel against Anna-Karin's forearms. The world spins as she gets to her feet.

All over the schoolyard, people have stopped to watch. She feels their stares. She has tranquilizers in her bag but won't take a tablet until she is away from here. The last thing she needs is to be seen popping pills in front of everyone. It would just add fuel to the rumor that she is a junkie.

'I'll take you home,' Anna-Karin tells her.

Linnéa shakes her head again. She doesn't want to be there because her apartment will remind her of that night and, besides, she's afraid that Julia and Felicia will come to try and scare her to silence now that they know how weak she is. She can't take anymore; she shouldn't have said anything to Patricia; she should have denied everything . . .

'Then we're going to my place,' Anna-Karin says, but Linnéa doesn't want that either.

I don't want to meet Minoo's family.

Her mother is in Stockholm and her father usually comes home late, Anna-Karin thinks.

But Minoo herself . . .

'She usually comes home late, too.'

If only she had had Vanessa here. If only she hadn't . . .

She is sweating again.

'Are you OK to walk?' Anna-Karin asks. 'Or I could easily call a taxi.'

'It's fine. I'll manage.'

Anna-Karin looks worried.

'Would you like me to phone Vanessa?' she asks gently.

'No, don't say anything to her.' Linnéa shakes her head.

She feels as if she's run a marathon. The next wave of panic is just below the surface. Waiting. Before it strikes, they must get to Minoo's house.

CHAPTER 71

Swirls of black smoke hang in the air in front of Minoo. The smoke is still and expectant.

Walter was right. As soon as she stopped being frightened and accepted her powers, her strength grew. The magic of the guardians is deeply rooted inside her and anchored by tendrils that reach everywhere, are *part* of her.

During these last few weeks, Minoo has learned more and more about how her magic is structured. How she can use it. Walter has often left the others to practice on their own and taken her aside, spent hours with her and encouraged her to go deeper into her concentration.

This is the first time she has demonstrated the results of her work to the rest of the circle.

The last of the twilight is fading from the sky now, and the bulbs in the chandeliers cast a warm light over the ballroom. Minoo stands in the middle of the circle of chairs and looks at the small table in front of her. She has taken a handful of feathers from a black velvet bag and scattered them over the table top. Then she placed a cube of glass in the center.

'I want you to lift the cube without a single feather moving,' Walter says.

Minoo sees him out of the corner of her eye. He is sitting in the folding chair, looking very relaxed. She sees his aura. His magic has grown much stronger. The others have stronger auras, too, except for Felix, even though he has been putting in more effort than anyone else.

For Minoo, this involves no effort at all.

She lets the smoke wind itself around the table, sensing its every shift in position. She observes the feathers, which lie perfectly still while the smoke slides over them and loops itself around the cube, envelops it.

She lifts the cube. Slowly, slowly, until it rises about a yard above the table top. She rotates it a couple of turns in the air before putting it back in its old place.

'Excellent!' Walter says.

Minoo makes the smoke twist above the table and the feathers take off into the air and circle around the cube in a leisurely dance. Then she stops the smoke so that the feathers hang still before she loosens her hold over them and lets them float back down.

'Thank you for that,' Walter says with his boyish smile. 'You gave us an extra bonus.'

Minoo pulls the black smoke back and looks at the others. She feels triumphant and has to try to force the self-satisfied smile from her lips.

She only just succeeds.

Walter, Viktor, Clara and Sigrid look frankly admiring, Nejla and Felix envious.

The Chosen Ones only showed fear when she used her powers.

'This is to give you an idea of what we have been up to so far,' Walter tells them. 'Minoo has advanced in a way that's beyond my expectations. As you can see, she can mimic elemental magic and affect physical reality.'

He glows with pride when he looks at Minoo.

'Please sit down, by the way.'

Minoo sits down on the empty seat between Viktor and Sigrid. Tiredness, as heavy as molten lead, spreads throughout her body.

The first day in the manor house, Walter had spoken about the importance of rest, but that seems so long ago. They usually start at seven in the morning and sometimes keep working until midnight. They haven't had a single day off. But she can't object. The world might end at any time. She is aware of what her priorities must be. They definitely don't include sleeping in. Or spending time with the Chosen Ones and Nicolaus. Or Dad.

Or Gustaf.

'I hope you will all feel inspired by this display,' Walter says.

Minoo notes that Felix glowers at her. She is too exhausted to be bothered. When you are constantly deprived of sleep, when you are always this tired, you can only concentrate on one thing at a time. She can only focus on what is in front of her. And just now, that is Walter who is talking about how they will practice during the rest of the week, how they will start training together as a circle.

She wishes that the other Chosen Ones could meet him. Maybe he could make them understand. And trust that it is the Council's circle that is supposed to close the portal.

Minoo regrets more and more that she agreed to search for the box and examine it. She promised for one reason only, which was to prove that she hadn't gone over to the enemy as Linnéa claimed; that she was still loyal to the Chosen Ones. But she can't believe that they will be able to close the portal. She remembers what Walter said when they met for the first time.

You cannot turn your back on the world because you feel you can't disappoint your friends.

Above all, she is angry with herself for dragging Viktor into this mess and exposing him to an unnecessary risk.

She is just putting off the inevitable. Sooner or later she must tell Walter about the box. Sooner or later she must give him the cross and the skull.

'Tomorrow morning, we start at five,' Walter says.

Minoo tries to tell herself that she'll be able to sleep in the car on the way to Västerås. She looks quickly at the others. Sigrid is moving about uneasily on her chair. Clara stares fixedly at the floor. The lack of sleep seems to affect her more than the others. She seems paler every passing day, and Minoo has begun to really worry about her. But she doesn't dare ask her how she feels. Clara has been very distant these last few weeks.

'Sorry, Walter,' Felix begins. He sounds nervous. 'But must we really? Lots at stake and so forth, of course I understand that, but I can't help thinking about what you said on day one. How important it is to have time to recover.'

Minoo stiffens. This is precisely what she thought herself, but she still gets irritated with Felix for speaking up. Doesn't he realize how out of order he is?

Walter looks at him. His silence makes Minoo's whole body tense up.

'Like I said,' he repeats, now looking away from Felix. 'I expect to see you all here at five o'clock in the morning.'

Nejla groans loudly.

'That's not even morning,' she says. 'It's night, I need to fucking sleep sometime.'

Walter laughs. 'Just what I felt at your age.'

Felix looks at the floor. He had said more or less the same thing, but got a quite different response.

'But I can't do anything about that,' Walter continues. 'And we shall have to go on until late. Viktor, you have other things to deal with tomorrow, but you can join us for a while in the morning, and then later, after the court case.'

Minoo tries to catch Walter's eye. He had promised that she could have some time off tomorrow to attend the court hearing. It doesn't matter that she and Linnéa are at loggerheads. Minoo wants to be there for her all the same.

'I will also provide you with personal evaluations,' he continues. He glances at Felix, making him shift position on the chair. 'And, Minoo . . .'

He turns his gaze to her at last.

'I want you to sleep here tonight since we're starting so

early. I've had a room made ready for you. There may be more nights, so you had better go home and pack what you will need.'

He must have forgotten, Minoo thinks. But how can he have forgotten?

'Viktor will drive you home now and pick you up when you're ready,' Walter says. He gets up and pulls his cell phone from his pocket. 'Let's call it a day now.'

'I'll be fucking dead tomorrow,' Nejla mutters as she leaves with Clara and Felix.

Sigrid remains in the room, looking for something in her handbag.

'Are you coming?' Viktor asks Minoo.

'I'll meet you at the car,' she says. He leaves, too, and Minoo walks up to Walter who is writing on his cell.

'What's the matter, Minoo?' he asks without looking up from the phone.

'I was just wondering about tomorrow.'

Walter's thumbs are flying across the display.

'About what?'

'I asked you if I could take time out to attend court . . .'

Walter looks up with an uncomprehending expression. For a moment, Minoo thinks she might be too tired to remember right. Did she dream it all? Surely she asked Walter's permission? Surely he gave it?

'Do you actually fulfill any function in court?' Walter asks.

'Sorry?'

'Well, in what capacity are you needed?'

'I'm not sure how . . .' She is uncertain of what he means. 'I just . . . you told me it would be all right. And Viktor is going.'

'Viktor is called as a witness. He *has to* be there.'

'I . . . I wanted to support Linnéa.'

Sigrid is still rooting around in her handbag. She is obviously eavesdropping.

'Will you be able to support her in any effective way?' Walter asks.

'Well, no, I just wanted . . . to be there.'

'*Be there?*' Walter repeats. 'So you're off to Västerås just *to sit* in court? And you consider that more important than our work here?'

He looks so disappointed. She feels as if she had been caught out trying to sneak away. And as if what she's asking for is unreasonable. But it isn't. Or is it?

'Of course, I can't prevent you. You have to decide yourself what your priorities are,' Walter tells her, and starts walking toward his office. 'Sigrid, would you come with me, please?'

Minoo walks quickly through the ballroom and continues through the rooms and hallways that have grown so familiar to her now.

She can't understand what has happened. She can't entirely shake off the feeling that she imagined asking Walter's permission. Could he really have forgotten? Anyway, why would he change his mind like that?

It would've been easier to sort out if she hadn't been so tired.

Minoo winds her scarf around her neck and puts her jacket on in the reception area. A strong, cold wind hits her face when she steps outside. She plunges her hands deep into her pocket as she crosses the yard to Viktor's car. It's only September, but it feels like November.

She takes her seat and Viktor starts the engine.

It's become a habit that Viktor drives her to and from the manor house every day. Walter doesn't allow anyone belonging to the Council's circle to walk the streets of Engelsfors alone while Olivia is still on the loose.

The beams from the headlights cut through the darkening air.

Walter had said it was for her to choose. And so it is. But the way he said it made her feel that she was about to commit an unforgivable act of treachery. But perhaps her guilt comes from inside herself? Because she's so keen to please and be a good girl?

Miss one day in the manor house? Or the court case against Linnéa's would-be murderers? It shouldn't be a hard choice. But the disappointed look Walter gave her seems to matter more than anything else.

'I've fixed what you wanted,' Viktor says. 'A copy of the key to Adriana's room.'

Minoo is surprised.

'It wasn't easy,' he continues. 'She's there practically all the time. I had to ask Clara to help me.'

'Right.' She tries to keep her voice neutral. She doesn't want him to notice her panic at the thought of Clara being dragged into this pointless mission.

'If you trust me, you must trust Clara,' he says, completely misunderstanding her.

Minoo isn't entirely convinced that she trusts Clara. But that's not what worries her. What does worry her is that Clara might get into trouble because Minoo can't say no to the Chosen Ones.

Viktor pulls the key from the inside pocket of his jacket. The metal is still warm from his body.

'Thank you . . .' Minoo is almost suffocated by guilt.

'I know that attending the court case matters a lot to you,' Viktor says. 'But as it happens, tomorrow Adriana is due to assist Walter with the personal evaluations he spoke about, so she'll be busy all day.'

She looks at the key. It gleams in the streetlight.

Linnéa would accept that Minoo rated getting into Adriana's room to investigate the box higher than turning up in court. She wouldn't just accept it, she would want it.

'I'll think about it.' She puts the key in her pocket.

'If they catch you and suspect that someone must have helped you, don't say anything about Clara,' Viktor says. 'Just blame everything on me. Promise me that.'

'I promise. But I won't say anything about you either.'

He glances at her as he pulls up at a stop sign.

'And you still won't tell me what you're planning to do?'

She shakes her head. After all, she can hardly explain to herself why she should do this. The key almost burns a hole in her pocket.

They drive into the residential area. A familiar figure is jogging along the roadside. Gustaf. Minoo's heart beats faster.

'Stop!' she says. Viktor stamps on the brake.

'What's up?'

'Sorry.' Minoo's ears are burning. 'I . . . I'd just like to walk the last bit. Thank you for driving me. And for the other thing.'

She hasn't told anyone in the Council's circle that she and Gustaf are together. She is afraid that they will start asking questions about how much he knows.

'No problem,' Viktor says. 'Give me a call when you want me to pick you up.' He drives off as soon as she has climbed out of the car.

She calls to Gustaf. He turns around and comes running toward her. She might be the most powerful witch in the world, but no magic power can match being the one who is able to make Gustaf smile like that. There is no magic like being this much in love.

They have been a couple ever since they kissed in Kärrgruvan. Even the impending apocalypse has a silver lining. If she had had time to think, she might well have ruined everything with her usual overanalyzing.

She had never grasped how easy it can be to love someone. She had believed that she was in love with Max, before she realized that he was blessed by the demons. But she confused love with obsession; what she feels now is completely different.

With Gustaf, everything is so easy, the only easy thing in a difficult world.

He reaches her now and she feels his body against her own. Feels his lips against her temple and turns her face up to his. Kisses him, then leans her head against his shoulder and holds him tightly so she can reassure herself that he is really here.

'I'm so happy to see you,' he says, caressing her hair.

'And I'm happy to see you.'

'How are you?'

'Tired, as usual. And you?'

'Same. I'm so sick of those caves. Once you're out of them, all you want to do is sleep. But at least it's all over now. We explored the last two tunnels today and they were both dead ends,' Gustaf tells her.

Minoo feels sorry for Anna-Karin. She had been so convinced she was on to something.

'What a shame.'

'It is,' Gustaf agrees. 'I mean, what do we do now? Wait for more portents?'

She realizes that he is wondering about the box but doesn't want to press her.

'I've got hold of a key to Adriana's room,' Minoo says. 'And she's busy tomorrow and won't be in her room. Trouble is, I'll miss the court hearing.'

'Linnéa won't mind,' Gustaf assures her. 'She, more than anyone, wants you to look for the box.'

Just looking at him makes her calmer.

She always thought the cliché 'drowning in each other's eyes' was silly, but now she knows better. She is the most enthusiastic deep-sea diver in the world.

'My parents have left now,' Gustaf says.

Minoo is about to ask where they've gone, but knows that she should know because she has asked before. Gustaf would hardly get mad that she forgot, given how intense these last few weeks have been, but she still feels bad about having such a poor grip on what is going on in his life. Her thoughts are dominated by her everyday routine at the manor house.

'Perhaps you'd like to stay over?' he asks.

They both know perfectly well what his real question is. And, even though she finds the prospect unnerving, there is nothing she wants more.

Reluctantly, she shakes her head.

'I'm just going home to pick up a few things and then I have to get back to the manor house.'

Gustaf pulls her close again.

'I had been looking forward to going to Västerås with you tomorrow morning,' he says. 'A road trip. You and me.'

'Together with Rickard and Anna-Karin. On the road to the courthouse,' Minoo says with a smile. 'Not exactly the most romantic set-up.'

'Yeah, I know,' Gustaf agrees. 'But at least I would be with you. I'm so jealous of the people who get to spend all day, every day, with you.'

Minoo clings tighter to him. She knows that it isn't what he intended at all, but it frightens her to hear him say things like that. She fears losing him. And that makes her think of Vanessa and Linnéa. If bonds of love as strong as theirs can tear . . .

'I miss you too,' she tells him.

He strokes her cheek. Sometimes she worries that her uneven, blemished skin will disgust him. But all she feels now are the tingles that his hands trigger throughout her body. His hands wander now, down her arms to her waist.

'I love you,' Gustaf says.

It is the first time he has said these words.

And Minoo doesn't hesitate at all before she utters them, too.

CHAPTER 72

When Minoo comes home, Dad has just stopped in front of the house. The lights on the back of the car turn dark and the muffled newsreader's voice is silenced. All her thoughts about Gustaf end just as abruptly.

She stops by the car. Dad climbs out and she is struck again by how much healthier he looks. And how wonderful it is not to have to worry about him any longer.

'Hello, darling,' he says. 'Did I drive past you just now?'

'I don't think so.'

Or, if he did, she had been far too absorbed in Gustaf to notice.

She is glad that Dad didn't see them. Her parents know by now that she is going out with Gustaf, but she would rather not make out with him in front of them.

'How did you get on at work today?' Dad asks.

'Fine.' Minoo avoids his eyes.

It has been amazingly easy to get her parents to accept her taking a year out. The 'job' she told them about made them rather more doubtful. *It's a kind of intern placement. With Alexander Ehrenskiöld. Yes, that's right, him. The day trader from Stockholm who moved into the manor house. His son, Viktor, joined my class for a while. No, mostly as an assistant. Well, yes, I've always been interested in economics and the stock market and all that because it's . . . there's a lot of math in it . . . and of course there aren't that many job opportunities here . . .*

'I don't like how hard he works you. He should at least pay

you a wage. Which he can well afford, I hear,' Dad says. 'Well, at least he hasn't kept you late again tonight – that's something, I suppose.'

'Yeah,' Minoo agrees, staring at the car, which glistens in the outdoor light. 'But I must leave in a while. I'm sleeping over at Gustaf's place.'

Her face immediately goes bright red because Dad must assume that she is going to sleep with Gustaf, and she doesn't want to think about him thinking that, but what else could he think? Especially when she is blushing like this.

'Okay,' is his only response. 'But could you hang on and not disappear until I'm back from my evening walk?'

'Sure.'

She smiles quickly at him and hurries into the house. The first thing she sees is Linnéa's fake fur coat hanging among the other clothes in the hall. Her boots are standing below. Minoo hasn't seen her since their confrontation in Kärrgruvan. And now she's here. In Minoo's home.

She listens hard. The house is silent. Light from upstairs slightly illuminates the staircase. She hangs her jacket up, glancing at the fake leopard fur. Then she goes to the kitchen.

She pours herself a glass of juice. It's too cold. Or is it that her mouth is still too warm?

She can still feel Gustaf's kisses. It's as if he has become part of her. She suffers phantom pains the moment they are separated.

She wishes she could just put off going upstairs and seeing Linnéa, put off finding the box, put off *thinking*. All she wants is to be with Gustaf, close to him in every way.

But, my life right now isn't like that, she thinks, putting her glass down on the sink.

Minoo knocks lightly on the door to Anna-Karin's room.

Anna-Karin opens the door. She is wrapped in a blanket. The only light comes from the reading lamp next to the small armchair. A chemistry textbook is on the floor and Peppar is sniffing it thoughtfully.

'Linnéa is here,' Anna-Karin whispers, and points at the bed. All Minoo can see is a black mane of hair spread out over the pillow. Linnéa has pulled the duvet up over most of her face and is lying turned to the wall. Minoo hears her calm, regular breathing.

It's rare to see her so vulnerable.

'What happened?' Minoo whispers.

Anna-Karin goes out into the passage and closes the door behind her. Then she quietly tells the story of how they met Julia and Felicia. It's a nightmare. If Robin retracts, then . . . what? Will he and Erik walk free? Return to school as if nothing happened? Declared innocent by society?

With her insight into Erik's consciousness, Minoo doubts that he will be content with that. He will plot his revenge.

'She fell asleep as soon as we came home,' Anna-Karin whispers. 'It was so scary to see her like that.'

Minoo nods. She had a taste of Linnéa's panic attacks when the Chosen Ones exchanged bodies.

'Have you talked to Vanessa?' she asks.

'No, Linnéa didn't want me to. But Minoo, what should we do?'

Minoo remembers when Walter said that Alexander was far too fixated on obeying rules. Could she talk to Walter about this? Explain the situation? Apply for dispensation for using magic in court?

Yesterday, she might have, but after their last talk today she no longer feels so positive.

She has deliberately not thought about the fact that Walter must know that Alexander plans to oversee what they do during the court proceedings. But now it's so obvious that she can't ignore it. Alexander would never dare do anything that Walter hadn't sanctioned.

'Hello?' calls a sleepy voice.

Anna-Karin and Minoo exchange a quick glance and go back into the bedroom.

Linnéa is sitting up in bed. Her eye make-up is smeared over her face and she has red pillow-marks on her cheek.

'Hi,' Minoo says. She stays near the door in case she isn't wanted.

'Hi,' Linnéa responds dully. She wraps her arms around her knees. 'I've slept for fucking ages.'

'You needed it,' Anna-Karin says, sitting down in the armchair. 'Is there anything you'd like? Are you hungry?'

Linnéa shakes her head, then drinks the whole glass of water on the bedside table. 'I must go home soon. I'll just wake up properly first.'

'Stay here,' Minoo suggests. 'I don't think you should be alone tonight.'

Linnéa looks at her with eyes as lifeless as her voice.

'Fine.'

Peppar stretches and prances away.

'I've talked to Ludvig, my lawyer,' Linnéa says. 'Obviously I couldn't say that I'd been reading Felicia's mind. But I told him that those two are friends again and that they wouldn't be unless Robin and Erik were on good terms again. He tried to hide it, but I could tell he was worried.'

She stares at the glass in her hand.

'Later on, the prosecutor phoned me to ask, had Julia and Felicia threatened me in any way. If they had, it would've been victim intimidation and he might even have got them arrested. But they didn't threaten me . . . And then he said not to think about it any more. That I mustn't worry.'

She looks at Minoo.

'He clearly thinks it's hopeless.'

She sounds desolate. Minoo doesn't know what to say to make her feel better. The only comforting words she can think of would be an insult to Linnéa's intelligence.

Too much depends on Robin's statement. They are all aware

of that. The only corroboration is Viktor's statement that he saw 'two guys with balaclavas on' whose voices he 'recognized from school'. At a distance. In thick fog.

Linnéa puts the glass down.

'I will make Robin confess,' Anna-Karin says.

Minoo wants to protest that Anna-Karin mustn't put her life on the line. But the idea that Erik and Robin might walk out free men is too much to bear. If she had had Anna-Karin's power she would've used it too, regardless of the risk.

'Why should Alexander even notice that I've done something?' Anna-Karin goes on stubbornly. 'He'll expect Robin to confess anyway.'

'Maybe he'll sense the magic,' Minoo says.

Anna-Karin looks annoyed.

'Hang on a minute,' Linnéa looks up. 'We need to get things in perspective. Alexander has threatened to kill anyone who uses magic to affect the hearing. You're needed to save the world, Anna-Karin. That's much more important than what happens to Erik and Robin. Besides, I don't want to have to worry about you tomorrow. Promise that you won't do anything.'

Anna-Karin looks at her, jaw clenched.

'Promise!'

'All right,' Anna-Karin agrees.

Linnéa nods. She looks very tired again.

Minoo realizes how much she'd like to be in the courtroom and how bad she will feel about not being there. What Walter said isn't true. It wouldn't be 'just to sit'.

Suddenly, she longs to be back with the others. She so much wishes that she has been wrong.

She releases a wisp of the black smoke.

She hasn't only studied the Council's circle. On the few occasions she has been with the Chosen Ones, she has studied them as well. And now she confirms her observations. While the members of the Council's circle have become stronger, the

Chosen Ones have not. On the contrary, they even seem to have weakened.

It doesn't matter that they're her friends. That she even loves them. She can't ignore the facts.

'What's the matter, Minoo?' Anna-Karin asks.

Instantly, Minoo pulls the smoke back. She tells them that she has a chance to look over Adriana's room tomorrow, but withholds everything about Viktor and Clara.

Linnéa reacts exactly as expected.

'You must go for the box,' she says.

The box.

If Minoo finds it tomorrow, she will examine it and tell the other Chosen Ones what she has seen. But that will be the last thing she does for them. They won't understand, but she can't ignore what she has observed. She knows that deep inside her.

The Council's circle is the strongest. They are the ones who must close the portal. And she must hand the skull and the cross over to Walter.

'I'll put the kettle on,' Anna-Karin says, and goes downstairs.

Minoo looks at Linnéa and wonders if they ought to talk about the fight in Kärrgruvan. But it seems so unimportant now.

'I heard about the caves,' she says instead. 'Such a shame that you didn't find anything.'

'Yeah,' Linnéa says. 'It was pretty much a waste of time.'

She looks sad.

'I really wanted to be in court with you tomorrow, I want you to know that,' Minoo tells her.

'I know,' Linnéa replies. 'I wish you could've.'

She sounds as if she genuinely means it. Minoo wishes that they could stay together in this moment and escape all the looming betrayals.

* * *

533

Anna-Karin watches the kettle. The burbling noise of simmering water gets louder.

Linnéa is right. She shouldn't have to worry about Anna-Karin tomorrow.

Which is why Anna-Karin will do it without telling her.

She'll do it not only for Linnéa's sake, but for her own. And Elias's. She wants to act on behalf of all those who have been tormented by Erik and Robin, year after year and day after day. Now there is hope of exposing them and making sure that they're punished. Anna-Karin can't let this opportunity pass.

Alexander will surely sense the magic. She would be deceiving herself if she thought otherwise. But he will not use his own magic in the courtroom. That would mean breaking the council's rules. Any consequences will come afterward. And she will be ready for him.

Time to oppose the Council, once and for all. The Chosen Ones are powerful witches; they are not helpless. Together, they will find a way to gain victory over the Council again.

The kettle vibrates as the water starts boiling.

Anna-Karin taps in a number on her cell phone.

CHAPTER 73

Vanessa opens the chest of drawers in the hall, finds a pair of thick socks and pulls them on. When she and Evelina came home from the caves, she fell asleep under double duvets. Despite that, and a long hot shower, the raw, chilly damp remains in her bones.

She goes into the kitchen, sits down at the table and pulls the hood up on her bulky gray hoodie.

'Why are you hiding inside that thing?' Mom asks.

'I think I'm catching a cold.'

The water is running in the bathroom where Evelina is having a shower.

It had felt absurd having to pretend to Gustaf that they hadn't found anything today. As soon as he and Rickard left the tunnels, Vanessa and Evelina went to have a look at the cave that seemed to be an anteroom to the portal. Vanessa felt panic rising when she saw the signs of the elements and the glowing circles. She panicked because they don't know what to do next. And because they're supposed to keep all this a secret from Minoo.

Vanessa wishes she could feel as convinced as the others that the Council's circle shouldn't close the portal. She can't get away from the possibility that Minoo might be right. Minoo is the only one with a direct link to the guardians. And the only one who knows the witches in both circles and has observed their magic.

Mom pours boiling water into the teapot. The fragrant scent of vanilla and flowers fills the kitchen. She sits down and pushes the jar of honey toward Vanessa.

'It's terrific against a cold,' she says. 'Boosts the immune system. I'll buy you some echinacea as well.'

The light in the ceiling fizzes, goes out, and comes on again. Their Alsatian, Frasse, who is lying under the table, moans a little in his sleep. Vanessa can't wait for the tea to infuse, she needs warming up from inside. She spoons honey into her mug and pours tea on top.

'I had almost forgotten how Evelina loves to shower,' Mom says.

Vanessa smiles a little wearily and Mom laughs.

'Do you remember when Nicke "fixed" the shower?'

She shakes her head and laughs again, but somehow looks sad at the same time. Vanessa suspects that they are both thinking about when Vanessa moved out to live with Wille and Sirpa. She and her mother didn't speak for several months. Vanessa learned later that Mom had phoned Sirpa daily to ask if her daughter was all right.

She simply can't get her head around everything that's happened since then. How many changes there have been. How much *she* has changed. And Mom, too.

'You know, Nessa,' Mom says, twirling a teaspoon round and round. 'There are times when it's hard to comprehend that you are almost a grownup. Soon, you'll move out, perhaps even leave Engelsfors and . . . you know, I'm so glad that we're getting on so well now. That the difficult times are behind us.'

'I was thinking of that, too.'

Mom smiles at her and seems almost embarrassed. She puts the teaspoon down.

'Have you talked to Linnéa lately?' she asks.

'No.'

'Maybe things will be easier for you once this dreadful trial is over.'

'Mom, it's over between us.'

Vanessa's cell phone rings in the pocket of her hoodie. It's Anna-Karin.

'I have to take this,' she says, getting up.

She answers in her room. And stops in the middle of the floor. She feels as if a black hole is opening up to swallow her while Anna-Karin tells her what has happened.

'Vanessa, are you still there?'

Vanessa looks at herself in the mirror and meets her own shocked eyes.

'Yes, I am.'

'Linnéa made me promise not to do anything to Robin,' Anna-Karin whispers. 'She said the risk was too great. But if one of us had been in trouble, Linnéa wouldn't have given a shit about the Council and its threats. She would've done whatever she could anyway. Isn't that right?'

'Yes, that's exactly what she would've done,' Vanessa says.

It's the truth and she can't believe that Linnéa doesn't see it.

'But you mustn't act on your own,' Vanessa continues. 'I'll help you.'

'That's why I phoned,' Anna-Karin says, sounding relieved. 'I don't know how strong my magic will be in Västerås.'

Evelina comes in, wrapped in Vanessa's old dressing gown, and starts to dress.

'If you hadn't asked me, I'd never have forgiven you,' Vanessa says.

Evelina looks inquisitive.

'We won't tell anyone, will we?' Anna-Karin asks.

'I must tell Evelina,' Vanessa says, and Evelina looks even more curious. 'How is Linnéa?'

'Better,' Anna-Karin says.

In her mind, Vanessa has a clear picture of Linnéa. She knows precisely how brave she'll pretend to be. And how frightened she is. All Vanessa's anger toward her suddenly feels meaningless. She only feels love. She must see Linnéa, must hold her in her arms.

'I'm coming over,' she says.

'No, you can't,' Anna-Karin says. 'She didn't even want me to phone you . . .'

Vanessa ends the call and pockets the cell.

'What's up?' Evelina asks.

Vanessa tells her and, while she talks, she becomes even more certain. She must go to Linnéa. This instant.

'I'm off to Minoo's,' she says.

'No, Nessa. It's a bad idea.'

'But I have to.'

Evelina shakes her head. Then she goes to the door and stands in front of it.

'Move over,' Vanessa says. 'Linnéa needs me.'

'I'm sure she does, but tonight you must let her decide.'

'No. I don't want to.'

It is a Melvin-style argument. *Don't want to.* And, just like Melvin, she would like to lie down on the floor and scream and cry and hit out and kick the floor.

'I've got to get out of here,' Vanessa says.

'Fine,' Evelina says. 'We'll walk. Anywhere, but *not* to see Linnéa.'

They walk through Engelsfors.

Frasse pulls at his leash, nosy and eager to pee on every bush, lamppost, electrical box and fence.

Above them, the moon glows and the stars glitter in a clear sky.

Many of the stars are dead, extinguished millions of years ago. Vanessa thinks about the demons' earlier experiments on other worlds. Experiments that have all ended the same way.

Complete extinction of all living things on the planet. In a dead world, nothing is left to offend the demons' sense of order.

In the empty, dark shop windows of long-since bankrupt shops, Vanessa can see her own and Evelina's images. Ghosts in a ghost town. Nobody has moved into Anna-Karin's old house. There is no light on in any of the windows in the building. And the old center for Positive Engelsfors is still abandoned.

Suddenly, Vanessa's arm is forced back. The tug is so strong it feels as if her arm is about to be twisted out of its socket. She turns and stares at Frasse, who has stopped cold at the wall of a house and is sniffing it noisily.

'Come on, how interesting can it be?' Vanessa sighs.

Right now, she detests him. It's like all her frustration focuses on his block-headed doggyness.

'Please, you take him for a while,' she says. She hands the leash to Evelina.

Evelina is right, she knows that. She has already texted Anna-Karin to say she won't come tonight. But she must get in touch with Linnéa.

She makes a few attempts at texting, but it's difficult to express everything she wants to say. In the end, she just sticks to the basic truth.

ANNA-KARIN TOLD ME. I'M HERE IF YOU NEED ME.

Vanessa puts the cell phone away and takes over the leash. She glances at Evelina. Her best friend.

Perhaps everything would have worked out differently if only Linnéa also had friends to talk to. Friends who would have told her at times that she behaved like an idiot.

'Do you think she'll answer?' Evelina asks.

'No, she won't, which might be just as well,' Vanessa says. 'It was stupid of us to get together in the first place.'

She doesn't mean it, of course. Nothing will ever make her regret Linnéa. She will never stop loving her, even if she can't be with her.

The window of what used to be Café Monique is covered in graffiti – mostly swastikas and spraying cocks. Where there once was an outdoor part of the café, a man in blue overalls stands, involved in a lively discussion with himself. He slaps himself, first once, then again. Frasse whines. Vanessa and

Evelina speed up. But the man doesn't notice them; he is immersed in the drama inside his head.

'Do you mind if we walk for a little longer?' Vanessa asks. 'It would be good if Mom was asleep when we get back.'

They leave the center of town behind them and walk on.

Now and then, Vanessa checks her cell phone in case she has somehow missed a text or a call, even though it is set to maximum volume.

'Please, say something, anything, to make me think about something else,' she says.

'Okay,' Evelina says. 'I think Rickard is really hot.'

Vanessa snickers a little. 'I never thought he'd be your type.'

'But there's something really sexy about him. Terrific body, for a start.'

'And when did you just happen to notice?'

'Once when he pulled his sweater off and his T-shirt came up with it. He has a six-pack. You can see all the lines, you know.'

Vanessa laughs, a little too loudly, just because it feels so good to laugh. They have reached the fence surrounding the yard of Engelsfors High School.

Frasse starts growling.

'Now what's your problem?' Vanessa asks.

'Shit . . . Nessa, look.' Evelina points to the sky.

Vanessa looks. And catches her breath.

The sky above the school undulates and glows in an intense shade of green, as if painted with sweeping strokes of a giant paintbrush dipped in a shining, phosphorescent color.

Northern lights.

The pattern of light is like a fan with the school at its center.

Vanessa and Evelina walk through the gates and stop in the schoolyard.

The green veils in the sky are drifting and billowing.

Vanessa feels every hair on her body standing on end. It's the sensation you get when you walk across a carpet-covered floor until your body is so charged with static electricity that, when you touch something, you know you will get a shock and it will *hurt*.

'Don't northern lights have something to do with electricity?' Vanessa says. 'Like, magnetic particles in the air?'

'I'll check,' Evelina says, opening her cell phone. 'Shit, there's no signal.'

Vanessa looks at her phone.

'I'm not connected either,' she says, thinking that this is no coincidence. 'It must be the metal element that's gone live.'

She remembers the cave under the school and thinks that the sign for metal must be lit up now. Only three elemental signs to go.

When darkness falls I will open.

'Are you sure that you want to be in on all this?' Vanessa asks. 'I mean, closing the portal with us, even though we have no clue how to do it?'

'Wow, you're really tempting me,' Evelina says.

They smile at each other and Evelina puts her arm around Vanessa. As they watch together, red streaks begin to mingle with the green, and then deepen to violet.

'It's so beautiful,' Evelina says. 'How can a portent for the end of the world be so beautiful?'

CHAPTER 74

The car bounces gently and gravel crunches under the tires as Viktor drives across the yard in front of the manor house. Illuminated by outdoor lights, the building is ghostly white against the dark night sky. Viktor parks and turns the engine off.

Minoo thinks she smells snow when she steps out into the cold air.

She follows Viktor inside and, after hanging up her coat in the reception cloakroom, they walk the same route that Viktor took when he first led the way to Clara's room.

The hallway looks spooky in the moonlight. Minoo knows by now that everyone in the circle, except Walter, has a room along this hallway.

Viktor escorts her to the room at the far end, the one with the red clover-patterned wallpaper. She is pleased that she has been put here. At least it feels familiar.

She switches on the bedside light and puts her backpack next to the big double bed.

'Recognize it?' Viktor asks.

'I wasn't that far gone.'

'You were when I carried you in here.'

Minoo feels herself blush. She had never thought about how she transferred from Clara's room to this one.

'Just kidding,' Viktor grins. 'I couldn't carry you alone. I had to ask Adriana to help me.'

'That makes me feel so much better,' Minoo says as she imagines them heaving and dragging her floppy body. But she has to smile at him.

542

'Right,' Viktor says. 'Sleep well. Breakfast will be laid out in the dining room by four in the morning.'

Minoo sighs. She has almost managed to forget that she'll have to get out of bed after only a few hours. She changes, brushes her teeth and washes her face, then crawls into bed. She sets the alarm for quarter to four and then tries to send Gustaf a text, but there's no signal. She puts the phone down and turns the light off.

The bed is wonderfully soft but she still can't sleep. She feels as though she is carrying the weight of the whole world on her shoulders. Probably because she is.

Moonlight pours in through the flimsy curtains and the trees cast spidery shadows on the walls. Minoo tries to think about Gustaf. If only he was lying next to her. If only they had time for each other.

There's a light knock on the door. Minoo sits up. Another knock.

The floor is cold under her bare feet when she goes to open the door, wrapped in her long cardigan.

'Hello,' Sigrid whispers. 'Can we come in?'

She tiptoes into the room without waiting for an answer. She is wrapped in a dressing gown of bone-colored silk. She is wearing her glasses and carrying a bottle of something alcoholic. Clara follows her. She has pulled a big knitted sweater over the top of her nightdress.

Clara smiles quickly at Minoo, her first smile in three weeks.

'Hi,' she whispers.

'Hi,' Minoo says, and then feels even more confused when Nejla follows the other two.

'Hey,' Nejla says as she marches into the room. She is wearing soft leisure pants and a T-shirt with a picture of a figure wearing a hockey mask and waving a machete.

Minoo closes the door. Sigrid and Clara have already settled down on her bed. Now she sees that Sigrid has also brought a stack of plastic glasses.

'Come here.' Sigrid pats the bed.

Minoo sits down with her legs crossed under her, trying to hide her big feet and the fact that she hasn't shaved her legs for ages.

'Here, one for you,' Sigrid says, handing Minoo an empty glass.

Minoo takes it and glances at the bottle.

'I'd rather not,' she says.

Nejla sits down next to her. 'Yeah you do!' she grins.

Sigrid pulls a small silver bottle from the pocket of her dressing gown and empties a cloudy liquid into the alcohol. She shakes it while the others sit in total silence. There is something solemn about the whole procedure.

'Beginners first,' Sigrid says, and pours a slug into Minoo's glass.

Minoo hasn't got the energy to protest. All she has to do is not drink it.

Sigrid pours everyone else a couple of fingers of the mixture and puts the bottle on the bedside table.

'Okay then. Minoo, are you ready?'

'I'm sorry, but I don't really feel like it,' Minoo says.

She doesn't even like any ordinary alcoholic drinks. And the fluid in Sigrid's little bottle looked far too much like the truth serum.

'It isn't dangerous,' Clara says.

'Just whisky with a twist,' Sigrid says.

'What's in the twist?' Minoo says.

Nejla snorts with laughter.

'You don't want to know,' she says. 'I was with some of the guys once when they held a ritual and made this stuff and . . . fucking hell. I could hardly drink.'

Minoo wishes she hadn't asked. She remembers the dried eyeballs that Adriana kept a jar of in her office. And all the spit, blood and nails the Chosen Ones have used in their rituals.

'So it's magical?' Minoo says.

'Oh yes,' Sigrid says. 'No question about that.'

'It makes you relax.' Clara's eyes are shining.

'Best of all, you don't get a hangover,' Nejla says.

'But, you see, the magic only works if everyone drinks,' Sigrid says.

Minoo wonders if that's true, or if it is old-fashioned peer pressure disguised as magic rules.

'Are you with us?' Sigrid asks. 'Bottoms up!'

Minoo takes a deep breath. They are all going to drink the same amount of the same cocktail. It can't contain truth serum. The others wouldn't expose themselves to that. And if what Clara says is true, that it really does relax you – well, that's just what Minoo needs.

'Why not?' she says.

'Great!' Sigrid says. 'Welcome, Minoo! And cheers!'

They all join in and Minoo drains her glass with the others.

CHAPTER 75

The drink burns her palate, her throat and all the way up into her nose. Minoo picks up a faint taste of vomit. Should it taste like that, or is she about to throw up?

But then the taste fades away.

Everything fades away.

What had been burning moments ago turns into pleasant warmth that spreads from her stomach into the rest of her body. She can feel tense muscles relaxing. Her shoulders droop. She can take a deep breath. And another. She feels so calm. Calm and content, simmering with a quiet kind of euphoria. A feeling that things will be sorted and that all will be well in the end. Absolutely everything. Having the drink was the right thing to do.

Minoo looks around.

Clara's long, ash-blonde hair falls over her shoulders. Her eyes are closed and her lips curled in an indulgent smile. She looks almost supernaturally lovely in the moonlight. It must be so special and important for her to be with friends of her own age after having spent all these years alone and isolated. No wonder she seems a little standoffish at times. Minoo's heart goes out to her. She ought to become a much better friend to her. They are friends, aren't they? It feels like it.

She gazes at Sigrid, who is leaning back against the headboard, and studies the movement of the trees' shadows in the ceiling. Her face, surrounded by blonde curls, is wonderfully pretty. Minoo gets a kick out of just gazing at her. Sigrid looks just as happy as Minoo feels. And she thinks that she really likes Sigrid and has since the first time they met. How stupid to feel threatened by her style and the elegance of her movements. Instead of wallowing in self-pity, she should ask Sigrid for advice about how to be more like her. Maybe she can finally learn to understand clothes and how to dress? And maybe Sigrid could show her how to paint her nails without ending up looking like a four-year-old has done them.

And then, Nejla. Nejla, who always behaves as if she didn't give a damn about anything. But she does, of course. Nejla loves her boyfriend, loves music and loves magic. Come to think of it, of all the members of the Council's circle, Nejla is probably the one who is most passionate about magic. And she doesn't care one bit about what people think about her. And that is beautiful. *Nejla* is beautiful.

Sigrid laughs.

'Not bad, eh?'

'Not bad at all,' Minoo says.

She realizes that she has a foolish grin all over her face and, also, that she simply can't be bothered worrying about it. Sigrid tops up all the glasses.

'We've hardly had a chance to get to know you, Minoo,' Sigrid says. 'You don't live here, of course. And you practice alone with Walter all the time—'

'Are you jealous?' Nejla interrupts, and giggles.

'Come off it,' Sigrid replies. 'All I'm saying is that this is our opportunity to get to know Minoo better. Let's go a round or two of "I never".'

'What's that?' Clara asks.

Minoo is grateful that Clara asked first. She has every reason not to know about group games, after all.

'Somebody claims never to have done something,' Nejla says. 'Like "I've never stolen anything". And if you have, you must drink.'

547

'So everyone who has stolen something must drink then?' Minoo asks.

'That's right,' Sigrid says.

Minoo feels elated, which is not what she expected. The mere thought of games like this one used to scare her. Now she's excited.

'I'll start,' Sigrid says. 'I never envied anybody else's powers.'

Minoo raises the glass and drinks. This time she doesn't notice any off-putting taste. The mouthful goes down easily and warms pleasantly. A sidelong glance at the others tells her that they are also drinking.

'Oh my God, Minoo, who have *you* envied?' Sigrid asks her.

'Like . . . everyone, I guess?' she laughs. 'At first I thought I had no power at all. And then, when I discovered it, it scared me.'

'That's fucked up,' Nejla says.

Minoo giggles. It *feels* fucked up.

'I suspect we were all thinking of you when we drank in this round,' Sigrid says. 'I mean, when you listen to Walter . . . all those things he tells us that you can do . . .'

'It would be fun to watch you doing some of that,' Nejla says. 'I've already seen witches levitate objects and all that shit. But you've never shown off any of your specials.'

This is a challenge, and Minoo can't resist it.

'I could enter into your memories and then describe something I've seen.'

'What? You mean like, *right now?*'

'Sure,' Minoo says. 'Why not?'

Nejla grins broadly. 'Why not? Go for it!'

Sigrid tops the glasses up again and Minoo has a preparatory sip. Then she releases the black smoke and puts her hand against Nejla's forehead.

The sense of quiet euphoria doesn't disappear, it is just dampened down.

Minoo slips into Nejla's memories easily and follows the weave. She avoids memories that seem heavy and painful, searching for one that feels brighter yet strong.

The music is deafening and it sucks. Nejla can't think why she went to this shit party at all, with this lame crowd. They think it's so exciting to pile into this old barn a few miles away from the school and be eaten alive by midges while they get drunk and high and listen to this shitty music, thinking they're being cool and rebellious.

'Hey,' a voice says. She turns and sees a guy standing there, dressed in black from head to toe. Nejla has seen him around in school. He's new.

'You're Nejla, right?' he says. 'I'm Marcus.'

'So?' she says and drinks some more beer.

'They're heavy.' He is pointing at her Bathory T-shirt.

'Sure,' she says, convinced he's lying and has never heard of them. 'What's your favorite album?' she asks.

'*Blood Fire Death*,' he tells her. 'The runner-up is *Under the Sign of the Black Mark*.' Nejla is gobsmacked. She would have said exactly the same. Actually, he is quite hot. So she kisses him.

Minoo pulls the smoke in, looks at Nejla and smiles.

'Your boyfriend, is his name Marcus?'

'Yes.' Nejla lifts one eyebrow. 'Not too hard to find out, though.'

'The first time you met him was at a party in an old barn a couple of miles away from your school. You thought it was a dull party, but then Marcus came up to you and told you how much he liked Bathory. You thought he was lying at first and tested him. It turned out you have the same favorite album and the same second-best choice. The top one is *Blood Fire Death* and the next best *Under the Sign of the Black Mark*.'

Nejla's eyes widen. 'Fucking hell, that's cool,' she says.

'You will *not* do that to me,' Sigrid tells Minoo.

Clara says nothing, just smiles a little at Minoo.

'But let's go on, I've got a good one,' Nejla says. 'I never . . . had sex with someone who is in the house now.'

Sigrid is the only one who drinks.

'Who with?' Nejla asks. 'Walter?'

'Stop it!' Sigrid goes beet-red. 'With Viktor, of course.'

'I'm not listening.' Clara presses her hands to her ears and starts humming to herself.

'It was years ago. *Once,*' Sigrid says, holding up one finger. Then she turns to Minoo with a smile. 'I thought we had Viktor in common?'

'No,' Minoo says. 'Definitely not.'

'Seriously? Viktor is such a total slut,' Sigrid says. 'Surely at least one of the Chosen Ones has slept with him?'

Clara is humming loudly now. Minoo shakes her head.

'Come off it!' Sigrid says. 'Made out?'

'None of us were into him,' Minoo says.

Nejla laughs. 'Seems like Viktor's not the right type for Engelsfors.'

'Actually, a lot of girls at school were interested in him at first,' Minoo says. 'But he kept to himself, so in the end everybody decided that he had to be gay.'

Sigrid laughs out loud.

'That sounds like Felix's dream. Though he doesn't want Viktor to be *homo*sexual. *Felix*sexual would be more like it. My personal take on Viktor is that he's simply not capable of deciding to go for one person or one thing. Too greedy.'

'But has he had sex with Felix?' Nejla asks.

'I don't know.' Sigrid shrugs. 'Probably.'

'Please, everybody,' Clara whimpers. 'I can hear every word!'

'I've never actually thought of Viktor as a sexual being at all,' Minoo says. 'He's so . . . not physical.'

Sigrid and Nejla laugh.

'He's always so, you know, freshly ironed and never sweaty or anything,' Minoo goes on, although she has a vague feeling she should follow up this line of thought inside her own head. 'I can hardly imagine him having any bodily functions. Like he was one of those Ken dolls underneath his clothes. As if there was nothing down there.'

Sigrid giggles. 'There is. Trust me on this.'

'Come on!' Clara says, lowering her hands. 'Please stop discussing my brother's sex life.'

Everyone bursts out laughing.

'We're sorry, Clara,' Sigrid says. 'Let's drink to that.'

They empty their glasses and Sigrid fills them again. Minoo can't stop smiling. It reminds her of when the Chosen Ones swapped bodies, though this is the other way around. It is like she has swapped her soul with somebody. Somebody who doesn't worry. Someone who talks easily about boys and sex with friends, and who doesn't feel at all shy or weird about it.

'I think I've got another one,' Sigrid says.

She seems to be thinking it over, rocking the glass in her hand so that the amber-colored liquid threatens to spill.

'Here we go. I've never had sex.'

She and Nejla drink. Minoo and Clara look at each other.

Clara goes pink and Minoo feels sorry for her. How could Clara have had a sex life?

'Have you made out with someone?' Sigrid asks Minoo.

'Well, yes.'

'How long ago?' Sigrid asks, smiling.

Now Minoo can't help blushing. And suddenly she can't help herself at all.

'A couple of hours ago. With my boyfriend.'

It is the first time she's used the word. She's not been in a situation where she's had a reason to call Gustaf anything but 'Gustaf'. But she is pleased to say it now. And Sigrid responds just as Minoo has always imagined one's girlfriends should.

'Oh my God, oh my God!' She bounces a little on the spot. 'Why haven't you said anything? Who is it?'

'You don't know him,' Minoo says.

'Is it Gustaf?' Clara asks.

Minoo looks at her in surprise.

'I saw you together once,' Clara says. 'You seemed to like each other a lot.'

'How did you meet?' Sigrid asks.

'It's a little complicated,' Minoo says, and blushes even more deeply. 'We started going out together three weeks ago, but we've known each other for a long time.'

'And when did you realize that you actually loved him?' Sigrid asks eagerly.

Minoo has a vision of Gustaf, and happiness explodes inside her. Her boyfriend is fantastic. And she has these lovely new friends who want to listen when she speaks about him.

'I'm not sure . . . maybe six months ago, something like that.'

'You've liked him for half a year and you still haven't had sex!' Sigrid exclaims. 'But I suppose you haven't had much time to spare?'

'They've had time to make out, for fuck's sake.' Nejla looks at Minoo. 'Just do it.'

It sounds so simple the way Nejla puts it. Suddenly, Minoo can't understand why she ever thought it was any more complicated than that.

'Tell us more about him,' Sigrid says. 'Is he hot?'

'Yes, he's quite . . . perfect.'

'That's true actually,' Clara says and lies down, closes her eyes and smiles.

'What's his element?' Nejla asks.

Minoo looks up. Clearly, Nejla takes for granted that Gustaf is a witch, too. This is a dangerous direction for their talk to take.

'Water,' she says. At least she isn't lying.

'That's Marcus's as well,' Nejla says with a dreamy expression.

'There's something special about the water element,' Sigrid says, giggling.

'Let's do another round,' Minoo says quickly, to change the subject.

'I've got one,' Nejla says, looking at Sigrid. 'I've never had a sexy dream about Walter.'

No one drinks but Sigrid goes bright red again.

'Oh my God, Nejla, what are you after?'

'Nothing,' Nejla smiles.

'You know what?' Sigrid fills Minoo's glass again. 'Time to stop this silly game. Let's just listen to Minoo. Come on, tell us about what's been going on here.'

Minoo looks at her and anxiety wells up inside her, pushing through the soft, cozy feeling of being wadded in cotton wool. She has promised Walter not to tell the others too much.

'I'm not sure I want to talk about it,' Minoo says, sipping cautiously.

She glances at Clara, who has fallen asleep.

'Too many fucking secrets around here,' Nejla says. She burps and adds, 'Like this garbage about how you're hardly allowed to talk to Adriana.'

'I know. And what's this about her losing her memory. Is it true?' Sigrid asks. 'Does it have anything to do with that court case? Everybody was going on about the rumors last winter. What actually happened?'

'It was so bad, I'd rather not think about it,' Minoo says.

'Don't be like that, Minoo,' Sigrid says. 'There must be something you can tell us. Just a hint. Please.'

'Lay off, Sigrid,' Nejla says.

Sigrid looks annoyed but, after a quick glance at Nejla, she smiles. 'Sorry.'

'It's OK,' Minoo tells her.

She twirls the glass in circles, making the liquid swirl around. She glances sideways at Sigrid, who looks thoughtful.

'Minoo, I must say one more thing,' she says. 'I shouldn't have listened in, I know, and I'm sorry, but I thought it was awful of Walter not to let you go to that court hearing.'

'He didn't exactly forbid me,' Minoo says.

'Hello, guilt trip? It was obvious that he had given you permission and then changed his mind. Am I the only one who thinks we're driven far too hard? I mean, we never get enough sleep . . . '

'Could be because we do this every night,' Nejla says, and drains her glass.

'. . . and he's awful to Felix all the time,' Sigrid continues. 'It started with breaking his finger, and since then it's been one thing after another. Like today, when Felix said we needed rest. I can't be the only one who has noticed the way Walter treats him?'

'No,' Minoo says, feeling relieved that Sigrid has seen it as well.

She feels it's easier now to admit to herself that Walter's behavior follows a pattern.

'Walter has said he doesn't have time to coddle us,' she adds. 'So, maybe he doesn't realize quite how harshly he treats us.'

'I'm sure you're right,' Sigrid says. 'But if it happens again, we really should speak up. Do you all back me on that?'

'I can't be bothered,' Nejla says. 'If Felix thinks it's a problem, he should deal with it himself.'

The mattress bounces a little when she gets up.

'Good night,' she says, wandering off into the hallway.

'What about you?' Sigrid asks.

Minoo meets her eyes and remembers how Walter said they must all be honest.

'Yes, I'm with you,' she says.

Sigrid smiles, takes her hand and squeezes it gently.

'You're such a wonderful person, Minoo,' she says.

Part Four

She wakes Clara gently and collects the plastic glasses.
'Sleep well,' she says as they leave.
This time, Minoo has no trouble going to sleep.

CHAPTER 76

Anna-Karin wakes and looks around the room. She is confused; the smell of the bed linen is unfamiliar, and then she remembers that she is sleeping in Minoo's bed.

She has been dreaming about her mother. They were in the kitchen in the farmhouse. Mom's hands were red and blistered, like that time when she had pushed her hands into boiling water. In the dream, she was reaching out for Anna-Karin, her fingers so swollen that her rings were digging into the flesh. Anna-Karin ran from her. And then she was in a hallway in the Västerås courthouse. Even though she has never been there before, she knew where she was. And it was no longer her mother who was chasing her. It was Alexander.

Anna-Karin tries to go back to sleep, but it's impossible. And then, hunger begins to obsess her.

She staggers out of bed and puts her fleece top on. When she steps out into the passage, she hears noisy snoring from Minoo's dad. She listens outside the door to her own room, where Linnéa is sleeping. Not a sound.

She tiptoes down to the kitchen and pours herself a glass of milk. Drinks it standing by the sink. Then she takes a slice of the whole wheat bread that Minoo's dad buys for himself. It tastes like compacted bird seed and is only edible at all with a thick layer of cream cheese.

Anna-Karin jumps when Peppar meows shrilly. She puts her snack down and looks around. He is meowing again and the sound comes from the living room.

'What is it, sweetie?'

She walks in. He has leapt up on one of the sofa's armrests and stands there, arching his back. His green eyes are fixed on something outside the window.

Anna-Karin follows Peppar's eyes.

The garden is bathed in moonlight. A breeze stirs the branches of the maple and some of its leaves flutter to the ground.

Someone is walking toward the house.

Anna-Karin backs away from the window instinctively. Hits the sofa. Peppar hisses and arches his back even more.

Olivia stops in the middle of the lawn.

She is wearing a black parka. She looks exactly as she used to before magic ruined her.

And she keeps standing there. The wind swirls some of the leaves on the ground around her and plays in her blue hair.

Anna-Karin doesn't know if Olivia has seen her. She sneaks out into the hall as quietly as she can and picks up the phone on the hall table. The line is dead. Is that because of Olivia?

She goes back upstairs and looks out through the window in Minoo's room. Olivia is still there, in exactly the same position.

Anna-Karin turns her cell phone on. No signal. She goes to the window and tries to stay out of Olivia's sightline.

If she comes any closer to the house, Anna-Karin must wake Linnéa. But not until then. Linnéa needs her sleep, in order to be as sharp as possible for tomorrow.

Olivia's eyes gleam in her pale face. She stands so still it is unnatural.

But I can wait as long as you can, Anna-Karin thinks.

CHAPTER 77

When Minoo's alarm goes off, she sits straight up in bed. Her heart is pounding, as if someone has chased her out of her sleep. Fumbling for her cell phone, she drops it on the floor. She picks it up. Bending down makes her head feel as if it's about to explode.

She silences the alarm.

It is still dark outside. She turns on the bedside lamp and screws up her eyes against the light. She has to lean against the doorframe on her way to the bathroom. It is like the worst attack of flu she has ever experienced. She bends cautiously over the tap and drinks a few mouthfuls. After all that effort, she has to sit down on the toilet lid and hold her head in her hands.

Best of all, you don't get a hangover.

Nejla's assurance feels like mockery. Perhaps it was meant to be. Minoo suddenly grasps the essence of all representations of hangovers that she has read about or watched. The cotton wool she had felt padded in last night is replaced by glass fiber now.

I won't be able to handle today, Minoo thinks. But she knows that she doesn't have a choice.

She gets into the shower and allows the hot water to massage her body. Her headache retreats a little, only to leave space for anguish.

Last night's scene and their talk replays in her head. It is like being forced to watch the same movie clip over and over again. An everlasting loop where she becomes more and more embarrassing each time.

How drunk was she? And how sober were the others, really?

She staggers back to her bed, then checks her cell phone because she has no idea of time. Still no signal. Her text to Gustaf has not been sent.

Gustaf. She shouldn't have told everyone about him. And what else did she say that she can't remember?

She puts her clothes on, anxiety simmering in her mind.

Breakfast is laid on the long table in the dining room. Adriana is up and about. She is aligning the spouts on the big thermos flasks containing tea and coffee with military precision. She is wearing a green dress in a 1960s style. Minoo recognizes it from her time as school principal. Adriana wore it when the Chosen Ones had been called to her office so that she could tell them who she really was. And who *they* really were.

Next to the bread basket, she has provided a few dishes with sliced cheese. The slices look dried at the edges. There is another plate with rows of sliced cucumber and tomato. Sometimes, Minoo suspects that the Council regards food as something too worldly to be of any interest whatever.

Sigrid, Felix and Nejla are seated at the table already and tucking into breakfast. Sigrid looks up and, as usual, seems alert and neat. Minoo wonders if she really feels that fresh, or if she's even better at doing her make-up than Minoo imagined.

'Hi!' Sigrid says. 'Did you sleep well?'

Nejla turns to Minoo. 'Are you even awake?' she says with her mouth full of cheese sandwich.

She is wearing the same T-shirt as she was last night.

Felix looks curiously at Minoo, who tries to look away. Unfortunately, it makes her focus on the lynx. It is gnawing on a skinned hare carcass, placed on a newspaper on the floor.

She pours herself a cup of coffee and fixes herself a cheese sandwich for show. She has no desire to eat it. Or anything else.

'Good morning.'

It's Viktor.

The memory of the Ken doll makes Minoo splash coffee on the tablecloth. She can hardly look at Viktor when he comes to the table, followed by Clara.

She moans inwardly. Clara heard all that and even had to ask them to stop.

'You're not a morning person, are you?' Viktor sounds amused as he looks at Minoo.

'I guess not.'

Minoo sips at her coffee, drinking it in tiny mouthfuls. At least she doesn't feel sick. Or, at least, as long as she can ignore the squelching noises from the lynx's corner.

Minoo glances surreptitiously at Clara. She is pale and very quiet, but that's how she is most of the time.

Walter enters. He is wearing his dark gray winter coat.

'Could I please have your attention for a moment?' he asks.

As if he had to ask.

He smells of shower gel and his hair is damp. A few strands of hair tumble onto his forehead as he leans forward, resting his hands on the table.

He looks troubled. Minoo wonders if he has heard of the little bedroom party last night and is going to give them hell.

'A new portent occurred last night,' he says.

Felix, Nejla and Sigrid sit up, as if keen to hear more. As for Minoo, her coffee wants to come back up. Yet another sign of the approaching apocalypse. Only Clara looks as worried as Minoo feels.

'So, which element is it this time?' Viktor asks nonchalantly.

'Metal,' Walter says. 'It showed up as northern lights. It is very worrying that the portents are coming in such rapid succession. And, even if it's a relief that no one got hurt this time, this portent has had exceptional effects. All cell phone networks are down. And television. And Internet and landlines. The only functioning media seem to be radio channels.'

'In the whole of Engelsfors?' Felix asks.

'Yes, Felix,' Walter says impatiently. 'In the whole of Engelsfors.'

Minoo exchanges a look with Sigrid and is certain that she too is thinking about their talk last night.

'When will the phones come back on?' Nejla asks. 'If the world is ending, I'd like to call my boyfriend one last time.'

Walter laughs.

'That's prioritizing for you!' He straightens up. 'Joking aside, what happened last night is confirmation – if confirmation were needed – that we must work harder than ever.'

He doesn't ask Minoo if she is going to the court hearing. Is it because he has already understood that she has decided to stay? Or does he assume that she will go and therefore is punishing her by giving her the silent treatment?

'Get your coats,' Walter says. 'Time to start.'

Sigrid gulps down her coffee. Everybody rises from the table. As Minoo leaves the room, she sees Adriana stacking cups and plates on a tray.

Minoo remembers the key, and another wave of anxiety sweeps through her.

Walter ushers them into the ballroom. Two large ectoplasm circles are painted on the floor. Alexander stands nearby with an ectoplasm tube in his hand.

Walter takes the tube from him and uses it to draw the sign for wood inside the inner circle. He hands it to Viktor, who adds the water sign. The others draw their signs while Minoo waits. She passes the time winding the scarf around her neck, buttoning her coat and pulling on her gloves.

When all six signs are in place, Walter opens the double doors wide and they all walk outside.

Nejla was right. It is still night and it is so cold that Minoo's breath turns into clouds of frozen vapor. The outdoor lights are on and spotlights glow here and there on the lawn. Walter leads the way into the green room between the hedges.

They stop just inside the outer stone circle. The inner circle glows with ectoplasm and their faces are lit from below by its blue light.

'We will connect our magic now,' Walter says. 'Work as a circle.'

Everyone automatically bares their hands. Minoo pulls her gloves off, too, and glances at Viktor on her right side and Nejla on her left. She wonders if they knew what to expect as soon as they saw the circles in the ballroom.

'Teleportation can be managed in different ways,' Walter says. 'But, whichever way, it will be complicated. And dangerous. This is why, to begin with, we won't use any living things. Have you all seen *The Fly*? The film?'

Minoo hasn't and the others also stare blankly at Walter, who smiles ruefully.

'Sorry,' he says. 'I sometimes forget how terribly old I am.'

He walks up to the inner circle and pulls an object from his coat pocket. It is the glass cube that Minoo used for her demonstration. It seems to glow from within when he places it in the inner circle. Then he returns to his place between Clara and Sigrid and takes their hands. Minoo reaches for Viktor and Nejla.

'This exercise is about strength and precision,' Walter says. 'Release your powers, but listen to each other at the same time and adjust. The group energy must be calibrated to a common, steady level or else things will not go well. Think of it as a choir that is supposed to hit the same note.'

Minoo releases the black smoke. Now she can see the auras belonging to the others, shining in the dark like colorful lights.

'Ready?' Walter says. 'Let's do it.'

CHAPTER 78

L innéa opens her eyes. She looks at the strange room in the pale daylight.

Anna-Karin's room. In Minoo's home. The hearing is today. Robin will retract his confession.

Her cell phone alarm starts and she turns it off. Only one hour to go before Diana comes to pick her up to drive her to Västerås.

No network coverage. But Vanessa has sent her a text. She is glad she didn't see it last night, because she probably wouldn't have been able to stop herself from answering it.

She must get up now if she is to change and be ready in time. Her clothes for the court are ready at home, hanging on the wardrobe door, freshly washed and ironed. White blouse. Pale blue cardigan. Navy blue skirt. She got the whole outfit from Ingrid's Hidey-hole. When she tried them on, she scarcely recognized herself.

And that is precisely the point. She has to dress as someone else. Someone who is a credible victim.

'Remove all the rings from your ears,' Ludvig had advised her. 'We can be pretty sure that Erik's representative will paint a picture of you as a mentally unstable, antisocial junkie. Unfortunately, we've been allocated a decrepit old judge and some of the magistrates could be even more bigoted. Your looks must remind them of their children and grandchildren. I wish I didn't have to tell you this, but I'm just being realistic.'

And he said all that at a time when they still believed Robin would confess.

563

The Key

Linnéa steps out into the passage. She hears the voices of Anna-Karin and Minoo's father from downstairs, but the radio is on and she can't make out what they are talking about.

She washes off yesterday's make-up in the bathroom. She smells of sweat but will shower at home. Her face still carries lines from the pillow and her eyes look hollow. It might be an advantage if it makes her look more like a trustworthy victim. Or a disadvantage because it makes her look more like the headcase she'll be portrayed as.

Anna-Karin sits in the armchair in her room and waits for Linnéa. She looks even more tired than Linnéa feels.

'How are you?' Anna-Karin asks.

'How are *you*?' Linnéa responds, closing the door behind her.

Anna-Karin looks deeply uneasy and Linnéa realizes that something has happened.

'What's wrong?' she says. She doesn't want to know, but can't bear not to.

'Olivia,' Anna-Karin says. 'She was here last night, I saw her in the garden.'

Linnéa slumps down on the bed, still warm after her sleep. She has known all the time that Olivia would show up. And now, she's here.

'What did she do?'

'Nothing. Stood there and stared at the house.'

'Did she see you?'

'I don't think so.'

'How did she look? I mean . . . same as last winter?'

Anna-Karin shakes her head. 'She looked well again, her old self. She had even dyed her hair.'

So totally Olivia, Linnéa thinks. She wants to look cool while she kills us.

'Why didn't you wake me?' she says.

'You needed to sleep. I kept watching her. She left at dawn.'

It's heartbreaking to think of Anna-Karin staying awake all night so that Linnéa won't be disturbed. She must have been so frightened.

'Have you talked to the others?' Linnéa asks.

'No. I tried but the cells don't work. No signal. Landlines are disconnected, too. No Internet, no TV. Only the radio. The local news said this morning that "work on normalizing the situation is in hand".'

Linnéa has a vision of Vanessa. Her apartment building on Törnros Road. Jannike and Melvin.

'But the others must be told that Olivia is here!'

'I don't think Olivia will do anything to anyone in full daylight,' Anna-Karin says, as if she has guessed what Linnéa thinks. 'We'll see everyone in Västerås except for Minoo, and she should be safe enough where she is. Olivia has escaped from the Council and I don't think the first thing she'll do is hang around the manor house.'

Linnéa nods and tries to breathe normally.

'But we must be extra careful,' Anna-Karin says. 'Erik is off to Borlänge for a conference so he can drive past your house and drop you off.'

Linnéa goes cold at that name, before she realizes that Anna-Karin is talking about Minoo's father.

'That's good,' she says. 'Thank you. And thank you for yesterday, for looking after me.'

Anna-Karin looks embarrassed. 'You would've done the same for me,' she says.

And Linnéa knows that it is perfectly true.

* * *

When Linnéa has left with Minoo's dad, Anna-Karin showers and blow-dries her hair. The scent of freshly washed, warm hair fills her room.

Then she sits down on the bed and slips into the fox's consciousness.

565

He is half asleep, curled up under the floor of the dance pavilion in Kärrgruvan.

She wants to spend a little extra time with him. When she is so much further away in Västerås, the bond between them will be weaker.

The doorbell rings. She checks the time on her cell phone. Gustaf is early.

She goes downstairs and opens the door. When she sees Alexander, she takes an instinctive step back.

He fills the entire doorway.

'You're going with me to Västerås,' he says.

'The others are coming to collect me—'

'Leave a note on the door,' Alexander interrupts. 'Tell them that you've gone with me.'

'But—'

'Just do as I say.'

Anna-Karin tears a page from the notepad on the hall table. While she writes she considers refusing. But if she starts resisting, he will surely become even more suspicious.

She knew already that his mission in the courtroom would be to keep an eye on her and the others. The only new factor is that she'll have to sit in a car alone with him.

Anna-Karin gets her jacket and shoes, then locks the door and hangs the note on the door handle.

Alexander places his hand on her shoulder and almost shoves her toward his dark green car, which is parked right outside the house. He closes the door as soon as she has sat down on the passenger seat.

Maybe she should escape. This is her last chance. But where to? And how is she supposed to get away from Alexander? She has no choice but to come with him quietly.

Anna-Karin becomes aware of the fox. He is wide awake now and feels her unease. She tries to calm him, but it's hard when Alexander seats himself behind the wheel and starts the car.

CHAPTER 79

Vanessa considers her clothes critically in the full-length mirror in the hall. Black jeans, white knitted sweater. She has already changed several times. As if what she wears would have the slightest influence on Linnéa's chances.

The doorbell rings. It's Nicolaus, wearing a dark blue trench-coat that looks new. Underneath, suit and tie.

'Good morning,' he says. 'Are you ready? Evelina is waiting in the car.'

There's a quick patter of little feet behind Vanessa.

'Hello poo!' Melvin's shout booms around the stairwell.

Nicolaus stares at Melvin, clearly baffled that the child isn't kept locked up in a cage.

'Melvin, that's naughty!'

Mom comes running to get him. When she sees Nicolaus, she smiles apologetically.

'Sorry, he's a little fixated.'

'Please, don't apologize,' Nicolaus says. 'No need for that at all. I was just taken by surprise. How nice to meet you . . . I'm Nicolaus Elingius.'

He holds his hand out and Mom takes it.

'Jannike,' she says, looking curious.

No, she is a little more than curious, Vanessa notices. When her mom's hand is free again, she pulls her fingers through her hair in a gesture that is unselfconscious and self-conscious at the same time. Vanessa recognizes it only too well.

'You're Linnéa's uncle, right?' Mom says.

567

'Yes,' Nicolaus says. 'Shall we go?'

'We should *definitely* go,' Vanessa agrees.

She pulls her jacket on. While she ties her shoelaces, Melvin grabs hold of the belt on Nicolaus's coat and starts humming his new favorite word, *poo, poo, poo*.

'That's enough,' Mom says, pulling him away and putting her hand over his mouth.

Melvin thinks it's great fun and carries on spitting out the word between Mom's fingers.

'Oh, dear, that hearing. I won't be thinking about anything else all day,' Mom says to Vanessa. 'I hope they'll get the phones up and running again. I want you to call me when it's all over.'

'I'll try, promise,' Vanessa says, and gives her a quick kiss.

'Very nice to meet you, Nicolaus!' are the last words she hears her mother say as she closes the door.

'Your little brother is a very . . . lively child,' Nicolaus observes as they get into the elevator.

'I know,' Vanessa says, pressing the button, hoping that he didn't notice her mom making lively eyes at him.

The elevator chugs down.

'I must admit I haven't slept all night,' Nicolaus tells her. 'I have worried incessantly about what will happen to Linnéa, and to Minoo, if they catch her out. And I've been worrying about you.'

'About me?'

'Yes, because I do understand how much Linnéa means to you. Even though you have . . . broken up,' Nicolaus says.

Vanessa is touched. She would like to tell him about their plan, but reckons it would make him even more worried.

'I'll be fine,' she says as they leave the elevator. 'We'll all be fine.'

She intends to adopt this as her mantra for as long as possible.

They walk toward Nicolaus's mustard-yellow Fiat. Evelina

sits in the back seat waiting for her and they hug each other, while Nicolaus starts the car.

All Vanessa wants is for this day to be over. She wants it to be evening when she will know the outcome of the hearing. She so much wants to know something for sure.

Once they have crossed the Engelsfors town limits, the cell phone networks function again. Vanessa considers texting Linnéa.

But what should she write? Linnéa hasn't answered her text from last night and she must have seen it by now. She looks out through the window as they drive past the monotonous fir forest.

Her cell rings. It is Gustaf.

'Anna-Karin wasn't in when I called,' he says. 'There was a note on the door to say she had left with Alexander, who was driving her to the courthouse. I called her as soon as I had a signal but she didn't answer.'

'Perhaps she didn't dare talk to you,' Vanessa says. 'You know, scared that Alexander would understand how mixed up you are in all this. I'll try calling her.'

Both Evelina and Nicolaus are looking puzzled, but she has no time to explain. She finds Anna-Karin's number and Anna-Karin replies almost instantly.

'Are you with Alexander?' Vanessa says.

'Yes,' Anna-Karin says.

'Has he hurt you?'

'No. But, Vanessa . . . I saw Olivia last night. She was standing in the garden outside Minoo's house.'

So, Olivia is in Engelsfors now? How long has she been here? Has she been in hiding? Spying on them? Biding her time?

'We'll deal with her later,' Vanessa says. Maybe it's wrong of her, but she actually hopes that the Council will find her first. 'I'm here if something happens. Take care.'

'You, too,' Anna-Karin says. 'See you soon.'

They end the call. While she tells the other two what Anna-Karin said, Vanessa tries to think.

'We knew already that Alexander was planning to monitor the hearing,' Nicolaus says. 'I don't think we need to be concerned about her.'

'I hope you're right,' Vanessa says.

She exchanges a glance with Evelina, knowing that she is also thinking about the plan and how much hangs on it.

* * *

Minoo has lost any sense of passing time.

Her presence inside the smoke is total. Her concentration is absolute. She is perfectly attuned to her magic. The auras of the others are all glowing evenly and strongly. Only Felix's flickers now and then. Together, they try to adjust and find the perfect balance. And to focus all their energy on the glass cube in the center of the inner circle.

And, suddenly, the cube is gone.

Minoo blinks.

She looks to the right and sees Viktor's dark blue aura. It is almost the same color as his eyes. His eyes look at her. She notes how thick his eyelashes are. She notes the size and shape of small leaves in the hedge. Every detail of the stone flags they are standing on. The thin film of sweat on Clara's face where she stands on Viktor's other side.

'Well then,' Walter says. 'That was it.'

Minoo reluctantly separates herself from the grip of the smoke.

The sun has risen. She didn't even notice when it happened. Everything looks too sharp, too vibrant. Like a photo in which the contrast has been maxed out. Gradually, Minoo becomes aware of her body again. How stiff it feels. But, strangely enough, she doesn't feel cold, even though she can see her breath turn to vapor in the cold morning light. She watches the others stretching, trying to shake life into arms and legs.

Only one of them looks unaffected. Walter.

'One might have hoped for a better time,' he says. He looks at his wristwatch. 'Let's hope that it worked at least.'

He walks out into the garden. When Viktor glances at his watch, Minoo sees that they have been doing this for almost three hours. Now her sore head is back, like a dull throb.

'I must go soon,' Viktor says.

She senses that there is something else he wants to say. They hang back until the rest of the group has left the green room one by one, Felix last of all.

'Please remember what I said about Clara,' Viktor says in a low voice. 'She mustn't be involved.'

She nods.

'I'm so worried about her,' he continues. 'She is driving herself too hard.'

Minoo thinks that Viktor is right, but doesn't want to say so to him. And she most certainly doesn't want to let on that she and Clara were drinking last night.

'I'll keep an eye on her,' she says.

They leave the hedge enclosure and walk through the garden. The morning sun paints the manor house's façade in a rich shade of gold.

'And, if you get to talk to Linnéa . . . please say hello from me,' Minoo says. 'Tell her that I'm . . . that I'm thinking of her.'

It sounds so inadequate. Suddenly, Minoo wishes that Linnéa had allowed Anna-Karin to try to change the course of the proceedings.

'I will,' Viktor tells her.

When they come into the ballroom, they can only see the backs of the others; they are all standing in front of the ectoplasm circles. Minoo comes closer.

There is a pile of broken glass in the center of the inner circle. It is smoking a little.

Minoo notices how disappointed Sigrid and Nejla are, and how tired Clara is.

571

And, then, how afraid Felix is.

He assumes that it is all his fault, Minoo thinks. And he might well be right.

Walter's face reveals no emotion at all.

'Viktor, I believe you have to leave now?' he says.

'Yes, I'm on my way,' Viktor replies.

He glances at Clara. Minoo suspects that they're sending thoughts to each other. Clara looks irritated and waves at him to go. Viktor frowns and leaves the ballroom without another word.

'Well, everybody, let's settle down.' Walter gestures to the folding chairs that are lined up along one of the walls.

He still makes no comment about Minoo's presence. Doesn't even give her a special look to show that he is aware of her choice to stay.

Everybody pulls up a chair to the outer ectoplasm circle and sits down after removing their coats. Minoo happens to be opposite Walter. His face does not change when their eyes meet.

Maybe her being here wasn't so important for him after all. Had she imagined the whole thing? Overinterpreted what had been said out of sheer nervousness?

If only she was allowed to sleep. She might think more clearly afterward.

'I've given serious thought to our assessment talks,' Walter says. 'You're all aware of the speed of the portent sequence. And you must realize that we must make quicker progress. It is no secret that our chain has a weak link. The consequences are right in front of us.'

He fixes his gaze for a moment on the splintered glass. A few twists of smoke still rise from it. Minoo suddenly feels an anguish so strong that she almost falls off her chair.

'Felix, what the hell . . . ?' Walter says.

Minoo's wave of anguish dies away. Nejla shakes herself a little.

Felix looks devastated.

'Sorry,' he says. 'I didn't mean to do that.'

'I don't believe you did,' Walter says. 'That's the problem. You do what you shouldn't and don't do what you should.'

'I know.' Felix looks at his hands.

Minoo tries to catch Sigrid's eye, but Sigrid doesn't notice. She is stroking Henry, who has turned up from nowhere.

'However, I've had an idea about how to solve this problem.' Walter turns to Minoo. 'You were able to help Clara with her powers. Perhaps you could help Felix with his?'

Minoo is aware that everyone is looking at her, but Walter's gaze is so intense that she feels as if the two of them are the only people in the room.

'I don't know,' she says.

'Why not?' Walter says. 'It can't do any harm. After all, we can't carry on as we are, can we?'

'Walter is right,' Felix says. 'Please try to help me.'

He looks pleadingly at her. And she knows that she has to try, for his sake. She doesn't think she can do much for him, but she might be wrong.

'I'll try,' she agrees.

Nejla leans forward to watch them, full of expectation.

Minoo allows the black smoke to seep out of her again. The sympathy she felt for Felix is fading away. Now he is turning into something to study. An interesting object.

She walks across the ectoplasm circles and hears glass crunch under her feet.

Felix sits stock still when she puts her hand on his forehead. She investigates his magic scrupulously and her suspicions are confirmed.

There is nothing wrong with his magic. But something is wrong with him.

She takes her hand away, turns and goes to sit down again. She pulls the smoke back.

The others look at her intently. Felix is clutching the seat of his chair so hard his knuckles have gone white.

'What's wrong?' he asks.

She meets his eyes.

'Maybe it's best if we talk somewhere more private,' she says.

'This concerns us all,' Walter says. 'And matters that concern us all should be openly discussed.'

Minoo desperately wants to disappear into the unemotional world of the black smoke.

'It's more of a private thing, really,' she says.

Felix looks at her unhappily.

'I don't see what you mean by "private",' Walter says. 'We all trust each other. Don't you agree? We support each other.'

But Minoo can't bring herself to say that Felix's problem is being Felix. It doesn't feel right and, besides, won't help him. If anything, it might make things worse for him. The error is deeply rooted in his personality. He tries too hard – so hard that he suffocates his magic.

'Very well, we will ask Felix himself to decide,' Walter says. 'Since he is the one who is chiefly concerned.'

Felix looks like a child trying to be brave, trying to be a grownup.

'It's best if everyone hears this,' he says. 'Perhaps we can find a solution to my problem together.'

'There you are,' Walter says to Minoo. 'Felix is aware that his performance is an issue for the whole group. Of course he'd like to improve. Isn't that so, Felix?'

'Yes. Please tell us what you saw,' Felix says.

Minoo wants to say to Walter that he can't do this to Felix. That he is unfair to Felix, that he is unfair to him all the time.

But, apart from the time when Walter broke Felix's finger, all her examples suddenly seem petty and ridiculous. What can she say? *Walter, it's mean of you to become irritated every time Felix says anything, and to act as if he is stupid and to make jokes at his expense. And sometimes you don't look at him when he speaks!*

Minoo tries to catch Sigrid's eye, but she's apparently engrossed in Henry.

Minoo hesitates. Felix wants her to speak out, or so he says. Is she making things harder for him by refusing? Perhaps he doesn't mind all that much? Maybe she should stop projecting her own feelings onto everything. Actually, she has no idea of what Felix is really like as a person.

'Just say it,' Felix says. 'Please, Minoo.'

She tries to focus entirely on him.

'I can't help you, Felix. There is nothing wrong with your magic. You block it yourself.'

The room is very still. Felix stares at the shattered glass.

'Now you know,' Walter says. 'With you in the group we don't stand a chance. Not how you are now. Whatever you need to do to fix this, I expect you to do it soon.'

Felix can't hold his tears back any longer. Minoo feels like crying, too. At first, she thinks that Felix's emotions have invaded her again, but then she realizes that the tears are her own. And that they are tears of fury.

What Walter is doing to Felix cannot be right. Whatever she told herself a moment ago is neither here nor there.

Sigrid holds up her hand, to Minoo's relief. They will speak up together.

'I'd like to say something,' Sigrid says when Walter turns to her. 'Look, I don't mean this nastily, but shouldn't we replace Felix?'

All Minoo can do is stare, speechless.

'Wouldn't that be for the best?' Sigrid continues. 'This situation isn't much fun for anyone. Especially not for Felix. There must be stronger earth witches around. What about Anna-Karin?'

'Don't think I haven't considered it. But, this is the group that the guardians helped me to select,' Walter says with his eyes fixed on Felix. 'Which is not intended to reassure you that they are satisfied. On the contrary. They are very worried. And so is Minoo.'

Minoo's face goes hot. She can't look at the others. The fragile friendships they have been building will come crashing down if Walter tells them that . . .

'Minoo has studied everyone's magic,' Walter continues. 'And, already after our first training session, she had noticed that Felix's magic was by far the weakest.'

A wave of intense hatred flows through Minoo. It's Felix's emotions for her, and this time he wants her to feel them.

'Now let's move forward, guys,' Walter says. 'Today is the day for personal assessments and talking about how we can improve. Take some time now to rest and then we'll meet in the dining room at ten o'clock for something to eat. The assessments will start at eleven. Adriana is going to assist me. We will be in here, and the time per individual will be about one hour. Sigrid, we'll begin with you. Next, in this order, Nejla, Felix, Clara and Minoo. Keep practicing while you wait for your turn.'

Minoo still doesn't dare look at anyone.

'You can go now,' Walter says. 'All of you except Minoo.'

Minoo hears the others get up and troop out of the room. Then Walter comes to sit down next to her. She can smell his aftershave.

'That was quite unnecessary, don't you think?' he says.

He looks calm and relaxed leaning back in his chair with one arm draped over the back.

'You put Felix in a really awkward position when you made such a big deal out of telling us.'

Minoo can't object. When you're with Walter, his view is all that matters. Everything Minoo usually believes in or thinks, suddenly appears irrelevant and naïve, almost delusional. It's as if he invalidates her perception of reality simply by being so confident in his own.

'You're such a strong witch I sometimes forget that you haven't grown up inside the Council and don't know how it works,' he continues. 'But here we're open and frank with each other. That shows much more respect than tiptoeing around sensitive subjects. Do that and, in the end, *everything* will seem sensitive.'

He smiles at her, clearly pleased with himself.

'May I leave now?' she asks.

'Of course,' he says. 'We'll meet up again for the assessment.'

She leaves through the double doors.

Sigrid is waiting for her. Henry dashes around her feet doing figures eights.

'What did Walter say?' she asks.

'Nothing special,' Minoo says, and keeps walking.

'It was awful, what he did to Felix,' Sigrid whispers as she follows Minoo.

Minoo stops and turns to her. 'I thought we were going to raise the issue together,' she says.

From the corner of her eye, she notices Henry shooting off and disappearing like a shadow around a corner.

'I tried,' Sigrid says. 'That's why I said maybe we should replace Felix. Then he wouldn't have to put up with Walter being so mean to him all the time.'

Minoo decides there and then never to trust Sigrid again.

'I'm going to rest a while,' she says, and walks away, ignoring Sigrid who is calling after her.

CHAPTER 80

Diana casts a sidelong glance at Linnéa as she drives into the large parking lot in front of the Västmanland courthouse in Västerås. It is a large, square building of light concrete and glass, with a wide set of steps leading to the front doors. Already, people are waiting on the steps. Many of them are likely to be journalists. On the way, Linnéa has seen the newspaper posters.

THE CASE THAT DIVIDES A TOWN – COURT HEARING TODAY

She is trembling. She would like to take one of the tranquilizers she has brought in her handbag, but doesn't dare. What if the court concludes that she is too calm and too disengaged to be believed?

'Don't be afraid to show your emotions,' Ludvig has told her. 'It does no harm if you burst into tears. Not at all. But whatever you do, Linnéa, don't lose your temper. Erik's lawyer will try to provoke you into showing aggression. Don't let him.'

'We'll go in when you're ready,' Diana says.

It's the first words she has said since they left Engelsfors. She must have understood that Linnéa didn't want to talk.

'I need a cigarette first,' Linnéa says.

The pack is ready in her hand when she and Diana get out of the car.

Linnéa's first drag on the cigarette is so deep her throat hurts. The car park looks out onto a mustard yellow factory building with tall chimneys and she can hear the loudspeakers at Västerås central station.

'Linnéa?' says a voice. She turns around.

A woman comes walking briskly toward her. She has blonde, coarse hair and seems vaguely familiar, but Linnéa can't place her.

Something about the woman's face, together with her almost maniacally alert eyes, makes Linnéa think of some kind of rodent that has spotted a tasty piece of cheese.

'My name is Cissi Larsson.'

Linnéa blows out smoke. She doesn't answer. So this is Cissi; she was an intern at the *Engelsfors Herald* who went on to make a name for herself by using the town's series of spectacular tragedies.

'I'm here to report on the hearing,' Cissi continues. 'Naturally, I'd appreciate a chat with you. Get your angle on the case and so forth.'

'I'm not interested,' Linnéa says.

'Would you please leave her alone?' Diana says.

'Erik Forslund claims that he was in the PE Center that whole evening,' Cissi says. 'I believe the police have examined the cell phone records and say that the boys' phones were in the center all that time. What's your comment to that?'

'I guess they forgot their phones,' Linnéa says. She throws her cigarette away. 'Or they left them there on purpose.'

'The question seems to make you uncomfortable,' Cissi says.

Linnéa picks up Cissi's thoughts. They match the intensely alert look in her eyes.

Cissi has talked to Nicke. It didn't take her long to get him to talk about the police investigation. Cissi flattered him, made him feel important and, of course, he also felt bitter about the reprimands he received for his handling of the case: *One thing I can tell you is that Linnéa Wallin is a pathological liar.*

Cissi wants to believe him. Erik being guilty is too predictable for her taste. A conspiracy or mystery to solve is much more interesting. A conspiracy driven by Linnéa would be just the thing. Cissi wants that very much.

'According to eyewitnesses, you were celebrating on Olsson's Hill on the evening of Erik Forslund's arrest,' Cissi says. 'Are you pleased that he has been in prison for over three months? Do you know what it's like to be locked up like that?'

'Go to hell, you repulsive fucking vulture,' Linnéa says.

As soon as the words pass her lips, fear contracts her stomach.

But whatever you do, Linnéa, don't lose your temper.

'Let's go, Linnéa,' Diana says, taking her arm and walking her toward the courthouse.

'Some people believe you're out to frame Erik!' Cissi shouts.

'Don't listen to her,' Diana says quietly. 'She isn't the judge.'

The glass panes above the front doors reflect the blue skies and the slowly drifting little clouds. Linnéa spots a TV camera among the small crowd on the steps.

Ludvig almost runs out to meet them. He is in his mid-thirties, wears a suit and has combed his blonde hair straight back from his forehead.

'Hello, Linnéa,' he says. 'Unfortunately, there are quite a few people here but Diana and I will be with you all the time. You don't have to answer any questions or even look at anyone. All right?'

Linnéa nods and takes Diana's hand, wishing that it was Vanessa's. Ludvig moves in to cover her other side. Cameras start clicking as the three of them walk up the steps. A journalist holds out a microphone and tries to block their passage, but Ludvig firmly moves him to the side.

Together, they enter the building. The moment she sees the number of people inside, Linnéa lowers her eyes. She tries to ignore their voices, but their thoughts, charged with anger, excitement and curiosity, are harder to shut out.

*. . . does she really believe that anyone will take her word
for anything . . . know her type, fucking man-hater . . . shit,
if I don't get an interview with her they'll never put me on
permanent staff . . . she actually looks quite hot when she's
dressed normally . . .*

They pass through security but Linnéa is barely aware of
what's going on. When she is given back her handbag after
passing the metal detector, she suddenly sees a triumphant-
looking Felicia, whose eyes follow her. She stands in a group
with Robin's parents and his brother. Their eyes are full of
pure hatred.

She hasn't a hope . . .

Then, Linnéa catches a glimpse of Erik's representative, the
well-known lawyer. He is giving an interview to a reporter
from a radio channel, who keeps nodding as if he agrees with
everything he hears in his large headphones.

Tindra stands a little further along, but hers is the only
friendly face Linnéa sees. All the rest belong to enemies.
Enemies everywhere.

Linnéa lowers her eyes again and allows Diana and Ludvig
to escort her. All her energy is consumed by trying to shut
everything out. Her every instinct urges her to get away from
here, at once. Her grip on Diana's hand tightens.

They lead her into a small room, barely wider than the
green sofa that is the main piece of furniture. Diana sits down
next to her. Ludvig shuts the door, cutting out the murmur of
voices from outside. Linnéa dares to look up now and sees a
silver-haired man with glasses standing in front of her.

'Hello, Linnéa,' he says, holding out his hand. 'I'm Hans-
Peter Ramström. We have talked on the phone.'

Linnéa presses his hand and says 'hello' quietly.

'I understand how trying this time must have been for you.'
He smiles comfortingly. 'And I can't pretend that today will be
easy.'

His calm voice is full of authority.

The Key

'Of course it won't,' Ludvig says. 'Only remember what we've talked about.'

'Not angry, only sad,' Linnéa mumbles.

She listens as they talk about the hearing and the possibility of a new statement by Robin.

And now Linnéa regrets that she forced Anna-Karin to promise. If she hadn't, there wouldn't be any new statements by Robin. But it would have been selfish. It would have been wrong. Besides, she never believed she would win this case.

Linnéa wishes she could cling to a hope of some kind, however slight. She wishes that she had Vanessa with her now.

But most of all, she wishes that she was someone else. Anyone other than Linnéa Wallin.

* * *

When Minoo comes into her room, she is struck by how stale the air is. She doesn't know if she is imagining the smell of alcohol or not.

She opens the window to let the fresh, cold air in. She knows she should try to sleep for a while but doesn't think she'll be able to. Instead, she makes the bed, sits down on it and takes the key from her pocket. For a while, she stares at it.

The throbbing backdrop of her hangover is making it difficult to think clearly. But she doesn't need to think, she needs to act. And she will, while Sigrid has her assessment.

A knock on the door. Minoo pockets the key.

'Come in.'

The door opens and the draft makes the thin curtains flap. Clara quickly closes the door behind her.

'Hi, Clara.'

'Hello, Minoo.'

Clara sits down on the edge of the bed next to Minoo. Kicks off her slippers and crosses her legs underneath her. Minoo wonders why she is here.

'So, you've been checking up on us?' Clara says.

'Not in the way Walter made it sound,' Minoo says. 'I didn't spy on you like that. Or, I guess I did . . .'

'Relax,' Clara says with an ironic little smile. 'I've no right to be judgmental about spying.' Then her smile fades completely. 'And I know what Walter is like.'

Minoo doesn't dare to ask what she means. She isn't sure if she can trust Clara when it concerns Walter – she doesn't even trust herself entirely.

'I despise him,' Clara says quietly.

Minoo feels that eyes and ears might lurk among red clover flowers on the wall; that the whole house is observing them.

'And I hate the way I act when I'm with him,' Clara continues. 'How we all act.'

'Me too.'

Minoo is so relieved to get this out in the open, but at the same time she is terrified that she might have said too much.

Clara traces the seam on her jeans with her finger. Her profile is timelessly beautiful, as if on a statue. Her skin looks almost transparent. Once again, Minoo is reminded of the pale, fragile women idolized by the Pre-Raphaelites.

'How are you?' she asks.

Clara looks irritated.

'Are you going to nag me as well? Has Viktor put you up to this?'

Minoo says nothing. Clara's face softens.

'Sorry,' she sighs. 'It's just that I get so fed up with being watched over. It's nice of you. But I'm fine. Truly.'

'Good,' Minoo says.

'Besides, I don't think I'm the one who's the most worn out today,' Clara says with a smile that makes her look more like Viktor than ever. 'You look absolutely exhausted. You probably needed a rest. I know I do.'

They sit in silence for a while. A dog barks somewhere outside.

'I hope the court hearing goes all right,' Clara says. 'Those bastards need to pay. But Erik will never confess. I had no illusions about trying to appeal to *his* conscience. He doesn't have one.'

Minoo agrees. She remembers what it was like to be inside Erik's mind.

'You'd be amazed about the things I imagined doing to them,' Clara says. 'One idea I had was to slip into one of their hockey practices . . . the sharpened blade of a hockey skate would be a good murder weapon.'

Minoo must have looked shocked, because Clara laughs at her.

'I wouldn't have done it, not really. But it was fun to fantasize about it.'

Something about her smile makes Minoo less than convinced that Clara would never have made her fantasies a reality.

Suddenly, Clara wraps her arms around herself. She looks cold despite her knitted sweater.

'Shall I close the window?' Minoo asks.

'No, I'm not cold, I just feel really horrible about something I need to confess.'

She gives Minoo a quick glance.

'You might have seen it already in my memories, but I was there when you opened Nicolaus's grave. I watched when Cat died. And I told Alexander that Nicolaus had stored his memories in his familiar. If I hadn't told him, he would never have worked out that Adriana had done the same with her raven. What happened to her is my fault.'

Minoo can't see why Clara should blame herself, and says so. Clara sighs.

'You're wrong. I was Alexander's spy. I hated it but . . . he and Viktor made up my whole world. And when Viktor was away at school I was alone with Alexander. He was only at home for a couple of evenings a week but he was always kind to me. He taught me what I should have learned in the Council's school. And he always brought me gifts. New books.

Films and video games. Nice clothes, even though most people would think it a waste of money for an invisible person. We spent the summers together on his island in the Stockholm archipelago. Viktor would be there during school holidays and I was almost able to pretend to myself that I led an ordinary life. That I was normal.'

She is silent for a moment and then continues.

'It was only after I came here that I began to see other sides of Alexander. That's when I started to understand . . .'

She looks at Minoo.

'I think he cares about Viktor and me. At least, as much as he is able to care about anyone; it was thanks to him that we could get away with not taking the Council's oath for so long.'

Alexander. Obsessed by the Council and its rules. And yet he helped the twins to avoid becoming its slaves for as long as he could.

'He has done unforgivable things,' Clara continues. 'Terrible things. The fact that he isn't bad through and through makes his evil actions almost worse. I don't understand how he fits these things together in his own mind. I truly don't.'

She pushes a strand of hair back behind her ear. Minoo silently compares the Alexander described by Clara with the Alexander she knows. She doesn't understand either. Still, some people seem to be like that. They don't make sense.

'I feel like such a hypocrite,' Clara says. 'I have joined this circle. I take orders from a man I hate. I don't even have a good reason. Viktor believes that we can save the world. I don't. All I wanted was . . . to belong. Just for once.'

Clara's eyes are glistening with tears.

'I know exactly how you feel,' Minoo says quietly. 'And I am not particularly proud of how I've behaved either.'

She holds on to her question for a moment but then she asks Clara.

'You really don't believe that we can save the world?'

'You mustn't listen to me,' Clara replies. 'I always believe the worst. It is as if Viktor got all the optimism and I all the pessimism. You know, like the light and the dark twin.'

An ironic smile comes and goes again.

'Besides, it doesn't matter what I believe or don't believe now. I have sworn the oath to obey the Council. Do you know what they do to defectors?'

Minoo nods. She knows it far too well.

'Anyway,' Clara says. 'I'm glad I can finally do some good. However small.'

'What are you talking about?'

'I know you won't say what it's for,' Clara says. 'But we'll do it together once the assessments are under way. I'll make myself invisible and stand guard in the hallway while you're in Adriana's room. If someone comes I'll knock on the door.'

Minoo doesn't want Clara to take any more risks. And she promised Viktor.

'It's too dangerous. Being invisible isn't going to protect you. Animals can see you. What if Walter's familiar—'

'I'm going to do it,' Clara interrupts.

'Viktor would never forgive me.'

Clara looks very serious.

'I love my brother more than anything. But I'm stronger than he thinks. There is no need for him to behave like my personal nurse. And I can say this thanks to you, Minoo. I owe you.'

'You don't understand. What I'm doing isn't so important. It's not worth—'

'I don't care,' Clara says. 'I'm doing it because I want to.'

* * *

Anna-Karin sits silently next to Alexander and stares straight ahead. She clutches her cell phone. The car radio is on and running a report on the inexplicable breakdown of all communication links in the Engelsfors area. Alexander is just about to end yet another call to tell his contacts that Anna-Karin saw Olivia last night.

She remembers the scene in the gym hall, when Alexander carried Olivia away. And wonders if he feels personally responsible for her escape.

'Thank you,' he says. 'I will be back in touch later.'

He pulls his hands-free set from his ear.

'What will you do if you catch her?' Anna-Karin asks.

'What is required,' Alexander replies.

Anna-Karin is relieved that he doesn't go into details.

She keeps an eye on the road signs for Västerås. By now the miles are down to single digits. Suddenly, they pass the slip road to Västerås city center and Alexander pulls the cell phone from her grip.

'I'll drive you back to Engelsfors later,' he says. 'Just keep calm.'

Anna-Karin panics.

STOP!

Of course he saw it coming. Her power bounces back and the impact is so strong she feels as though her skull is cracking. She tries to keep her eyes focused but everything is spinning, as if in a kaleidoscope. Then darkness closes in around her.

CHAPTER 81

Vanessa walks into the hall of the courthouse. It is a white-walled atrium, flooded with daylight through its high glass ceiling. Looking up, she can see the clouds floating past. The courtroom doors are large rectangles of light wood. Sofas are placed here and there on the polished, stone-flagged floor.

There are people everywhere. Far too many people. Vanessa worries that she and the others won't get seats in the courtroom. They don't allow more than thirty people in, and most of the crowd have come to support Erik, Robin and Kevin. Or to report on the proceedings. Linnéa needs to be able to see that her friends are there.

Vanessa, together with Evelina and Nicolaus, go quickly along to stand outside the door where some journalists have already clustered.

She scans the faces. Many are familiar from school. Linnéa's father sits alone on one of the sofas. But there's no sign of Alexander's tall figure and no sense of Anna-Karin's energy either.

'Where are they?' she says. 'They left before us so they ought to be here already.'

'I'm sure they're just stuck in the traffic,' Nicolaus says, but he looks concerned.

Vanessa takes her cell phone out of her bag.

'Hi, Vanessa!' a voice says behind her.

She turns and sees a tall, gangly young man with a thin beard. He wears a keffiyeh around his neck and clutches a microphone.

'Someone here pointed you out as the claimant's girlfriend. Must be tough to date another girl in a small town. Can you tell us a little about your relationship? Were you dating when the alleged events took place? Do you think that it was a hate crime?'

Vanessa barely hears.

What if Alexander won't allow Anna-Karin to come here at all? What if he has injured her in some way?

Dear God, Vanessa thinks. Don't let anything bad happen to her. Don't let him hurt her.

'Julia!' Felicia calls. Vanessa turns to the front door.

Julia has just come in with Erik's parents and his older brother. Her blonde hair is neatly pinned up and her make-up is discreet. She is wearing a gauzy white dress under a pale pink cardigan. She comes across as a nice, ordinary girl, only better looking than most. Someone who has been caught up in this dreadful business through no fault of her own. Someone who would absolutely not go out with a boy capable of appalling acts of violence. Her bearing is proud. Sad yet courageous.

And Vanessa knows just how much Julia adores this role.

Cameras go off again and the guy in the keffiyeh gallops off toward Julia together with the other reporters.

'We believe Erik!' a middle-aged lady shouts. Her cheeks are as round as a baby's. 'Be strong! They'll get through this!'

Disgusted, Vanessa turns her back and calls Anna-Karin.

'We just want to be able to put all this behind us,' she hears Julia say while she waits for the signal to get through. 'We want to go back to our normal lives. She has stolen so much of our time together. It's perhaps the worst thing she has done to us.'

Another signal. And someone replies.

'Hello, Vanessa.'

It's Alexander's voice. Vanessa can't find her own.

'I have agents in place in the courtroom. They will contact

me immediately if they even suspect any of you of trying to manipulate the conduct of the hearing. And if they do, Anna-Karin will pay a high price. I will not hesitate. Do you understand me?'

Vanessa's face goes cold with fear.

'Yes,' she whispers.

'You will have to put your faith in justice,' Alexander says, ending the call.

Gustaf and Rickard have just come to join them. People behind them in line mutter angrily.

'What's wrong?' Evelina asks.

Vanessa is scrutinizing the people in the hall. Who is spying for Alexander? Of course, the bit about 'agents' might be a lie. She sees Viktor at a distance, but he won't be in the courtroom until it is his time to take the witness stand.

'Vanessa?' Nicolaus says.

She tries to think logically but her thoughts are bouncing about. Anna-Karin might be in danger. They can't do anything about Robin. Erik will be freed. What if Alexander has killed Anna-Karin already?

'Nessa?' Evelina says.

'They're not coming,' Vanessa says. 'I think Anna-Karin is all right but . . .'

She can't say any more than that in this crowd. Nicolaus looks very worried. But not as worried as Evelina, who understands the full implications of Anna-Karin not being able to be here.

A voice on the intercom announces that it is time for the public to take their seats and the doors open automatically. Vanessa and Evelina walk in and find seats next to each other in the front row.

The room is divided by a glass wall, confining the public to one half, while the court sits on the other. The judge is a man in his sixties. When he bends to check something in his documents, Vanessa notices that he has a comb-over, evidence that he is refusing to accept the truth about what is happening to his own head. And Vanessa wonders if that means anything regarding his approach to his job. His deputy sits next to him, a young woman who looks not much older than the Chosen Ones. Vanessa wonders what she thinks about the case. Not that it matters. She isn't going to deliver the judgment.

That is up to the judge and the magistrates, a woman and two men of the same age as the judge. The four of them are to decide if Erik, Robin and Kevin are guilty and, in that case, what their sentence should be.

The woman wears a gray suit, has short, white hair and a face with almost as many smoke-wrinkles as Mona Moonbeam. She looks distracted, as if she is planning tonight's dinner. One of the men has crew-cut gray hair and a military bearing. Vanessa suspects he is ex-army. The other man is the complete opposite. He is so fat his features seem blurred and his eyes have an uncertain look as he scans the crowd in the galleries. He seems stressed by all the people.

This is the court that they are supposed to put their faith in.

Then Linnéa comes in, walking between two men. One of them must be the prosecutor; the other Vanessa recognizes as Linnéa's lawyer.

Vanessa's eyes fill with tears as she watches Linnéa on the other side of the glass wall. Her head is bent and her arms crossed. She isn't wearing any make-up and the clothes she's wearing obviously don't belong to her.

Linnéa, Vanessa thinks, hoping that Linnéa can pick up her thoughts. *I'm here.*

Linnéa meets her eyes for a brief moment.

Is Anna-Karin here? Linnéa asks.

No.

Vanessa won't tell her why because Linnéa mustn't be troubled now.

Good. I was worried she'd try something.

It will go all right anyway, Vanessa thinks. *I promise.*

No reply now. Linnéa sits down to the left with her back to the public.

Then the defendants enter from the right. They are escorted by three prison guards each. All three defendants are wearing a suit and tie, their hair is neatly combed and they look serious. Despite their handcuffs, they look more like victims than criminals. That is especially true of Erik and Robin, who have missed out on the summer sun, and no longer look like sporty hockey dudes with rosy cheeks. Vanessa hears a broken sob from Erik's mother. The boys sit down with their representatives on the right-hand side of the court.

The judge starts talking to introduce the hearing. The prosecutor outlines the case and reads out a description of the alleged events. Vanessa can't concentrate properly, and instead becomes fixated on the way he keeps using the phrase 'by means of'. Why can't he talk normally? She hates this overly complicated language.

'How do the defendants plead?' the judge asks.

Erik's lawyer speaks into the microphone.

'Erik Forslund pleads not guilty.'

Vanessa looks at Robin or, rather, the back of his neck with its short, blonde hair. And, even though she knows it is hopeless, she still hopes.

* * *

Not guilty. Erik. Robin. Kevin. All three. Innocent.

Linnéa already knew how they would plead, but to hear it in open court makes her feel as if she stands accused. That she is the one to be judged. And punished.

She regrets not taking a tranquilizer but it's too late now. She can't start swallowing pills in front of the court.

Not guilty.

They have just taken a short break and Hans-Peter Ramström is about to question her. His voice is kind when he asks her if the perpetrators are present in court. And, if so, can she point to them?

Kevin doesn't meet her eyes when she points at him. Robin doesn't either, but Erik looks straight at her and, even though she doesn't want to hear his thoughts, she can't stop them all from entering her mind.

Just wait, you fucking whore. Just wait.

His face remains completely calm.

The prosecutor asks Linnéa to give an account of what happened that evening. He leads her through the events with his questions. Linnéa tries to be coherent, tries to focus on what he says. But she is constantly aware of the public on the other side of the glass wall, of the video camera pointed at her by the deputy judge and of the eyes of the judge. Now and then, she senses some of Kevin and Robin's anxious, fluttering thoughts as well as Erik's powerful fantasies of what he'll do to her once all this is over.

Then, suddenly, it is the turn of Erik's lawyer.

The famous lawyer looks different from the photos. He is shorter. His brown eyes are almost jovial. A perfectly ordinary, friendly man. Until he opens his mouth.

Now, Linnéa becomes even more certain that she is the accused.

He calls into question everything she has said.

How could she be certain that the man on the bridge was Erik? He was masked, wasn't he? The water was ice cold at the time, so how did she manage to get out? Why didn't she tell the police? Who made the anonymous call to emergency services? How did she explain the curious coincidence that the cell phones belonging to both boys were in the PE center all night?

She tries to answer, to explain, but she feels as if she is just making things worse. Now and then, the lawyer's thoughts get through to her. He is positive that he'll win and get one up on that old sod Ramström. She also senses the doubts in the minds of the judge and the magistrates. Her story is unconvincing. *She* is unconvincing.

At least she doesn't lose her temper. She is too preoccupied with surviving.

Does Linnéa have a police record? Contacts with social services? She is actually subject to a Child Protective Custody Order? Foster care? And the apartment where she lives now belongs to social services? Does Linnéa have a history of alcohol abuse? Cannabis abuse? Dependence on any other classified substances? If so, which substances? Would she please list for the court the drugs she has consumed, or perhaps that is too hard to remember? Does she have any psychological problems? Has she seen a psychologist? Twice a week, is that so? Did she tell her psychologist about the alleged events by the canal? No? Why not? Perhaps there wasn't all that much to tell?

And Ludvig says to the judge: 'Is this really relevant?'

And, one time, the judge responds: 'Could counsel rephrase his questions so that they are less provocative?'

But another time he says: 'I think it's highly relevant to examine closely the relationships between the claimant and the defendants. It's not like the claimant has a monopoly on the truth.'

That makes some members of the public titter.

The lawyer continues.

Is it correct, as reported, that Linnéa has been in a physical conflict with Erik Forslund before? Is that so? But only in 'self-defense'? In other words, he attacked you without any provocation? Out of the blue? In the middle of the day and at school?

Has Linnéa ever seen things that don't exist? Could it be that Linnéa has developed a psychotic condition? Or, perhaps, she is consumed by a lust for revenge? Or envy perhaps?

'But in that case, why should Robin have confessed?' Linnéa asks. Her voice is weak and a little breathless.

'He hasn't confessed,' the lawyer says, and his brown eyes glitter. 'He hasn't confessed to anything.'

When Erik's lawyer has finished with her, Robin's representative will take over and, after him, Kevin's.

And the question is: will there be anything left of Linnéa after that?

CHAPTER 82

'Hurry,' Clara whispers.

Her voice comes out of empty air.

Minoo is grateful for the carpet that muffles the sounds of her footsteps, and tries to avoid looking at the grand portraits as she walks along the hallway. Adriana's and Alexander's ancestors seem to stand guard, ready to step out of their frames.

She tries the key in the lock of Adriana's door. It works. She turns and whispers into empty space.

'If someone comes, warn me, but then you have to leave at once. Please.'

Minoo opens the door and sneaks inside.

In front of her is what must be Adriana's study. The curtains are drawn, leaving the room in a dull half-light.

Minoo takes a couple of steps into the room. The parquet floor creaks. She recognizes the desk, which used to be kept in the locked room in Adriana's house. The desktop is empty, apart from a letter knife of shiny steel and a couple of fountain pens in a rack next to the lamp.

Adriana's books, mostly worn, leather-bound volumes, are arranged behind locked glass doors in the bookshelves. Two stuffed owls sit on top of the shelves. Their dead eyes are dull. When Vanessa and Minoo sneaked into Adriana's house, there was a live raven as well. What happened to Adriana's familiar after the court case in the manor? Was it thrown in the trash?

Minoo scans the room for the box but can't see it anywhere.

She opens a pair of double doors. The bedroom is on the other side. The blind is pulled down here. On the windowsill she sees the lamp, with the shade of dragonflies made of glass mosaic. The bed is neatly made.

Minoo opens the door to the next room.

The thick curtains are drawn and only admit a thin strip of light. A large, white rug covers most of the floor. It is furnished with a sofa, two armchairs and a table, placed in the middle of the room. The only object on the table is the box. It feels almost as if it has been waiting for her.

Minoo goes closer to the table while listening intently for any warning knock. The box is perfectly centered on the table. She lifts it, weighs it in her hands. It is surprisingly light. She tries to open it but the lid doesn't shift, not a single millimeter. She shakes it gently, looks for another way of opening it, but finds nothing.

When she last saw this box, she and Vanessa had been terrified that they might be caught snooping among Adriana's things. When the air began to tremble with a deep, thumping noise that made the whole house vibrate, they reached out for each other and held hands. They barely knew each other, but they knew that they needed each other.

Minoo is suddenly overwhelmed by a huge sense of loss. It is an almost physical sensation. For the first time, she *understands*. And she doesn't try to close her eyes to the truth.

Her place is with the others.

She has made the wrong choice. An utterly wrong choice.

What Nicolaus said is true. *If we switch off our doubts and our emotions, and excuse ourselves by insisting that we are acting rationally . . . that is when we make some of our most dangerous decisions.*

In order to get along here in the manor house, she has had not only to switch off her critical mind, but also her empathy.

Still, Walter was right about one thing he said to her.

Eventually, one must stop messing around. For her, the time has come. What other time is there? By the time darkness falls over Engelsfors, she will know no more than now. She already knows what she needs to know. And, deep inside, she has known it all along.

Perhaps the Council's circle also has a chance, but she believes in the Chosen Ones. The Chosen Ones will close the portal.

Minoo has the box now. If there is any more information to be had from Walter, she will find out about it; she will have to do as Linnéa suggested, take it out of his head and make him forget about it afterward. It could be done during their assessment talk this afternoon.

She dreads the thought of attacking him. But surely she is stronger than he is? He keeps saying so himself.

A knock on the study door.

And Minoo panics.

She puts the box back on the table and dives down behind the sofa. Holds her breath; she hears nothing but the beating of her pulse.

Someone enters Adriana's study. High heels tap on the parquet. The steps continue into the bedroom.

Minoo hopes that it is Adriana who has just come by to pick something up.

The heels come closer now. Then silence. Such complete silence that any sound, even breathing would be audible.

Minoo wants to put her hands in front of her mouth but doesn't dare move a finger.

She was no good at hide-and-seek when she was little. The others always found her.

The heels tap along a few more times: three, four, five, then silence.

'I see you,' Adriana says.

* * *

Anna-Karin comes to gradually. She glances out through the window. Yellowing fields against a backdrop of forest. The car is gliding softly, silently along the road. She has been lying slumped in the passenger seat and the seat belt is cutting into her belly.

She sits up straight, feeling completely alert. She starts looking for her cell phone and then remembers that Alexander has got it.

'You've only got yourself to blame,' he says without looking at her. 'The power you fired off in my direction was very strong.'

Linnéa.

Anna-Karin checks the time on the dashboard clock. The hearing has been going on for two hours.

They are still driving along a highway and the speedometer needle is steady at 70 miles an hour.

How far have they traveled and where to? What can she do?

She must do something.

Alexander was prepared for her attempt to control his mind. But he probably doesn't know about her new physical strength. What if she struck his head, rendered him unconscious? Or grabbed the wheel and forced the car off the road?

She has no idea. They might end up in a ditch. Or swerve into the opposite lanes and crash into oncoming traffic.

She must not risk the lives of innocent people.

Anna-Karin looks out again.

Alexander drives in the outside lane.

Would her new strength protect her if she leapt out?

She hadn't been hurt at all when she fell in the gym hall, or when she cracked china with her hands. Not even when she moved the heavy, sharp-edged boulders in the caves.

But does any of that compare to throwing yourself out of a car at 70 miles an hour?

Anna-Karin glances at Alexander. His eyes are fixed on the

road. Every passing second she is taken further and further away from Västerås. She must do it now.

She cautiously undoes the safety belt.

'What are you up to?' Alexander says as he turns to have a look.

Anna-Karin fumbles for the door handle, pushes the door open. The noise of tires against asphalt becomes loud and cold air rushes in. Alexander grabs her shoulder but she releases her strength and jumps out with her arms around her head.

She hits the ground so hard that the air is driven out of her lungs. She rolls across the asphalt. The world rotates. Then all is still.

Anna-Karin lies on the shoulder. She draws breath once, then again. Becomes aware of a burning pain in her right arm and hip. She hardly dares to look, afraid of seeing torn skin, or a stump of her broken bones protruding from bloody flesh.

She sits up. Her duffel coat and the sweater underneath it are both ripped. Her skin is red but there are no open wounds anywhere. No blood. No broken bones.

Anna-Karin hears a car door slam. Alexander's car has stopped a ways ahead. The rear lights glow, the engine is idling. He is coming toward her and has already covered half the distance between her and the car. She must hurry.

When she stands, her legs are shaking so much she almost falls over. A few cars drive past but none of them stops.

Alexander will reach her soon.

Her power has protected her. Now, it must come to her aid again. She mustn't hesitate, or worry about damaging him. Alexander shall not stop her from doing the right thing. Alexander, who tried to get her convicted in the Council's trial; Alexander, who has threatened to kill her if she tries to help Linnéa.

He is close to her now.

'What the hell do you think you're doing now?' he says.

Anna-Karin hits him in the chest with the flat of her

hand and he flies backward. He lands in the tall grass of the field.

She runs to the car, hoping she will remember enough from the practice sessions with Grandpa on the farm. Alexander's car is an automatic. She releases the brake and pushes the gear lever to Drive. And accelerates. Nothing happens, and she almost panics before realizing that the parking brake is still on. She releases it and the car shoots away.

She glances in the rear mirror and just has time to see Alexander get up.

The car is so large it feels like driving a tank. The engine is responsive and she nearly panics again when she sees that the needle has jumped to 90. She eases her foot back off the accelerator.

The palms of her hands get sweaty as she looks for an opportunity to turn around. Scared that the wheel will slide out of her hands, her grip tightens.

A glance at the clock makes her increase the speed again.

* * *

Minoo gets up, supporting herself against the back of the sofa. Adriana observes her, and then looks at the box. The box that no longer stands perfectly placed in the exact center of the table. It is only a few inches out, but Minoo knows it's enough for Adriana to see that it has been tampered with.

'I didn't find my keys the other day,' Adriana says. 'I knew exactly where I had put them. Then, a little later, they turned up again in the right place.'

She looks at Minoo.

'Was it only the box you planned to steal?'

'I didn't plan to steal anything.'

Adriana looks at her carefully. Minoo forces herself not to start blabbing. Mustn't say stuff like, *I got lost, door happened to be open, I'd come to look for you and just as you came in, I thought I saw something behind the sofa and must have*

601

nudged the table so the box moved, what box anyway? I don't know anything about any box . . .

'I don't care why you want it,' Adriana says. 'You can have it. But I want something in exchange.'

Minoo stares at her and tries to think ahead.

'I'm bound to the Council,' Adriana continues. 'And not only through the oath.'

She unbuttons the top two buttons on her dress. Minoo wants to say that it's unnecessary, that she knows about the scar already, but how would she explain that to Adriana?

'I broke the laws of the Council when I was young and this was my punishment.'

Her tone is calm, explanatory, as she points with one of her long, slender fingers to the burn scars where the sign of fire has been branded into her skin just below her left collarbone.

'Ever since, I can't defy the will of the Council. If I try to escape, they'll locate me as easily as if I had a built-in radio transmitter.'

She buttons up her dress.

'You can manipulate magic. You did it for Clara. Please . . . I can't say it explicitly. I truly *can't*. But . . . do you understand what I want?'

Her eyes are full of desperation. And Minoo does understand.

'Walter said he didn't need me to be there for the assessments after all,' Adriana says.

'He'll be busy all day. And Alexander isn't here . . . Please, Minoo. You can have the box. Take it.'

'It's not about the box. I want to help you. I truly do,' Minoo says, thinking: *You've no idea just how much.* 'But I've never done anything like this before. And I don't know if I can.'

Adriana comes closer to her.

'I've never met anyone with powers like yours.'

She pauses, then starts again.

'You're a young witch with exceptional powers and born in Engelsfors.'

She looks pleadingly at Minoo.

'You are the Chosen One, aren't you?'

Minoo sees the frail hope in Adriana's eyes. Must she kill it? Is she even capable of doing that?

'Yes,' she says. 'I am Chosen.'

Adriana puts her hand over her mouth. She looks as if Minoo has just returned from the dead. Which, in a way, she has, because Adriana's dream is alive again now. Her dream of finding the Chosen One. The dream that once lit a spark of hope and life inside her and helped her on the way to find her true self. That was before Alexander took everything from her again.

'Then I was right?' Adriana says breathlessly. 'Did I . . . did I find you?'

'Yes,' Minoo says, speaking through tears. 'You found me.'

'Oh my God,' Adriana says.

She sits down on the sofa and leans her head in her hands.

Minoo watches her. Adriana now knows for certain that she has been deceived. Minoo can't think what to say and is not sure that she should say anything.

When Adriana straightens up, her eyes are red-rimmed.

'What has happened, truly?' she asks.

Minoo sits down next to her.

If she can free Adriana from her magic chains, she won't have to live under the tyranny of the Council; she will have a genuine chance of escape and, if she does, her memories will no longer be a danger to her. She can have them all back.

As a bonus, Minoo will have the box. Everyone will believe that Adriana took it with her when she escaped.

'I can't explain what happened,' Minoo says. 'But I can return your memories to you. And I will try to remove your bond.'

603

The Key

'I don't know how to thank you,' Adriana says.
'I can't promise anything.'
Adriana only nods and sits back on the sofa.
'What would you like me to do?' she asks.
'Nothing at all,' Minoo says and releases the black smoke.

CHAPTER 83

Vanessa returns to the courtroom and sits down in her old place. Her eyes are still brimming with tears. She knows she should be strong for Linnéa's sake, but she can't stop crying.

After listening to the cross-examination of Linnéa, the judge announced that it was time for a lunch break.

Lunch.

As if the whole trial is nothing more than a normal day's work and now it's time to pop around the corner for a burger and fries.

Vanessa felt like screaming.

She thought her view of the judicial system was cynical, but now she sees that she has been utterly naïve. She had never dreamed that anyone would be allowed to do what Erik's lawyer has just done to Linnéa in a court of law. He systematically scrutinized her life, took it apart, twisted and distorted what he found and used it to make *her* seem like the guilty one.

Compared to Erik's top-class lawyer, the performances of Robin and Kevin's representatives were neither as polished nor as aggressive, but by then it didn't matter. Linnéa was already in so much pain, so every question they asked was like probing raw wounds.

Vanessa felt her pain. Literally, for the bond between them hasn't disappeared even though they are no longer a couple.

Once the questioning had finished, Linnéa was escorted from the courtroom by Ludvig. She didn't reply when Vanessa tried to send thoughts to her. Now, as she is brought back into court, her face is as blank as before.

Evelina takes Vanessa's hand and squeezes it.

It is time for Erik's cross-examination.

Vanessa watches him as he sits down. From her position she can see his profile. During the questioning he kept looking at Linnéa gravely, sometimes a little pityingly.

Vanessa is in no mood to listen to his lies but, above all, she doesn't want Linnéa to hear. *I'm here,* she thinks to Linnéa. *I'm here all the time.* Vanessa hopes that she hears her.

* * *

Linnéa hears Vanessa's thoughts, but it's as if they come from a very great distance. She looks down at her hands. They lie on the table in front of her, balled into fists. She feels that they don't belong to her.

When Robin's lawyer started asking her questions, she had been hurting so much she simply shut off. Answered as if on autopilot. Linnéa doesn't know what she said. It could've been anything. It doesn't matter. They will go free, all three of them. All Engelsfors will regard them as innocent victims and Linnéa will be the crazed liar.

And she knows what Erik is thinking. How certain he is that he'll get away with it next time. He has been fantasizing around several different scenarios, but with the same end point. Linnéa dead. It will look like suicide.

I'm not alone, Linnéa tells herself. *I have powers. I'm a witch. One of the Chosen Ones.*

But the gut-wrenching fear is all that is real to her now. And the look in Erik's eyes.

Just wait, you fucking whore. Just wait.

Ramström clears his throat. The court will now listen to Erik's statements.

* * *

Anna-Karin has been in Västerås many times. But she has never driven a car and, as for the court, she only has a vague memory of Gustaf saying that it is near the railroad station. And Alexander still has her cell phone.

She parks the car near the station, wondering how she managed to drive it all the way here. She gets out, feeling as if she is still holding the wheel in a frantic grip.

Anna-Karin looks around. She sees a bearded man in a leather waistcoat coming out from the station.

'Excuse me!' she says. 'Can I ask you something?'

The man glances nervously at her and walks on. Anna-Karin realizes that with her torn, filthy clothes and wild hair, she must look deranged.

Tell me where the district court building is, she commands.

'On the other side of the tracks,' he replies tonelessly, and points to a covered footbridge.

Anna-Karin runs into the station, past the newsstand. She pushes people aside on the narrow escalator, speeds across the footbridge, almost slips on the terracotta tiles as she runs straight through a group of girls wearing identical tracksuits and carrying large duffel bags. On the other side, she takes the stairs two steps at a time.

She enters a parking lot. Spots a large building with a sign in front.

VÄSTMANLAND DISTRICT COURT.

Maybe she'll get there in time. She must.

She runs inside and gives the guards at the security gate a straightforward order.

Let me in.

* * *

Ramström leafs through some of his documents. Linnéa wonders if he believes he has any hope of winning. She can't read his mind. Earlier, she couldn't keep other people's thoughts out of her head. Now her power seems to have jammed.

'Could you tell us in your own words and with as many

607

details as possible, what you did and where you were during the evening when the alleged crime was committed?' Ramström says. He looks up at Erik.

Linnéa tries to detach herself completely but it's not working.

'I had dinner with my family and my girlfriend, Ida,' Erik says. 'She . . . passed away last winter.'

He pauses. Linnéa doesn't need to look at him to know how well he does 'grieving boyfriend'. She has seen it before. His big thing is bravely fighting back tears.

'Then we went to the Positive Engelsfors Center,' he finally continues. 'Helena Malmgren had asked us to help set things up for their special Spring Equinox party. She and her husband, Krister.'

Two more dead people, another reverential pause. A long one. Linnéa counts to five seconds. Then to ten.

'And what happened afterward?' Ramström says.

Erik still doesn't reply. The silence is growing unbearable. Linnéa has to have a look. Erik is staring at the table in front of him.

'Erik?' Ramström says.

'Sorry,' Erik says. He looks at the prosecutor. 'I don't know what I'm doing.'

'What do you mean?'

'I don't know why I'm lying about everything. I take responsibility for what I did. One hundred percent.'

Linnéa is confused. And it looks as if Erik's star lawyer feels just as lost. Robin and Kevin look uneasily at each other. But Erik seems confident as he faces Ramström.

'Helena and I had talked about it for a long time. We felt that it was time that someone put Linnéa in her place.'

Is she hearing this? Or is she out of her mind and hallucinating? Maybe this is the psychosis Erik's lawyer was talking about?

'Could you explain what was meant by "put her in her

place"?' Ramström asks. He seems to be the only one who has the new situation under control.

'Helena wanted us to wait until we knew Linnéa wasn't at home. Then we'd go there and wreck her apartment.'

* * *

Vanessa hears Julia and Felicia moan. The reporters are scribbling frenetically.

'What the fuck are you doing?' Erik's older brother shouts, and tries to stand up, but his father pulls him down onto his seat again.

The judge demands silence. 'This is no way to behave in a court of law,' he says.

Vanessa senses her energy and turns her head. Anna-Karin is pushing her way through the aisle. Eventually she manages to squeeze herself in to sit next to Vanessa. She is very dirty and her clothes are in tatters. Her breathing is forced, as if she has been running.

And her eyes burn with a dangerous glow. They are fixed on Erik.

The judge is still talking.

'I am aware that cases of this type arouse strong emotions, but you must show some respect.'

Anna-Karin holds out her hand and Vanessa takes it. She gives Anna-Karin all her strength, doubles Anna-Karin's capacity, hoping that the Council's spies also feel the magic that radiates from them; that they realize they don't stand a chance against the Chosen Ones.

* * *

'Can you tell me what happened when you got into Linnéa's apartment?' Ramström asks.

'Sure,' Erik says.

Linnéa stares at him. He looks perfectly content. Relaxed. And suddenly she becomes aware of her energy. Linnéa turns around and sees Anna-Karin in the front row. She looks like the angel of wrath. Vanessa is at her side, boosting her power.

And Alexander is nowhere in sight.

Linnéa can breathe again.

'Helena had given us a key so we just walked straight in,' Erik continues. 'We brought liquor and beer cans. The idea was to make it look as if Linnéa had thrown a party that got out of hand. Helena said that social services would kick her out of the apartment and lock her up somewhere.'

'That's quite enough, Erik,' his lawyer says in an authoritative voice, and then turns to the judge. 'I request a break at this point.'

'I don't want a fucking break,' Erik snaps.

'Neither do I,' the judge says. 'This defendant clearly has a tale to tell, and I for one want to hear him out.'

'Thank you, sir,' Erik says. He settles back in his chair. 'Anyway. The slut came home earlier than we expected.'

'Erik!' his lawyer hisses.

'Is he allowed to interrupt me all the time?' Erik asks.

'No, he isn't,' Ramström says, and can't quite hide his smile. 'He will have to wait his turn. Please continue, Erik. I assume that you were referring to the fact that Linnéa came home?'

'Yes, that's it.'

You could hear a pin drop in the court. The judge and the magistrates observe Erik with interest. Linnéa is fascinated, too. He is completely calm, completely himself. He seems convinced that he is talking to a bunch of friends.

'Suddenly she was just standing there,' Erik says. 'First I was worried because she saw our faces, but then I realized it didn't matter.'

'Why didn't it matter?'

'No one would believe her. I knew Helena would back us with an alibi if something went wrong. And, just in case, we had left our cells in the center. It would be Linnéa's word against ours and Helena's . . . a no-brainer, don't you think?'

He laughs a little.

'You mean that nobody would have believed Linnéa if she accused you of vandalizing her apartment?'

'Not a soul. I might as well have let her call the cops and gone back to the PE Center,' Erik says.

'So, why didn't you?'

Erik's complacent smile is replaced by a chilly expression.

'I wanted to take the opportunity.'

'What opportunity?'

'To kill her.'

Erik's words hang in the still air of the courtroom. Everyone has heard him; everyone knows who he is now.

'I was disappointed with Helena, who just wanted us to trash the apartment. I sort of *hoped* something like that would happen. You know, that Linnéa would show up.'

'So that you could kill her?' Ramström asks.

'That's right,' Erik replies. 'So, when she ran off, I set out after her. And when we had trapped her on the bridge . . . it was just perfect. I would have liked to carry on messing around for a bit longer, but someone might have come by, a car or something. I got such a kick out of seeing her so scared. And then, to see her do what I told her to. Just jump . . . and sink. I felt so fucking powerful!'

Minoo had described Erik's memories just along those lines. Now Linnéa can pick up Erik's thoughts. He is loving every minute of this. Anna-Karin is making him *enjoy* telling the truth.

'How did you feel when you learned that Linnéa had survived?'

'I was disappointed. But hoped for better luck next time.'

Linnéa hears a long-drawn-out whimpering noise. She sees that, on the other side of the glass, Julia is having a breakdown. Her face is swollen with crying. Next to her, Felicia sits with her head almost resting on her knees.

Erik sighs loudly when he sees Julia.

'Get over it,' he says wearily.

'This behavior is quite unacceptable,' the judge says. 'One more incident like this and I will call the guards. Anyone who causes a disturbance will be asked to leave.'

He nods to the prosecutor to continue.

'Erik, I want to establish that I've heard you correctly,' Ramström says. 'When you heard that Linnéa had survived your attempt to drown her in the canal, your reaction was to start planning other ways of murdering her?'

'That's right,' Erik says, leaning back in his chair. 'I would have done it, you know. Should have done it ages ago.'

'Could you develop that thought further?'

Erik chuckles.

'Robin, Kevin and I have always got off on beating the shit out of the freaks. But Linnéa is special to me. I can't think of anyone I hate more.'

He looks at her with that smile of his. And though she knows he can't do anything to her now, fear still rises inside her.

'Why do you hate Linnéa Wallin?' Ramström asks. His voice is almost seductive.

'Because she's a stuck-up little whore who thinks she's so special. That sort of thing cannot be tolerated.'

His cold smile again.

'That kind of person needs to be exterminated.'

Robin and Kevin look shocked. Linnéa wonders if even they have ever heard him speak so frankly.

'I'm only sorry about one thing. I should have spoken out long before now. And I shouldn't have threatened to kill Robin and Kevin to make them take their confessions back.'

'I see,' Ramström says. 'You told them that you would murder them unless they lied to this court?'

'That's right. But, apart from that, I don't regret anything. I'm proud of it and would do it again.'

He turns to the public galleries.

'When you leave today you'll be like, *Oh my God, I had no idea.* But you'll be lying. Because you've always known. You've always known who I am. You've always let me get away with it.'

He grins and turns to face the court again.

'Am I correct in assuming that you're changing your plea?' the judge asks him.

'Guilty,' Erik says, and crosses his arms.

CHAPTER 84

Adriana's connection to the Council does not consist of just one bond.

It is more like hundreds of fish hooks. When Minoo takes them out, she must carefully remove each barb so that they don't cause any tears. She is endlessly thorough and cautious. The task is not particularly difficult, but it is very time-consuming. Though time, she knows somewhere in the back of her mind, is in short supply.

But it is hard to keep in touch with the world outside when she works with her magic. The hooks require all her concentration.

One by one, they are removed. Until, finally, they are all out.

Adriana is free.

She is reclining on the sofa, her magic a faint red glow around her. Her bondage is over. When Minoo has returned her memories to her, she will be a whole person again.

It isn't as easy as it was with Gustaf. It is not just a matter of a few hidden hours. Minoo has to reinstate each junction, each detour that she created last summer. Unstitch the seams made in the memory weave, unravel it and allow it to take on its original shape.

It is satisfying work.

Now, soon, she'll be done.

* * *

Anna-Karin leans against the wall near the entrance to the courtroom. The sky has become overcast; a grayish light floods into the atrium.

She folds the sleeves back on Nicolaus's coat, which she is wearing on top of her own messed-up clothes. She has washed her face and hands and eaten a bar of chocolate that Evelina had brought. But she still feels drained. Vanessa, who is standing next to her, is exhausted too. Even though their powers are almost as strong here as in Engelsfors, they run out of strength faster when they are away from its source.

But their tiredness feels good. It is the fatigue that comes after working hard and achieving a fantastic result.

She looks around the hall. The atmosphere is morose, except among the journalists. The parents and siblings of the boys seem unable to face even each other. Julia and Felicia have vanished.

Anna-Karin is very aware of how Erik's words will stick in everyone's mind.

. . . You've always known. You've always known who I am. You've always let me get away with it.

Anna-Karin made Erik lie just once. It was when he claimed that he had threatened to kill Robin and Kevin. They of course repeated the lie as a reason for retracting their confessions, topped with plenty of assurances about how scared they had been of Erik.

Their lawyers were utterly confused. After a break for consultation, both sides informed the court that they wouldn't call any witnesses. Viktor could go back home. The prosecution and the defense lawyers gave their closing remarks and then the court withdrew to deliberate.

Anna-Karin has no worries about the outcome because she has already instructed the members of the court. They are to sentence along the lines indicated in the prosecutor's submission to the court. And make the actual sentences as tough as possible.

The Key

The loudspeakers announce that the court is in session again.

'Ready?' Anna-Karin asks Vanessa.

She nods and smiles a tired smile. They walk back to their seats, hand in hand.

'The defendants have admitted to criminal acts as charged, and confirmed collusion with each other. Their admissions of guilt are supported by all available evidence in this case,' the judge announces. 'Because of the defendants' youth, and because two of them have already spent two months in custody, this court will deliver its sentences immediately.'

All is still now. Anna-Karin turns her eyes to Erik and squeezes Vanessa's hand. Concentrates. Earlier, she made him love speaking out. Now, she wants him to understand what he has done.

Listen to your sentence. Say nothing. Realize that you have confessed, that everyone here knows what you have done.

Anna-Karin observes Erik. He freezes as the judge utters the words *five years*. Red streaks on his skin rise up from underneath his shirt collar. Robin bursts into tears when he hears his sentence: *four years*. Kevin just nods when he hears *three months*.

Anna-Karin focuses on Erik again.

Turn around.

Erik turns his head.

Look along the first row. Look at me. The BO Ho.

Erik scans the row and catches sight of Anna-Karin.

Understand that I am making all this happen and that I'm not alone.

Slowly, all color drains from Erik's face.

Understand that we will do much, much worse things to you if you ever try to appeal against your sentence. Or if you ever try to hurt Linnéa again. Or if you ever hurt anyone else.

616

Erik's face has gone white as chalk. He looks nauseous with sheer terror.

Anna-Karin feels completely calm. They have won.

* * *

Minoo opens her eyes.

The light that finds its way into the room is dimmer now, and she wonders how long she has been operating inside the black smoke. Next to her, Adriana is reclining on the sofa and staring at the ceiling.

'Adriana?' Minoo says.

No answer. Adriana's eyes are blank, unblinking. Minoo is frightened.

'Adriana! Can you hear me?'

She touches her arm, then shakes her lightly. No response. Minoo places her fingertips on the large artery in the neck and registers a pulse. Adriana is alive but she doesn't respond. Why isn't she responding?

The study door is pulled open and quick, heavy steps are crossing the floor. Minoo can't move. She is shivering all over.

Alexander enters the room. His black coat is very dusty and the skin over one cheekbone is scratched. He stops and looks at them.

'What's going on here?' he says. 'Adriana?'

She doesn't react. Alexander hurries to her side, takes her pulse, tries to wake her.

'What have you done?' he screams at Minoo. 'What have you done?'

Drops of spit hit her face. She is speechless. She can't stop her trembling. She is shivering, as if the room has turned arctic.

'Alexander,' Walter says calmly from the doorway. 'Let me try.'

Alexander backs away and Walter bends over Adriana and

617

holds her head with both hands. He closes his eyes. It takes only a few seconds before he opens them again.

'I'm very sorry,' he says. 'I can't help her.'

Alexander looks murderously at Minoo. She is certain that if Walter gave him free rein, he would kill her.

'Take your sister away from here,' Walter says. 'I'll have a look at her later on.'

Alexander lifts Adriana and carries her out of the room, much as he once carried Olivia from the gym hall. Minoo just has time to glimpse him as he lowers Adriana onto the bed in the bedroom. Then Walter shuts the door.

Minoo clutches herself in an attempt to stop the shaking. Where did she go wrong? Was it too much for Adriana? Perhaps she'll get better after a little rest? Or has Minoo completely burnt out her brain?

She feels the sofa give when Walter sits down next to her. He leans forward, rests his elbows on his knees.

'Well, now, Minoo,' he says.

She hears Alexander moving about in the next room, saying Adriana's name. No response.

'Will she be all right?' Minoo asks in a voice that trembles as much as the rest of her.

'How can I answer that?' Walter says. 'I don't even know what kind of damage you've caused.'

He sits back, puts his arm along the back of the sofa and looks at her.

'It wasn't too hard to get Clara to talk,' he says. 'Her pain threshold is quite low. What about yours, Minoo?'

She feels sick. The room vibrates in time with her heartbeats.

'What did you do to her?' she asks him.

'It wasn't that bad. And I can always fix any damage I do. Unlike you, it seems.'

'I didn't mean to—'

'That's enough,' Walter says. He fixes his eyes on her.

'You're only to listen and answer my questions. So, what is your pain threshold like, Minoo?'

He looks so calm. What has he done to Clara? What does he plan to do to Minoo?

'Forget it,' he says and sighs. 'You'd just retreat into your magic. Pointless. I'm sure you'd respond better to other methods. You know that we have our headquarters in Stockholm, don't you?'

'Yes,' Minoo whispers.

'It is not unusual for people to fall off metro platforms. Not to mention all those lethal traffic accidents. Sometimes muggings go awfully wrong. And then there are fires. Bad things could happen to anyone. Even to hospital consultants. If you get my meaning?'

The shaking is intensifying and her teeth are chattering. All Minoo can do is nod.

'Good,' Walter says. 'I take it you've understood that Alexander isn't my only subordinate here in Engelsfors?'

Minoo hasn't given it much thought. She always trusted Walter's sincere-sounding assurances that he didn't want to involve too many others.

Now she realizes just how gullible she has been.

'Alexander isn't the only one, far from it,' Walter continues. 'So, there's every reason to have a chat about bad things that might happen in Engelsfors. Let's leave your family out of it for the moment. Take Vanessa's little brother. Do you think he could defend himself?'

Minoo shuts her eyes tightly and tries not to vomit.

'Answer my question, Minoo. Do you think Melvin can defend himself?'

'N-n-no.'

It feels as if she has lockjaw.

'Do you think Gustaf can defend himself?'

'Please . . .' Minoo stammers as her eyes fill with tears.

The courage she felt when she held the box, the sense of

control she experienced when she was inside the black smoke, all of it is gone. Walter is in charge. He has all the power and she can't think how she could ever believe otherwise.

'It's come to my attention that Anna-Karin Nieminen, together with Vanessa Dahl, manipulated the court hearing today,' he says. 'Also, that Anna-Karin attacked Alexander . . . '

'Please,' Minoo says again. She forces herself to look at him. 'I understand. I fully understand where you're going with all this . . . I'll do what you want . . . anything you want.'

Walter wipes away the tears running down her cheeks with the sleeve of his sweater. First her right cheek. Then her left.

'I thought you wanted to save the world, Minoo.'

'I do.'

'Then, why go behind my back? Why have you recruited new witches to your circle, even though you haven't the faintest hope of it being effective? Why try to deceive me and the guardians?'

She has no answers.

'As for the box, you don't even have a clue how to use it,' Walter adds.

She looks at him. Of course he knew. He knew all along.

'I hoped you'd come and talk to me of your own accord. We really thought you would, the guardians and I.'

'I had planned to do it,' Minoo says.

Walter nods. 'I believe you,' he says. 'You're intelligent. You're able to see the big picture, to look beyond your own immediate needs. But the others are dragging you down. "The Chosen Ones". Christ.'

He picks up the box from the table and weighs it in his hands.

'Chinese craftwork from the 1400s. Carved, lacquered wood and some magic. What you see are only the surface features, of course. The object inside the box is a good deal older. It dates from the period of the first Council.'

His finger follows the carved figures on the lid.

'There's a story here linked to the conspiracy. A reason why they stole these objects.'

Minoo tries but fails to take a deep breath. She can't get enough air into her lungs.

'They believed the demons were ancient gods who ruled this world in the beginning. The conspirators also believed that they would be elevated if they let the demons in. They thought that they would be given a new civilization. The plan was to keep these objects concealed and hand them over to the demons' Blessed One when the next portal was activated.'

Walter points to the male figure in the center of the lid. Then he puts the box back on the table.

'People are capable of believing anything,' he says. 'No matter how many facts one presents to them. They'll always find a way to twist what is true and simple.'

He looks hard at Minoo.

'It is very simple, Minoo. The Chosen Ones can't save the world. But we can. Our circle is the strongest.'

'Yes,' Minoo whispers.

'You've seen it yourself.'

She nods. She has seen it herself.

'You don't like me,' he says. 'And I understand why you don't. It's actually quite charming how *young* you are. That you still believe you can keep your hands clean. That it's possible to be idealistic and still get on in the world. That love and friendship will conquer everything.'

'I don't believe that,' Minoo says.

Suddenly she can't get her head around how she could ever have believed that. Reality looks different. Reality is sitting in front of her.

'But I hate you,' Minoo says.

The words come out of her mouth just like that. She can't stop it. But Walter just grins, his usual boyish smile.

'Always something,' he says.

He places his hand on her cheek. His fingertips are cold as ice when he turns her head and locks his eyes onto hers.

'We want the same thing. That's what matters now. I'm the enemy of your enemy and hence your friend. Hate me as much as you like. But you will stay here. And you will obey me. Understood?'

'Yes,' Minoo whispers.

'Excellent,' Walter says. 'You still have the key to Nicolaus's apartment, I hope? And the cross is still kept at your place?'

'Yes.'

Walter lowers his hand.

'I understand that this is hard,' he says gently. 'But you're doing the right thing.'

CHAPTER 85

Ludvig and Ramström accompany Linnéa to the small room and she sinks down on the sofa. Was it really this morning they met in here for the first time? Now it seems all that happened in a different life. In a different universe.

Diana hurries in, sits down next to Linnéa and gives her a hug.

'Christ,' she says. 'It's all over.'

Awkwardly, Linnéa returns the hug. She still can't quite believe it's true.

'You were incredibly brave,' Ludvig says when Diana lets go.

'I must say, I've never experienced anything like it,' Ramström says, sounding almost exhilarated. 'I think the court would've agreed to·anything after that confession.'

He and Ludvig carry on talking about the damages that the court has awarded Linnéa. A hundred thousand dollars. A lot of money.

'Would you like me to get you something?' Diana asks. 'A glass of water, perhaps?'

'Vanessa,' Linnéa says. 'Please, could you find Vanessa and Anna-Karin?'

'No problem,' Diana says, and leaves.

Linnéa just sits quietly, listening to the two men. They are talking about the sentences.

Erik's five years and Robin's four. Years that they'll never get back. And they will always be known as the guys who tried to murder somebody.

Linnéa senses Vanessa's energy coming closer and Diana opens the door.

'They are on their way,' she says. 'Do you need a ride later?'

'No,' Linnéa replies. 'I'll go back with the others.'

Diana nods and smiles. Diana, who has always trusted Linnéa, always done more for her than her job required. Much more. Linnéa can't blame her for what she did while Olivia controlled her. She has known that for a long time, but now she feels it as well.

'Thank you,' Linnéa says. 'For everything.'

Diana looks touched.

'You take care,' she says. 'We'll talk soon.'

Ludvig and Ramström shake hands with Linnéa. She thanks them both, as usual feeling awkward and stiff when she tries to be polite. But her gratitude is real enough and she hopes they will realize that.

They leave just as Vanessa and Anna-Karin enter.

Vanessa's cheeks are streaky with tears. Linnéa walks toward her and straight into her arms. Suddenly she is surrounded by the scent of coconut shampoo.

Vanessa's emotions flow into Linnéa. She feels Vanessa's happiness and relief and they become her own happiness and relief. Now, she dares to believe that it actually happened. They won.

She wishes she could kiss Vanessa and tell her that not a day goes by when she does not regret what she did. Tell her how much she needs her. But she reminds herself that history would only repeat itself. She would hurt Vanessa again.

She lets go and gives Anna-Karin a quick hug.

'You got them', Linnéa says. 'You fucking got them.'

Anna-Karin smiles.

'Erik won't try to appeal,' she says. 'And he won't try to harm you or anyone else again.'

'It feels like we've won against the whole of Engelsfors,' Vanessa says. 'Against everything that's rotten in the town.'

Linnéa laughs. That's exactly how it feels.

'What happened to Alexander by the way?'

Anna-Karin and Vanessa glance at each other.

'He did his best to stop me from getting here,' Anna-Karin says. 'But I dealt with him.'

'The Council probably had spies in court today,' Vanessa says. 'We have to assume that they know what we did. But, Linnéa, it was worth it. You mustn't ever think any different. Not for one second. We're not going to be scared of them anymore.' Vanessa's eyes shine defiantly and Linnéa doesn't feel afraid anymore. She feels how strong they are together.

'Having said that, we shouldn't be alone tonight,' Vanessa continues. 'Not while both the Council and Olivia are after us. Evelina is sleeping over at Rickard's place. They have already left with Gustaf.'

'The three of us can stay at Minoo's,' Anna-Karin says.

Linnéa agrees, glad not to be left on her own tonight.

'Does anyone know how things panned out for Minoo?' Linnéa asks. 'Did she find the box?'

'We don't know,' Anna-Karin says. 'It's still impossible to phone Engelsfors.'

'Nicolaus has gone for the car,' Vanessa says. 'Do you want to leave now? Or stay for a while?'

'Let's go now,' Linnéa replies.

The crowd in the hall has thinned. Tindra comes along to give Linnéa a hug and congratulate her. Ramström is talking to some journalists. Linnéa catches a glimpse of Cissi's blonde hair in the group.

Near the doors, a guy wearing a keffiyeh is waiting with a microphone at the ready.

'Congrats, Linnéa! How are you feeling?' he says.

'Like maybe there's some justice in the world after all.'

Then, fresh air at last.

He stands at the bottom of the steps.

Dad.

Linnéa stops on the top step.

I'm just going to talk to him for a moment, she thinks to Vanessa, who nods and walks on together with Anna-Karin toward Nicolaus's car.

Linnéa walks down the steps.

He isn't drunk today.

'Have you been here all day?' she asks.

'Yes, I have.'

She wonders how she would have felt if she had spotted him in the public gallery. Would it have made her feel worse? Or better?

'I'm so very sorry about the last time,' he says. 'I've joined AA now. But you don't have to listen to any more about that. There is just one thing I want to tell you, for your sake. Not mine.'

What he is saying sounds prepared, but his eyes tell her that he really means it.

'You were so wrong,' he says. 'You're not ruined. You're not like me. You're like your mother. Emelie was the bravest, strongest person I've ever met. If she hadn't died in the damned accident, she would have made a future for herself. As you will, Linnéa. You must never believe that you can't.'

Linnéa opens her mouth to say something, until she realizes that her voice wouldn't carry.

Her mind goes to the box back in the apartment, full of letters that her mom and dad wrote to each other when they were young. And the cassette tapes they exchanged. TO BJÖRN FROM EMELIE. Two kids from foster care who married and tried to build a life together.

What is it that decides who gets on and who is dragged down? Is it inherited? Or in the environment? Willpower? Good luck and bad?

She hears the reporters swarm down the steps. Cissi calls her name.

'I have to go,' Linnéa says.

She isn't sure that she wants to see him again. Or if she will ever forgive him.

But she is grateful for what he has just said.

'Take care,' she says.

'And you,' Björn Wallin replies.

She gives him a brief smile.

'Bye, Dad,' she whispers.

And then she sets off at a run toward Nicolaus's car.

Chapter 86

Walter's car is parked outside an abandoned townhouse. The FOR SALE sign is so dirty you can barely make out the real estate agent's phone number. Minoo sits in the passenger seat, wrapped in the black smoke. It soothes her, makes her feel pleasantly numb. Thoughts and memories come and go without hurting her.

Adriana's lifeless eyes.

Alexander's furious gaze.

Walter's threats.

Do you think Gustaf can defend himself?

She doesn't even feel anything when she looks at Walter, who is sitting next to her with an old copy of the *Engelsfors Herald* spread out across the steering wheel. The pages rustle as he turns them. The heater is humming. The stereo quietly plays old tunes that seem to belong in black-and-white films.

A car slows down and stops behind them. Walter checks the mirror. Minoo hears a car door open and close.

'All right,' Walter says, folding the newspaper. 'I can allow you two hours.'

'Thank you,' she says, not feeling the humiliation.

'Of course, with Olivia snapping at our heels, we'll have to be extra careful. I'll stay here and watch until you've gotten in safely.'

Outside, the air is icy, as if the temperature has fallen to zero. The sky is covered in dark clouds. She walks quickly to Gustaf's house. Rings the doorbell. His face opens up in a surprised smile when he answers the door.

'Hi there,' he says. He takes her in his arms.

Now that she is inside the smoke, it feels meaningless to kiss him, but she does it all the same. He must not think that anything is wrong. That is why Walter allowed her to come here. She must make Gustaf believe that all is well with her.

'I've just come back home,' Gustaf says. 'It's so good to see you. I've been worried about you.'

'Because of Olivia, you mean?'

'Yes,' he says.

'You mustn't worry,' she says. 'I got a ride here.'

She walks ahead of him into the kitchen, feeling his eyes on her. To give herself something to do, she grabs a glass from the rack and fills it with water.

'Tell me about the court hearing,' she says.

Gustaf tells her and she listens. There is so much that should make her feel something, but all she can do is note the facts, and try to look happy or worried in the right places. Not that she thinks she can fool him. It is obvious that he notices that something is wrong.

'Where are the others?' Minoo says.

'Evelina is sleeping at Rickard's tonight, and the others have all gone to your house,' Gustaf says. 'Special precautions, because we know that both the Council and Olivia are on the warpath.'

'But what about you?'

'It's cool. Olivia is chasing natural witches. And the Council aren't likely to be interested in me either.'

Do you think Gustaf can defend himself?

She has to release a little more black smoke to dampen down her fear.

'Has the Council said anything?' Gustaf asks. 'I mean, about what they might do to Anna-Karin and Vanessa?'

'No, they haven't said anything.'

Gustaf looks concerned.

'How are you feeling? Did you find the box?'

'No,' Minoo says. She drinks a little water. 'Shall we go to your room?'

'It's a crazy mess. Hang on.'

He walks ahead of her up the stairs and, after a while, calls to her that all is clear and she can come up.

The bed has obviously been tidied up in a hurry. The wardrobe door is slightly open and she can see he's thrown a pile of clothes inside. The Venetian blinds are pulled down and the only light comes from the bedside lamp.

She notices the photograph of Rebecka and Gustaf. It used to hang on the wall above his bed, but now it has been moved to the windowsill, next to a photo of Gustaf's family. He moved it in the spring, saying that Rebecka would always be a part of his life, but that she couldn't be his girlfriend anymore.

'You're using your magic,' he says. 'I can see it in your eyes.'

She turns toward him. He sits on the bed and she can see the tendrils of smoke float in the air between them. It's so strange that he can't see them, even though they almost touch him.

'It feels as if you aren't here,' he says. 'Please, Minoo. Stop it.'

She hesitates. Without her magic, she risks breaking down. But she must try to draw strength from something else.

She pulls the smoke back. Gustaf looks relieved.

And she realizes that he truly sees her. That he can tell how she is, even when she tries to hide it.

'Why did you use your magic? Has something happened?'

Adriana's lifeless eyes.

Alexander's furious gaze.

Walter's threats.

Do you think Gustaf can defend himself?

Fear is lurking, ready to leap at her. But she will not let it. She has less than two hours with him.

These might be their last moments together.

She wants them to be filled with happiness.

'Tons of things have happened,' Minoo says.

She goes to the bed and sits down next to him.

'But is it all right if we don't talk about it now? Can't we forget all the bad things? Just for now?'

She looks at him and he nods. And so she slams the door shut on all her fears, on all the problems. All that will be waiting patiently for her the moment she steps outside this house.

She kisses him and Gustaf pulls her close. She feels the scent of him. And how much she loves him. It makes her dizzy.

She has always wondered about sex. Like, how do you even begin? Does one have a discussion and reach a joint decision? Or, is it supposed to kind of *happen*, wordlessly?

But now, all these questions are unimportant. There's no time.

'Gustaf,' she murmurs. 'I've never . . .'

And she feels herself blushing.

'You know . . .' she says.

Gustaf nods.

'But I want to,' Minoo says, and her face goes hotter still. 'If you do.'

He smiles. Then kisses her again, lingeringly. His lips move down her neck and on to kiss her ear. It tickles wonderfully. He pulls his T-shirt off and throws it on the floor; she slides her hand through his tousled hair, along his neck, his shoulder, down to his waist. Feels his warm skin under her hand.

Gustaf starts unbuttoning her cardigan. She pulls it off, and her top. She moves closer to him, feels the warmth of his naked skin against her body. It's a new sensation.

They kiss awkwardly while they fumble to get jeans and socks off. Then she lies back on his bed and he kisses her neck again. His lips move down her collarbone to her breasts. She unfastens her bra. He takes it off.

She had always thought that she would be shy and stiff;

631

that her many body fixations would distract her. Now, she feels that she can't do anything wrong because there is no such thing as wrong. All she wants is to continue.

Gustaf's fingers wander down to her waist, leaving goosebumps in their wake. He touches her hips and pulls down her panties. She kicks them off, then slips her hand down the small of his back and tugs at the elastic of his underpants. He pulls them off and lies down next to her so she can rest her head on his arm.

He looks at her.

'You are so lovely,' he says.

The way he says it makes her believe it.

'You, too,' she whispers.

He smiles a little and kisses her again. The kiss is deeper this time. His free hand moves up the inside of her thigh.

The way he caresses her feels different from when she has done it herself, and she wonders if she should do something for him, but then she relaxes and allows herself to be swept along by his touch.

Gustaf has condoms in a drawer and she realizes that he had hoped that this would happen, that he wanted to be prepared.

It doesn't hurt. It mostly feels strange but in an enticing way. She would like to find out more. Everything is so new. Just being close to him like this is overwhelming.

Afterward she lies close to him and he holds her; he laughs a little.

'What's so funny?'

'Your cheeks are burning,' he says.

Minoo smiles. She feels so calm.

'Why did we wait so long?' she asks.

'You never had the time,' he says. She hears the smile in his voice.

She hasn't got time now either. But she refuses to think about that. Her arm rests on his chest. Her leg is lightly

632

hooked around his. She wishes she could stay like this for all eternity. That nothing would ever happen, not ever.

She used to be baffled by people who said they'd like to stop time.

Now she understands. Now, she is happy.

Chapter 87

'Vanessa?'

It's Anna-Karin's voice. Vanessa opens her eyes. She and Anna-Karin are sitting on the back seat of Nicolaus's car.

'We've arrived.'

Vanessa massages her neck. It is stiff and tender. She looks out at Törnros Road. She has slept the whole way, ever since they left the fast-food place just outside Västerås. It was only an hour or so ago, but she feels as if she has slept forever and would like to keep sleeping forever more.

'I'll come with you,' Nicolaus says.

Vanessa opens her mouth to say something like, *Isn't that a bit over the top?*, but changes her mind. Where Olivia is concerned, no security measures are over the top.

Linnéa opens the passenger door to the cold outside world. She folds the seat back to let Vanessa crawl out.

'It's fucking freezing,' Linnéa says. She pulls out a pack of cigarettes. Vanessa feels calm radiating from her. It has been there ever since they left Västerås. It is wonderful to share it. To simply look at each other and let all questions rest for a while.

Something cold lightly touches Vanessa's forehead and she looks up.

'Wow,' Linnéa says.

Large snowflakes fall from the dark sky and dance toward the ground. Snow in September.

Vanessa looks at Linnéa. A few white flakes have landed on her black bangs. Everything is so quiet.

Part Four

'Vanessa?' Nicolaus says from the other side of the car.

'Coming.'

As she walks with Nicolaus toward the front door, the snowfall gets heavier. She stretches to bring life into her body.

'What a day,' Nicolaus says as they step into the elevator.

'You can say that again,' Vanessa agrees. 'Do you think the Council is going to kick our doors in tonight and lock us up?'

The elevator doors close slowly. Vanessa presses level 5.

'They won't let it pass,' Nicolaus says. 'But what you did was right.'

The elevator shudders and starts.

'I have lived for four hundred years,' Nicolaus continues. 'Very rarely have I seen justice being done in society.'

He looks seriously at her.

'You and Anna-Karin were very courageous today. You are very brave, Vanessa. I don't remember ever having told you that I think so.'

'I don't believe you have.'

'High time, then.'

'Come to think of it, I've never apologized to you for calling you "creepy" the first time we met,' Vanessa says.

'I have a feeling I didn't make a good impression,' he smiles.

The doors open to the landing.

'Perhaps you had better wait here,' Vanessa tells him. 'Then you don't have to play Linnéa's uncle, I mean.'

Nicolaus looks embarrassed. She understands that he's as reluctant as she is to watch her mom trying to chat him up.

'Ring the doorbell if something happens,' she says.

She walks into the apartment, closes the door, turns the light on, kicks her shoes off, but keeps her jacket on. She tries to make a list in her head of what she should pack to take with her to Minoo's.

The light is on in the kitchen and there's a strong smell of frying. Mom is listening to an old power ballad that's playing in the living room.

The Key

'We won!' Vanessa calls out. She walks toward the music. 'They've been put away!'

She steps into the darkened living room. The stereo is giving off a faint, greenish light. Mom is asleep on the sofa. Frasse lies on the floor at her feet. The smell of frying is stronger in here.

Frasse.

He is far too still.

His eyes are wide open.

His tongue is hanging out.

The smell is coming from him.

Not frying food. Burnt flesh.

Vanessa stands as if frozen to the spot.

'Mom,' she whispers. 'Mom . . .'

'Calm down,' a voice says.

In the corner of her eye, Vanessa sees something moving in the darkness between the windows. A figure, dressed in black, steps into the light from the hall and pulls back her hood. Her face is covered in white powder and framed by blue hair.

'Your mom is alive,' Olivia says. 'So far.'

She holds out her hands, turns her palms up and makes blue sparks flash between her fingers. Her face looks ghostly in the cold light.

Vanessa's terror seems to make her skin shrink and tighten around her.

'I'm sorry about the dog,' Olivia says. 'I like animals a whole lot better than people. But he tried to bite me.'

She aims a flash at the stereo. It crackles and dies.

'Do you have any idea what a pain it's been, waiting for you and having to listen to your mom's shitty music?'

Vanessa looks at Mom. Her eyes are closed and her mouth is open, but she is breathing.

'She's asleep. Sort of,' Olivia says. 'She seems like a really nice person. Pretty stupid though. I just said that I'm a friend of yours and she let me in, just like that. She'll wake up again if you stay cool.'

'You mean, if I stay cool until you've murdered me?'

Olivia smiles and Vanessa notices that new teeth are filling the gaps where the old ones had fallen out. The Council has looked after its prisoner very well.

'Let's talk a little first,' Olivia says. 'It's been ages since I spoke to anyone at all. Apart from the demons, of course, and they aren't exactly a laugh a minute. Just now they're furious with me for not getting on with it. Killing you, that is.'

Vanessa is so grateful Melvin isn't here tonight; that he is with Nicke this week.

'You're V, aren't you?' Olivia says.

'What are you talking about?'

'V. In Linnéa's diary. I managed to get my hands on it a few times. She was totally obsessing over this V. I've been think- ing about it ever since. And figured it must be you. She was so worried about you at the Spring Equinox party.'

'I know nothing about all that.' Vanessa tries to empty her voice of emotion.

Olivia laughs a little.

'Whatever. The point is, I know that Linnéa is in love with you. And that's why I'm going to kill you first. Then I can tell her about it.'

She smiles in a superior manner. It looks so ghoulishly theatrical that Vanessa half expects Olivia to throw her head back and burst into evil laughter any minute now. She would be ridiculous if she wasn't so dangerous.

'Olivia, listen,' Vanessa says. 'The demons tricked you.'

'I know that,' Olivia says, making little flashes run up her wrists. 'They tricked me and then they dumped me. And left me alone with the Council. But then I started dreaming about them again. They wanted me to return and I decided to forgive them.'

The flashes leap up her arms and run down her body.

'I don't give a shit that they lied. The power they give me is real. And I'll use it to help them open the portal.'

The blue light dances over her face and magic fills the room. The hall light flickers.

'If you do, you'll start the apocalypse,' Vanessa says. 'You won't survive.'

'I know I won't. But I'll take the whole world with me when I go.'

Olivia smiles and Vanessa knows there's nothing she can say to stop her. She needs to stall until she can figure out what to do. Olivia must keep talking. It's lucky that she is in such a chatty mood.

'But why do you want that?'

'There's nothing left for me here. Elias is dead and sooner or later the Council will trap me again. I don't want to spend the rest of my life as Walter's guinea pig.'

'Walter?'

The flashes of lightning swarm down Olivia's arms again and collect in her hands. The light is so intense that Vanessa's eyes hurt.

'The boss of the Council. For a while he wanted me to be the metal witch in his circle. He's obviously an idiot.'

Vanessa agrees. How could Walter think that Minoo would join the same circle as Olivia?

'I mean, it's not like you can replace the Chosen Ones,' Olivia says.

Vanessa stares at her. She tries to get her head around what Olivia is saying.

'In that case, you and the demons might as well give up. Three of us are already dead, if you haven't noticed.'

This time there is nothing theatrical about the grin on Olivia's face. It's genuine.

'So you don't know?' The sparks around her hands are growing ever stronger and more intense. The lights in the kitchen go out.

'And now you'll never know,' she adds.

Vanessa is blinded by the bolt of lightning coming toward her.

* * *

Vanessa's scream fills Linnéa's head and puts her into a state of total shock. Then the scream stops abruptly.

Through the falling snow, she sees the lights go out in all the windows in Vanessa's building.

Then, blue light illuminates the living-room window of Vanessa's house.

She understands and drops her cigarette.

'Anna-Karin!' she shouts in the direction of the car. 'It's Olivia!'

She runs toward the house, her stupid preppy shoes slipping on the thin layer of snow. She bursts into the dark stairwell, and finds her way upstairs in the light of her cell phone display. She clings to the handrail as she speeds up, slips again, hurries on.

Vanessa! She shouts in her head. *Vanessa, answer!*

There is an answer.

Olivia is here! Be careful!

Vanessa is alive.

When Linnéa reaches the fifth floor, she tastes blood in her mouth. Nicolaus is standing outside Vanessa's door. He has turned on his cell phone display.

Olivia is in there, Linnéa thinks.

He looks shaken. The sound of Anna-Karin's steps echo in the stairwell.

Linnéa tries the door handle. Locked. Of course. At Vanessa's place, the door locks automatically when you shut it.

Anna-Karin, Linnéa thinks. *Hurry up!*

* * *

Vanessa smells burning. Where the lightning struck the wall just to the left of her head, the burnt scar is smoking.

Olivia didn't miss her. She's just having fun. Now she makes more electrical discharges crawl up her arms.

But Olivia doesn't know that the others are here.

Vanessa senses Linnéa's energy outside the front door; Anna-Karin's is halfway up the stairs.

Vanessa releases all her power. It grows inside her into a howling storm that she can hardly control.

Press the doorbell, she thinks to Linnéa.

The sound of the bell slices through the air. Olivia turns toward the sound and Vanessa hurls the storm at her.

Olivia is thrown violently backward, hits the base of her spine against the windowsill and sinks to the floor. The window-pane behind her is blown out by the gust. Shattered glass and bits of broken flowerpots whirl in the darkness outside.

Vanessa rushes to her mother but stumbles on Frasse's body. She mustn't think about him now. Mustn't think at all. She slides into invisibility, leans over and places one of her Mom's limp arms around her neck, pulls her into invisibility and away from the sofa.

'Nessa?' Mom mutters faintly.

Vanessa shushes her, although Olivia shouldn't be able to hear them.

A lightning bolt strikes the sofa and forms a black, smoking crater in the upholstery.

Olivia has got up and is standing in front of the empty window opening; snowflakes are spiraling into the room.

'Where are you?' she screams.

She sends a bolt at the doorway to the hall and Vanessa realizes that she mustn't try to get Mom out by that route.

Somebody is thumping on the door. She senses Anna-Karin's energy just outside on the landing.

'Get your fat friend to stop sending me goddamn control thoughts!' Olivia shouts.

She can resist Anna-Karin, Vanessa thinks, as she drags Mom toward her own room. *Don't come in.*

Part Four

We're fucking well coming in! Linnéa thinks.

Lightning zooms just above Vanessa's head and hits a framed photo of herself as a little girl. It crashes to the floor. Vanessa hauls Mom into her room. Mom has fainted again and her limp body is so heavy that Vanessa isn't sure she can handle it. She drags Mom by her arms across the floor and shoves her under the bed, hoping that she's not hurting her. The moment Vanessa lets go, Mom will become visible again, but at least she's hidden.

'Come out!' Olivia screams. Vanessa hears the sizzling electric sound; sees lightning fill the living room.

A crash from the front door, then another one. The others will soon get in. Vanessa can't let Olivia injure them.

She runs back into the living room. When she is invisible, her footsteps are inaudible. Olivia is walking toward the hall with the lightning twisting around her arms like glittering snakes.

Vanessa's fist hits Olivia's face. She hears the satisfying *crack!* as something breaks, and then feels a shooting pain from her own hand, so sharp that she is jolted out of invisibility. Olivia's face is contorted by rage and blood is rushing from her nose down over her bared teeth. She looks grotesque.

Sparks fly around Olivia's hands. Before she has time to create full-scale flashes of lightning, Vanessa leaps at her and shoves her up against the wall between the windows. Olivia is flailing wildly, but Vanessa grips her wrists and presses them against the wall, ignoring the pain from her own hand.

Olivia screams, then head-butts Vanessa.

A wave of pain and the world goes black. She hears Linnéa call her name, but isn't sure if Linnéa is in the apartment or only projecting thoughts. Something wet is pouring into her left eye and obscuring her vision. Blood.

Olivia takes hold of Vanessa's shoulders and swings her around toward the window opening. The windowsill is pressing into the small of Vanessa's back. She tries to fight and releases her power, but she is too dazed and her magic is too strong. The howling wind comes at both of them and tears at their clothes and hair. The blood is pouring over Vanessa's face. She tries to push Olivia away, but Olivia won't let go. Her fingers dig into Vanessa's upper arms as she presses her toward the window.

Then, suddenly, Vanessa knows that she will fall.

Her feet leave the ground.

The wind tears them both out into the cold night, into the still-falling snow.

* * *

Linnéa enters just in time to see the storm wind heave them out through the window.

A second of stillness follows.

Then there is a heavy thud far below. The hall and kitchen lights come on again. The snowflakes blowing in through the window melt as soon as they land on the floor.

And then Linnéa sees first Vanessa's blonde hair and then her bloodstained face as she hovers in the air outside.

CHAPTER 88

Minoo is woken by a sudden sense of panic. Gustaf is not in bed with her. She grabs his phone from the bedside table and checks the time.

Only ten minutes to go. How could she *fall asleep*?

Gustaf comes in with a towel around his hips. His hair is damp and there is a smell of soap around him. He smiles when he sees her awake.

She loves him so much. And what she will do now will hurt terribly.

'I could kill for something to eat,' he says. 'Want a grilled cheese? It's the only thing I can offer, I'm afraid.'

'I'm sorry, but I have to go.'

She can't bear even to look at him as she gathers up her clothes, goes to the bathroom and gets ready. When she returns he is sitting on the bed. The silence weighs heavily on them both.

'I truly want to stay,' Minoo says in the end. 'But I can't.'

'I know,' Gustaf says.

He gets up and comes over to kiss her. She kisses him, too, but all she can think about is that this might be the last time. Their last kiss, ever.

'I'll come downstairs with you,' Gustaf says.

She puts on her shoes and jacket, then takes an envelope from her jacket pocket and hands it to him.

'What's this?' he asks.

'It will explain everything,' she says. 'Please try to make the others understand.'

The Key

Before he has time to do or say anything else, she runs outside. Into a shimmering whiteness, a world covered in snow.

'Minoo!' Gustaf cries.

Walter's car moves smoothly along and stops. She runs toward it. The last thing she hears before shutting the door is Gustaf calling her name once more.

* * *

Anna-Karin had almost forgotten how much she hates the hospital. Now and then, she has to be in touch with the fox. He is padding through the snowfall in the forest. Being with him reminds her that there are places where the smells don't make her think of illness and death.

There are four beds in the room, and three of them are empty. Jannike lies in the fourth and Vanessa sits on the edge of the bed, holding her mom's hand. Her other hand is swollen, she has a large bandage over her left eyebrow and her white sweater is soaked in blood. Mother and daughter are both in tears.

Jannike recovered a little on the way to the hospital. She has been examined, declared in good shape, but is kept in for observation.

'Poor Frasse,' Jannike says, sniveling with each breath.

She is so beautiful, still so young. She could almost be Vanessa's older sister. And it's obvious that she and Vanessa love each other.

'I don't get it,' Jannike continues. 'Who was she? She said she was a friend of yours.'

'She wasn't,' Vanessa says.

'The whole business is so mixed up in my mind; things went black and . . . she must have hit me. And then you turned up, Nessa. I was so scared. I must have blacked out. I dreamt things . . .'

She falls silent and looks anxious.

She saw Olivia's magic, Linnéa thinks. *But of course she can't believe what she saw.*

'Everything will be all right,' Vanessa says.

Anna-Karin wishes they could tell Jannike the truth so she doesn't have to worry about hallucinating. But the truth would be even more upsetting.

Nicke comes in, together with a woman police officer with short dark hair. Both look uncomfortable when they see Vanessa and Jannike. And Nicke looks more uncomfortable still when he realizes that Linnéa is with them.

'Christ,' he says, and turns back to Jannike. 'I had no idea it was you two who . . . This is one hell of a chaotic evening. How are you?'

He glances at Vanessa's bloodied sweater.

'We'll live,' Jannike says dourly. 'Where's Melvin?'

'With my mom,' Nicke says. 'All police have been called in. It's this effing weather that's messed it up. Nobody has changed to winter tires yet. And the communication . . . I don't know what we would have done without the police radio . . . I wonder sometimes what's going on in this town.'

'That's what you keep saying,' Jannike says. 'Hi, Paula.'

'Hi,' she replies.

Nicke clears his throat. Paula shifts from one foot to the other. The snow on their uniform jackets is melting and dripping on the floor.

'Sorry, but I think you must be Linnéa Wallin?' Paula says, looking at Linnéa. 'I just want to say congratulations. It was good news that those boys got punished. It usually doesn't turn out that way.'

'No,' Linnéa says, with a glance at Anna-Karin that warms her heart. 'It usually doesn't.'

'Good thing that they confessed,' Vanessa says. 'If they hadn't, Linnéa wouldn't have had a chance. Right, Nicke? I seem to remember that you didn't even believe that there had been a break-in.'

645

'You know, Nicke, I think you owe Linnéa an apology,' Jannike says.

She and Vanessa stare at him. He seems so ill at ease that Anna-Karin has to stifle a smile.

'It's possible that the case could've been handled differently,' Nicke says. 'Though it's a fact that these two lied to me. And that the boys had alibis.'

'Is that all you've got to say?' Jannike asks.

'We're here to talk about you.' Nicke produces a notepad and a chewed pencil. 'Vanessa, we'll want to talk to you as well later on.'

'We'll go away for now.' Vanessa gives Jannike a kiss on the cheek.

'Bye, Jannike,' Linnéa says.

'You take care, sweetheart.' Jannike looks close to tears again. 'I'm very, very happy for you.'

Linnéa nods and leaves the room quickly with Vanessa just behind her. Anna-Karin waves to Jannike and as soon as she turns her back, Nicke starts to speak.

'Now, tell me what happened, from the beginning?' he sounds kinder than before.

'Frasse is dead,' Jannike starts sobbing. 'She killed him.'

Anna-Karin turns just as the door closes, catching a glimpse of Nicke's face crumbling with grief.

Out in the hallway, hospital misery comes over her again. It makes her feel nauseated. Further away, in the waiting room, a woman screams. Anna-Karin pities her. And pities Nicolaus, who is waiting for them there.

They go to the stairwell. Outside, the snow falls thickly now, flakes as large as down turning yellow in the light from the streetlamps.

Vanessa fingers her bandage – Olivia broke the skin under her eyebrow. Anna-Karin will never forget the moment when she saw Vanessa thrown out of the window. And never forget the next moment, when she floated back up, still dripping

646

with blood, hovered outside and then climbed in through the window.

'It was so easy,' she'd said. 'As easy as in my dreams.' And then she'd collapsed to the floor and fainted. They had to carry both her and Jannike down to Nicolaus's car because it was no good trying to phone for an ambulance.

'I killed her,' Vanessa whispers. 'I have killed someone.'

The figure lying on the pavement in front of Vanessa's house is part of another memory Anna-Karin will keep all her life. A lifeless body, already covered by a thin layer of snow. Around its head, a dark halo of blood.

Linnéa looks intently at Vanessa. Anna-Karin knows that they must be thinking to each other. The magic between them is so strong it's palpable.

'You didn't kill her,' Anna-Karin says. 'She fell.'

'But I wanted her to die,' Vanessa says, looking at her with frightened eyes.

'Stop it,' Linnéa says. 'She attacked you. And your mother. And she killed Frasse.'

Vanessa nods but doesn't look entirely convinced.

'There's something else,' she says quietly. 'Olivia said that Walter wanted her to join the Council's circle. And she went on to say that of course it was a useless idea because "it's not like you can replace the Chosen Ones".'

'What did she mean by that?' Linnéa asks. 'Was she saying she didn't think she could open the portal?'

'No,' Vanessa says. 'That's the thing. She thought she could.'

The stairwell is silent.

Anna-Karin tries to get a grip on what Olivia has said, what it means. But she can't. All she can think of is that Walter wanted to use Olivia in his circle, despite knowing what she had done. What she was capable of. It surely says all you need to know about Walter? Anna-Karin worries about Minoo. She has hardly had time to think about her today, but Minoo has also taken risks. Did she find the box? Did they catch her looking for it?

Anna-Karin hopes that Minoo will be at home when they arrive.

'I can't make sense of it,' Vanessa says.

'I can't either,' Linnéa admits. 'But we have to talk with Minoo about it.'

'Yes,' Vanessa agrees. 'But, Linnéa, don't be so hard on her.'

'I know,' Linnéa says. 'I won't.'

Vanessa hugs Linnéa and then puts her arms around Anna-Karin, who almost bursts into tears.

Anna-Karin would like to say to her that she hasn't forgotten that Vanessa held her when Mom was dying in this hospital.

And she would like to tell Linnéa and Vanessa that they must find each other again. She almost feels like using her magic to make them understand they belong together, that they love each other.

They leave the stairwell and Anna-Karin and Linnéa carry on to the waiting room. The room is full of people. The screaming woman sits on the floor. She wears a thick quilted coat. Now and then she opens her mouth to let out another anguished howl. Everybody else in the room is busily looking anywhere but in her direction.

Nicolaus gets up from one of the sofas and comes to meet them.

'How did it go?' he asks.

'They're fine,' Anna-Karin says with a nervous glance at the screaming woman.

'But there's lots to talk about,' Linnéa says. 'We'll tell you in the car.'

The woman in the quilted coat starts crawling between the rows of seats. Her dirty scarf is trailing on the floor.

'It's coming!' she says, looking straight at Anna-Karin. Her eyes are burning with despair. 'It's coming!'

CHAPTER 89

L innéa sits next to Nicolaus as they drive at a snail's pace through the streets of Engelsfors. The snow is falling as quickly as ever and the large flakes stick to the windshield. The wipers are struggling.

Linnéa looks at the snow and thinks of the flakes that landed on the floor of Vanessa's living room. And the snow that slowly covered Olivia's dead body.

It's not like you can replace the Chosen Ones.

But Olivia believed she could open the portal all the same.

Nicolaus parks outside Minoo's house. Linnéa sees someone waiting on the steps. It's Gustaf. She feels a knot of anxiety inside her.

She climbs out of the car. Gustaf's jacket is far too thin for this weather. He has snow in his hair, on his shoulders, all over him. His face bears signs of tears.

'I've got to talk to you,' he says.

They settle down in the living room. Anna-Karin hands Gustaf a blanket and he wraps it around his shoulders.

'Minoo came to see me,' he says. 'When she left, she gave me this.'

He holds out a scruffy envelope, damp with snow, and Linnéa takes it from him. She unfolds the letter inside it.

I have to leave you for a while.

I know you won't understand, especially not you, Linnéa, but I have no choice. The time for closing the portal is near now and I must spend all my time practicing with the Council's circle. I will move into the manor house and stay there. I must not be in contact with you or with my family until this is all over.

I will tell my parents that I live in the manor house in order to assist my boss Alexander with an important project that he has to complete. Anna-Karin, please make them accept this explanation.

Do not attempt to contact me by any means. And keep away from the manor house at all times. The Council will not punish Anna-Karin and Vanessa for their intervention at the court hearing, on condition that you leave us all in peace.

I have already packed everything I need. That includes the cross and the skull. You have no use for them.

I am so sorry that it turned out like this but there is no alternative.

Minoo

Linnéa folds the letter and hands it to Anna-Karin and Nicolaus, who are sitting side by side.

'I noticed something was wrong,' Gustaf says. 'She used her magic at first but then she stopped and I thought . . . she said something had happened but that she didn't want to . . . I didn't get it.'

Linnéa feels a heavy sadness. Minoo has chosen sides. She wishes that she could be surprised at Minoo's final decision.

'Minoo would never do this willingly,' Anna-Karin says.

'Yes, she would,' Linnéa says. 'If the guardians have told her to—'

'For fuck's sake, how can you say that?' Gustaf says. 'Read the letter! She's frightened! They've threatened her!'

'I agree that all this sounds as if she is under undue pressure,' Nicolaus says.

He is studying the letter.

'It reads as if each word has been chosen too carefully,' he continues. 'As if she is afraid of saying too much.'

'She *wants* us to believe that she has deceived us so that we don't come after her,' Anna-Karin says. 'She wants to protect us! Don't you see that, Linnéa?'

Anna-Karin is blushing with indignation. And Linnéa feels ashamed because she can't believe in Minoo as much as the others do.

'Never mind if she's there willingly or not,' Linnéa says. 'She shouldn't be there at all. Especially not after what Olivia told us.'

'What are you talking about?' Gustaf asks.

Anna-Karin starts explaining but Linnéa isn't listening.

It's not like you can replace the Chosen Ones.

The souls of the Chosen Ones make up the Key.

The souls of all the Chosen Ones.

All are needed.

'They're not gone,' Linnéa says straight out in the air.

The others stop talking and turn to her.

'They haven't passed,' she says. 'Elias, Rebecka and Ida must be caught between worlds, just like Matilda.'

They look dubious but Linnéa grows more convinced as she speaks.

'Think about it! The demons carried on, even though Max didn't manage to hang on to the souls of Elias and Rebecka. They must've known somehow that those souls were not completely lost.'

'But Matilda said—' Anna-Karin begins.

'That's it,' Linnéa interrupts. '*Matilda* said that Elias and Rebecka weren't left. And she works for the guardians and the guardians usually lie to us.'

It's all crystal clear now, and Linnéa could hit herself for not seeing it earlier. She has accepted far too much, even though she thinks of herself as so cynical and questioning. Unbelievable that she hasn't even *tried* to contact Elias. It feels as if she has abandoned him and the thought is enough to make her panic.

'Is Rebecka in the same place as Matilda?' Gustaf says.

'She could well be,' Nicolaus says thoughtfully.

'And she might have been stuck there ever since she died?'

Linnéa meets his eyes and knows exactly how he is feeling.

'But if their souls are there,' Anna-Karin says, 'why wouldn't the guardians tell us? And why would Matilda say they had passed on?'

Nicolaus looks uncertain.

'I can't understand that either. Perhaps she didn't know.'

'I don't give a fuck about why,' Linnéa says. 'We will never understand why the guardians and Matilda do what they do. Olivia was planning to open the portal. She must have thought that she could get hold of the souls of Elias, Ida and Rebecka. And, if she thought she could, then surely we must be able to as well.'

'If what Olivia said is true, that is,' Nicolaus says.

'Yes,' Linnéa says. 'The first thing we must do is confirm that they really are stuck between worlds.'

'And what will we do for Minoo?' Gustaf asks.

Linnéa doesn't want to hurt him again. But she has to.

'Nothing,' she says.

Gustaf goes red in the face.

'You'll just leave her with the Council?'

'Of course not,' Linnéa says. 'But we can't do anything right now. If you're right and she is being kept captive there, we can't just barge in. We need a plan. Or else we might all die. And if she's there willingly, as I think, then we must find some evidence to persuade her to come with us.'

'I don't like this,' Anna-Karin says. 'We have no idea what goes on in the manor house.'

'I think Linnéa is right,' Nicolaus says. 'An unplanned attack could put both Minoo and ourselves in danger. Also, remember that Minoo is an exceptionally strong witch. She is far from helpless.'

Anna-Karin nods, but looks unhappy.

'I'm going there,' Gustaf says, getting up and pulling off the blanket.

'No!' Anna-Karin says. 'You can't!'

'I agree with Anna-Karin,' Nicolaus says. 'The other circle is powerful and they wouldn't hesitate to hurt you. And that would not help Minoo.'

Gustaf says nothing, just stares at the decorative vase in front of him on the table. Linnéa hears his thoughts. He realizes that Nicolaus is right – he is just as helpless as ever. Just as useless. He can't help the ones he loves. Not Rebecka. Not Minoo. There is nothing he can do. Nothing.

Linnéa jumps in her seat when Gustaf sweeps the vase from the table. It crashes to the floor and shatters.

The room is very silent after the crash.

Gustaf's hands are clenched. He is breathing quickly as he stares at the broken glass.

'Gustaf . . .' Linnéa begins.

'Tell Minoo's parents that I'll pay for it,' he says as he leaves the room.

They hear the door slam. Linnéa looks at Anna-Karin and Nicolaus.

'I'm so sorry for that boy,' Nicolaus says, shaking his head. 'Feeling powerless is dreadful.'

'But we aren't powerless,' Linnéa says. 'Let's have a séance. Tonight.'

'But it isn't a Saturday,' Anna-Karin says. 'Mona says that you should hold séances on Saturdays and at midnight and—'

'Fuck Mona!' Linnéa interrupts. 'We'll try every night. Until it works. Until we get in touch with them.'

* * *

They are in the hall, waiting for her and Walter.

Sigrid, Nejla, Felix and Viktor have formed a semicircle in front of the reception. Neither Alexander or Clara are there. Fear is scratching away inside Minoo's mind and she wants to calm it. But Walter has forbidden her to use magic during the ceremony. He wants her to be fully present.

How is Adriana? And Clara? What did Walter actually do to her? Minoo tries to catch Viktor's eye but he refuses to look at her.

'Now then,' Walter says. 'This is the situation. Minoo managed to get into Adriana's room, intending to steal an object that her friends thought was important. Adriana caught her red-handed. Minoo tried to escape and there was an accident. We can't be sure yet that Adriana will recover.'

Minoo isn't sure if the others believe Walter's story. Sigrid looks shocked, Nejla uncomfortable, but Felix almost pleased as he stands holding the *Book of Patterns*. Minoo can't blame him. This time, he isn't the one to be publicly humiliated.

'It's a tragedy in many ways,' Walter says. 'Even so, I feel some measure of sympathy for Minoo. She acted out of misplaced loyalty to her friends. And now she's full of remorse. Isn't that so, Minoo?'

'Yes,' she says, staring at the floor, where the melting snow on her shoes is forming a small puddle.

'And you have understood where you belong?'

'Yes.'

Walter takes the *Book of Patterns* from Felix and turns to her. She places her right hand on the worn leather surface and touches the embossed circles with her fingertips. Walter rehearsed the words with her on the way back and, by now, she knows them by heart.

'I, Minoo Falk Karimi, swear to serve the Council in thought, word and deed. To always uphold the laws of the Council. I will not practice magic without the Council's express permission. I will not use magic to break non-magical laws. I will not reveal myself as a witch to the non-magical public. I swear to be faithful to the Council unto death.'

She takes her hand away.

There is nothing magic about this oath of allegiance but, all the same, it feels as if a band of iron has tightened around her chest.

Her life belongs to the Council now.

'Thank you, Minoo,' Walter says. 'I would of course have wished this to take place in different circumstances, but I would still like to welcome you into our community.'

'Thank you,' she says.

'As I have said already, I understand the motives for Minoo's recent behavior,' he continues, turning to face the others. 'Nonetheless, some disciplinary steps must be taken. From now on, Minoo will stay in her room and she will practice only with me. No one must speak to her without my permission.'

No one looks at her. She is already invisible. A pariah.

'Minoo, you may leave,' Walter says. 'Your bags will be delivered later.'

Moving like a sleepwalker, she wanders through the hallways, up the stairs and along to her room with the red clover wallpaper. Her new home.

She takes off her shoes and her jacket. Goes to her bed, switches the bedside lamp on and sits down. The silence is like a distant roar in her ears.

She wonders if the others have read her letter by now. Hopefully, they'll hate her as someone who has betrayed them and who is now lost to them. The last thing they must do is come here and try to rescue her.

Footsteps are approaching and her stomach turns when the door opens. It's Viktor, carrying her suitcases. The door closes behind him.

'I'm so sorry,' she whispers. 'I tried to make Clara stay away.'

Viktor ignores her completely, turns his back to her and puts her cases near the wardrobe.

'What did he do to her?' Minoo asks him. 'How is she?'

Viktor's back goes rigid.

'You promised,' he says, in a barely audible voice. 'You promised to keep her out of it.'

'I tried.'

Viktor faces her now. His face is full of anger.

655

'Do you want to know what Walter said to her?' he says quietly. 'He said, "I won't do anything to you that you haven't done to yourself already".'

Minoo feels sick.

'He opened her scar,' Viktor whispers.

Minoo remembers the white band across the inside of Clara's wrist and is almost overwhelmed with nausea.

Her pain threshold is quite low.

'I'm sorry,' she says. 'I'm sorry, I never thought—'

'Stop it,' Viktor interrupts, but he no longer sounds angry. Only weary. 'I know it wasn't your fault.'

He stares at the floor.

'I want to kill him. Kill him, take Clara with me and leave. I'd take you, too. And Felix. But we must save the world. And they would come after us. They wouldn't kill us for as long as they needed us, but there are other things . . .'

He looks at her now and his eyes are haunted.

'Only three portents to go now. It can't be long until we can close the portal. Don't you think?'

'No. I think you're right.'

'We must stick it out. Just for a while longer.'

Minoo nods. Stick it out. That's exactly what they must do.

'I've already disobeyed his orders by talking to you.' Viktor looks pleadingly at her. 'I can't do it again. You understand that, don't you?'

'Of course,' she says.

He takes a step closer to her and touches her shoulder lightly.

'We'll get through all this,' he says.

Then he walks out into the hallway and Minoo hears the key being inserted in the door lock and turned.

She lies down on the bed and releases her magic. Then she directs it toward herself. She disappears into her memories, becomes engrossed in them.

And everything is perfect again.

Her arm rests on his chest. Her leg is lightly hooked around his. She wishes she could stay like this for all eternity. That nothing would ever happen, not ever.

She used to be baffled by people who said they'd like to stop time.

Now she understands. Now, she is happy.

The Borderland

CHAPTER 90

'Wake up!'

A voice.

The silence has lasted for so long.
So long he can't remember if there was a before.
Before the silence.
Before the darkness.

'Come on, wake up!'

Someone touches him.

'Oh, please, come on, why don't you wake up?'

Awake.
Everything is blurred.
A pale face.
Blonde hair.
Blue eyes.
Her features come into focus. He knows her face is familiar.
Who is she?
'I thought you'd never come to!' she whispers. 'Follow me.
Hurry up!'
She takes his hand and pulls him along. The world around
him is completely gray, and wrapped in the thickest fog.
Moving his legs feels odd, unusual.

If only he could remember where he is.

If only he could remember *who* he is.

Surely you are supposed to know that when you are dreaming?

'Why don't you say anything?' she whispers. 'Just say something!'

She has a silver heart on a chain around her neck. This is familiar, too, something he recognizes. Did he give it to her? *Who is she?*

He is sure now that he has seen her face lots of times. Both close-up and at a distance. Is she his sister? No, he never had any sisters. He is certain about that. Girlfriend? No. Definitely not his girlfriend. He never had any of those either.

A friend?

There's a bond between them. They belong, somehow. He feels that.

She stops and turns toward him.

'What's the matter with you?' she says. 'Elias?'

Elias.

Elias.

Elias Mikael Malmgren.

That's him.

And now he knows who she is.

He pulls his hand out of her grip.

'Calm down,' Ida says. 'I know this is confusing—'

'It's a dream,' Elias interrupts.

'No,' she says. 'You're dead. And so am I.'

She looks perfectly serious but what she says is utterly absurd. Elias bursts out laughing.

'And what's this place, then?' he says. 'Hell? Must be, since you're here.'

Of course, he doesn't believe her. Of course not. Obviously. But, even so, anguish is swelling inside him like a big, black balloon.

He tries to stay detached and analyze what his subconscious

is trying to tell him with this dream. Must ask Regina next time he has an appointment for psychological counseling.

'I thought it was a dream at first,' Ida says. 'But you've got to believe—'

'Believe what?' he interrupts. 'That I'm *dead?*'

'What's the last thing you remember?'

He doesn't want to talk about this. He starts walking, searching the grayness for some kind of landmark, but it's pointless. There is nothing there. Nothing at all. Nothing to distract him from the memories that begin to stir and come alive in his mind.

'The school bathrooms,' Ida says. Her voice comes from just behind him.

Shiny white tiles.

'No idea what you're talking about,' Elias says.

Pale blue sky outside the window.

'You went there after seeing the principal,' Ida says. 'And you heard a voice in your head. It made you break a mirror, take one of the shards—'

The sharp edges cutting into his hand.

'I don't want to talk about this!'

Blood drops on the gray-tiled floor.

'Then the voice made you go into one of the stalls,' says Ida. 'It forced you to cut—'

'Shut up!' Elias screams, and turns around quickly.

Everything becomes blurred again, a blur of grayness and mist.

It will soon be over, Elias. Just a little more. Then it will be over. It'll be better like this. You've suffered so much.

Black spots are dancing in front of his eyes. Footsteps approach in the hallway outside.

Forgive me.

And Elias screams. He screams and screams as the pain burns inside now, scorching everything as he is being torn apart, as everything that is *him* is being ripped out.

Hands are gripping his shoulders and shaking him.

'Be quiet!' Ida's voice says. 'Elias, you must be quiet!'

He opens his eyes and meets Ida's terrified ones. He looks at his forearm. The sleeve of his sweater is whole. When he pulls it up, all he can see are his old scars. But all the same he knows that . . .

He frees himself from Ida's grip and wraps his arms around his body. Cannot understand how his body can feel so solid, so real.

It's no use denying it.

He died in that school bathroom.

Bled to death.

Dead.

He catches a glimpse of a bright light and turns around.

A blinding light is piercing through the gray veils of mist.

'What's that?' he asks. 'Is that . . . the light at the end of the tunnel?'

Ida doesn't reply, only pushes him toward the light.

CHAPTER 91

T he fog is gone.

Elias stands on ground covered in snow and lit by yellowy light from outdoor lamps.

The schoolyard. The bulky, brick-built monstrosity that is Engelsfors High School towers against the dark sky.

'What did you do?' he asks Ida, who stands next to him.

'I got us out of there.'

Elias looks at the snowy steps leading up to the front doors. The last time he walked through those doors was in late summer. It feels no longer ago than this morning.

'How long have I been dead?'

'Depends on when this is, doesn't it?' Ida says sharply.

Elias stares at her.

'Well, excuse me for not having all the answers all the time!' she says.

It's weird to see her alone, without her gang. And he suddenly understands something about Ida. She hides her fear behind anger.

'Time is, like, totally messed up when you're dead,' she continues, and her voice is high-pitched now. 'Once, I was dumped in fucking ancient Greece. At least, I think it was.'

'*Ancient Greece?*' Elias repeats, feeling overwhelmed. 'Did you travel back in time?'

'I haven't traveled,' Ida says. 'I've jumped. Back and forth, back and forth.'

'But that's amazing!'

'Maybe it sounds amazing,' Ida says. 'But it totally sucks.'

Elias can't get on board anymore with what she says. It's weird enough that he's dead. And that he's dead together with Ida Holmström.

Dead.

He takes a few steps. His boots leave no marks in the snow. But he can feel it under his feet all the same. He bends to pick up a lump of ice.

'There's no point,' Ida says. 'Believe me.'

Elias's hand goes straight through the lump, but when he puts his hand against the ground, he can feel the hard surface under his palm. He leaves no mark on the snow, though.

Ida sighs impatiently as he straightens up.

'What if we simply *imagine* that we have bodies?' he says. 'Maybe, if we didn't, our minds couldn't deal with this state.'

'All I know is that it's annoying as hell,' Ida says. She might as well have been speaking about a spell of especially bad weather.

'Don't you find this at all fascinating?'

'What's so fucking fascinating?'

'This!' Elias throws his arms out. 'It doesn't just end! There is life after death! How can you *not* think it's amazing?'

'Maybe I'm not as easily impressed as you are!'

'Easily impressed? Here's the answer to one of humanity's biggest questions and you don't even care!'

'Maybe it's because I already know much more than you!' Ida shouts. 'Maybe it's because I already know that there are souls and demons and guardians and fucking familiars and people who are blessed by demons! Remember the school janitor? His name is Nicolaus and he's a clergyman from the 1600s! He's four hundred years old! So, no, I'm not so fucking impressed by all this crap!'

Her voice goes shrill and she stops instantly. Looks at him, her lips still slightly parted. Then her lower lip starts trembling, tears fill her eyes and trickle down her cheeks.

Elias doesn't know what he finds more incomprehensible, what Ida just said or the fact that she is crying.

He can't remember ever seeing her cry, not even when they were little. If Ida fell off the jungle gym, she'd kick it and call it names.

'I've been so lonely,' she sobs, speaking with her hands pressed to her face. 'I've been so alone, you have no idea how lonely I've been. And I was so happy when I found you, but you just hate me. You *hate* me!'

She's so different. But she's still Ida. The teachers' favorite. Excellent student, excellent singer in the choir. Chair of the Students' Committee, active in the school's anti-bullying program. Ida, who always spread the filthiest rumors. Ida, who could ruin anyone's life at will. Ida, who ruined his life.

'Can you give me one good reason why I should *not* hate you?'

Ida lowers her hands. And stares down at the snow-covered schoolyard for what feels like an eternity.

'No,' she says in the end. 'I understand why you hate me.'

It's utterly unexpected to hear her say this. It's impossible to believe.

'All right,' he says. 'It's all very well to say that now when we're both stuck in some kind of limbo. But if your friends were here—'

'They aren't my friends anymore,' Ida interrupts. 'As a matter of fact, I suspect they hate me as much as you do. Perhaps even more.'

She snivels.

'A great deal has happened since you died,' she says. 'And I want to say . . . not because I think you care but . . .'

She glances quickly at him.

'I'm sorry. I'm sorry for . . . everything.'

She is ashamed. And her shame is real.

This doesn't make his hatred disappear, nor all the memories of what she did.

But it does make a difference.

'I can't forgive you just like that. But it matters that you said it.'

They stand side by side in silence. The sky above them is dark. No stars in sight. There's a distant rumble of traffic, but not a car anywhere. No human passersby either.

Elias looks at Ida. She ought to be freezing in her thin jacket. But neither of them will ever freeze again.

Dead.

When he was little, he used to wonder about death and dying. He tried to imagine the heaven that Mom and Dad believed in.

Later, he stopped thinking about heaven. Instead, he told himself that death was the end of everything.

At least, that's what he hoped.

That the pain would end.

That was what he longed for each time he considered letting the razor blade cut a little deeper. That was his goal when he walked to the canal and thought of jumping in. And he would have jumped, if it hadn't been for Linnéa turning up, grabbing hold of him and phoning his parents. She had saved his life.

Uselessly.

'What happened to me?' Elias says. 'That voice in my head . . .'

'That was Max,' Ida says. 'The math teacher.'

'The young one?'

He almost said 'the hot one', but saying that sort of thing about another guy in front of Ida goes against his every instinct.

'Yes, him,' Ida says. 'He was blessed by the demons and he murdered you and took your soul. But then Minoo liberated you by breaking the blessing. And then your soul, like, flew away. And we all thought you'd passed on because Matilda said so, but it seems she lied about that as well—'

'Slow down,' Elias interrupts.

Ida looks impatient. Elias had almost forgotten how hopeless she is at explaining things. In school, her oral accounts were always impossible to follow. And now, Ida is the only one who can explain the mysteries of life and death to him.

'Please, one thing at a time,' he says. '*Demons?*'

Ida sighs. 'Are you saying that you don't remember anything from when Max kept your soul? For like, six months?'

'No. The last thing I remember is how badly it hurt. And then everything was dark. Until you woke me.'

'Are you absolutely sure?' Ida says. 'So, you don't remember, say . . . your memorial assembly at school?'

'No? Was there one?'

Does Ida look relieved? He isn't sure.

'Yes, there was,' she says. 'But I'll start from the beginning. You see, witches and magic exist for real—'

'*What* exists?'

'If you're going to interrupt me every time I say something that sounds weird, this will go on for hundreds of years,' Ida says. 'Just listen. I am a witch. You are a witch. We are very special witches. Two of the Chosen Ones. The Chosen Ones are supposed to stop the demons from taking over the world. There are seven of us: you, me, Vanessa Dahl, Minoo Falk Karimi, Anna-Karin Nieminen, Rebecka Mohlin and Linnéa Wallin.'

Elias stares at her. What she has said is reasonably coherent. Still, it's no easier to understand.

'So Linnéa has something to do with all this, too?'

'Yes, that's what I just said,' Ida sighs.

'And magic is for real?'

'And so are witches. You and I both. We all have magic powers. Your element is wood. Your power is that you can change your appearance to look like other people.'

Elias recalls the days before his death. How he saw his reflected face change in mirrors and shop windows, and gradually became convinced that he was going mad. Was so convinced that he had to go to Jonte and buy weed to dampen down his terror.

But it wasn't madness.

It was magic.

And just how mad does that sound? Elias thinks.

'OK,' he says aloud. 'Max . . . he had something to do with these . . . demons, right? Did he kill you, too?'

'No. Your friend did.'

'*Linnéa?*'

'No,' Ida sighs. 'Though I'm sure she wanted to, lots of times. It was Olivia who killed me. She is a witch too and she also worked for the demons. She's back in town now and I don't even know if the others know. I've tried to warn them but I can't.'

What if Ida is inventing all this stuff? What if she's lying to him and everything is a sick joke; what if they've drugged him or if he's drugged himself and this is a psychosis . . .

But he recognizes this as just his usual paranoia. She is telling him the truth. And this is really happening.

'I don't know if this is the right time to tell you,' Ida says. 'But Olivia killed your parents as well.'

Elias recalls Olivia as he knew her. Her round, slightly childish face and large brown eyes. Olivia, who always wanted to listen to the same music as he did; who dyed her hair blue because he mentioned once that he thought it looked good on girls.

He tries to imagine Olivia as a murderer. It is just as difficult as imagining his parents dead. Murdered by Olivia.

'I don't get it,' he says. 'Why would Olivia want to kill my parents?'

'It's complicated but, basically, your parents were evil too. I'm sorry, but they were. And I can guess at how that makes you feel. Mine aren't exactly wonderful either, but I still love them.'

A fox runs across the schoolyard and disappears behind a plowed-up pile of snow.

'You can't help it,' Ida says quietly. 'Even when you aren't so sure that they love you back.'

Mom. Dad. He did love them. He did.

Did they love him? They said so, but they made him feel as if he constantly disappointed them. As if they always hoped he could become someone else, someone better. Someone more like them.

At times, he felt that they only loved the son they imagined that they *might* have had.

'Have you seen my parents?' he says. 'I mean, in that gray place where we met?'

'The Borderland,' Ida says. 'No. I don't think we are meant to be there either. I think we've got stuck there. Other souls pass on.'

'Pass on to where?'

'I don't know. I don't think anyone knows that.'

Elias looks at the school.

It has gone. Disappeared.

He blinks. Looks away, then turns back to the school.

All he can see is a large, dark rectangle in the snow. As if a giant has removed the entire building.

'Ida . . .'

Ida looks in the same direction. She seems startled, though not as startled as she should be.

'Can you explain this?' Elias asks.

'No,' she says. 'But I'm not exactly surprised.'

They hear footsteps from behind them coming nearer and Elias turns around.

Two people come walking along, a man and a woman. Both are leaving tracks in the snow. So they are not dead. The man might be in his fifties. His hair is turning gray. He is wearing a dark gray coat and a stylish black scarf. He is looking at the building-free site with interest. The woman is in her early twenties, and is wearing a red, old-fashioned coat and a matching beret. Her curly blonde hair reaches her shoulders. She is almost absurdly pretty.

Little Red Riding Hood out for a stroll with the Wolf, Elias thinks as he watches them. They stop near the gates.

'The air element,' the man says as he looks toward the vanished building. His breath turns into vapor clouds as he speaks. 'Exactly what you predicted, Sigrid,' the man continues. 'I'm impressed. Your clairvoyance has developed in leaps and bounds during these weeks.'

Sigrid smiles modestly. He puts his arm around her shoulders and they walk away.

'Those two, are they witches too?' Elias asks.

'Yes, they are.'

'Good or evil?'

'The other Chosen Ones have been fighting about that forever. But, if you ask me, I'd say evil.'

Elias turns back to the school.

There it is. As if it had never disappeared.

And then he is somewhere else altogether.

CHAPTER 92

The light in the unfurnished room is dim, but Elias instantly recognizes where he is. He and Ida stand in the middle of the living room in Linnéa's apartment on either side of a mirror. Around them, several people sit on the floor holding hands.

One of them is Linnéa. He calls her name but she doesn't react at all. He goes to kneel in front of her. Her bangs almost hide her eyes, which are fixed on the mirror. Her expression is tense, as if she is waiting for something to happen.

'Linnéa!' he says again.

He reaches out for her, tries to touch her. Dread grows inside him when his hand passes straight through her cheek.

'It's no use,' Ida calls to him. 'Come here!'

He tries to touch Linnéa's knee. Nothing. Nothing.

She is so close. And he can't reach her.

Dead.

He lowers his hand.

He died. He died and Linnéa was left behind, alone. His sister in all but blood. She was his last thought before he died.

She is as he remembers her and yet she is not. She has grown older and she has changed. Elias can see that.

He will never laugh with her again, never share her sadness.

Dead.

Only now does he begin to understand the true meaning of the word.

Nevermore.

'What the hell, Elias!' Ida calls sharply. 'You've got to help me!'

Elias turns to her without caring that she'll see him cry. She has settled down on the floor, too, near the mirror.

'What do you want?' he snaps.

'Are you blind?' Ida says. 'This is a séance! They're trying to contact the dead!'

Elias looks at the mirror, which reflects neither him nor Ida. And now he sees that someone has scribbled all over it. Lots of letters inside circles. An upside-down glass has been placed in the center of the mirror. He should have known immediately. He has played spirit-in-the-glass himself.

'Have you tried touching the glass?' he asks.

'Guess!' Ida hisses. 'Here. Come and hold my hand.'

She holds out her right hand and Elias takes it, a little hesitantly.

'It will make us stronger,' she says.

Oddly enough, Elias understands what she means. He *feels* it, like warmth slowly filling his whole being.

'It might be that we have to accept that it won't work tonight either,' the man who sits behind Ida says.

The school janitor. His ice-blue eyes are fixed on the glass. He was the last person Elias saw before he died. And Ida's story is that this man is four hundred years old.

'No,' Linnéa says tersely. 'Let's try for a little longer. It has to work.'

'Shit, they mustn't stop now,' Ida says. 'You try touching the glass, Elias.'

Elias cautiously touches the bottom of the glass.

He can feel the hard surface.

'It works!' Ida says, and places her fingertips on the glass. 'OK, let's start with the *I*!'

But the glass won't shift.

'Linnéa, it isn't working,' Vanessa Dahl says.

'Shut up! It does so work!' Ida almost shrieks. 'Elias, focus!'

Elias focuses on the glass. Focuses on feeling its surface. It will work. It has to work.

And the glass moves. Just one inch. It leaves a white trail.

Anna-Karin Nieminen draws breath.

'It moved!' Linnéa exclaims. 'It moved!'

'I saw it, too.' That's from a guy with glasses who sits between the school janitor and Vanessa's friend Evelina.

Elias tightens his grip on Ida's hand. They move the glass across the mirror, adding letter to letter.

I-D-A

E-L-I-A-S

H-E-R-E

And then the mist sweeps in and thickens around them.

Elias and Ida face each other in the Borderland, still hand in hand.

And they are beaming at each other like two crazy people.

'Now they know we exist!' Ida says.

'How do we get back?' Elias says as he lets go of her hand.

'I don't know,' Ida says as she starts walking. 'But we can't hang around here.'

'Isn't it better to wait?'

'No,' Ida says. 'Believe me.'

Elias is past asking any more questions by now and just follows her, full of conflicting emotions.

He thinks back on seeing Linnéa again. He knows her so well and can sense every feeling she tries to hide. She looked so alone.

'How has Linnéa been?' he asks.

'Not so great,' Ida says. 'I mean, it wasn't like she called me when she was feeling low. But it was pretty obvious that she missed you. A lot. And lots of other tough things happened . . .'

She pauses.

'But good things as well. Like Vanessa. They seem to have

broken up now but they were really in love.'

'Has Linnéa been together with *Vanessa Dahl*?'

Now he has to smile. Linnéa, who always used to make fun of him because he had a thing for blondes.

'You must tell me everything,' he says. 'From the beginning.'

'Yes,' Ida sighs. 'I suppose I must.'

Part 5

CHAPTER 93

Sharp snowflakes burst from the clouds, patter against Vanessa's jacket and find their way in under her scarf. The world is made up of whirling white spots against the pale gray sky and brilliantly white ground. Autumn came and went before anyone had time to notice it. Now, in October, mid-winter has arrived.

Vanessa is invisible where she stands on the roof, looking out over the other apartment buildings along Törnros Road, all identical to the one where she lives with Mom and Melvin. She goes to stand at the edge of the roof and looks down at the place where Olivia died three weeks ago.

Vanessa doesn't want to think about what Olivia's parents and siblings must have been going through this past year. Olivia had begun by dropping out of school and then physically declined. Her family must have feared that she was seriously ill. They must have feared much worse things when she suddenly vanished without a trace for six months. And then she died breaking into the home of an old schoolfriend and throwing herself out of a window. The official explanation was 'psychosis'. 'She said that she wanted to be with Elias,' Vanessa had told Nicke, and felt quite sick when she saw this quoted in the evening papers.

She touches the small scar above her left eyebrow.

She knows that what happened wasn't her fault.

Olivia had pushed her toward the window, not the other way around. Then Vanessa lost control of her magic and they both fell. In mid-air, they lost their grip on each other. Vanessa hardly had time to notice that she was hovering by the time Olivia's body crashed into the pavement. There was nothing she could have done.

But what if she had had a chance to rescue her? If she could have grabbed Olivia's hoodie and stopped her from hitting the ground, would she have done it?

Would she have let Olivia live?

In her nightmares, she lets her die.

And every time she wakes up, she longs for Linnéa.

The dense snow means that Vanessa can't see Linnéa's apartment building. She imagines Linnéa in her living room. She won't have slept, just smoked one cig after another while brooding on how much she misses Elias; Elias, whom they got in touch with last night.

Matilda had said that Elias had passed on. Had she lied? Or didn't she know? She did say once that the demons at times seem better informed than the guardians.

They must find out more.

Nicolaus thinks that to avoid the contact being broken again, they need a stronger and more experienced metal witch than Rickard. And they have only one alternative. An alternative they will try to find today. The door of the Crystal Cave has had the same sign in place for six weeks now. CLOSED FOR HOLIDAY. But the last time Mona vanished, she was actually in Engelsfors all the while. She had just been lying low. She must have a home somewhere, even if the Chosen Ones have never been able to work out where.

The wind tears and pulls at Vanessa. She closes her eyes. The snowflakes are blasting her face and sting like pinpricks on her eyelids and lips.

She releases more of her power. She feels the magic fill her, an energy that radiates from within her body, makes her feel so light. During these last three weeks, she has been practicing every day. But always safely, on the ground or at low heights. It is time for the real test.

Part Five

Vanessa opens her eyes, lifts one foot and puts it over the edge of the roof. It should be all right. This is what birds do to fledglings, after all. Push them out of the nest to make them fly.

She looks at her foot. The ground is so far away.

Her power is strong inside her. It is so obviously a part of her. And yet, it's against every instinct to do this.

She steps straight out into empty air.

It holds. She is hovering.

She lets the wind carry her upwards. Upwards. Leans into the wind so that it takes her in a wide arc around the residential area.

The snow stops falling as suddenly as it began. A last flurry of flakes and then the view clears.

Engelsfors lies spread out underneath her. The railroad and the national road divide the town and the forest surrounds it. The snow-covered ice on the canal turns it into a wide, white road.

Vanessa looks down on the closed gas stations. The industrial park with the steel plant where no smoke has risen from the chimneys during her lifetime. The burnt-down sawmill. She allows herself to be carried even further. The manor house looks like an extravagant doll's house. Among bare trees, the church spire sticks up. Then, the area with the grand villas, the 'Beverly Hills of Bergslagen' as Mom calls it. There is the center of Engelsfors, with Storvall Park and the huge block of gray cement that is the City Mall.

There, in the distance, she sees Engelsfors High School.

Last night, the fox watched as the school became invisible. The air element. Only two portents left now, earth and water. And then, darkness will fall in Engelsfors. The wall of rock underneath the school will open. What will the portal look like? How are they going to be able to close it?

Vanessa looks at the manor house again and wonders if the doll's house is Minoo's prison or if she stays there of her own free will. What is going on in there now? Has Minoo found out how to close the portal? And what will she say when they tell her that their dead friends have not passed on?

Vanessa suddenly becomes acutely aware of how high up she is. What if her power stops?

She forces her panicky thoughts out of her mind and listens to the wind. Her body understands, in a way her mind can't grasp, how to lean against the wind so that it carries her back to the only roof where there are deep footsteps in the snow.

* * *

It has stopped snowing. Minoo's room is bathed in the pale morning light. Everything looks chilly, even the yellow and white striped wallpaper, which usually adds warmth to the room. The desk, usually a busy mess, is cleared. The bed is tidily made. No one has slept in it for three weeks.

And, last night, no one slept in Anna-Karin's bed either. She has been awake.

I-D-A

E-L-I-A-S

H-E-R-E

They haven't passed on.

Today, they must try to find Mona and get her to help them contact the dead Chosen Ones again. They need answers to so many questions. But Anna-Karin knows one thing for sure. They must get Minoo out. They should do it now. She mustn't stay in the manor house. She should never have set foot in there in the first place.

'Good morning.'

Anna-Karin turns to see Minoo's father standing in the doorway. His creased shirt and stubbly cheeks and chin tell her that he hasn't slept either, just sat up all night in his study.

'Good morning,' she says.

Erik looks around the room, takes his glasses off and rubs his eyes.

'I'm really looking forward to the day Minoo finishes that damned project,' he says.

It is obvious that he misses her, but he doesn't sound bothered at all by not having heard from his daughter for three weeks. Anna-Karin used her magic to convince him and Farnaz that everything is fine and that Minoo will come back home as soon as her boss has gotten his project up and running.

'How are you getting on with the articles?' she asks to change the subject.

'As well as can be expected, I suppose. It would be so much easier if I didn't have to commute to Fagersta.'

When all the communication networks went down, the *Engelsfors Herald* moved back to the office of the *Fagersta Gazette*. Minoo's father is working on a series of articles about 'the Engelsfors situation', about what happens to a town when landline and cell phone links, Internet and television transmission have broken down. All the expected and unexpected problems that crop up.

Credit cards don't work. ATMs don't either. Emergency services are no longer at the end of a phone call. The town council has set up community aid centers around town, where people can go for information and assistance. It is heartening to hear of how many people have worked together to do things like look after the elderly whose safety alarms no longer work. It is rather less cheering that vigilante committees had been formed, once rumors about unchecked crime started making the rounds. The stories were mostly about criminal gangs from outside, drawn to the newly vulnerable Engelsfors. Already, the police have arrested several old boys from the civil defense who had taken it upon themselves to go out on armed patrols.

'I don't know how much more this town can take,' Minoo's father says, shaking his head. 'To be honest, I don't know how much more *I* can take. I have enough contacts to survive on freelance work and I'd very much like to write the book about Engelsfors before Cissi does it . . .'

He pauses. 'It could be that Farnaz has been right all along,' he says quietly, as if to himself. 'Staying here is like staying on a sinking ship.'

Anna-Karin doesn't know what to say to that.

'Goodness, I sound quite morose,' Erik says, and smiles. 'I'll just clean up and then I'll be on my way. Would you like a ride to school?'

'No, thanks, I'll be fine,' she tells him, and he wanders off to the bathroom.

Nicolaus will pick her up but not to drive her to school. They are off to the Crystal Cave to try a little breaking and entering. The need to find clues as to where Mona might be.

The doorbell rings and Anna-Karin hurries downstairs. An ice-cold blast of wind hits her as she opens the front door and she shivers.

'Hi,' Gustaf says as he steps inside and takes his wool cap off. 'How did it go yesterday?'

He has asked the same question every day for three weeks and, for every day, looked less and less hopeful.

'We got in touch with Ida and Elias,' Anna-Karin says.

Gustaf looks surprised.

'It lasted only a moment before breaking off,' she continues. 'But we're going to try to find Mona and ask her to help us.'

'Did they say anything about Rebecka?'

'No. But it doesn't mean that she isn't there.'

Gustaf's face has a closed-off look. Anna-Karin would so much like to say something to make him feel better. But she can't even begin to understand how he feels. His dead girl-friend is probably caught between worlds and his living one is held in the clutches of the Council.

'Then we know that Olivia did speak the truth,' he says. 'The Chosen Ones who died are still there and you are the ones who will close the portal. So, when do we go and get Minoo?'

'I'd like to do it now,' Anna-Karin says. 'But the others want to find out more first.'

She sees his jaw clench.

'I'm coming to the séance tonight,' he says. 'I'll come with Rickard and Evelina.'

She nods. No one could deny him the right to be there.

When Gustaf opens the door, Anna-Karin sees Nicolaus's car slow down outside.

Time to go to the Crystal Cave.

CHAPTER 94

Linnéa crosses the parking lot outside the City Mall. The sky is a cloudy gray and the colorless morning light almost blinds her. They have only just got out of Nicolaus's car but her face is already numb with cold.

Anna-Karin has pulled her hand-knitted cap well down over her forehead and Nicolaus has wound a thick scarf around his neck. Vanessa has put on her mom's old padded jacket. It glows bright pink against the whiteness outside.

Linnéa does her best to keep her distance from Vanessa because she doesn't want her to feel her anxiety.

After the others had left her apartment last night, Linnéa couldn't sleep. She stayed in the living room, smoking and thinking about Elias. How did the glass move? Was he in the room? If he was, why didn't she sense his presence?

'I must admit I feel uncomfortable about breaking in,' Nicolaus says.

'Mona has only herself to blame,' Linnéa replies.

The automatic doors to the mall open infinitely slowly. Linnéa squeezes through and starts jogging across the tiled floor with the others following her.

The mall is dark, all the lights are off. The further in they get, the murkier it becomes. Linnéa can't even see the sign of the Crystal Cave. And then she realizes that it isn't there. It has been taken down.

'Fucking hell!' Vanessa says behind her.

Linnéa goes to look in through the dirty glass pane in the door. Just outside the shop the smell of incense still hangs in

686

the air. Inside, the shelves are empty. The cash register has gone and so has the red velvet curtain.

Linnéa releases her power and searches for contact with Mona's thoughts. She hopes to hear a hoarse cackle in her head. But the only thoughts getting through to her are Vanessa's.

Fuck, fuck, fuck, fucking, fuck.

Linnéa is close to tears. She kicks the glazed door and it rattles on its hinges.

'Fuck!' she says. 'She's taken off! That old bitch!'

'I don't get it,' Vanessa says. 'I came by yesterday and everything looked the same as usual. How could she clear out overnight?'

'Let's stick to our plan,' Anna-Karin says. 'She might have left some kind of clue.'

Linnéa steps back to give Anna-Karin room, but wishes she was the one doing it. She is in the mood for destroying something.

Anna-Karin puts her gloves away in her pockets and then drives her fist through the glass. With a creaking sound, a network of cracks spreads from the point of impact. She prods the pane and shards of glass tumble onto the floor inside the shop.

Nicolaus looks around nervously, but there is nobody around in the deserted mall and there is no sound of a burglar alarm going off.

Linnéa walks inside with glass crunching under her boots. The mixed smell of incense and cigarette smoke is the only trace of Mona.

'We know there must be another entrance,' Vanessa says. 'I think it's in here.'

She walks into the room where Mona used to predict her customers' futures.

* * *

Vanessa turns the light on. The room is quite different now. The table looks naked without its dark purple tablecloth. A mug with the text ENGELSFORS – CROWN JEWEL OF BERGSLAGEN stands on the worn table. A lipstick mark has dried on it. The red curtains that covered the walls have been taken down. The worn, curling edges of the peach-colored plastic flooring are exposed along the baseboards. But the walls are quite smooth. There is no sign of a secret door anywhere.

'She would never let me into this room alone,' Vanessa says. 'Do you think the door might be protected by magic?'

'That's perfectly possible,' Nicolaus says.

He closes his eyes and moves his hands slowly over one of the walls. Takes a step, explores again. Vanessa notes how Anna-Karin intently observes his every move.

Linnéa shifts from foot to foot and Vanessa senses her impatience.

'Can't you listen out for Mona's thoughts?' Vanessa asks.

'What do you think I'm doing?' Linnéa replies curtly.

Vanessa looks away, feeling Linnéa's frustration all too sharply.

Linnéa has been like this ever since she understood that Elias's soul probably hadn't passed on after all. Constantly tense, always on the brink of anger. Edgier than ever on the outside, and on the inside filled with a despair that pierces through Vanessa.

Vanessa tries to show her sympathy because she really is sympathetic. But it's so tiring to be invaded by both Linnéa's external anger and her internal desperation. And she can't even tell Linnéa to stop. What could she say?

Please stop feeling so much.

She still loves Linnéa but, just now, she can't bear being around her more than absolutely necessary. Her defense against magic doesn't work against the bond between them.

'Here it is,' Nicolaus says.

He reaches out with his hand, grabs hold of empty air and pulls back, looking like a mime artist pretending to open a door. And suddenly Vanessa sees a gray-painted steel door open, squeaking on its hinges.

She looks behind it. A steel staircase disappears downwards. A red light button glows in the darkness. She presses it. Strip lighting comes on and shows that the stairs lead down to a tunnel.

'I can hear her!' Linnéa exclaims. 'She's . . . fuck, she's discovered me!'

She pushes past Vanessa and runs down the rickety staircase. Vanessa sets out after her. Large, white-painted pipes run along the ceiling of the tunnel. Linnéa's stress flows into Vanessa; she can't tell it from her own. Mona must not vanish again.

They pass several stairs and steel doors still bearing the names of long-since shut local shops. FASHION GIRL. CHEAP CHARLIE'S. LILY'S MOVIE HOUSE.

They turn a corner and Linnéa stops outside a door marked BOMB SHELTER.

'She's in here,' Linnéa says. 'She's still blocking me but I can sense her.'

'Fuck off!' Mona shouts.

Anna-Karin goes to stand by the door and pulls off her thick cap.

'If you don't open the door, I'll rip it off.'

She says this in her mild-mannered, Anna-Karin-style, but leaves no doubt that she means it seriously.

It takes a moment, then another one.

And then the heavy door opens with a screeching noise.

In the doorway, Mona appears in all her glory. She wears a neon-yellow tracksuit with the pants crammed into her cowboy boots. Her curls are newly permed and she has a cigarette in the corner of her mouth. She looks utterly fed up as she examines her visitors.

'The bunch of you are about as welcome as a boil on your ass on a cycling holiday,' she says as she lets them in.

Vanessa scans the large room. Along one wall, boxes are stacked all the way to the ceiling. One of them has fallen over and china fairies have spilled on the floor. The fairies seem to be making a dash for freedom.

A chandelier hangs above an unmade bed. The bedframe has wrought-iron end-boards. There is also a red velvet-covered couch and a bookshelf packed full of Harlequin novels. A clothes rack stands next to a large mirror with an ornamental gilt frame. Mona's denim suit with golden butterflies is on the front hanger on the rack. Mona was wearing it the first time Vanessa met her.

'What are you doing down here?' Vanessa asks.

'I had to move my business activities,' Mona tells her. 'The Council-vibes were getting too strong for my taste.'

'But do you *live* here?' Anna-Karin asks.

'Not for much longer.' Mona taps the ash off her cigarette. Gray flakes float to the floor. 'I plan to spend my last days some place where the beer is cold and the men hot.'

Then she smiles at Nicolaus, looks him up and down, and then back up.

'Do you want to come? I could do with some company on the trip.'

Nicolaus looks ill at ease.

'We are here because we need your help,' he says.

Mona's smile dies away and she pulls on her cigarette.

'What a boring guy. Still, I prefer younger men. A couple of hundred years old or thereabouts, max.'

She goes to stub out her cigarette in a red marble ashtray left among the rumpled sheets on her bed. Only now does Vanessa grasp what Mona said.

'What do you mean, "your last days"?' Vanessa asks. 'What have you seen in the future?'

'Tell you what, I see hardly anything anymore. The veil between worlds has grown so thin. Everything comes across completely bonkers.'

'But if you've "hardly" seen anything, it means you've seen *something*,' Vanessa persists.

Mona reaches out to take a strand of hair that has come loose from Vanessa's ponytail and gently pushes it behind her ear. It's a gesture completely unlike Mona and Vanessa realizes that she is moved by it. But it scares her, too.

For what has Mona seen to make her feel that Vanessa deserves sympathy?

'Just say it,' Vanessa says.

'You have a chance of closing the portal,' Mona says. 'I don't know how you're supposed to do it, but there is a chance and you must go for it.'

She clears her throat and looks distracted.

'And now I'll go straight to Stockholm Arlanda and take the first flight southwards. Business class, one way. No point in being thrifty, not now. *Carpe diem.*'

She glances knowingly at Nicolaus.

'We need your help,' Anna-Karin says.

'What do you want? Ectoplasm? Sure, I'll give you a jar. Or three.'

Vanessa feels nauseous. If Mona is giving stuff away, the prognosis must be terrible.

'We need you to help us out with a séance,' she says. 'We're trying to get in touch with the Chosen Ones who have died. We just got through yesterday, but then the contact was broken. We need them. To close the portal.'

Mona takes a cigarette from the pocket of her tracksuit top. Lights it, inhales and blows out a cloud of smoke. Vanessa waits for her.

'The dead members of the Chosen Ones are stuck between worlds, are they? And does that include that stuck-up little blonde miss who came into the shop on the day of the Spring Equinox?'

'Yes,' Vanessa says.

A pleased grin spreads over Mona's face.

'So that's why I saw that the year ahead would be dark and hard for her. I was flabbergasted when I heard she had been killed that same night. Almost did it for my self-confidence.'

'Ida should have been more considerate and not had herself murdered like that,' Linnéa says.

'But if she exists between worlds, she isn't properly dead.' Mona goes on as if she hadn't heard Linnéa. 'So I was right after all.'

'Yes, you were,' Vanessa says. 'What you saw was right. Because you're the strongest metal witch in Engelsfors . . .'

'In the whole of northern fucking Europe,' Mona says.

'Exactly,' Vanessa says. 'You're the only one who can help us. And you know it.'

Mona smiles.

'I enjoy the sweet-talking, but it won't wash, dearie. I'm not going to stay for a second longer than necessary, not in this hellhole.'

She walks over to the bed, bends down and pulls out a leopard-skin suitcase.

'I don't believe you,' Vanessa says.

Mona straightens up.

'You're psychic,' Vanessa continues. 'You must have seen that we'd show up here. But you stayed all the same. Because, in your heart of hearts, you want to help us. I don't believe you are such a coward that you'd leave town now.'

Mona walks slowly toward her.

'*Coward?*' She nearly spits her cigarette out. 'Who are you calling a coward, honeybun? I'm not the one who has left my friend in the clutches of Walter Hjorth.'

'She went of her own free will,' Linnéa says.

Mona snorts. Vanessa has a nasty sinking feeling about all this.

'I happen to know a thing or two about that bundle of charm Walter,' Mona goes on. 'Why do you think I've crawled into a cellar and stayed there?'

'What has he done?' Anna-Karin asks.

'I don't want to give you nightmares, sweetheart.' Mona

blows out a cloud of smoke. 'What you need to know isn't what he's done, but who he is. He doesn't care for anybody else. No one matters to him. You can't bribe him, you can't tempt him with sex. He isn't afraid of anything. He is only interested in one thing.'

She pauses. The only sound is the hissing in the ventilation system.

'Power,' she continues. 'It is his only motivation. Power over others. He will use any means to control other people. If necessary, he works them over until they break down. His type is dangerous, even without magic powers. As it happens, he is one of the strongest natural witches in the world. You shouldn't have left her there. You ought to be ashamed of yourselves.'

Vanessa *is* ashamed. They have abandoned Minoo.

'You, in particular,' Mona says, pointing at Nicolaus. 'You, if anyone, should have known what the leaders of the Council are capable of.'

'Yes, I should have,' Nicolaus agrees. He has turned deathly pale.

'We must get her out,' Anna-Karin says. Her voice is filled with panic.

Mona stubs her cigarette out on the floor.

'You must,' she says. 'But, first you must chat with your dead friends. I'll pack a few things and see you in a couple of hours.'

'So we don't have to wait until midnight?' Anna-Karin asks.

'Not when the levels of magic are this high. We could have done it straightaway, but you all have got to go to the school first.'

It can hardly be concern about truancy that is motivating Mona, Vanessa thinks. And the sinking feeling returns.

'Why?' Anna-Karin asks.

'You'll find out,' Mona says.

Linnéa roots around in a pocket and then throws her key-ring to Nicolaus.

'You and Mona can go to my apartment and prepare everything,' she says. 'But make sure she doesn't vanish again.'

Nicolaus weighs the keys in his hand. He looks profoundly unhappy.

'Sorry,' Vanessa says, turning to go. 'But Mona is usually right.'

'Exactly!' Mona calls after her. 'And take your time. Nicolaus and I will entertain each other.'

CHAPTER 95

Anna-Karin walks into the entrance lobby of the school and looks around while she catches her breath. The place is empty. Distant voices from the classrooms reach her.

They ran all the way to the school. Only two elements left: earth and water. Anna-Karin imagined a hundred different scenarios, all devastating. But somehow, this silence is worse still. It is as if the school is brooding. Waiting.

She looks at the others. Vanessa wipes a dribble from her nose with her glove. Linnéa's eyes dart everywhere.

Do you sense any magic here? she thinks. *I don't.*

Both Anna-Karin and Vanessa shake their heads. Linnéa closes her eyes and looks focused.

Evelina hasn't noticed anything either, she thinks next. The small crease between her eyebrows deepens.

And I can't pick up anything odd from other people's thoughts. At least, no odder than usual.

She opens her eyes again.

If Mona sent us off here so she could have a sexy afternoon with Nicolaus, she'll be in trouble.

'Oh *please*,' Anna-Karin says. She doesn't want to think about Nicolaus like that, and definitely not with *Mona*. 'What do you think we should do?'

'Let's keep an eye on things,' Vanessa says. 'Go to our classes and see if something happens.'

Linnéa nods.

I'll get in touch now and then, she thinks.

Anna-Karin walks up the stairs and remembers all the

times she and Minoo have walked here together. Minoo, who is in the manor house. With Walter.

He will use any means to control other people. If necessary, he works them over until they break down.

How could they have left her there?

* * *

When Vanessa enters her classroom, it is silent apart from the rasping sound of pens on paper. Everyone sits bent over their desks. It must be a surprise test.

Or . . . not. When Patrick, her English teacher, puts his book down and looks wearily at her from behind the teacher's desk, she remembers. They had been told about the test. Evelina mentioned something about it more than a week ago.

Vanessa collects a set of stapled sheets from Patrick and goes to sit down between Evelina and Michelle.

Evelina grabs hold of her hand under the desk and gives it a quick squeeze. They walked home together with Rickard last night. He and Evelina made an effort not to show how relieved they were that they weren't going to have to help with the closing of the portal. Although both kept saying how keen they were to stay around and do what they could to help the Chosen Ones. Vanessa doesn't doubt it.

Michelle stretches and yawns. Her test sheets are decorated all over the margins with flower garlands drawn lovingly in pencil. The pre-printed lines for writing on are almost completely empty. She nods to Vanessa and adds a few buds to a garland.

Vanessa looks around. Liam's breathing is strained and he snivels now and then. Patrick has picked up his book again and licks a finger to turn the page. Someone titters at the other end of the room. A gust of wind blows snow at the windows. The only thing Vanessa can do is wait, without knowing for what.

* * *

'I thought you were off sick today,' Petter Backman says when Linnéa comes into the art class.

'I got better,' she tells him, and sits down at the back of the room.

Restlessness is crawling inside her. She doesn't want to be here. She wants to be in her apartment preparing for the séance.

E-L-I-A-S.

She looks around the classroom. Petter leans against his desk and stares at Tindra, who is bending over her sketchbook. Linnéa knows that little smile of his only too well.

Just to have something to do, she takes out her sketchbook and puts pen to paper.

'Bet she lets guys do what they like with her.'

Linnéa's pen jerks across the paper and she looks up at Petter. He is still ogling Tindra. His thought was so clear it was almost as if he had said it aloud.

'Wonder if she'd be down for some webcam scenes. She needn't know it was me watching.'

It takes Linnéa a moment to realize that Petter didn't think it. That his lips had been moving. He has said it out loud, but he doesn't seem to have understood that himself.

'What the fuck did you say?' Tindra asks, getting up from her seat.

Petter blinks.

'You're so repulsive,' she goes on. 'Last autumn, when I was pregnant, I had this nightmare where you were the father. And I puked extra when I got up that morning.'

The rest of the class is alert now. And Linnéa senses the water magic coming toward her. She instinctively sets up her defenses.

The fifth portent. This is what Mona warned them about.

'I fucking knew it,' Petter says. 'I knew this would happen sooner or later. Sometimes it feels like you can read my mind.'

He glances at Linnéa.

'I'm so fucking lucky that I'm not a chick so I can't get knocked up,' Pascal says loudly. He usually doesn't speak at all and he always wants to make collages. 'It must be disgusting, I mean they look like sows.'

He fingers the waistband of his jeans.

'I'd like to have proper anorexia,' he goes on. 'I don't care that it's dangerous. It's worth it. I need to have more self-discipline.'

The disgust in his voice is so intense it sounds almost as if he found it pleasurable.

Linnéa has heard the disgust before, but in Pascal's thoughts. She picked it up in the beginning, when she had just got her powers but didn't know how to control them.

Anna-Karin, Linnéa thinks. *Is this happening in your class, too?*

But her thought won't transmit now. The air is too thick with magic. She gets up to go to Anna-Karin. She is the only one who can put a stop to this.

* * *

Anna-Karin sits in the front row in her classroom. She feels tense and looks around from time to time. Everyone is working at their math problems. Everyone except her. The book is still in her locker.

Ylva glances irritably at her. 'You might at least pretend you're interested.'

'I'm actually busy saving the world,' Anna-Karin says.

The words just slip out. She tries to understand how it happened. Why did she say what she thought? And then she senses the magic. It is welling into the classroom and she sets up her defense quickly.

'God, I've had it with you, Anna-Karin,' Ylva says. 'I've had it with all of you. I keep trying and trying. What's in it for me?'

'Shit, I hope she goes crazy again,' a boy's voice says somewhere behind Anna-Karin. 'It's so much fun.'

Water, Anna-Karin thinks. This is the next portent. The water element.

'I am so sick of the others in the guild,' Levan says. 'And this doesn't work for me anymore. I must go to bed earlier at night. I must prioritize school.'

Anna-Karin turns to look at Levan, who is now drinking from a can of Coke and seems unaware that he has said anything out loud.

'What if I've caught AIDS,' Lina says from the other end of the room. 'His stubble scratched my cheek. What if he has AIDS and I got his saliva into my blood.'

'He could easily be infected,' Anchalee says. 'He's a bouncer at Götis and bound to have had sex with tons of people. I don't get how you could sleep with him.'

'She's so repulsive,' Hanna H says.

Anna-Karin turns to look. Notices Hanna H glaring at Hanna A who has the desk next to hers.

'Who?' Hanna A asks.

'Who do you think?' Hanna H says. 'You, of course. If you would only wash your hair sometimes, you wouldn't smell of *scalp* all the time. Soaking yourself in perfume doesn't exactly help.'

Hanna A begins to cry quietly.

'I know we'll stop being friends after the finals,' she says. 'You'll leave town. And I won't go anywhere. I'm terrified of leaving Engelsfors because if I move to a new place I'll never get to know anyone and I'll be completely alone. I wish I could spend my whole life living with Mom and Dad. At least, until I move in with a boyfriend. If I ever find a boyfriend. Maybe I'll be one of those people who ends up on their own.'

'Shut up,' Hanna H says, giving her a shove. 'I'm so fucking tired of your whining. And your perfume.'

Someone starts to sing very badly, repeating the chorus of a song over and over, getting only half of the lyrics right.

'God I'm hungry,' Anchalee says to no one in particular, while Lina stares fixedly at a point in front of her and mutters *AIDS AIDS AIDS AIDS*, non-stop.

Anna-Karin senses the magic growing in strength continuously. By now, everyone is speaking out loud. There are no barriers left between what they think and what they say. Some people respond to what is being said, but others seem absorbed in what is going on inside their heads.

'I must get up earlier so I've time to have a shit at home, I hate the school bathrooms.'

'She'll dump me. She always adds a smiley. Why didn't she add a smiley?'

'My name is so weird. August. August. August. What kind of name is that? It doesn't sound like me. August? August . . . August!'

Anna-Karin tries to listen for Linnéa's thoughts but the magic is too strong. She gets up from her seat.

'I hate you,' Ylva says. 'I'd like to kill every one of you.'

Anna-Karin sees how the teacher's thin blonde hair has gone moist at her temples and her salmon-pink blouse has developed damp patches under her armpits.

'It's all a waste of time. You're as thick as two short planks, all of you. The only ones I cared for were Minoo and Viktor. And you, Anna-Karin, once. But not any longer.'

Ylva looks miserable.

'I have to stay up all night to correct tests, compile new tests, prepare lessons. In the breaks, I sit in the common room with colleagues who are as stupid as all of you. The only time I enjoy their company is when we talk about how awful you are. But I can't tell them that I fantasize about killing all of you. It would be so easy. Just to lock the classroom door and hack everyone to death with an axe.'

'Ylva,' Anna-Karin says, 'you must calm down a bit.'

'Some people count sheep, I count heads rolling on the

floor,' Ylva continues. 'Shame Kevin is locked up. Beheading him is always the best bit of my fantasy.'

She sighs.

'I wonder what Ylva looks like naked,' Levan says.

'Adults' bodies are disgusting,' August says. 'They're so flabby. Bet you Ylva is a virgin and lives with four cats.'

'I can't take it anymore,' Ylva says.

She walks along to one of the windows. When she pulls it open, a blast of cold wind tears through the classroom. For a little while, everyone falls silent.

'She's going to jump,' Hanna A says, pulling at Hanna H's hair. 'She's going to kill herself.'

'Like Rebecka,' Hanna H says.

Ylva tries to clamber up onto the windowsill. Everyone is talking louder now.

Anna-Karin struggles to release her power while at the same time defend herself against the water magic.

CLIMB DOWN AND SHUT THE WINDOW

Ylva holds still in the middle of her efforts.

'I must climb down and shut the window,' she says.

Anna-Karin watches with relief as Ylva slams the window shut so vigorously that the panes rattle.

LEAVE SCHOOL NOW. GO HOME. HURRY UP.

'I must leave school now,' Ylva says, straightening her blouse, which has escaped from the waistband of her skirt. 'I will go home. I must hurry.'

She walks obediently to the door.

PUT YOUR JACKET ON BEFORE YOU LEAVE, Anna-Karin orders. She reckons Ylva would freeze to death otherwise. *AND DON'T FORGET YOUR KEYS.*

'I'll kill you!' Hanna H screams, grabbing Hanna A's neck.

GO HOME! Anna-Karin thinks, and turns around, allowing her power to sweep across the classroom. *TAKE YOUR JACKETS AND BAGS AND GO HOME.*

Hanna H relaxes her grip on Hanna A's neck.

'I am to go home,' the class choruses. 'I am to take my jacket and my bag and go home.'

Everyone begins to move toward the door. Linnéa forces her way in against the flow.

'Help me,' Anna-Karin says. She holds out her hand to Linnéa.

* * *

Vanessa and Evelina look at each other when a piercing scream echoes in the hallway outside their classroom.

'Just you wait,' Liam says, sniveling loudly. 'One day I'll write a book about this town. I'll show you all.'

The strong water magic actually *feels* like water. Water flowing strongly enough to tear up whole villages and burst through great dams. And drown everything.

'Shit, I'm *so* hot.' Michelle pouts and studies her face in the mirror in her powder compact. 'If I were lesbian too, I'd definitely want to sleep with me.'

'They don't understand how quickly time passes,' Patrick says. 'They believe their youth is like a personal trait, something that belongs to them. Can't get their heads around the fact that they'll all wake up one day and it will be gone. Forever.'

Downstairs lobby! Linnéa shouts inside Vanessa's head. *Now!*

'I'll expose everyone I hate,' Liam says. 'And I hate almost everyone.'

'We must get out of here,' Vanessa says to Evelina. She gets up and pulls her jacket on.

'Yes, absolutely. Or I'll blurt out that we're witches,' Evelina says, getting ready.

'What are they talking about?' Michelle says. She snaps her powder compact shut.

'What are you talking about?'

'I'm trying not to think about it because then I'll say it,' Evelina says as they walk toward the door. 'I'm trying not to think about the apocalypse. I am *not* thinking about the apocalypse. I am *not* thinking about the apocalypse.'

The babble of voices in the classroom is deafening.

'They never ask me to hang out with them anymore,' Michelle says loudly behind them. 'Shit, Nessa's ass looks terrific in those jeans. Why does she always find the best jeans?'

'Linnéa will meet us in the lobby,' Vanessa says as soon as they are in the hallway. 'Can't you . . . sorry, but can you please hold your hand over your mouth?'

Evelina does as Vanessa suggested.

They walk quickly along the row of lockers. Two freshmen, a boy and a girl, are kissing each other in one of the sofa groups. And then they start laughing.

'Why didn't you say anything before?' she says.

'Why didn't *you* say anything?' he asks. 'I've been crazy about you since summer camp. But you were going out with Mikko and Mikko is better-looking than me.'

'I know,' the girl says. 'But I like you more than him anyway.'

They keep making out and Vanessa increases her pace. Evelina is mumbling furiously but pressing her hand to her lips so it's at least impossible to hear what she is saying.

They meet a junior guy who stares straight at Vanessa.

'She is so fucking sexy,' he says. 'Lucky Jari who shagged her before she turned dyke. It sucks that I didn't get a chance.'

'Like you'd ever have one,' Vanessa sneers.

'Fuck, I'm sad now,' he says. 'I'll never get to have sex.'

Tommy Ekberg stands in the hallway, together with the music teacher Kerstin Stålnacke and the biology teacher Ove Post.

'I'm drunk,' Ove says.

'I'm gay,' Tommy says.

Kerstin stares sadly at him.

703

'I'm in love with you,' she says, and bursts into tears.

Vanessa and Evelina carry on walking quickly through the school. It's like a nightmare. Some people talk straight out into the air. Others are deeply engaged in utterly bizarre conversations that remind Vanessa of how Wille, Jonte and Lucky could ramble on after they had smoked themselves into near-unconsciousness.

'. . . I guess he has to be right, I could learn to like it . . .'

'. . . would love to go on a helicopter ride. It seems so fucking cool. How do helicopters even fly? I have to find out . . .'

'. . . why doesn't she turn me on? She wants it. Why don't I . . .'

'. . . caviar, how could anyone face creamed smoked roe in the morning, it smells foul . . . and black pudding. Christ, black pudding is like eating scabs . . . and blue cheese, how can you willingly eat something that's moldy . . .'

Vanessa glances at Evelina, who seems to be in control. She has taken her hand away from her mouth so she can pull her jacket on.

Hurry up, she hears Linnéa's thought. *There are too many of them. Anna-Karin and I can't handle it alone.*

Vanessa starts running and Evelina follows. They pass a group of junior girls who are arguing noisily.

'Cousins are even allowed to *marry* in this country!' one of them screams. Someone pushes her hard and she bangs her head against the wall.

The lobby is full of students. More making out. More fights. Vanessa catches sight of one boy insanely beating up another boy.

Anna-Karin and Linnéa are waiting for them just inside the doors.

'Evelina, you go home to Rickard and tell him,' Vanessa says. 'And then go around to Linnéa's.'

'Will do,' Evelina. 'But we'll fuck first.'

She slaps her hand over her mouth and leaves quickly.

Vanessa looks at Anna-Karin and Linnéa. They join hands. Anna-Karin's control thoughts are so powerful they boom through their minds.

STOP FIGHTING! BE QUIET! EACH ONE OF YOU, TAKE YOUR JACKET AND GO HOME. TAKE IT EASY. GO TO THE HOSPITAL IF YOU THINK YOU NEED IT AND HELP OTHERS IF THEY NEED IT.

Vanessa watches as people stop in their tracks. Some set out for the doors. She sees one boy with half his face dripping blood and bloodstains all over his light quilted jacket.

'Shit,' Linnéa says. 'What would have happened today if we hadn't been here? Just think about it.'

Vanessa doesn't want to think about it. People would have ended up tearing each other apart.

She has never before been properly aware how many students there are. It takes a long time before everyone is through the front doors. Some are bleeding, others limping. Many are weeping, but no one seems seriously injured.

'I wonder if they'll remember what happened,' Anna-Karin says.

I don't know, Linnéa thinks. *It's impossible to tell. Just now, their minds only contain your control thoughts.*

The stream of students thins out. Lollo, the PE teacher, walks through the door with an intense expression on her face. Vanessa hardly recognizes her with her hair loose and tousled.

All around them, the magic is ebbing away.

It seems to be over now, Linnéa thinks. *Do you feel it, too?*

'Yes,' Anna-Karin says.

Tommy Ekberg walks past them, munching a Kit Kat. Vanessa watches him as he wanders away and disappears. The school is silent. They wait for a while but nobody else turns up.

'Seems they've all left,' Linnéa says, letting go of Anna-Karin's hand. 'Unless there's a dead body lying around somewhere.'

The Key

Vanessa shudders. She also lets go of Anna-Karin's hand and listens hard to the silence. She has a feeling it's not quite over.

'Shit!' Linnéa says. 'That was just about the sickest—'

Vanessa picks up a vibration in the floor. She turns to the others. And then, the whole world starts shaking, as the magic of the earth element wells up from the ground.

'Run!' Anna-Karin screams.

The lamps in the ceiling are swinging on their chains. Vanessa leaps at the door, stumbles and falls down the steps. Someone pulls her upright. Anna-Karin. A dull rumble fills the world around them. Vanessa sees the steps crack in front of her feet as the three of them run down to the schoolyard. Ahead of them, the pavement is bulging and the snow swirling in the air. The dead trees are falling, torn up, their roots exposed. The soccer goal collapses. Car alarms howl in the parking lot.

They rush out through the gates, then stop and look back at their school. The mortar is crumbling. Bricks are coming off and crash to the ground. Suddenly, all the windows explode. Broken glass showers the yard.

And then, silence.

The crack in the schoolyard, which appeared on the night of the blood-red moon, has opened again. A black, jagged tear in the snow.

Earth. The last portent.

'It looks as if there's a war on,' Anna-Karin says.

'There is,' Linnéa says.

Chapter 96

Anna-Karin is walking along the gravel road to the Sunny Side home for the elderly. She ought to be utterly exhausted, but keeps going on sheer adrenalin.

The apocalypse will be here soon. She must see Grandpa.

When the front doors open, she walks into a mad cacophony of ringing, beeping and howling. She pulls her cap off and takes the elevator to Grandpa's floor.

Here, the sounds are even stronger. The bulb in a wall light blows as she steps out into the hallway.

A birdlike little old lady is sitting in a wheelchair with her bony hands pressed against her ears, shaking her head and moaning *no, no, no*. Even her voice is like a bird's, shrill and a little hoarse. A care assistant comes out from one of the rooms and runs toward her.

'Now, now, Boel. It will be all right,' he says. 'Not to worry.'

He tries to sound calm but can't hide how stressed he is. He looks up and catches sight of Anna-Karin.

'Hello there and welcome to Armageddon,' he says. 'Every single telephone in the place is ringing. We are taking the receivers off the hook.'

Anna-Karin hurries along the hallway, goes into Grandpa's room and shuts the door. The phone is ringing here too, a tinny shrieking that hurts your ears.

In the small living room, Grandpa sits in his wheelchair. He has fallen asleep with a crossword magazine open on the little table attached to his chair.

How can he sleep in this racket? Is he really asleep? His

707

lower jaw hangs slackly. But then he snores and Anna-Karin breathes again.

She lifts the receiver of the gray, wall-mounted phone next to his bed and listens. All she can hear is hissing static that comes and goes in waves. Almost like breathing.

Then the noise stops. The signals from the other rooms die away.

She goes back to the living room. Grandpa snores once more, then opens his eyes and looks surprised.

'My sweet girl,' he mumbles and smiles at her. 'What brings you here?'

'How are you, Grandpa?'

'Can't complain, my dear. Is it cold again today?'

Anna-Karin nods and tries to smile.

'It's brass monkeys out there,' she says, using an expression Grandpa was fond of. It reminds her of skiing trips, thermoses full of hot chocolate and sandwiches made with cream cheese.

'Fetch me a glass of water, please,' Grandpa says.

She goes out into the small kitchen and runs the tap for cold water while she listens to him busying himself with something in the living room. Grandpa has his own things here, his own china and glassware and cutlery. It just makes her realize how far this is from his proper home. It smelled of green soap, coffee, wood, fresh air and, when Grandpa had done the laundry, freshly ironed cotton. The Sunny Side smell is artificial and stale, with a tinge of urine. She remembers what her mom said one day after they had been visiting.

I'd rather die than end up in a home like this.

At least she didn't have to go through that, Anna-Karin thinks, and feels a pang of grief.

She goes back to the living room and puts the glass of water on the wheelchair table. Grandpa has an envelope in his hand.

'I have a letter for you here,' he says.

Anna-Karin sits down next to him.

'I didn't want to say anything until I was sure I'd get an answer,' Grandpa continues. 'But I've found Staffan. Your father.'

Anna-Karin notes the sloping handwriting on the envelope. Her name but her grandfather's address. It says SUECIA on the last line.

So that is his handwriting. The man in the photographs, who came to Kärrgruvan one night and met Mom. He was good-looking and a great dancer.

If I had known how bad he was at everything else, I would've run as fast as my legs could carry me, Mom used to say.

Grandpa fingers the envelope nervously.

'I hope you don't think that I've been interfering?' he says.

Anna-Karin shakes her head as she takes the letter from him. Inside, a sheet of lined paper is covered in the same handwriting.

Hello Anna-Karin!

This letter has been very difficult to write. Taisto wrote to me and told me what had happened to Mia. It is very sad news and I am truly sorry. I hope you feel as well as you possibly can in these circumstances. I understand that you have many questions about me, and who I am. Perhaps you wonder most of all about why I disappeared. I regret to admit it, but I have no good answer to give you.

Mia was a very kind person and she always stood by me. I had a difficult background and she made me believe that I could settle down with my family in the countryside and lead a simple, stable life. I liked your grandparents very much, too, and thought it would work. But that kind of life was not for me. I wish it had been. And I wished all the time that I could be a good father as well. It seems I simply haven't got it in me. I haven't had any role models, and that might have something to do with it.

I live on Gran Canaria these days. The town is called Maspalomas. I work in a Swedish restaurant called Skansen and live alone, sharing my home with a dog. I'm happy enough and enjoy the sun and the warmth. Living in a place where few people stay for long is, I think, perfect for someone like me.

I come home to Sweden once or twice a year and stay with relatives in Västerås. It would give us a chance to meet. I hope you don't expect too much. I will never become a proper father for you. But if you have questions I will answer them as best I can.

Kind Regards, Staffan

Anna-Karin reads and rereads the letter. It doesn't make her feel any closer to him. Rather the opposite.

She tries to imagine him on Gran Canaria but, as she has never been there, she can't. Strange that he might be in that restaurant now, maybe chatting to a drunken tourist with a peeling, red nose. It's easier to imagine the tourist than her father. Dad.

Anna-Karin folds the letter.

'Would you like to talk about it?' Grandpa asks.

'Not just now,' Anna-Karin replies. 'But thank you for finding him.'

She puts the letter down on his table. 'Please, look after it for me.'

'The time has come, hasn't it?' Grandpa asks.

Anna-Karin nods, she can't find the voice to speak.

'You will do very well,' he continues. 'Everything you've been through will have prepared you for what is to come. You are ready.'

The light flickers.

'I don't feel ready,' Anna-Karin says. 'I'm scared.'

'Don't you think heroes feel fear? Courage is facing the things you are afraid of.'

He takes her hand and holds it tightly between both his.

'Today, you will walk into battle. But I'm not worried about you. Not in the slightest. Are you listening to me?'

710

She meets his eyes. And, in a crystal clear moment, she believes him. She believes him completely.

She is ready.

* * *

Vanessa sits on the floor in Linnéa's living room, leaning back against the wall. The solid, unlit red candles are placed in the corners of the room. The rectangular mirror lies in the middle of the floor, where it has been for the last three weeks.

Linnéa stands at the window smoking a cigarette in the pale sunlight. She has opened the window a crack and is trying to blow the smoke out through the gap. She shivers in the cold wind.

'You might as well shut the window,' Vanessa says. 'The smoke blows straight back in again anyway.'

Her voice echoes. All the furniture has been crammed into Linnéa's bedroom. It looks like Gym-Lollo's extreme obstacle course fantasy.

'I know,' Linnéa says dully.

Vanessa watches her and thinks about when they prepared for their first séance here. She hadn't realized that she was in love with Linnéa back then, but Linnéa already loved her.

Linnéa flicks the cigarette out into the blizzard and closes the window, then shivers again. She turns to look at Vanessa and seems to hesitate for a moment before she goes to sit down next to her.

In the kitchen, Mona is snickering coquettishly at something Nicolaus has just said. Vanessa imagines his posture growing even more rigid. She finds herself wondering if Nicolaus has had sex since the seventeenth century.

'Are you sure you don't want to see your mom?' Linnéa asks.

Vanessa nods. Anna-Karin has gone to see her grandpa and she had wondered herself if she should visit Mom at work. Or drop in at Melvin's day nursery. But she couldn't cope with the thought that it would be like saying farewell.

She mustn't let her fear take over. They will deal with this. Will save the world, will survive and then . . . never mind what happens then.

They will survive.

Linnéa wraps her arms around herself.

Vanessa is very aware of how close she is. Linnéa's energy is so strong that it vibrates in Vanessa's chest. And Vanessa shares her determination.

She wonders if there is a chance for them after they have closed the portal. She has no answer. All she knows now is that she misses Linnéa. And that, if she just reached out her hand a little, she could touch her.

But what would happen if she did? She couldn't bear it if Linnéa backed away. And, even if she didn't, all wouldn't be well. Sooner or later they would hurt each other again. For now, they must concentrate on saving the world.

It would be so much easier if she didn't want to kiss Linnéa quite so much. Lose herself in her arms. But she mustn't risk beginning something without even knowing what she really wants.

'What are you thinking about?' Linnéa says quietly.

'Nothing special. What about you?'

'I'm thinking about Elias.'

Obviously, her mind is full of Elias, her best friend – she had thought of him as dead for two years. Now, she might get to talk with him again.

Vanessa is so glad she didn't touch Linnéa. The timing would have been terrible.

In the kitchen, Mona cackles loudly.

'Relax, darling,' she says. 'If this isn't the moment to have a good time, I don't know what is.'

Nicolaus pops his head around the kitchen door.

'Linnéa, would you be kind enough to give me a hand?' he says stiffly.

* * *

712

Linnéa doesn't want to get up and go to the kitchen. She is full of Vanessa's presence and doesn't want to leave it.

In the kitchen, Nicolaus is stirring ectoplasm in a bowl. Mona stands next to him and pours in iron filings now and then. Her breasts nudge his arm. She grins at Linnéa.

'I told Vanessa it wouldn't be a picnic,' Mona says. 'But I couldn't have foreseen quite how chicken you'd be.'

Linnéa is stunned. Then she wonders if Vanessa heard what Mona said.

'I've no idea what you're talking about,' Linnéa says.

Mona cackles, then produces her pack of cigarettes.

'I expected a better comeback from you,' she says.

Naturally, Linnéa can't think of a single thing to say. She hates Mona wholeheartedly. And hates herself for letting Mona make her look like a fool.

Mona grins at her before going off to the living room to light a cigarette.

Linnéa and Nicolaus exchange glances.

'That woman . . .' he begins.

'I can't think how you can resist her,' Linnéa says.

Nicolaus laughs. It takes her aback completely. She can't remember ever seeing him laugh before. His teeth are remarkably white, especially given that they've been around since the seventeenth century.

'What can I help you with?' she asks.

'Can we speak privately?' Nicolaus asks quietly and points at his head.

Linnéa nods and releases her power.

There's something I must tell you, Nicolaus thinks. *Do you remember the night we opened my grave and I got my memories back?*

Hard to forget, she replies. He smiles faintly.

You and Minoo wondered why I hadn't opened the grave earlier. I think you said that it would have been 'pretty useful' if I had remembered everything when you were called.

Linnéa nods again. She hasn't thought about it since, but remembers how weird she thought it back then.

You said you didn't know, she thinks.

Nicolaus sighs and pulls his fingers through his hair. *I didn't want to worry you at that stage. I had planned to tell you. But, that very same night, Matilda told me I had to leave Engelsfors.*

It can't be good news if he thought it would worry them.

Tell me now then, she thinks.

The magic that preserved my memories in the grave was also preserving me, allowing me to live for such an unnaturally long time.

Nicolaus looks as though he hopes he has said enough, that she has understood. But she doesn't want to take it in.

For hundreds of years, I've lived on borrowed time, he continues. *The repayment will be swift. As soon as the grave was opened, the last of my life energy began to drain away. I only hope that I have enough time left to complete my task as guide of the Chosen Ones.*

The inscription on Nicolaus's gravestone read MEMENTO MORI. *Remember you must die.* And Nicolaus did remember.

She looks at him. He seems his normal self – not dying in the least. If anything, he has looked healthier since he came back from his journeys. More alive.

Don't tell the others, he thinks. *Not yet.*

The feeling driving his thought is so full of pleading. It is hard to meet his eyes. She feels overwhelmed.

Why tell me? she thinks. *Why me?*

Because you understand what must be done, he thinks, looking pained.

What do you mean? she thinks.

I might not have the time to say farewell as I would like to, Nicolaus thinks. *And if so, you must tell them, Linnéa. Assure the others that I was prepared and that I have felt honored to be at your side, even though I wish I could have done more to help you. Above all, tell everyone that what I did, I did out of love.*

Linnéa is too shaken to answer, even in her thoughts, and only nods.

She senses Anna-Karin's energy in the stairwell and hurries out into the hall.

On the landing, Anna-Karin is waiting, together with Rickard and Evelina. And Gustaf.

'What are you doing here?' Linnéa says.

She sounds far too harsh, but what Nicolaus has just said has thrown her.

'Why shouldn't Gustaf join us?' Anna-Karin says.

'Let's check with Mona,' Linnéa says, avoiding Gustaf's gaze.

Four people getting out of their winter clothes and shoes in her small hall is more than enough to crowd the space, so she backs into the living room.

And almost walks into Mona.

'Good that you turned up, sweetheart,' Mona says to Gustaf. She drags on her cigarette. 'Both the girls were crazy about you. You being here will probably strengthen the connections. I want you to sit on my right.'

She looks at Linnéa.

'And you on my left. For the boy's sake.'

It takes a second before Linnéa realizes that Mona means Elias. Her heart starts beating faster.

Mona turns to Rickard and scrutinizes him.

'Well, well,' she says. 'So you're the metal witch? All right then. We'll draw the circles now. Keep your eyes open and you might learn a thing or two.'

CHAPTER 97

The sun is flooding the room. In the corner, the pale flames of the candles are fluttering. Linnéa's eyes are fixed on the upside-down glass placed at the center of the mirror, the edges of which are smeared with ectoplasm.

Linnéa has Mona on her right and she holds on tightly to Vanessa with her left hand. Mona might have put her and Vanessa next to each other to tease them. It would be just like her, but Linnéa is glad she did. Glad to have Vanessa so close.

Because, something will happen. She is certain of it.

From the corner of her eye, she sees Mona lean forward so that her blonde hair hides her profile.

'We are trying to make contact with three souls,' Mona says in a solemn voice. 'Ida Holmström, daughter to Carina and Anders Holmström. Elias Malmgren, son to Krister and Helena Malmgren. Rebecka Mohlin, daughter to Isabelle and Jörgen Mohlin. Are any of you here?'

The glass doesn't move. The room is as silent as the grave.

Please, Elias, Linnéa thinks. Please Elias, come. Please come. Talk to us. Talk to me.

A slight grinding noise. The glass begins to move. Linnéa presses Vanessa's hand harder when it stops at yes.

'Within this circle, we meet with mutual respect and deference,' Mona continues.

Then she coughs, straight out. An abysmal, slimy wheezing that would scare off the most enthusiastic would-be smoker. Gustaf leans sideway as far as he can without letting go of Mona's right hand. Mona falls silent. Linnéa feels the hairs on her arms standing up. Across the circle, she meets Nicolaus's gaze.

'Hello?' Mona says.

It sounds like a poor little bleat. She straightens her neck and looks around the room, apparently confused.

'What's the matter?' Linnéa says.

'It worked!' Mona says. 'I'm in her! I'm in Mona!'

She leans forward, looks at herself in the mirror, then turns her head to sniff her shoulder and looks disgusted.

'Oh my God, she stinks!'

Linnéa stares at Mona. It's so obvious, but she still can't believe it.

'Ida?'

'Yes!' Ida says in Mona's voice. 'It's me! You can hear me!'

'Is Elias here too?' Linnéa asks.

'No,' Ida says.

The disappointment is so bitter that Linnéa can't speak.

Ida catches sight of Gustaf. Looks down at their clasped hands.

'Hi, G,' she mumbles.

'Hi, Ida,' he replies uncertainly.

Large tears start trickling down Mona's cheeks, leaving oily trails of mascara.

'You guys have no idea how happy I am to see you,' Ida says. 'Or, rather, I have seen you lots of times, but you haven't seen me. Apart from that one time when you glimpsed me in your mirror, Linnéa.'

It takes a moment and then Linnéa understands. In her bathroom, just before the court hearing.

'I hadn't slept for – like – forty-eight hours,' Linnéa says. 'I thought I was hallucinating.'

'Really? Even though you know ghosts exist?' Ida says irritably. 'Seriously? You have no idea how frustrating it was for me. I tried to warn you that Olivia is in town.'

'Olivia is dead,' Vanessa tells her.

'Oh,' Ida says with audible relief. 'Good.'

Linnéa and Rickard glance at each other. He had wept when she told him what had happened and, since then, they haven't mentioned Olivia again.

A thin string of ectoplasm dribbles from one corner of Mona's mouth. Ida lifts the hand that holds on to Linnéa and quickly wipes the white goo off with the sleeve of Mona's track-suit. Then she glances at Gustaf to see if he noticed. He has.

'Where's Minoo?' she suddenly asks, looking alarmed. 'Did Olivia get her?'

'Minoo is with the Council,' Anna-Karin says. 'But we're going to get her out.'

'You really should,' Ida says. 'All that stuff about the Council circle that you were talking about in Kärrgruvan, it seemed so totally wrong.'

'How often have you been around, really?' Vanessa asks.

Linnéa wonders, too. How often has Ida been in her bath-room? In her bedroom? In her life?

'It's hard to explain,' Ida says. 'I've sort of jumped back and forth. It might feel like five minutes to me, but for you, months can have passed . . . what's the month now?'

'October,' Linnéa says. 'We're seniors now.'

'Did you ever watch me?' Evelina asks her. Rickard looks ill at ease.

'Mostly, I end up in places that have to do with the Chosen Ones,' Ida says.

'Because of the bond between you.' Nicolaus nods thought-fully. 'It's only natural.'

'Natural?' Ida sneers. 'There isn't anything natural about it.'

'Where is Elias?' Linnéa asks, because she needs to know now.

'He is waiting for me in the Borderland. I've only found him quite recently. Or, well, recently for me but . . . everything is so different when you're dead.'

There are so many questions that Linnéa wants to ask, so

much she wants an answer to that she doesn't know where to begin.

'He is fine,' Ida says. 'And he has asked tons of questions about you.'

It's so unfair. Ida gets to talk to Elias and she doesn't.

'Ida,' Nicolaus says, 'what do you mean by the Borderland?'

'It's what Matilda called the place where we are,' Ida says.

'You have met her then?'

'Yes, I have,' Ida says. 'I've met her and I've seen both her and you. And there's a great deal I could say about certain events.'

Linnéa looks at Nicolaus and wonders if he understands what Ida refers to.

'But I don't know how much time we have,' Ida continues. 'All I can say is that her behavior has been so weird. I don't think we can quite trust her and the guardians. But I guess you've worked that out already.'

'Yes.' Nicolaus looks down. 'We've understood that.'

'Is Rebecka there as well?' Gustaf asks. 'In the Borderland?'

'I don't know.'

Gustaf nods, obviously suppressing his feelings.

'But we can look for her,' Ida continues. 'I mean, I found Elias, after all.'

'You must find her,' Linnéa says. 'We need her to close the portal. And we need you and Elias as well.'

Ida looks triumphant.

'I knew it!' she says. 'We are the Key. We are chosen to close the portal. I just knew that no damn Council circle could replace the Chosen Ones! The guardians tricked you, just as they tricked me!'

'How do you mean?' Vanessa asks.

Ida purses her mouth. The effect is to deepen Mona's tobacco-induced wrinkles. Linnéa recognizes the expression as typical of Ida when she had to tell them something she didn't want to.

'You remember that I wasn't exactly keen to be in the Circle,' she says.

Linnéa has to laugh.

'It would've been hard to miss it,' Vanessa says, smiling.

'Whatever,' Ida snaps. 'The thing was, the *Book of Patterns* promised me that I didn't have to. I mean, it said that if I cooperated with you, I'd get out of it later on. And it also said that if I did that, then . . .'

She sighs. 'The guardians gave me a vision,' she continues, glancing at Gustaf. 'They showed me that you . . . that you kissed me. But it was no kiss.'

She stares at the floor and tears fill her eyes again.

'It was when you tried to save me,' she says quietly. 'In the gym hall. Just after my pathetic declaration of love.'

Gustaf looks tenderly at her. 'Ida . . .' he begins.

'I know. You didn't like me in that way. Actually, not at all.'

'Ida,' Gustaf says gently, 'you saved my life.'

'You saved us *all*,' Linnéa says, suddenly feeling her own eyes fill with tears.

'But why did the guardians want me to die?' Ida sobs. 'I know they're trying to read the future, but did I really have to die?'

'We can't know that,' Nicolaus says. 'But we do know that you must try to find Rebecka.'

Ida opens her mouth to reply but Mona's head drops forward.

'Ida?' Linnéa says.

Mona doesn't move.

'Ida, are you still here?' Vanessa says. Mona moves now and looks up. Unmistakably Mona now. She clears her throat and spits out the ectoplasm. It lands on the mirror like a large, slimy lump of mucous.

'Oh, hell.' Mona lets go of Linnéa's and Gustaf's hands. 'I need a smoke . . .'

She fumbles in the front pocket and finds a cigarette.

'Who does little Miss Up-herself think she is? Just jumping into me like that! How rude!'

But Linnéa can tell that she is shaken to the core.

Linnéa feels strangely numb. Outside, a cloud drifts in front of the sun and the candle flames in the corners brighten.

'Now what should we do?' Linnéa says. 'We know they're there, but how can they help us close the portal?'

Vanessa releases her hand, gets up and walks over to the window. She looks out.

'I think Minoo is the solution,' Nicolaus says. 'She has the power to handle souls.'

The light in the room fades a little more.

'Shit,' Vanessa says and points toward the window.

* * *

Vanessa hears the others rise from their places and come to look out of the window. Linnéa appears at her side; Vanessa wants to shout to her not to go near the window, just as her mother used to when Vanessa was little and scared of a thunderstorm.

This is no ordinary twilight.

There are no changes of color in the sky, no gradual turning of dusk into night.

It is as if the whole world is being rapidly drained of all light. The eye can hardly follow the speed of the invading darkness.

Suddenly, all is black.

Pitch-black.

No stars in the sky. No moon. No streetlights.

All of Engelsfors seems to have vanished. Only their faces, lit by flickering candlelight, are reflected in the windowpane.

Vanessa feels Linnéa's terror. Feels how she is trying to keep it under control, but it is like a maelstrom just below the surface, a maelstrom that threatens to suck them both down.

'I feel so strange,' Gustaf says. 'I think I'll have to . . .'

Vanessa turns to look at him just as he slumps heavily to the floor.

'Gustaf!' Rickard calls out.

He kneels at Gustaf's side and shakes him gently. Gustaf's head rolls limply from side to side.

'He's asleep,' Mona says.

They hear a loud bang from the street. Metal crunching, glass splintering.

'And he isn't the only one,' Mona says.

'Anna-Karin, can you make him wake up?' Rickard asks.

Anna-Karin shakes her head. 'I've already tried,' she tells him.

'I've heard that this can happen when the magic levels rise to very high values very quickly,' Nicolaus says. 'Only natural witches can cope with the readjustment.'

Vanessa glances at the window as a chilly sensation runs down her spine.

'So, that car crash . . .' She stops to swallow.

'Is likely to have been one of many,' Mona says.

Vanessa suddenly remembers *Sleeping Beauty*. Everyone in the castle fell asleep when the princess pricked her finger on the enchanted spindle. The cook at his pots, the horses in the stables, the ladies of the court in the throne room.

What is happening in Engelsfors? Have truck drivers nodded off at the wheel? Surgeons in the middle of an operation, with their scalpel lifted ready for an incision? Have people out for an evening stroll fallen unconscious onto the icy pavements?

'The boy is at least sleeping safely here,' Mona observes.

Vanessa looks at Gustaf. His breathing is calm and regular.

'You must go to the manor house at once,' Nicolaus says. 'You must get Minoo and the three objects too. And then you must go directly to the cave under the school.'

'He's right,' Mona says. 'You have to hurry.'

Part Five

Vanessa has never seen Mona so serious.

'But what about all the people who have fallen asleep?' Anna-Karin asks.

'They will be sleeping for all eternity unless you close the portal,' Nicolaus says.

Vanessa looks at the black window. Mom has been at work and will be indoors. But Melvin . . . what if he was outside playing in the snow when the darkness fell? Then he'll be lying in a snowdrift now.

'Evelina and I can drive around in my car,' Rickard says. 'And help people if we are able to.'

'Yes,' Evelina says. 'And we'll check on Melvin's nursery.'

Of course, Evelina would understand. Vanessa puts her arms around her and holds her tight. She is close to tears, but she mustn't give in now. Must stay focused.

'I love you,' she says.

'And I you.'

'See you after we've saved the world,' Vanessa says as she lets Evelina go. 'And then we will celebrate!'

'Hell yeah!' Evelina smiles through her tears, then turns to the others. 'Good luck, everyone.'

'Yes,' Rickard says. 'Good luck, everyone.'

He looks one last time at the sleeping Gustaf and then they leave the room. Vanessa hears them putting their things on in the hall. Then the door slams.

Was this the last time she would see Evelina?

'I'll go ahead to the caves,' Nicolaus says.

Anna-Karin asks, 'Where is Mona?'

They all turn around to have a look and suddenly they all realize it: Mona has gone.

'Shit!' Vanessa says.

'Is anyone surprised?' Linnéa asks.

No, Vanessa isn't. What surprised her is that Mona stayed for as long as she did.

'I'll get flashlights.' Linnéa heads into the bedroom.

The Key

'I'll find Gustaf's car keys.' Anna-Karin goes out into the hall and starts going through his jacket pockets.

'With magic levels this high, your powers will be exceptionally strong,' Nicolaus says, looking at Vanessa.

'But that's true of the Council's witches as well,' she says.

'Exactly,' Nicolaus says. 'Be very careful. I don't think there's any chance of Walter letting Minoo go willingly.'

CHAPTER 98

Anna-Karin drives through the streets of Engelsfors with great care.

It is so dark.

No streetlights were on when darkness enveloped the town. Cars weren't using their headlights. In the residential areas, most of the houses are dark.

She thinks about Grandpa. Hopes that he sits in his wheelchair now, or is safely in bed. And that the dark didn't come just as a member of staff was lifting him.

The car headlights pick out a woman lying curled up on the pavement. She lies on her side with a couple of ICA carrier bags next to her. One of them has toppled over and tins have rolled out.

At least she is warmly dressed in ski pants and a thick jacket.

Anna-Karin turns a corner.

A bus has stopped halfway across the road. She has a glimpse of the driver, hunched over the wheel, and of the passengers sleeping in their seats.

She gets around the bus by driving in the wrong lane and then up on the pavement.

'Do we have anything like a plan?' Linnéa asks. She is in the passenger seat.

'We find Minoo first. Hopefully she knows where the objects are,' Anna-Karin says.

'I think I can make both of you invisible,' Vanessa says from a seat in the back. 'I feel mega-strong.'

They cross the dark Canal Bridge. A little way along the

track to the manor house, Anna-Karin stops and parks the car.

They close the car doors quietly and Linnéa shines her flashlight down at the snow.

Anna-Karin is struck by the silence, now that the constant roar of traffic from the highway is gone. She thinks of all the long-distance trucks and hopes no one has been seriously injured.

Then she slips into the consciousness of the fox. He is curled up under the dance pavilion; he is afraid. All his senses are alert. And Anna-Karin feels that the whole forest is waiting with him.

But she is not afraid.

She seems to have found a place beyond fear after her talk with Grandpa. A fixed point inside her.

They hear snow creaking under walking feet. The footsteps come toward them from the direction of the manor house. Linnéa turns the flashlight off at once.

Anna-Karin releases her power and realizes how strong it is. The beam of a flashlight is coming closer. Anna-Karin doesn't care who it is. She is prepared.

* * *

Linnéa watches the approaching flashlights intently.

Make us invisible, she thinks to Vanessa.

And then she is dazzled when light shines into her eyes.

Linnéa!

It's Viktor. Linnéa's grip on her own flashlight hardens.

It's only me and Clara, he continues quickly. *We were on our way to you. We want to help you. You can read my mind if you don't believe me.*

He leaves his mind wide open. His thoughts are chaotic, full of conflicting emotions. But she can't pick up any hint that he is hiding something. And they need all the help they can get.

'It's Viktor and his sister,' she tells Anna-Karin and Vanessa.

She turns her flashlight on again and watches as the Ehrenskiöld twins walk along the plowed track. Viktor is wearing his black winter coat and Clara a sand-colored quilted jacket. This is the first time Linnéa has seen Clara. She owes her such a lot. Brother and sister are strikingly alike, but Clara looks very fragile. It is hard to imagine her systematically terrorizing Robin into confession.

'What are you doing here?' Vanessa whispers when the twins have come close enough.

'We were coming to find you,' Viktor says. He blinks against the light.

Linnéa lowers her flashlight.

'Walter called us to a meeting. He told us that the last portent had shown itself,' Viktor continues.

Clara takes up the story. 'When the others had gone, I stayed behind and asked if he knew how we were to go about closing the portal. And he said he did.'

'But I had hung around just outside the door and sensed that he lied,' Viktor adds.

'We didn't know what to do,' Clara says. 'We were hoping that you would know more.'

Their sentences join up and overlap, almost as if a single individual is speaking.

'We only know that we have a shot at closing the portal,' Linnéa says.

'But you need Minoo, don't you?' Clara says.

'Yes, we do,' agrees Linnéa.

'She's in Walter's office,' Viktor says. 'Walter and Alexander are both there. And Walter's lynx.'

'We need three objects as well,' Anna-Karin says. 'A skull, a silver cross and a round box.'

Viktor closes his eyes.

'They're in the office,' he says when he has opened his eyes again. 'My familiar is perching on the outside windowsill.'

'Is Minoo all right?' Anna-Karin asks. Linnéa waits fearfully for Viktor's answer.

'I think so, but I can't quite make out her face.'

'We haven't seen her for three weeks,' Clara explains.

'Has she stayed on . . . willingly?' Linnéa asks.

She picks up a sudden burst of shame in Viktor's mind and her fears grow worse.

'Walter forced her to swear the oath,' he says. 'And, ever since, he has kept her isolated from the rest of us.'

It comes back to Linnéa that when they had that fight in Kärrgruvan, she had told Minoo she might as well swear allegiance to the Council. She wishes she could take it back.

'Let's go to Walter's office,' she says. 'Anna-Karin, you order him to stay put while we get Minoo out.'

'Wait, don't forget about Adriana,' Clara says. 'We must get her out of there, too. Walter might do something terrible to her if Minoo disappears.'

Linnéa observes Clara, senses how afraid she is of Walter and how much she hates him.

'OK, we'll get her out,' Linnéa says while looking at Viktor. 'I don't know if you've noticed anything about Alexander, but everyone who isn't a natural witch is knocked out cold by all this magic. We'll have to carry her out.'

'Clara and I can do it,' Vanessa says. 'We'll go invisible, of course. At least it isn't a worse idea than our usual plans.'

Viktor's eyes are glued to her while she speaks.

Should I tell her? If we're all going to die soon . . .

And then he glances at Linnéa and, for the first time tonight, slams shut the gateway into his mind.

But it's too late and she knows now that he loves Vanessa. Linnéa is surprised, but actually not very. How can one *not* be in love with Vanessa?

I know how you feel, she thinks.

Viktor smiles a little sadly at her and then looks away.

'Minoo has told us about the others and their powers,' Anna-Karin says. 'Is everyone loyal to the Council?'

'Alexander, definitely,' Clara says. 'But he is likely to be asleep.'

Viktor shuts his eyes again.

'I can't see him from this angle. He's sitting in an armchair with his back to the window. But he hasn't moved for a long time.'

'What about the others?' Vanessa asks.

'Sigrid is completely loyal. And her familiar is a mink, so be careful even when you're invisible. It's harder to tell where Felix and Nejla stand.'

'I think we know where Felix stands,' Clara says, giving Viktor a sidelong glance. 'With you.'

There is a sound of an explosion in the town. Just as they turn to have a look, a cloud of fire flares up in the center. The fire lights the sky. Car alarms start howling.

'Shit!' Vanessa says in a small voice. 'Shit.'

Linnéa looks away. Doesn't want to think about what might have happened, how many might have been injured or dead.

She has no time to feel anything now. No time to be afraid.

'Come on,' she says. 'We have to hurry.'

CHAPTER 99

M inoo hears the explosion.

She knows that it came from a third-floor apartment in a brick building on Malm Road downtown. Rut Olsson fell asleep at the kitchen table and overturned a lit candle that fell on the rag-rug. It was her eighty-third birthday and she was celebrating it alone. Her beloved children, grandchildren and great-grandchildren all live in Göteborg. Her greatest fear was that she would end her days hidden away in a home for the elderly. But she died quickly, and so did her neighbor, after the kitchen fire reached the bottled gas tubes feeding Rut's cooker.

All very regrettable. But it could have been worse. Minoo understands that now. There are no perfect decisions. Every time, advantages and disadvantages must be weighed against each other and, every time, sacrifices have to be made.

There is always someone who must be sacrificed.

This insight has grown during these last few weeks, as she has grown stronger.

At last, she has grasped what her vision in the spring actually meant.

It showed her that the power of the guardians would come to her. That all their power would be vested in her. Now, the transfer is almost complete.

She has spent three weeks inside the black smoke. It feels like an essential part of her now, as much as her arms and legs. She has been exploring her magic on her own, but also under Walter's guidance.

Not that she has told him of all her new discoveries, far from it. Walter knows incredibly little.

'Minoo!' he says.

He is of no interest to her right now.

The other Chosen Ones are on their way here. The Ehrenskiöld twins as well. She can see them walking across the snow-covered yard in front of the manor house, which is glowing with lights. They are close to the main entrance now.

She sees Nicolaus, flashlight in hand, hurrying toward the opening of the tunnel in the mountain.

At the same time, she can see the new, gaping hole in the cave. The wall with the ectoplasm circles has crumbled. The wall that the other Chosen Ones tried to keep secret from her. When the darkness fell, Minoo had watched as the cracks spread until it collapsed.

Everything is progressing as it should.

'Minoo!' Walter says again.

Her body sits on his office sofa. Alexander has fallen asleep in an armchair. The lynx is padding anxiously up and down near the window. It can sense danger in the air.

'The world will end soon,' Walter says. 'Are the guardians just going to let it happen?'

She looks thoughtfully at him, her head tilted a little to the side. His aura is a matte yellow, like the fur of a lion, and stronger than ever. It pulsates around him.

He has placed the box, the cross and the table between them. The box that is not a box. The cross that is not a cross. More sacrifices will be required.

All for a good cause. It must be done to let them close the portal and create harmony in the world, once and for all.

The Chosen Ones and the twins are in the hall now. Everything is progressing as it should.

Minoo sees herself reflected in the glass covering the framed picture behind Walter. A magnificent three-masted ship against a richly colored evening sky. She sees herself smile blandly. Sees her own eyes, black and glowing. Eyes that no one else can see.

'We had an agreement!' Walter says. He can barely keep himself from yelling. 'They gave me a mission to fulfill. And then they cut me off! The same day that the portal must be closed! I must know what is going on!'

He has been following the guardians' directives for four years. He has operated in the shadows. He saw to it that Adriana's application to do her research in Engelsfors was approved. He encouraged Alexander to organize the trial. He chose to overlook the fact that the Chosen Ones outsmarted Alexander and then told him to use Adriana as a scapegoat. He assured Alexander that his sister wouldn't be harshly punished and then ordered the judges to condemn her to death, so that Minoo would try to rescue her and learn more about her own powers. Walter's combined efforts have triggered the sequence of events that has led to this exact moment. He has been invaluable.

So has Alexander, in his own way. Minoo observes him as he sits, deeply asleep, his head slumped sideways. She has been inside his memories and had a good look around. He is obsessed with Walter. He is chained to him by fear and shame and admiration and hatred. Again and again, Walter has used and betrayed him. And yet, he trusts Walter blindly. Some people have that kind of power over others.

Walter doesn't anymore. Not over Minoo.

She has taken it from him, and that is the most unforgivable thing anyone could do to him. She can feel his rage, his hatred. He would like to make her suffer and then kill her. But he doesn't dare do anything now, because he knows that she is strong. Even though he has no idea just *how* strong.

Minoo could neutralize him, easily.

But, for now, Walter is necessary. Just for a little while longer.

* * *

Follow me across the floor, Viktor instructs Linnéa. *Some places creak less than others.*

Linnéa passes the warning on to Anna-Karin, then looks around at the enormous dark room.

A few heavy crystal chandeliers hang from the ceiling. Six folding chairs are arranged in a circle in the middle of the floor. It is eerily silent. The bars in the tall windows cast long shadows on the parquet. Outside, the snow glitters in the light from the outdoor lamps.

They follow Viktor to a door at the far end of the room. Now and then, the parquet groans under their feet. Linnéa stops every time it happens and holds her breath. She knows that Walter's office is on the other side of the door.

Walter.

Linnéa feels a surge of terror. What has she exposed Minoo to by leaving her here?

Then she thinks of Vanessa, who is somewhere else in the building trying to rescue Adriana. She would so much like to send her a thought and find out if she's all right. But she doesn't dare to.

She looks at the door again.

Are you positive they're still in there? she thinks.

Viktor turns to Linnéa and nods.

Don't try to read Walter's mind. He will notice. You have only one chance to take him by surprise.

They reach the door. Linnéa stands in front of it, next to Anna-Karin.

Thanks, Linnéa thinks, looking at Viktor.

You were right, he replies. *You can't change a rotten system from within. All that comes of it is that you become rotten yourself.*

Linnéa realizes just how big a risk Viktor and Clara run by doing this.

At least you tried, she thinks.

He smiles ironically.

Good luck, he says, then nods at Anna-Karin and wanders away across the parquet.

Are you ready? she thinks to Anna-Karin.

Anna-Karin nods, a grim look on her face.

Remember how strong you were in school today, Linnéa thinks. *We can do this together. We're stronger than ever and—*

I know, Anna-Karin interrupts. *I am not afraid.*

Linnéa meets her friend's green eyes and feels her own terror fade. They hold hands.

Wait.

A new voice in Linnéa's head. And seeing how confused Anna-Karin looks, she must have heard it, too.

Do nothing until I tell you to.

It is Minoo.

OK, Linnéa replies hesitantly, and feels the thought arrive.

When did Minoo learn to do this? And what is going on in there?

* * *

Vanessa and Clara walk hand in hand as they enter a hallway with a brownish-red carpet and dark red wallpaper. If this is how the manor house looked when it was a hotel, no wonder the owners went bankrupt. It looks like the set of a horror film. Who'd sleep here willingly? The walls are hung with portraits that don't improve Vanessa's mood.

Clara points at one of the doors further along the hallway and squeezes Vanessa's hand. For as long as their bodies are in contact, they can see each other. Otherwise they are as invisible to each other as to everyone.

Almost everyone. In this place, a roving mink or lynx can turn up at any minute.

Vanessa glances at Clara from the corner of her eye. Her first impression was that Clara looks frail, but now she has a feeling that Clara is much tougher than she looks. And there is so much Vanessa would like to talk to her about.

When Vanessa came inside, she carefully scraped the snow from her shoes to avoid leaving a trail and noticed that Clara had the same routine. Both are used to the little problems of invisibility; Vanessa hasn't met anyone before who is.

She wants to tell Clara how grateful she is because Clara made Robin confess. That she wishes she had thought of it herself. But there is no time to talk now.

Vanessa looks around. No familiar is around, sniffing the air and transmitting information to its owner. She hopes that it doesn't mean that they're sneaking after the others.

They stop outside the door to Adriana's room. It is locked. Vanessa lets go of Clara's hand, and Clara seemingly dissolves into nothingness. Vanessa starts fiddling around with a bent hairpin. Picking locks was one of the few useful things that Wille taught her. She thinks gratefully of him and his career as a petty criminal. When the lock gives, she fumbles for Clara's hand and finds it. She can see her again.

They enter Adriana's study together. The lamp on the desk is on and casts a faint light. She recognizes quite a few of the things she saw two years ago, after another hairpin job.

The double doors in one corner of the room are closed. Vanessa is sweating in the thick jacket.

'It's just Viktor,' Clara says.

Vanessa is just about to ask what she means when the door opens behind them and Viktor enters from the hallway. They both go visible again and Viktor looks relieved. He doesn't say anything and Vanessa hopes that no news is good news. She opens the double doors.

And chokes back a scream. Someone is sitting on a chair in the dark bedroom. She turns the light on and sees that it is Adriana. Her eyes are closed and she is sitting in a wheelchair.

Vanessa turns and sees that Viktor and Clara look just as shocked.

'What has happened to her?' she whispers.

'All they told us was that she was ill,' Viktor replies quietly.

Vanessa is glad that Adriana is sleeping; glad that she doesn't have to find out right now exactly how ill she is.

She tries to push the wheelchair but the brake is on. It takes her a moment to work out how to operate it.

'Hold on to me,' she says to Viktor. 'I think I can make both you and Adriana invisible.'

Viktor puts his hand lightly on her shoulder and she releases more of her magic to envelop them all in the cloak of invisibility. Next to them, Clara also disappears.

Vanessa pushes Adriana into the study when the door to the hallway suddenly opens wide.

The young woman in the doorway must be Sigrid. She wears a white, knee-length dress patterned with tiny cherries. The full skirt swings around her hips as she walks into the room. The mink is perched on her shoulder and watches them with its tiny, beady eyes.

A boy and a girl follow Sigrid into the room. They've got to be Felix and Nejla.

Nejla checks the room. Then she puts out her hand and a fireball flares up. It hovers above her palm.

'It's pointless to stay invisible,' Sigrid says. 'My familiar sees you!'

'Yeah, we know,' Clara says wearily. She becomes visible.

Vanessa follows her example. Felix looks upset when he sees Viktor. Vanessa doesn't feel convinced in the slightest that Felix will be on their side.

Sigrid is clearly furious. The low-cut dress shows off the blush spreading up to her neck.

'Step away from Adriana!' she orders Vanessa.

'Sigrid . . .' Viktor begins.

'Let go of the wheelchair!' Sigrid says. 'And step away from Adriana now!'

The fireball in Nejla's hand is growing. It is a warning.

Vanessa steps away from the wheelchair. The mink runs down from Sigrid's shoulder, shoots across the room and climbs up on the bookshelf behind Vanessa.

'Adriana is not permitted to leave the manor house,' Sigrid says, looking at Viktor and Clara. 'And neither are you. What are you doing? We are meant to be closing the portal!'

'No, you're not,' Vanessa says. 'The Chosen Ones are to close the portal. And we must do it now.'

She fixes her eyes on Nejla and Felix.

'Please,' she says, trying to keep her voice calm and determined. 'You can pretend you never saw us.'

Nejla looks inscrutable. Her fireball is still burning steadily. Felix's gaze is lost somewhere behind Vanessa's head, as if she is still invisible.

'Let's go,' Viktor says.

Vanessa is just about to take hold of the wheelchair handles when something hard hits her in the chest. Her back slams into the bookshelf and the glass doors break. A stuffed owl hits the floor next to her. The mink is hissing from somewhere just above.

'You're going nowhere,' Sigrid says. She stands in precisely the same spot where Vanessa just stood.

Vanessa knew that Sigrid could move very quickly, but she is still shocked. She pats her back for injuries, grateful for Mom's thick jacket. At least she's not skewered on a shard of glass.

'Have you gone fucking mad?' Viktor shouts. Sigrid backs away. 'You have to let us go! The world is on the brink of destruction and only the Chosen Ones can save it!

'He's right,' Clara says. 'Walter doesn't even know how to go about closing the portal.'

'He does so! Walter—'

'Is lying to us!' Clara says sharply.

'No, he's not!' Sigrid says, staring angrily at her. 'He is our leader and leaders have to make tough decisions and—'

'We're going.' Vanessa gets up from the floor. 'We haven't got time for this.'

She turns to Nejla.

'Go ahead and set us on fire. But then there'll be no one who can stop the apocalypse.'

Vanessa sees movement out of the corner of her eye. Suddenly Sigrid is standing next to Adriana, pressing the sharp tip of a silver-colored letter opener against her neck. There is a small depression in the skin just where the knife tip rests. If Sigrid presses a little harder, the skin will break. The mink is scratching excitedly on top of the bookshelf.

'I'll do it,' Sigrid says. 'I'll kill her if you leave.'

Vanessa looks at Viktor, who is frowning.

'She isn't lying,' he says. 'She is desperate enough.'

Sigrid *looks* desperate. Her eyes are darting all around her.

'You must do what Walter tells you!' she says. 'He's the only one who knows how to save the world, don't you get that?'

Vanessa is close to panic. How much time do they have? Sigrid is keeping them here just because she can't admit to herself that Walter is wrong.

'Bullshit,' Nejla says.

The fireball goes out. She lowers her hand. 'I'm fucking sick of this,' she continues. 'I'm fucking sick of you, Sigrid. You're so false. You spy on the rest of us, and then run off to Walter with the information. Don't you think we've worked out what you're doing? And what you and he are doing?'

She sounds disgusted.

'It's not true!' Sigrid says.

'Let go of the knife,' Viktor says.

'No!' Sigrid screams, and Vanessa sees her press the knife so hard on Adriana's neck that the skin is going white. Sigrid doesn't even seem aware of what she is doing. She could easily puncture the large artery in the neck by mistake.

'Felix, go and get Walter!' she says.

He stares at his clenched right hand. He seems not to hear Sigrid.

'Felix!' she screams.

He takes a deep breath and drives his fist into the wall.

Vanessa feels a terrible pain in her hand, as if she has broken it. Clara screams. The knife drops from Sigrid's hand to the floor. Viktor leaps forward, pushes her away from the wheelchair so hard that she stumbles and falls. Grimacing with pain, Viktor grabs the knife and begins to push the wheelchair toward the door.

Vanessa follows and feels the pain in her hand fading. Clara is wiping away a few tears.

Nejla backs out of the room with them. She lets the ball of fire flare up again and keeps her eyes on Sigrid. Felix follows them. His face is contorted with pain and he holds his injured hand against his chest. Vanessa feels sorry for him. She knows exactly how much it hurts. She turns around to have a last look.

Sigrid is getting up. Tears, heavy with mascara, are pouring down her cheeks. The mink clings to her tights, trying to climb up her legs.

Vanessa dislikes her enormously but can't forget what Mona said about Walter.

'You can't trust Walter,' she says to Sigrid. 'You ought to get out of here, too.'

Sigrid says nothing, just shakes her head, and Vanessa knows she can't reach her. She lets the door close between them.

* * *

Minoo studies Walter. It's almost time.

'Have you forgotten our deal?' he says.

The deal? He means his threats. That he would hurt those she loves.

Love.

She likes the feeling, in theory. It makes her curious, interested. It is simultaneously so simple and so complex, so predictable and so unpredictable. She can still experience it when she returns into her own memories of being with Gustaf. She would very much like to explore it more. And she would prefer that neither Gustaf nor the others were harmed. It would be a shame.

'I haven't forgotten that you threatened me,' she says. 'But what can you do now? The darkness has fallen.'

Walter leans forward.

'I know I can't get at you,' he says. 'But I can get at Viktor and Clara. Would you like to have that on your conscience?'

Minoo looks at him. The moment is here. Now, he will be told.

'Your role will soon be over,' she says. 'The guardians have used you. Your circle never had a hope of closing the portal. The Chosen Ones are the Key.'

Walter goes rigid.

'Are the guardians telling you all that?' he asks.

It takes a moment for her to understand the question, and before she knows it she's answering.

She meets his eyes. His gray eyes that used to frighten her so much.

'I am saying it,' she says. 'The guardians are saying it. It is the same thing.'

* * *

Now.

Minoo's order arrives in Linnéa's mind.

She releases her power simultaneously with Anna-Karin and they look at each other in surprise. Their joint magic is stronger than ever before.

Anna-Karin's control thoughts ring out inside Linnéa.

DO NOT MOVE. DO NOT SPEAK.

Anna-Karin opens the door and they step into Walter's office hand in hand.

Linnéa sees him at once. He sits absolutely still, leaning forward a little. He doesn't look at all like the man she had imagined. His hair is grayer, but at the same time he looks younger, more athletic. And, even when paralyzed by Anna-Karin's magic, something about him makes Linnéa sense danger.

'Minoo!' Anna-Karin whispers.

Minoo, sitting relaxed on the sofa, turns her head to look at them. Linnéa feels suddenly cold. There is something wrong with the look in Minoo's eyes. It is like when she was examining their magic in Kärrgruvan. Only worse.

Minoo gets up and calmly picks up the three objects from the table. She walks past the armchair where Alexander is sleeping and stops in front of Linnéa and Anna-Karin.

'Come with me,' she says.

It is Minoo's voice, and yet it is not. She doesn't wait for them to answer, only walks out of the room. Linnéa exchanges a glance with Anna-Karin, who looks alarmed, but follows Minoo.

Linnéa casts a last glance at Walter.

He smiles, a barely noticeable twist of the corners of his mouth. And then he looks at her.

Panic freezes her to the floor. Walter gets up and the lynx emerges from behind the desk. The fucking lynx. She had forgotten about it.

'You are Linnéa Wallin, aren't you?' Walter's voice is deep and melodious.

She runs into the ballroom, crashes into Anna-Karin and gives her a push.

'Run!' she screams.

Minoo is standing at the door on the other side of the room. The light from one of the windows falls on her and makes the silver cross in her arms gleam.

741

'Come,' she says. 'This way.'

Linnéa runs toward her and doesn't dare look behind her. What if Walter is chasing them.

They know we're here! she calls out to Vanessa.

Chapter 100

Minoo hurries though the manor house with Anna-Karin and Linnéa at her heels. She is clutching the silver cross, the box and the skull to her chest.

Any moment now, Walter will follow them.

Everything is progressing as it should.

She runs through the hall and opens the front door. When the cold hits her, her magic immediately resets and coats her whole body with a layer of protective warmth.

Vanessa has responded to Linnéa's warning. She and the Ehrenskiöld twins are waiting in the yard.

At the same time, Nejla and Felix run toward the canal.

At the same time, Sigrid, crying and holding Henry in her arms, hurries through the hallways of the manor house.

At the same time, Walter is approaching the hall.

Everything is progressing as it should.

Minoo carries on walking across the snow. Linnéa and Anna-Karin are close behind her. She stops a few feet away from the others.

'Where is Walter?' Clara asks.

'Don't know,' Linnéa replies. 'But we must get out of here.'

Vanessa, Minoo thinks. *Come here.*

Vanessa looks surprised, but does as she is told.

Stand in a circle, Minoo thinks to the other Chosen Ones. They all look bewildered but obey her instruction.

'What are you doing?' Viktor says. 'We must leave now!'

Minoo considers him. And Clara. And the sleeping Adriana. What is about to happen is indeed regrettable. But necessary.

She turns, catches a glimpse of Walter in the open front door, outlined against the hall light. Then she wraps the Chosen Ones in her magic and they are on their way.

* * *

It feels like being thrown into a centrifuge, being whirled around at a breathtaking speed. All the air seems to be squeezed out of Vanessa's lungs.

Then, suddenly, she is lying on her back in the snow.

Her head is still spinning. She takes a deep breath. Tries to focus on the blue light that is dancing above her.

She sits up, feeling the cold snow against her hands. Linnéa and Anna-Karin are also about to get up. Minoo stands in front of them, her face looking like a strange mask in the light of a blue fireball hovering above her. She is dressed in jeans and a cotton sweater but doesn't seem to feel the cold.

'What did you do?' Vanessa asks her.

'Moved us.'

Vanessa tries to orientate herself and realizes that they are on the ledge outside the opening to the tunnel. The steep rock face is right behind her. The forest below is rustling quietly but it is too dark to see anything.

'Did you . . . *teleport* us here?' Vanessa asks.

'Yes,' Minoo confirms.

It is not just *how* they got here, but the fact that they got to this particular place. Minoo obviously knows about the tunnel leading to the portal.

'Come along,' Minoo says. 'We haven't got much time now.'

She takes Anna-Karin's hand and pulls her toward the opening in the mountain. Vanessa notes that the snow is melting in front of Minoo's feet.

'Hurry,' she tells them, without turning to look at them.

The fireball divides in two so that one floats along to light the way for Vanessa and Linnéa. The other one escorts Minoo and Anna-Karin into the tunnel.

Are you all right? Linnéa thinks to Vanessa.

Vanessa nods as she gets up on shaky legs, then helps Linnéa to stand and brushes the snow from her fake fur coat.

What's up with Minoo? she thinks to Linnéa. *How come she has all those new powers?*

I don't know, Linnéa says as she looks toward the tunnel. *I tried to read her mind a moment ago, but she's so deep inside her magic I'm not even sure how much of Minoo is left.*

Their fears flow from one to the other. The darkness is drawing closer, surrounding them.

If we follow Minoo now, we will be following the guardians, Vanessa thinks.

Do we have a choice?

Linnéa's dark eyes glitter in the light from the fireball. And Vanessa remembers when Mona traced the lines in her palm and talked about the love of her life, she who turned out to be Linnéa. *These two lines are intertwined all the way to the end.*

Is this the end?

At least they are together.

'Let's do this,' Linnéa says.

* * *

Minoo walks through the underground spaces. The blue light is there to guide Anna-Karin through the tunnels. Minoo would find the way without it. She no longer needs her eyes.

She makes the cross, the skull and the box float along in front of her. Her fingers touch the stone walls and she senses echoes of pain. So many of the guardians have existed in these tunnels for hundreds of years. They have waited. Tried to husband their waning powers. They never wanted to hurt, but now and then they have had to entice people into the caves to gain strength from their souls, their life-forces. All those who have disappeared over the years in the forests around Engelsfors have ended their lives here. Sacrificed for the good cause.

And when the Chosen Ones and their friends explored the

tunnels, the guardians had to take a little of their energies, too. Keep them weak, so that Minoo would think that the Council's circle was the stronger one. She had to be persuaded to believe that in order to make the choices that have ultimately taken her here. She understands all that now.

Anna-Karin is silent as she walks behind Minoo. She has stopped asking questions. But Minoo can read her mind anyway and sense her feelings. Anna-Karin is frightened about what will happen next but, most of all, she worries about Minoo. Which would have been touching, if Minoo had been able to feel touched.

The tunnel widens and they enter the first cave, the antechamber. The wall has collapsed. On the other side she picks up the beam of Nicolaus's flashlight. She senses the portal's vibrations and how they sing inside her.

The struggle will soon be over.

She walks through the antechamber, climbs over the low wall of broken stone, feels the sharp edges against her hands. When she steps down into the enormous cave on the other side, she makes the blue globe expand, glow more strongly and hover higher up, near the ceiling.

The walls and the floor of this space are completely smooth. The floor is an almost perfect circle, like a circus ring. This cave was created when the tear appeared. When they got in, thousands of years ago. They were strong, then. And they will be strong again. Stronger than ever.

The floor slopes toward the center. And there the circles are laid out, as perfect tracks in the perfect stone. The outer circle is four yards across. The inner circle is little more than a hollow, its diameter not much greater than Nicolaus's foot. He is standing next to it and is putting his flashlight away in his coat pocket. Minoo makes the objects float along to him.

She turns to watch as Anna-Karin enters the cave and looks around, wide-eyed. She takes a step forward. Another one. And then she stops.

Part Five

'I can't . . . I can't move,' she says.

'Don't worry,' Minoo says. 'It has to do with the levels of magic. Soon, I'll tell you some more, but first there is something Nicolaus and I must do.'

'What are you going to do?' Anna-Karin asks. 'And how did you know the portal is here?'

Minoo glances at her and turns away. So pathetic, really, that they thought they could hide it from her. But she forgives them. They understand so very little.

She walks across the smooth, shiny stone floor. As she crosses the outer circle, the vibrations become stronger. She can glimpse the tear as a faintly shimmering lightness.

She senses Linnéa and Vanessa entering the cave.

'What are you doing?' Vanessa calls out.

Minoo takes the box out of the air. Caresses the lacquered surface of the lid, traces the carved motif with her fingers. Walter is right. The craftsmanship is exquisite.

She bends and places the box in the inner circle, then pushes it down into the hollow. A click. Then a shudder runs through the stone floor. The wooden outer shell of the box cracks in front of her eyes, then crumbles and evaporates. A silver bowl with the elemental signs engraved in its flat bottom is left in the hollow.

The bowl.

Used six times.

This is the last time.

Linnéa tries to scream something but can't make herself heard. The magic is far too strong.

Minoo straightens up and allows the skull to settle inside the bowl. Once it was part of a woman who belonged to the Florentine Council in the fifteenth century. She volunteered. It was a glorious task. It still is. But the Chosen Ones of this time would never understand.

Minoo takes the cross. The silver dissolves, becomes a glittering swarm, like sparks from a bonfire. And then vanishes into thin air. The dagger hidden inside it is now resting in her hand. Despite the thousands of years that have passed since it was forged, its edge is still as clean and sharp as a razor blade. The ebony handle has not the slightest scratch.

The dagger.

Used six times.

This is the last time.

She gives it to Nicolaus.

'Are you afraid?' she asks.

'No,' he says. He grips the handle of the dagger.

He thinks about his daughter. He hopes that he will meet her again. But he is anxious about how the other Chosen Ones will react.

'They will understand,' Minoo says.

Nicolaus nods. Pulls off his scarf and puts it away.

Then he kneels with his back turned to the others. Minoo is the only one who sees him put the blade against his throat.

* * *

Anna-Karin can't see what Nicolaus is doing.

And then he collapses on his side, with the dagger still in his hand. A moist, gurgling sound comes from him as a dark liquid flows from his body. It doesn't look like blood in the blue light but it is. It flows, dark and oily along the sloping floor toward the bowl in the inner circle.

Anna-Karin can't move. And Minoo does nothing. Just stands there and watches Nicolaus bleed to death. Anna-Karin wants to force her to help him but her magic doesn't work either. She has to make an effort just to breathe. She doesn't understand. She cannot grasp why Nicolaus did this. Or how Minoo can look so calm as she walks toward them.

The air inside the circle has grown hazy. The haze thickens and becomes a mist.

Nicolaus's body twitches a few times and then the grayness swallows it. Anna-Karin can't see him anymore.

She wants to cry but her body lacks the strength. Vanessa and Linnéa stand on either side of her, just as immobile.

Minoo steps in front of them.

'The tear begins here,' she says. 'From here, it runs all the way to the limits of our world. The portal is there. We must get there in order to close it.'

She points to the thick, swirling mist inside the outer circle.

'We must travel into the Borderland. Strong magic was necessary to set up a stable link. A sacrifice. Nicolaus's task as our guide was precisely that. To sacrifice himself and guide us into the Borderland.'

Guide.

Their guide.

'He lived on borrowed time,' Minoo continues. 'He has been dying ever since he opened the grave and his memories returned. He told Linnéa about this.'

Anna-Karin glances at Linnéa, who confirms it with a barely perceptible nod.

She knew, then. Nicolaus knew. And neither of them told anyone else.

'Linnéa didn't know of his sacrifice,' Minoo tells Anna-Karin, as if she has read her mind. Then she points at the circles.

'It is time. We must go in.'

Anna-Karin looks at the mist, swirling ever faster in the blue light. She doesn't want to enter it. It's just about the last thing she would ever care to do. But she knows she will. That she must. This is what Grandpa spoke about. To be brave even though one is afraid.

Minoo places one of Anna-Karin's hands in Vanessa's, and the other in Linnéa's. Suddenly they can all move again.

'Now go,' Minoo says. 'Hurry. Wait at the outer circle. There is one more thing I must do.'

The three of them start moving forward. They struggle, as if against a strong headwind. They could have talked now but none of them speaks. They walk until they reach the edge of the mist. And stop.

Anna-Karin turns around.

Walter is entering the cave.

* * *

The black smoke is twisting around Walter. His black bird's eyes are fixed on Minoo.

Ever since he arrived in Engelsfors, the demons have been whispering to him, urging him to accept their blessing.

He has resisted them. The guardians had already promised him what he wanted.

But once Minoo had revealed the truth to him, he didn't hesitate. When Linnéa had run off, he invited the demons. 'The guardians have offered me all the power I can imagine in this world,' he told them. 'And I can imagine a great deal. How will you bid against that?' The demons replied that there are many other worlds, many other realities – you can take your pick.

Walter crosses the smooth stone floor and aims straight for Minoo. She senses the terror felt by the Chosen Ones.

His shirt has lost two buttons. Sigrid gripped his collar when he killed her in the hall. Until the very last moment, she refused to believe it was happening. He ripped out her soul and her life-force. Her lifeless body sagged and collapsed. Walter felt no remorse, only impatience. When he opened the front door, he caught a glimpse of the Chosen Ones just before they vanished into thin air. Now that he had added Sigrid's power to his own, it was easy to catch up with Viktor and Clara. He broke Viktor's neck with a touch, then took his powers and his soul. Clara made herself invisible and threw herself at him, but he simply shoved her away, opening up a deep wound as he did so. Deep enough to kill her. But he didn't bother with her frail life-force and her soul. He wanted to get to the caves and meet the Chosen Ones.

Now, Walter is only a few yards from Minoo. He is intoxicated by his own strength and can't wait for the victory he knows will be his. He wants to test Viktor's power in a way Viktor never did. Walter is considering the large amount of water in the human body. What if one froze it? Or made it boil?

'I should've done this long ago,' he says, reaching for Minoo.

She sees the blood spattered over his shirtfront and jacket. Clara's blood. She grabs his wrist and holds it firmly. The dial of his wristwatch cracks under her hand. She forces him down; his knees slam against the stone floor. He looks shocked.

'Yes,' she says. 'You should have killed me in my sleep. Maybe then you would have had a chance.'

Walter is afraid, for the first time.

He is not a worthy opponent.

No one is.

But she needs him. The demons have staked all their expectations on Walter and made him as strong as they possibly can. Their magic is in him. Magic that she intends to take from him.

Minoo sets Viktor's and Sigrid's souls free. Unlike Walter, she isn't a monster. Besides, she doesn't need them. Taking Walter's soul will be more than enough. He fills her. Makes her even stronger. She observes his memories as they pass. All the lives he has destroyed, all the pain he has inflicted, all the pleasure power has given him.

She feels the weight of his soul, pulls, and it comes loose. Walter doesn't scream. His pain is too intense. His mouth gapes, his eyes are wide open.

Minoo doesn't take his soul, she incinerates it. Turns it into pure energy. The final boost of energy that she needs.

Walter's eyes roll back so that only the whites are showing. She lets go of his wrist and he slumps sideways.

Around her, the magic grows. All the powers of the guardians are concentrated inside her now. She is their anchor.

She turns to face the other Chosen Ones, who are staring at her.

'What happened?' Anna-Karin asks.

'The demons had blessed him,' Minoo says.

'Is he . . . ?' Linnéa begins. 'Have you *killed* him?'

'Yes,' Minoo says.

She has in fact done more than kill him. She has obliterated him. But the others would hardly see the distinction.

Minoo walks toward them, then takes Linnéa's hand. The four of them form a chain now. She turns to the swirling mist.

'Now,' Minoo says.

Together they walk into the Borderland.

The Borderland

CHAPTER 101

Rebecka feels hands gripping her shoulders and shaking her. I survived, she thinks. I survived. But how?

She opens her eyes.

It is Ida who is holding her shoulders. Now she lets go and throws her arms around Rebecka, hugging her tightly.

'We found you!'

Rebecka hugs Ida, but awkwardly. She is so confused. Everything around them is gray.

And then she sees him.

Large, blue eyes. Black, unruly hair. Rings in his eyebrows, his ears, his lower lip. A leather strap around his neck. Black T-shirt with the word NIN on it, worn over a long-sleeved top. Torn jeans and large black boots.

Elias.

Elias, who is dead.

Suddenly, Rebecka isn't as certain that she has survived.

'It wasn't G,' Ida says in that falsetto tone of hers that always hurt Rebecka's ears. They let go of each other. 'I mean, it wasn't G who killed you. It was Max. He had murdered Elias and taken his power to look like different people. So G didn't do it, it was Max disguised as G. But no one suspected G – at least, the police didn't. Everyone thought you had jumped because you wanted to, except the Chosen Ones—'

'Calm down,' Elias interrupts. 'Give her a break.'

He glances worriedly at Rebecka.

'Do you even know who we are?' he asks.

755

Rebecka nods, feeling confused. She is still trying to grasp what Ida has just told her.

Gustaf pushed her off the roof. But it wasn't Gustaf. She didn't believe it was him and it turns out she was right. She feels so relieved that she almost forgets about being dead.

Dead. Murdered by Max. Max, who Minoo had a crush on.

'How do you feel?' Ida asks.

'I'm not sure. Am I really dead?'

'We all are,' Elias says.

Rebecka looks at Ida. And she remembers the night of the blood-red moon, when Ida was levitating above the graveled area in Kärrgruvan. And remembers, too, the warning they were given not to trust anyone. Then something else comes back to her. The figure in a hoodie who observed her on Olsson's Hill. And then followed her to the City Mall.

'Was Max the evil we were warned against?'

'Yes, he was,' Ida says. 'But not just him. It's such an insanely complicated story . . .'

Abruptly, she stops speaking, and instead scans the grayness behind Rebecka.

'What's wrong?' Elias says. 'Is it the thing you told me about?'

Rebecka turns to look but sees nothing. Then she shudders. There is something out there. Something that wants to get at them.

'Run!' Ida screams.

* * *

All that was needed was one step.

Everything in front of Linnéa is still and gray.

'Do you feel it?' Vanessa asks.

'Yes,' Linnéa says.

It is a note so deep it is not heard but felt as a vibration. She became aware of it as soon as she stepped into the round cave room with the circles. Now it has grown more powerful.

Looking back, she can see the lit cave through a whirling haze.

Minoo lets go of Linnéa. Linnéa looks at her hand. Minoo used that hand to hold Walter down when she killed him. Minoo *killed* him.

'Is this the Borderland?' Vanessa asks.

'Yes, it is the outermost limit of our world,' Minoo says. 'A territory between our world and others.'

Linnéa scans the grayness. Is this where Elias is? Where he has been for two years? She tries to comfort herself with what Ida has said about how time passes more quickly when you're dead.

'Where is the portal?' Anna-Karin asks.

Minoo points.

At first, Linnéa feels that this place lacks all perspective. But then, far away, she sees a black dot. The portal.

Vanessa shrieks when Nicolaus emerges out of the grayness in front of them.

He looks the same as he used to. It is impossible to imagine that he slit his throat with a dagger some moments ago. That he bled to death on the floor of the round cave. It is impossible to think of him as dead.

But it isn't hard at all to be angry with him, Linnéa realizes.

'*Memento mori,*' she says. 'Now I understand what you meant by that. For how long have you known what being our guide would mean to you?'

Nicolaus pulls his fingers through his hair.

'It was part of my original pact with the guardians,' he says. 'The one that was set up between them and me just after Matilda's death.'

Linnéa is aware that he has sacrificed everything for their sake, for the sake of the world. That his entire long life, as well as his death, has been a sacrifice. Even so, she is still angry.

Anna-Karin's eyes are full of tears. 'You lied to us.'

'Yes,' Nicolaus says, looking pained. 'I've lied even more than you know.'

Anna-Karin takes a step backward, as if she has been hit.

No. Not him as well.

Vanessa's thought pierces Linnéa. She feels the same. Not another betrayal.

'I've lived for hundreds of years, knowing that I caused my daughter's death,' Nicolaus says. 'I couldn't let her down once more.'

'What do you mean?' Linnéa asks. 'You told us that you didn't trust Matilda.'

'That is what she told me to say to you,' Nicolaus says. 'I've been following her instructions ever since she appeared to me in a dream. The night when my memories returned.'

'You owe us a fucking explanation,' Linnéa says.

Nicolaus looks helplessly at Minoo. She radiates patience, perhaps boredom.

'You had to be made to distrust Matilda and the guardians,' she says. 'You had to make all the choices you did so that you would end up just here, just at this time. So that you're able to save the world.'

Linnéa remembers how, in the dream, Matilda had explained that the guardians were always trying to read different futures and determine what different choices might lead to. That they were always trying to foresee the effects of every little detail.

All the time, Linnéa had believed that she had resisted. Questioned. Followed the course she herself had set.

But she had been doing what the guardians had wanted.

All the time.

They had directed her and the other Chosen Ones through the *Book of Patterns*, through Matilda, through Nicolaus and through Minoo. And Linnéa had reacted throughout just as the guardians had calculated that she would. She had been utterly predictable.

'I realize that this is difficult to accept,' Minoo says. 'But now we're all here.'

She points.

It takes a moment before Linnéa understands what she is seeing. Who they are, the people who are running through the Borderland.

Rebecka is first. And, behind her, Ida and Elias.

Elias.

She can't move. And then she can. She runs toward him and throws her arms around him, feels him holding her and pressing her close. She picks up a light in the corner of her eye, hears Ida scream something and then she feels someone give her a push in the back. But she doesn't care.

Because everything is all right again.

She closes her eyes and breathes in his smell. All the memories she thought she might have lost wash over her again.

She has missed him so much she thought she would also die. But it is not until now that she really understands how great her loss has been. Now that he is with her again.

'Linnéa,' he says.

His voice. How could she even for a second believe that she had forgotten it? It is part of her. He is a part of her.

Linnéa looks into his blue eyes. He is crying. And she realizes she is crying, too. The tears just flow. With him she was never afraid of crying.

'How did you get here?' he asks. 'You're not dead, are you?'

'No,' she says, and shakes her head. 'I've missed you so much. And I never believed that you killed yourself.'

Elias strokes her hair. Such a familiar touch.

'Ida told me,' he says. 'And she said that it was you who found me . . .'

He hugs her again and she clings to him, to his washed-out T-shirt, feels his shoulder blades through the material.

'It's OK,' she says. 'You're here now. I'm here.'

And, in that instant, she wonders what 'here' is.

Because they are no longer in the Borderland.

They are standing in a room with white-limed walls and a dark, stone-flagged floor. A gloomy light filters in through the small windows. Outside, it's pouring with rain.

'Where are we?' she asks.

'I have no idea,' Elias says.

* * *

Minoo's irritation is growing.

This isn't going according to plan.

She looks at the spot where Elias, Linnéa and Ida stood before they disappeared. The area of light has already faded away. Black smoke is whirling around over there. The others can't see it but may be aware of it as an invisible something, a whisper at most. It's the guardians that inhabit the Borderland and have kept the souls of Ida, Elias and Rebecka under control.

Minoo sends the guardians away and watches as they flit through the zone. They have really become lax. And stupid as well. The idea was that they should bring Ida, Rebecka and Elias here, not frighten them away.

But now Ida has dragged Elias and Linnéa along to some other place. They could be absolutely anywhere. In *any time*. And the portal must be closed. Closed soon.

'Where did they go?' Vanessa says. She looks alarmed. 'They just vanished!'

'They will not be in any danger,' Minoo says. 'They will be back.'

They will be back because the Chosen Ones are always drawn to each other. Sooner or later, they will turn up. But it must not be too late.

Minoo watches while Rebecka hugs everyone in turn: Anna-Karin, Vanessa and Nicolaus. Now and then, Rebecka glances at Minoo.

This isn't going according to plan.

But events in the Borderland have always been the hardest to read. The zone is very unstable. It has always been the weakest link in their plans.

Minoo looks back at the cave. The blue light over there is growing fainter all the time.

'Minoo?' Rebecka says.

Minoo looks at her. She hasn't changed. She looks like the same Rebecka to whom they gave the task in Kärrgruvan.

You must lead them, Rebecka. They won't like it, but they need you. It is your task to deepen the bond between you. But it is our secret. No one else must know that I have given you this charge. Do you understand?

That was what she had to believe. Until she had to die.

Minoo is taken by surprise when Rebecka puts her arms around her. She quickly reminds herself what you're meant to do next. She hugs Rebecka because it's quite unnecessary to worry her in any way.

'Minoo, what's the matter?' Rebecka says as she pulls away.

'It's the magic of the guardians,' Vanessa says behind her.

Rebecka looks baffled. She died long before the Chosen Ones were told anything about the guardians. She doesn't know that they are the ones who have kept her here.

'Come with me,' Minoo says. 'We have to go to the portal.'

'But what about Linnéa and—' Vanessa begins.

'They will find us,' Minoo says. 'I promise.'

She starts walking toward the black dot.

'Where is Matilda?' Nicolaus asks as he follows her. 'The guardians assured me that I would meet her one last time.'

'You will,' Minoo says.

To tell the truth, she isn't sure. Not sure at all. Only a small discontinuity could be enough and then everything could go wrong. They have taken such huge risks. Staked everything on one card.

'How are you?' Nicolaus asks. He sounds concerned. 'The magic of the guardians seems to affect you a great deal.'

'Yes,' Minoo says. 'It makes me stronger.'

Vanessa and Anna-Karin walk a bit behind them. Minoo hears them both trying to explain to Rebecka what has happened since she died.

Suddenly, their voices are cut short. Vanessa's and Anna-Karin's energies disappear.

Minoo turns to look.

They are gone. Only Rebecka is left. And she seems stunned.

'What happened?' Minoo asks.

'This freckled girl turned up out of nowhere,' Rebecka says. 'She . . . took them.'

Nicolaus looks baffled too and glances from Rebecka to Minoo.

'Was that Matilda?' he says. 'But I don't understand . . . why?'

Minoo doesn't reply.

For the first time in a very long while she no longer feels in control. She hates it.

* * *

Linnéa goes to one of the windows and looks outside. Rain is running down the bulging panes of glass and makes the details of the outside world blur. She can just make out a dark forest.

'How did we end up here?' she asks.

'Something was chasing us and—'

'Chasing?' Linnéa interrupts, immediately worrying about Vanessa.

'I don't know what it is but there is some kind of thing around in the Borderland,' Elias says.

Linnéa shivers. But surely Minoo will protect the others?

'I think Ida pushed us,' Elias says. 'She did it to me once before and we ended up outside the school . . . Where is she, by the way?'

They look around the room. There isn't much in it. An open hearth. A table and, next to it, a simple wooden armchair. A door that is half open. The only sound is the rain.

Linnéa walks along to the chair. She can't think why it should make her feel so ill at ease. She reaches out for it and shrieks when her hand passes straight through the back of the chair.

'What the fuck was that?' she asks Elias.

'The same thing happens when I try to touch something,' Elias says, pushing his hand through the table top to make the point. 'But you're alive, so maybe we are in another time? Ida said it could happen.'

Another time? Linnéa looks around. When could it be? She doesn't see any wall sockets or light switches.

'How do we get back to the Borderland?' she asks. 'We must close the portal.'

'I don't know. Last time, we just ended up there again,' Elias says. 'I think all we can do is wait. And if we're in the past, maybe there's no need to rush.'

He tries to smile. Linnéa knows she should worry more, but it's hard to think about anything except that she is with Elias. She studies him, trying to take in every detail. He looks exactly as he did the day he died, and at the same time she thinks he looks younger. He is, in a way. He has stayed sixteen while she is two years older.

Two years.

How much does he know about what has happened?

'Ida has told me everything,' he says.

She had almost forgotten that he used to do that. Start to speak about what she had just been thinking about. And he didn't need magic, either.

'She told me about my parents,' he continues.

A blast of strong wind hits the window; the rain is drumming hard against it.

'It's so fucked up,' Elias says. 'How could they believe that I wanted them to murder people? And that Mom would do that to you . . .'

He falls silent. Tugs at the sleeves of his top. Linnéa recalls

763

what she had said to Helena and Krister in the gym. *How can you believe that he is the one who drives all this? Your son Elias? Elias, who took care never to hurt anyone? Who never even hit back?* They had looked as if they might begin to understand. Seconds later, Olivia killed them both.

'Grief does strange things to people,' Linnéa says.

'Like, to Olivia?'

'Yes,' Linnéa nods. 'And me, too. When I found out that it was Max who had killed you, I went to his place ready to shoot him.'

'Ida told me,' Elias says. 'Fucking stupid thing to do.'

'I know.'

'I would've done exactly the same.'

'I know,' Linnéa says. 'And you wouldn't have been able to pull the trigger, either.'

They are silent for a while. She thinks about the others in the Borderland. Wonders if they're even there anymore. How much time do they have?

'Ida told me about what happened on Canal Bridge,' Elias says finally. 'And she said that Erik was caught.'

'All three of them were convicted,' Linnéa says. 'Erik got five years. But, you know, the best thing was that Anna-Karin made him confess everything. Now everyone knows what he is really like.'

A huge smile breaks out on Elias's face. His beautiful smile. She must smile back.

'I wish I could have seen that!' he laughs.

'I wish you could have too,' Linnéa says.

'There's so much I've missed. Like this thing with *Vanessa Dahl.*'

Linnéa's smile dies away and she no longer meets his eyes. Just watches the raindrops run down the windowpanes.

'I'm sorry,' he says. 'I didn't think. Ida did say that you aren't together anymore.'

Linnéa wonders again how many scenes from her life have

been witnessed by Ida. Was she even around that time, on the gravel road?

'What happened?' Elias asks.

Linnéa shrugs.

'I had to end it. For her sake. Look, you know what I'm like. A fucking mess.'

'Aren't you in love with her anymore?'

'Yes, I am.' Linnéa studies the rain running down the window. 'We are in love with each other. But sometimes it doesn't work out. You have to accept it.'

'Bullshit!'

She stares at him and is stunned to see how angry he is.

'You love her and she loves you . . . and you simply chicken out?'

Linnéa is frustrated. She had thought he'd understand. He of all people.

'She could never stand being with me in the long run.'

'So you dumped her so you wouldn't be dumped? Brilliant!'

Yes, Elias does understand her. Better than anyone. And it hurts.

'I'd just ruin Vanessa as well! She deserves someone better than me!'

'Isn't that up to Vanessa? You wrecked a chance of being happy because you were scared of becoming unhappy. You must see how totally fucked up this is!'

'Yes, it's fucked up!' Linnéa says. '*I* am fucked up!'

'Yes, you are!' Elias says. 'But you're amazing, too. You have always been there for me. Why couldn't you be there for Vanessa? Sure, it might end one day. But, Linnéa, *everything* ends. Sooner or later. Don't you get that?'

His voice breaks.

Linnéa can't argue with him because what he says is true.

'Excuse me . . .' a familiar voice says.

Linnéa and Elias turn to face Ida who stands in the doorway.

'I just have to say that Elias is absolutely right,' she says as she walks into the room. 'I've seen you and Vanessa together and, seriously, Linnéa . . .'

She falls silent while she quickly dries her eyes.

'I don't even have a chance to experience all that!' she continues. 'Elias doesn't either. And you're throwing it all away! I mean, seriously! Get your act together and sort this out!'

'Exactly,' Elias says.

Linnéa stares at the two of them.

'I'm glad you two agree,' she says.

Elias puts his arms around her and she leans her head against his shoulder. She is thoroughly shaken. Elias's words have hit her hard. She feels as if she has been running toward an abyss and he has made her stop right at the edge.

She has been such an idiot.

'Oh no,' Ida says. 'Not him.'

Linnéa straightens up.

A man with shoulder-length blonde hair and a blonde moustache comes into the room. Linnéa notes how expensive his clothes look. At a guess, seventeenth-century style. Member of the nobility.

He stands and stares blankly at the room, obviously not seeing them.

'Who is he?' Linnéa asks.

'Baron Henrik Ehrenskiöld,' Ida says with obvious distaste. 'Alexander's and Adriana's great-great-great-whatever.'

Henrik Ehrenskiöld walks into the room, stops at the table, touches it with his hand and then he gazes at the chair. He looks pained. Then he bursts into tears.

'Nicolaus told us about him,' Linnéa says. 'He is the one who promised to see to it that Matilda would live and then sent her off to burn at the stake.'

'I thought it must be him,' Ida says. 'What an asshole.'

'Yes, it was he who did it,' a voice says. 'But it wasn't his idea. He just obeyed orders.'

They all turn toward the voice.

The Borderland

And see Matilda in front of the window. Vanessa and Anna-Karin stand next to her. Vanessa looks completely confused. And then she and the others vanish behind the mist that sweeps into the room. Linnéa clings to Elias and feels Ida grip her arm.

'Vanessa!' Linnéa calls out as the mist closes in around them.

Lively dance music at a distance. Laughter; drunken voices shouting.

'What's happening?' Linnéa whispers as she tries to see through the veils of mist.

'This is what I've had to put up with all the time,' Ida says.

The mist clears. Vanessa is there and Linnéa takes her hand. Anna-Karin and Matilda are facing them.

'Where are we?' Elias says.

Linnéa has never seen the place so alive.

It is a light summer evening. A smell of grease is coming from the hot dog stand. The mosquitoes are humming. People are criss-crossing the yard where the Chosen Ones stand. Now and then someone runs straight *through* them.

Five guys in shiny, baby-blue shirts are playing on the bandstand in the dance pavilion. They have all had their hair dyed blonde. Couples and groups of girls are dancing to the music. Two women with white T-shirts under long, flowery dresses stroll past just behind Matilda.

'Kärrgruvan,' Anna-Karin tells them.

'That's right,' says Matilda. 'And we have a lot to talk about.'

CHAPTER 102

Rebecka looks at Minoo and Nicolaus, who are walking in front of her through the grayness. Neither has said a word since Vanessa and Anna-Karin disappeared.

She fixes her eyes on the black dot they are walking toward.

It is the portal that Minoo mentioned. And Vanessa talked about guardians and said that it is their magic that makes Minoo so weird. Anna-Karin got around to explaining something about stopping an apocalypse, and something about demons.

Rebecka tries to understand but feels as if she is doing a thousand-piece jigsaw without a clue what it's meant to look like.

'Minoo!' she calls.

Minoo doesn't reply. Rebecka stops walking.

'You've got to tell me something about what's going on.'

Minoo turns and looks at Rebecka with her empty eyes.

'I understand that you feel at a loss.' She comes a little closer. 'There's so much you don't know. After all, you've been dead for two years.'

It feels like being struck across the face. Rebecka feels dazed.

Two years.

Moa must be five, and Alma will have started proper school. Anton and Oskar are teenagers.

She has missed two years of their lives. And she will never see them again. Never see them grow up; never learn what happens to them. These thoughts are indescribably painful and lead on to other thoughts that she has tried to keep at bay.

Mom and Dad.

They believe that she took her own life. Are they blaming themselves? The last time she spoke to Dad she more-or-less hung up on him.

Gustaf.

It doesn't hit her until now that he must believe it as well. That she wanted to die. Wanted to leave him.

Her pain is so overwhelming that she doesn't know what to do with herself.

Then she feels Minoo's cool hand against her cheek. The pain is dampened down, and then goes away altogether.

'Did you do that?' Rebecka asks.

'Of course,' Minoo says. 'You were suffering. It seemed unnecessary.'

Rebecka can't believe her ears.

'Those were my feelings! You can't just change them!'

'Feelings are very interesting, but just now, too much is at stake. You must be focused.'

'I can't be focused when I don't know what all this is about! And what's the matter with you, Minoo? I don't recognize you at all!'

Minoo blinks. Rebecka hasn't seen her do that since their arrival here.

'You want to know what has happened?' Minoo asks.

'Yes!'

Minoo nods. Then, before there is time to react, she has put her hand on Rebecka's forehead and Minoo's memories flood into her mind.

* * *

Ida is so glad that she wasn't around at the time when Kärrgruvan was where all Engelsfors went to have a good time. The place is disgusting. Everything is gross: the music, the way people behave.

She looks at Matilda. 'I think you should explain yourself.'

769

'At last I can,' Matilda says. 'You know those invisible beings that were chasing us? They were guardians. I've been their hostage since I died.'

Ida's irritation feels wrong now. Hostage?

'I hated them at first,' Matilda continues. 'Later, I learned to hide my hatred and pretended to collaborate with them. I waited and watched. And hoped I'd have a chance to contact you, the next Chosen Ones, and warn you about their plans. The first time I tried was at the ball for the eighth-graders in middle school.'

She looks straight at Ida. All the others do, too.

Ida rummages in her memory. It had been a horrible evening. She had made up her mind to go all out to get G, but because the food was so vile she hadn't eaten a thing and had passed out on the bathroom floor. And when she'd left the bathroom, she'd seen Rebecka and Gustaf kissing.

An evening she'd rather forget. But she has no memory of what Matilda is talking about.

'The guardians caught me afterward,' Matilda says. 'They kept me captive. I managed to escape a few times and tried to reach you again. Once was in the dining area when you managed to keep me out. And once in your bathroom, when I warned you of dangers to come. And, just at the start of the séance, when you called me. I tried to warn you of the *Book of Patterns* and the guardians. I tried to warn all of you.'

Ida looks at Matilda, remembering how she hated it when Matilda tried to get into her head. But she had wanted to help all along. To save her.

'The séance, it was really you who was moving the glass then?' Linnéa asks.

'Yes, but the guardians got hold of me again. That was when the glass exploded. Afterward, all my words were really theirs.'

Her ice-blue eyes darken.

'The guardians used me as a puppet to communicate with you. They realized that you would be more likely to trust another Chosen One. Everything that you and my father have heard me say has been dictated by the guardians.'

She sounds so bitter. Ida understands perfectly. She knows what it's like to lose control of yourself and be manipulated by someone else.

'By now, you know the truth about most things,' Matilda says. 'And I'll tell you the rest.'

A meltingly romantic saxophone solo drifts out from the pavilion. And, nearby, the sound of someone throwing up. Ida turns away, revolted.

'The guardians gave Henrik Ehrenskiöld his orders through the *Book of Patterns*,' Matilda continues. 'They wanted me to be burnt alive. Or else, the ritual wouldn't be complete.'

'What ritual?' Vanessa asks.

'The ritual I had to undertake to give up my powers. The guardians took me through the first steps. But never mentioned that my death was the last step in it.'

The music stops and the singer asks if there are any singles here tonight; tells them that the next dance is for them.

'Henrik was not evil,' Matilda says. 'But the guardians came up with their usual threat. That the world would end unless he did what he was told. That's what they told me to make me give up my powers. But it wasn't true. I *could* have closed the portal. All this could have been dealt with when I was alive.'

* * *

Rebecka blinks.

She feels the same as always. Yet, everything is different.

Rebecka has Minoo's memories of all that has happened between her own death and up to three weeks ago. Minoo's memories and the memories of others. Rebecka's own terrified face, seen through Max's eyes. The bird's-eye view of Engelsfors, seen through the eyes of Adriana's raven. Erik Forslund's reflection in Linnéa's window, seconds before he smashes it with a baseball bat. A pale boy with ash-blonde hair and blue eyes whose name is Viktor. Rebecka has never met him, but Minoo has, and Minoo has also seen his sister's memories of him.

Rebecka knows it all.

She knows far too much.

Gustaf, crying after Rebecka's funeral. *She was the best thing that ever happened to me. I'm so fucking alone without her. I don't recognize my own life anymore.*

Gustaf.

He and Minoo are together now.

They have kissed and they have had sex. And Rebecka knows exactly how much Minoo loves him.

The knowledge is tearing Rebecka apart. She knows how Gustaf has suffered and how bitterly he has missed her. And how much he has needed someone's love. She also knows how guilty Minoo felt and how irresistible the attraction proved in the end. Rebecka is aware that Minoo and Gustaf need each other.

Still, for her, it feels as if it was only a few hours ago that she was standing on the school steps facing Gustaf.

I love you. You won't forget that, will you?

Conflicting emotions pull at her. She envies Minoo, who is still alive, and she is wildly jealous of her being with Gustaf. At the same time, she has experienced Minoo's happiness and feels relieved that Gustaf isn't alone and that Minoo isn't either. And she is grateful to Minoo for taking the risk of telling him the truth. Now he no longer has to struggle with the thought that she killed herself.

'Is it too much?' Minoo scrutinizes her with her head tilted a little to the side. As if Rebecka is some kind of guinea pig. 'I can take something away if you'd rather,' she adds helpfully.

'No,' Rebecka says. 'I'm not going to let you do anything else to me.'

'As you like.'

The Borderland

The last memory transferred to Rebecka was of Minoo being locked into her room in the manor house. Rebecka guesses that she has been inside the black smoke since then. And she understands why. She has also felt the pain Minoo experienced and sensed the relief that the magic of the guardians could give.

She understands Minoo.

But she is convinced that this isn't right. Minoo is being devoured by the magic of the guardians. She is disappearing.

'We must go,' Minoo says.

Together with Nicolaus, they walk through the Borderland. Minoo seems to be listening to voices that Rebecka can't hear.

They come closer and closer to the black dot. Now, Rebecka sees that it is a gaping hole opening into blackness.

A hole that is slowly expanding.

* * *

Anna-Karin tries to ignore the music and the loud voices. She wants to grasp what Matilda has just told them.

'But, why didn't the guardians let you close the portal?' she asks. 'Do they *want* the demons to enter?'

'Not at all,' Matilda says. 'The demons hate the guardians and would like to destroy them together with the rest of this world.'

A group of middle-aged women are running toward the dance pavilion. They are yelling wildly and one of them rushes straight through Anna-Karin. She doesn't feel a thing; just catches a whiff of cigarette smoke and mosquito repellent. And then the woman is gone.

'I shall have to start from the beginning,' Matilda says. 'Magic is a form of living energy. It's part of nature. Once, the magic in our world was like a working ecosystem. It was based on balance. Earth and air. Fire and water. Wood and metal. But when the demons got here and brought their own magic, the balance was disturbed. The first Chosen One was our magic's attempt to restore balance. The system had been disrupted by the portals and now there was a chance to close them. A Key.'

She pauses briefly.

'The guardians decided to use the Key,' she continues. 'They too wanted the portals closed but failed to foresee a side effect. They tend to be blind to their own weaknesses. Only in the fifteenth century, when the sixth portal was closed, did they begin to see the connection.'

Matilda looks very serious.

'The guardians don't belong in this world. For each closed portal, a connection to their original world disappeared, and with it some of their power. That's why they've grown weaker and weaker through the millennia. If I had closed the last portal, they would have died.'

'Last thing they'd have wanted,' Linnéa says.

'Indeed,' Matilda agrees. 'They became completely obsessed with finding a solution to their dilemma. How to close the portal to the demons without losing the last of their power. And they found an answer. Their new insight was that, if they split my powers, by the next magic epoch, a new aberration would occur. Instead of one Chosen One, a Circle would make up the Key. One witch for each element. And one who would have none. A witch without any connection to the magic system of this world. Someone in whom the guardians could invest all their power. A kind of magic anchor.'

'Minoo,' Anna-Karin says.

Matilda nods.

Anna-Karin already knew that Minoo was unique in that she could handle the magic of the guardians.

But it makes a great difference to know that the guardians *created* her for that purpose. Not to save the world but themselves. To hang on to their powers through her. As if Minoo was an object, a tool they could use.

A tool that they're using right now, Anna-Karin thinks.

'It wasn't enough for her to exist,' Matilda goes on. 'The

guardians had to persuade Minoo to let them in, to accept their powers willingly. To make her give in fully, they had to isolate her from you.'

Anna-Karin is sick at heart. The guardians have manipulated them and got their own way every time.

'The guardians can remain in this world if Minoo is with you when you close the portal,' Matilda says. 'When you do, the magic balance will be disturbed again. The elemental magic will be further weakened and the power of the guardians stronger than ever before. Next, they will take over mankind as they have taken over Minoo. Every human being will become a toy for the guardians to play with until they get bored. They will become fed up with their games, sooner or later. Nothing is as boring as absolute power.'

Matilda falls silent and Anna-Karin suddenly becomes aware of the song that is playing. She recognizes it. Mom used to play the record when Anna-Karin was little.

'Look, I'm pretty new to all this,' Elias says. 'But can't we just leave the portal?'

'I'm afraid not,' Matilda says. 'Once Minoo entered the Borderland, she brought with her *all* the power of the guardians. Now the magic balance has shifted in the Borderland as well. And that makes it possible for the demons to get in. Which is precisely what they are trying to do now.'

Anna-Karin tries to make sense of all this. The Chosen Ones should save the world. But now they have to choose between two types of destruction. Either let the demons ruin the world straightaway, or let the guardians do it when they have had enough of their puppets.

'It seems the guardians have won, then,' Linnéa says. 'And we are just pawns in their game.'

'That's not true and you must never think that!' Matilda sounds very determined. 'The guardians have taken risks throughout. They have forced you into practically impossible situations and, every time, you've got out of them on your own merits. They haven't been able to predict everything you've done and you have a free will! It is thanks to your skills and courage and solidarity that you have succeeded in—'

'What does all that matter?' Linnéa interrupts. 'We still have no other options!'

'Yes, you do,' Matilda says. 'Close the portal without Minoo in the Borderland.'

'How do we do that?' Ida asks. 'Do we shove her into one of the lit-up spots and hope she doesn't get back from wherever before we've closed the portal?'

'There is only one way to deal with this,' Matilda says gravely. 'Together, you are stronger than the guardians. Together, you can kill Minoo.'

A wind blows through the trees in the parkland and rips a straw hat decorated with sunflowers from the head of a young girl.

'Never,' Anna-Karin says.

'Not a fucking chance,' Linnéa says.

'The guardians have taken her over completely,' Matilda says. 'I believe there mightn't be anything of your Minoo left—'

'Listen,' Ida butts in. 'This isn't up for discussion.'

'And Minoo is still somewhere in there,' Anna-Karin says. She refuses to consider anything else.

'We'll think of an alternative,' Vanessa says. 'You can help or not.'

'There's nothing more I can do for you,' Matilda says. 'Or for the world. I gave up my powers long ago.'

Gray veils of mist are gathering around them.

'I hope you can find that alternative,' Matilda tells them. 'I truly hope so. Just remember that the fate of the world hangs on what you decide.'

The mist is rising.

Then, suddenly, Anna-Karin catches sight of something through the haze.

The Borderland

A couple, a man and a woman, are leaving the dance pavilion. They walk close together, with their arms around each other.

He looks better in real life than in the photos. He is a little shorter than her, his wavy hair is dark blonde and his eyes a deep, clear green. Her long hair is pulled back in a ponytail and her smile is the same as Anna-Karin's own.

He whispers something in her ear and she laughs. Deep inside Anna-Karin a memory awakens. That, sometimes, when she was very little, Mom would laugh like that.

They pass by so close that she can smell Mom's perfume. She watches as they walk, wrapped up in each other, toward the gate.

And then the mist closes in around her.

Chapter 103

The tone from the portal vibrates in Minoo's body. She stands in front of it and could reach out with her hand into the opening. Take a step forward into it. It is as tall as she is and widening steadily. Inch by inch, the grayness of the zone is corroded and replaced by blackness.

Only Minoo can see the movement in the deep dark. Inside the portal, the demons are writhing, desperate to get in. And they will; it is only a matter of time. Now, after thousands of years, they have a chance to enter without the help of one of their blessed ones.

Minoo is attracting them, as a positive charge attracts a negative.

Once, they were the same.

Rebecka and Nicolaus have stopped behind her.

'I hear them,' Nicolaus says quietly.

'Me, too,' Rebecka says.

Minoo senses their fear. And she registers the whispered messages the demons send into the heads of Rebecka and Nicolaus. They try to frighten them by saying that they can't close the portal, that the guardians are tricking them, that all they need to do is to do nothing at all.

'Don't listen to them.' Minoo blocks the demons' magic so that it can't reach Rebecka and Nicolaus.

Now she hears the voices of the demons inside her own head and senses their loathing.

You betrayed your own kind. You permitted yourselves to change, to become degraded. You formed alliances with beings that were far below you. You gave yourselves a name. You even dared give us a name. How can we be named? Perfection can't be contained within a name. Your very existence is an insult to us. We will destroy you. We will destroy the pathetic world you are hiding in. We will exterminate you and then forget that this failed experiment ever existed.

Minoo knows that it could happen.

They have seen it happen in innumerable possible futures.

She remembers one of these futures that didn't come to pass.

The gym in the school. Olivia smiles. The glow of the ecto-plasm circles brightens and she holds out her hands. Sparks and flashes of lightning criss-cross the hall. The Chosen Ones die, pinned to the floor. Olivia feels their souls and their powers flow into her and now the PE members, her slaves, are fall-ing like dominos. Their combined life-force is so strong that it opens up the tear and allows free passage into the Borderland. Filled with the souls drawn from the Chosen Ones, it is easy for Olivia to find Rebecka. And the demons keep their promise to her. She does meet Elias again. She meets him only to dis-cover that it means nothing to her anymore. Nothing at all, for something in Olivia has died. So, when she has taken his soul and let the demons in, all she wants is to be wiped out.

There have been many possible futures in which the demons have won. There still are.

Minoo sees them now. She sees what the outcome will be unless the Chosen Ones come back in time to close the portal.

The demons will pour into the Borderland as clouds of black smoke that only she can see; that she will glimpse only for a moment before the demons consume her. Then they will rush through the Borderland, through the tear, and flow through the world like an invisible wave. They will suck up the energy of all living things. It won't take them long, a few days at most. And the world will be dead, down to the smallest microorganism.

But there is still hope.

Suddenly, Minoo senses familiar energies.

She turns to look.

The others are back and Matilda is with them.

Nicolaus calls out when he sees her and Minoo registers his feelings. Joy, grief, guilt. This sense of guilt that people seem to carry around always.

He goes to Matilda.

'I did everything you asked.'

'I know.' Matilda looks tenderly at him.

She will not tell him that the words were never her own, Minoo realizes.

But she has told the Chosen Ones. She has told them everything that Minoo didn't want them to know. She has even suggested to them that they should kill Minoo.

As she stares at Matilda, anger grows inside her.

How could the guardians in the Borderland have allowed themselves to become so useless? It was of the utmost importance that they should keep Matilda under strict surveillance but, no, they let her run away and now she has disturbed all their plans. This very moment, Minoo hears Linnéa tell Rebecka everything by thought-transfer. Minoo would like to punish Matilda by annihilating her, but she doesn't want to alienate the others more than she already has. They are so short of time.

'But I'm not sure if I did the right thing,' Nicolaus says. 'I'm not sure that the guardians want what's best for us.'

'You only wanted to do good, Father,' Matilda says. 'We must leave now.'

Tears are trickling down Nicolaus's cheeks as he looks at the Chosen Ones. He doesn't dare ask them to forgive him. And they haven't forgiven him for lying to them, Minoo senses that. But they try to, especially Anna-Karin.

'We understand why you did it,' she tells Nicolaus, because she can't let him go believing that they don't.

Nicolaus looks at her with loving eyes, then at the others. But when gazing at Minoo, love is mixed with worry.

'Do not lose yourself,' he says.

'He is right,' says Matilda, who is standing next to him. 'If you're there, Minoo . . . you must resist.'

You understand nothing, Minoo thinks to her.

Matilda doesn't show any fear. She turns to the others.

'You are stronger together. Don't forget what I told you.'

They won't kill me, Minoo thinks.

Then why do you look so scared? Matilda replies without pausing.

Then she goes to Nicolaus who takes her in his arms. She leans her head against his chest and he puts his hand on her head. Both close their eyes and an expression of peace spreads across their faces.

Then, they are not there anymore. From one moment to the next, they are gone.

Somewhere, deep inside Minoo, there is a vague feeling of grief. That was the last time she would see Nicolaus. But the feeling soon fades.

She looks at the other Chosen Ones.

Anna-Karin. Elias. Linnéa. Vanessa. Ida. Rebecka.

All seven of them. The Chosen Ones. Together for the first time.

* * *

Linnéa watches Minoo as she watches them, with her back to the portal. Her black hair somehow merges with the dark interior of the gaping hole behind her and her eyes . . . they look as if the same blackness has invaded them. As if it is seeping out from her students.

'Closing the portal is not a problem,' Minoo instructs them. 'All you have to do is form a circle, release your powers and focus them. Listen to each other, adjust to each other. Think of it as a choir that is supposed to hit the same note.'

Take each other's hands, Linnéa thinks to the others. *We are stronger together.*

She takes Elias's and Vanessa's hand and they all form a chain.

'Matilda has told us the truth,' Linnéa says to Minoo. 'We know what the guardians are planning.'

'I know that you know,' Minoo says. 'We don't want you to come to any harm.'

Linnéa feels rattled when she hears Minoo talk about herself and the guardians as 'we'.

Then it hits her that perhaps this is just the guardians talking about themselves. Perhaps Matilda was right. Maybe there is no Minoo left. And, if that's true, if Minoo is only a shell, a vessel for the guardians . . .

Then it wouldn't be Minoo we killed, Linnéa thinks.

Still, the idea feels impossible. This can't be the way to save the world. It mustn't be.

'All we want is to improve you,' Minoo says.

'By removing our free will?' Linnéa asks. 'Taking away our personalities?'

'And our feelings?' Rebecka adds.

'No,' Minoo says. 'Of course you will keep all that. Only it will be . . . controlled.'

'Controlled free will? That really makes sense,' Elias says sarcastically.

'If the guardians only mean well, why have they tried to hide their plans from us?' Vanessa asks.

'Because you don't understand,' Minoo replies. 'I know from my own experience how long it takes to understand. But, once I did . . . it's an amazing experience. Does it look like I'm suffering?'

Linnéa observes Minoo's chilly, superior gaze. Her expressionless face.

'No, it doesn't,' Linnéa says. 'That's what's so fucking scary about it.'

Minoo crosses her arms.

'It seems I must motivate you a little more,' she says.

* * *

Anna-Karin stands in a kitchen. It smells of green soap and coffee. The checked curtains are drawn. She recognizes the furniture. It belongs to Grandpa. But she has never been in this room before.

'It can become yours,' Minoo's voice says.

Anna-Karin turns toward the voice. Minoo stands in front of the fridge with her arms crossed.

'Look out of the window,' she orders.

Anna-Karin pulls a curtain to the side. It is a summer day. Cows are grazing in the meadows. On the other side of the view, she sees a barn and a few outbuildings.

And then she sees Grandpa.

He is walking from the barn toward the house. He *walks*. He looks vigorous and moves with energy. It is astonishing to see him like this and makes Anna-Karin realize how much he has aged since the fire.

'In our new world, there will be no illness,' Minoo says.

Grandpa doesn't look as if he is a slave to the guardians. He looks just normal. Any second now, he'll open the front door and call her name. And then he'll step into the kitchen and look at her with his bright, warm eyes.

Grandpa.

She hears the front door open.

* * *

Vanessa lies in Linnéa's bed, covered by Linnéa's duvet and close to Linnéa. Skin against skin, so very close. And Vanessa feels how much she has longed for this and how much she needs it.

Linnéa turns to her and meets her eyes.

Vanessa is so calm. All the wounds are healed now. She feels fine and Linnéa feels fine and they will stay together forever, without hurting each other, without tearing everything beautiful apart. She knows it in the depths of her soul.

'This isn't happening, right?' Vanessa says. 'It's just the guardians messing with our heads.'

'Yeah,' Linnéa says. 'It's not for real.'

They both know it. But it doesn't matter. Not when Vanessa slides her hand around Linnéa's waist. Not when Linnéa moves a little closer still, nor when her lips are just about to touch Vanessa's.

* * *

Elias sits on the sofa in Linnéa's living room. Sunlight is pouring in. It is all very familiar, and yet not. The furniture has been changed and so have most of the pictures and drawings. The panther's head has been glued on. Linnéa sits on the sofa, too, but at the other end. She looks at him and seems surprised.

'Where is Vanessa?' she says. 'I was with her a minute ago.'

Elias can't reply. He is too absorbed by *sitting* on the sofa. He is able to touch it with his hands. It feels as if he really is here, in this room.

He catches a glimpse of movement and turns to look. Minoo has materialized on the other side of the table in front of the sofa.

Minoo is one of those people he has known all his life but never got to know properly. He has only heard her speak during school lessons. This Minoo is completely alien to him. How can the others be so sure that there is something human left inside this figure? Are they blinded by their friendship with her?

Is it up to him to be rational, to say that they should consider the possibility that Matilda is right?

He doesn't want it to be like that. He doesn't want to save the world at all. All he wants is to stay here. With Linnéa.

'This is not for real, is it?' he says.

784

'No,' Minoo says. 'But it could be. You could return to life.'

He doesn't believe her. But, at the same time, he desperately wants to believe her.

It's so unfair that everyone else gets to go on, but not him. That he will miss out on everything, just as he felt life was getting better.

'You're lying,' Linnéa says. 'You can't resurrect the dead.'

But Elias can hear that she isn't completely convinced. She wants to believe. She wants it at least as much as he does.

'True, not if a soul has passed on,' Minoo says. 'But Elias's soul is still in the Borderland. In a world where the guardians are all-powerful, Elias can live again.'

* * *

Linnéa looks at Elias, sitting on her sofa.

Elias. Alive. Vanessa. Together with her.

'You can have it all,' Minoo says to Linnéa. 'You can be with the love of your life and your best friend. You will never have to part from them again.'

Never part again.

Elias.

It is too unbearably painful to think that they would have to say goodbye to each other again. She couldn't take it. She must be allowed to keep him. He must stay.

* * *

Above Ida's head, the canopies of the trees merge to form a green tunnel. Sunbeams filter through the leaves, create patterns on the ground and on Troja.

He stands next to her and she can touch him. She reaches out and feels his warmth under her stroking hand, then leans her cheek against his muzzle and inhales the smell of horse and safety.

She has missed him. So much.

'Troja,' she whispers.

He snuffles.

'Ida, he could be yours again,' Minoo says. 'You could become alive again.'

Ida takes a step back. Minoo stands on the other side of Troja; she is patting his mane.

'The guardians can make your dream come true,' she continues. 'And this time around, everything will be so much better for you than last time.'

Ida looks at Minoo's fingers. She doesn't want her to touch Troja. Minoo takes her hand away.

'I understand why you love him,' she says. 'He is the only one you can be yourself with. He doesn't judge you. When you're with him, you feel free. You can have that feeling every day, Ida. And not only when you're with Troja.'

Ida wants to capitulate. Saying yes would be so easy.

She wants to live again. Of course she does. Live and be happy. And the feeling that Minoo described is exactly what she wants. More than she wants G. More than anything else.

Just to be.

* * *

Rebecka stands next to Gustaf's bed. He is lying on his back, deeply asleep.

Gingerly, she sits down on the edge of his bed. She is close enough to sense the warmth radiating from his body. She places her hand on his chest and feels his skin. His calm breathing; the beating of his heart.

She sees the photo of both of them that Gustaf took down by the canal. It hangs in its usual place above his bed, but she remembers seeing in Minoo's memories that Gustaf had moved it.

Now, it seems it hasn't happened. It is Rebecka and Gustaf again. She wants to lie down next to him. Wake him. Look into his eyes again.

Would it really be him? Would it matter?

'You could become alive again,' Minoo says.

Rebecka sees Minoo standing at the other end of the bed.

'You can be with him again,' she continues. 'You can be with your family again.'

All of this is fake.

Or so Rebecka's brain tells her. But her longing for him, for them, for life, all tell her something different.

And then, suddenly, she is back in the Borderland.

She looks around at the other Chosen Ones. They all seem shaken and Rebecka wonders what the guardians have tempted them with.

'We can give you all that you dream about,' Minoo says. 'And I can take your pain away. If you collaborate with us.'

Rebecka turns toward Ida and Elias. The guardians must have offered them the same choice as her.

An impossible choice.

A choice that is too impossibly grand and too cruel.

A choice that really isn't a choice.

She feels the rage and the bottomless grief at being dead.

But she knows that she can't accept the guardians' offer. It would be wrong. And it would not be a real life, anyway. All she needs to make her feel certain of that is to look at Minoo.

'No,' Rebecka says. 'We can't accept that.'

'Then you will die,' Minoo says.

'We're dead already,' Ida sobs.

'And this isn't only about us,' Elias says. 'It's about the rest of the world as well.'

Rebecka gazes at the other Chosen Ones and realizes that none of them has fallen for the guardians' temptations. It makes her proud to be one of them.

But what can they do?

'What can you do?' Minoo asks, and Rebecka wonders if her mind has been read. 'Are you going to let the demons in?'

She gestures toward the portal, which is twice her height by now and still growing.

'Or maybe you're going to kill me, as Matilda advised?' She looks accusingly at Rebecka.

'Of course not,' she replies.

'Did Matilda tell you what would happen if you do?' Minoo says. 'The guardians will of course vanish from the world. Which is what you want. But the magic balance will shift again.'

She gazes at them all in turn.

'It will start on a small scale. The magic will grow slowly at first and spread across the world. Non-magical places will become magical. And then the levels will rise. A magical flood all across the world. The earliest consequence will be that more natural witches will be awakened, many more than ever before. Do you think they'll just sit quietly and wait for some authority to allow them to use their powers?'

'You're lying,' Linnéa says.

'No, I'm not,' Minoo says, 'and it won't stop there. The levels will continue to increase. Becoming a trained witch will become easier and easier. And by the time the levels finally stabilize, you will have a world where anybody at all can learn to handle magic.'

She takes a few steps toward them.

'The outcome of all this will be chaos. All existing political, economic and religious systems will crumble. Magic will equal power. Those with the most magic will rule over everyone else. Let's narrow the perspective to make an obvious point . . . can you imagine someone like Erik Forslund with magic powers?

* * *

Erik Forslund with magic powers.

Anna-Karin can imagine it only too well.

A world drowning in magic.

It is a frightening thought. But not as frightening as one where the guardians rule and have made playthings out of human beings.

As they have done with Minoo.

'If you close the portal now, you can truly save the world,' Minoo continues. 'Together with us, you can make it into what it should be. You could correct all the wrongs, all the injustices.'

Anna-Karin looks at Minoo and realizes that they have only one chance.

Together, you are stronger than the guardians.

She leaps at Minoo and grabs her right hand. She calls out to Rebecka, who takes Minoo's left hand.

Now, Minoo is part of the Circle.

Anna-Karin feels how Minoo struggles and tries to use her powers to free herself. But the Circle holds her.

'Let go of me!' Minoo screams.

Anna-Karin senses how the others stare at her in utter surprise.

But she fixes her eyes on Minoo.

'Use the guardians' powers against yourself. Break your own blessing!'

* * *

Break your own blessing.

Minoo hears Anna-Karin's words. She hears them but they somehow don't sink in. There is a barrier that stops them.

And suddenly she becomes aware. Aware of the barrier between herself and the guardians. It is still there, even though they would like to eliminate it.

Anna-Karin's hand squeezes her own.

'You can make it,' she says. 'We'll help you.'

'We're here,' says Rebecka, who is holding her other hand.

Rebecka.

It is only now that Minoo truly realizes she is here. Emotions try to surface, but they don't reach her.

'We're here for you,' Vanessa says.

'Pull yourself together, Minoo!' Ida says.

Ida. She is here as well. And Elias, whose grave eyes are fixed on her.

They are all here and Minoo is aware of the bond between them. Of the tremendous power they have when they are together, all seven of them. All are individuals yet they belong together. She belongs with them. The guardians have tried to make her forget that.

Don't do it.

The guardians are whispering to her now.

You are the Chosen One, Minoo. Chosen by us. We have given you all this power because we believe in you, believe that you are the right one to exert it. It is a huge responsibility, but you are a good human being, Minoo. You will do the right thing. You can save the world.

Then Minoo recalls what Walter said about how one must not be afraid of power.

She realizes that he was wrong.

One must be afraid of power, always. Power is dangerous and must be handled with caution, carefully examined and cared for. Above all, it must be shared.

There is no human being who is so completely good that she can rule the world alone. And no one who can save it without the help of others.

For the first time in weeks, Minoo becomes aware of the black smoke pulsating around her. And then she realizes that she controls it. Not the other way around.

If you do this you will lose all your magic. The world will become ever more magic but you will never be able to take part in it. All your friends, Gustaf, your mother, your father – everyone will have access to that magic. Everyone except you, Minoo. You will go from being the most powerful witch in the world to nothing.

She hears the whispering from the other side of the portal as well. The demons.

You don't have to do it, Minoo. Just do nothing. Do nothing for a little longer and we will give you another world. We will let your friends come with you. Think about it. Think about it for a while. Then you won't even have to make the decision yourself.

'Minoo!' Linnéa says. 'Do it now! You must do it now!'

'I will,' Minoo whispers, holding tightly to Rebecka's and Anna-Karin's hands. 'But you must close the portal while I . . . The demons . . . they're coming . . .'

The others nod.

And Minoo senses when they release their powers.

* * *

Vanessa opens herself up completely to her power.

She is holding on to Anna-Karin and Linnéa but is just as aware of the other four members of the Circle, as conscious of them as she is of herself.

Magic flows freely through the Circle, like a beating pulse. As if they shared the same blood circulation.

Now Vanessa experiences a bond that she hasn't been aware of before. It connects her to the air element that permeates the whole world. This magic is so strong and pure that she realizes it would have obliterated her if the Circle hadn't been there. But together they can focus the power and direct it toward the portal to heal the wound.

The Circle is the answer. The Circle is the weapon.

The portal has stopped widening.

It is shrinking.

Inch by inch, grayness oozes, covering the black void.

And Vanessa keeps an eye on Minoo, hoping that she, too, will win her battle. Otherwise, all their efforts have been in vain.

* * *

Minoo senses the fury of the demons when the portal gradually narrows. They are furious but impotent. They are losing and they know it.

Magic keeps flowing through the Circle.

The six elements. United. Strong. They strengthen Minoo as well.

She has turned the black smoke toward herself and tries to find her blessing.

The magic auras of the others glow brilliantly strong, clear, intense and beautiful. Rebecka's ruby-red. Ida's silver. Elias's warmly golden. Linnéa's sapphire blue, Vanessa's aquamarine blue. Anna-Karin's emerald green.

Suddenly, she sees her own aura. Like a dazzling black sheen surrounding her whole body.

Don't do it, the guardians' voices urge her again. *You will lose everything! You will become powerless!*

Yes, Minoo thinks. *But I'm not powerless now.*

And she turns her power against herself.

The guardians can't resist her. Minoo is their most powerful weapon and their most vulnerable point. They took a risk when they allowed her to hold all their magic. And now, they will regret that they did.

Behind her, the portal is shrinking, becoming smaller and smaller at an increasing speed.

And Minoo chokes the blessing, extinguishes it completely and breaks the bond with the guardians once and for all.

The black smoke flares up and is sucked into the dark void behind her, together with the guardians who have inhabited the Borderland. A piercing scream fills her head. A scream from innumerable voices that have fused into a single one.

And then it stops abruptly.

Silence.

Minoo can no longer make out the auras of the Chosen Ones.

She turns toward the portal. No darkness there. Only the gray nothingness.

'We did it,' Rebecka says next to her. 'We closed the portal.'

But no one cheers. No one moves. Everyone is looking at Minoo.

'Did you do it?' Anna-Karin asks. 'Did you break their blessing?'

'Yes,' Minoo replies. 'They're gone. All of them.'

She isn't sure yet if she feels relieved or empty.

'I can see it in your eyes,' Rebecka says. 'I recognize you now.'

'And your thoughts seem like yours,' Linnéa says. 'Sorry, but I had to check.'

'I understand,' Minoo says.

The members of the Circle let go of each other's hands.

'Is what the guardians said true?' Vanessa asks Minoo. 'Will the whole world turn magic now?'

'Yes, it will,' Minoo says.

She knows it's true. When she was with the guardians, she could see what they saw and she could understand it as they did. She was able to find coherence in the innumerable impressions, and possibilities. All that is far beyond her now. But she still knows what she knew then.

Minoo looks at Vanessa, Linnéa and Anna-Karin. Together, they found their way here.

She looks at Elias, Ida and Rebecka. Something seems to heal inside her when she sees them like this. Elias with his arm around Linnéa erases the image of the dead, bloody Elias. Ida, playing with the silver heart on her neck chain erases the image of the lifeless Ida in Gustaf's arms.

And Rebecka. She is wearing what she wore on the day she died. Jeans. A pale blue, long-sleeved top. Minoo looks at the long reddish-blonde hair, the kind blue-gray eyes that gaze back at her. She is as beautiful as ever.

'We won't be able to stay for very much longer,' Elias says. 'I feel it.'

'So do I,' Ida says. She looks very scared.

Minoo looks at Rebecka, who nods.

'Something is pulling at me,' she says.

Tears well up in Minoo's eyes. She wants to protest, hold on to Rebecka. But she knows that she can't. What will happen must happen. And she has been given a chance that the rest of mankind can only dream of. To be able to say some of the many things that were not said in time.

'I love you,' Minoo says. 'You were my first friend. My first true friend.'

Rebecka smiles through her tears.

'And you were mine,' she says. 'And I wish so much that . . . It could have continued.'

'So do I.' Minoo can hardly get the words out.

'Minoo,' Rebecka says. 'About Gustaf and you . . .'

It is a shock to hear her say this. At first, Minoo can't think how Rebecka knows. And then she remembers.

She gave Rebecka her memories. How could she do that? Expose her to such a wrench?

'I'm so sorry,' Minoo says. 'I—'

'I was glad to know,' Rebecka tells her. 'It's fine.'

She sobs.

'Rather, I mean . . . it's not fine. Of course not. I don't want to be dead. I don't want to . . .'

She sobs again. Minoo puts her arms around her and holds her tight, feeling Rebecka's tears against her neck.

'I don't want to be dead,' Rebecka whispers. 'But I am. And I know you love him.'

Minoo can't answer her because she is crying too much. She can smell Rebecka's scent. Feels the bond between them. It is still there. It will always be there.

'When the whole world becomes magic, you must tell my family what really happened,' Rebecka whispers. 'And tell Gustaf . . . tell him that I love him. And that I want him to be happy.'

'I will,' Minoo whispers back. 'I promise.'

* * *

Linnéa looks at Elias. She cannot move, cannot speak. She knows this is their last moment together and she can't think what to do with it, because all she can think of is that it will end.

'Linnéa,' Elias says softly.

She realizes that he understands and her paralysis disappears. She bursts into tears.

Elias slips his hands in under her fake fur coat and pulls her to him. She feels his arms around her and clings to him. She doesn't want to let go. She can't. Not again.

'You must stay,' she says. 'You must.'

'I can't.' He too is crying.

'I should have told you,' he says. 'Those last few days . . . I thought I was going mad. But now I know that it was my powers, that they were awakening. If only I had spoken out . . . then I would never have bought that stuff from Jonte. And you and I would never have had that fight . . .'

'I was also getting my powers at that time and thought *I* was going mad,' Linnéa says. 'I should have told you too. But we can't stand here regretting stuff we can't change.'

She feels so hypocritical because now she regrets not accepting the guardians' offer. How could they say no? Elias could have lived. They could have been together again. Who cares if it hadn't been for real.

'I can hear your thoughts,' Elias says. 'You know it's not true.'

'I know,' Linnéa says. 'It's just . . . I can't think how I'll survive without you. I don't know if I can go on.'

Elias grabs her by the shoulders and looks at her. His eyes are red-rimmed and the kohl has smeared.

'You have to go on,' he says. 'For my sake.'

He smiles. She knows what an effort he is making, even though he is being torn apart.

795

'Do all the things I never got to do,' he says. 'Go to Japan. Make out with some blondes for me too.'

She laughs and he caresses her hair.

'You're not alone, Linnéa,' he says quietly. 'You have friends. And you have Vanessa. They will be there for you. Let them be there for you. Promise me that.'

'Yes.' Linnéa clings to him again.

* * *

Ida closes her eyes. She hears the others crying. Linnéa and Elias. Rebecka and Minoo.

She tries to concentrate. Tries to resist what is pulling at her. It is hard. Almost impossible. As hard as it is to resist sleep when you fall into the softest, nicest bed after having been up all night.

But Ida is a strong person. Plenty of self-discipline. Mom always said so. She can resist. She must. She doesn't want to disappear. If only she can fight back for long enough, maybe whatever it is will give up pulling.

Don't want, don't want to, don't want to.

'Ida?' Anna-Karin's voice says near her.

She opens her eyes. Anna-Karin and Vanessa stand in front of her.

'I just wanted to tell you that I went down to the stables to check on Troja,' Anna-Karin says. 'He is fine. Really well looked after by a girl there. She's called Lisa.'

Lisa. Ida remembers Lisa. One of those annoying younger girls who used to swarm around Troja. But at least she was a good rider.

She looks at Anna-Karin. She had promised to make sure that Troja was looked after. She remembered. She cared.

'Thank you,' Ida says.

'Is there something else we can do for you?' Vanessa asks. 'Do you want us to talk to your family? Would you like them to know?'

Yes. Ida would like them to know the truth about everything. There is so much she has understood herself and she would like them to understand too. She finds it hard to believe that they ever would. But they should have the opportunity to. Lotta and Rasmus perhaps don't have to grow up to be like she was, before she changed.

'Tell them everything,' she says.

There it is again. The tug. It is stronger now. So strong that she realizes that she will not be able to resist it.

Terror flares up inside her again.

What if she ends up in hell and is tortured for all eternity? Does she really deserve that? Surely it will count for something that she helped save the world?

What if she ends up in an über-boring heaven. What is she supposed to do for an eternity there?

What if she is reborn as some disgusting little animal?

What if everything just ends?

'Is there anything more we can do?' Anna-Karin asks.

'I think I need a hug,' Ida says.

Anna-Karin puts her arms around Ida.

She is so soft, so warm. Ida feels herself relaxing a little. Just a little.

'I'm sorry,' she says. 'For everything.'

'It's okay, Ida,' Anna-Karin says.

'Okay,' Ida says.

And then she doesn't think anymore.

Part 6

CHAPTER 104

Vanessa has no time to react.

Suddenly, she is in the school dining room. She and the other Chosen Ones. The ones who are alive.

The chairs are upside-down on the tables. Daylight filters in through the plastic sheeting that is used to cover the windows. Vanessa picks up the sounds of people moving around outside. Voices. Life.

And for a moment all she can feel is a huge relief.

The world is still there. They saved it.

She turns to Anna-Karin, Minoo and Linnéa.

'We did it,' she says. 'It's over.'

The others nod and look at each other. And suddenly it's so obvious that they are incomplete.

A moment ago they were seven.

A moment ago they were all together.

One single time they got to experience the Circle as it was meant to be.

Vanessa sees that Linnéa has cried so much her make-up has turned to mush. She has lost Elias again. One day, Vanessa will tell her how glad she is to have met him. During the moments it took them to close the portal, she knew Elias. She understood who he was and why Linnéa loves him.

She touches Linnéa's hand lightly and receives a faint smile in return.

Vanessa thinks back on how the guardians tried to lure her with the vision of a harmonious Linnéa and love without any obstacles.

The Key

It hadn't been hard to say no, because the price was too high. But can they make that vision come true anyway, on their own?

Now they have saved the world, Vanessa knows what she wants. She wants to be with Linnéa. She loves her. But that isn't enough. Linnéa must also decide what she wants. Show that she trusts Vanessa. That she dares to be loved by her.

Minoo staggers and Anna-Karin takes hold of her. Vanessa pulls one of the chairs from a table so that Minoo can sit down.

'Deep breaths,' Linnéa says, and Minoo lets her head droop between her knees.

Vanessa places her hand on Minoo's back and exchanges worried glances with the others. When Minoo broke Max's demonic blessing, he ended up in a coma. What actually happened to her when she broke her own?

'Thanks,' Minoo says after a while. She straightens up.

'How are you?' Anna-Karin asks.

* * *

Minoo can't think how to answer Anna-Karin's question.

She looks around the dining room. It smells faintly of old cooking, cleaning materials and stale air. The dust is dancing in the light from the windows.

It is almost *too* real. And at the same time, nothing feels real at all.

Rebecka is gone again.

Ida and Elias, too.

And Minoo was about to help the guardians enslave mankind.

Fragments of memories from the last three weeks surface in her mind. Then, everything felt clear and logical. But, looking back, it is as if she is watching someone else do what she did and think what she thought. Perhaps this is what it feels like after a psychotic episode.

802

She feels the others gazing at her and knows she must say something.

'I feel fine,' she lies.

She had never realized how deeply ingrained the guardians' magic was in her. But, how could she, because it is only now that she can compare before and after. Now that the magic is gone, it is as if a white noise has been silenced.

She will never again be able to lose herself in the black smoke. Without it, she is weak. Vulnerable. Emotions can get at her at any time.

And they will. Sooner or later.

She allowed Nicolaus to take his own life, actively helped him to do it. She killed Walter, obliterated him and wiped out his soul. She abandoned Sigrid and Viktor to their killer. She can still hear in the echoes of Walter's memories the last gurgling breath Sigrid took when he stopped her heart. The sharp crack when Viktor's neck broke.

Minoo let them die. She let *Viktor* die.

She closes her eyes to escape those memories but, beneath her eyelids, she can still see the bloodstains on Walter's shirt. Clara's blood.

Clara. What happened to her? Did she survive?

Minoo knows that she must tell the others. But not now. Not yet. She is too afraid about how it will affect her if she says it out loud.

Then she remembers the explosion in the center of town. It caused the deaths of an old lady and her neighbor. What has happened in Engelsfors while they've been away? Have more people been injured? Killed?

Gustaf.

'We must go and find the others,' she says.

'Yes.' Vanessa looks worried. 'Shit, I hope everyone is OK . . .'

She suddenly stops talking. Stares at the clock on the wall. Minoo follows her eyes.

It feels as if they have been away for perhaps a couple of hours, at most. But it must have taken them a whole night. It's ten to eleven now.

'One thing,' Linnéa says. 'All the windows exploded in the earthquake . . .'

Minoo grasps at once what she means. She had watched the earth portent from the vantage point of the guardians and saw the broken glass shower the schoolyard.

But the panes in the dining area windows are all in one piece.

'Maybe these ones weren't affected,' she says.

'Maybe,' Linnéa says. 'But doesn't everything look quite freshly painted?'

* * *

Anna-Karin scans the big room and has to admit that Linnéa is right. It does look freshly painted and the walls are several shades lighter than they used to be.

An unpleasant suspicion begins to make itself felt.

'How long have we actually been away?' she asks.

'If they've had time to put in new windows and paint the place . . .' Vanessa begins, but she doesn't complete the sentence.

'Does anyone have a cell phone?' Minoo pats her jeans pockets.

Anna-Karin checks, too. But of course she didn't bring it. When she left home in the morning, the networks were still down in Engelsfors.

This morning. It can't have been this morning.

Her heart beats faster now. Grandpa. He will have worried so.

If he is still alive.

She isn't fast enough to block the thought.

'There are so many people in the yard their thoughts just add up to a headache,' Linnéa says. 'But they seem to be waiting for something to happen.'

'I must go to Grandpa,' Anna-Karin says.

Part Six

She quickly leaves the dining room. The others follow her upstairs to the entrance lobby.

There are wooden boards across the windows and the glazed parts of the front doors. The air smells strongly of paint. The floor looks new. And so do the lamps in the ceiling.

Anna-Karin hears the buzz of voices in the yard and opens the front doors.

* * *

The cheering hits Vanessa full force. Whistles, horns, applause and shrieks echo across the schoolyard.

It is crowded with people in light summer clothes. Above their heads, a forest of boards with messages in bright colors. Blue and yellow streamers. Pictures of children. Vanessa recognizes several. Michelle, still in nappies, has covered herself with blue finger paint. Liam is blushing sweetly, wearing a princess dress and with his feet stuck into a pair of large, high-heeled shoes.

It's graduation day.

It should have been Vanessa's graduation too.

Then, the noise dies down. Everyone looks at the Chosen Ones standing on top of the steps. Now, the only sound is the rustling of the sheets of plastic that enclose the scaffolding along the façade of the school.

Eight months, Linnéa thinks. *We have been away for eight months.*

'It's them!' a girl's voice screams from somewhere in the crowd. 'They're back!'

The noise grows again. People press close to the steps and some stretch to see better, waving their cell phones and cameras in the air to get good shots.

Vanessa is sweating in her thick winter jacket. She just stands there, as if paralyzed.

It was October when they went into the cave. And now, it's June.

Eight months.

She glances at Minoo, Anna-Karin and Linnéa and sees the shock in their faces.

There is the sound of running feet inside the school. Raucous voices, louder and louder.

'Cause we have graduated! 'Cause we have graduated!

The doors behind them are opened wide and the band of white-capped graduates rushes out and surrounds the Chosen Ones. Vanessa is pushed, stumbles, but grabs the handrail. She turns and searches for a glimpse of Evelina and Michelle.

'Cause we have gradua-a-ated!

The first ones catch sight of the Chosen Ones and stop in their tracks. It causes a multiple pile-up among the white caps and irritated shouting from further back. Inside the school, those who haven't yet noticed the blockage carry on singing.

'Vanessa is back!' screams some guy she has never exchanged one word with before.

Several people start calling out their names. The singing inside the school stops. Vanessa sees Linnéa's head disappear under Tindra's black and purple dreads. Behind them, Julia and Felicia watch the chaos, obviously upset that their dream of the perfect graduation is going up in smoke.

Vanessa picks up the familiar smell of Michelle's hairspray and perfume a fraction of a second before she is jumped.

'You're back!' she yells. Vanessa notices that she's quite drunk.

She doesn't have time to say anything before Evelina has pushed through the mass of bodies. She is crying black mascara tears and her white cap falls off her head as she throws her arms around Vanessa's neck.

'Nessa!' she sobs.

They are both hugging Vanessa so hard she can't breathe. Michelle is sniveling damply in her ear. Vanessa is pouring with sweat under her winter jacket. People are crowding in from all directions.

'Evelina said you're witches,' Michelle whispers. 'But I haven't told anyone, honest.'

Vanessa thinks about Mom. Mom and Melvin. They must think that she's dead.

'I must get out of here,' she says. Evelina nods.

Tommy Ekberg has turned up on the top of the steps. He wears a brilliantly blue shirt with a pattern of ice-cream lollies. He stretches his arms up in the air and is shouting to the graduates to calm down and stay where they are.

Come to the parking lot, Linnéa thinks to Vanessa. *See you at Rickard's car.*

* * *

Minoo is pushed back and forth by the people on the steps. They all want to talk to her, touch her, and the light is so strong. So terribly strong. She is sweating in her black sweater.

She saw Linnéa just moments ago but now she can only see her friend with the dreads. Anna-Karin and Vanessa have vanished, too. She is alone with her fear and her thoughts about Mom and Dad and Gustaf.

They've been waiting for her for eight months.

'Anybody got a phone?' she shouts.

But nobody listens; they only carry on yelling things like, 'Where have you been?' and other questions Minoo can't answer.

'Minoo!' Rickard calls to her.

Just at the bottom of the steps, she sees the sun glint in his glasses. She needs to get to him and doesn't care who she annoys as she elbows her way through the crowd. She reaches out her hand and he pulls her down the last bit. Linnéa stands next to him, without her fake fur coat. She has swept her bangs from her sweaty face.

'Let's go. I've got my car parked around the back,' Rickard says.

Vanessa will meet us there, Linnéa thinks. *Anna-Karin has gone to see her grandpa.*

Minoo clutches Rickard's arm as they plow on across the schoolyard. She stares fixedly at the ground. Cell phones are clicking around them.

'Minoo!' calls a voice that sounds like Ylva's, but she ignores it.

Eight months.

When they are clear of the throng, she starts running to the back of the school, together with Rickard and Linnéa.

'What do they think happened to us?' she asks Rickard.

'The authorities claimed that it was an unidentified gas leak that made the whole town fall asleep,' he replies. 'The police thought you were involved in some kind of accident at the time. But there have been tons of rumors. And your parents have kept searching for you.'

Vanessa, Evelina and Michelle are already waiting near an old red Nissan. Vanessa has taken off her jacket and folded the sleeves of her top so that it looks like a tank top.

'What shall we do?' she says. 'I must phone Mom, but we've got to agree on a story!'

Minoo glances nervously at Michelle.

'No problem,' Michelle says slowly. 'I know that you do spells and stuff.'

Minoo wonders if more people have learned the truth while they've been away. And then it strikes her that it's only a matter of time before *everyone* will learn it.

'What the hell do we say, Minoo?' Vanessa says.

There is only one option.

'We've got to tell them,' Minoo says.

The others look baffled.

'Everything will change now,' Minoo continues. 'We must tell them the truth so that they're prepared.'

But she has no idea how to go about it. How can she convince her parents? Get them to believe the unbelievable?

'I don't think I can deal with that on my own,' Vanessa says. 'Can't we do it together?'

'Yes, that'll probably be best,' Minoo agrees. Linnéa nods.

Vanessa hugs Michelle and leaps into the back with Evelina and Linnéa. Minoo settles down in the passenger seat and Rickard hands her his cell.

She draws a deep breath before phoning home.

* * *

Anna-Karin pulls off her jacket as she cruises between the festive graduate carriages. There are all sorts, cars and trailers and trucks, all decorated with balloons and birch branches covered in green leaves. The decorations sway in a gentle breeze and Anna-Karin enjoys the cool wind against her overheated body.

Just ten minutes from here to Sunny Side if she runs.

So, she starts running. And while she's running, she reaches out for the fox.

She finds him at once. He has waited for her. Pure joy flows through their link, a joy that should surely be too great for a small fox. She shares it and promises him that she will soon meet him in the forest.

Just now, she is running along the streets of Engelsfors.

The sun is shining strongly from a clear blue sky that is arching high above the town. She smells the warm asphalt, the newly mown grass in the gardens, the lilac. Hears the buzz of the insects dancing among the Queen Anne's Lace and forget-me-nots. A dog barks somewhere in the distance; the owner shouts at it but it doesn't stop.

Anna-Karin is breathing, her heart is beating. Her feet run lightly on the ground.

She is alive.

The world is alive.

It will become magical and Anna-Karin can't begin to imagine what this will mean. But it is still here.

She hopes that Grandpa is, too.

CHAPTER 105

Minoo ends the phone call and wipes the tears off her cheeks. The air conditioning in Rickard's car makes her shiver. She looks out at the gardens in their June greenery. Several doors are decorated with birch leaves, flags, ribbons and balloons, welcoming a graduate home. How the sight of every such door must have pained her parents.

Dad hadn't been able to get a word out when he first heard Minoo's voice. She said she'd be back home soon, that she was well and that she'd explain everything. Then Mom wanted the phone but she simply wept. And Minoo began to weep with her. Just as Vanessa does now, speaking to her mother.

'I love you,' she says. 'See you soon.'

She hands the cell phone back to Evelina and meets Minoo's eyes in the mirror.

'Mom will be along at once. She says she has seen a lot of your parents since we disappeared. They've tried to support each other . . .'

She cries even harder and Evelina puts her arm around her.

'Sweetie,' she says.

Minoo runs through Rickard's contacts, and selects Gustaf's number. The recorded voicemail answer is new, more grown-up and formal. *Hello, you've reached Gustaf Åhlander. Please leave a message and I will call you back as soon as I can.*

'Hi,' she manages to say. 'I'm using Rickard's phone . . . I'm back.' She doesn't know what she should say next and ends the call.

'He must keep his cell switched off at work,' Rickard says.

810

Minoo wants him to explain.

'He has got himself a job in a hotel in Borlänge while he does a distance-learning course in law,' Rickard says. 'You mustn't feel bad about him. He has known all along that you'll be back.'

'How could he?' Minoo asks.

'Rickard had this vision,' Evelina says behind her.

'Just after the town had woken up,' he says, 'I saw that you had succeeded and that you would be back. But there was no warning that you'd take so long.' He smiles.

Minoo's fears are calmed a little. At least Gustaf had hope to cling to during all these months. Unlike her parents.

'How long was the town asleep?' Linnéa asks.

'A few hours,' Evelina replies.

It had taken them roughly that long to close the portal. It had been the saying goodbye afterward that had lasted for eight months.

'It was pretty bad,' Rickard says. 'We drove around and tried to help where we could. But there were tons of things we couldn't do anything about . . . thirty-four people died or disappeared, not counting you guys.'

But Minoo is hardly listening. Rickard has stopped outside her house and her parents are waiting for her on the drive.

* * *

Vanessa watches as Minoo rushes out even before Rickard has had time to turn the engine off. She is almost hit by a cyclist who shouts angrily at her.

Minoo and her parents are running toward each other.

Vanessa doesn't want to see them fall into each other's arms; doesn't want to start crying again.

'In that vision of yours, did you *see* us as we closed the portal?' she asks Rickard.

'I didn't,' he says. 'But Mona did.'

'Mona?' Vanessa exchanges a glance with Linnéa. 'So, she came back?'

'Yes, the next day,' Evelina says. 'She said she couldn't miss a golden opportunity like this.'

'What opportunity?' Linnéa asks.

'Engelsfors will become like, world famous, when everything goes magical,' Evelina says.

They already know. And when Evelina says it, it seems real for the first time. Real and mind-boggling.

'Nessa, I need to tell you something,' Evelina says. 'When we drove around to the nursery to check on Melvin, he was the only one who wasn't asleep.'

It takes Vanessa a moment to understand what that means. Melvin is a natural witch.

'Shit,' she says. 'Has he developed any power yet?'

'I don't think so,' Evelina says. 'I've tried to keep an eye. You know, done babysitting and helped Jannike pick him up from nursery and things . . .'

Now, Vanessa can't stop the tears.

'You're the best friend in the whole world, you know that, don't you?'

'I so wish I could have told your mom everything,' Evelina says. 'But I thought of the Council and simply didn't dare.'

Linnéa and Vanessa look at each other again and sense that neither of them can bear to think about the Council just now.

'Good that you didn't,' Vanessa says.

She realizes that she is looking forward to telling their story. To stopping lying to Mom at last. Besides, if Melvin is going to develop magic powers any time soon, Mom had better be prepared.

'Nessa, look,' Evelina says.

Vanessa looks in the same direction and sees a taxi stop just in front of them. Mom is sitting in the back.

Vanessa opens the car door and runs.

* * *

Part Six

Linnéa looks at the two of them. Jannike, still in her care assistant's blue overalls, leaps out of the car. She screams when she sees Vanessa and it hardly sounds human. They fall into each other's arms in the middle of the street.

Linnéa starts fiddling with her cuticles. Her nails are varnished green and look just as freshly painted as they did when she entered the Borderland eight months ago. It's past all understanding.

She probably doesn't have anywhere to live anymore. She hasn't paid any bills for more than half a year. Or met up with social services.

Still, the thought leaves her strangely unmoved. Perhaps that's what happens when you've stopped the apocalypse and met your dead best friend and learned that the world will soon be flooded with magic.

The pain of losing Elias is still with her, but it is different now. It is as if he had left a piece of himself in her heart. Something she can keep with her, always. Something that might make her braver. Brave enough to get Vanessa back.

Vanessa is still hugging her mother. And Minoo is with her parents. She ought to phone Dad. And she ought to phone Diana.

'Thanks,' Evelina says.

Linnéa looks up. 'For what?'

'For, like, us still existing.'

'Yes,' Rickard says. 'Thank you. You saved the world.'

'It's huge,' Evelina says.

'It is,' Linnéa agrees, wondering if she will ever grasp quite how huge it is.

Evelina takes Linnéa's hand between both hers and looks seriously at her.

'Maybe you'll think that I should mind my own business, but I don't give a shit. Now you've another chance. And I know you love her.'

Linnéa stares at Evelina. Can't come up with an answer. Rickard rather transparently pretends that he hasn't heard.

'I must go to my reception,' Evelina says. 'Mom and Dad will have strangled each other with streamers by now.'

Rickard smiles at Linnéa in the mirror. 'Talk to you later,' he says. 'You must tell us everything.'

'We will,' Linnéa says. She climbs out of the car with the feeling that everyone can see right through her – and it's kind of a relief.

* * *

Minoo looks around the living room. Everything looks so familiar and, at the same time, alien. The bright summer sun shines through the windows. She sees the well-filled bookshelves, one with a built-in TV cupboard. The large armchair, where Vanessa's mother sits with her daughter on her lap. Another chair, where Linnéa sits with one leg folded under her.

Mom sits next to Minoo and holds on to her as if she will never let go again. She has stopped crying now, but she doesn't seem able to stop stroking Minoo's hair, and kissing her cheek.

As far as Minoo is concerned, she and Mom spoke on the phone just a few weeks ago. But to Mom, eight months have gone by. Eight months of nightmares and self-reproach.

Minoo wishes Anna-Karin's hold on her parents' minds had lasted for longer so that Mom and Dad could have carried on believing that Minoo was nicely looked after in the manor house.

But when Anna-Karin, Vanessa and Linnéa disappeared, they finally came to the conclusion that something was very wrong. The police arrived and wanted to speak to Minoo, and, when they looked for her in the manor house, they found it had been abandoned.

Mom moved back to Engelsfors. Since then, she and Dad have been waiting. And their hopes have faded with every new day of waiting.

Minoo glances toward the kitchen, where Dad is pacing up and down on the dark wooden floorboards. He is on the phone to the police, informing them that the girls are back, in good condition, and have not been victims of any kind of crime.

'Linnéa,' Mom says. 'You should know that we have contacted your father.'

Linnéa's focus is on the side table.

'We've been in touch since you disappeared,' Mom continues. 'And I called him as soon as we heard from Minoo.'

'Thank you,' Linnéa says quietly.

'And your furniture and other things are stored in our cellar,' Mom adds cautiously. 'You see, your apartment . . .'

'Thank you,' Linnéa whispers again.

Minoo can see that she is close to tears. She wishes that Linnéa had someone to hold her, too.

A bird is chirping just outside the living-room window. Minoo catches a glimpse of a blue tit flitting past. What if Viktor is still alive? If it was only her imagination that . . . ?

No, she tells herself, cutting the line of thought. Viktor is dead. She knows it.

The chirping goes on happily. What happens to a familiar when the witch dies? Perhaps it was Viktor's blue tit she saw, after all? Perhaps it is searching for him? Where is Sigrid's mink now? Does Walter's lynx haunt the forests around Engelsfors? Have they become ordinary animals again?

And what happened to Clara? And Adriana? Felix? Nejla? Will Minoo ever find out?

Dad finishes the phone call to the police but the phone immediately starts ringing.

'No comment,' he says, turning it off.

'I so hope the hacks won't trace Anna-Karin to the Sunny Side home,' Dad says when he comes back into the living room.

'Her grandpa is in very poor shape,' Mom says. 'We've visited him a couple of times but . . . you know, I'm not even

815

sure he understood that Anna-Karin was missing. He was strangely calm.'

We must go and see her later.

Minoo hears Linnéa's thought in her head. She looks up, meets her eyes and nods.

Dad sits down on Minoo's other side and takes her hand.

'Minoo,' he begins. It's obvious he is trying hard to restrain his feelings. 'None of us are accusing you. But you turn up from nowhere after eight months and insist that you've stayed away willingly . . .'

'*Man nemifahmam,*' Mom says. 'Couldn't you have phoned us just once and told us you were alive?'

She sounds angry now and Minoo sympathizes.

'Has anybody harmed you in any way, or threatened you?' Dad asks.

'You know, don't you, that you can tell us everything?' Jannike adds.

Minoo glances at Vanessa. Jannike has no idea how hard she'll be tested.

Let's do it, Linnéa thinks.

Minoo feels a little queasy now that the moment has come.

'We will tell you,' she says.

The silence in the room is broken only by the birdsong and music blasting out from a graduate's carriage somewhere far away.

'It's a very long story,' Minoo says.

'For us, it began in our first year,' Vanessa says. 'Though the real beginning was much earlier.'

'You already know that a lot of weird things happen in Engelsfors,' Linnéa says. 'What we're going to tell you will sound much weirder but, in fact, it will explain everything.'

Mom has stopped holding on to Minoo now. She, Dad and Jannike look, if anything, even more concerned. It strikes Minoo that there's only one way to make them understand.

'We have to show them,' she says. 'Vanessa, could you . . . ?'

Vanessa understands at once, gets up and looks at her mother.

'Don't be scared now,' she says. 'It's not dangerous, I promise.'

Dad and Jannike scream in unison when Vanessa becomes invisible. Jannike lifts her feet off the floor.

Vanessa becomes visible again.

Minoo gives her mom a sidelong glance. Mom has put her hands against her temples, as if she is trying to stop her brain from exploding. She has just watched scientific laws being broken right in front of her medically trained eyes.

'I can fly as well,' Vanessa says with a hesitant smile.

'What . . . what is this?' Mom looks at Minoo.

Minoo meets her eyes and gives her the only possible answer.

'It's magic, Mom.'

* * *

Anna-Karin sits on a chair next to her grandpa's bed. Members of staff have told her that his health has declined a great deal during the last few months. He sleeps almost all the time and seems confused when he is awake.

But they assure her that he hasn't been suffering in any way, that he doesn't seem to understand how poorly he's doing. He is not at all anxious.

Grandpa has been sleeping ever since she arrived and Anna-Karin is grateful for that.

Because she hasn't been able to stop crying for a single minute.

She cries because she hasn't been with him for Christmas and New Years and Easter. Without her, he has been completely alone. Grandma dead; Mia dead.

She cries because she has lost so much time with him.

She cries for Nicolaus who sacrificed himself for them. She

feels she can forgive him now because she can truly understand why he acted as he did.

She cries for Matilda who was alone for so long. If it hadn't
been for her, the world would have fallen into the guardians'
possession. Her only reward was death.

She cries for Rebecka and Elias.

She cries for Ida.

She cries for the stranger in the Canaries.

And, finally, she cries for Mom.

She cries for the woman she saw in Kärrgruvan. And she
cries for the woman Mom became. She can see her more
clearly now. She can see that she tried, and that she knew that
it wasn't enough.

Anna-Karin cries because she has finally realized that she
must not hate herself for not missing her mother more. Mom
was never a mother to her. To take that on board is a relief in a
way but, in another, the saddest thing of all.

Anna-Karin has no idea how long she has been sitting there
when she senses the energies of the others in the hallway. She
doesn't turn around when they enter the room.

We didn't want you to be alone, Linnéa thinks.

'Are we disturbing you?' Minoo asks.

'No,' Anna-Karin says. 'I'm glad you came.'

Minoo stands behind her and puts her hand on Anna-
Karin's shoulder. Vanessa and Linnéa stand at the far end of
the bed.

'My dear child,' Grandpa mumbles.

Anna-Karin takes his hand. He sounds as if his mouth is
dry.

'I'm here, Grandpa.' She quickly wipes her tears away with
her free hand.

'I knew you'd come back,' he mutters, opening his eyes. 'I
knew it all along.'

He gives the others a curious look.

'This is Minoo, Linnéa and Vanessa, who I've told you about,' Anna-Karin says.

She notices that he has problems focusing his eyes, but he nods as if he could see perfectly well.

'I would have smartened myself up a bit if I'd known I'd get such grand visitors,' he says with a little smile.

Then he turns his head to Anna-Karin again.

'It's very nice to meet your second family.'

All Anna-Karin can do is nod, because she has started to cry again. She tries to do it quietly so he won't notice.

'Run along now,' he says. 'There are other people waiting to meet you.'

'I don't want to go now that you've just woken up,' Anna-Karin says.

'I promise I won't disappear,' he tells her. He closes his eyes.

Anna-Karin gets up, though she doesn't want to. Takes a tissue from the bedside table and wipes her eyes and cheeks.

'I'll come back tomorrow,' she says.

'You do that, *lapsikulta*.'

Grandpa goes back to sleep and they tiptoe out of the room and then walk to the elevators.

We have told Minoo's parents and Jannike now, Linnéa thinks as they reach the ground floor.

How did it go? Anna-Karin asks.

Linnéa smiles faintly.

It was mad.

They walk toward the exit. When the automatic doors slide open, Anna-Karin picks up a waft of incense.

Someone is waiting just outside the door. Someone who stands with her hands on her hips.

819

CHAPTER 106

'Took your effing time, didn't you?' Mona Moonbeam says.

Vanessa looks wearily at her. She is dressed in a white denim skirt and a white tank top decorated on the chest with a crocodile sitting in a beach chair drinking a cocktail with an umbrella in it. Her hair is bigger and blonder than ever and she is chewing gum with her mouth open.

'Nice to see you too, Mona,' Vanessa says.

But she can't quite manage to sound sarcastic, because she actually means what she says. Mona almost smiles.

'Good thing you got rid of that crap,' she says to Minoo.

'Do you mean the guardians?' Minoo asks.

'Whatever you want to call it,' Mona says. 'Come on, we can't hang around this place. The hacks are sniffing around for you.'

She walks across the car park toward a flash 1950s American car, all white leather seats and shiny pale blue paint.

'Have you even got a license?' Vanessa asks her.

'Listen, baby face, I was burning the asphalt when your mom was still in diapers,' Mona snaps, climbing into the car and slamming the driver's door.

Vanessa glances at the others, then goes to sit in the passenger seat. The others settle in the back.

'Where are we going?' Anna-Karin asks.

'Well now, if you're not psychic you'll just have to wait and see,' Mona says.

Part Six

The engine starts with a piercing howl and Vanessa fumbles for the seat belt. But there isn't one. When Mona steps on the gas, Vanessa is flattened against the back of her seat.

A couple of crows that have been pecking on the asphalt fly away, clearly terrified.

'I had just settled down at a bar at the airport and had a couple of shots when I had this vision of what you all had been up to,' Mona shouts at the top of her voice. Her hair is flying in front of her face and Vanessa wonders if she can see anything at all. 'That was it. All I could do was try to get a refund for that goddamn business-class ticket.'

The traffic lights go from green to yellow and Mona puts her foot down. Vanessa hopes that Mona is psychic enough to know for certain that she won't kill them all today.

'Not that I'm complaining!' Mona yells. 'No way! Not just new rules to play by! It's a completely new *game*!'

She leans on the steering wheel, using her body weight to turn it. They drive into Lilla Lugnet on screaming tires. Out of the corner of her eye, Vanessa sees Minoo, Anna-Karin and Linnéa slide along the leather seats.

'Been quite a migration to this place recently,' Mona howls. 'Both real witches and tons of loonies who are waiting for the next UFO to land!'

They zoom past the burnt-down house where the locals claim someone used to run a sex club at one point. The lawn is full of dandelions.

'I've opened the Crystal Cave again, in the old Positive Engelsfors Center!' Mona screams. 'I need staff, so let me know if you want to do some moonlighting.'

The car stops with a jerk outside the white wooden house where Adriana used to live. Mona looks at Vanessa and grins.

'I'd say you're going to need the cash. You'll hardly get paid doing your other job.'

'What do you mean?' Vanessa asks.

821

The Key

'Never mind what she means,' Linnéa tries to climb out of the back seat.

'Hang on now,' Mona says. 'Wait.'

She sounds so serious that Linnéa stops moving and sits back on the seat again.

'This is a house in mourning,' Mona says. 'So you'd better tell them about Viktor now, sweetie.'

She glances at Minoo through the rear-view mirror.

* * *

Minoo meets Mona's eyes and then looks away. She turns to study Adriana's old home. The elaborate carvings look like piped decorations on a wedding cake. The branches on the birch trees sway gently in the breeze.

'Viktor is dead,' she says.

'Dead?' Linnéa says. She sounds confused. 'But . . . when did he die?'

'Just after I teleported us all,' Minoo says. 'Walter killed him and took his powers. He had already murdered Sigrid. And I don't know if Clara . . .'

She falls silent.

'Clara survived,' Mona says. She sounds almost kind. 'Adriana too.'

Minoo looks at her via the mirror.

'Is she . . . ? Is she all right?'

'You'll meet her in a minute,' Mona says. 'I just wanted everyone to know about Viktor first, so that none of you puts your foot in it. It's a sensitive subject for some of the people in there.'

Minoo gives her a surprised look.

'What are you looking at? I do have my sensitive moments, you know,' Mona snaps, and jumps out of the car. 'Come on!'

She slams the car door and starts walking in her white court shoes toward Adriana's house.

Minoo looks at the others. Anna-Karin is tearful.

'Minoo, I'm so sorry,' Vanessa says. 'I mean . . . everything to do with Viktor was so fucking complicated. But he was your friend, wasn't he?'

'Yes,' Minoo says.

He was her friend. And her grief is just under the surface, waiting to emerge and overwhelm her. But, right now, she can't let it.

Why didn't you tell us? Linnéa thinks.

Minoo doesn't know where to begin, so she doesn't answer. She just follows Mona through the garden. She hears voices and laughter coming from the other side of the house.

Mona rings the doorbell and they hear steps approach.

Felix opens the door. His black hair has grown longer and almost covers his eyes. He looks at them, Minoo for a little longer.

'Hi,' he says.

'Hi,' she replies.

'How is your hand?' Vanessa asks.

Felix makes a fist of his right hand and then opens it again.

'I broke it,' he says. 'But it's okay now.'

'Thank you for doing that,' Vanessa says.

'I should be thanking you,' Felix says stiffly.

He looks at Minoo again. She would like to say something about Viktor, but this is hardly the right time. Felix turns abruptly and disappears into the house.

Minoo walks into the hall. The rack is full of jackets. Lots of pairs of shoes on the floor. The same heavy, old-fashioned furniture fills the living room, but the oil paintings of gloomy landscapes and portraits of ancestors have been removed. The unnaturally clean smell is gone, too. On the table by the sofa, a half-drunk mug of coffee stands next to a pile of books and newspapers. Someone has even used the open fireplace.

The windows are open and Minoo hears a laugh she recognizes. She goes to have a look.

The Key

Nejla lies on the lawn with her head resting on a guy's lap. Minoo has seen him before in Nejla's memories. His name is Marcus. His raven-black hair is as long as Nejla's by now. There are two other guys sitting next to them. One of them is about twenty, with purple hair and a ring in his nose. He is blowing at a dandelion puff and then freezes the seeds in mid-air. The other guy looks younger and wears a gold chain around his neck. He snaps his fingers and the seeds fall to the ground. Nejla laughs again.

Minoo takes a step back before they can spot her watching them. She is pleased that Nejla seems to be happy, but doesn't feel she can cope with talking to her just now.

When she turns to move away, she almost walks into Mona.

'I know,' Mona says. 'It's like a fucking witches' day nursery. And there are more of them. They don't all live here, but they're running in and out all day long. How Adriana stands it is a mystery.'

Then, Minoo sees her.

She walks barefoot across the creaking floorboards. Her dress is low cut and exposes the scarred skin on her upper chest. Her gaze is calm and alive.

She comes straight up to Minoo and puts her arms around her. Minoo smells her perfume, rich with the scent of roses. She is close to tears again.

'Thank you,' Adriana says.

'I thought I had destroyed your mind,' Minoo almost whispers.

Adriana holds her tightly.

'You removed my bond to the Council. I'm free now. You gave me my life back.'

Minoo closes her eyes. Maybe, after all, she has used her powers to do at least one wholly good thing.

Adriana hugs the other Chosen Ones and they all sit down. Felix comes in carrying a tray with glasses and a jug full of iced tea. He clears the table and then pours tea for everyone.

'I could hardly believe my ears when Evelina called and told me you were back,' Adriana says.

'Evelina?' Vanessa says.

'Rickard and Evelina have joined our small group here,' Adriana smiles. 'Gustaf, too. But we had better tell you everything from the beginning. That is, what happened after you vanished.'

Felix puts the jug down and goes to sit next to Adriana.

'I don't know how much you already know,' he says. 'But Walter murdered Sigrid. And then he murdered Viktor.'

'We know,' Minoo says quietly.

She senses his pain, and notices that the others do, too.

Felix waits until his feelings have ebbed.

'Nejla and I ran back to the manor house when we heard Clara scream. We took her and Adriana to the hospital. We had no idea what to do next, or where we could go. But then Gustaf, Rickard and Evelina turned up, looking for you.'

He stops speaking and glances at Adriana, as if he wants her to take up the story.

'I started to come to after a couple of days and then recovered quickly,' Adriana says. 'We decided to move in here. Nejla's boyfriend joined us and, a little later, more witches turned up. The rumor had spread, you see, that there was a haven in Engelsfors for witches who wanted to leave the Council. Most of them are young.'

Minoo thinks of the group on the lawn and the risks they have run to come here.

'We practice every day,' Adriana says. 'They're all doing very well. Evelina is such a good student.'

Minoo can't help smiling because she remembers the talent she saw in Evelina when she watched everyone's auras in Kärrgruvan. Nejla must really enjoy having another high-powered fire witch to train against.

'I'm so happy to see you again,' Adriana says. 'And so proud of you.'

She looks at them all in turn.

'Mona told me about the choices you faced in the Borderland. I can think of many people who would have thought they could save the world by accepting the deal the guardians offered you. But you saw through them and had the strength to resist the temptations. You have given humanity a new chance.'

Minoo recalls what she told the Chosen Ones while she was blessed by the guardians.

The outcome of all this will be chaos. All existing political, economic and religious systems will crumble. Magic will equal power. Those with most magic will rule over everyone else.

'So, you do believe we have a chance?' she asks Adriana. 'It won't all end in chaos?'

'It probably will be chaotic,' Adriana says in a matter-of-fact tone. 'The Council will have a frightening advantage over everyone else. They are well organized and exhaustively well informed about magic.'

The Council. Minoo hadn't even begun to think about its role in this new world. Obviously, they'll try to take over as much as possible. In the end, to take over *everything*.

'We'll have to get organized,' Anna-Karin says.

'And tell the world the truth,' Vanessa says.

Adriana smiles, and Minoo is proud of their courage, even though it does nothing to make her feel less anxious.

'That's exactly what I had in mind,' Adriana says. 'The only way to keep the chaos from escalating is to enlighten everyone about what's going on. That's where I need your help. You're the strongest witches in the world. And you've saved it from extinction.'

'This is the unpaid job I was mentioning earlier,' Mona grins.

'Sign me up,' Vanessa says. 'Listen, who will people trust most, once they know exactly what's happened? Us or the Council?'

'Sadly, people tend to go for whoever provides the most simplistic answers and the most unambiguous guidelines,' Adriana says. 'It's especially tempting when one's afraid – and many will be. And, as always, some people will grab any chance for personal gain at the expense of others.'

'There will always be jerks,' Vanessa says. 'Lots of them. It's not great that they will have magic powers sometime soon. But, hopefully, the non-jerks will be in the majority.'

Minoo hopes that Vanessa is right. But, even if the proportion of non-jerks is larger, they must find a way to get on with the jerks. Minoo still believes that power must be shared, but she can see that it will be an enormously complicated process.

It's all very well to save mankind from the guardians and the demons. But how is one to save mankind from itself?

'How long do you think we'll have before people start noticing the change?' she asks.

'We've already noticed a few odd phenomena,' Adriana replies. 'Events that we think are linked to recently awakened natural witches. I'm planning to travel and try to reach as many witches as possible before the Council does.'

'The levels are rising, slowly but surely.' Mona is trying to make her chewing gum stick to the edge of her glass. 'I'm stocking up as best I can. There'll be a run on ectoplasm, mark my words.'

She glances at Minoo.

'Though I guess none of that will be of much use to you, honey-bun. Because you're absolutely non-magical now, aren't you?'

'Yes,' Minoo admits.

She feels that they are all looking at her and wonders if they pity her.

'No powers at all,' Mona says. 'Never again.'

She doesn't say this nastily. Instead she sounds thoughtful. Suddenly, Minoo finds herself hoping that Mona will start chuckling and saying something like, *You've got it all wrong again, baby face; you'll get powers just like everyone else.* But Mona is quiet.

'Have you taken care of Nicolaus's body?' Anna-Karin asks.

'What was left of it,' Mona says. 'A small pile of ashes and some clothes, basically. That's what happens when you've been alive for centuries.'

Minoo thinks about his sacrifice, a sacrifice that she allowed him to make. Without it, they would never have been able to enter the Borderland and close the portal.

'Was there a dagger anywhere?' Minoo asks. 'And a bowl and a skull?'

'A dagger and a bowl, yes, we found those,' Adriana tells her. 'But no skull.'

The skull belonged to the last-but-one guide. Nicolaus was the last. The last sacrifice so that the last portal could be closed.

Minoo still can't get her head around the idea that it is all over. Is it really over?

'Is there any risk that they will try to come back to this world? The demons and the guardians, I mean.'

'Not as far as I can see,' Mona says.

No one speaks for a while. Minoo takes a sip of the peach-flavored iced tea.

'How much does the Council know about all that's been going on?' Linnéa asks. 'And about what's going to happen next?'

'I'm not quite sure.' Adriana pauses before she continues. 'Alexander is the new chairman.'

Minoo feels a mixture of weariness and sadness. Alexander let his fear win though, in his heart of hearts, he longed to be free. Minoo saw that in him when she could still use the powers of the guardians.

'The last time I met him was just before Christmas,' Adriana continues. 'He led a delegation that came to take Walter's body away. I tried to appeal to him but . . .'

She stops and Minoo understands why. Alexander chose Walter's side, even in death.

'We haven't heard much from them since,' Adriana continues. 'But we know they have spies around town.' She looks at Minoo. 'I'm especially worried about you. The Council doesn't know for certain that you killed Walter, but they suspect it. And they know of course that you have taken the oath. Like me, you're a defector.'

There is a sadness in her eyes when she looks at Minoo. Minoo suddenly feels as though there is not enough air in the room. She has no powers and the Council will be hunting her for the rest of her life.

'It seems you'll have to take on being my bodyguards.' She tries to smile.

No one else even tries.

'We will be,' Anna-Karin says gravely. 'They won't get anywhere near you.'

A cell phone pings and Minoo has time to think that it's hers and that it might be a text from Gustaf. But Felix is checking his; he frowns before turning to Minoo.

'Clara would like to talk to you,' he says, and Minoo gets up at once.

* * *

Linnéa looks at Minoo as she leaves to follow Felix upstairs.

She knows that she had better speak to her soon about everything that happened in the Borderland and before. She will not allow Minoo to withdraw into herself as she had done after breaking Max's blessing.

Adriana carries on talking about the new witches in Engelsfors and Linnéa notes a new self-assurance in her. Perhaps it is as Adriana said to Minoo, that she is truly free, not only from the Council, but from the image of herself that the Council had forced her to accept. The organization that despises weakness more than anything else had made

Adriana believe that her lack of magical ability meant she was worthless.

In the end, there will be some kind of organization opposing the Council, and Adriana for sure will be one of its leaders. She will be good at it. A worthy opponent to her brother.

But what will become of me? Linnéa thinks.

Being one of the Chosen Ones was all very well. She didn't have a choice. But now there will be others to take the fight further.

Vanessa will, for one. She, if anyone can, will be able to inspire others.

'I'm going out for a smoke,' Linnéa announces.

'You do that,' Mona says. She chews gum ostentatiously and looks unbearably smug.

And now, for the first time, it dawns on Linnéa that she hasn't seen Mona have a single cigarette since they met at Sunny Side.

'What, have *you* stopped smoking?' Vanessa asks.

Linnéa feels Vanessa's shock.

'You bet,' Mona says. 'I wasn't going to survive the end of the world just to die of lung cancer. Besides, it's so very passé.'

She pulls up her top to show off her midriff. It glows with a rich tanning-salon brown where it isn't covered in nicotine patches.

'These cutie-pies and plenty of chewing gum make all the difference.'

If even Mona can stop, I've got no excuses left, Linnéa thinks.

She pulls her pack of cigs and her lighter from the top of one of her boots and sets out for the front door.

'If I said it has been all fun and games I'd be lying,' Mona says. 'But, you know, people do change sometimes. Right, Linnéa?'

Linnéa stops in mid-step.

'We've all got bad habits we're fed up with,' Mona says behind her.

Linnéa's hands are shaking so much when she finally lights up in the garden, she almost drops the cigarette. She tries to think straight, but this seems too much. Too big for her. But, at the same time, so simple.

She must get Vanessa back.

CHAPTER 107

Felix stops outside one of the doors on the upstairs landing. His face is lit from a skylight as he turns to Minoo.

'Would you care to come with me to Viktor's grave later on?'

He sounds formal but Minoo realizes what a huge deal it is for him to ask this.

'Yes, I would, very much,' she says.

Felix nods, opens the door and closes it behind her when she has stepped inside.

At first, Minoo thinks Viktor is sitting on the bed.

Clara has cut her ash-blonde hair short and is wearing one of Viktor's pale blue shirts with her jeans. Minoo wonders what it does to her to look at herself in the mirror; if it is like glimpsing Viktor again.

'Hi,' Minoo says gently.

Clara doesn't reply.

An ugly scar runs from the base of her throat and down across her chest. It disappears under the tank top she's wearing underneath the unbuttoned shirt.

In the garden outside the open widow, Nejla is laughing.

'Could you close the window?' Clara says. 'Felix keeps opening it all the time.'

Minoo goes up to the window. She sees Vanessa, Anna-Karin and Adriana come out into the garden and walk along to join Nejla and the two guys.

Minoo closes the window and turns to Clara. She tries to avoid staring at her scar, but it is hard not to.

'Nejla saved my life,' Clara says. 'She stopped the blood flow using fire. I had thought that the pain couldn't get any worse. I was wrong.' Her smile is bitter.

. 'Do sit down,' she says next.

Minoo sits down next to her on the bed. Clara's room in the manor house had always been wildly untidy, but in this room everything is compulsively neat. Perhaps that's another way in which Clara has taken after her brother.

'Mona told us that you killed Walter,' Clara says.

Minoo looks at her hands. They rest, lightly clasped, on her lap. Harmless. She will never again release her black smoke. This world no longer contains the potential.

'I did,' she says.

'Good,' Clara says.

Minoo looks up and almost backs away from the hatred in Clara's eyes.

'I murdered him,' Minoo says. 'I *obliterated* him.'

The memory is so vivid. If she closed her eyes now, she could relive the moment she burnt his soul.

'Better still,' Clara says.

'No,' Minoo says, shaking her head.

'Did it feel wrong at the time?'

'No,' Minoo says once more. 'But that was because the guardians wanted it. They controlled me. I would never have done it as myself.'

She wishes Clara had Viktor's powers so she could determine if Minoo was telling the truth, because she isn't quite sure herself.

She hears steps on the ground floor and a door closing.

'The guardians could see the future,' Clara says. 'Did you know that Viktor would die?'

The direct question shocks Minoo. She wonders for how long Clara has pondered on this and how long it took her to understand it all.

'Did you?' Clara asks.

Once again, Minoo wants to say that she had lost her own self. That she couldn't fight the guardians. But is that really true? And, even if it were so, would she not sound as if she was making excuses for herself?

'Yes,' she says.

She can't find the courage to look Clara in the eyes. Clara's eyes, which are cornflower blue, just like Viktor's. Minoo had done nothing to save him. As she had done nothing to protect Clara from near-fatal injury. She allowed these things to happen because the guardians had wanted it, so that their plans would not be upset.

'Thanks for being honest,' Clara says. Her thumb is sliding up and down the scar on her wrist.

'I hated you for a while,' she continues. 'But I know that you would have saved us if you could. I don't blame you anymore.'

Minoo notices that, on the bookshelf, on top of a row of books, *The Secret History* has been jammed in. She can almost hear Viktor's voice say: *I only ever read books in the original language.*

'The only one I blame is myself,' Clara says. 'I should have persuaded Viktor not to take the oath to the Council. We should've gotten the hell out. I knew we weren't in the circle that was meant to save the world. I felt it all along.'

She stops touching her scar and clenches her fists.

'I keep going over what happened again and again in my head, thinking of all the things I could have done differently . . . It should have been me.'

'You mustn't even think that,' Minoo says. 'Viktor wouldn't want you to blame yourself.'

Clara looks at Minoo and her eyes are shiny with tears.

'Right,' she says. 'Tell me, then, how I'm supposed to stop.'

Minoo can't. They sit in silence for a while.

'I think I'm broken,' Clara finally says. 'All I can think about is revenge.'

'But Walter is dead.'

'The Council is still there. And so is Alexander.'

The hatred returns to Clara's eyes. She has not only lost her brother, she has lost her father, too. Lost yet another part of her childhood.

'There are other ways of fighting the Council,' Minoo says.

'You mean Adriana's idea?' Clara asks contemptuously.

'Viktor believed in an organization that could help people—'

'I loved my brother more than anything,' Clara interrupts. 'But he was naïve.'

Her eyes pierce Minoo's. 'There is going to be a war. More will die. As for the survivors, how much is left of them? How much do you reckon is left of me?'

'Clara . . .'

'And, even when the war ends, the problems won't be solved. Power corrupts. You, if anyone, should know that.'

'I know that very well,' Minoo says. 'Which is precisely why I think we have a chance. Just because we are so aware of the dangers.'

She is not at all sure that she believes all this, but she can't let Clara disappear.

'Don't give up. We need you.'

'I'm not going to help anyone else ever again,' Clara says. 'I am my own person and no one else's.'

She gives Minoo another piercing look.

'And I have not given up. Alexander got away after his last visit in town. He won't next time. And don't preach about how Viktor wouldn't have wanted me to avenge him. He would have done the same for me.'

'And you would have tried to persuade him not to,' Minoo says.

Clara looks at her with a sardonic little smile. Viktor's smile. Clara's smile.

835

The Key

'I'm glad you're back.'

She leans toward Minoo and places a light kiss on her cheek. And then she lies down on the bed, with her back turned.

Minoo stays for a moment before leaving the room.

* * *

Linnéa sits with her legs crossed on the lawn outside Adriana's house, leaning against the trunk of one of the birches. She has smoked her last cigarette and is collecting the butts in her empty pack.

She hears the voices of the others from the back garden. Laughter is rising toward the cloudless sky. One of the voices is Vanessa's.

Then Minoo comes outside. She stops when she catches sight of Linnéa.

'The others are in the back garden,' Linnéa says.

'I know.'

Minoo walks along to sit next to Linnéa. She takes care when she settles down to avoid grass stains on her clothes. Careful Minoo, who almost laid waste to the entire world.

How was Clara? Linnéa thinks.

Not well, Minoo thinks. *She's completely set on taking revenge. And she doesn't think much of Adriana's organization.*

'Do you?' Linnéa asks.

Minoo tugs at a few grass stems.

'I don't know.'

'I don't either,' Linnéa says. 'I want to believe in it . . . only, it seems so fucking complicated. I keep thinking about how hard it was to get the Circle to agree and act together. There were only six of us, but now we're talking about billions of individuals who suddenly have to start handling magic powers . . .'

She looks at Minoo.

'It frightens me,' she admits.

'Me, too,' Minoo says. 'I'm scared about what will happen.

Part Six

And how we will change. What kind of people we will become.'

She sits quietly and concentrates on pulling up long blades of grass that she divides lengthwise.

'Remember when we all went to the cemetery after the final day assembly in our first year? What I said then, when we stood near Elias's and Rebecka's graves?'

'You said, "They're where they should be",' Linnéa remembers.

Minoo pulls up more grass.

'I felt so sure,' she says. 'I knew it with my whole being. And, it was true. Elias and Rebecka were where they should be. Where *the guardians* thought they should be.'

Linnéa shudders. She hasn't thought about it like that. She can't imagine how it feels for Minoo.

'Before, I didn't feel that my power was part of me,' Minoo continues. 'The reverse was true. It has been a much larger part of me than I ever understood. And now it's gone.'

She pulls up an entire fistful of grass and tears the blades into tiny pieces.

'When was it me? When was it the guardians? Which of my instincts were my own and which were theirs? For how long have they been influencing me? I allowed people to die, and I've killed someone. And, I don't even know if I did those things to save the world or to save the guardians. And I don't know—'

'Stop it,' Linnéa interrupts.

She takes Minoo's hands in hers. The torn grass falls to the ground.

'If you carry on like this, you'll go out of your mind,' Linnéa says. 'It wasn't your fault.'

Minoo meets her eyes.

'If only I had fought back . . .'

'It wasn't *you* who was at fault,' Linnéa insists. 'The guardians *possessed* you. They took you over.'

'But I let them in,' Minoo says stubbornly.

837

'What else could you do? You trusted them.'

Tears are flowing down Minoo's cheeks now.

'But I loved it,' she mumbles. 'I had absolute power and I loved it.'

'Who wouldn't have? Why should just you be some fucking saint?'

Minoo sobs.

'The guardians knew just how to manipulate you, Minoo. Don't be ashamed of falling for it. We all fell for it. Me too. None of what happened was your fault.'

Minoo smiles at her through tears.

'It would've been so much easier to believe if it hadn't been about me.'

Linnéa laughs a little. The voices of the others are coming closer.

'I'm sorry I was such an asshole to you,' Linnéa says.

'I wasn't much better.'

They look at each other.

'And I'm so sorry for what happened to Viktor,' Linnéa says.

Linnéa's eyes fill with tears when she says this. She remembers the last words she thought to him the night he died. *At least you tried.*

Yes, Viktor tried. And now, all is over for him.

'I'm going with Felix to the cemetery later on,' Minoo says quietly.

Linnéa almost gives her a hug, even though neither of them is the hugging type.

Minoo's cell phone rings. She almost rips it out, and Linnéa just catches sight of Gustaf's name on the display before Minoo gets up, answers and walks into the house.

Linnéa senses Vanessa's energy coming closer and gets up too.

Vanessa strolls toward her across the grass and Linnéa's heart beats in double time. As it did in the beginning, when she was secretly in love.

'There you are,' Vanessa says.

'Here I am,' Linnéa says.

Vanessa pulls her hand through her hair.

'I was thinking of going home,' she says.

Linnéa makes up her mind.

'Would it be all right for me to come, too?' she says. 'I'm homeless after all.'

'Sure,' Vanessa says and smiles.

CHAPTER 108

Viktor's gravestone is a rectangle of black marble with an elegantly chiseled pattern around the inscription.

Minoo's and Felix's shadows fall across it.

VIKTOR EHRENSKIÖLD. BORN ANDERSSON

The grief that overwhelms her is so deep that she wonders if it is Felix's or her own. And then she wonders if it matters.

'Clara wanted it just to say "Andersson",' Felix tells her. 'But I don't think Viktor would've wanted that. This was part of his life as well.'

'I think you're right,' Minoo says.

These are the first words they've exchanged since they arrived. They have been sitting together in the grass, quietly listening to the wind playing in the crowns of the lime trees. Hearing the odd cry of a child from the rectory, where a new family has moved in. And lots of drunken yelling from Olsson's Hill.

'If you still had your old powers, I would have asked you to use them on me,' Felix says.

'Would you have wanted to lose your memories of him?'

'No, on the contrary. I would have liked to show you what Viktor meant to me.'

He touches the gravestone lightly.

'You, Clara and I were probably the only people who knew what he was truly like,' Felix continues, glancing at her. 'I was jealous of you. Not only because you had those incredible powers, but also because I was convinced there was something between you and Viktor.'

840

That explains the way Felix looked at me at first, Minoo thinks.

'When I arrived here, I hadn't seen him for more than a year,' he continues. 'I hoped . . . Never mind what I hoped. As soon as I met him, I realized that he was in love with someone. I saw the two of you together and there seemed to be something special between you. On your first day in the manor house, he took your hand when we saw the sun going dark.'

'There never was anything between us. Not like that.'

'I know', Felix says. 'You weren't exactly Viktor's type.'

The way he says it makes her feel mildly offended, but he doesn't seem to realize that she might mind.

'I wasn't either, of course,' he adds, trying to smile. 'He liked me well enough. But he never loved me.'

The pain Minoo feels now is definitely Felix's. Grief. Unrequited love for someone who is gone forever.

'Was there ever anything between you?' Minoo asks.

'Do you have any idea how many times Sigrid tried to find that out?'

Minoo feels her ears going hotter. She doesn't want to be like Sigrid. Ever.

'I'm sorry.'

'It's OK,' Felix says. 'Yes, there was something. A couple of times. But he ended it. He didn't think it was fair on me since I had feelings for him. I couldn't exactly hide it, you know. I hated that he was so fucking considerate.'

Another wave of grief hits her.

'I can't believe he's gone.' Misery distorts Felix's face.

He turns a little away from her and they sit like that for a while. He takes a deep breath and seems to pull himself together. The grief inside Minoo dies down a little.

'Sorry,' he says. 'It seems I'll never be able to control my powers. But I'm trying to learn to accept that.'

She hopes that will make it easier for him.

'At least it's some comfort that Walter is dead,' Felix says. 'There's some justice after all.'

841

Minoo can't see what she did as an act of justice, but doesn't want to discuss it with Felix just now.

'You have no idea how I worshipped Walter,' Felix continues. 'At school, I was nothing but a great big disappointment. Even though all the tests showed that I was very talented, I could never perform. And then *the chairman* asked me to help him save the world.'

He wipes the tears from his cheeks.

'He was really nice to me sometimes, but only when no one was watching. So when he made a fool of me in public, it made me feel even more of a loser. The worst part of the humiliation was that I looked up to him. Walter was everything I dreamt of becoming. Or, so I thought. Now I know that he was a monster.'

'Yes, he was,' she agrees.

Felix gets up and Minoo goes to stand next to him. Somebody is playing music on Olsson's Hill. A heavy bass beat echoes across the town. She doesn't recognize the tune.

'I keep trying to persuade Clara to come to the grave,' Felix says. 'But she refuses. I hope she'll be able to move on one day.'

Minoo hopes so, too, but isn't sure what she believes.

'Have you moved on?' she asks him.

'I suppose one never does, not completely. But I have met someone ... Maybe you saw him at Adriana's? Guy called Sanke.'

Minoo remembers the name. Nejla's boyfriend's big brother. She guesses he must be the older of the two guys in the garden. The one with purple hair.

'And it's great to have something to aim for now,' Felix continues. 'I really believe we can accomplish great things with Adriana. And we could use someone with your strength.'

'Me? I haven't even got the slightest power.'

'You were offered all the power in the world,' Felix says. 'And you rejected it. I would never have been able to resist.'

He fixes his dark eyes on Minoo.

'I don't believe you realize how strong you are, Minoo. It's time you did, because the world will need you.'

CHAPTER 109

Vanessa sits on the floor in the living room and looks at Melvin's soft toy, a penguin that's lying between her and Melvin. It has lost an eye since she last saw it.

She reaches out with her finger and tickles the penguin's tummy.

'But he must remember a little about me?' She fights to keep her voice steady.

'No, he really doesn't remember you at all,' Melvin says.

Vanessa still can't get over how well he speaks now, and how much he has grown. She has tried to pick up hints of magic energy from him, but not sensed anything so far.

Mom cries, seated on the new sofa behind Vanessa. She wonders how many times Melvin has had to watch Mom cry while she's been away.

'Maybe Pingu remembers when we used to sing "Twinkle, Twinkle Little Star"?' Vanessa suggests.

Melvin looks inquisitively at her, then purses his lips and shakes his head.

Vanessa gave him the penguin for his second birthday. Melvin treated her as a stranger then as well. She had been staying with Wille and his mother and had been away for quite a long time. When she moved back home, she had promised herself never to do this to her little brother again. And now she has been away for even longer.

'Mom, why are you crying?' Melvin asks.

'I'm crying because I'm so happy,' Mom says. 'I'm happy because Nessa is with us again.'

Melvin doesn't comment. But he hugs the penguin closer. Then he turns to point at Linnéa, who is in the kitchen talking to her father on the phone.

'Why is she here?' he asks.

Vanessa wishes there was a simple answer to his question. 'She's my friend,' she says.

Linnéa ends the call, puts the phone down and stares out through the window.

'Mom, I want to watch the rest of *The Little Mermaid* now,' Melvin says.

'Of course you can,' Mom says. 'Are you all right with watching on your own if we go to sit in the kitchen?'

'Yes, if you don't talk too loudly,' Melvin says. 'It's annoying.'

Vanessa aches with longing to pick him up and hug him, but instead she just gets up from the floor while Mom puts the film on for him. Melvin curls up on the sofa together with his penguin and loses himself in the story immediately.

Vanessa goes to sit next to Linnéa at the kitchen table. They look at each other as the little mermaid's underwater friends start singing at the bottom of the sea.

'You must give him time,' Mom says as she sits down on Vanessa's other side. 'And don't disappear again.'

She smiles, but tears still trickle down her cheeks.

'Sorry,' she says, drying her eyes. 'I've actually stopped crying. It's more like I'm leaking.'

Vanessa scans the kitchen. New wallpaper. Mom had thought it was as well to do that at the same time as the living room had a complete overhaul after Olivia's attack.

There are more pictures of Vanessa on the fridge than ever. Frasse's bowls have gone. When she opened the front door, she missed his coming to greet her. The kindly, daft Alsatian they had rescued from a home for stray dogs. He had tried to defend Mom. Vanessa will never forget the stench of scorched meat.

'How is Björn?' Mom asks.

'He . . . was pleased that I called,' Linnéa replies. Vanessa notes the effort she is making not to withdraw.

He was sober today. Always something, Linnéa thinks, looking at Vanessa.

'You know, getting my head around all your stories is so hard.' Mom shakes her head. 'I know you think I'm a bit New Agey, Nessa. But this is hard to believe, even for me.'

'I understand that,' Vanessa tells her.

'We had a hard time believing it too, in the beginning, even though we were in the middle of it,' Linnéa says.

'I thought I was hallucinating when Olivia was here,' Mom says. 'But I suppose I wasn't.'

'No, you weren't,' Vanessa says.

Mom nods and pops her head around the living-room door to make sure that Melvin can't hear them.

'What are we to do with him?' she asks.

'Are you sure you haven't noticed anything?' Vanessa says. 'If you really think about it?'

'No, nothing. Except, he has started to sleepwalk, but you did the same when you were little and—'

Mom's phone starts ringing and Vanessa is grateful for the distraction. Usually, this is the point at which Mom tells the anecdote about how little Vanessa squatted and peed on the rug in the hall.

Mom only listens for a minute before clicking to end the call.

'Another journalist,' she says. 'What are you going to tell them?'

'Nothing just now,' Vanessa says. 'But we must tell them something. Later.'

'That Council you spoke about. They won't be best pleased when you go public.'

'True,' Linnéa says. 'But they don't like us anyway.'

Mom shakes her head again. 'How did you *cope* with all the terrible things you experienced?'

She looks at Vanessa. They hear Melvin laugh.

'I don't know,' Vanessa says. 'We simply had to.'

She checks the time. They're going to meet the others in the park and Linnéa has suggested that they walk there. Vanessa is expectant. And nervous.

'We'd better go now,' she says.

Mom looks at her and lightly touches the scar above her eyebrow.

'I will be back.' Vanessa gets up and gives her a hug. 'Solemn promise. I'll take the longest shower in the world and then sleep for a week. At least.'

She kisses her Mom's head and wanders off to the living room.

'Bye bye, Melvin,' she says.

And stays in the doorway, as if nailed to the floor.

Melvin has got down on the floor and is dancing to the music.

Behind him, his penguin is leaping about on the sofa, as if dancing with him. His wings bounce in a crazy rhythm against the bulky little penguin body.

* * *

Minoo sits on her bed with the *Book of Patterns* in her hands. It is empty now. One blank page after another. The guardians will never again talk to anyone through its pages.

They will never talk to her.

A sense of loneliness lurks somewhere inside her.

She had become used to having them within her reach, just beyond her consciousness. It made her feel safe. Just as she will miss the power, so she will miss that safety. Both helped her to feel strong. But perhaps she has another kind of strength. Felix thinks so.

The door to her room opens and Mom pops her head in. She doesn't speak, only smiles. Just now, that is enough. Minoo knows that they have a great deal to talk about. But it can wait.

The doorbell rings and Minoo wonders if it's yet another journalist. But when the front door is opened, she hears Gustaf's voice. She gets up. Running footsteps on the stairs. Another second or two, then he comes in.

Minoo hardly has time to see him before he has taken her in his arms.

She doesn't know how long they stand like that.

She hears the beating of Gustaf's heart: fast at first, then slower. She looks up at him and their eyes meet.

He knows most of what has happened already. They have talked on the phone. And she has told him that she loves him. He has said he loves her and that he has missed her. He has said it over and over again.

Now he bends to kiss her and she realizes how much she has feared that something between them would have changed while she was away. That he would have grown fed up with waiting. Or perhaps that something about her had been ruined by the guardians.

But everything feels all right.

They sit down on the bed and he puts his arm around her shoulders.

She has told him everything. Almost.

'I know that you want to know about Rebecka.'

He nods but doesn't say anything.

'She is no longer in the Borderland,' Minoo begins. 'She has passed on. But I had time to speak to her before . . .' She sobs, then tells herself to be strong for Gustaf's sake. 'She knows that it wasn't you who killed her. And I told her about us. She asked me to tell you . . . that she loves you. And that she wants you to be happy.'

Gustaf bursts into tears. Minoo holds him and cries with him.

* * *

It is a perfect summer evening and the sky is clear. The sun still warms Linnéa's face. She left her fake fur coat at Vanessa's and is wearing only T-shirt and jeans. Vanessa has changed to a tank top and shorts. Linnéa reckons she has never before had such pale legs in June.

They walk through the deserted industrial plots in Engelsfors. Linnéa catches sight of the grim old community hall where they had their spring dance in the last year of middle school. She had been outside with Elias and Olivia, checking people out. She must have seen Vanessa that night. Linnéa doesn't even want to think about the comments she would have made back then. She used to be so judgmental. Working on the assumption that absolutely everyone else was stupid. It had taken mind-reading and threats of apocalyptic doom to make her realize that people were a bit more complicated than that.

'I always wanted to get out of Engelsfors as soon as possible,' Vanessa says suddenly. 'But, just now, it seems all right to hang on here for a while. And there's a chance that I'll be traveling with Adriana to look for witches.'

She smiles and Linnéa smiles back at her.

Elias was right, Linnéa thinks. I must be there for Vanessa and let her be there for me. Ida was right. I need to get my act together and sort this out. Matilda was right. We have free will. We aren't pawns.

'Do you remember when you said that you wanted to understand what it's like to feel the way I do?' Linnéa asks. 'It was before we . . . before I broke up with you.'

'Yes,' Vanessa says.

'I'm not sure how to explain it,' Linnéa says. 'But it's kind of like this. It's like being wrongly . . . wired, as if all the leads are all over the place . . . Sometimes I don't even know why I react the way I do.'

She's talking quickly without daring to look at Vanessa.

'I think I get it,' Vanessa says.

They have reached the old steel plant now and are walking

along the overgrown rail tracks. They pass an abandoned freight wagon.

'I used to think that, you know . . . that it was just who I was,' Linnéa says. 'I figured there was nothing I could do about it. And perhaps some things can't be fixed. But I think I can learn to understand them better. That I can learn to understand *me* better.'

She balances on the rails that have been worn shiny. Vanessa is silent. Paranoia is rushing into Linnéa's mind. Maybe she won't fix anything by speaking like this; maybe she is ruining their relationship even more.

'Remember when Mona said that people do change some- times?' she says. 'At first, I didn't believe it. Then I thought she was talking about my dad. And then I thought she was talking about you. But now I think she was talking about me.'

'Do you think she's right?' Vanessa asks.

'I know that I want to change. And yes, I think I can. But it's not going to be easy. And I'm not saying this to get you back. I mean, I want to . . . I want to change for my own sake. So I can handle being me.'

She stops. Glances at Vanessa, who is looking straight at her with her large brown eyes. What do these eyes see when they are looking at her?

'But I'd like to change for your sake, too,' Linnéa continues. 'I know very well that I've got no right to ask you for anything. I just want you to know that if you ever . . . If you should want to . . .'

She takes a deep breath. A chorus of her internal voices screams that this is going straight to hell. She asks *them* to go to hell.

'If you ever want me back, I'm here,' says Linnéa. 'This time I won't be such a fucking coward. But if you don't want to . . . and, believe me, I'd understand only too easily . . . I'll be happy anyway that you're in my life.'

She forces herself to look at Vanessa. Their eyes meet.

She knows at once that Vanessa gets it. She got it from the start.

* * *

Vanessa can find no words to express what she feels. Instead she takes Linnéa's hand. She lets her feelings flow into her. She lets her know.

And she feels that Linnéa receives her love.

Vanessa takes a step closer and puts her arms around Linnéa, touches her lips with her own. Little stars begin to burn in Vanessa's body. Whole galaxies of them. She feels them light up in Linnéa, too.

They kiss.

Vanessa wraps them in invisibility. Air magic flutters across her skin and she feels it caress Linnéa. Then they both levitate a few inches above the ground.

'I've never done this with anyone else before,' Vanessa says. 'Do you dare to do this?'

'I do,' Linnéa says.

They take off together. Invisible to the world. Barely a part of it anymore. Linnéa holds on to Vanessa's waist. Vanessa senses both her fear and her fascination. Above all, she feels her trust.

* * *

Anna-Karin sits on the steps leading up to the dance pavilion. There are a couple of empty beer cans on the ground next to her. The townspeople have obviously remembered Kärrgruvan again.

Gustaf's car stops just outside the gates. He and Minoo climb out and walk into the park hand in hand.

The fox rubs itself against Anna-Karin's legs when she gets up. He has refused to leave her side since she met him in the forest.

She walks along to the place she has marked beforehand by

kicking the gravel away to expose the soil underneath. Minoo and Gustaf come along and then stop at the bare ground in front of their feet.

'Is this where she is?' Gustaf asks.

Anna-Karin nods. It had been so easy to find her; she just asked the earth and it answered.

'This is the exact spot where we all met on the night of the blood-red moon,' Minoo says. Anna-Karin nods again.

'We would never have had a chance without her,' she adds.

'But we wouldn't without you either,' Minoo says. 'It was you who took my hand in the Borderland. You told me what I had to do. If you hadn't . . .'

'We did it together,' Anna-Karin says.

'That's true,' Minoo says. 'But that's not everything. There is so much I couldn't have done without you.'

'I feel the same,' Anna-Karin mumbles.

She doesn't know what more she can say. But when she looks at Minoo, she knows that she has said enough.

Suddenly, she senses Vanessa's and Linnéa's energies approaching. But from the wrong direction. They're coming . . . from above.

Vanessa and Linnéa become visible the moment they hit the ground, spraying gravel and dust into a cloud around them. The wind has made a mess of their hair.

'So sorry!' Vanessa says and laughs. 'Must improve my landing technique.'

'Yes, please.' Linnéa gives her a kiss.

Anna-Karin feels warmth spread in her chest. At least one thing in this world is as it should be.

'Well, here we are again,' Linnéa says.

'We are,' Minoo says.

Gustaf puts his arm around her and she leans against his shoulder.

They stay silent for a while. The park is so beautiful.

The Key

Anna-Karin is pleased that people in Engelsfors have found their way here again.

They hear another car coming closer on the gravel road.

Anna-Karin looks toward the gates to Kärrgruvan, where the dark blue Mercedes stops. Rickard and Evelina come in first. Behind them come Mona, Felix and Adriana. Adriana carries an urn in her arms. Mona chews gum so vigorously she could dislocate her jaw at any minute.

They join the others. Anna-Karin bends down and places her hand on the ground. Releases her power and feels it flow through the soil. She can shape it according to her will. It obeys her, and a round pit with firm walls is formed.

She can't see anything at the bottom of the pit, but knows that this is the place where Nicolaus buried Matilda. This is where he will be laid to rest.

Adriana hands the stone urn to Anna-Karin. It is cold against her hands. She wishes she could think of something to say, something beautiful and suitably solemn.

'Such a damn shame,' Mona says. 'Fair enough, it was high time for him to pack up, but he was one handsome fellow despite his age.'

'Are you sure you have no idea where they end up?' Anna-Karin says. 'The ones who die for real?'

Mona stops chewing and her features seem to soften a little. 'No, sweetheart. I don't think we're meant to know.'

Anna-Karin nods. Maybe it's such an amazing place that people would refuse to live on if they knew where they would end up. She hopes that's how it is.

She takes the lid off the urn and gently scatters the ashes into the pit. Then makes the ground heal itself.

She puts the urn down and straightens up.

And faces Minoo, Vanessa and Linnéa.

Grandpa was right. She has a family. They have been through so much together. The magical bond between the

Chosen Ones is thicker than blood. But that's not the only thing that connects them now.

It's who they are.

And it's not only the Chosen Ones anymore, Anna-Karin thinks.

She looks in turn at Adriana. Evelina. Rickard. Felix. Mona. There will be more of them. And what's to come will be harder than anything Anna-Karin can imagine.

She is afraid. But she is ready. And she is not alone.

'What shall we do next?' Minoo asks.

'Keep on saving the world,' Anna-Karin says.

Acknowledgments

As we write this, we are listening to the playlist from the release party for *The Circle*. It feels like yesterday. It feels like a whole lifetime ago. Engelsfors has changed everything for us and we have so many people to thank, more than we can fit here.

As usual, we want to start with Marie Augustsson, our publisher, who showed such an unconditional belief in us that we too dared to believe that we could pull off this huge project. Thanks also to our editor Ylva Blomqvist who fearlessly moved into Engelsfors, made herself at home and allowed herself to be held hostage during a crazy week of going through the proofs. Thank you to Anders Bergström who stepped in when time was running out. Thanks to Heléne Jensen and our proofreaders, also those who read *The Circle* and *Fire*. A big thank you to everyone else at Rabén & Sjögren Norstedts who worked so hard for the trilogy. Many thanks to Pocketförlaget who have made our books do so well in the smaller format.

A big thank you to the unparalleled team at Grand Agency –Lena Stjernström, Lotta Jämtsved Millberg, Peter Stjernström, Maria Enberg and Umberto Ghidoni. A special thanks to Lena, also called Lena – Warrior Princess. Your loyalty and integrity have been a huge support for us during both our ups and downs. You always have our back and we have yours.

Måns Elenius and Gitte Ekdahl: Words cannot express how reassuring it has been to have you reading through all the different versions of the book. Thank you for your comments, both big and small, and for taking our universe so deadly seriously.

A huge thank you to other beta readers, who all contributed unique perspectives and insights: Anna Andersson, Johan Ehn,

Acknowledgments

Linnéa Lindsköld, Margareta Elfgren, Mathilda Elfgren Schwartz, Mikael Sveding, Minna Frydén Bonnier, Siska Humlesjö and Sofie Neckmar Arvidsson.

Three other readers are Karl Johnsson, Kim W. Andersson and Lina Neidestam, the brilliant people who created the comic book album *Tales from Engelsfors* with us. You have shared our world and inspired us more than you can imagine.

We have done a great deal of research for this book. Thanks to all who gave up their time to answer our questions, whether large or small. All errors are our own or Engelsfors' (and that goes for *The Circle* and *Fire* too).Thanks to: Alexandra Nordlander (MSB), Anna Bonnier, Anton Bonnier, Björn Bergenholtz, Cecilia Brors (BOJ), Emil Larsson, Erik Petersson, Göran Parkrud, Hannes Salo, Johan Öhman, Katarina Scding, Kekke Stadin, Lars Rambe, Lina Ljung, Liza Hermeline Andersson, Maria Turtschaninoff, Margit Strandberg, Mats Jonsson, Micko Strandberg, Nene Ormes, Stian Raneke, Tara Johansson, Torgny Hedström and Ulf Karlsson. A special thanks to Patrik Engström who probably had to answer more dumb questions than anyone else.

We also want to give an extra special thanks to Christel Rockström, for help with research and huge support. Thank you for going beyond the call of duty, and doing it with such humor and warmth in a hard, cold world. A big thanks also to Hans-Jörgen Riis Jensen for all the good advice that came from your Danish head and for your big heart.

Thanks to Julia Dufvenius who gave Engelsfors a voice for the audio books.

Thanks Erika Stark for being awesome.

Thanks to Cecilia Norman Mardell and Johan Mardell.

Thanks Peter Danowsky.

And regarding the elves and orcs that Minoo and Linnéa speak of, there are two people whose goodness we don't doubt and would rely on at every escape from Mordor. Their names are Benny Andersson and Ludvig Andersson. We very much look forward to our further adventures.

Levan Akin. There has never been anyone else but you. You are part of *The Circle*. Thank you for your friendship, your strength,

Acknowledgments

your courage, your solidarity and your one-liners. *'Can we get an Amen up in here?'*

Sara would like to thank Micke. This is the fourth book in which I have thanked you. The fourth book in three years, and I don't know how I could have done it without you by my side. You are the most magical person in my life. I love you.

Sara would also like to say a special thanks to Mamma Margareta for her unfailing support and care. Thanks also to my beloved father Claes, and sister Sofia and everyone else in the family. Thanks Annika Berger, Alexander Rönnberg and Hélène Dahl for holding my hand and listening to my rants. Love to Lina and Kalle for being there and sharing in the tears and laughter. Thanks to the Malmö gang!

Mats would like to thank Johan, who was the voice of reason when my own reason was very silent indeed. You make me appreciate the good even more, and you give me perspective on the annoying stuff (sometimes including myself). I love you.

Thanks also to Mom and Dad, who always believed in me. How lucky that I ended up with you. Thanks also to Margareta Elfgren for providing a matriarchal utopia during the first round of edits. And for Sara, of course. Thank you Pär, Anna A and Anna TS, and thanks to Kulturkoftorna for good conversation and sacrifices of goats.

Thanks to our friends. You wonderful, patient people who have forgiven us for all the canceled dates, and all the times that we have shown up at parties and then left after an hour. Thank you for putting up with us while we have been living in Engelsfors and unable to talk about anything else, and not really that either because of our fear of spoilers.

Many warm greetings and thanks to Fagersta, which is a much nicer place than Engelsfors.

Thanks to all our readers who have supported us and cheered us on during this time. Your enthusiasm has given us so much energy and inspiration. It's a bittersweet feeling for us to finish this trilogy, and we hope that we have given you something to dream further about.

We dedicate this book to you, especially to the teenagers.